TWILIGHT'S LAST SCREAMING

Black Shuck Books
www.blackshuckbooks.co.uk

First published in Great Britain in 2022 by
Black Shuck Books
Kent, UK

All content © Sean Hogan 2022

Cover art © Graham Humphreys 2022

Set in Electra and Courier
Interior design © WHITEspace, 2022
www.white-space.uk

978-1-913038-84-7

TWILIGHT'S LAST SCREAMING

SEAN HOGAN

BLACK
SHUCK
BOOKS

Cast of Characters

Prologue

13 | Damien Thorn (redux)

Book One

21 | Thomasin
35 | F. W. Colqhoun
51 | Jesse Hooker
65 | Lizzy Macklin
85 | The Stranger
95 | Daniel Plainview
115 | Stanton Carlisle
123 | Michael Myers
135 | Andy Brooks
147 | Jessica
159 | David Mann
171 | Arletty Long
181 | Eric Binford
203 | Wendy Torrance
221 | Jimmy Quinn
235 | Rhoda
251 | Paul Hackett
269 | Patrick Bateman
283| The Narrator

Interlude

295 | Nikki Brand
303 | David

Book Two

313 | Katherine
327 | R. J. MacReady
335 | David Norliss
357 | Jay Height
367 | Dr. John Markway
401 | Candice Carveth
423 | Adam Cramer & Liz Wetherly
451 | Fred Madison
463 | Dean Corso
487 | Lily Saylor
501 | Travis Bickle
523 | Greg Stillson
551 | Alice Spages
579 | Rosemary Woodhouse
595 | Kendra
605 | The Creature
613 | Tasya Vos

Epilogue

639 | The Boy

AUTHOR'S PREFACE

Here it is: the sequel to a book I never thought I'd write. So how did it come to this? Well, somehow, *England's Screaming* went from being the book I wasn't going to write, to a book I thought might be barely released (doomy thoughts were pretty much the norm in early 2020, remember), to a book whose warm reception took me utterly by surprise. And if you're one of the people who read and enjoyed *England's Screaming*, you're basically the reason this current volume exists, so thank you.

If you *didn't* read it, however, you might want to go back and do so before we go any further. This isn't intended as a hard sell; merely a warning that this is very much a direct sequel to the earlier novel, picking up exactly where we left off. There are a host of different stories contained within this book: some entirely self-contained, some not, but the seeds of the overarching narrative that reaches its culmination here were planted back in *England's Screaming*, and I'd hate for you to only hear half of the tale.

Right. Let's begin again, shall we? And the end does seem like a perfect place to start…

For Ian and Giles (the Jolly Boys)

PROLOGUE

DAMIEN THORN (redux)

Sam Neill in Omen III: The Final Conflict, *1981*
written by Andrew Birkin
directed by Graham Baker

As he gazed into his opponent's eyes, Damien Thorn realised he was about to be defeated for the second time. Not only that, but should he lose this particular battle, there would be no possibility of reprieve. He now faced an opponent as implacably powerful as himself. Not the hated Nazarene, not Count Dracula nor any of his father's other malefic princes, but a mere man.

John Morlar.

Only minutes before, Morlar had swept into Damien's country estate, a lunatic wind at his back, and with nothing but the power of his mind, cut down the Antichrist's two most faithful supplicants: his consort Julia Cotton, and his manservant Hugo Barrett. Damien was weak, crippled and caught completely unprepared by the assault. Despite supposedly enjoying the protection of his Satanic father's near-omnipotent power, he knew nothing of this new foe. The man standing before him recognised no gods or leaders; he acted alone and entirely of his own volition.

And seemingly, his only desire was to see the Antichrist utterly destroyed.

It was true that John Morlar cared nothing for the world and its people – despised them, even – but he would rather see the planet razed to ashes than for it to fall under the control of Hell and its legions. His loathing for humanity was only surpassed by his absolute hatred of those who would seek to preside over it. In order to save Earth, he meant to destroy it.

So now Damien was left alone to face this madman, this fanatical nihilist. And although Julia had nursed him back from near-death to a semblance of health, he was still confined to a wheelchair, his diabolical strength much diminished from what it once was. After his first defeat, Damien had retreated from the world like a cowed and beaten dog, and in response, Lucifer had abandoned him. The Antichrist knew how much his father despised weakness, and understood that he would have to prove himself many times over before he would ever be permitted to wield the same level of power he had enjoyed during his first ascendancy.

Still, he was far from powerless, and normally the force of his unholy will would easily be enough to crush any mortal assassin. But Morlar was *not* mortal, not quite. Although the figure that stood facing him appeared to be nothing more than a somewhat unremarkable-looking middle-aged man, to Damien's preternatural senses Morlar resembled a great black tsunami of rage and power, relentlessly swelling to fill the confines of the country mansion that served as their gladiatorial arena. Probing with his mind, Damien could discern no weakness in the dark tide that threatened to engulf him, no possible means of holding it back. It seemed to him as though Morlar might have been anticipating this moment for his entire life, and now that it had finally arrived, he meant to relish every second of it, permitting Damien no mercy nor respite.

Morlar took a step towards him. *Killing you almost seems like a kindness, Mr Thorn. Not a quality you're overly familiar with, I imagine.*

Something flared in the man's eyes, and Damien felt a crushing weight slam into him, as though a huge fist had just smashed into his ribcage. With a winded gasp, he spasmed in his seat like a pinned insect, the force of the impact sending the wheelchair toppling over onto its side and its occupant thudding down onto the marble floor of the hallway.

Damien lay helpless on his back, hands clutching weakly at the empty air, his useless legs crumpled underneath him. He gazed up at his opponent, anticipating the death blow that would surely arrive at any moment. To think that he, the dark prince of Hell, his father's anointed Earthly scion, should fall to this man! This lunatic who craved only destruction and death! True, he and Morlar were both harbingers of apocalypse, but Damien's holocaust would, in time, see a new ruling class rise from the ruins of the world to create its kingdom anew, only this time in Lucifer Morningstar's image. While if Morlar had his way, only blackened earth would remain.

So which of them was truly the greater evil?

The Antichrist closed his eyes. In his final moments, he found himself remembering the Bible verses he had studied so assiduously all his life, believing they held the key to his eventual triumph over the Nazarene. Instead, he too had been brought low by mankind. He and the hated Christ had that much in common, it seemed. But whereas the Nazarene had triumphantly ascended to his Father's heavenly kingdom after His sacrifice, His divine purpose fulfilled, Damien knew that should he be cast back into the pit that had spawned him, his only reward would be eternal scorn and torment.

He let out a bitter laugh. *My God, my God, why hast thou forsaken me?* he croaked.

Damien expected no reply to his sardonic prayer, but in the next instant, he felt a faint pulse of energy somewhere deep within him, flickering like a dying candle flame. It seemed his appeal had been granted after all.

Desperately, the Antichrist turned his concentration inwards, focusing on the power, trying to nurture the tiny spark back into life. If only he had just a few more seconds…

Morlar's empty eyes stared down at him, two black holes in the blasted wasteland of his face. In the moment of his victory, the man seemed almost disappointed. *I've been watching you and your kind for years,* he murmured. *Following your every move. Listening to you scurry around behind the walls of this rotten country like vermin. No one really believed me, of course, but then they never did. It didn't matter. I knew this day was coming. And now, to find you like this…*

Damien's opponent was given to speechifying, it appeared. Perhaps that might just gift him the opening he needed…

The Antichrist reached out with the last reserves of his strength and probed Morlar's defences once more, searching for the smallest chink, the tiniest weakness. Anything to allow him a fingerhold.

Agonising moments passed, and still there was nothing. Damien felt as though he were trying to bring down a castle wall using only his fists.

He was on the verge of abandoning all hope when he found it.

A small electronic device, nestled deep in the man's spine. No bigger than the head of a nail, but what would happen if Damien gave it the smallest nudge…?

A split-second later, he received his answer.

John Morlar exploded.

Damien lay motionless as blood and flesh rained down on him, his opponent's crimson remains baptising him as the victor of their duel. As the last of Morlar splattered to the marble floor, Damien howled in triumph.

The Antichrist had no way of knowing precisely who had implanted the explosive within Morlar's body, nor why. Some kind of safeguard, perhaps. Did it mean the man was originally some kind of government operative, or an assassin created by the corporate sector? He supposed he might never learn the truth of it.

But really, what did it matter? Weakened and alone, Damien had nevertheless defeated his enemies once again. He had survived his own Stations of the Cross, and now, at last, he would ascend to his throne.

Rolling over onto his side, Damien surveyed Morlar's shattered remains. The man's skull had been ripped in half by the explosion, and Damien could see his jellied brain glistening within. Remarkably, he could still sense a life force pulsing within it. A powerful, seething hatred, still centred at the organ's core, gathering itself for another opportunity, another assault.

Morlar was even more dangerous than he had first imagined. Damien considered simply crushing the brain between his fingers, but a warning voice in his mind stopped him. If bodily destruction could not fully dissipate the man's power, what good would obliterating his brain do? It might even release Morlar's energies from the anchor of his flesh. And thus freed, what would then stand in the way of his nemesis achieving omnipresence, even omnipotence? No, far better to keep him caged and helpless.

Damien dragged himself over to the corpse and carefully scooped the brain out from its cavity, holding it up to the sunlight. He almost fancied he could feel the force of Morlar's loathing throbbing wetly beneath his touch. Holding the organ in his palm, Damien suddenly remembered reading of a scientist named Cory, who, some years ago, had taken the brain of a dead tycoon named W.H. Donovan and kept it alive in an electrified saline solution. Rumour had it that Cory had almost succumbed to the malevolent psychic will of the brain, but, after all, he was just a man, weak and mortal. If Damien could do the same with Morlar's brain, he could keep his opponent safely locked away in a vault, rendered powerless and helpless. Imprisoned within the useless remnants of his destroyed flesh, forever tormented by the knowledge of his own failure.

The idea had a certain sadistic appeal, Damien had to admit.

Reaching for his toppled wheelchair, Damien righted it, then managed to heave himself back into its seat. He propelled himself over to the top of the staircase, marking the floor with twin trails of John Morlar's blood. Looking down over the house that had once been a sanctuary to him, he wondered how many more enemies might attempt to seek him out here. The estate had kept him safe throughout the long years of his seclusion, but on the heels of Morlar's assault, now seemed horribly exposed. The lifeless bodies of Hugo Barrett and Julia Cotton lying before him served as ample testament to that.

Perhaps it was at last time to set out for more distant shores. After all, Damien's work in England was almost complete. Soon, the isle would be lost to its deluded fantasies of sovereignty and empire, reduced to little more but an irrelevant mudpile just off the shores of Europe. There was nothing more for him here. Damien could now abandon England to the rest of its monsters and proceed with the next stage of his plan.

He had always known that the time would come for him to leave behind his adopted country and return to the homeland of the family that had raised him as one of their own. The Thorn dynasty, blithely accustomed to the aspirational dreams of wealth and influence that served as the bedrock of their country, had never questioned the means that such inherited power might one day be put to. Now, their cherished legacy lay in ruins, as Damien Thorn, the Great Beast and last of the Thorn line, conquered and prospered in their name.

And their homeland, the country that had long prided itself on its own virtue and exceptionalism, would soon prove itself to be as compliantly craven in the face of the Antichrist's blandishments as any other.

America.

BOOK ONE

A CITY ON A HILL

Is a dream a lie, if it don't come true,
Or is it something worse?

– Bruce Springsteen, "The River"

THOMASIN

Anya Taylor-Joy in The Witch, *2015*
written & directed by Robert Eggers

*T*HE TASTE OF BUTTER, A PRETTY DRESS…
Before young Thomasin left her home behind forever and disappeared into that accursed dark forest, she was promised a great many sinful treats. But she was little more than a child in those days, and such forbidden fancies meant a good deal more to her then.

As it was, she never did receive her pretty dress, and was obliged to taste much viler substances than butter during her long exile in the woods. Still, when all was said and done, it hardly mattered, for what she discovered there instead was incalculably precious, far more valuable than countless wardrobes full of finery. When Thomasin finally re-emerged from the forest, she was as naked as when she first entered, without a stitch of clothing or a single possession to her name, but she was wealthy beyond measure all the same. Rich with power and esoteric knowledge, the only two currencies that would prove to be of any lasting worth in this New World over the decades and centuries to come.

Her education was not without a steep price, however. When Thomasin first entered into her dreadful covenant with Lucifer, signing her name in His Black Book and giving herself over to His dark tutelage, the year was 1630. But by the time she stumbled hesitantly from the treeline and stood blinking in the early morning sunlight, over a hundred years had passed. She'd sat at Satan's knee for more than a century, gorging herself at His unspeakable banquet, drinking her fill of His blasphemies and wicked wisdom. And although time has little meaning in His black realm, Thomasin found she had nevertheless left her youth far behind her, abandoned somewhere within those shadowed trees. The angel-faced young girl she used to be had now grown into a mature woman. Still handsome, even bewitching in the right light, but a forfeit had been extracted all the same.

Regardless, what did such vanities mean to her now? She could take on a multitude of forms just as she pleased, transforming into a hare or a cat as easily as blinking an eye, so it was hardly beyond her powers to appear young and beautiful again if she so desired. No, all Thomasin truly craved was to be free. Her parents had brought her to this strange new country claiming it represented freedom and Divine Providence for them all, but their notion of liberty had only meant repression and grinding misery. Worse yet, her father's fanatical devotion to his faith had led him to turn against a close neighbour, a wealthy merchant named Charles Croydon. He'd accused Croydon of witchcraft and vampirism, but the elders of their settlement had sided with the merchant and banished Thomasin's family into the wilderness, where only madness and death awaited them. Fleeing these torments had brought Thomasin stumbling unwittingly into Satan's path, resulting in these long decades of servitude and study.

She had been exiled to these devil-haunted woods for far too many years. Now, she demanded clean air, bright, warm sunshine, and an open blue sky.

Extending her right hand, Thomasin concentrated for a moment. Within seconds, her broomstick appeared at her side. She ran her hand along its length, remembering the atrocities she'd committed in order to gain the miraculous power of flight. The infant child she'd snatched from its parents, just as her baby brother Samuel had been so cruelly snatched from her. The gory paste she'd made of the babe's flesh and bones, applying it to every inch of this same broomstick. Still, none of those horrors had given Thomasin the slightest pause. She had no doubt that the child would only have grown up to experience the same sort of suffering and deprivation she herself had been subjected to. And as for any question of moral or spiritual reparation, she had left such petty considerations far behind her. Her earthly father had betrayed her, abjectly laying the blame for his own weakness squarely at his eldest daughter's feet. Even her heavenly Father had averted His gaze when she needed Him the most, abandoning her to the sin she had spent her entire young life vainly attempting to expiate.

So be it, then. She had but one patriarch now.

Straddling the broomstick, she rose slowly into the air, exulting in her emancipation from the tyranny of solid ground. As she ascended into the heavens, she began to head away from the woods and towards the New England coast. Thomasin knew she would return to the forest in time – she was a dark thing now and where else do dark things dwell if not in the depths of the forest? – but for now she wished to taste the salty tang of the sea on her lips, feel its cool spray on her skin. Shrieking her defiance into the fathomless blue sky, she sped away into the aether.

Upon reaching the ocean, she followed the coastline for a time, darting in and out of the breaking waves and chasing bewildered gulls around the sky. Thomasin revelled in her newfound liberty, but understood that such pleasure could only be short-lived. She possessed neither clothes nor means of sustenance, and despite all her supernatural power was still tethered by the physical demands of her flesh.

Not only that, but the era she now inhabited had no idea she even existed. She had no name, no identity. As far as this new century was concerned, the girl who had once been named Thomasin was dead and long forgotten, her bones mouldering in an unmarked grave. At best, she supposed she might be a bedtime story to scare small children: Thomasin the witch, who murdered her entire family and was spirited away to Hell by the Devil Himself. *Now, follow the word of thy parents, little ones, or the same will happen to thee.*

Skimming across the waves, she caught sight of a distant ship, bound for the shores of America. Thomasin thought back to her own passage to the New World, and the long weeks of sickness and misery she had endured at sea. *We must ascend to Heaven,* her father had always stubbornly insisted, *and so shall be content to travel uphill, though the journey be hard and tiresome.*

As it turned out, he'd spoken the truth about the quality of her journey, but had, it seemed, been quite mistaken about his daughter's final destination.

She flew closer to the ship, muttering an incantation under her breath so that she might veil herself in invisibility. Thus shielded from prying eyes, Thomasin circled the vessel, a three-masted fluyt named the *Reliant*. It was quite similar in appearance to the ship that had first transported her to this country over a century before, she realised.

Thomasin decided to take this small coincidence as a good omen.

She followed the vessel into port, a bustling harbour town she quickly ascertained was named Baltimore. Descending back to solid ground, she waited upon the dock, still cloaked from sight, until a long line of travel-weary passengers began to disembark. Many were married couples or small families, and as such were of little use to her. But eventually she noticed a sour-faced woman, apparently travelling alone. A sack containing her few belongings slung over one hunched shoulder, the woman shuffled stiffly down the gangplank and wandered away into the crowded streets. She paid little heed to anyone around her, heading straight for the nearest tavern and ordering some stew and ale.

Thomasin lurked in a darkened corner of the tavern and observed the woman as she messily devoured her meal. She was middle-aged, unencumbered by family or companions, a complete stranger to this country.

She was, Thomasin decided, perfect.

After the woman had finished eating, she wandered back out into the afternoon sunlight, entirely unaware that she was being closely followed. As far as Thomasin could tell, the woman's arrival in America did not seem to be accompanied by any particular intent or plan of action; perhaps she too had been swayed by honeyed promises of Providence and now expected this new country to simply pile fresh opportunities at her feet. She needed to act quickly, before the woman's disorientation faded and she began to think more clearly about where her destiny might lay, for it was a destiny that Thomasin meant to claim for herself.

Little did the unfortunate woman know that her whole life, past and future both, was about to be prised away from her, as simply and swiftly as if it had been a coinpurse.

Leaving the docks behind, the woman ventured further into the town. Now the streets around her were growing less populated, granting her unseen pursuer the opportunity she needed. Picking up her pace, Thomasin ran ahead of the woman and darted into a nearby alleyway. Doing her best to ignore the filth and trash piled there, she dropped to her knees and shrugged off her veil of invisibility, curling herself into a tight ball and whimpering piteously.

When the woman passed by the mouth of the alleyway moments later, Thomasin looked up at her and began to wail. *Oh please! Oh help me!*

The woman stopped in her tracks and gazed down at her, astonished. Thomasin could tell she was considering whether to ignore her pleas and simply hurry on with her business. Wasting no time, she stretched out a beseeching arm towards her saviour.

Please, canst thou help me! Thomasin implored the woman, quickly adding for good measure: *My husband is a wealthy merchant and will reward thee handsomely for thy aid!*

That was enough to settle the matter. The woman hurriedly looked around, then scuttled into the alleyway and knelt down besides Thomasin. Removing her shawl, the woman wrapped it around her naked body. *Hush now, I am here*, she said, in a broad accent Thomasin recognised as Irish. *What in God's name has happened to you?*

Three sailors, Thomasin sobbed. *They didst set upon me while I was out walking. They robbed me of my clothes and money, then ravished me most brutally.*

Animals, the woman spat. *I see men remain the same filthy dogs in the New World as they were in the old.*

Thomasin clutched desperately at her rescuer's sleeve. *Willst thou help me, good samaritan? The price of thy mercy is surely beyond measure, but I will see to it that my husband dost tip the scales in thy favour nonetheless.*

The woman looked at her curiously. *Do all women here talk like you?*

For the first time, it struck Thomasin that a great many things must have changed in the preceding century, manners of contemporary speech being foremost amongst them.

F-forgive me, she stuttered. *My family are old-fashioned in their customs, and I fear I am sadly unaccustomed to the ways of normal folk.*

That much I can tell, the woman said bluntly. *Well, Mrs whoever-you-are, my name is Elly Kedward, and I am a stranger to this country of yours. I will need you to advise me on where we must go from here, and how best we can get there.*

A look of sly satisfaction flickered across Thomasin's face. She suddenly sat upright, her eyes fixing the startled Elly in place.

As soon as I have finished my business here, I shall go where I please, she whispered. *But thou, Elly Kedward...thou shallst go nowhere.*

Before the other woman could react, Thomasin's hands had snaked out and seized her around the throat, firmly enough to choke off Elly's frightened cry.

Thou shouldst not have travelled here, Elly, she murmured, her voice oddly gentle. *This land was old and evil before the settlers came, before even the Indians. T'is not for such as thee.*

In the next instant, she began to squeeze.

The woman that departed the alleyway some minutes later, scowling at the unclean clothes circumstances had required her to don, so scratchy and unfamiliar against her skin, was not Elly Kedward, whatever she might have claimed to the contrary.

But in all truth, neither was she Thomasin; that scared, angelic girl who had stood by and watched as her entire family were claimed by darkness, until darkness was all that was left to her. In a very real sense, although only one corpse lay abandoned in the alley, the woman now calling herself Elly Kedward had left two lifeless bodies behind her.

Still, it was not the last name, nor the most infamous, that history would come to know her by.

The legend of Elly Kedward is by now a familiar one, and we need not concern ourselves with the elements of the story that have already been well-documented by others: Elly's banishment from the town of Blair after accusations of witchcraft had been made against her, and her subsequent revenge against the townsfolk, a terrible vengeance that would extend across centuries. No, our purpose here is to chart a shadow history of America, to map the unrevealed trails and pathways that criss-cross this great continent's past. As such, this particular account only requires us to return to Thomasin twice more, to detail fateful, hitherto-unrecorded encounters that would lead to her assuming her final and most dreadful identity of all.

—

The first encounter occurred on a freezing winter's night in 1775. The snow was piled high in the streets of Blair, the vicious bite in the air enough to rip the meat from a man's bones. To look at it, Blair might have seemed like a ghost town, a memory of a once-living settlement preserved in ice. A portent of what was yet to come.

But then a figure appeared out of the blinding, howling white. Wrapped in a red hooded cloak, the figure moved swiftly and easily through the frozen drifts, almost as if it were gliding inches above the deep layers of ice and snow.

Moving the length of the street, it came to a halt outside a small, neatly-maintained cottage. Extending a slim, pale hand from within its cloak, the figure knocked upon the cottage door with a force that seemed incongruous with the obvious delicacy of the limb itself.

Long seconds passed, and although it was already little short of a miracle that the figure had made it this far, one might now have expected it to buckle under the relentless assault of the wind and cold. But the visitor remained resolutely upright, standing firm against the elements and waiting for its summons to be answered.

Finally, the door was wrenched open, revealing the face of the woman her neighbours knew only as Elly Kedward.

Wariness and suspicion were etched upon Thomasin's features, for an unnatural thing such as she understood full well that only *another* unnatural thing could possibly have made it all the way to her threshold in such treacherous conditions as these.

Glancing down, she quickly found proof of this assessment: the visitor had left no visible footprints in the snow during its passage to her doorway.

Who are you? she demanded, bellowing against the force of the gale. *What do you want here?*

The figure reached up and lowered the hood of its cloak, revealing itself to be an eerily beautiful young woman. As Thomasin gazed into the woman's eyes, she saw that the endless, desolate winter which howled there was a thousand times colder than the blizzard currently raging upon her doorstep.

My name is Mater Lachrymarum, the woman told her. Her voice was soft, and yet it seemed she hardly needed to raise it to be heard above the storm. *And I am here to warn you, sister Thomasin.*

After hearing the identity of her visitor, it came as no surprise to Thomasin that the woman knew her real name. Mater Lachrymarum and her two sisters, Mater Suspiriorum and Mater Tenebrarum, were the oldest and most feared of all witches. Some practitioners of the Dark Arts claimed they were merely a myth, a bedside story intended to frighten those who were themselves bedside stories, but Thomasin was both old enough and wise enough to know that there was often a great deal of truth in such tales.

Bowing her head, she stood back and allowed the visitor to enter her cottage. *I am humbled by your presence,* she murmured reverently.

Stepping across the threshold, Mater Lachrymarum nodded in silent acknowledgement of the tribute. The cottage interior was bathed in an orange glow, lit only by the flames burning in the grate. Clumps of dried herbs dangled from the rafters, and the air inside the room was thick and pungent with their scent.

Mater Lachrymarum crossed to the hearth, allowing the heat of the crackling flames to dry her sodden cloak. *Come, sit by me,* she instructed her host.

Thomasin hurried over and took a chair by the fire. *You have a warning for me, Mother?* she asked quietly.

Her visitor stood and gazed into the roaring fire, which did little to warm the cold gleam of her eyes. *You are familiar with the Book of Revelation?* she asked Thomasin. *The prophecies concerning the Great Beast?*

Of course, Thomasin said. Having been raised in the Puritan faith, she had been more than sufficiently schooled in the Good Book.

The other woman nodded. *It has come to our attention that Lucifer Morningstar is seeking to sire an heir, so as to fulfil the Biblical prophecy and seize control of the Kingdom of Earth.* Mater Lachrymarum picked up the poker and stabbed viciously at the fire. *It is as yet unknown by what foul means He might achieve this, as it remains to be seen whether congress with a human woman will result in a suitable offspring. Regardless, He means to try.*

Her eyes rose to study Thomasin. *It is our understanding that He has chosen you as the prospective mother of His son.*

Me? Thomasin gasped. *Surely this cannot be. I am too old to bear His child!*

Lucifer knows your power, sister Thomasin. Did He not instruct you in the Dark Arts Himself? He knows you are not a helpless prisoner to the cage of your flesh. If you wished to carry a child to term, it is well within your magical ability to do so.

At the sound of Mater Lachrymarum's words, a vast emptiness welled up inside Thomasin. After so much time spent winning her freedom, the prospect of having it torn away from her, of once more being placed in thrall to a man's unyielding demands, filled her with horror.

He owns me, body and soul, she muttered, sinking back into her chair. *How can I possibly defy Him?*

Mater Lachrymarum tossed the poker aside and whirled round to face Elly. Her face had grown bloodless with rage, and yet was somehow all the more beautiful for it. *You must defy Him!* she screamed. *He cannot be allowed to claim the Earth! It will only mean subjugation and misery for our kind!*

Outside, the wind redoubled its assault on the little cottage, shrieking and battering against its roof and walls.

Thomasin cowered before the force of the witch's terrible anger. Her fury quickly subsiding, Mater Lachrymarum took a step back, willing herself to be calm. In response, the wind duly ceased its hideous shrieking, content once more to merely howl its discontent.

Elly's visitor moved to the window and stared out into the night. *As long as He reigns only in Hell, we can resist Him here,* she said quietly. *But should He gain a foothold in this realm, all will be lost. My sisters and*

I have gazed into an infinity of futures, and we have glimpsed the untold horror and devastation of the End Times. Such a future cannot be permitted to transpire, sister Thomasin.

Turning away from the window, Mater Lachrymarum glanced back at her host. And perhaps it was simply a trick of the firelight, but Thomasin thought she at last glimpsed a trace of human feeling in the other woman's cold eyes.

You must resist Him, for all our sakes, she begged Thomasin, who needed no reminding as to just how unaccustomed to begging the entity standing before her must be.

Very well, she said quietly. *I do not know if I have sufficient power to resist Him, but I will try.* Thomasin rose from her chair, then knelt in supplication at Mater Lachrymarum's feet.

The other woman reached down and gently stroked her hair. *I know you have suffered much, sister Thomasin,* she murmured. *And you may yet suffer again. But I promise you this: you will have your vengeance, and the song of a woman's vengeance is the sweetest song that has ever been sung, sweeter than the call of a thousand nightingales.*

Thomasin closed her eyes, leaning into Mater Lachrymarum's touch. They remained like that for some time, until Thomasin finally realised she could no longer feel Mater Lachrymarum's soothing hand on her scalp.

She opened her eyes to find herself alone in the cottage once more.

Sighing, Thomasin climbed to her feet and moved gingerly back to her chair. As she sat, she began to think upon the other witch's warning, and all at once a verse from Revelation sprang unbidden to her lips: *Then the third Angel blew the trumpet, and there fell a great star from heaven, burning like a torch, and it fell into the third part of the rivers, and into the fountains of waters. And the name of the star is called Wormwood.*

Why this particular verse had come to mind, she did not know.

For a time, Thomasin had found peace and contentment in Blair, despite the persistent rumours of her true nature she often heard whispered behind her back. But now it seemed as though she was about to be caught up in a battle of wills waged between two powerful masters, and Thomasin feared that King Solomon had been quite correct in his judgement that there was but one way to settle such a dispute. A settlement which, irrespective of the prophet's much-vaunted wisdom, could hardly be viewed as any sort of a satisfactory outcome for her.

Thomasin remained huddled in her chair for the rest of that long, fearfully cold winter's night, staring into the capering flames and thinking about the various hells she had known, and those she might yet have to endure.

———

The second of the two encounters came several years later, on the day of Elly Kedward's banishment from the town of Blair.

In the midst of another severe winter, Thomasin had been taken from her cottage by the vengeful townsfolk and dragged into the nearby woods, where she was tied to a tree and left to perish. Helpless against the freezing elements, it was not long before she began to succumb to hypothermia, her body teetering on the verge of unconsciousness.

As her vision began to darken, Thomasin imagined she heard two childish voices, carried to her ears atop the cruelly biting wind.

Look, Mercy! T'is the wicked Witch of the Wood!

Aye, but she dost not appear half so wicked whilst bound helpless to that tree!

With the last of her strength, she forced her eyes open.

Before her stood her younger siblings, the twins Jonas and Mercy. Thomasin had not laid eyes on them since the day of their disappearance, more than one hundred and fifty years before. But they appeared just as she remembered them from that day, save for two dreadful details: their blood-red eyes, and the forked serpents' tongues that flickered from between their lips.

Devils, Thomasin moaned weakly. *Begone from here.*

The twins chittered with glee. *Art thou not touched with joy to see us, sister?*

She felt herself slipping back into the past, a frightened young girl once more. *Thou art evil wretches, and thou always were.*

T'is not we who art evil, Thomasin, Jonas chided her. *We must perform our master's bidding, t'is all. And the scale of our deviltry is but a mote of dust before His.*

Glimpsing movement in the corner of her eye, Thomasin looked around to see an ebony goat emerging from the trees nearby, the same malefic avatar she had once known as Black Philip.

Pausing to tramp its hooves against the frozen earth, the goat fixed her with a baleful, inhuman glare.

Black Philip saist thou belongst to Him, sister, Mercy told her. *We must free thee from thy bonds and deliver thee unto His grace with all haste.*

Moving to Thomasin's side, the twins began to poke and pry at the ropes binding her to the tree. Thomasin closed her eyes as they worked, allowing herself to sink back into semi-consciousness. A part of her even welcomed the encroaching darkness, believing it might be better to simply perish now, rather than face whatever further trials Black Philip intended for her.

But before she could succumb, the twins at last succeeded in their efforts. Thomasin's bonds gave way, sending her sprawling gracelessly to the earth.

Her cheek pressed against the icy forest floor, Thomasin listened to her siblings jeer and caper around her. She knew she should try to move, to get up and seek shelter, but she was tired, so very tired, and even resting upon this bed of frozen mud seemed a far preferable prospect than attempting so herculean a task as climbing to her feet.

Blackness enfolded her, and she knew no more for a time.

The next thing Thomasin was aware of was a growing sensation of cold around her thighs and rump. As her consciousness slowly returned, it brought with it a gradual realisation that her skirts had been pushed up around her waist, exposing her nether regions to the elements.

Then, her senses were suddenly assailed by an animal stink of dung and filth, and to Elly's horror, she felt a furry body nestling in between her thighs, attempting to mount her.

Glancing back over her shoulder, she saw Black Philip's face looming into view, its teeth bared in a horrible expression of bestial lust and triumph.

No! Thomasin screamed, and attempted to wriggle away from the goat. But she quickly felt her attacker's front hooves slam down into her back, winding her and pinning her in place against the earth.

She heard the goat grunting in excitement, readying itself to enter her.

Closing her eyes, Thomasin thought back to the night Mater Lachrymarum had visited her. *Please, Mother,* she prayed. *Help me resist Him.*

Blindly scrabbling about in the frozen dirt, her hand suddenly closed around a jagged rock. Whether its presence was down to witchcraft or mere happenstance, it represented her last chance to escape.

Seizing it, Thomasin summoned every last ounce of strength she possessed, and with a scream of rage, twisted around from underneath her attacker's hooves. With both hands clasped tightly around her makeshift weapon, she thrust its jagged point into one of Black Philip's eyes.

The beast let out a loud wail of pain and rage, and immediately leapt away from her. Disorientated, it blundered away through the undergrowth and was quickly lost to the shadows of the forest.

Thomasin collapsed down to the earth. Her ordeal had already taken much out of her, and she was still a long way from deliverance. But she had fought for, and won, her freedom. All she needed now was a moment to reclaim her breath.

However, even that one small mercy was denied her. The next instant, she heard the seething hiss of a voice in her ear, the sound of it filling her skull like a tumour. A terrible, all-powerful voice she remembered only too well from her long years of instruction.

Thou wouldst defy me? the voice demanded.

Arms trembling with exhaustion, Thomasin slowly raised herself to a sitting position, eyes searching the surrounding woods. *I will not bear thy child!* she shouted into the shadows. *That was not our bargain!*

Impudent sow! the voice snarled back. *If t'is my will, then t'is thy bargain.*

With my last breath I shall reject thee! screamed Thomasin, flinging the bloodied rock impotently into the trees.

There was absolute silence in the forest for a moment, before the voice spoke again, this time in a capricious, satisfied purr. *So be it, child,* it told her. *If thou willst not lie with beasts, thou shallst be as one.*

With those words, a sudden jolt of agony coursed through Thomasin's flesh, as though every nerve in her body had been set aflame. Looking down, she saw her limbs beginning to warp and shift, fingers and toes curling into talons, a coarse dark fur sprouting from her pores. She screamed in fear and pain, but could do nothing to resist the diabolical transformation that had been visited upon her.

It took some minutes for her metamorphosis to be be completed, but when the agony finally stopped, the creature that lay motionless and spent on the floor of the forest bore no resemblance to the girl Thomasin, nor the woman Elly Kedward.

She was now a nameless, dreadful thing, whose infamy would soon cause history to bestow another title upon her.

The Blair Witch.

Consumed with rage and hatred, the witch would in time make a new lair for herself in the deepest, darkest corner of the forest. From there, she plotted to enact her vengeance upon the townsfolk of Blair, a vengeance she swore would continue for centuries to come. Even when that settlement finally died out in the face of her relentless fury, the Blair Witch's thirst for retribution was not sated, and so she simply waited until another town, Burkittsville, sprang up in its place. Given the circumstances of the curse that had been laid upon her, the witch reserved a particular animus for children, and generation upon generation of the town's unwary offspring quickly learned to fear her.

But even as the long centuries passed, there was one who continued to remember the woman the Blair Witch had once been, and respected her for the bravery she had shown in defying the maleficent will of the Devil.

So it was that, on the same night every December, when the wind screamed fit to wake the dead and the world was a whirling blur of cold and whiteness, Mater Lachrymarum would venture into the depths of the forest, to visit the home of the Blair Witch and sit with her awhile.

It was said that, on those black nights, if you stood on your front porch and listened hard enough, you might catch the terrible laughter of the two creatures carried aloft on the storm. And so, however much Burkittsville may have feared the Blair Witch's wrath during the remainder of the year, on those particular midwinter evenings, the townsfolk made sure to take extra care in locking their doors and windows, and never once dared set foot on the streets after dark.

F. W. COLQHOUN

Robert Carlyle in Ravenous, *1999*
written by Ted Griffin
directed by Antonia Bird

ITS CALL RESOUNDED DEEP WITHIN THE EARTH, AWAKENING COLQHOUN from the black sleep to which he had been consigned. The Wendigo's appetite was fathomless, insatiable; it would not permit its servant to rest so easily.

There was still so much feeding to be done.

He opened his eyes, to no avail; the smothering, choking darkness had pursued him into waking. Fearing he had been somehow struck blind, Colqhoun inhaled a panicked lungful of air, his juddering breath ringing hollow in his ears. He could smell mud and damp lingering in his nostrils, and mingling with them, the sweet aroma of pine.

Realisation slowly dawning, he reached up with his hands, only to encounter the unyielding barrier of a wooden coffin lid, weighed down by six feet of rich Californian soil.

Bollocks, he hissed.

Concentrating, he opened himself to the mystical power of his master, allowing the Wendigo's energies to flow into his body. Colqhoun knew that the price for channeling such power would be an awful, all-consuming hunger, more insidious than any opium craving, but he could deal with that later, as soon as he had freed himself from his not-so-final resting place.

An inhuman strength coursed through him. Howling with the force of it, Colqhoun began to batter at the lid of his prison, quickly reducing it to splinters. As the cold mud cascaded down upon him, he thrust his body upwards, hands scrabbling furiously at the earth like some infernal demon digging its way free from Hell itself.

Within minutes, the ground had given up its formerly dead. Spitting out dirt, Colqhoun scrambled to his feet and roared his triumph at the watching moon. His grave marker confirmed that he had been buried under his assumed identity of Colonel Ives, in the small military graveyard to the rear of Fort Spencer, and as he strode from the enclosure, Colqhoun noted with quiet satisfaction that Captain Boyd, the soldier responsible for his demise, had been laid to rest in the unconsecrated soil outside its boundaries. Clearly the U.S. Cavalry still believed Boyd to be responsible for the recent wave of anthropophagous murders that had swept through Fort Spencer. That credulity would soon cost them dearly.

Colqhoun's mouth watered at the thought of it.

Still, first things first. Ignoring the hunger that was already starting to gripe at his belly, the cannibal planted his feet on either side of Boyd's burial plot, whipped out his cock, and let his contempt rain down onto the soil, the steaming arc of reddish urine quickly darkening the grave dirt to black.

His thirst for petty retribution slaked, Colqhoun was now at liberty to tend to the matter of his appetite. Fort Spencer had never been anything more than a military stopping point, a remote purgatory manned by a motley selection of drunks and cretins, all of whom were now dead. Until a new garrison could be posted there, a mere handful of soldiers had been left to oversee the outpost. Already bored almost to the point of madness by the relentless tedium of everyday life at the fort, the men were passing the time the only way they could: by getting absolutely soused. Colqhoun could hear their drunken singing and shouting from where he stood, carried outside on the night breeze. Dull-witted cattle, helplessly ignorant of the great wolf watching them from the shadows.

He sauntered off to pay the soldiers a welcome visit, whistling a jaunty tune as he went.

Later, after he had eaten his fill, the cannibal settled down in front of the fire with a pipe of good tobacco. He'd once considered making Fort Spencer his lair, using it as a snare to trap unwary travellers passing through the Sierra Nevada. Alas, Boyd's damned meddling had now ruined that delicious possibility. Colqhoun would simply have to find somewhere new to set up camp, somewhere he was free to feed to both his and his master's satisfaction.

But where should he go?

Inhaling deeply upon the pipe, the cannibal closed his eyes and allowed his consciousness to drift free of his body, becoming one with that of the Wendigo.

Show me, he murmured.

Floating high above the world, the ageless spirit guided him to a remote desert valley, many miles from Fort Spencer. The terrain appeared almost devoid of life, barely able to sustain even the wilderness creatures who lived there, let alone a preternaturally hungry cannibal. But Colqhoun could feel the presence of a primal power, tugging at him from deep within the soil, and decided to investigate further.

Descending closer to the earth, he came across a primitive-looking burial site. Seen from above, it immediately became clear to him that the ground markings linking the graves formed an ancient mystic pattern, one the cannibal recognised immediately. Whoever had constructed this site worshipped the very same master as he.

With a flash of cold fire, Colqhoun's mind rejoined his body. He sat up with a start, a name seared into the meat of his brain.

The Valley of the Starving Men.

Plotting the journey on a map, he estimated it would take him a good couple of weeks to ride to the valley's location. While he dared not dally at Fort Spencer for too long, Colqhoun knew he would need to be well-prepared for such a trek, given that the opportunities for feeding en route might be scarce. Going to work upon the corpses of the soldiers, he carved himself plenty of meat for the journey, leaving it to cure for several days afterwards.

Finally he was ready. Selecting the best of the horses left behind by his victims, the cannibal rode out from the fort. Surveying the landscape, he could see a dust cloud billowing in the distance, thrown up by the hooves of approaching horses. No doubt they belonged to the replacement garrison; he had scheduled his departure just in time. Imagining the faces of the arriving troops once they discovered the half-eaten bodies of their comrades, not to mention the hastily-vacated grave outside the fort, Colqhoun cackled with malevolent glee and urged his steed forwards. By the time the cavalry reached their destination, he was nowhere in sight.

Colqhoun rode for many days, the Wendigo forever screaming at his back, its ravenous howls driving him further and further into the unknown territories. The cannibal knew he needed to be frugal with his food supplies, but his limited stash of cured meat was scarcely enough to satisfy his master's infinite hunger. Colqhoun did not consider himself a bastion of sanity – given the long list of atrocities he had to his credit, it would be exceptionally difficult to make such a case – but even he found himself driven to the brink of absolute madness by the Wendigo's incessant shrieking. Its unearthly cries swirled round and round inside his skull like a maelstrom, threatening to suck his body and soul down into oblivion. He was only saved by the intrusion of two bushwhackers into his camp one evening; thinking the lone traveller an easy mark, the unsuspecting bandits quickly found themselves at the wrong end of Colqhoun's blade. He feasted well that night, enough to keep his master sated for a few more days at least.

The bushwhackers were the last living souls he would encounter on his journey; truly living, at any rate. As the cannibal ventured further and further into the unknown, he could sense his surroundings altering around him. Not in their outward appearance; to the naked eye, the terrain remained as bleak and desolate as it had always been. Rather, Colqhoun's heightened perceptions told him that the innermost aspect of the landscape was rapidly changing, a black corruption blooming ripely at its core. This was a haunted, liminal place, filled with inexplicable forces and hideous creatures entirely beyond the understanding of the white man's so-called civilisation. As much as he was a full-blooded proponent of the theory of manifest destiny, Colqhoun began to wonder whether lands such as these could ever really be tamed.

Shortly afterwards, he came across further evidence of the unbridled malignity of the territory, this time physical rather than spiritual. Noticing something that looked like a human form hidden in the long brush, the cannibal dismounted and moved to investigate, weapon at the ready. What he discovered was a young woman lying half-buried in the soil, her pallor pale and grey. At first Colqhoun thought her to be a lifeless corpse, sloppily buried by her murderers. But upon closer inspection, he realised the woman was still alive, albeit adrift in some form of catatonic stupor. For a moment, he considered making good use of her flesh, until his keen nose told him that whatever unknown poison had placed her in this state was also slowly rotting her from within.

As he abandoned the sorry wretch to her terrible fate, Colqhoun wondered exactly what manner of creature could do that to a human being. He would need to be on his guard.

That night, he learned – almost to his cost – the hideous answer to his question. Dozing by his campfire, the cannibal was jerked into wakefulness by the frightened whinnying of his horse. Upon opening his eyes, what Colqhoun beheld stunned even his debased sensibilities. Several creatures – no, *abominations* – were emerging from deep within the earth and quickly closing in on where he lay. Their long bodies snaked swiftly towards him, multitudes of grasping limbs contorting at impossible angles. Staring into their blank eyes, Colqhoun could tell the creatures possessed little or no sight, but they greedily sensed his proximity all the same. One of them loomed up before him, its great maw opening wide, like a tunnel leading inexorably to his own damnation.

Bellowing in shock, the cannibal grabbed his rifle and began to fire upon the burrowing monstrosities, to no avail. Conventional weaponry seemed to have little effect upon them.

Colqhoun had nowhere to run. Was this really to be his fate, the merciless predator falling prey to something far deadlier than he? Where was his master the Wendigo now? He looked up to the black heavens and screamed. *Damn your fucking eyes!*

The next moment, he heard a whizzing sound, and looked around to see a heavy white object speed through the air and embed itself in the hide in one of the creatures. A high-pitched shriek of triumph filled the night, followed by a further barrage of the vicious-looking projectiles. Whoever the attackers were, their aim was unerring and deadly, and within seconds, all of the burrowing creatures were left writhing and screaming in pain.

A thunder of hoofbeats announced the entrance of Colqhoun's saviours; a posse of inhuman-looking savages, their skin entirely daubed with white pigment. Their presence was hardly any more reassuring than that of the burrowers, but his current predicament was such that the cannibal had little option but to gamble that their rescue was motivated by sheer altruism alone. So, when one of the savage riders galloped towards him and held out a hand, Colqhoun grabbed for it, allowing himself to be yanked up onto the horse. They sped off into the night, leaving the abominations to fade into the shadows like a fevered nightmare.

With the Wendigo as his guardian, there was little enough Colqhoun feared in life, but this feral tribe gave even him pause. The savages, while humanoid in appearance, differed from normal men in some unusual and alarming ways. The larger and more dominant of them had hog-like tusks sprouting from their faces, but the curious feature they all shared was the fact that none of them communicated via normal speech. From what Colqhoun could ascertain, their mouths were designed only for ingesting food, and their 'speech' – a mixture of screeches, whistles and roars – emanated entirely from some form of mutated appendage located in their throats. Accordingly, they could not communicate with him, nor he with them, and so the cannibal had to spend the rest of the long ride wondering exactly what fate the tribesmen intended for him.

They rode for the rest of the night and into the following day, finally arriving at a stretch of mountainous desert wasteland. The savages guided their horses through the winding nooks and crannies of the rocks, Colqhoun noting the array of sun-bleached human skulls that had been displayed – as markers, warnings? – along their route.

If he was not very much mistaken, they had now entered the Valley of Starving Men.

The desolate moan of the desert wind blowing through the mountains put in the cannibal in mind of his master's dreadful song, and he could feel a low vibration humming in his bones, the product of the ancient energies that flowed through the valley. By now, Colqhoun was certain that this site was a place of power for the Wendigo, a locus of absolute malignity and horror. Thinking back to the burial site he had glimpsed in his vision, he realised that it must have been constructed by these same creatures: fellow disciples of the same terrible deity he himself served.

They finally arrived at the tribe's lair, a series of interlinked caves situated deep within the mountains, and they led him inside to a large central chamber, littered with skeletal remains. In the centre of the space, a large and ornate throne had been constructed entirely out of human bones and sinew. Although grisly in its aspect, Colqhoun had to admire the painstaking craftsmanship that had gone into the throne's making; it demonstrated a level of morbid artistry that he would not previously have considered these creatures capable of.

The largest of the tribe, doubtless their chieftain, took Colqhoun's arm and guided him insistently towards the throne, barking loudly and gesturing for him to sit. But as much as he ascribed to the notion of his own natural supremacy, something still held the cannibal back. For if he took the proffered place upon the throne, what *else* might he be accepting…?

Letting out a squeal of discontent, the chieftain grabbed him by the shoulders and shoved him forcibly down onto the seat.

Apparently, Colqhoun's kingly destiny had already been decided for him.

The assembled creatures prostrated themselves before their new ruler, letting out a chorus of shrieks and bellows that Colqhoun decided must be intended as a song of devotion, however gratingly discordant it might be. It seemed as though his master had guided him to this valley with the express intention that he should rule over this monstrous tribe; they recognised that he bore the indelible mark of the Wendigo, and as such, viewed him as the entity's divine avatar.

Thankfully, the musical tribute did not last for too long, and as soon as it had climaxed, two of the savages left the chamber, returning with an offering for their newly anointed king: the freshly-killed corpse of a small boy. Reverentially, they placed the body at his feet and withdrew. It had been some time since Colqhoun had dined on fresh meat, and his mouth began to water uncontrollably. Somewhere in the back of his mind, he could hear the Wendigo howling its approval.

Very well, then. He would accept the tribute, and all that came with it.

He ate.

Time passed, and Colqhoun learned more about his new kingdom. The tribe numbered only about a dozen warriors, with two females kept as brood mares. The males were strong, fast and completely without mercy, and the cannibal began to fantasise about what he might accomplish at the head of an army comprised of such creatures. Surely nothing could stand against such a force; he could expand the limits of his realm far beyond this godforsaken valley and realise his own manifest destiny.

But much to his chagrin, Colqhoun discovered that birthing rates in the tribe were far too low to support such ambitions. The two females were sickly, crippled things, the males having blinded them and amputated all of their limbs. And although the tribesmen saw to it that they were kept in an almost continual state of pregnancy, very few of the offspring were ever carried to term. More often than not, the deformed, stillborn fetuses were delivered and deposited straight into a stew; a delicacy relished by the savages but which Colqhoun, demonstrating an uncharacteristic squeamishness, habitually declined.

Before long, the cannibal began to chafe at the limits imposed upon his rule. While his kingly belly always remained full – a regular procession of unwary travellers kept the tribe's dining table well-replenished – in most other respects, he was more of a prisoner than a ruler. Although Colqhoun liked to believe he possessed an appropriate disdain for his fellow man, such misanthropy soon wore thin when you were surrounded by brutish abominations that were, for all intents and purposes, entirely mute. He also found himself plagued by a persistent carnal itch that he had no way of scratching – the warriors had offered him the use of their females, but despite his nagging compulsion, it was a moral and ethical leap even Colqhoun was quite unwilling to make.

He therefore decided to set out for the nearest town, some three days' ride from the valley. He would steal away in the dead of night, take one of the tribe's horses, and be away before they ever realised he had gone. Colqhoun told himself that he was not necessarily abandoning his kingdom for good; he merely required a few days of sociable drinking and whoring to recalibrate his mental and spiritual wellbeing. Once he was fully restored, he could then begin to properly consider his situation and make some important decisions about his future.

The initial stages of his scheme went exactly as planned, but things fell apart quickly after that. After escaping the tribe's lair, Colqhoun rode for the rest of the night and half of the following day before exhaustion eventually claimed him. Concealing himself and his horse within a thicket of trees, he settled down to snatch a few hours' sleep. However, he soon found his dreams interrupted, awakening to find two of the savages standing over him with weapons poised. Before he could do any more than let out a startled yelp, one of them brought the butt of his tomahawk crashing down onto Colqhoun's skull, and the cannibal knew nothing more until he finally came around the next night, to find himself back in his bed of furs and straw at the tribe's lair.

He would mount various other escape attempts over the following years, but always found his efforts stymied, no matter how cunning he thought them to be. Colqhoun supposed this was the price he must pay for being the Wendigo's catspaw; the entity wanted him to remain precisely where he was, receiving the worship and tributes it believed were its due, and always saw to it that any plans he entertained about interrupting that particular state of affairs were unerringly quashed.

Utterly trapped, the cannibal sank into a deep, unrelenting melancholy. Suicide seemed to be the only possible means of escape available to him, but Colqhoun knew his master would only drag him forcibly back from the grave once again if he attempted it. Unsurprisingly, his chronic melancholia led to a much dulled appetite, but even his attempts to refuse food were met with furious reprisals by the Wendigo, who would scream and claw inside Colqhoun's skull until he thought his head might burst.

It appeared as though his only remaining option might simply be to wait to die of old age, but the restorative qualities of his obscene diet meant that the cannibal aged at a far slower rate than normal human beings. So it was that even after nearly half a century serving as the tribe's king, Colqhoun still had the appearance of a healthy middle-aged man.

After so many long years, he had all but given up hope of escaping the dread bargain he had made. He moved through each day as a sheep might meander across a meadow; slow and dull-witted, occasionally pausing to graze at whatever morsels it found under its nose. The recklessly depraved life Colqhoun had once led, his once-fervent ambitions to slaughter and conquer; all might have been dimly-remembered childhood stories for what little they meant to him now.

And then, one day, everything changed.

Two bushwhackers had stumbled upon the tribe's sacred burial site, lingering long enough to attract the attentions of the tribesmen themselves. Unsurprisingly, their ill-starred transgression was swiftly met with murderous reprisal. But although one of the men perished at the hands of the warriors, the other managed to escape. Terrified by what he had seen in the valley, the thief fled for the nearest settlement: the small town of Bright Hope.

Colqhoun berated the savages for their failure. *They will hear about us now!* he screamed. *Men will come here with their guns to kill us all!* Secretly, he hoped it might even be the case, but apparently his tirade had been compelling enough to provoke the tribe into sending out a raiding party. Several warriors departed for Bright Hope in pursuit of their quarry, and when they returned, they had captured not only the luckless thief, but also a deputy and a young woman. Not wishing to be seen by the captives, Colqhoun waited until they were asleep, then went to peer at them through the bars of their cages.

The woman was attractive, and wore a gold band on her finger. That was enough to tell the cannibal all he needed to know. No one in Bright Hope would have given a damn about the thief, and even the deputy's abduction might have been regretfully deemed a hazard of the job. But the woman? Her vengeful husband would doubtless come after her, and bring others with him.

Perhaps this was the opportunity Colqhoun needed, after so many years spent in a black daze.

He did not have to wait very much longer. Some days later, more intruders arrived in the valley – Bright Hope's sheriff, and two other men. However, although they had come prepared to fight, the posse had not reckoned with the ferocity of the monstrous tribespeople. A fierce skirmish broke out, and while three of the savages lay dead at the end of it, one of the townsfolk had also been killed, and the other two captured.

Colqhoun cursed his ill-fortune, although he was certain more men would follow in time. The tribe had foolishly drawn the attentions of western civilisation down upon them, and would now pay the price. A new age was dawning, an age in which dark things such as he and the savages would be forced to conceal themselves in the shadows, lest they be exterminated, just as America's native tribes had been exterminated.

Such was the price of civilisation.

In the end, Colqhoun did not have to wait very much longer for his deliverance. It turned out that the woman's husband had not been amongst the initial posse, and although crippled by a broken leg, he had followed them to the Valley of Starving Men. His cunning, and the resourcefulness of the surviving captives, enabled them to overcome the rest of the tribespeople.

The cannibal had made sure to absent himself from the battle, and when he emerged from his hiding place, it was to find all of the Wendigo's monstrous disciples dead, save for the two unfortunate females. He could hear his master screaming in rage over the loss of his congregation, but what could Colqhoun do? There was no sense in him remaining here now, not if he was to continue satisfying the Wendigo's hunger. Gathering up his few belongings, he prepared to depart the valley. Over the preceding years, he had at least possessed the wherewithal to amass a tidy nest egg of cash and other valuables taken from the tribe's victims; the savages themselves had no need of such things, and had been happy enough to present them as offerings to their king.

Colqhoun had money in his pocket, and the fresh taste of freedom in his lungs. A new world awaited him.

As he made to vacate the lair, he came across the sheriff of Bright Hope, mortally injured and on the verge of expiring from his wounds. The man stared at Colqhoun in amazement, and not a little disgust, the cannibal having let his standards of personal hygiene slip during his long decades with the tribe.

Who the hell are you? the dying sheriff wheezed. *You're not one of those goddamn monstrosities.*

I was their king, Colqhoun said, a trace of sadness in his voice.

Their king?!? Appalled, the sheriff struggled to sit upright. *Those hell-spawned bastards killed some damn good men. I should crown you with a bullet for such talk!*

The man fumbled for his revolver, only to find he had already emptied it during the fighting. *Goddamn it,* he bellowed, flinging the useless weapon in Colqhoun's direction.

I must be leaving you now, sheriff, the cannibal told him with a mocking bow. *It's been a great many years since I last set foot in the outside world, and I must go forth and preach my gospel.*

Leaving the wounded man raging hopelessly behind him, Colqhoun set out on his journey. He had no particular destination in mind, content for now to reacquaint himself with the benefits of civilisation – a hot bath, a stiff drink, a comfortable bed, preferably with a loose woman to help keep it warm – but also mindful of the fact that one such as he could never truly be part of such a world. When it came time for him to feed again, he would have to retreat to the wilderness, but that particular realm had become vanishingly small in comparison to what he remembered; the American frontier having now been all but conquered.

For months he drifted, observing the various changes that had come to the country during his enforced absence. The more he saw, the more Colqhoun began to think he should finally make a home for himself; somewhere private enough that he could continue his activities unhindered. Despite his unnatural longevity, he could feel the frost of old age beginning to settle into his bones, and knew he could not continue to roam as freely as he once had done. Perhaps he could even start a family; find a wife to bear him sons he could raise in the ways of the Wendigo. In this fashion, he could gift his master with a whole new clan of disciples; one far better equipped to survive in this rapidly-changing modern world.

Sitting alone by his campfire one night, Colqhoun became aware of a stealthy presence observing him from the shadows. He instantly sprang to his feet and pulled his revolver, aiming it into the darkness. *Announce yourself!* he bellowed. *Announce yourself or I shoot!*

There was silence for a moment, and then a man stepped into the glow of the firelight, his hands held in the air. He was tall and dressed entirely in black, his face so pale it gave Colqhoun the impression that it might melt like snow if he moved too close to the flames.

My name's Robey, the man said. *Drake Robey.*

What's your business here, Robey? Colqhoun demanded.

The man smiled, although it seemed to Colqhoun he was very careful not to display his teeth. *Just some companionship,* he said. *Perhaps a bite to eat, if you can spare it.*

I don't have any food to share, but you're welcome to warm yourself by my fire, Colqhoun said, all the while thinking to himself, *Once you're dead, I won't have to share you with a soul.*

Robey squatted down opposite his host, watching Colqhoun carefully through the flames. His eyes gleamed silver in the firelight.

Neither said a word, but after only a few moments in each other's company, both men quickly recognised they each carried a whiff of the grave about them.

Colqhoun laughed at the irony of it. *I guess we'll both go hungry tonight.*

Robey smiled again, this time displaying the sharp canines he had so deliberately concealed. *I guess so.*

Now that the two predators had ruled each other out as prospective prey, there seemed little more for them to discuss. Robey climbed back to his feet, his face thoughtful. *Which way are you headed, friend?* he suddenly enquired. *It occurs to me it might be wise if we chose separate feeding grounds.*

Colqhoun couldn't argue the wisdom of this, but as yet, had no particular destination in mind. *Right now, wherever the wind takes me,* he replied. *I'm looking for someplace to settle down.*

The other man considered this. *Go to Texas, would be my advice,* he finally said. *The eating is good, and folk there know how to mind their own business.*

Colqhoun nodded. *Thank you for your counsel, friend. I'll certainly consider it.*

The words had barely left his lips when Robey faded into darkness and was gone, like the moon vanishing behind a cloud.

The cannibal slept on the matter, and when he awoke the next morning, decided to follow Robey's advice. After all, it was not often he had the opportunity to confer with someone conversant with his particular proclivities. Packing up his camp, he set out for Texas.

Upon entering the state some weeks later, Colqhoun decided to visit its capital city for a few days. Wandering the streets of Austin, he quickly grew convinced that he had indeed found an appropriate location for him to settle. Texas was still wild enough to accommodate men of his dubious ilk, not to mention obsessed with somewhat questionable notions of personal liberty; notions that would inadvertently serve to shelter Colqhoun's true nature from the unwelcome attentions of the law.

The cannibal left Austin and headed out into the surrounding territory first thing the next morning. He could feel the land calling to him; so much blood had been spilt here that Colqhoun could feel the primal power of it coursing through the soil. There was a magic in man's lifeblood, the same dark magic that had sustained him throughout the long decades of his unnatural existence.

And so the matter was decided; he would settle here and continue to feed the land, and trusted that it would do the same for him and his kin in return.

Encountering a homesteader named Hardesty, Colqhoun learned that the acreage next to the man's property was up for sale. Although he disliked the idea of having a neighbour, both properties were large and isolated enough to permit the cannibal to operate in complete seclusion; not to mention that Hardesty was a Texan born-and-bred, and as such, understood the sanctity of another man's privacy.

Colqhoun strode out into the empty fields, imagining the life he would build here. First, a large comfortable house for his family, pristine and white and outwardly respectable, all the better to conceal the horrors its four walls would contain. Then, a business to support his kinfolk; perhaps a slaughterhouse, he thought. After all, who understood the ways of meat better than he?

He lay down in the tall grass, allowing his mind to drift free of his body. As his consciousness rose into the aether and merged with that of the Wendigo, the entity permitted Colqhoun a glimpse into the distant future, at a time when everything he imagined had come to pass.

He saw a ghastly house, festooned with blood, bone and sinew; its four walls suffused with dying screams, the air reeking of carrion and torment.

He saw his family gathered together at the dinner table, laden with a unspeakable feast of glistening human meat.

He saw his two devoted grandsons; one a deranged fool, the other a lumbering masked brute.

And finally, he saw himself: aged beyond all comprehension, his cankerous skin shrivelled like a fruit left out in the sun. But still breathing nonetheless; still thirsting for the blood of man.

As the grisly vision unfolded before his eyes, the Wendigo howled its approval, and embracing the bestial madness that lay festering at his core, Colqhoun howled along with it.

JESSE HOOKER

Lance Henrikson in Near Dark, *1987*
written by Eric Red & Kathryn Bigelow
directed by Kathryn Bigelow

WHEN CAPTAIN WISHBONE CUTTER CAME CALLING AT HIS WOODLAND cabin on that hot July morning, Jesse Hooker was in the midst of trying to sleep off a howling bitch of a rotgut hangover. Even on his better days, which were admittedly few and far between, Jesse had a well-earned reputation as being meaner than a rabid wolverine, and under normal circumstances, any unfortunate soul who had the effrontery to wake him after a heavy night's drinking would be put straight to sleep themselves. Only difference being, they'd never wake up.

Still, Jesse would never dream of raising a hand to Captain Cutter, no matter that his head was shrieking like a bobcat in heat. For one thing, he'd served under Cutter in the Confederate Army, and while they might have lost the damned war, Jesse had the captain to thank for not having lost his miserable life into the bargain. And besides, you didn't raise a hand to the likes of Wishbone Cutter, not if you wanted to keep wiping your ass with that hand you didn't. Even Jesse, who'd been in an ill temper ever since the moment he slithered from between his mother's loins, had to admit he'd learned a thing or two about the art of being a sadistic bastard during the years he'd spent serving under the man.

Cutter prodded Jesse's prone body with the tip of his boot. *Is this how you greet your superior officer, Hooker?* he bellowed. *Lying on your scrawny ass in bed? Jesus H. Christ, it's no wonder we lost to the bluebellies.*

Jesse rolled over onto his side and spat onto the floorboards, hoping that the act would improve the foul taste in his mouth. It didn't. *Unless you're planning to fight the war all over again, Captain, I got no better place to be than here,* he replied.

The other man grinned, and extended a hand towards Jesse. His own hand trembling like a dandelion, Jesse accepted the handshake. Cutter's grip was strong as a bear trap, but his eyes brimmed with a bitter loss. He sighed. *The war is lost, Hooker. It was a noble cause, but nobility alone doesn't win battles. I have my eye on bigger prizes now.*

Jesse struggled to an upright position, fumbling for the bottle of moonshine placed next to his mattress. Taking a drink of the tepid liquid, he swished it around his mouth for a few seconds, then swallowed with a grimace and offered the bottle to Cutter. *To the South,* he croaked.

Accepting the bottle, Cutter raised it in the air. *To the South,* he said quietly, before taking a mouthful.

The shot of moonshine finally helped to cut through the cacophony inside Jesse's skull. He glanced up at the captain, his heavy-lidded eyes blinking warily. *Now, what's all this about prizes?*

He listened as Cutter told him a story about a cache of lost diamonds, hidden away somewhere on a haunted mountain in Arkansas. As he continued with his tale, Cutter kept pulling on the bottle, his face growing increasingly ruddy and excited. A part of Jesse wished he could get swept up in the captain's fervour, but what he saw standing before him was a desperate man who had lost everything that had given his life meaning: a war, a wife, a house. All that was left for him now was to go on some damn fool treasure hunt.

But to what end? Those diamonds weren't going to buy Cutter's woman back from the bluebelly who'd stolen her heart, nor win the goddamn war. As far as Jesse could see, all they were likely to do was get Cutter killed. And maybe that was the real point of it, when all was said and done.

As the captain finished his story, he handed the bottle back to Jesse. *So will you join me?* he asked.

Jesse took a long swallow of moonshine. *I've heard stories about that mountain*, he said finally. *That's Indian territory.*

Injuns, Cutter said dismissively, spitting the word out like it was a curse.

But even the Indians won't set foot up there. They call it The Mountain of Demons.

The captain cackled. *Don't tell me a no-good murdering bastard like Jesse Hooker is scared of haints!*

I ain't scared of nothing, Cutter, Jesse murmured. *What I am is smart enough not to go any place bad enough to scare an Indian. Those sons of bitches don't scare easy. But what they know, and any good Southerner knows, and what the fucking Yankees never will, is that this is old, old country, Cutter. And old, old things still live here. Now you take my advice, Captain, and you leave them be.*

So you won't join me? Cutter gazed at him, incredulous.

Jesse shook his head. *I'm sorry, Captain. I got better things to do than risk my body and soul over a few rocks, no matter how pretty.*

Such as? Sitting around this shithole drinking that rotgut until your liver bursts?

Jesse fixed Cutter with a lizard stare. *No. I guess I just ain't done killing yet.*

The captain turned and kicked out at a nearby stool, sending it flying off into the corner. *Damn you and damn your killing, Hooker! We lost the war, understand? Don't matter how long you lie around in this cabin and dream, you ain't gonna make it otherwise. Men like us, we need to take something for ourselves now.*

Jesse raised the bottle of moonshine in a sardonic toast. *The South will rise again, Captain.*

Fuck you, and fuck the South, Cutter snarled, before turning on his heels and stalking from the cabin.

As Jesse watched him exit, he knew he would never see Cutter again. He supposed it would have been far better for everyone if the captain had simply fallen in battle. That way, he would've died a hero, at least to the people who cared about such things. Maybe one day they'd even have erected a statue in his name. But now, he'd just ride off into the wilderness and disappear without a trace. And if Cutter's name did survive, it would only be as a cautionary tale whispered amongst impressionable children. *Cap'n Wishbone Cutter rode up that trail and never came back. I hear his unquiet ghost still haunts Demon Mountain.*

Regardless, the captain had a point. Jesse couldn't just sit around here drinking for the rest of his days. Sure, he had a powerful thirst for booze, but no amount of moonshine could hope to slake the *other* thirst that gripped him, the thirst for blood that had been heightened by all the war and all the killing he'd seen over the past few years. On the other hand, he wasn't dumb enough to go renegade. His old buddy Amison had tried that, banding together with a gang of degenerate ex-soldiers to rob and kill bluebellies, and had ended up in front of a Yankee firing squad for his trouble. Or there was that gunfighter Josey Wales, who everyone said was the fastest draw alive, but being fast hadn't saved him from being chased halfway across the country by Captain Terrill and his Red Legs.

No, there had to be a better way.

The next week, Jesse rode into town and hitched his horse outside the sheriff's office, where he began to inspect the wanted posters hanging on the noticeboard. His eyes scanned the assembled faces, mostly petty criminals with bounties of a hundred bucks or less. But Jesse Hooker didn't risk his neck for no one hundred goddamn dollars.

Then he saw it: an image of a dark-featured man staring back at him from the wall. Underneath, the poster read: 'WANTED: $1000 REWARD'

There was something about the man's eyes Jesse couldn't shake; even in the poorly-printed reproduction, they were piercing enough that the outlaw might have been standing right there before him. Close enough for Jesse to smell his cologne, close enough for the man to gaze mockingly down into his soul, taunting him with forbidden secrets. *Are you man enough to take me, Jesse? Are you evil enough? It takes an evil man to fight real evil, did you know that?*

Jesse snatched the poster from the wall. For a thousand bucks, he'd be evil enough to shame the Devil. Christ, if someone had that big of a bounty on their head, it didn't matter what the hell you did to them, as long as they were dead at the end of it.

Then he heard a voice from behind him; a deep, weathered voice that sounded like it had been left out in the rain too long. *Son, you fixing to go up against Drake Robey on your own?*

Jesse span around to discover a skinny old preacher watching him, an amused smirk creasing his already deeply-lined face. *And what business is it of yours if I am, padre?* he snarled.

The preacher raised his hands placatingly. *Just wanted to make sure you knew what you were fixing to go up against, son. They say he's in league with Satan, you know. They say he can't be killed.*

Ain't never come across man nor beast that can't be killed, Jesse scoffed. *All you need's a steady hand and a cold heart.*

The old man gazed up to the heavens. '*Do not be lifted up in pride, but have fear.' Romans 11:20.* He took a step towards Jesse, his voice taking on a businesslike tone. *Son, if Robey is even half as dangerous as they say, does it not strike you that a partnership might be of considerable benefit to us both?*

Jesse goggled at him. *Me, partner with you? A goddamn preacher?*

Son, do not be fooled by these shabby vestments, the preacher replied. *Even a man who dedicates himself to the Lord's work has to get his hands dirty occasionally. 'And I shall bring a sword upon you, that shall avenge the quarrel of my covenant…'*

Jesse cut him off with a curt gesture. *Spare me the sermon, old man.* He considered the offer for a moment. The preacher might have a point, he decided. And when it came to splitting the reward, well. An old fool who'd swapped his brains for the Bible would be a hell of a lot easier to deal with by himself than a stone killer like Robey.

His eyes met the old man's. *Okay, you got yourself a deal. We cut everything straight down the middle, right?*

The preacher doffed his hat and bowed. *It shall be thus,* he murmured.

And so began the curious partnership between Jesse Hooker and the man known as the Reverend Simms. As Jesse was soon to discover, his new partner was not an ordained priest at all, but merely an eccentric bounty killer who felt the need to justify his murderous vocation with constant recourse to biblical quotes, of which he possessed a seemingly never-ending supply. For his part, Jesse didn't give a damn what excuses the Reverend made; they were both killers, pure and simple, and as far as he was concerned, the pleasure of sending one more asshole off to whatever reward awaited him in the afterlife was all the justification he needed.

After all, Jesse reasoned, there were an awful lot of assholes in the world.

One thing that did give him pause was the old man's morbid habit of removing the heads of his kills and preserving them in a barrel of brine attached to the side of his wagon. As someone well acquainted with the boundless horrors of war, Jesse had seen more than his fair share of atrocities in his time – hell, he'd committed several dozen himself – but even he drew the line somewhere. Simms defended his ghastly predilection by arguing that he needed to provide proof in order to claim his bounties, and he could hardly be expected to drag an entire rotting corpse across the prairies for weeks on end, now could he?

It was a convincing enough story, Jesse supposed, but he knew there was more to it than the preacher admitted. He'd watched Simms take the heads out late at night, when he thought Jesse was safely asleep, and hold lengthy conversations with them, putting on a different voice for each head. In all honesty, it gave Jesse a hefty fucking dose of the creeps, and he fervently looked forward to the day he could send the Reverend off to meet the heavenly Maker whose Word he was so fond of quoting.

They rode in pursuit of Robey for several weeks, crossing the Southern States without finding a trace of him. During this time, the Reverend Simms was much given to muttering darkly about the supernatural abilities of their quarry. Jesse might've thought Wishbone Cutter a fool for disregarding the old Indian legends, but neither did that mean he believed every last wives' tale Simms told him about Robey during their long journey. *Drake Robey rose from the dead. Drake Robey doesn't cast a shadow. Drake Robey drinks the blood of women and children.* As far as Jesse was concerned, Robey was just another man, albeit a dangerous one. And while dangerous men often saw fit to burnish their legends with outlandish tales, they died just as quick as anyone else once you sank a few bullets into them.

Still, he was forced to admit that it did at times seem as though they might be chasing a ghost. All they ever heard of Robey was a whispered rumour here, a drunken saloon story there. No one ever seemed to have clapped eyes on him; no one still living, anyway. By the time they reached Alabama, Jesse was about ready to give up the chase. They were no closer to finding Robey, and he was growing pig sick of the old man and his constant preaching.

One cloudless night, the two bounty killers were sitting quietly by their campfire: Simms contentedly smoking a cigar, Jesse relishing the momentary peace afforded him by the preacher's wordless pleasure. But the next moment, the old man turned to him and fixed him with a flinty stare. *You know, son, I think we are drawing close to him*, he announced. *I can feel the chill of evil in my bones.*

Horseshit, Jesse said simply.

Simms climbed to his feet. *You must repent*, he told Jesse. *If we are to triumph in the battle ahead, we must engage the enemy with a clear conscience and a soul that is free from sin. Let us both confess to the Lord now, and seek His absolution for our crimes.*

Jesse spat into the flames. *Who says I'm a sinner?* he demanded, before adding sarcastically: *I thought we were out here doing the Lord's work, old man.*

The preacher squinted in the firelight. *You fought for the South, did you not?*

Proudly, said Jesse, leaping upright and going eyeball to eyeball with Simms. *And I would gladly do so again. You telling me that's a sin?*

Simms raised his wizened fist in the air. '*Stand fast therefore in the liberty by which Christ has made us free, and do not be entangled again with a yoke of bondage!*' he thundered. *Galatians 5:1!*

Jesse pondered the preacher's words for a moment. He couldn't really make head nor tail of them, but supposed they had something to do with slavery.

I don't recall the Bible saying nothing about niggers, he said finally.

The preacher thrust his face angrily into Jesse's. *For we were all baptized by one Spirit so as to form one body – whether Jews or Gentiles, slave or free – and we were all given the one Spirit to drink!* he bellowed.

His patience finally at an end, Jesse punched Simms squarely in the nose.

The old man collapsed to the dirt, barely missing the fire. He gazed up at his attacker, mouth silently opening and closing like a landed fish.

Jesse pointed a finger at him. *I don't want to hear one more word outta you, old man,* he instructed Simms. *Nothing more about liberty or bondage or spirits. And certainly nothing about goddamn niggers.* His face twisted with loathing. *You breathe another single fuckin' word, and I leave your skinny ass behind, to repent all on your lonesome. And you can see how far you get with Drake Robey then.*

Nothing more was said between them for the rest of the night, nor the following morning. When they reached the next town, they each took separate rooms in the hotel, Simms immediately retiring upstairs for the rest of the day. Jesse remained down in the saloon, working his way through a bottle of whisky and growing steadily meaner with every sip. He knew he should just get the hell out of here and head straight back to his cabin, where he didn't have to suffer anyone else's damn fool talk. The whole journey had been a fucking waste; next time he'd settle for a quick and easy hundred dollar bounty on some drunken cowhand and be done with it. Tonight, he'd treat himself to a whore and a hot bath, and be on his way in the morning. Let Reverend Simms chase his damn ghosts all the way into Hell, if he pleased.

He sat drinking for a while longer, until the sky outside began to darken and his bladder had started to swell uncomfortably. Jesse eased himself down from his barstool and staggered off in the direction of the outhouse. He already regretted having had so much to drink, but he'd piss out what he could now, sweat the rest of it out in the bath, and leave himself in fine fettle to spend the rest of the evening entertaining whatever the local whorehouse had to offer in the way of female company.

As Jesse exited through the saloon's back door, he caught sight of a shadowy figure creeping towards him, and his hand flew to the butt of his gun. *Who's that there?* he demanded. *Speak up, or I'll shoot!*

A sallow-faced man emerged from the darkness, his hands raised in the air. Jesse saw that both the man's hands and his gun holster were empty, and relaxed somewhat.

My name's William, the man said in a soft, papery voice. *I hear you're hunting Drake Robey. Well, I know where he is.*

Is that so? said Jesse carefully. *And how do you know I'm hunting Robey?*

Look, do you want him or not? William hissed. *I don't have much time!*

Jesse suddenly noticed how empty the other man's eyes looked. He'd seen more life in a rattlesnake's gaze. *I want him,* he said finally. *How much is it gonna cost me?*

William laughed, a hollow, emotionless sound. *I got no use for your money,* he said. *Robey's holed up in the old plantation outside of town. Take him or don't, it makes no odds to me. I'm just delivering a message.* With that, he immediately began to melt back into the shadows, ignoring Jesse's shouted imprecation. *Hey, wait! What message? Who told you to send it?*

But William had vanished into nothingness, like a footprint in a howling blizzard.

All thoughts of whores and personal hygiene gone from his mind, Jesse quickly pissed against the back wall of the saloon, then hurried back inside to speak to Simms. Stumbling up the staircase, he arrived at the reverend's door and began to beat upon it with his fist. *Simms! We got him, ya hear? We got the sonofabitch!*

There was a pause, before the door slowly creaked open to reveal the old man's gaunt, expressionless face. He gave Jesse a searching look. *Son, you smell of drink,* he said finally.

Never mind that! Jesse snapped. *Robey's hiding out in an old plantation, just outside of town. If we leave now, we can get him before he even knows we're coming.*

Simms considered this. *If Robey is a creature of darkness,* he murmured, *then his powers will be at their height now. We should wait until morning. And that way, you'll have a chance to sleep your drunk off.*

Fuck that! Jesse shouted. *We wait till morning and we might lose him again!*

I've made my decision, son, the reverend replied, before firmly closing the door in Jesse's face.

Fuckin' coward! Jesse screamed, unleashing a volley of blows and kicks upon the woodwork. But the door held fast, and did not reopen.

There was nothing else for it; he would have to take down Robey alone. It was a shame the old buzzard wouldn't be there to draw the outlaw's fire, but at least it would save Jesse the price of an extra bullet had Simms survived. And hell, Robey would never even know what hit him. Like old Wishbone Cutter always said, the element of surprise is half the battle. Jesse could almost smell that thousand bucks now. It smelt good, better than sweet young pussy even.

He mounted up and rode out of town, encountering nothing but shadows on his way. It took him less than an hour to ride to the plantation. Upon his arrival there, Jesse found a gloomy old mansion house, surrounded by a field of dead corn. Dismounting at the periphery of the property, he hitched his horse to a rotting fencepost and began to creep through the rows towards the main house, the dessicated husks of the plants whispering in unison around him.

As he moved deeper into the field, he came across a crucified scarecrow, suspended over the corn as if it were Christ the Redeemer gazing down at his flock. The damned thing looked so lifelike that Jesse almost thought it might start crying up to the heavens at any moment: *My God, my God, why hast thou forsaken me?* Simms would probably have loved it.

Maybe it was just the old man's superstitious nonsense preying on his nerves, but the plantation was starting to get to Jesse. The whole place felt *bad* somehow, as if whatever had killed the corn had spilled up into the air and polluted the entire atmosphere. He could feel his nerves beginning to fray, like a row of embroidered stitches being slowly unpicked, one by one. The sooner he dealt with Robey and got the hell out of here, the better. Doing his best to ignore the constant whispers of the corn, and the stealthy rustles that gave the impression of something moving through the rows alongside him, keeping pace with his every step, Jesse continued onwards.

When he reached the mansion, he drew his pistol and began to circle the house, peering through the windows for any sign of Robey. But he saw no lights burning, heard no sounds of occupation. He might as well have been walking through a bone orchard. The damn place couldn't be any more than thirty years old and it had just been left to rot. What in God's name had happened here?

Fuck it, Jesse decided. If Robey was somewhere in the house, he must be sleeping the sleep of the dead. In which case, it would be an awful shame to wake him.

Or maybe he's just sitting in the dark waiting for you, a voice whispered in the back of his mind. *Hungry eyes gleaming silver in the moonlight.*

Bullshit, Jesse murmured to himself. Mounting the steps to the back porch, he tried the rear entrance to the house and found it open. His heart slithering into his mouth, he plunged into the darkened interior.

The air inside the house was dry and unpleasant, a faint coppery taste lingering on Jesse's tongue. He stifled the urge to cough and spit, and instead pressed on with his search, moving from room to room like a prowling coyote, finding each one deserted. Jesse began to wonder whether he was simply barking at a knot. The place felt abandoned, utterly without life, as though no one had so much as drawn breath here in years. As he moved through the downstairs rooms, he came across various discarded items – a set of saddlebags, some old clothes – that suggested people had once stayed in the house, but the sheer amount of dust on them told him their visit had not been recent. Jesse could feel a hot coal of anger igniting in his belly. By God, if that pale-faced freak William had chiseled him, he would ride back to town and take it out of the boy's hide. And maybe he'd plug a bullet in the Reverend Simms too, just for the pure satisfaction of it.

Finding the door to the cellar hanging open, Jesse paused and peered down into the darkness below. If Robey was in the house, it was surely more likely he was sound asleep upstairs, rather than hiding out in a cold dirty basement. But what if the whole thing was an ambush? Maybe William had been setting him up all along, and Robey was just waiting down there, biding his time. And as soon as Jesse turned around and headed upstairs, Robey would creep up behind him and...

The darkness from the cellar suddenly seemed to envelop him, filling Jesse's skull until his thoughts felt like they were receding away to nothing, adrift in an abyssal void. He could feel his guts dissolving to water, and immediately recoiled at his own weakness. Jesse Hooker wasn't no yellow-bellied coward; it was this godforsaken place putting idiot notions in his head. There was deviltry in the air, he was sure of that now. He thought of Wishbone Cutter riding off to his doom on Demon Mountain, and suddenly wished to God he'd gone with him. At least then he'd have died with a good man by his side, damn fool treasure hunt or not.

Because he *was* going to die here, wasn't he? If there was one thing Jesse was now certain of, it was that his own end was imminent. That's all this damned plantation was, he finally realised: a killing floor for the unwary.

Whimpering, he stumbled back from the cellar doorway and turned around, only to see a demonic face come screaming at him from out of the darkness. Eye sockets black and empty, mouth yawning impossibly wide and bristling with long sharp teeth.

Jesse screamed.

Throwing his arms up in front of his face, he felt a wave of irresistible force buffeting him, sending him flying backwards into the cellar. Down and down he fell, spiralling down into blackness until he was lost to the shadows and knew no more.

When Jesse eventually came to, the world was still dark. He could taste dirt on his tongue, feel cold earth pressing against his cheek, but his eyes might have been plucked from their sockets for all that they could tell him about his surroundings.

Then he heard a low chuckle from the darkness. *I understand you've been hunting me, Jesse.*

Blindly, Jesse began to fumble around for his gun. Striking lucky, he found it lying a few inches away from his right hand and immediately snatched it up. Aiming towards the voice, he fired once, then twice.

The two muzzle flashes briefly lit up the cellar interior, but there was no one standing in the bullet's path. The shot thudded harmlessly into the cellar wall, prompting a muttered curse from Jesse. But as the light faded away and he was plunged back into shadow, he heard the chuckle again, closer this time.

Or maybe you should be asking yourself whether I've *been hunting* you *all along,* the voice said. *Seeing as how it was me who sent that poor lost soul William out to bring you here.*

Show yourself, damn you! Jesse shouted.

There was silence for a moment, then he heard the scratch of a match. A light flared, then grew in intensity as the match was held to a lantern wick. Gradually, the cellar was filled with a warm, greasy light.

There, before him, stood Drake Robey. Dressed head to toe in black, skin white as virgin snow, eyes burning silver in the glow of the lantern.

His revolver still warm in his hand, Jesse raised it and fired again, directly at Robey this time. There was very little he was certain of in this terrible place, but he was at least still sure of his own aim, he knew that much.

But nothing happened. Robey merely smiled, showing a hint of teeth that were far too long, far too sharp.

Jesse heard the preacher's voice in his mind. *They say he can't be killed…*

It's all true, then? he croaked, the pistol falling from his limp fingers.

I'll allow that some of it is, Robey said modestly. *After all, a story never gets told the same way twice, and there have been quite a lot of stories told about me.*

Jesse heard a hideous screech coming from somewhere upstairs in the house. He couldn't decide whether it was the sound of a demon's ecstasy or that of a soul in torment, but realised that it probably mattered very little either way.

The next thing he realised was that he had pissed himself without noticing. *What is this fucking hellhole?* he moaned to Robey.

The gunfighter shrugged. *Evil was called up out of the earth,* he told Jesse. *Many men have died here. You can taste it in the air, can't you? But it wasn't my doing. No, it just called to me, as evil places will call to evil men. The creatures that dwell here leave me well enough alone. They know we serve the same master.* He smiled again. *But you? Well, that's quite another matter.*

Bastard! Jesse spat. *What's to become of me?*

Robey sauntered over to where he lay and squatted down beside him. *The way I see it, Jesse, you have two choices,* he murmured. *These devils will never let a single living soul leave this place. You were quite right to call it a hellhole. It's their very own private hell, and any soul unfortunate enough to stumble into it will be trapped here and tormented for all eternity. Just like poor William.*

Suddenly overpowered by an aching weariness, Jesse closed his eyes. *And the second choice?*

The second choice allows you to walk out of here. But you have to take my communion first. Live as I live. Feed as I feed.

Jesse opened his eyes again and glanced up at Robey, becoming lost in the gunfighter's silvery gaze, allowing himself to drown in its glittering waters. It felt good. Everything that was perplexing elsewhere was simple here; everything that was rotten and stinking in his life was suddenly rendered of no consequence whatsoever.

So when it came down to it, there was really no choice at all, was there? *Fuck it,* Jesse said.

As Robey bent down towards him, Jesse leant his head back, baring his throat. And when the world turned red a few short seconds later, it was the sweetest thing he had ever known.

When he awoke a few hours later, Jesse found himself alone. He could tell at once that Robey had gone from the house; somehow, his senses had been magnified to a state of almost unbearable acuteness. From down here in the cellar Jesse could hear the creak of the eaves in the attic; smell the vinous scent of kudzu carried aloft on the night breeze.

He climbed to his feet, revelling in the unholy strength flowing through his body. Everything they said of Robey was now also true of him, Jesse realised. He need fear no one, for how can you kill what's already dead?

Alongside his newfound power, he also felt a black craving seething in his guts, an unspeakable hunger he knew would have to be satisfied soon, and on every night to come. But that hardly mattered to Jesse; spilling other men's blood had never been a matter of any great consequence to him.

Ah, there would be so much blood, gushing redly forth in rivers and torrents, and what he did not take to fill his belly he would gladly give back to the earth. He imagined them running before him like frightened sheep, all the hated Yankees and niggers and the rest.

Jesse's dark laughter echoed through the empty cellar.

Oh yes, the South had risen again, all right.

LIZZY MACKLIN

Caitlin Gerard in The Wind, 2018
written by Teresa Sutherland
directed by Emma Tammi

IT WAS JANUARY IN NEW MEXICO, AND WITH THE PRAIRIE WIND CAME THE snows, blanketing everything in a pristine white silence that was as cold and lonely as death.

America had never seen anything like this great blizzard. Temperatures across the country plummeted to well below freezing, crops were decimated, and the waterways and railroads ground to a standstill. Those blessed with families and loved ones huddled together for warmth, and prayed for the coming of spring.

Alone in her prairie cabin, Lizzy Macklin had no one to keep her warm, and no longer saw any use in prayers. So she simply waited; either for death or the snow to thaw, whichever came first. In truth, the outcome mattered little to her. The only reason Lizzy had not already taken her own life was the fear that her unquiet spirit would then join the other shades doomed to wander the surrounding plains: those of her husband Isaac, and his young lover Emma. She could hear them singing to her at night, their voices mingling emptily with the wind that wailed incessantly around her cabin. Lizzy had killed them both; not, she would stubbornly insist (had there been anyone left alive to insist to) because of their adultery, and the unborn child it had spawned, but due to the plain and simple fact that they had both been possessed by prairie demons. She could not say whether the voices she heard at night belonged to their damned souls, or simply to devils maliciously imitating them, but reasoned that it hardly made any difference; either way, Lizzy had no wish to spend the rest of eternity in their company. She would therefore not rush to hasten her own demise, and should she eventually freeze to death in this hellish cold regardless, she only hoped that dying a natural death would allow her to finally find the peace she craved.

For two weeks, Lizzy barely moved from her place in front of the hearth, where she sat wrapped in a patchwork quilt, gazing into the flames and remembering. During that time, she ate and drank little, her limbs growing as thin as the kindling that she would intermittently feed to the fire. *Perhaps*, she thought, *if I sit here for long enough, my body might burst into flame too, and burn into ashes that would then rise up through the chimney spout and ascend to heaven.*

It was, Lizzy decided, about the only way she would ever get there.

January moved into February, and still the frozen purgatory outside her windows remained. She began to wonder whether she had in fact died without realising it, and if this was to be her final punishment, forever tormented by cold and loneliness and the cries of those she had murdered. Surely neither God nor Devil could have condemned her to a fate that was any more fitting.

But then, late one evening, she heard another voice calling to her from outside; a desperate voice, shivering audibly in the freezing wind, but irrefutably *alive*.

Hello in there! Hello!

Suspecting trickery, Lizzy snatched up her rifle and crossed to the front window. Through the gusting snow and darkness, she could just about make out a small hunched figure, visibly staggering against the force of the wind.

I need help! the figure cried. *My horse is dead, and I'll freeze to death out here if you don't let me in!*

Despite the blood already on her hands, Lizzy did not consider herself to be any sort of murderer. Killing Isaac and Emma had merely served to release them from their demonic thrall, and therefore hardly constituted so base and vile an act as murder. But to leave this man out in the blizzard – if man he was – would be tantamount to simply pointing her rifle at him and shooting him where he stood.

On the other hand, if this was yet another demon, allowing it into her home could be to invite her own damnation across the threshold.

Lizzy marched to the door, lifted the bolt, and hauled it open, straining to hold it firm against the force of the elements. Freezing shards of ice immediately began to pepper her face. Squinting through the storm, she raised her rifle in the man's direction and bellowed: *Identify yourself! Tell me your name and where you hail from!*

For an moment she thought her question had been lost to the wind, but then she heard his faint reply. *They call me Loco! I was riding down from Utah when I got caught in this damn blizzard!*

She gestured for him to come forward, keeping her gun raised. Holding his empty hands in the air, the man named Loco trudged heavily through the piled snow and stepped into the faint glow being cast through the open doorway. He was a small man, dressed in what looked like a priest's hat and a woman's fur coat. Stopping a few yards in front of Lizzy, he slowly lowered one hand and wiped the crusted snow from his face, careful not to make any sudden movements.

Lizzy kept the gun aimed at his chest, saying nothing.

Eventually, the man spoke again. *You must be getting cold, standing there without a coat,* he said. *Careful you don't catch a chill.*

I'll soon be a damn sight colder if I invite a killer into my home, Lizzy retorted.

Loco laughed. *I won't lie to you, madam. It's true, I have killed men. But only those who broke the law. You have nothing to fear from me.*

You're with the law?

Yes.

Lizzy gazed at him for a few more seconds, then lowered her rifle and nodded her head. Stepping back into the cabin, she allowed Loco to enter, then shoved the door closed once more.

Stamping his feet heavily, Loco thumped over to the fireplace and began to warm himself. Lizzy watched in silence as the little man marched up and down in front of the flames, the snow encrusting his hat and coat quickly melting and puddling around him on the floor.

When the heat had finally restored him, he turned to face Lizzy and took off his hat, revealing a shock of blond hair and a face as gaunt as a corpse. At the sight of him, Lizzy let out a small gasp. If Loco were indeed just a man, he looked more like a demon than any hellspawn she had yet encountered. His blue eyes were colder and crueller than any ice storm and possessed not an ounce of human feeling that she could discern. Instinctively, her hands tightened around the rifle.

Loco looked at her closely. *You look startled, madam,* he said quietly. In contrast to his malevolent appearance, his voice was soft, almost girlish.

Well, you *don't look much like a lawman,* Lizzy snapped back.

The man smiled and gave a knowing shrug. *I do serve the law, but not in any elected capacity,* he admitted. *And I'm afraid the rigours of my chosen profession may have coarsened me somewhat. But believe me when I say that I work harder to uphold justice than any of the good-for-nothing lawmen I've crossed paths with.*

Realisation dawned. *You're a bounty hunter,* Lizzy said flatly.

Loco nodded. *Or was, at least. Times are changing, and I fear my kind may no longer be welcome in the West.*

This concern did not prevent Loco from making himself welcome in Lizzy's cabin, however. As she looked on silently, he brushed off his coat and settled down into a chair in front of the fire, before finally resuming his spiel. *My plan was to head back east and seek a quiet place to retire, until I was set upon by this devilish blizzard. When my horse succumbed to the cold, I believed my days were numbered. For a moment, I felt a black figure at my shoulder, beckoning me.* A look of fear flashed in the bounty hunter's eyes, and he gave a fleeting glance towards the cabin window. *A man in my profession cannot be afraid of death, but to meet it in such a helpless fashion…*

Loco shivered, and bent to rub his hands in front of the fire. *And then I spied your home in the distance. For a moment I feared I was imagining it! A lone cabin, out in this godforsaken wilderness! Truly it must be Divine Providence.*

There is another cabin nearby, Lizzy told him. *But no one lives there any more.* She crossed to the window and gazed out into the night. For a moment she fancied she saw a dark figure lurking off in the distance, as if her guest had abandoned his shadow and left it standing out in the snow. She quickly averted her gaze and turned back towards Loco.

Then you are all alone out here? he asked her.

My husband died recently, Lizzy replied, hefting the rifle in her hands. *But make no mistake, I can take care of myself.*

My profoundest sympathies, madam. Loco's eyes crept to her firearm. *And yes, I have no doubt that you are an extremely capable woman.*

Lizzy turned and walked towards the stove, reaching up to take a bowl down from a shelf. *I will warm you some stew. You can stay here tonight, and sleep there by the fire. This rifle will keep me company in my own bed, and it is a very short-tempered companion, understand?*

Loco chuckled wryly. *You are most kind, madam.*

She waved him away. *In the morning, if the storm has passed, you can make your way over to the other cabin and shelter there for as long as you need. I'm afraid I have very little desire for company these days.*

Little more was said between them that night. Loco gratefully ate two bowls of Lizzy's stew and then proclaimed himself exhausted by his travails. His host gave him a blanket to wrap himself in, and within minutes he was snoring in his chair by the hearth.

Lizzy, however, did not sleep. She kept her rifle close, and one eye trained on her uninvited guest at all times. She was, by now, reasonably convinced Loco was no demon, but that hardly equated to trusting him, despite his courteous manner. She had looked deep into his emotionless eyes, and the many hours she had spent in front of the mirror studying her own reflection had taught Lizzy to recognise a killer when she saw one.

When dawn finally arrived, the blizzard had not abated; if anything, its fury had redoubled. Lizzy began to resign herself to the fact that her houseguest might be with her for quite some time yet. As much as she longed to send

Loco off to the empty cabin once inhabited by Emma and her husband, she knew the odds were that he would simply lose his way in the storm and perish in the attempt. And as their hours together passed, she was forced to admit he was at least polite and respectful towards her at all times. While Lizzy did not consider herself any sort of a beauty, she was all too aware that such things hardly mattered to most men, certainly not one who found himself cooped up with a helpless woman miles from anywhere.

And yet Loco seemed to have no carnal interest in her whatsoever. Her body might have been carved from stone for all the attention it elicited from him. Eventually, Lizzy decided that the bounty hunter was the type of man who cared nothing for the company of women, and this conclusion finally allowed her to relax in his presence somewhat. She still did not trust him, but had come to believe he had no vested interest in doing her any sort of harm. After the first day or two they spent together, she stopped carrying the rifle with her everywhere she went, and the pair of them settled into a routine that was, if not entirely friendly, at least companionable.

A week went by, and Lizzy began to despair of the blizzard ever ending. And even if it did, what would become of her then? She would still be trapped in this hell she had fashioned for herself, and while the snows might have passed, it would be no less desolate for all that.

Perhaps Loco intuited something of her lingering dread, for as they sat together in front of the fire one night, the wind screaming around the house like a chorus of the damned, he turned to Lizzy and quietly asked, *Do you mean to remain out here all by yourself?*

Lizzy was startled by the question, but tried to mask her surprise. *I do not have any choice in the matter,* she said finally. *This is my home, and I have nowhere else to go.*

It doesn't seem like much of a life for you, Loco replied.

It is the life I made, Lizzy said simply.

Perhaps, the bounty hunter said. *But that should not prevent you from making a new one. Much as I intend to do.*

These days, Lizzy had little tolerance for men who didn't say what they meant, and grew impatient at the unspoken question she sensed dallying on Loco's tongue. *What are you suggesting?* she demanded.

Loco gazed at her for a moment, the firelight lending his icy blue eyes a warmth they did not normally possess. *I have a proposal that might be to our mutual advantage,* he said softly. *To be entirely honest with you, it is not solely my desire for a new life that caused me to leave Utah. I encountered a little trouble there, and although it was not trouble of my own making, in time, men will doubtless come after me. It would therefore suit my purposes to travel incognito. As for your situation, madam, it seems to me that for you to stay here would simply be to surrender to madness. However, I can offer you protection and passage out of this wasteland.* The flames danced in his eyes. *All you would have to do is travel with me for a short while posing as my wife.*

Your wife? Lizzy exclaimed, without bothering to conceal her distaste.

Loco smiled mirthlessly. *In name only, I assure you. I have no interest in trying to take advantage of you. No, the pretence would simply serve to make me less conspicuous.*

Lizzy got to her feet and crossed to the window. The blizzard seemed at last to be dwindling, and once again she thought she glimpsed a black figure watching from the distance. She thought of the demonic preacher that had once paid her a visit, and her stomach clenched. Maybe this lurking presence outside her window would come calling as soon as she was left alone once more. What should she do? The thought of travelling with this cruel stranger hardly appealed, but then neither did the alternative.

She turned back towards Loco. *I shall have to sleep on the matter,* she announced.

The bounty hunter accepted this without comment, merely inclining his head by way of a reply. They both retired shortly afterwards, Loco shrouding himself in his blanket and turning his chair towards the fire, so that his back was to Lizzy's bed.

For her part, Lizzy tossed and turned restlessly for the next several hours. Her soft mattress might have been a pile of filthy straw in a jail cell for all the comfort it accorded her that night. But of course, she *was* a prisoner here, no matter that the cabin windows were not barred and her hands and feet were not chained. And yet she had now been offered a means of escape. If she fled the cabin with Loco, she might be able to find a new life. Perhaps the devils and the dead would finally leave her be.

However, Lizzy still did not trust Loco, and certainly didn't believe his protestations that whatever trouble he was in was not of his own making. Anything might happen to her if she chose to travel at his side. He would doubtless abandon her at the first hint of danger, and what then?

She would be left at the mercy of others, very possibly men who were more inclined towards the company of women. Men who would be far less prissy than Loco about the prospect of taking advantage of her.

Lizzy rose early, and brewed a pot of coffee on the stove. Outside the cabin, the snowfall had finally stopped, and the sun shone bright and clear in the sky. When Loco awoke, she presented him with a steaming cup of coffee, and after he'd taken a few bleary sips, announced that she'd made her decision.

I cannot go with you, Lizzy told him. *Believe me, I wish I could, but it's impossible.*

Loco shrugged. *That's unfortunate,* he replied, before draining his cup and climbing to his feet. *May I have some more of this excellent coffee?* he asked her, holding out his empty cup.

Of course, Lizzy said, taking the cup from his hands.

The next moment his fist lashed out and struck her on the jaw, knocking her senseless.

When Lizzy came to, she found herself on the floor of the cabin, her hands and feet securely bound. On the other side of the room, Loco stood before the mirror, drawing a straight razor carefully across his skull. Piles of his blond hair lay clumped around his feet.

Seeing Lizzy stir in the mirror, he glanced around. *I apologise for striking you,* he said calmly. *But your rejection of my quite reasonable proposal left me no choice. Now, I'm afraid I shall have to compel you to travel east with me as my wife. As long as you don't resist, I shall have no cause to hurt you again, and once I've safely reached the coast you will be free to do as you please.*

He turned back to the mirror, slicing away his last few locks of hair. To Lizzy's eyes, Loco's face now appeared to be little more than a skull, his frosted blue eyes lending it whatever rudiments of life it still possessed. But the bounty hunter seemed satisfied. *Not bad,* he murmured. *Once my beard grows a little longer, they won't know who they're looking at.*

Turning away from the mirror, he walked over to where Lizzy lay and squatted down beside her. *What do you think of your new husband, my dear?* he said mockingly.

Go to hell! Lizzy spat, writhing in her bonds.

Loco looked thoughtful. *That reminds me. We'll need to make sure our marriage appears convincing in every way. Where is your husband's wedding ring? I have no doubt that you still have it.*

I don't! Lizzy shouted. *I buried it with him!*

The bounty hunter scratched at his jaw with the edge of his straight razor, then slowly lowered the blade and rested it against Lizzy's cheek. She could feel the chill of the honed metal prickling at her flesh. It would only take the slightest exertion of pressure…

Would you rather I cut you? Loco whispered. *Believe me, I'm not at all squeamish about such things. Your looks aren't anything much, my dear, but I can soon make them a great deal worse. It's entirely your choice.*

Lizzy screwed her eyes shut, willing herself not to cry. *In my jewellery box,* she hissed. *Underneath the mattress.* She'd hidden it there on the night Loco arrived; now she wished she'd simply cast it out into the snow.

The bounty hunter snapped the razor closed and went to inspect the bed. Shoving the mattress aside, he found the box hidden exactly where Lizzy had said. He opened it and rummaged around inside, before producing Isaac's wedding band. With a flourish, Loco placed it on his finger and waggled the digit in the air. *Perfect!* he exclaimed. *And what was your late husband's name, might I ask?*

She told him, at which point he bowed mockingly and said, *Then it shall be my very great pleasure to be Isaac, for as long as it suits me.*

Lizzy turned her head away. What the bounty hunter did not know was that she cared very little for the ring. Its symbolism had been a sham and a lie, just like so much else between her and Isaac. So what better place for it than on the finger of another liar?

She began to wonder whether all men were lying, inveterate tricksters. Or worse still, were they all secretly demons in human form?

Loco tossed the jewellery box down into the bed. *You can take the rest of your valuables with you when we leave in the morning,* he told Lizzy. *I'm not a thief, whatever else you may think of me.*

He left her tied up on the floor for a few more hours, finally relenting when Lizzy begged him to let her use the outhouse. Afterwards, he told her to prepare for their journey, bringing only that which she could carry on foot. They would have to procure a horse along the way somehow, but until then, Loco assured her he had no intention of burdening himself with any feminine baubles or trinkets. For the rest of the day, he watched her as an owl might watch a mouse, keeping her rifle and his pistol within easy reach at all times. And when night fell, he tied her tightly to the bed, much as her own husband had once done. If the bounty hunter had intended to ravish Lizzy, now would have been the perfect time. But he might have been tying up a barnyard hog for all the interest he showed in her. In that much, at least, he had been telling her the truth.

Other women might have spent the night sobbing pitifully or attempting to free themselves, but Lizzy saw little point in either. She had no means of escaping the cabin and nowhere to escape to, and even if she managed the impossible and killed the bounty hunter, she entertained little doubt that his unquiet spirit would simply join the others already tormenting her. And Lizzy's instincts told her that any torments Loco's vengeful revenant might devise for her would be hellish indeed.

No, if her life up until this moment had taught her anything, it was that an opportunity would present itself eventually. It might do so unexpectedly and entirely without warning, but she would be ready when it did.

Ready to do whatever was necessary.

Her determination was such that she managed a reasonable night's sleep despite the discomfort of her bonds, and when dawn broke the next morning Lizzy felt energised and ready to match her captor stride for stride on the long walk that lay ahead of them. She did not intend to gift him with any reason to berate or punish her by falling behind, and while Loco was undoubtedly stronger than her, Lizzy's hardscrabble prairie existence had nevertheless given her enviable reserves of strength and stamina.

They set out without delay. The surrounding prairie was a vast white blur, the colourless sky indistinguishable from the land lying beneath it. Although the snow had stopped falling, it was still piled high enough to make for slow and exhausting progress. The cold and exertion soon set Lizzy's bones to aching, but she refused to let the pain impede her. One advantage she did enjoy over her captor was her longer legs, and so despite the relentless strain of the journey, she managed to keep pace with Loco as they struggled onwards. She was aware of him throwing her sidelong glances as they walked, and felt sure they were now locked in a silent battle for supremacy. Once or twice she heard Loco muttering curses to himself, and while Lizzy feared what the consequences of his temper getting the better of him might be, she was also well aware that anger tends to cloud man's judgement. So by all means, let him fume and rant as much he liked.

When Loco finally called a halt to their weary march later that day, Lizzy thought her limbs might burst into flame. But when he ordered her to gather firewood, she made no complaint, merely banished all thoughts of rest from her mind and did as she was instructed. She was aided in this by the knowledge that they had already put some fair distance between themselves and the purgatorial existence she had previously known; that simple fact alone lent her strength enough to carry out the task at hand.

Later, after darkness had fallen and they both sat huddled around the campfire, Lizzy felt a sudden chill on the back of her neck, as if a cold exhalation of breath had prickled the flesh there. Shivering, she whipped her head around, but could see nothing lurking in the deep shadows behind her.

Noticing her disquiet, Loco sat up. *What is it?* he demanded.

Lizzy's eyes strained against the gloom, to no avail. *Nothing,* she said eventually. *Just someone walking over my grave, I guess.*

Her captor seemed unaccountably alarmed by this statement, and spent the next few minutes staring into the darkness himself, one hand placed on the butt of his revolver in readiness. But there was seemingly nothing out there but the night, and eventually he gave up and told Lizzy to turn in, making sure to bind her hands and feet before she slept. Still, before sleep finally claimed her, she noted that Loco seemed very ill at ease, tossing and turning under his blankets like a child plagued with bad dreams.

The following morning, after they had packed up their camp and resumed their journey, Lizzy once again felt that telltale prickle on the nape of her neck. When she glanced around on this occasion, she was greeted by the sight of a dark rider, following in their footsteps some ways off in the distance behind them.

Spotting her looking backwards, Loco once again demanded that Lizzy tell him what she was staring at. When she tried to point out the rider, he promptly lashed out with one hand and knocked her to the earth. *There's no one there*, he spat. *Don't try playing games with me, woman, or it'll be the worse for you.*

Once she'd picked herself back up off the ground, they continued on their way in silence. The black rider kept pace with them for the rest of the day, but Lizzy never mentioned him again. And later that night, when Loco was once again seized by uneasy dreams, she thought she knew exactly what he was dreaming of, and took quiet satisfaction from it.

On their third day of walking, they encountered a lone farmer riding a wagon, who noticed their weary state and offered them a ride to the nearest town. Loco thanked the man for his kindness, then drew his pistol and shot him dead. As he buried the man's body in a snowdrift, he flashed Lizzy a wolfish grin and told her, *What good fortune! I do believe you're my own little good luck charm.*

Unhappily, she pondered whether this might even be true. If so, it could only serve as further confirmation of the utter godlessness of existence, given the misfortune normally suffered by those luckless enough to make her acquaintance: the murdered farmer merely being the latest example.

However, whether it was down to Lizzy's influence or not, the bounty hunter's professed good luck continued to hold. Over the days that followed, the snow finally began to thaw, and that fact, combined with their acquisition of a means of transport, enabled them to pick up speed considerably. Less than three weeks later, they had crossed Texas and Arkansas and entered into Mississippi.

Loco had given Lizzy no clue as to his ultimate destination, and she began to despair of ever escaping him. Even if she managed to endure the perdition of his company for however much more remained of their journey, what was there to stop the bounty hunter from shooting her dead once she had finally outlived her usefulness to him? She had already witnessed first-hand how little Loco respected human life, and he did not strike Lizzy as the kind of man who liked leaving loose ends.

But on one fine March morning, as she once again sat silently obsessing over her dire predicament, fate at last saw fit to smile upon her.

They were riding through a quiet wooded grove when a violent jolting suddenly jerked Lizzy from her bleak reverie. The next instant, one of the wagon wheels parted company with its axle and span off into the undergrowth, tipping the vehicle onto its side and sending her and Loco tumbling to the earth.

Cursing, the bounty hunter picked himself up off the dirt, and, without checking to see whether Lizzy was hurt, rushed to inspect the damage to the wagon. *Shit!* he bellowed, turning to punch ineffectually at the flank of their bewildered horse. *I don't have any tools to fix this! Shit!*

Winded, Lizzy lay on the ground and gazed up into the heavens. Over the distant treetops, she could make out a plume of woodsmoke snaking into the sky. She let Loco rage until her breath eventually returned, and then pointed towards the smoke and said, simply, *There.*

The bounty hunter gazed in the direction indicated and grew quiet. Finally, he turned and helped Lizzy to her feet, at which point his uncharacteristic act of chivalry immediately shifted into violence. Grabbing his captive by the hair, he pulled her close and hissed, *Don't forget our arrangement, madam. Or I might just forget myself and shoot you and anyone else within range, understand?*

Lizzy nodded silently.

Taking her by the arm, Loco guided Lizzy through the trees, heading towards the source of the smoke. Eventually they came upon a dirt road, which led them to a walled plantation estate, shut off from the world by a locked iron gate. Beyond the wall, Lizzy could see a large antebellum mansion house, neatly maintained but showing the visible deprivations of age.

A brass plaque mounted next to the gate read "The Miss Martha Farnsworth Seminary for Young Ladies', a bell pull dangling beside it. Wasting no time, Loco reached up and tugged vigorously at the rope, sending a chorus of jangling ringing out across the estate grounds.

Within moments, a middle-aged woman emerged from the main house and hurried down the path towards them. She had brown hair, a long nose, and small furtive eyes. As she moved closer and caught sight of Loco, her expression hardened, only to soften again when she noticed Lizzy standing at his side.

Upon reaching the gate, she made no immediate move to open it, gazing at them warily through the iron bars. *How may I help you?* she said primly.

Loco removed his hat and stepped forward. *I'm very sorry to trouble you, ma'am,* he told her apologetically. *A wheel came off our wagon back in those woods and I have no way of repairing it. We were wondering if anyone here might be able to assist us?*

The woman stiffened. *We don't normally allow visitors here, sir. We've had…trouble in the past, you see.*

I quite understand, Loco said. *You can't be too careful. But my wife and I have been travelling for several weeks and we're quite at our wit's end. So any help you offer us would very gratefully received.*

The woman's eyes moved to Lizzy. Careful not to do anything that Loco might interpret as an attempt to signal her predicament, Lizzy met the woman's gaze and tried to communicate the force of her despair through nothing more than a look. *Please help,* she thought desperately, willing the woman to understand.

Each stared at the other for a few moments, then the woman nodded and stepped forward to unlock the gate. *Very well,* she said. *Come on up to the house and meet the other ladies. We'll get you some food and drink and see what we can do about helping you on your way.*

She ushered them inside the grounds and introduced herself as Amy, prompting Loco to take her hand and bow his head in courtly gratitude. *My beloved and I thank you from the bottom of our hearts, Miss Amy,* he said unctuously. *I'm Isaac and this is my wife Lizzy. And may I take this opportunity to say what a pretty little school you have here.*

Lizzy thought she saw a hint of regret flit across Amy's face, like a rabbit dashing for the safety of its warren. *It's no longer a school, I'm afraid,* she replied softly. *A lot has changed around here over the years, and Miss Martha is sadly no longer with us. But those of us who once studied under her loved it so much here that we never wanted to leave.*

She took them up to the main house, where the putative couple met the rest of the ladies of the school: Edwina, Carol, Doris, Abigail, Lizzie and Janey. They were all middle-aged, and had apparently been resident at Miss Farnsworth's ever since the conflict they habitually chose to refer to as the War Between the States. Edwina was the oldest, grey-haired and withdrawn in nature, and although Carol was not much younger than her, she had retained a youthful spark of mischief in her eye, and persisted in flirting with Loco until the wall of his disinterest became too steep for even her to scale.

Lizzy and Loco were given food and drink, after which a couple of the ladies helped them to go back out into the woods and retrieve their horse and wagon. Loco was granted access to the school's toolshed, and laboured for the rest of the day fixing their vehicle. Amy asked Lizzy whether she might like to lay down and rest while her husband worked, but when Loco heard this, he insisted that his wife's place was right by his side. So Lizzy was forced to sit underneath a nearby tree and watch Loco struggle and curse all afternoon, and when any of the ladies approached, she was careful not to fall into anything but the most cursory of conversations with them.

By the time Loco had finally fixed the wagon, the sun was dipping beneath the horizon, and Amy emerged from the house once more, this time to invite them to stay the night. *It's far too late for you to think of leaving now*, she insisted, *and I'd forgotten how nice it is to have some fresh company around. We have plenty of room, and the quality of our home cooking is second to none.*

Lizzy could tell that Loco was hugely reluctant to accept the invitation. Burying her loathing as deep as she could manage, she forced herself to embrace him and kiss his cheek. *Please, darling, say we can stay!* she pleaded girlishly. *We've been travelling for so long. Just one night in a warm soft bed would do us both the world of good.*

She could feel him instinctively recoiling from her touch, but the bounty hunter had little option but to continue the agreed charade. *Very well*, he muttered. *But we must be on our way at dawn tomorrow.*

Lizzy suspected she might pay dearly for this provocation once they were alone together once more, but some intuition told her this might be the best chance she would ever have to escape Loco. Exactly why, she could not say – after all, what help would a group of ageing spinsters be against a hardened killer? – but such was her desperation that she persisted all the same.

That night at supper, her captor's mood had improved considerably, and he began to display some of the same reptilian charm which had originally enabled him to coax his way across Lizzy's threshold. Loco entertained the ladies with many tall tales of life in the West, and some even more outlandish stories of his and Lizzy's fictitious courtship. All the while, Lizzy sat quietly seething. Surely these apparently sensible women could not believe such lies! But one look at their faces told a different story. Carol in particular seemed almost puce with envy, as though the prospect of a life with the likes of Loco was her fondest dream. A black pit of misery opened under Lizzy's feet, threatening to drown her in its nebulous depths.

Perhaps sensing her distress, Edwina turned to Lizzy and quietly asked her, *And how was your journey here from New Mexico? You appeared exhausted when you first arrived, and forgive me for saying, seem little better now.*

Lizzy's eyes dropped to her plate. She was certain that if she met the older woman's gaze, she would simply dissolve into helpless sobs. A lump formed in her throat. *It was…hard,* she croaked. *Yes, very hard.*

Edwina's hand closed gently over her own. *Then you must stay as our guest as long as you like.*

Unable to prevent herself, Lizzy looked up into Edwina's eyes. *Do you really mean that?* she whispered.

Of course, Edwina assured her. *You will find us to be very understanding company.*

Lizzy squeezed her hand. *I would…like that very much.*

Suddenly, Loco's voice cut sharply through the bond the two women had just established. *What did you just say, woman?*

Lizzy stared across at the bounty hunter, clutching tightly at Edwina's hand for support. *I said that I want to stay,* she said defiantly. *You are free to leave, of course. 'Husband'.*

In the next moment, all of Loco's politeness and charm instantly dropped away, as if a playing card had been flipped over to reveal the malign joker lurking underneath. Erupting from his seat, he lashed out across the tabletop and struck Lizzy across the cheek, drawing shocked gasps from the other women.

Do not dare defy me! he snarled at her.

No one said a word. Crossing to Lizzy's side, Loco grabbed her by the arm and roughly pulled her to her feet. *I am afraid that when my wife becomes overtired, she sometimes forgets herself,* he announced to the table. *We will retire for the night and be on our way at dawn, after which we shall trouble you no longer. I thank you again for your hospitality, ladies.*

Lizzy felt her eyes burning as her captor dragged her from the room. She longed for one of the assembled women to say something, anything, before she vanished from their lives forever, but they remained as silent as the dead. Still, what on earth could she expect them to say? They were all as helpless as she.

After they had reached their bedroom, Loco proceeded to beat Lizzy viciously. She tried not to cry out at first, but after the assault had continued for some minutes, she gave into her pain and misery and let loose an almost animal howling, the accumulation of all the long months of suffering she had endured ever since she and Isaac had first made their home on the prairie. As Loco's blows continued to rain down, Lizzy closed her eyes and began to imagine that all of her ghosts were gathered around her, Isaac and Emma and the rest, assembled together to enact the vengeance they had craved for so long.

At last, she sank gratefully into oblivion.

The next thing Lizzy was aware of was Loco's snoring, hoarse and sonorous. Opening her eyes, she found herself lying on the floor next to the bed, her hands and feet bound. Her body throbbed all over, and she could feel dried blood caked upon one side of her face. This was her captor's brand of justice, the sort of sadistic retribution that left him sated and sleeping like a carefree babe. Listening to him snore, Lizzy decided she had never hated him more than at that very moment.

The next instant, she heard a stealthy creak from the doorway, and glanced up to see the door to the bedroom being carefully opened. A second later, Amy's head slowly peered around the door. Seeing Lizzy lying tied and beaten on the floorboards, her eyes widened, and she immediately raised a warning finger to her lips.

Lizzy watched silently as the rest of the women followed Amy into the room, moving as swiftly and soundlessly as shades. Taking care to avoid stepping on Lizzy, they clustered around the bed like mourners gathering around a grave.

Amy produced a bottle of chloroform and a rag. Dousing the material with the pungent liquid, she leant down and clamped it firmly over Loco's snoring mouth and nostrils. A second or two elapsed, and then the bounty hunter's body buckled violently, twisting like an electric current was coursing through his limbs. He opened his eyes and began to thrash around, but the other women jumped forward in unison and held his limbs down. Had he had more time, their victim might have been able to break free, but the drug was quick to take effect, and very soon Loco was unconscious and carefree once more.

Producing some lengths of rope, the other ladies hurriedly began to tie the bounty hunter to the bedposts, while Amy knelt down beside Lizzy and helped her escape her own bonds. When the former captive was finally free, she threw her arms around Amy and buried her face in the other woman's shoulder. *I'm sorry, I'm so very sorry*, Lizzy moaned.

Hush now, Amy told her, stroking Lizzy's head. *It wasn't your fault, none of it. And the women here are well accustomed to men and their trickery and violence. We learnt the hard way, much as you did. We could tell that much about you the moment you set foot in this house.*

They sat like that for a few moments, Amy holding the younger woman safe and tight, until Edwina announced that Loco had been secured. Then Amy leant to Lizzy's ear and whispered, *Now, do you want to see how we deal with such men?*

Lizzy did, very much.

Amy helped her to her feet, and Lizzy took up a position at the foot of the bed. Next, Edwina went and fetched a saw from the toolshed, the very same saw Loco had used to help fix the wagon earlier that day. Testing the blade with her finger, she commented, *It's not as sharp as it once was, but that's more his problem than mine.*

Lizzy gazed at them all with a kind of appalled glee. Amy leant in to kiss her cheek and murmured, *Trust me. He'll never lay a hand on a woman ever again.*

The operation took quite some time, and by the time Edwina had finished, the air in the room was thick with blood and screams. The ladies were all dripping head to toe in gore, like the participants of some ghoulish bacchanal. Having parted company with his four limbs forever,

Loco writhed on the bed like a plump worm, shrieking insanely to the heavens.

Suddenly feeling quite overcome, Lizzy crossed to the window and opened the shutters to let in the night breeze. Gazing down across the estate grounds, she could see a mounted figure in the moonlight, waiting patiently outside the gate. At this distance, she could finally make out the black rider more clearly: a handsome man, his face partly obscured by his long hair, a bandana tied tightly around his throat. Seeing Lizzy watching him, he gave her a single slow nod.

From the bed behind her, she heard Loco scream. *No! Noooooooooo!*

She turned away from the window and approached the bedside, the bounty hunter's eyes imploring her. *Silence!* he gibbered. *Silence! The great silence!*

What's he making so much noise about? Edwina said crossly.

I think he's afraid of dying, Lizzy replied.

Well, said Amy, wiping the blood from her eyes. *He won't be there for a little while yet. He'll have some time to think about what he's done first.*

The ladies abandoned Loco to his madness and filed downstairs into the garden. There, in an overgrown corner, they took some picks and shovels and began to dig. Luckily, enough time had elapsed since the recent blizzard that the ground had begun to soften again, and although the work was hard going, by the time dawn began to creep across the sky the eight women had managed to dig a grave several feet deep.

Taking a short break to catch their breath – none of them were quite as young as they used to be – Edwina and Carol then went into the cellar to find a crate, while the rest of the ladies went upstairs to fetch Loco. Upon seeing them enter the bedroom, the bounty hunter set to shrieking all over again, and Amy was minded to take the chloroform to him a second time until one of the others reminded her that they didn't want their patient to miss the best part. Relenting, she directed them to pick Loco up from the bed, and although he struggled and writhed in their arms the whole way downstairs, they managed not to drop him more than once or twice.

Taking him into the garden, they carefully deposited him inside the crate. Loco immediately began to giggle, a gratingly feminine sound that quickly began to wear on their nerves.

All right, Edwina snapped, bending down to pick up the lid of the crate. *I think that's quite enough of that noise.*

Lizzy gazed at them in awed wonder as they lowered the lid into place and began to methodically nail it down. It was hardly the first burial she had been a party to, but it was certainly the first where the body being buried was not entirely dead. But after all, as Amy told her afterwards, *We're not cold-blooded murderers, not like him. We're quite content to let him go to Death in his own good time.*

After the crate was placed into the grave and the earth filled back in, blessed peace was once again restored to the grounds of the Miss Martha Farnsworth Seminary for Young Ladies. The assembled women stood in respectful silence for a few moments, before Edwina announced that it was bedtime. *I'm quite exhausted,* she said, *and I'm sure all you ladies are too. So off to bed with you, before we all end up in our own graves.*

Lizzy was the last to leave the garden. Glancing over towards the school entrance, she once again glimpsed the black rider waiting patiently outside the gate. This time, she nodded back to him. She knew he would no longer be waiting there when she awoke the next day.

After she had gone back inside the house, silence fell upon the garden, save for the distant cry of the whippoorwills. The house stood quiet and still, jealously guarding its secrets from the world outside. It appeared then much as it appears today, over a century later; and although the grounds are by now wild and overgrown, the house itself is still remarkably well-preserved, almost as though it still has tenants living within its walls and minding its upkeep.

Of course, the building has been abandoned for years, but rumours persist that the women of the Miss Martha Farnsworth Seminary for Young Ladies still live on there…in whatever fashion they can be deemed to be living. Some have whispered of lingering outside the house on a quiet summer night and hearing the sounds of feminine laughter and conversation coming from inside.

But the ladies have rightfully earned their peace and seclusion, and so of course, no one would ever contemplate intruding upon them.

Certainly not any of the local men who occasionally have cause to pass by the property, and who know far better than to risk arousing the ire of those dwelling within.

THE STRANGER

Clint Eastwood in High Plains Drifter, *1973*
written by Ernest Tidyman
directed by Clint Eastwood

H E WAS NOT THE FIRST NAMELESS KILLER TO RIDE OUT OF THE DESERT; at times, it almost seemed as though the Old West was full of them. Silent men with empty eyes, a pistol draw as quick as a viper's strike and a sliver of ice in their hearts. But it was obvious to everyone in Lago there was something different about the Stranger. Something unearthly, and unspeakably cruel.

Some whispered that he was the Devil himself, arrived to claim the townspeople's souls. Others were heard to venture that he was the vengeful ghost of the federal marshal Jim Duncan. Duncan had been horsewhipped to death on the main street of Lago by three outlaws; vicious criminals who had been hired by the townspeople themselves, after the lawman had discovered the town's silver mine lay on what was rightly government land.

TWILIGHT'S LAST SCREAMING

Desperate to protect their sole source of income, the inhabitants of Lago had conspired to rid themselves of Duncan, and had stood by and watched silently as Stacey Bridges and the two Carlin brothers had murdered him in cold blood.

Now Duncan mouldered in an unmarked grave at the edge of town, and wasn't it true that the dead would not rest without a marker? Moreover, didn't the Stranger somewhat resemble the deceased marshal? Some agreed that he did, while others scoffed at such an outlandish notion. After all, memory was a treacherous thing, especially when the entire town had done their level best to banish Duncan's bloodied, dying face from their minds and forget he had ever even existed. So the speculation continued unabated, spreading throughout Lago like a contagion, and in the meantime the Stranger simply sat on his hotel room balcony and stared down at them all with his wintry eyes, as though the townsfolk were nothing more than scurrying termites, erupting onto land that was rightfully his.

For the town of Lago belonged to him now, no one could dispute the fact. Much as they had betrayed Marshal Duncan, the townspeople had then turned on Bridges and the Carlins and handed them over to the law, thinking their – decent and God-fearing! – way of life would finally be safe. But now the outlaws were returning to Lago to seek revenge, and the town's only hope of salvation lay with the Stranger. If anyone noted the irony of relying on a demonic killer for deliverance, they did not publicly remark on it; it would hardly be the first time the inhabitants of Lago had made a deal with the Devil, after all. In exchange for his protection, the Stranger simply took whatever he wanted in return – alcohol, comfortable lodgings, any woman that happened to take his fancy – and there was nothing the townspeople could do about it. Why, he had even stripped the sheriff and mayor of their titles and awarded them to Mordecai, the town dwarf! His contempt for Lago and everything right and proper it represented could hardly have been made any more evident, the townsfolk muttered. But they reminded themselves that men such as the Stranger were still unfortunately necessary; after all, had their great country not been forged by pioneers of a similarly ruthless ilk? What was important above all else was the greater good of America, and when the people of Lago and decent citizens like them had finally succeeded in bringing civilisation to this untamed land, it was reassuring to think that such brutal men would no longer be needed.

Still, when the Stranger subsequently ordered them to paint the entire town red and rename it Hell, even the most pragmatic of the townsfolk had cause to doubt their chosen course. Most shockingly, he'd insisted on including the church in his wanton blasphemy – and when the town's preacher had attempted to exclude their place of worship from the Stranger's infernal scheme, the man had fixed him with that chill, deathless stare and hissed, *Especially the church.*

(Such was the Stranger's scornful godlessness that, amongst those superstitious souls who ascribed to him some manner of supernatural origin, some privately began to wonder whether he perhaps knew something they didn't.)

But when all was said and done, the various indignities suffered by the townsfolk might have been worth it after all. Although they initially feared the Stranger had abandoned them to the returning outlaws, when the hour came, he had materialised out of the black night like some conjured abomination and claimed the lives of the three men. The killers had been helpless in the face of his implacable fury. Silhouetted against the flames of the burning town, the Stranger had mercilessly cut them down, one by one. Stacey Bridges had been the last of them left standing, and, without even knowing it, he'd spoken for the whole of the town's population when he screamed at his executioner, in abject, witless terror, *Who are you?!?*

If the Stranger dignified him with a reply, it was not recorded.

The next morning, he rode out of Lago, never to be seen by its inhabitants again. Thinking their own crimes were now consigned to history, the townspeople had at last instructed Mordecai to carve Jim Duncan's name into the hitherto unmarked grave, and for a short time, they all believed that might be the end of it. Be he man or devil or ghost, the Stranger had avenged Duncan's death, and with the marshal now properly laid to rest, surely their erstwhile saviour could have no more business with Lago or its (unquestionably decent and God-fearing) population.

The Stranger rode for the whole of the day, heading south towards the Californian coast. As night descended upon the land, he came upon a small campsite, occupied by two men: one dead, and one living; after a fashion at least. The man in question was dressed as a preacher, although he comported himself like no priest the Stranger had ever seen. As he approached the campsite, the Stranger could make out the priest hunched greedily over his companion's corpse, his mouth slathered with dark blood, helping himself to glistening sweetmeats from the dead man's disembowelled belly.

And yet, even in the face of such monstrosity, the Stranger did not immediately draw his weapon. The truth of it was that the two men quickly intuited they had much in common. Perhaps their respective natures were not exactly the same, but they nevertheless both came from an entirely similar place.

The preacher wiped daintily at his bloodied mouth and stood up to greet his visitor. *Greetings, stranger,* he said politely. *If you'd like to join me by the fire, I can offer you a warm place to sleep and a fresh meal.*

Thanks for the offer, but I reckon I'll be moving right along, replied the Stranger with a wry half-smile. *I was just wondering where you might be headed?*

No place in particular, shrugged the preacher. *Everywhere and nowhere. I'm spreading the Word of my God, as you can see.*

The Stranger gazed down at the expression of horror on the dead man's face. *Yep. Looks like he heard you, alright.*

The preacher reached down and tenderly brushed a lock of the man's hair away from his face. *Stranger, allow me to introduce you to Mr Harold Callaghan, from Sacramento. That was his birthname, anyhow. But now he has been born again into my flock, nameless and made anew. Many more will join him before my work is done.*

Well now, said the Stranger. *As it happens, I can point you towards a large congregation, all ready and waiting to be converted. All decent, God-fearing folk, so I'm sure the soil of their faith will prove to be extremely fertile. If you head south from here, you'll find a town called Lago, right next to Mono Lake. I know the people there very well, and you have my word that they're entirely worthy of your deliverance, preacher.*

The preacher tipped his hat. *I'm very much obliged to you, stranger. I can tell it was ordained, us meeting like this.*

The Stranger nodded, and without another word, rode away into the darkness, satisfied that the people of Lago would soon meet the messiah they so richly deserved.

In that, he was to be proven correct, as far as anyone can tell. For, by the close of the nineteenth century, the town of Lago had simply ceased to exist. It no longer appeared on any maps, and any travellers who rode that way reported nothing but the skeletal remnants of a few burned-out buildings and an eerie wind blowing off the lake, sounding like the keening of a hundred damned souls. Before long, the area acquired a sinister reputation as a place best to be avoided.

As for the Stranger, one might have thought he had finally earned his rest. He could have returned to whichever shadowed place he first came from, his thirst for vengeance slaked. But the more he thought on it, the more the Stranger began to view the pious hypocrisy he'd discovered in Lago as symptomatic of a wider blight, a disease lurking at the root of this young country which might yet rot it from within, should it be left to spread unchecked.

The Stranger decided he still had much work left to do. Realising it might be beneficial for him to have a name and pass as a seemingly normal man, he thought back to the preacher's unfortunate convert. After all, a corpse had very little use for a name, and Callaghan was as good a one as any. And so it was settled: the nameless Stranger became Harold – although he quickly came to prefer the abbreviated 'Harry' – Callaghan. Under the circumstances, he decided to forego a Christian baptism (and if any of the whispered stories about the Stranger's origin were indeed true, that was probably a prudent decision.)

He continued to drift for a time, leaving a trail of dead men and ravished women in his wake. But eventually, his deadly talents led him to more gainful employment. Harry had stood by and watched as America continued to inch painfully towards the state of civilisation that had been so prized by the townspeople of Lago, as if a land founded upon theft and murder could ever truly be called *civilised*. This, Harry mused, was merely another example of the hypocrisy he loathed so much, a hypocrisy that was quickly becoming the favoured currency of the times. Nevertheless, he was but one man, and one man could hardly stand in the way of so-called progress. The inhabitants of Lago had been right about one thing: there was less and less call for men of his particular nature, unless of course they were acting in service of the country's own laws and institutions. Harry had always believed that there was a very clear distinction to be made between *law* and *justice*, but accepting that this was a battle he would perhaps be wise to concede for now, he duly took an oath and was sworn in as an officer of the peace.

And if anyone had dared look Harry in the eye as he placed his hand on the Bible and solemnly vowed to uphold the law, they might have glimpsed a hint of cold, bright amusement there, like a diamond glittering at the bottom of an icy lake.

So it was that Harry Callaghan joined the ranks of American law enforcement. Early on in his career, his superiors chose to turn a blind eye to his, shall we say, occasionally disproportionate use of force, reasoning that while Callaghan might have been an exceptionally blunt instrument, he was at the very least an instrument of the law. Callaghan was thereby freed from his previous qualms about joining America's nascent legal system, satisfied that he was now at liberty to solve any contradictions between the thorny question of law vs justice in his own particular manner.

The years passed, and while America gradually grew older, the ageless drifter did not. In order to avoid any suspicion, Harry would drop out of sight every decade or two, before surfacing to rejoin the law somewhere else; a new county, a new city. This road eventually brought him to San Francisco, where he joined the city's police department and quickly rose through the ranks to become a plainclothes detective.

But as much as Harry tried to tell himself he was still the merciless lone wolf, called forth from the wasteland to dispense divine justice, unencumbered by any notions of remorse or phoney morality, the rot he'd observed all those long years before in Lago had at last begun to blacken the foundations of the country. No longer was he permitted to administer his favoured form of Old Testament retribution; now, guilty men somehow had *rights*. Not only that, but Harry was even expected to inform them of those (allegedly God-given, although he knew better) rights when he apprehended them, instead of simply dropping them where they stood. He was assured by his lieutenant that to do so now would risk an official reprimand, if not suspension or worse.

So, when he gunned down a violent rapist on the street (even Harry had, by now, begrudgingly accepted that rape was no longer permissible in these more enlightened times), he was summoned into the lieutenant's office to justify his actions, as though he were somehow guiltier than the degenerate he'd wiped from the earth.

An unfamiliar despair now gripped him. He understood that he was losing the battle he'd begun to wage in Lago almost a century before; a battle against lies and insufferably polite evasions; against double standards and despicable liberal hypocrisy.

A rubicon was finally crossed when the Scorpio Killer appeared in San Francisco, materialising out of the lawless urban jungle just as the Stranger himself had once materialised out of the Californian desert. In quick succession, the maniac murdered a young woman and a small boy, before kidnapping a teenage girl and threatening to rape and kill her unless the city paid him two hundred thousand dollars. Harry looked on in disgust as his superiors – the weaselly district attorney, the unctuous mayor – wrung their hands and slunk around their plush offices like the lost, cringing dogs they were. In a simpler time, Harry might have set the whole city ablaze, forcing the killer out onto the streets where he could be dealt with properly, but instead he was ordered to act as a grovelling errand boy, scurrying around San Francisco to deliver the killer the blood money he'd demanded.

In the face of such wilful ineffectuality, Harry snapped. Tracking Scorpio to his lair, he wounded and tortured the man, only sparing his life in a bid to learn of the whereabouts of his teenage victim. But he was too late – the girl was already dead, and in a final, pathetic display of cowardice, the city promptly released the maniac from custody, claiming that Harry had infringed the man's preciously inalienable rights.

That night, Harry dreamed of blood and fire, of a lawman being whipped to death on the street while an entire town stood by and watched. Now, it was happening again.

When he woke from the dream, he went to his bedroom window and stared out at the red dawn seeping across the sky. His whole existence had been a bitter refutation of what he had witnessed in Lago. So would he stand by and do nothing now, simply because a bunch of soft-bellied men in grey suits had ordered it?

He would not.

Harry began to stalk Scorpio, the hunter and the hunted, slyly goading the killer into action. If this was the game he must play, then so be it. Harry understood the nature of his prey better than anyone; some men are born simply to kill, and can only achieve the rare perfection they seek in doing so. By hounding Scorpio, he knew that the man would inevitably be provoked into revealing his true nature once more.

The policeman's predatory instincts, honed over the course of the century, were correct. One afternoon Scorpio kidnapped a busload of schoolchildren and demanded another ransom from the city. And once more, San Francisco's snivelling officialdom agreed to pay. When they asked Harry to deliver the ransom, he refused.

Instead, he tracked the school bus down and forced a final confrontation with Scorpio. Gazing down the barrel of his gun at the giggling murderer, he was suddenly reminded of Stacey Bridges' final moments on that long-ago night in Lago: the outlaw desperately pleading to know the identity of the man about to kill him, unable to bear the fact that, deep down, he knew exactly who his killer was.

But Scorpio *didn't* know who he was; no one did. Harry was just another impotent cop in a broken-down city that was full of such men, not allowed to be any better or more effectual than the rest of the poor bastards.

He shot Scorpio dead, leaving the man's body floating in a river, a look of astonishment fixed on his face. But Harry felt no surprise; in truth, he felt absolutely nothing. He could no longer participate in this cheap charade. Taking out his detective's badge, he tossed it into the river, to be swept away along with the dead man. Neither of them meant anything; they were merely abstract symbols of the country America was fast becoming; a country he found increasingly, unbearably alien.

Returning to the city, Harry sought out a titty bar and sequestered himself in a corner booth, drinking beer after beer. Perhaps he should return to wraithlike anonymity, at last freed from the shackles of the justice system. But what could he achieve in a land that preferred to believe it no longer had a use for him? He might as well be dead.

For a moment, he wondered whether Duncan's grave was still there, looking out onto that desolate, haunted lake. Perhaps the Stranger had finally earned his rest, after all this time, after all the blood he had so righteously spilt.

Harry gazed blankly up at the hollow-eyed women onstage. He began to imagine them as living corpses, their sallow bodies stiffening as they danced, their movements becoming jerky and spastic, threatening to rupture their decaying flesh and spill their ripe insides out onto the walkway.

The next moment, a man slid into the seat across from him.

Harry stared over at the new arrival. He was a small, unassuming man, dressed in an anonymous-looking suit. Was this meant to be some kind of faggot pickup, he wondered?

The man smiled, in the wry manner of someone well practiced in divining exactly what other men were thinking. *Don't look so worried,* he told Harry.

Could be you're the one who should be worried, replied Harry.

Please, it's nothing like that, the man assured him. *My name's Younger. Jack Younger. I have a business proposition for you. One which I think you'll find interesting.*

He extended a hand in greeting, which Harry pointedly did not take. Unfazed, the man withdrew it and continued with his pitch. *We've been keeping an eye on you for quite some time, Inspector Callaghan. We think you're a man of very rare gifts. We also think those gifts are not currently being put to good use. We – my employers and I – would like to offer you the chance to change that.*

And who the hell's 'we'? Harry hissed.

Younger pulled out his wallet and produced a business card, handing it to Harry. The card was plain, unfussy black lettering on white, nothing so fancy as to call attention to itself. Studiedly unobtrusive, much like Younger himself.

I believe you'll find the kind of work we do very rewarding, Younger told him.

Harry looked down at the card. It read:

Jack Younger
Recruitment Executive
THE PARALLAX CORPORATION

DANIEL PLAINVIEW

Daniel Day-Lewis in There Will Be Blood, *2007*
based on the novel by Upton Sinclair
written & directed by Paul Thomas Anderson

1
From the journal of Daniel Plainview

An unexpected visitor today: Hubie Marsten from Boston. It must have been well over twenty years since I saw him last, but time has not improved his low character any. This estimation is not down to any hypocrisy on my part, mind. I have never been under any misapprehensions as to Hubie's preferred line of work. He is a diligent, efficient man and there were certainly occasions when I had cause to call on his rather rarefied talents. Such is the unsparing nature of the world we live in, and I will say without any particular guilt or shame that this great country is none the worse off for having had certain people quietly removed from it.

No, my assessment of Hubie Marsten's character is based upon something far more nebulous. I have never been quite able to put my finger on the reason for it, but he carries with him an aura of <u>wrongness</u>, of complete and utter depravity. Whenever Hubie enters a room, it is as though a rotting, flyblown animal carcass has been suddenly dumped in the middle of the floor, the very air around him growing thick with foulness and corruption. I have no idea why this should be the case, but my instincts about people have always served me well, and so, despite our intermittent professional interactions, I have always been careful to keep him at arm's length.

His visit today therefore came as something of a surprise.

When Hubie turned up unannounced, I immediately anticipated some kind of chicanery - perhaps an attempt at blackmail or extortion - but when he was shown through to my study he greeted me like an old friend, and over a couple of whiskies spent some time telling me about the course his life has taken over the last few decades. Apparently he is now retired, and he and his wife have moved to a small Maine town named Jerusalem's Lot. I cannot begin to imagine how someone like Hubie will ever make a home in such a sleepy little backwater, or indeed how he might choose to occupy his days there. It is probably best not to think about it too closely.

When he finished his account, I offered him another drink, which he declined. I poured myself another, and when I looked up again I caught him looking at me oddly.

There was something in his gaze I did not like. 'What are you staring at, man?' I demanded.

Hubie smiled. 'I heard you had some recent troubles, Daniel,' he replied. 'Something concerning a preacher? I believe his name was Sunday, wasn't it?'

'A freak accident,' I informed him. 'A few too many drinks and the Reverend Sunday slipped and smashed his skull open. Obviously the law looked into it thoroughly but there was no implication of any wrongdoing.'

He smiled again. 'Men like us always make our own law, don't we, Daniel?'

I told him I had no idea what he meant. Eli Sunday was someone I'd known and respected for many years, and his sudden death was both a shock and a tragedy.

Hubie looked at me oddly again. 'Forgive me for saying so, Daniel, but it seems to me that I've come here to find you in somewhat questionable health.'

I was starting to grow impatient. 'There's nothing wrong with my damn health,' I said. 'What are you referring to, Hubie?'

'The drink, for one,' he replied. 'Two whiskies have still not allayed the visible tremor in your hands. And your state of mind seems...troubled.'

'I'll thank you to keep such thoughts to yourself,' I told him. 'I welcomed you into my home as a show of hospitality, not to listen to some half-assed amateur medical diagnosis.'

But he did not seem at all abashed by my rebuke. Instead, he grew thoughtful. 'Daniel, what if I were to tell you that, just as men like us are unrestricted by conventional laws or ethics, we can also throw off the burdensome shackles of mortality?

'And you say I am the one with a troubled mind,' I scoffed.

'Hear me out. There is a gentleman of my acquaintance named Breichen, a European nobleman. He now resides in Austria, but it is my understanding that he was originally born somewhere in Romania, under the name Orlok.'

'And why does this foreigner concern me?'

'No reason, save for one small detail that you may find of some interest. Breichen was born several centuries ago, Daniel.'

I began to laugh. 'I'm surprised someone like you would fall for such old world superstition, Hubie. I suppose you're now going to tell me he sold his soul to the Devil in exchange for eternal life?'

'Not quite,' Hubie said. 'There was a bargain, of sorts. An exchange. But nothing that an experienced businessman such as yourself would balk at.'

'And you wanted to offer this so-called bargain to me, is that it?'

Hubie looked grave. 'It's not my place to offer it. But as I say, Breichen is a trusted acquaintance of mine. In time, he intends to relocate to America, and I am helping him with the necessary arrangements. Now, I feel sure that he would be very interested in a man like yourself.'

'Interested how, exactly?'

'Breichen is an important man in Europe. A man of power and influence. But here in America, he knows very few people, and is keen to be introduced to more. An influential man should have influential friends, don't you think?'

I drained my glass. 'I'm not looking for friends. I've worked my whole damn life to get away from people. I see the worst in them, Hubie. You and everyone else who ever crossed my path.'

Now it was Hubie's turn to laugh. 'You worked your whole life to wind up rotting in this vast tomb of a house, is that it? What sort of an ending is that for a great man like yourself? Think about how much more you could accomplish if you were gifted with another lifetime, several lifetimes even.'

'Horseshit,' I told him. 'I see retirement has already turned your mind to pigswill, Hubie.'

Unruffled, he got up to leave. 'I will tell Breichen to write you,' he said. 'He can explain matters better than me. In the meantime, I wish you very good health, Daniel.' He gazed around at our surroundings, a mocking expression seeping into his features like an infection. 'You do have a very beautiful home.'

After he left, I poured myself another whisky and sat staring into the fire. I must have dozed off for a moment, for I swear I heard Eli's voice whispering softly in my ear. When I opened my eyes and looked around I was quite alone in the room, but I could still hear his girlish whine lingering in my ear. 'You will never be saved if you reject the blood,' it said.

I have told the servants that from this day forth they should admit no more visitors to the house without a prior appointment.

2

Letter from Kurt Breichen to Daniel Plainview

My dear Mr Plainview!

Firstly, let me say how delighted I am to make your acquaintance, even at this small remove. I have, over the years, taken a great interest in the development of your young country, so full of life and youthful potential. Europe, I am afraid to say, increasingly reminds me of an ageing courtesan; riddled with pox, her blood beating slow and heavy in her veins. Soon the time will come where I shall be forced to discreetly seek my pleasures elsewhere.

As you know, my good friend Hubert Marsten has already been assisting me in this regard. I greatly look forward to the day when I shall make the long journey to the New World, there to enjoy the company of men such as yourself, men who have availed themselves of the vitality of your virgin land and prospered mightily as a result.

You and I have much in common, Mr Plainview, much more than you know. Your thirst for oil is mirrored by my own particular appetites, of which you may learn more in time. Suffice to say that while the ceaseless pursuit of America's black lifeblood may have brought you great power and wealth, it is nothing compared to the power you could enjoy if you were to choose to enter my church. Now, do not misunderstand me - I do not refer to the Christian faith. I am reliably told that you are as scornful of the White as I. No, my faith is far, far older. I am not the serpent, but the father of serpents. Christ promises his followers eternal life, but all He truly has to offer is a dream of happiness, nothing but a heavenly fantasia. A lie. What use is life everlasting when your physical shell lies mouldering in the grave? No, the eternity I offer is a tangible one; this world and everything in it can be yours forever.

Now, my good friend Hubert tells me that you were sceptical, nay, <u>scornful</u> of this proposition. I quite understand your reluctance to believe, and only wish I could visit you in person to convince you of the veracity of my claims. Ah, how I would relish that! You have not seen the night until you have viewed it through my eyes, Mr Plainview.

Alas, circumstances preclude such a meeting for now. Instead, I beg a trifling indulgence of you. There is a book, a scholarly, monumental work named *De Vermis Mysteriis*. Quite a rare item these days, but still obtainable by those with sufficient wealth and influence. You have known Hubert Marsten for several decades, I believe. So, if his word means anything to you, if what I have said in this letter piques your curiosity even slightly, please do me the small service of purchasing the book. Many unknowable secrets lie within its pages. Trust me when I tell you it is the key to unlock the entrance to an entirely new, entirely different world. So will you not at least open the door for a moment and peer inside?

BREICHEN

3

<u>Letter from Walter Paisley to Daniel Plainview</u>

Dear Mr Plainview,

Please find enclosed the copy of *De Vermis Mysteriis*. A particularly unique and unusual volume. (To my knowledge, there are only three other copies existing in the country.) I do not know how deep your interest in esoterica runs, so please do not take offence when I say that this is not a work for the layman to dabble with. (I know of one account that suggests an entire Maine township fell under a curse simply due to the book's presence in its midst.)

You will also find that *De Vermis Mysteriis* is written in a curious hodgepodge of dead languages – Latin, Druidic, and others – and accordingly, may necessitate a great deal of scholarly expertise to decipher properly. Nevertheless, to those of strong mind and determined character, the book is undoubtedly capable of repaying the considerable investment of time and resources required to unlock its secrets a thousandfold.

I hope you will find your purchase to your satisfaction, Mr Plainview, and please do not hesitate to contact me should you require any other volumes of a similar nature.

Yours,
Walter Paisley Sr.
Dealer in Volumes of the Occult and Esoteric

4

Letter from Daniel Plainview to Kurt Breichen

Breichen,

I bought the damned book, as per your instructions. I suppose that will teach me to think twice before ever taking the dubious word of lowlife hoods and kraut crackpots. It is written in complete gibberish, and filled with the most depraved, perverted illustrations. That might pass for 'scholarly reading' wherever it is you come from, but I assure you it does not in any decent American home.

As well as the considerable outlay of money it took to purchase the volume, I also had to privately hire a professor of ancient languages in order to translate the bastard thing. Well, he got through about ten pages of it before he lost his nerve entirely and quit on me. I thought he was going to vomit all over the rug, he looked so pale and ill.

So now I'm saddled with a ghastly, incomprehensible book that cost me a small fortune to acquire. If ever the day comes when we do meet, I look forward to taking the cost of it out of your worthless hide.

Do not contact me again.

Sincerely,
D. Plainview

5

From the journal of Daniel Plainview

It is almost 6AM, and the sky outside my study window is turning pink with the dawn. It is only the promise of the sun that has settled my nerves enough to set pen to paper. Despite my having emptied a decanter of whisky since he departed, all I can taste on my lips is the metallic sting of pure terror.

I am getting ahead of myself, I know. Very well. Before I attempt to set down the details of what I have experienced this night, let me just say this: all of the following happened. It was no nightmare, or delusion found at the bottom of a whisky glass. I know there are those who would gladly dismiss me as an eccentric recluse, or denounce me as a drunk or a madman, but my mind has never felt so clear since the day I first struck silver in New Mexico. The day I broke my leg and almost died in a dynamite explosion. Encountering death at close hand lends clarity to a man's thoughts, a clarity as cold and hard as diamond. And it is with exactly that kind of clarity that I commit these words to paper now.

Because - make no mistake - the reaper visited me here in my home tonight.

I had fallen asleep in my chair in front of the fire. One of the servants, assuming I would not awaken again until morning, had taken care to remove the whisky glass from my hand and to drape me in a blanket. But awaken I did, I would guess at around 2AM. Despite my wool blanket and the fact that the servant had placed another log on the fire, I found myself gripped by a sudden cold in my bones, and awoke with a violent shudder.

My visitor was sitting in the chair placed opposite this one, observing me carefully.

I sat unmoving for a few moments, staring at him. At first I thought he must be some manner of hallucination, or an escapee from a half-recalled night terror, and fully expected him to vanish within seconds.

But then I saw how the embers of the fire lit up his eyes, lending them an infernal gleam, and I knew that he was as real as I.

The visitor leaned forward in his chair. 'My name is Charles Croydon,' he told me. 'I have come to your beautiful home on the behalf of your recent correspondent Kurt Breichen.'

'Who is Breichen to you?' I demanded.

He smiled broadly, a harmless enough gesture which made me unaccountably wary, although I could not be certain why. 'Breichen is my mentor, one might even say benefactor,' he replied. 'I owe him everything. You could say he made me the man I am today.'

I wanted to get up and berate him, chase him from the room, but found myself quite unable to stand. 'I care nothing for you or Breichen,' I told him, playing for time until the strength returned to my legs. 'Whatever business has brought you here and prompted you to break into my home, I want nothing to do with it. You're fortunate I don't shoot you where you sit.'

He inclined his head politely. 'You could do that, Mr Plainview. And you would of course be well within your rights to attempt such a thing. You do own a firearm, I trust?'

Something in his voice compelled me to answer. 'There is a loaded pistol in my right-hand desk drawer,' I whispered.

Then, it were as though I had fallen asleep again for just a couple of seconds, for the next thing I knew Croydon was standing beside my desk some feet away. But I swear that I did not, and yet somehow my visitor crossed the room in the time it took me to blink.

He opened the right-hand drawer and removed the pistol, which he turned over in his hands. 'An amusing little toy,' he said. 'Quite deadly in the right hands, I suppose. Against the right sort of intruder, that is.'

The next moment, he pressed the gun barrel underneath his jaw and fired.

Instinctively, I recoiled and closed my eyes. But when I reopened them an instant later, Croydon's face loomed up before me, mere inches from my own. The bullet should have blown half his head off, but he was seemingly unharmed, the only evidence of the gunshot a blackened scorch mark on his throat.

However, while his face may have been unharmed, it was nonetheless horribly transformed. It resembled nothing more than a demon from the pit; eyes blazing crimson, teeth sharp enough to tear the flesh from a man's bones.

'NOW DO YOU BELIEVE?' he bellowed.

The shock of his sudden assault was such that I jerked violently backwards in my seat, sending the chair toppling to the ground. I landed heavily; hard enough to knock the air from my lungs, if only I had been in a fit state to breathe.

I lay there on the hearth rug, gasping and helpless, waiting for the demon to strike me dead.

Instead, Croydon took a step backwards. A knot flared in the grate, and the resulting blaze of firelight seemed to extinguish all signs of monstrosity from his features. Instantly, he seemed like a normal man again.

He walked back over to the desk, where he picked up that filthy book and began to thumb carefully through its pages. Within moments, a look of satisfaction crossed his face. Turning towards me, he moved to my side and proffered a hand to help me back to my feet. When I hesitated, he simply reached down, grabbed me by my lapel and hauled me upright. I will admit that my trembling legs could barely hold my weight, but Croydon quickly righted my chair and eased me back down into it, before placing the open book on my lap.

'Everything you must know is written down upon these two pages in front of you, Plainview,' he told me. 'Conduct the ritual detailed there and prove yourself worthy of my master's church. Tonight, I have permitted you a small glimpse of the power that could be yours. Imagine what you could accomplish with such a gift! Demonstrate to my master that you are deserving of it, and you shall be baptised and born anew.'

With that, Croydon turned and withdrew into the shadows. At no time did I see him exit through the study doorway, and yet within moments I knew he had gone from the room.

That was several hours ago. I have scarcely moved from this chair since, save to pour myself more whisky or throw another log on the fire. It seems to me that to venture any further would risk revealing myself to the world outside this room, a world that now appears fraught with unknowable threat and terror.

So here I sit, waiting for the servants to awake, in the hope that the dreadful loneliness that has suddenly gripped me might then abate.

I sit, and sip at my whisky, and wait impatiently for the sun to rise.

I sit, and I think about true power, and the lengths one might be willing to go to in order to achieve it.

6

Letter from Kurt Breichen to Daniel Plainview

My dear Mr Plainview!

Forgive my presumption in writing to you again. You made it quite clear that I should not do so, but I imagine much has changed since our last exchange. Charles can be quite persuasive when the mood takes him, as I believe you have discovered. His methods are sometimes coarser than I prefer, but he has been a trusted ally to me ever since he joined my congregation several centuries ago.

In deference to your previous request, I will keep this brief. You now have everything you need: *De Vermis Mysteriis* (Have you examined it yet? A fascinating work, is it not?), and the knowledge of the gift that awaits you, should you choose to accept the boon I have offered. (I should however warn you that if you continue to refuse my gracious invitation, it will not go well for you. My kind guard our secrets jealously, and will do whatever is necessary to ensure that our cherished *Silentium* remains unbroken.)

Regardless, the final choice remains yours. You may perhaps quibble that it is really no sort of a choice at all, but as a successful businessman of many years' standing, I have no doubt that you are quite familiar with the concept of - I believe this is the correct term? - 'driving a hard bargain'.

I suspect you are probably not a chess player, Mr Plainview. I myself have grown to appreciate the finer qualities of the game during the many long nights of my ageless existence. Perhaps, in time, you might choose to take it up too, in which case I would greatly look forward to one day facing you across a chess board. I imagine you are a worthy opponent.

But regardless, we must only concern ourselves with the game we are currently playing. In which it is now <u>your move</u>.

BREICHEN

7

<u>Letter from H.W. Plainview to Daniel Plainview</u>

Father,

I had not planned to write this letter, but Mary insisted that I should. Even after the mysterious - some might say suspicious - death of her brother Eli at your home last year, she maintains that you are family, and are therefore worthy of our love and respect. Well, she is a far better Christian than I. Our last encounter left me in little doubt that you no longer regard me as your kin, and that any love and respect I have previously accorded you will not be reciprocated.

But it is not my intention to reopen old wounds. On my wife's instruction, this letter is simply to inform you of the recent birth of our first-born son. He is a happy, healthy boy, and I look forward to fulfilling my paternal duties towards him for as long as I am able. He will never want for love in this house, that much I do solemnly swear.

We have named him Abel, after Mary's late father.

Yours faithfully,
H.W.

8

Newspaper clipping from *The Santa Fe New Mexican*

OIL PROSPECTOR'S CHILD ABDUCTED

Santa Teresa N.M., May 4 (AP) - The infant son of oil prospector H.W. Plainview and his wife Mary was taken from their home in Santa Teresa yesterday night.

The couple had just finished their evening meal when Mrs Plainview went to check on their sleeping son, only to find he had been abducted from his crib. There were no visible signs of entry anywhere in the house, and while Mr Plainview's hearing was irreparably damaged in a childhood accident, his wife claimed not to have heard a sound.

'Our nearest neighbour is a mile away,' the prospector said in a written statement afterwards. 'If anyone so much as sets foot on our property, Mary knows about it.'

Mr Plainview, the only son of famed oil tycoon Daniel Plainview, has offered a $5000 reward for information leading to his child's safe return.

Local police agree that kidnapping is by far the most likely explanation for the boy's disappearance, although no ransom demand has yet been received...

9
Letter from Charles Croydon to Kurt Breichen

Master,

It is done. Assuming successful completion of the ritual, I shall visit Plainview in his home tomorrow night and complete his induction into your sacred church. With his wealth and influence at your disposal, your future prosperity in the New World is assured. *Carpe Noctum!*
  Yours eternally,
  Charles

10
From the journal of Daniel Plainview

The house is silent and dark. I have sent all the servants away. I cannot risk discovery now, not when I am so close. Also, if Croydon is to be believed - and it seems like I have little choice but to believe him - I will soon have no use for them anyway.

I have been studying *De Vermis Mysteriis* for the past several hours. While Croydon directed me towards the relevant pages during his visit here, I still believed my task was hopeless. After all, the book is written in an incomprehensible slurry of languages. What hope did I have of deciphering it? But somehow, the more I look at its pages, the more I understand. It is as though the book itself is guiding me. I can almost hear its insinuating whisper at the back of my mind, like the slow hiss of methane escaping from the earth.

I now know what must be done.

It is no secret that I have ruined several men. Left their livelihoods in ruins, put them and their families out on the streets without so much as a second thought. And I would do it all again tomorrow if I had to.

I have also murdered a man in cold blood. Regardless, he was a liar and a cheat and sought to insinuate himself into my life and business as though he were a tick battening on a stag. And I can spare no more remorse for his death than I would if I crushed such a bloodsucking insect between my thumb and forefinger.

But _this_? Can I possibly do as the book instructs and ever sleep soundly in my bed again? How can a man live with such dreadful knowledge when he may have to live with it forever? Is Breichen's offer a blessing or a curse?

The infant reminds me of H.W. as a baby. Quiet and watchful, not much given to childish whining and wailing. He lays there and silently studies me, just as his own father used to. Of course, I now understand that what I simply took to be H.W.'s withdrawn and watchful nature was in fact him carefully assessing my strengths and weaknesses, patiently safeguarding his accumulated knowledge until the opportune moment arrived for him to strike. I tell myself this infant has doubtless inherited his father's sly cunning, his limitless capacity for betrayal. This is what children do; they seek to supplant us, to build their future successes on the foundations of their parents' bones.

I was a fool to ever allow H.W. into my life - now he seeks to compete with me, to destroy everything I have so assiduously built in order that he may prosper. What a delicious irony then, that his own offspring will provide me with the means to crush him and anyone else who would ever seek to stand against me!

So be it. One last whisky to quiet the tremor in my hands.

I go to perform the ritual now.

Later

It is done. In truth, it was scarcely any more difficult than carving a Thanksgiving turkey. The child's innards were rather small and slippery but I managed to arrange them in the configuration stipulated within the book's pages. When I spoke the invocation from *De Vermis Mysteriis* aloud - I had worried about pronouncing the words properly but again, it were as though the book itself were speaking through me - the bloodied organs burst immediately into flame and burnt away to ashes. I take that to mean the ceremony was a success.

Now I sit and await Croydon's return, filled with an elation I have not known since I first struck oil as a young man. I knew then that my life had changed forever, and that I could never go back; now I stand poised on the precipice of a similarly fateful juncture.

My fingers have stained these pages with blood, but no matter. This will be the last entry I ever make in this journal.

When I think back to the ritual, draining the child's blood was by far the worst of it. Drawing my blade across its plump pink throat, the choked wail as its lifeblood splattered into a waiting bowl. As I watched the crimson liquid bubble redly to the brim, I wondered if I could even bear to go through with the last part of the rite.

The strange thing was, the blood looked so thick and creamy that it scarcely resembled blood at all.

As I raised the bowl to my lips, I told myself that it would be just like drinking a milkshake.

STANTON CARLISLE

Tyrone Power in Nightmare Alley, *1947*
written by Jules Furthman
based on the novel by William Lindsay Gresham
directed by Edmund Goulding

THE WORST OF IT WAS, NO MATTER HOW MUCH WHISKEY HE DRANK, HE could never get the taste of chicken blood out of his mouth.

Once, Stan Carlisle had had it all. Fame, money, a beautiful dame. *You're looking at the American Dream made flesh,* he would tell his friends. *I used to be nothing, a carny grifter hustling for pennies. But now they queue around the block to see me. I'm living proof that, in America, even a little guy can make it big.*

But that was before he got greedy and stupid. Greedy enough to try and convince a grieving mark that he could summon up his wife's ghost, and stupid enough to trust that conniving bitch Lilith. She'd stolen Stan's money and sent him spiralling back down into the gutter he'd spent so many years climbing out of. And at long last, he'd understood.

Understood that you could have all the fame and money in the world, but you were never one of *them*, not really. When the beautiful people finally got tired of you, the very instant you weren't any use to them any more, you lost your seat at the big table. They'd toss you away without a second thought, like a cheap umbrella that had started to let the rain in.

And falling from such a great height, you'd fall *hard*.

Stan had fallen harder than most. Unable to bear the loss of the life he'd always dreamt of, he'd sought refuge in booze. But just like one of those dinky model ships, once you were in the bottle, there was no getting out. He'd tried to go back to the carny, but it was hopeless. He stank of whiskey, his clothes looked like he'd fished them out of a particularly deep sewer, and his timing was totally shot to hell. Christ, it wasn't so long ago that Stan had been able to hit a mark completely cold, colder than a nun's kiss even, and it didn't matter, before you knew it they'd be eating out of his hand like a goddamn pet pony. But now? Forget it. He could barely tell you his own name in the right order.

The pitiful state he was in, the only job he'd been able to get was in the freakshow, biting the heads off live chickens. Used to be he was the Great Stanton; now he was just the goddamn geek. Once he made audiences gasp in astonishment, now they simply moaned in prurient disgust. Back when he was on the up, Stan had always wondered what sort of pathetic loser could ever sink so low as to work as a geek. No one's life could be *that* bad, surely? Tomorrow was always another day, right?

But that was before all his tomorrows had been stolen from him. He'd been granted a brief glimpse of the paradise he would never be permitted to inhabit, before plunging screaming back down to earth, his ruined wings scorched to the bone. Stanton Carlisle would never fly that high again; grounded forever, just like the chickens he tore the heads off every night.

Oh, Molly had stuck by him, tried to help him as best she could. Poor Molly, so sweet and so kind. In the old days, Stan used to resent the fact that she seemed to be happy with her lot in life, that she figured people ought to be grateful for what they had, instead of constantly trying to chisel themselves a little extra. Secretly, he'd always thought that made her just another loser, and there was nothing Stan hated more than a loser. But it turned out she'd been right all along, and that burned him worse than anything.

So when Molly tried to help him, get him straightened out and off the booze so he could get the hell out of that geek pit, he'd pushed her away. Kept on drinking despite her pleas, even knocked her around a little bit when he got sick of her constant begging. She'd stuck it out for as long as she could bear, but eventually it had all gotten too much and she'd broken down in tears in front of the carny boss. The boss liked Molly a whole bunch, everybody did, and next thing Stan knew his contract had been sold to another outfit: Madame Tetrallini's circus. No one even said goodbye to him, they just left his cage behind when they moved onto their next engagement one morning. Stan was passed out as usual, so had been none the wiser. A few hours later, Tetrallini's circus showed up, hitched his cage to a horse and that was that. It took Stan a day or two before he even realised his old life had vanished into the distance, like it had never even existed in the first place.

More and more these days, Stan was starting to think that maybe it hadn't. Maybe he'd always been stuck in this cage, and had only imagined something better for himself. Maybe *that* had been the real American Dream all along.

And now here he was, his mouth forever tasting of puke and chicken blood, and with a pain behind his eyes that never quit. It was a kind of hell, he supposed, but he couldn't blame the Devil for it. This particular hell he'd walked into with his eyes wide open.

The truth of it was that Madame Tetrallini was actually a pretty decent sort, as far as circus owners went. The way Stan saw it, you could hardly call anyone running a freakshow a bleeding heart humanitarian or anything, but for what it was worth, the Madame got all sappy over her freaks, even treated some of them like they were her own kids. And they loved her back, because they'd never known any better. They were born losers, just like Molly and the rest.

But Stan *had* known something better, and even though he knew it was lost to him forever, the simple knowledge that it existed meant he would never be able to settle for the miserable sham of an existence he was living now.

So when the freaks tried to welcome him to the circus, even going as far as to throw him a welcome party, he couldn't stand it. The two German midgets, the pinheads, the Siamese twins and the rest, it made him sick to look at them. They even had some idiot song they chanted, *Gooble gobble, we accept you, one of us.* Like he was meant to feel honoured by *that*.

But deep down, he knew it was the truth. He *was* one of them. Christ, even lower than them.

Still, he wasn't the lowest wretch in the circus, not by a long shot. That particular honour went to a creature so pathetically hideous that even Madame Tetrallini and the freaks shunned her. She didn't seem to have a name, everyone just called her the Human Chicken. Stan had peered into her pit once and the sight had turned his stomach like a whirligig.

Just like her name suggested, she was nothing more than an unholy hybrid of human and chicken: face mutilated into an idiot rictus; the flesh of her arms melted into twisted parodies of wings; lower body amputated and torso covered with feathers. Stan couldn't begin to imagine how such a monstrosity could even exist. Black magic? Some kind of insane surgery? (Hadn't he heard stories about some crazy limey doctor who tried to mate men with animals?) Madame Tetrallini liked to say that her freaks were all God's children, but God had nothing to do with what he saw in the pit that day, Stan knew that much for certain.

The worst part of it was, when Stan had gazed into the creature's one remaining eye, he'd glimpsed something there he recognised. A look he'd seen in his own eyes, on the rare occasions he accidentally went anywhere near a mirror these days.

A look that said: *Please help me.*

That said: *I wasn't always like this.*

His gorge rising, he'd run straight back to his cage and downed the half-bottle of whiskey he'd been saving for after the show that night.

So the days turned into weeks, and the weeks into months, and Stan felt himself die a little more every day. He figured that death was really all he had to look forward to; the booze would take him sooner or later, and he only prayed that would truly be the end of it. He craved nothingness, total oblivion. On the really bad nights, he would dream he was dying and then wake up back in his cage, and start screaming because he was convinced this was the afterlife he had been consigned to; an eternity of iron bars and chicken blood and horrified eyes staring down at him.

And then one morning he saw her. He awoke in a puddle of his own puke and looked up to glimpse a beautiful woman drifting through the caravans nearby, like she'd just walked out of a dream. She was tall and slim and had that air about her, the one that says *I'm better than all of you schmucks and you know it.*

She looked like she should have been hanging in a gallery. She reminded him of Lilith so badly it hurt.

Stan didn't know what he wanted more, to fuck her or to kill her.

He watched as she bummed a cigarette from Hans, the German midget, who simpered over her like he did over any half decent-looking dame. She stood smoking for a minute, her cool gaze studying Stan from a distance. He wanted to stand up and scream, *I wasn't always like this! I used to be the Great Stanton! I went through stuck-up broads like you as though they were bubblegum!*

But he said nothing. Eventually, she finished her cigarette, dropped it to the ground and trod it into the mud with her heel, as though she were grinding away at the meat of his face.

The moment she'd gone, Stan called Hans over and asked him who the woman was.

Hans grinned. *The beautiful lady? Her name is Madame Zora. A gypsy fortune teller.*

Goddamn, but the midget was dumb. Anyone could see that broad was no gypsy. *Where's she from?* Stan asked him impatiently.

New York City, I think? But she is working her way south with the circus. She says she is going back to New Orleans, where she was born.

Hans couldn't tell him any more, so Stan told him to run along and play with his toys. He couldn't get Madame Zora's face out of his head for the rest of the day. Her presence in the circus was another affront, a reminder of how far he'd fallen. He hoped to hell he never saw her again.

But Stan forgot that he was fresh out of hope these days. The next day, the woman stopped by his cage to introduce herself. *Hello, Stan,* she said politely. *I'm Margaret.*

He stared at her dumbly, hardly able to believe she was talking to him. *I heard you were Zora.*

She affected a smile. *Just my stage name. Don't you have one of those?*

I used to.

I'll bet you used to have a lot of things, didn't you?

Before despair and the booze got him, Stan would have laid some snappy patter on the dame, but all that was long gone, flushed down the drain. So instead he just carried right on staring. The best he could hope for was that he wasn't drooling.

Margaret leaned in towards him, her voice dropping to a soft murmur. *You remind me of someone I knew back before the war. He used to be beautiful too.*

Stan's voice caught in his throat. *Beautiful?* he croaked.

Beautiful and talented. He had a wonderful voice. Johnny Golden Tonsils, they called him. But that wasn't his only gift. He had second sight too. Just like you did, before you drank it away.

Second sight? Did this dame actually believe the crap she was peddling? *What the hell are you talking about, lady?*

Oh, come on, Margaret sighed impatiently. *I'll bet you always used to know things about people, didn't you?*

Yeah, but —

And you thought you were so smart, because all the rubes thought it was magic, but you knew better; you knew it was only intuition. But they were right, Stan. And you were wrong.

Stan leapt forward and violently slapped the bars of his cage. *You don't know anything about me!*

She didn't flinch. *I know what I see.*

Go to hell!

Margaret smiled again, and Stan thought he glimpsed genuine amusement in her eyes this time. *Maybe I will, at that. And maybe I'll take you with me, Stan.*

With that, she turned on her heels and strode away.

Stan didn't see her again until a couple of nights later, when he spotted her amongst the crowd of people watching his act. As usual, the faces of the gathered onlookers ran the gamut of horrified to disgusted; all aside from Margaret's. Her face was like a mask, betraying nothing, even when he bit the head off a chicken and spat it right in her direction.

What the fuck did this bitch want from him?

Later that night, Stan was working his way through a fifth of whiskey when she came to him again. Seeing Margaret standing there, he let out a sour laugh and thrust the bottle towards her. *You looking for a drink, is that it? Cause I got nothing else for you, lady.*

I caught your act tonight, she told him quietly.

Pretty good, huh?

I thought it was appalling.

Stan cackled. *Well, that's what they pay me for.*

Is this what you want for yourself? Or do you want your old life back? Everything you used to have, and more. I can help you get it, Stan.

His stomach twisted. *Don't you taunt me, you bitch.*

I can.

Screw you! For a moment, he thought about dashing out of the cage and knocking her to the ground, fastening his hands around that elegant china neck of hers and choking the life from it.

Watch. Margaret raised her arm and extended a hand towards him. From her upturned palm a flame sprang into life, burning bright and steady.

If this was a trick, a carny illusion, he couldn't see it how she was pulling it off, and Stan thought he knew all the angles. *What the…?*

Look into the flame.

So he did, and he saw everything. The life he used to have, and the life he might yet have again. He saw himself restored, rich and healthy and happy, the circus and the cage and the geek act nothing more than a barely-remembered bad dream; the sort of thing that can be washed away with a pot of good coffee and a champagne breakfast.

Stan didn't know how long he sat staring into that flame, but by the end of it he was sobbing, the tears falling off his face like he was fit to melt away to nothing.

Eventually, he whispered a single word: *How?*

Margaret closed her palm, the flame instantly vanishing with a hiss. *The Prince of Darkness can grant you your life back. He has the power to do that, Stan. And I can help you make the bargain.*

The Prince of Darkness? The Devil? This was just about the craziest thing he'd ever heard, but Stan didn't care. Why should he? They could stick him in the nuthouse if they liked. It couldn't be any worse than this.

What do I have to do? Stan finally asked her.

It's very simple, really. You must carry out a blood ritual. One life for yours. I'll take care of the rest.

Murder? He slumped back against the bars of his cage, raising the bottle to his lips and drinking deeply. Stan had always treated the law as a trifling inconvenience in the past – Christ, everyone knew that laws were for suckers – but he'd never actually *hurt* anyone, not really. Could he do that, even to save himself? God knows he'd fantasised about it enough times. Sure, if Lilith were to walk by right now, he could see himself killing *her*, but that would barely even count as murder. Killing an innocent person, though?

Margaret gazed at him silently. In a way, she seemed more disgusted with him now than when she'd watched his act. She shrugged. *Of course, if you don't have the strength…*

He waved her away with an angry snarl. *Leave me be, dammit! I need to think about this.*

A nod. *When you've made your decision, I'll be here.*

The fortune teller slipped away into the shadows, leaving Stan alone in his cage. He stared up through the bars as the moon rose full and bright in the sky, and he drank some more and he thought some more. Jesus, thinking used to come so easy to him. How was it a man could even lose his own thoughts?

And then the answer came to him, clear as a baby's tears. Stan was so delighted that his hand reflexively jerked into the air, spilling the rest of his whiskey. But he didn't care. It was perfect, just perfect. Still, he needed to act now, right away, while he had the moxie to do it. He could finally be free of this cage, free of Madame Tetrallini and the rest of her goddamn freaks.

One of us, one of us.

No. Not any more, never again. No matter what it took.

He crept from his cage and stole through the clustered caravans, careful not to wake any of the freaks. When he arrived at her cage, he gazed down at her sleeping body, imagining it.

Stan told himself it would be a blessing. And hell, it wouldn't even be murder, not really.

After all, what was she but a big dumb chicken?

When they found him the next morning, he had almost gnawed the entire way through her neck.

MICHAEL MYERS

Will Sandin, Nick Castle & Tony Moran in Halloween, 1978
written by John Carpenter & Debra Hill
directed by John Carpenter

THE MURDERS THAT OCCURRED IN THE TOWN OF HADDONFIELD IN October 1978 have long since passed into American folklore, their perpetrator becoming immortalised alongside such other legendary monsters as Bigfoot and the Candyman. Children today tell each other whispered tales of the Boogeyman, or the Shape; a faceless, implacable evil that appears out of the darkness on Halloween night and cannot be stopped, not until its thirst for blood and murder has been assuaged.

But these killings *happened*, and within living memory at that; they are not simply the stuff of campfire stories or internet creepypastas. It is as though America has collectively refused to face up to the truth about that terrible night, preferring instead to banish it into the realms of myth, where it can be easily dismissed as merely another urban legend. But ask the families of Annie Brackett, or Lynda Van Der Klok; these were not fairy tale characters, but real people. Fun-loving adolescents who, as teenage girls are wont to do, once loved and laughed and bitched and argued, but now lie buried in Haddonfield Cemetery. Speak to their families, or to Laurie Strode, or to Tommy Doyle and Lindsey Wallace, and they will all tell you precisely the same thing: there is a black absence at the heart of the Halloween murders, and his name – his *real* name, not some horror story sobriquet – is Michael Myers.

Despite his spending fifteen years committed to Smith's Grove Sanitarium, very little is officially known about Myers. He was first taken into custody at age six, after the brutal and motiveless murder of his older sister Judith, and was assigned to the psychiatric care of one Dr. Samuel Loomis. Colleagues of the doctor described him as a conscientious, dedicated man, and yet for many commentators, the unavoidable truth of the matter is that Loomis failed utterly to gain any understanding of his young patient's particular pathology. In fact, some have even suggested that the doctor himself eventually suffered some sort of breakdown, abandoning all attempts to properly treat Myers and referring to him only as 'the Evil'. They point to this as an egregious systemic failure, one that fatally undermined our society's ability to comprehend Michael Myers and his crimes.

But the reality of it is far more simple: it was not truly Myers who committed the murders.

Let us first examine the known facts. Michael Myers's mother Edith Palmer eloped with her boyfriend Peter Myers when she was seventeen years old. By then she was already pregnant with Judith, but complications with the birth meant that she would not fall pregnant again for another ten years. The Palmer family had long been residents of the State of Washington, but when Peter and Judith ran away together, they chose to relocate more than halfway across the country, to Illinois. Peter's own family hailed from the Prairie State, and given how much the Palmers disapproved of their union, the newlyweds decided they would receive a far warmer welcome there. Edith would see very little of her parents over the following decade; her mother had recently given birth to another child herself, a son the Palmers named Leland, and during the years that followed, they all but disowned Edith and dedicated themselves solely to their son's upbringing. However, Peter Myers eventually managed to effect a *rapprochement* between parents and daughter, reasoning that the Palmers deserved the opportunity to meet their grandchildren Judith and Michael, much as Edith should be allowed to properly get to know her little brother Leland.

Although Judith Myers never really took to Leland and preferred to keep her distance (her parents reasoned that she was put off by the genealogical quirk of his being her uncle, despite being a mere one year older), Edith doted on the boy, treating him more like a son than a brother. As he grew older, he would regularly visit Illinois to holiday with the Myers family, and, never previously having known a sibling of his own, Leland began to take his young nephew Michael under his wing. By all accounts, Michael was a happy, gregarious child, and loved to play with his uncle, the two of them dancing to Peter's collection of jazz 45s or playing monsters in the backyard together. There would always be tears when it came time for Leland to leave, soon to be followed by frequent queries about exactly when 'Unca Leland' would be coming back.

The last time Leland Palmer visited the Myers family was during the summer of 1963. Leland was about to begin his law degree at the University of Washington, and confided in his older sister that he wasn't sure his studies would permit him to visit as regularly as he had done in the past. *I'm worried that Michael won't understand,* he told Edith. *He's still so young.*

Well, there's nothing you can do about it, she replied. *He'll just have to get used to the way things are. It's part of growing up.*

All the same, Leland said. *I'd like to make this summer special for him. If Peter doesn't mind me borrowing the car every now and then, maybe I can take Michael out on some day trips.*

Happy that their son had such an attentive uncle, Peter and Edith readily consented. The first outing, to the zoo in Peoria, was such a success that Leland agreed to take Michael on another day trip the following week.

Where we gonna go, Unca Leland? Michael asked.

This time is going to be a big surprise, Leland replied. *But it'll be really fun, I promise.*

Tell me, tell me! his nephew pleaded.

Leland refused. He wouldn't even reveal his secret to Edith and Peter, saying only that he was taking Michael to a magical place, a place most kids would never, ever get to visit.

It is here that we must depart from the recorded facts of the Myers affair. Because, unbelievable as it might sound, what no official case history of Michael Myers will ever reflect is that Leland Palmer was in fact telling them the literal truth.

Come the day, uncle and nephew set out bright and early. They soon left the town of Haddonfield behind them, and drove through empty expanses of prairie for what seemed like hours, enough time for little Michael to grow restive. *How much longer,* he whined, in the manner of all bored small children.

Soon! Very soon! Leland promised him, a broad grin stretching across his face.

And if Michael had been old enough to be cognisant of such things, he might have noticed that the grin remained there for just a couple of seconds too long.

But Michael's uncle was as good as his word. About fifteen minutes later, they drew up outside a large junkyard. A rusted sign hanging above the entrance read 'SIMON'S SCRAP'.

And here we are! Leland exclaimed.

Michael peered through the window, disappointment clouding his features. *It's just a bunch of old cars,* he mumbled.

Oh, no no no no no no no, his uncle replied, wagging an admonishing finger in the air. *Michael, have you ever heard the expression 'Things aren't always what they seem?'*

Still downcast, his nephew admitted that he had not.

Leland reached over and ruffled the boy's hair. *Well, if you follow me, I'll show you that this isn't just a bunch of old cars, very far from it. It may look like that right now, but it's actually a magic kingdom, full of fun and games. And if you come with me, I'll introduce you to my friend Simon, who can't wait to play with you.*

Somewhat mollified, Michael allowed Leland to lead him from the car and into the junkyard. It sure did look like a bunch of old cars to him, but he loved and trusted his uncle, and if Unca Leland said this dirty old place was magic, then Michael certainly had no cause to doubt him.

Of course, what Michael could not know, what no one would know for another thirty years, was that his Uncle Leland had long played host to the entity known only as BOB, a malefic spirit from the otherworldly realm called the Black Lodge. For years BOB had bided his time, waiting for Leland to come of age, so that BOB might finally be free to indulge his bestial appetite to rape and kill.

Still, even a crazed monster like BOB had certain responsibilities to his masters. One of them was to provide the other Lodge spirits with ample quantities of human pain and sorrow, the substance they called 'garmonbozia'.

The other, unfortunately enough for Michael, was to seek out possible hosts for other Lodge spirits to inhabit.

Leland escorted his nephew through the towering piles of corroding scrap, darting left, then right, then left again. Michael felt as though they were navigating a vast labyrinth, and became unaccountably frightened that his uncle might suddenly run off and leave him. He was sure that he would never find his way out, and be trapped here forever. This place wasn't magic, it couldn't be. Magic places didn't make little kids feel scared and unsafe, not in any of the bedtime stories he'd been told. And yet, Michael was convinced that, at any second, one of the towers of scrapped vehicles would begin to topple and come crashing down on him. Not to mention that the junkyard stank really bad. Michael guessed that the metallic scent hitting his nostrils was the smell of all the old cars rusting, but what could be causing that terrible burning stench underneath it?

He did not know, but it terrified him. Soon, he began to whimper.

Stop that silly noise, Michael! Leland jerked at his nephew's arm, much too hard. *It's not far now. You need to be a big boy now, otherwise Simon won't want to play with you!*

I don't wanna play, I wanna go home!

Leland gazed down at Michael, and his nephew saw that the grin his uncle had been wearing ever since they entered the junkyard had now frozen into a ghastly death's head grimace. *Shut up, you little bastard!*

Leland shrieked. *If you don't stop that fucking noise you'll never go home again! Do you understand me?*

As much startled by the forbidden obscenities as he was by his uncle's newly-revealed capacity for rage, Michael fell immediately into a shocked silence, allowing himself to be dragged ever further into the labyrinth of scrap metal. The noxious burning smell soon filled his throat and nostrils, to the point where he thought he might choke on it, but still Michael remained silent. Better to die than have Unca Leland scream those terrible words at him again.

Eventually, they emerged from the maze to find a small dilapidated shack, situated at the very heart of the scrapyard. Its windows were empty and dark, and the open entrance yawned like the mouth of some hungry beast. It put Michael in mind of the sorts of houses witches inhabited in fairy tales.

That's where Simon lives, said Leland, all anger now dispelled. *Let's go find and him.*

The very last place on Earth Michael wished to go was inside that shack, but all reserves of resistance had by now fled his body. His uncle's hand clasped tightly around his own, they stepped through the doorway and entered a small filthy room. A stained mattress lay shoved against one wall, and in the other corner an old rocking chair sat next to a rusty refrigerator, upon which a blackened hot plate had been placed. Lengths of yellowed plastic sheeting were tacked over the windows.

The burning smell was still strong in here, but now there was another scent mingling with it, Michael realised: the smell of pee-pee. Who would live in such a terrible place?

This way, Leland whispered.

There was another door set into the far wall, Michael saw, but surely that didn't make any sense. Seen from the outside, the shack hadn't been big enough to have another room inside it, of that much he was certain. But impossibly, when his uncle opened the door, there it was: a long dark passageway stretching off before them, leading to…where?

It could only be a Bad Place, Michael decided.

He whimpered in alarm, but found himself shoved inside by Leland's firm hand. *Don't be afraid*, his uncle said. *I told you, it's magic.*

They walked slowly down the passageway together. Michael could hear their footsteps echoing around them, as though they were in some huge cavern. It was all like some horrible dream and he just wanted to curl up on the floor and go to sleep, in the hope that he might wake up in his own bed back at home with Mommy and Daddy in the next room.

But he kept right on walking, because he knew if he didn't Unca Leland would get mad with him again, and nothing could be worse than that.

At the end of the passageway they reached a wooden staircase. *Nearly there*, his uncle told him. Humming gaily to himself, Leland began to tap dance up the stairs, pulling his nephew along behind him.

Upon reaching the top, they emerged into a large dimly-lit room. Some years before, the three tall windows set into the far wall had all been pasted over with sheets of newspaper, blocking most exterior light from the room. A dirty old couch had been placed in front of the middle window, upon which sat an old woman and a young boy of about the same age as Michael.

When he saw the other child, Michael looked desperately to him for help, but the boy's only response was to pick up a white *papier maché* mask and hold it in front of his face.

On the other side of the room, an old man sat alone at a green formica table, naked except for a pair of urine-stained long johns. His face and body were completely devoid of hair, and at the sight of Michael, his face split open in a wide grin, revealing a toothless mouth. His purplish gums clacked soundlessly together, sending a cascade of saliva drooling down his jowls.

Horrified, Michael looked desperately around for his uncle, but Leland had vanished. In his place stood a feral-looking man with long grey hair, dressed in dirtied denims. When Michael's eyes met his, the man let out a roar.

A friend in need is a friend indeed! he snarled, in a strange, garbled-sounding voice. *Friendly Simon wants to play until it's time for bed!*

Michael screamed and tried to run, only for the long-haired man to seize him by both arms. The little boy struggled, but could do nothing to escape his captor's grip. Wildly, he looked around to see Simon getting up from the table. The old man shuffled towards Michael, gibbering a slurry of nonsense, arms reaching out for his new playmate.

As Simon's shadow fell upon him, Michael was seized by a terrible inside-out sensation, as though the parts of him that were truly Michael Myers, the ones he kept tightly locked away in his brain and his belly, were being pulled out through his mouth. He could still sense the distant weight of his body tugging down on him, but increasingly, it seemed as though it was no longer really his.

All Michael could do now was watch as Simon's hairless face descended towards his own.

Dimly, he was aware of the other boy leaping down off the couch and beginning to jump up and down on the spot. *Is the glass half-empty?* the boy cried. *Or is it half-full?*

Simon opened his mouth, revealing the blackened stump of his severed tongue. It wiggled grotesquely, like a worm impaled on a fisherman's hook.

Then there was nothing.

By the time Michael emerged from the junkyard, the sky overhead was growing dark. His uncle Leland was sitting outside in the car, chewing rhythmically at a mouthful of gum. When Michael climbed inside, his uncle turned to him and asked, *Did you have fun?*

Michael nodded wordlessly, eyes fixed straight ahead. Reaching over to pat him on the shoulder, Leland started up the car and drove away. Glancing up into the rearview mirror, he watched as the reflected image of the junkyard began to warp and crackle, finally disappearing from sight completely. A barren stretch of wasteland was all that remained in its place.

When the pair of them reached home, Michael silently hugged his parents then went straight up to bed. When Edith queried her son's unusual behaviour, Leland merely laughed. *Oh, he's just tired,* he told his sister. *He played so hard today you wouldn't believe it. Come tomorrow, I bet he'll be right as rain.*

So where was it you took him? she asked.

Leland grinned. *I guess I'll let Michael tell you that himself. We can all talk about it at breakfast tomorrow.*

But Edith never saw her younger brother again. That night, after the Myers family had retired to bed, Leland crept out of the house and walked the three miles to Haddonfield's bus station, where he caught the first Greyhound heading east. Shortly after his arrival in Washington, he would leave home to commence his university studies. In the wake of the unspeakable tragedy that struck the Myers family that following Halloween, Edith desperately tried to contact her brother, certain that he might be able to shed some light on what had happened to Michael to transform him so utterly, but he simply never answered her calls and letters.

The morning after his excursion with Leland, Michael seemed little improved. Normally so cheerful and energetic, he had now become a silent, watchful boy, who would move soundlessly around the house and study his family from afar, without them having the faintest notion he was even there. Discomfited by her brother's sudden departure, Edith asked her son where his Uncle Leland had taken him. *To a magic place*, replied Michael, but would tell her no more.

His parents worried about the changes in their boy, but chose not to pursue the matter further. Perhaps it was just a phase. It wasn't until Judith caught her brother hiding in her closet, peeking at her undressing, that they finally decided to take Michael to a physician.

The doctor examined their son carefully, but could find nothing physically wrong with him. *He's a little quiet*, the doctor told them, *but that's hardly cause for alarm.*

But he never used to be this way! Edith insisted. *He was such a happy, loving child, and now all he does is stare. When I hug him, it's like I'm holding a mannequin in my arms. I swear, I hardly even recognise him anymore.*

The doctor shrugged. *He's young, he has a lot of growing up still to do. Give him another six months and he'll probably be a different person entirely.*

Well, what about him peeping at his sister?

Oh, he was just curious, the doctor said. *Listen. He's only six years old, he didn't understand what he was doing. I can understand your daughter being a little upset, but really, there's nothing at all to worry about.*

He's never been the same since he went off with his uncle that day, Judith murmured, barely able to face the implications of what she was saying. Her eyes gazed fixedly at the floor. *You don't think...?*

TWILIGHT'S LAST SCREAMING

There was no physical evidence of abuse, the doctor assured her. *But if you wanted to know any more, you'd really have to take Michael to a child psychologist. If you think you're ready for that step.*

Edith discussed the matter with her husband, but for the time being, they did nothing. Perhaps they decided to trust the doctor's advice, or perhaps they were simply unwilling to countenance the possibility that Leland might have harmed his nephew in any way. Whatever their reasoning, they simply chose to let Michael be. After all, he was not naughty, or unruly. And like the doctor said, everything could change again in a few months.

Come Halloween night, everything did change, but not in a manner that any doctor or parent could ever have foreseen.

In the years that followed Michael's committal for the murder of Judith Myers, Dr Loomis would conduct several more examinations of the boy, and interview both his parents at great length. Although the previous doctor's assessment that there was nothing wrong with Michael had obviously been disastrously misjudged, Loomis did concur that there appeared to be no real medical cause for his condition. Instead, the doctor eventually arrived at the – on the face of it, wholly unprofessional – conclusion that his young patient was not simply psychotic, but actively malevolent. As he would later tell people, *Whatever was lurking behind those eyes was, purely and simply, evil.* The weirdly matter-of-fact way in which he delivered this statement only made it easier for his listeners to scoff.

But although modern science lacked all capability to properly diagnose or comprehend the arcane truth of Michael Myers's condition, the doctor was nevertheless entirely correct in his intuition. He accurately sensed something *other* hiding behind Michael's eyes – the Black Lodge entity known only as Simon.

We cannot hope to ever understand such unknowable creatures, but it seems clear that, despite his host's immaturity, Simon had eagerly seized the first available opportunity to commit murder, and feed on the subsequent human pain and suffering. Temporarily sated after the killing of Judith Myers, he then lay dormant for several years (much as his brother spirit BOB had done with Leland Palmer) waiting for Michael Myers to reach adulthood.

Eventually, the time came when Michael, now aged twenty-one, was able to make good his escape from Smith's Grove. Driven by Simon's supernatural energies, he was by now practically unstoppable, immortal. He made his way back to Haddonfield, murdering another three people before Loomis was able to interrupt his former patient's killing spree.

When the two men finally stood face-to-face again, the doctor unhesitatingly shot Michael several times, at point-blank range. But seconds later, the killer had vanished completely. For a time, the police were certain their patrols would doubtless pick up the wounded man, or simply find his dead body somewhere.

Yet no trace of Michael Myers was ever found.

Under Simon's guidance, he had, of course, retreated back to the Black Lodge, content to remain there until the following Halloween. It is impossible to say whether the date has some mythological resonance for Simon and his fellow spirits, or whether the creature merely relishes the anticipatory terror caused by the knowledge that his host Michael Myers has, ever since the night of October 31st, 1978, returned to Haddonfield on that same date each and every subsequent year.

And once returned, he moves through the town's shadows as silently and unobtrusively as an plague, to kill and kill and kill again.

So yes, while the tale of Michael Myers has by now become a campfire story, an American myth, this account is the dreadful truth behind the legend. Little Michael has nothing to do with the ongoing evil being perpetrated in his name, no more than the real Leland Palmer did with the rape and murder of his own daughter Laura. In the absence of any real understanding of the Black Lodge and its vile denizens, it is perhaps as accurate as anything else to say that Haddonfield is doomed to suffer the curse of the *Shape*, or the *Boogeyman*, or whatever other name you might care to use. The chosen nomenclature simply does not matter; all that counts is that, every Halloween, he will return home. The residents of the town have long since accepted this, and it is why they no longer celebrate the holiday so beloved by the rest of the country, why you will not find a single trick-or-treater walking its streets.

Instead, each and every house will be securely locked come nightfall. Children will be tucked up safely in bed after dark, and worried fathers will stand guard until dawn, cradling pistols and shotguns in their laps.

And still the townsfolk know that several of their number will be found dead by morning.

Because you can't stop the Boogeyman, not ever.

ANDY BROOKS

Richard Backus in Deathdream, *1974*
written by Alan Ormsby
directed by Bob Clark

ANDY BROOKS HAD ALWAYS BEEN A GOOD BOY, RAISED TO BELIEVE IN GOD and country, to respect his elders and do exactly what he was told. So when he was ordered off to war, there was no question whatsoever in his mind that he would go. He wasn't one of those damn dirty hippies his father liked to rail against at the dinner table; he was a decent, all-American boy, and if the government told him that Communism was a threat to everything he knew and cherished, then who was he to say otherwise?

On the day he left, his mother broke down in tears. *Andy, tell me you'll come back*, she sobbed. *You've got to, you promised.*

And it was true, he *had* promised. His parents had instilled in him the need to always tell the truth and keep his promises, and so, as much as there had been no doubt that Andy would go to Vietnam, there was equally no doubt in his mind that he would return home to his family.

Whatever it took.

The last thing he remembered over there was joking around with his good buddy Jacob Singer. His unit had been grabbing some R&R in a village in the Mekong Delta, and for a short time, the war felt a million miles away. Everyone had seemed weirdly relaxed, almost doped even, and while that might have been true of some of the men, Andy would never touch the stuff. He'd been raised better than that.

Andy had been sunning himself under a tree and drinking a warm beer when Jacob ambled over to him. He was a tall, amiable-looking man in glasses, whom the rest of the unit called the Professor. They all wondered what the fuck a guy like Jacob was doing in 'Nam, although, truth be told, they were growing increasingly fucking baffled as to what any of them were doing there.

How's it hanging, Brooks? Jacob said.

Pretty good, Andy replied. *Every day above ground is a good day, right, Professor?*

If you say so. Jacob grinned. *Although there are definitely days where dying seems like a pretty viable alternative.*

Andy had laughed at the joke of course, although Jacob's wryly intellectual New York take on the world was almost completely alien to him. He knew that Jacob thought about death every single day they spent in-country, whereas Andy hardly ever did. Even in the middle of a firefight, he was filled with a calm assurance that he would see his home and loved ones again one day soon.

But not long after that, things had gotten completely FUBAR. Someone somewhere had started shooting, and within moments, the air around Andy was thick with the mingled smells of smoke and propellant and blood and shit. Not only that, but he found he couldn't even think straight. His mind, normally so clear and focused under fire, had been transformed into a whirlpool of fear and rage and confusion. He was so discombobulated that for one insane moment, it had seemed to him as though the attack had nothing whatsoever to do with Charlie, and that his fellow soldiers were actually firing upon each other.

Terrified by this sudden revelation, Andy had turned and fled into the surrounding jungle. The dense foliage had closed around him, time slipping away like a furtive lover. Day had quickly turned to night, light to dark, and when death came for Andy, it had struck from deep within the shadows of the jungle, taking care to conceal its true appearance. In that sense, his own demise did not seem at all real to him; if Andy could have looked upon death's face, even if only for an instant, perhaps he might have accepted it more readily.

As it was, he fell to the earth, bleeding from a bullet wound to the chest. He could feel blood seeping into his lungs, his limbs turning heavy and cold, but what truly appalled him in that moment was the realisation that he had broken the vow he had made to his mother. Andy could hear her grief-stricken voice echoing in his mind. *You promised. You promised.*

Staring up at the jungle canopy, he tried to whisper an apology to the air, but all that emerged from his mouth was a gobbet of crimson. When Andy Brooks died moments later, his last thought was that he had failed his family, failed his country, and that surely there was a special hell reserved for failures like him.

So when he found himself standing by the side of an empty highway, wearing his full army dress uniform, with no earthly sense of how he'd got there or ever found his way out of that dark jungle, Andy's first thought was that Hell must be right where he was headed. But this was like no hell he'd ever learned about in church – the air on his tongue was not the humid fug of Vietnam, but tasted sweet and dry, just like it did back at home. An overpowering dread seized him: wouldn't it be the worst kind of hell to have his old life dangled tantalisingly before him, only to be snatched away from his grasp the moment he eagerly reached out to take it back?

He was still attempting to process this thought when a truck pulled up beside him, the cab window rolling down to reveal the face of the driver. For an instant, Andy half-expected to see a horned devil leering back at him, but instead, he saw what appeared to be a normal man.

You need a ride, soldier boy? the trucker asked him.

Did he? Was he expected to hitch a ride all the way to the gates of Hell? Andy told himself it didn't matter. If this was Hell, this was clearly where he was meant to go. Even in damnation, his overriding instinct was to do precisely as he was told.

As it turned out, Andy had indeed entered his own personal hell, but not one he could ever have imagined for himself.

He climbed in besides the trucker, and when the man asked him where he was going, Andy simply shrugged and said, *I'll know when I get there.*

They continued on in silence for some minutes, until the driver felt the need to initiate conversation. *So, you just got back?* the man asked him.

I guess so, Andy said quietly.

Mind if I ask you a question? What the hell is going on over there?

Andy kept his eyes trained on the road ahead. *How exactly do you mean?*

What I mean is, our soldiers are the best in the world, right? The trucker rubbed at his mouth, as though trying to wipe away an unpleasant taste. *But all I keep hearing is how we're getting our asses handed to us by a buncha slopes in pyjamas. I mean, how is that even fuckin' possible?*

Andy reached into his kit bag, searching for the Gerber knife he knew lay within. Glancing across at the trucker, he smiled apologetically. *Would you mind pulling over a second? Call of nature.*

The trucker sighed, but did as he was asked. Once the truck was stationary, Andy leaned over and put a hand on the man's shoulder. *In answer to your question, it's like this,* he said softly. *Sometimes death just sneaks up on you, and you never really see it coming.*

In the next instant, when his hand whipped out and opened up a gaping red tear in the trucker's throat, Andy's first thought was not that he had just murdered a man, but of how very hungry he was. He lunged across at his dying victim, instinctively pressing his mouth to the spurting wound. He took several gulps of warm blood before his mind suddenly recoiled in disgust. Shoving the man's corpse away, Andy leapt from the cab and sprinted off down the highway, running as though all the demons of Hell were champing at his heels.

And for all he knew, they might have been, at that.

Eventually, he stopped besides a small stream and frantically washed the blood from his face. He still didn't know where he was or why he was doing these terrible things. Nothing made any damn sense. All he knew was he'd felt much better after drinking the man's blood, as awful as that was. Andy fought the urge to scream up to the heavens, *Why? Just tell me why!*

But then the headlights of a Greyhound bus had come into view, its destination reading BROOKSVILLE.

Andy's home town. Without thinking, he immediately raised his hand to flag the bus down.

When he climbed onboard, he knew straightaway that he had not been consigned to any sort of afterlife, of whatever description you might care to name. He could smell tobacco smoke, chewing gum, stale farts. The stuff of life. The vehicle was not filled with demons or damned souls, but living, breathing people.

Their proximity quickly prompted his next realisation: that he was no longer one of them.

When Andy settled down into his seat, he could feel the same chill torpor in his bones that had gripped him back in the jungle. He began to examine his own flesh, only to find it like clay; cold and bloodless, sculpted into a mere imitation of life. While the moment of his death was already fading like a bad dream, it appeared he had awakened only to discover himself inhabiting an entirely different kind of nightmare.

Gradually, Andy became aware of a presence sitting next to him, although he was quite certain he had selected an empty pair of seats. He looked around to see Jacob gazing quizzically back at him, still dressed in his bloodied military fatigues. *How's it hanging, Brooks?* he said.

Not so good, Professor, Andy replied. *Things are a little fucked up. I have the strangest feeling that I'm dead.*

That you are, my friend, Jacob informed him. *Which most definitely makes two of us. But you, sir, are a very special case. Hell, I couldn't accept that I was a goner for a little while back there, but this is a whole new ball game. Hauling yourself up out of the grave like that. Jesus, Brooks, I never would've thought you had it in you.*

I made a promise, Andy murmured.

That you did, my friend, that you did. Still, did you ever consider that some promises are made to be broken?

But that just wasn't the way Andy had been raised. So he just shook his head and said nothing, and the next time he looked, Jacob had vanished.

Andy knew he'd see his buddy again though. He dwelt amongst the dead now, and as a result, their lingering presence in the living world was no longer a secret to him.

As it turned out, he could see other things as well. When Andy arrived home, to be greeted by the dumbstruck parents who had been informed of their son's death only a few hours earlier, he discovered that they were not at all the same people he had left behind. In death, he could at last perceive them as they truly were. No longer was his father the stern-but-wise role model Andy had always looked up to; in his place, he found a boozy, ill-tempered reactionary. And his mother, whom he remembered as loving and attentive, had been replaced by a smothering, neurotic nag.

He couldn't bear it. His death in a foreign land had seemed like a terrible dream, but perhaps his whole life up to this point had been nothing but an oneiric illusion.

Andy fled out into the night, in search of the only person who might understand. He found Jacob sitting underneath the old tree in the backyard.

Andy sank to his knees in front of him. *It's all a lie*, he told his friend, the words bitter in his mouth.

Of course it is, Jacob replied. *'Nam and all the rest of it. Just a big old pile of bullshit. But when the shit gets stacked that high, no one can see how far it goes.*

I can see, Andy said. *I can see it all now.*

Dying sure does make things a lot clearer, doesn't it?

Andy's fingers clawed at the neatly mowed grass of the lawn. *What happened over there, Professor? I remember bits and pieces, but none of it makes any sense.*

I'll tell you exactly what happened. The Ladder happened.

What the hell is that?

An experimental drug designed to heighten aggression. They dosed us, Brooks. They dosed us with an untested drug and we tore each other apart.

Andy still didn't understand. *Charlie drugged us?*

Jacob laughed, a little unkindly. *Jesus, just listen to what I'm telling you, willya? Our own side did it to us. They wanted to make the perfect soldier, and we were their fucking guinea pigs.*

It sounded like stoner bullshit, some tinfoil hat theory conjured up by one too many hits on the bong, but Andy looked into his friend's eyes and knew Jacob was telling him the truth. The Professor was one hundred percent right on the money: everything Andy had spent his life believing in was nothing but a huge stinking pile of animal dung.

He left his friend sitting underneath the tree and went back indoors. Creeping up into his bedroom, he sat down in his old rocking chair and remained there all night, creaking back and forth and thinking. Now that he'd recognised his old life for what it was, Andy wanted nothing more than to die again, to seek refuge in that numbing, absolute darkness that held no memories or torment.

But he couldn't. His new state of being was like some awful form of insomnia, leaving him perpetually teetering on the edge of oblivion but never quite able to make the transition to that final dreamless sleep. In his agony, he took to visiting the local cemetery at night, pacing amongst the rows of the dead and envying them their eternal peace. He even tried to inscribe his own name on one of the gravestones, hoping that the symbolism of the act might serve to reverse whatever spell had brought him back to life.

Worse still was the constant pain: that dreadful tolling ache deep in his bones, like a bell marking the passage of his inexorable decay. Andy knew there was only one way to banish the pain, one way to hold his dissolution at bay. At first he tried to resist, but then the need grew to be too much. Visiting the Brooks family doctor at his surgery one evening, he viciously murdered the man. Afterwards, Andy drew some of the doctor's blood with a syringe and injected it into his own collapsing veins. The very act repelled him; heroin use had not been uncommon amongst the troops in Vietnam, and he'd loathed the junkies he'd encountered there, thinking them weak and un-American. But now Andy was one of them — no, even lower than them. As he lay on the floor of the surgery relishing the bliss of the blood hit, he could feel Jacob watching him.

I'm sorry, Professor, Andy moaned. *I don't know any other way to stop the pain, and it hurts so fucking bad.*

Jacob said nothing.

Andy opened his eyes. *Well, tell me what else I can do! You're the Professor, you're meant to be so fucking smart! Tell me!*

His friend's only reply was to fade away.

The doctor's blood helped, for a time, but once it wore off Andy found that the pain had redoubled. Crazed with agony, he attacked Joanne, the girl he'd been going with before the war, and his sister's boyfriend Bobby, killing them both. Andy had already been under suspicion for the murder of the trucker, and now there was no concealing what he'd done, what he was. As the police arrived at the Brooks home, Mr Brooks shot himself, appalled at the monster his son had become. Protective to the last, Andy's mother tried to help him escape, and they fled to the cemetery together. Deprived of the fresh blood it needed, Andy's flesh was rotting on his bones, driving his suffering to unimaginable heights. Stumbling to the grave he had claimed as his own, he collapsed to the ground and began to claw at the earth, praying that he might at last be allowed to die.

When the cops found them a short time later, Andy's mother had lost her mind entirely, while her returned son had lapsed into immobility, having seemingly achieved the peace he sought. Both of them were rushed to hospital; Andy's body was taken directly to the morgue, while his mother was placed in the psychiatric ward. A tragic ending, certainly, but one might have hoped that would at least be the end of it.

Alas, no. While Andy's mother still lived, so did her desperate need for her son. And while her need lived on, so did Andy.

He awoke once more to find himself lying on a drawer in the morgue cooler, his mind red with unendurable pain. Clambering from his stainless steel prison, he killed the surprised overnight morgue attendant and drank his blood until the agonies of withdrawal at last began to subside.

His vision clearing, Andy looked up to see Jacob sitting on one of the nearly slabs.

I thought you'd gone for good, Andy told him.

Look, you're my buddy, Jacob replied. *I can't say I'm down with all this* – he gestured at the lifeless attendant – *but a friend in need and all that.*

What am I gonna do now? Everyone knows what I am. I've got nowhere else to go.

I've found a place, Jacob told him. *We're gonna have to take a little road trip to get there, but I figure it's high time you got outta Brooksville anyway.*

Under cover of darkness, they set out. Despite Andy's repeated demands, his friend would not reveal their destination to him, saying only that they would have to travel cross-country to the West Coast, a distance of nearly three thousand miles. In all honesty, Andy doubted that they would ever make it; surely he would either be discovered by the authorities, or else succumb to the ravages of his condition.

But with Jacob watching his back, they made slow but steady progress. By day, Andy would conceal himself within dark woods, or abandoned barns and houses; by night they would walk America's lonely roads and highways, Andy occasionally stopping to feed if a likely victim presented themselves. At such times, Jacob was always careful to keep his distance. But as much as he disapproved of the murders, the Professor knew it was the only way of keeping his buddy's body and soul together until they finally got where they needed to go.

As they travelled, Andy marvelled at the amount of other dead folks they encountered en route. Ghosts, vampires, each and every manner of undead you could name; all could be found wandering across the cities and plains of America. For a country that was so fixated upon *living* – forever exhorting its population to strive for a new life, a better life – it certainly seemed to produce more than its fair share of the restless dead. For a time they rode with a predatory pack of vampires who prowled the highways in a blacked-out RV. Jacob hated them, thought they were redneck scum, but while Andy might have conceded his point, he also enjoyed talking military history with the leader of the group, an ex-Confederate soldier named Jesse. And of course, they made the killing easier. Their restless hunger almost matched Andy's, but they experienced nothing of the attendant guilt or self-loathing that plagued him. Killing was simply what they did to survive. *Just like you did in 'Nam*, Jesse reminded him one night.

Andy wondered if he should simply join up with the vampires and hunt alongside them; could this be a place for one such as him? But despite his constant need for blood, he was not *like* them, subject to none of their ancient laws or weaknesses, and in the end, they parted ways.

Finally, Andy and Jacob arrived at the shores of California, and began to wend their way up the coastline. Here they encountered yet more lost souls; as they passed the small town of Point Dume, Andy could smell the scent of decay on the warm sea air, hear the distant moans of the unquiet dead. *What about here?* he begged Jacob, desperate for their long journey to be over.

But his friend just shook his head. *It's not a place for you*, he told Andy.

Further along the coast, they stopped outside the town of Antonio Bay and watched a ghost ship sail past in the distance. *That wouldn't be so bad*, Andy mused. *Living out your death on the high seas.*

Jacob cackled. *What the fuck do you know about sailing?* he scoffed.

Another couple of hundred miles up the shoreline, they arrived at a small fog-shrouded town. To Andy's eyes, it looked quaint and curiously melancholy; half-forgotten by the rest of America, or perhaps just hiding from it.

This is the place, Jacob told him.

Andy gazed around. The streets were quiet, practically deserted. *Here?* he said. *Why? I don't get it. What's so special about this place?*

Let's take a walk, Jacob said.

The two friends walked slowly through the town. Andy hadn't fed for a day or so and his weakened body was starting to display the effects of withdrawal. He was worried about being spotted, but Jacob laughed off his fears. *You don't have to worry here*, he said.

And it was true: the few passersby they met looked at Andy not with fear or horror, but evident sympathy. *They're not frightened of me*, he said to Jacob with wonder.

Eventually they arrived at a small bench overlooking the ocean. *You look beat*, Jacob told Andy. *Why don't you rest for awhile?*

So Andy did. He closed his eyes and listened to the crashing waves, and were it not for the constant gnawing pain in his bones, he would have felt almost at peace.

Andy felt the touch of Jacob's reassuring hand on his shoulder, but when he next opened his eyes, his friend had vanished. However, he found that he was no longer alone on the bench. An old man sat next to him, gazing at Andy with a concerned smile.

You're not one of mine, are you? he asked.

Yours? Andy said, baffled. *What is this place? I don't understand any of this.*

Marvellous, the old man said excitedly. *You came back all by yourself? No one helped you?*

Andy looked down at his hands, grey and withered. *All by myself,* he murmured.

Well, you don't have to do it alone any more. I can help you. Get you fixed up.

You can help someone like me? Andy said, looking at the old man in disbelief.

Of course. Everyone *here is like you.*

Andy glanced back at the town. It seemed like a nice, quiet place, the sort of place where people would just let you be. He could already tell no one would ever bother him here; no longer would he have to bear the burden of expectations placed on him by family or country.

It could be a refuge, a home; even for a damned soul such as he.

The old man extended a hand in greeting, apparently unfazed by the prospect of touching Andy's decayed flesh.

My name's Dobbs, he said. *Welcome to Potters Bluff.*

JESSICA

Zohra Lampert in Let's Scare Jessica to Death, *1971*
written by John Hancock and Lee Kalcheim
directed by John Hancock

IT WAS FALL IN NEW ENGLAND, AND EVERYTHING WAS DYING.
Jessica couldn't remember a time when it hadn't been fall. Ever since the terrible events at the old house by the lake

(*what events jessica nothing really happened*)

it had seemed as though everything around her was perpetually fading away: the leaves on the trees were forever brown and withered; all vibrancy and colour had been leached from the sky; the pallid skin on her face pulled ever tighter and tighter, emphasising the contours of the skull beneath. She dwelt in a realm of constant twilight, a limbo of entropy and decay. How long had it been? How many weeks or months or years had passed since they'd first moved to the house, her and Bart and Woody, since they'd met...

(*i'm still here jessica i'll never leave you*)

Jessica couldn't remember that either. In truth, it was far easier *not* to remember. After years spent desperately clinging on to the tattered rags of her sanity, pulling them tightly around her to conceal her shame, she had at last chosen to plunge willingly into madness. Better that than the unadorned horror of everyday reality; a reality in which cold lifeless things lurked beneath the surfaces of lakes; in which the dead hungered and never rested.

She'd fled the old house in terror, with no real idea as to where she might go next. Where *could* she go?

(*back to the institution jessica back to your little white room*)

Her whole life had been back there. She and Bart had sold everything they owned to come to Connecticut, to start over. But now everything, *everyone*, was gone. Dead and gone. Her husband, Woody, all of them.

(*they haven't gone jessica they're waiting for you*)

Perhaps she'd died there too. At times Jessica thought it might be so. It was certainly true that she lived like a ghost now, drifting from place to place, the people she encountered never really seeing her, staring right through her. Could what she did even be thought of as living? Her flesh was numb and cold; it seemed as though she only ever drew breath when she remembered to. Perhaps she had become one of *them* after all; the only difference being she knew nothing of their insatiable hunger. Jessica had been emptied, hollowed out; she wanted for nothing any more.

In that sense, *they* were more alive than she was, because wasn't the essence of living to want, to desire, to need?

So she moved aimlessly from place to place, never really seeing faces or surroundings. Sometimes she would sleep rough, sometimes she let anonymous men fuck her in motel rooms, just to have a place to stay and the feeling of a warm body next to her. For a time, Jessica had kept company with a lesbian hitcher named Palm. She was kinder than the men at least, and although she was given to endless ranting monologues about *filth* and *crap*, Jessica did not really mind. It helped to drown out the other voices, the ones that never left her.

(*i'm in your blood jessica*)

But then one evening Palm had turned to Jessica in bed and told her, *You're rotting inside. I can smell it on your breath, like you're full of maggots.* Before Jessica could reply, the other woman had burrowed down into the covers and mumbled, *I don't even wanna talk about it.*

And when Jessica woke the next morning, Palm had gone, leaving her alone once more.

Not that she was ever truly alone. She could sense a dreadful presence forever at her heels, watching her, stalking her. Jessica knew that if she only turned around and looked, she would see *her* waiting there, hand outstretched, still wearing that old wedding dress…

(*say my name jessica*)

So her only choice was to keep moving, on and on and on, from Connecticut to New York to Pennsylvania, wherever the road took her. Now, she found herself back in New England, on the side of a lonely country road in Massachusetts, trees looming over her on either side, the surrounding forest filled with whispers. It was not a place Jessica wished to linger; she understood only too well what manner of things lurked in shadowed places. But what driver would ever pull over in such a place, and she was tired, so very tired.

Then she heard the distant purr of an engine, powerful enough to suggest a sports car. Jessica felt something crumple inside her. The sort of men who drove such cars – for they were *always* men – would not stop to help her.

Still, in sheer desperation, she turned around to face the oncoming vehicle, one arm raised limply in the air.

She saw a yellow Pontiac GTO approaching her through the gloom, its headlights pinning her in place like a dead butterfly. She fully expected the car to speed up and roar past in a blur of motion, just close enough to scare her, with the driver offering a contemptuous blat of the horn as his only response to her plight.

Instead, the vehicle unexpectedly began to slow. As it pulled up beside her, the passenger door opened to reveal the car's driver leaning across in greeting. He was a middle-aged man dressed in a green pullover and driving gloves, the sort of guy her erstwhile hippie friends would once have mocked as hopelessly square. But although he flashed her a broad, wolfish grin, Jessica could discern no malice behind it. If anything, she thought she glimpsed a buried, aching loneliness.

Hey there, little lady, the driver said. *You look like you might be in trouble.*

Jessica fought back a sour laugh. How could she even begin to explain her trouble? A hurried nod was all she could offer him in reply, but it was apparently enough. The man drew back to allow Jessica entrance into the car, and she climbed gratefully inside.

As they headed away down the road, the driver presented her with his hip flask. *This'll warm you right up*, he said.

Accepting the flask, Jessica took a sip of whisky, only for it to sear her throat like a corrosive. She began to cough and choke, and for one horrified moment, thought she might throw up on the car's upholstery. *I'm sorry, I'm sorry*, she cried, suddenly afraid that the man would kick her out of the vehicle.

But he merely grinned again. *I guess you got to acquire a taste for it*, he drawled, taking the whisky back. *So, whereabouts you headed?*

Jessica shrugged hopelessly. *Nowhere really.*

He nodded in apparent understanding. *I hear that. Well, you're not alone, let me tell you. There are a lot of us out here, believe me.*

She looked at him curiously. Surely everyone in a car was going somewhere?

Oblivious, the man continued. *I been driving awhile now. But the road, it wears on you. So I was thinking that I might take a break. There's a resort town, just a few miles up the coast. Pretty little place. That's where I'm headed, right now anyway. That OK with you?*

It made no difference to her. Jessica mumbled something unintelligible and sank exhaustedly back into her seat, her eyelids growing impossibly heavy. Next to her, the driver carried on talking, but it hardly seemed to matter to him whether his passenger was actually listening or not. For the moment, she felt safe, and tumbled gratefully towards sleep.

It was only when the man said, *Hell, here's another one. Lotta you ladies wandering around out here tonight*, that Jessica opened her eyes again, jerked out of slumber like a fish on a line.

The driver glanced over at her. *Whaddaya think, you want some company? Should we pick her up? Maybe we could have ourselves a little party…*

Rubbing at her eyes, Jessica peered out through the windshield. Up ahead, she could see a distant figure standing at the side of the road. Red hair, white dress. Waiting expectantly for Jessica…

Emily.

(*that's not my name jessica you know it's not my name*)

Jessica's hand snapped out and closed around the driver's, poised on the gearstick. *Don't. Please.*

He flinched in surprise. *Christ, what's the matter?*

Whatever you do, please don't stop.

For one terrible moment, Jessica thought the driver was going to ignore her, but then he pressed his foot down. Crazily, she suddenly considered grabbing the wheel and wrenching it over to the right, so that they might collide with Emily, sending her pirouetting into the air to land brokenly in the car's wake, nothing but roadkill in an antique wedding dress.

(*you can't hurt me jessica i'm already dead*)

But she did nothing, knowing it would not do any good. Instead, she merely stared out of the passenger window, watching Emily as they passed her by. The dead girl gazed back at her, her head resting drowsily on one shoulder, a poisoned smile on her lips. She reminded Jessica of a cottonmouth sunning itself on a log; seemingly idle, but if you got too close…

Mind telling me what the hell that was all about? the driver demanded.

The words were spilling from Jessica's tongue before she could stop them. *She's dead. She's dead, and she's following me. Her name's Emily. No, Abigail. She killed my husband, and my friend Woody. She killed all of them.*

Jessica clamped her hand over her mouth. But it was far too late, she knew. Now the driver would realise he had a crazy lady in the car and throw her out on the roadside.

And if he did, Jessica thought she might just lie right where she fell and wait for Emily to claim her.

Instead, the man merely nodded thoughtfully and helped himself to a swallow from his hip flask. *Dead, you say? Yep, they're the worst, alright. You pick up a dead hitcher and you'll never get rid of them. I had one in this car once and that motherfucker followed me clear across three states. You did me one helluva good turn there.*

Jessica had no idea whether the driver was telling the truth or not, whether he truly believed one iota of what he was saying. None of that mattered. The only thing that mattered was that she felt *listened* to, for the first time in months, years.

She began to laugh, surprising herself with the warm, unfamiliar sound of it. She hadn't known she still remembered how to. The driver glanced over at her and began to laugh too. He rolled down his window and hooted joyfully into the night, their laughter spilling out into the darkness like a fresh mountain spring bursting from the earth.

When they arrived at the ferry terminal, the car seemed to shrink around Jessica, enclosing her like a coffin. She hadn't realised they were going to an island. Ever since that dreadful afternoon by the lake, she had kept her distance from the water. Awful, unbreathing things dwelt there, waiting expectantly to claim anyone foolish enough to trespass in their realm.

So when the driver climbed out of the car to take in some air while they crossed, Jessica remained in her seat, despite the morbid claustrophobia gripping her. Another boat, another crossing. She was being ferried back to the land of the dead, she was certain of it. Her eyes sought out the ferryman; he seemed normal enough, at least. No visible marks on his face or neck. But how could you really tell? She had thought Bart was normal too, until he had leaned over to take her in his arms, his cold mouth seeking out the warmth of her neck…

(*he's mine jessica i'll make them all mine*)

When the driver got back into the car, he let out a hearty whoop. *Nothing like that sea air!* Oblivious to Jessica's distress, he grinned. *You're gonna love it here. Amity's a great little town.*

But when they pulled onto the main street a short time later, that was not at all what they discovered. What Jessica saw moving past the windshield was a procession of boarded-up shopfronts and long-vacant properties. Most of the windows in the town were dark, staring down at them like corpse eyes. Eddies of sand drifted through Amity's streets, as though the hourglass measuring the life of the little resort had shattered when its time finally ran out, spilling its contents to the four winds.

Goddamn it all to hell, muttered the driver.

Jessica said nothing. Part of her had always known what they would find here.

Eventually, they came across a solitary sign of life: a small neighbourhood bar, an illuminated neon beer sign in the window signalling the establishment was still open for business.

Here, Jessica said.

The driver reluctantly pulled over to the kerb. *I don't know about this, he mumbled. I gotta say, this place is giving me the willies.* He seemed to Jessica to be on the verge of tears. *I don't know what the hell happened here. This used to be a fine place. I know this whole goddamn country's gone to shit, but…*

It doesn't matter, Jessica told him.

The driver looked at her imploringly. *Let's keep heading up the coast. We can go to Cape Cod, anywhere you want. But I can't stay here.*

It's fine, Jessica said. *I'll be okay.*

Jesus! he exclaimed, his sad eyes growing desperate. *I can't wait around for you, lady. I've got no time, you understand?*

Neither do I, Jessica said softly, and climbed out of the car.

She moved towards the bar entrance, not looking back at the driver. After a moment, she heard the GTO's engine snarl into life and pull off into the distance, the sound of it gradually fading away like the last breath of a dying man.

Entering the dimly-lit bar, Jessica found it almost deserted, save for one man drinking alone in a corner. The bartender was sat reading a newspaper, and shot her a bemused look as she approached him. *I'm closing up soon, lady*, he told her.

A voice called impatiently from the shadows. *Give her a drink. It's on me.*

The bartender shrugged. *Sure thing, Chief.*

Jessica ordered a red wine, and while she waited for the bartender to pour it, her eyes moved to a framed news clipping that had pride of place on the wall behind the bar. 'Hero Cop Slays Killer Shark', read the headline. Underneath was a photo of a tanned, wiry-looking man, an embarrassed expression on his face, the mantle of hero seemingly lying heavy on his shoulders.

Accepting her drink from the bartender, Jessica moved to the corner. She immediately recognised the man sitting there from the clipping, only he no longer looked embarrassed, nor indeed like any sort of hero. He merely looked tired and drunk. A large glass of scotch sat on the table in front of him.

Thank you for the drink, she told him. *Do you mind if I join you?* He gestured soundlessly towards the seat opposite, which she duly took.

They both sat in a hesitant silence for a moment, before Jessica finally spoke again. *So, you're a hero?* She knew it sounded stupid, but had no idea what else to say.

The man snorted bitterly. *Yeah, that's me. Saved the whole damn town, can't you tell?*

What happened?

He took a long swallow of scotch. *There was a shark. A man-eater. People died, but we kept the beaches open. In the end, we managed to kill the bastard, but the tourists never came back, and the town died on its ass.*

They were afraid, Jessica said.

The man gazed over at her, his dark eyes like two black holes in his skull. *Damn right they were. And so they should be. How the hell do any of us know what else could be out there? There could be hundreds of those things swimming around in those waters. There could be anything down there.*

Jessica thought back to that day on the lake. *Yes,* she said.

I never liked the water, he told her. *But now I won't even go near it. I haven't even gotten on the goddamn ferry. My wife left me and took the kids back to New York, and I'm too scared to cross the water to go visit them.*

Jessica reached over and took his hand. *You're right to be scared,* she said.

The man's fingers closed around hers. *You're frightened too, aren't you?*

She nodded.

Raising his other hand to his mouth, he bit down on the knuckles. *You know what the most frightening thing was? I saw that mother right up close, as close as you are to me now. I looked right in its black eyes. And there was nothing. Just zero. I meant nothing to it. I was just food. Meat. And that's when I knew.*

Knew what? Jessica asked.

That there's no meaning to any of it. God and country, all that crap. We had six years with a crooked asshole in the White House and the man upstairs ain't home. We were lied to all along. We're not special. We're just meat, that's all. You, me, everyone. Meat for whatever hides in the dark places.

Yes, Jessica replied. It felt good to hear someone else say these things.

So what's the goddamn point? the man muttered, before gulping down the rest of his drink.

I agree with you, Jessica said. *But do you know what's even worse?*

What? he asked, his face growing bewildered. The thought that there could *be* anything worse had not occurred to him, she could tell.

Some of the things out there, they don't just want to feed on you, Jessica replied. *They want to make you just like they are. Cold and empty. So that all you want to do is feed too, just like them. For ever and ever and ever.*

Christ, the man said, absorbing this. *So is that what you're afraid of?*

Yes. And if you want to know what I think, you're right. There is no point. But I'd rather there be a quick end to it than no end at all. I'd rather be eaten than be like those things.

The man looked at her dumbly. Jessica got to her feet, at last knowing what she had to do. *Thanks again for the drink,* she told him. *Can I ask you one last favour?*

Sure.

Will you please go and see your family? For an instant, she pictured Bart and Woody, everyone she had lost.

The man looked uncomfortable. *Go out on the water?*

You'll be safe, I think. Sometimes we just have to give them what they want and they'll go away for a little while. Please say you'll see them.

He nodded reluctantly. *Okay.*

Jessica gave him a hesitant smile. *I'm very glad I met you....?*

Martin.

I'm Jessica. Goodbye, Martin.

Upon leaving the bar, Jessica turned and began to make her way towards the beachfront. Amity's streets were silent and empty, but she knew she was not alone.

(i'll never leave you jessica)

Still, she found that she was no longer afraid. After living in abject fear for so long, Jessica felt as though she had been released from a cramped and filthy cage. Her limbs felt lighter, the air around her tasted cleaner. She wished the feeling could go on forever, but knew that was impossible. There was but a short time left to her now.

When Jessica arrived at the beach, the dark ocean stretched away before her like a sheet of black glass. *Here be monsters*, she thought to herself. Walking through the dunes towards the sea, she passed an old wooden sign, lying upended amongst the sand grass: 'BEACH CLOSED. NO SWIMMING. ORDER OF AMITY P.D.'

She stood shivering on the threshold of the ocean for a moment, frail arms clasped to her chest. Could she do this? Was she even capable? For her whole life, Jessica had always been told exactly what to do, what was best for her. And now, this decision, this final, irrevocable choice, was hers and hers alone. Did she have the strength?

(*stay with me jessica don't go*)

Jessica glanced back, to see Emily

(*abigail*)

standing atop the sand dunes, gesturing to her. Impulsively, Jessica's feet began to carry her forward into the ocean, the tide kissing gently at her legs in greeting.

Emily would not have her.

(*JESSICA DON'T GO*)

She began to run as fast as she could manage, her wasted muscles barely able to force their way through the oncoming waves. But she would not, could not be driven back now. Jessica hurled herself into the ocean, rejoicing in the sting of brine in her eyes, the taste of salt on her tongue.

When her feet were no longer touching bottom, she glanced back towards land. She could still make out Emily's slumped figure, a distant smear of white in the darkness.

You can't have me! Jessica screamed. *You took all the others, but you can't have me!*

She continued swimming for a time, but her limbs soon began to tire. For a moment, Jessica began to panic, before telling herself this was what she'd wanted, what she'd *always* wanted.

Not to exist, not to remember.

Sinking below the surface of the ocean, she took in a lungful of water and slowly began to descend into the seemingly infinite depths.

Somewhere far below, she saw a pale shape rising to meet her.

At last, she thought.

And when the great fish finally swam into view, the jagged void of its mouth opening wide to envelop her, Jessica opened her arms in greeting, as if to embrace a long-lost lover.

DAVID MANN

Dennis Weaver in Duel, *1971*
written by Richard Matheson, based on his story
directed by Steven Spielberg

PICTURE THE SCENE: A SMALL TWENTY-FOUR HOUR ROADSIDE DINER, somewhere close to the ass end of nowhere, Bumfuck, Arizona. It's late, *very* late, and the smattering of customers and employees all look dead on their feet. And when I say dead, I mean doing an excellent impression of a bunch of three-day-old corpses. That might just be the unflattering effect of the overheard fluorescent lighting on their skin, or it could simply be down to the fact that anyone of a mind to set foot in this godforsaken formica hellhole at 3AM probably isn't too concerned with their bodily health and wellbeing.

Behind the counter, the middle-aged waitress is busily filing her nails, apparently all the way down to the quick. In the kitchen, the grill cook is reading a two-day-old copy of the *San Francisco Chronicle* that a previous customer left behind in a booth. A soldier boy in a military jacket is sitting at the far end of the counter nursing a cup of bitter black coffee and obsessively playing with a silver Zippo lighter emblazoned with a skull and crossbones insignia. To look at him, his skin is sweaty as warm meat and his eye sockets appear to have been dug out of his face. The waitress has the soldier boy down as a lunatic or a junkie, maybe both, and aside from occasionally refilling his cup, is giving him a wide a berth as possible.

Behind the soldier boy, an overweight trucker sits slumped in a booth, his sleeping face pressed up against the glass of the diner window. A half-eaten burger lies on the table in front of him, thick with congealed juices. But he's a regular, and isn't bothering anyone, so the waitress lets him sleep.

The only sound to be heard is that of a drowsily buzzing fan, and the occasional burp of the coffee percolator. The air in the room is uncomfortably close, sodden with liquid fat and humidity. Breathing it is somewhat akin to drinking a grease milkshake.

On the other side of the diner, a man sits alone at a table. His face is skinny and drawn, partly obscured by a wild salt and pepper growth of beard. He is busily consuming a cheese sandwich and a cup of coffee, and pays little attention to anyone else in the diner. If you were to get too close, the sour odour of unwashed clothes and stale sweat that hangs over him, hitherto masked by the heavy smell of fried food in the air, would suddenly become all too apparent.

But he seems entirely unthreatening, timid even, and was scrupulously polite to the waitress when he placed his order. So if there was ever going to be any manner of trouble tonight – and really, why the hell should anyone come to a place like this looking for trouble? – she would bet her evening's tips (and *there's* a joke in and of itself) that it won't be coming from his quarter.

Outside, it's raining like hell. Not that it ever rains in Hell, at least not as you and I understand the place, but if it *did*, it would come down exactly like this, like God had a million mouths and everyone of them was spitting at you with the force of a bullet fired from a gun.

So that's the scene. Nothing too remarkable about it, you might say, and you might even be right, at least without knowing some of the backstories of the four people currently occupying the diner. The soldier boy in particular has a doozy of a tale to tell, but that's another story entirely. No, the one who concerns us on this particular evening is the mild-mannered man in the booth, the very same man who's doing nothing but concentrating on eating his rather wan-looking cheese sandwich. Well, you might say, there isn't much to concern ourselves with *there*. Is this supposed to be an anecdote about a guy eating his lunch? Maybe I'll just skip ahead to the next story, or even put down the damn book completely.

Okay, okay. How's about we liven things up a bit? Let's see…

Right, how about this?

The next moment, the door to the diner opens, and Death walks in.

Not *literal* Death, you understand, not the guy in the hooded cloak carrying a scythe. This particular guy is wearing a long black coat, but that's about as far as the resemblance goes. Otherwise he's blond and handsome, with blue eyes so clear and sharp you could cut your fingertips on them. Maybe you'd take him for an actor you saw on a beer commercial once, or some kind of foreign tourist. Certainly not the kind of person you'd normally see in here, even if it wasn't gone three in the morning. But just a guy, all the same.

And you'd be as wrong as wrong could be, maybe for the last time in your poor misguided life.

Death wipes the rain from his eyes, pushes back his wet blond hair and slowly surveys the diner interior. He notes the slumbering trucker, the diner staff, and the soldier boy. The latter is the only one he pays any particular attention to, impassively studying the soldier as if he were a poisonous snake behind glass.

After a few moments, the soldier boy seems to feel Death's gaze upon his back, and shifts around in his seat to get a better look at the new arrival. Upon seeing the blond man, the soldier's face – well, not *pales* exactly, as he'd be hard pressed to get any paler. Let's say *curdles*, like his face is a saucer of milk that's been left out in the sun.

The two men lock eyes, and, very slowly and deliberately, Death shakes his head.

In the next instant, the soldier boy leaps up from his stool. He pockets his Zippo, drops a crumpled bill on the counter, and hightails it out of the diner without so much as a grunt of farewell.

The waitress watches him go with a look of mild astonishment on her face. As the diner door slams closed behind the soldier boy and he disappears into the rainstorm, she glances over at Death and raises a quizzical eyebrow. *Well,* she tells him. *I don't know what you did to that soldier but I thank you for it anyway. He sure looked like a whole mess of trouble to me and I'm glad to see the back of him.*

Death nods politely. *It's the rain,* he tells the waitress. *It brings them crawling in off the highway.*

With that, his blue eyes fix upon the meek-looking man sitting on the other side of the diner.

The waitress notes the trace of an accent in the new arrival's voice. He definitely sounds like some sort of tourist, although what a foreigner would be doing in here at this hour is entirely beyond her. Still, such things are far outside her pay grade. *What can I get you?* she asks him.

Just a coffee, he tells her with a faint smile, already setting off towards the meek-looking man.

While all this has been going on, the meek-looking man has barely even looked up from his sandwich. So either the sandwich is so delicious that it has entirely consumed his attention – which seems unlikely, judging by its enervated appearance – or else he is the type of man who likes to believe that if he concentrates hard enough on paying no attention to the world, it will in turn do him the courtesy of ignoring his presence in it.

Alas, he is about to be disabused of this particular notion.

Death stops by his table and gazes down at the meek-looking man for a moment, clearly anticipating some response. When the man does not look up, preferring instead to studiously focus on the last few bites of his sandwich, Death sighs, then slides into the seat opposite him.

Now, finally, the meek-looking man glances up at the new arrival, coughing slightly as he swallows the remaining morsel of bread and cheese.

Death smiles. *Mind if I sit here?* he asks the meek-looking man.

In response, the other man averts his head and gazes around the diner interior, noting the array of empty seats and tables. *Uh, n-no…I guess not,* he stammers.

Death settles back in his chair, his cold eyes unblinking. *Then I suppose we should be properly introduced,* he says, extending a hand across the table. *My name's Ryder. John Ryder.*

Warily, the meek-looking man accepts the handshake. *David Mann,* he mutters.

Oh, I know who you are, David, Ryder says softly.

Mann's eyes widen slightly. *I, er, I don't think we've met?* he says, before adding a hopeful *Have we?*

Never seen you before in my life. But don't be so modest, David. Everyone who travels the roads knows you. You're something of a legend.

Me? A legend? Mann lets out a disbelieving laugh. *D-don't be ridiculous.*

Ryder rests his arms on the tabletop and leans forward. *Listen,* he says, nodding towards the diner window. *Do you know how many people die out there each year? How many lives the open road claims? The highways and interstates of America are very dangerous places, David. There are more predators out there than in any foreign wilderness or jungle. But you know that. You met one of them.* His icy eyes grow warm with admiration. *And you survived.*

I'm sorry, w-who are you, exactly? Mann replies, visibly shaken by how much this stranger seems to know about him.

Another smile. *I'm a traveller, David. Just like you.*

Before Mann can say anything further, the waitress appears beside their table. She places an empty cup in front of Ryder and fills it with coffee. Glancing down at the two men, she asks, *You two know each other?*

Oh, only by reputation, Ryder tells her.

That so? She looks at Mann. *You famous or something?*

He immediately grows uncomfortable. *N-no, no, not at all. He's just joking with you.*

Huh, the waitress says. *Pardon me if I don't see the joke.* She gestures brusquely towards Mann with the coffee pot. *You wanna refill or what?*

Mann seems frozen in his seat, unsure of what to do next. Seconds pass, and the waitress's nostrils begin to flare impatiently. Eventually, he offers her a half-nod, and waits in silence as she fills his cup. Once the task is complete, the waitress shoots them both one final suspicious look, then promptly retreats back behind her counter.

Ryder picks up his cup and takes a sip of coffee, his eyes never leaving the man sitting opposite. Mann ignores his own beverage, his obvious discomfort mounting.

Finally, he leans towards Ryder and hisses, *What the hell do you want with me?*

The other man shrugs, a look of sly amusement on his face. *I just wanted to meet you, David. No more than that. We're in the same line of work, after all. Just two killers, passing the time of day.*

Kill--? Mann's face grows tight with sudden panic. *I'm no killer!*

Aren't you? They say it takes one to know one, and I know what I see.

Well then, what about you?

Ryder picks up a spoon and begins to idly stir his coffee. *I've been on the road a long time, David. A long, long time. I've seen and done a lot of things.* His voice drops to an urgent whisper. *God, do you even know what else is out there travelling those roads? You and I, we're just men, but those things? Ghosts, vampires, creatures that don't even have* names. *I've seen them all.*

You're fucking crazy, Mann tells him.

Ryder continues to stir his coffee, the spoon scraping audibly against the bottom of the cup and causing Mann to wince with discomfort. *Crazy? Maybe I am. Maybe we both are.* Smiling, he stops stirring and places the spoon on the table. His eyes drift thoughtfully back towards the window, staring out beyond the rain, beyond the darkness. *All those wide open spaces, all that nothingness*, Ryder murmurs. *Is it really any wonder people just lose their minds out there?*

As he gazes out into the night, there is a sudden bloom of light in the darkness. Ryder watches as a pair of car headlights draw closer, before pulling in off the highway and parking up outside the diner. He does not take his eyes away from the window until the car's engine has been shut off and the headlights extinguished, at which point he turns back to Mann and says, *Now we'll see who's crazy.*

Outside, a flashlight flares into life, moving around the parking lot, and soon it is Mann's turn to stare out into the darkness. He shifts uncomfortably in his seat, observing the movement of the flashlight and saying nothing. The silence between them continues until the light of the torch winks off and they hear the sound of wet footsteps approaching the diner entrance.

Moments later, the door opens to admit a sheriff's deputy, his uniform sodden with rainfall. *Raining like a sonofabitch*, he announces to the general populace of the diner, as though the fact had previously managed to escape everyone's attention.

People should have the good sense to stay home on a night like this, the waitress offers in response.

Well, some people ain't got the sense they were born with, replies the deputy. *Just had to attend to a wreck five miles up the road. Car was all smashed up. Young couple inside, both dead. Godawful mess, it was.*

That's too bad, says the waitress. *They just lose control in the wet?*

Maybe, maybe. The deputy silently surveys the diner. *Thing is, it seemed to me like they mighta been driven off the road. All signs pointed towards the presence of another vehicle at the scene.*

Well, shit, the waitress says.

The deputy sighs. *Anyone mind telling me who's driving that Plymouth parked outside?*

No one in the diner speaks. The deputy waits for a moment, then glances over at the waitress, who gives an imperceptible nod in the direction of Mann's table.

Keeping a measured pace, the deputy strolls over towards where the two men are sitting. When he reaches the table, Ryder looks up and gives him a friendly nod, while Mann busies himself with blowing onto the surface of his by-now lukewarm coffee.

Evening, gentlemen, the deputy says. *Say, either one of you own that Plymouth out there?*

I'm afraid it's not mine, deputy, Ryder tells him, before glancing over at his companion. *How about you, David?*

There is a pause, before Mann finally looks up, as if registering the deputy's presence for the first time. *I-I'm sorry, w-what?*

The deputy's eyes drill into him. *That Plymouth yours?*

Plymouth, what? Mann looks around wildly. *Oh right. Y-yes, yes it is. Why, is there a problem, officer?* He tugs nervously at his shirt collar and gives an uneasy smile. *I know the front tyres are looking a little bald. I'm gonna get those replaced just as soon as I can.*

I'm not concerned with the tyres, the deputy replies flatly. *Mind telling me how come the passenger side is all dented up?*

Mann gestures hopelessly at the empty air. *Well, since you ask,* he splutters. *Last town I was in, I left the car for an hour and when I got back, some asshole had run into it. Didn't leave his damn details or anything.*

That so? the deputy replies. *Because I don't know if you heard me just now, but I got two dead kids sitting in a car just five miles up the road. Cute little blue car, it was. Real banged up.*

No, *I didn't hear,* Mann says. *I'm sorry to hear that. Kids, you say?*

Two of 'em, yep. The deputy arches his back until it pops. *Thing is, there are traces of blue paint on your car, where it's dented up. Right where you say this other car hit you. Now, that's something of a coincidence, wouldn't you say?*

Well, now, says Mann, folding his fingers together. *Well, now. I'm sure you don't need me to tell you that there are an awful lot of blue vehicles on the road, officer.* He looks desperately over at Ryder, seeking some show of support.

But the other man merely smiles and takes a sip of his coffee.

I'm gonna have to ask you to get up out of your chair and come with me, sir, the deputy tells Mann.

This is crazy, Mann protests, although he does exactly as instructed. Nor does he resist as the officer quickly cuffs his hands behind his back.

The deputy turns to Ryder. *Are you travelling with this man, sir?*

Never saw him in my life until just ten minutes ago, Ryder replies.

The deputy looks at Mann. *That so?*

I have no idea who this man is, Mann squeals. *He just sat down at my table uninvited and started spouting insanity at me! Have you stopped to consider that he might be the one you're looking for?*

There's only one car in the parking lot, sir, and you already stated it belonged to you, the deputy replies patiently. *Now, you need to accompany me outside.*

As they start to move away from the table, Ryder raises a solitary finger. *Excuse me, deputy?* he says softly. *There was just one more thing…*

The deputy stops and sighs. It's late, he has to go back out in the sonofabitch pouring rain and he just wants all this to be over with so that he can go right on home and crawl into bed with his girlfriend. *And what's that, sir?* he asks Ryder wearily.

In the next instant, the room explodes.

Or that's how it seems to its occupants at first, anyway. The sound of the gunshot going off is so loud in the small, airless diner that, for a moment, everyone believes a bomb must have detonated somewhere.

That is, until they glimpse the smoking revolver in Ryder's hand, and the bloody hole he has just blown in the deputy's belly.

The officer makes a wet, disbelieving sound in the back of his throat, then turns and topples over onto a neighbouring table, his blood splattering the menus and napkins assembled there. The force of his fall sends the table crashing over to the floor, spilling condiments and cutlery and more of the deputy's blood everywhere.

As the roar of the gun slowly dissipates, there is silence in the diner for a moment, before the hush is broken by an appalled cry from the waitress. Perhaps she is just reaching for the first expression that comes to mind. Or perhaps she already suspects they are to be the last words she will ever utter on this earth, and they are in fact a heartfelt entreaty to her Lord and Saviour.

Oh sweet Jesus, she says.

Quick as a lizard, Ryder is up from his seat, gun poised in his hand. Without blinking, he aims and fires again, shooting the waitress in her chest. The woman crumples to the floor, thereby permitting her murderer a line of fire on the grill cook, who is now beating a hasty retreat towards the diner's rear exit. Ryder takes three strides forward, slightly narrowing the distance between them, and fires again, splattering the man's brains over the door he so desperately hoped would be his gateway to salvation.

Ryder then pivots and takes careful aim at the nearby trucker, only to find that the man has somehow managed to sleep through the entire massacre. An amused expression crosses the gunman's face, and he lowers his weapon, granting his target an indefinite stay of execution.

Beside him, Mann's legs buckle weakly and he slumps back down into his chair with a moan. Abject terror in his eyes, he stares up at Ryder. *Well, what the hell are you waiting for?* he shrieks. *Go on, do it!*

Instead, Ryder moves to the deputy's body, kneels down and removes the set of keys dangling from the man's belt. Finding the key to the handcuffs, he waggles it at Mann. *Do you want me to let you out of those cuffs, or not?*

Bewildered, Mann bends forward, allowing the other man access to his cuffed hands. Ryder quickly removes the restraints and tosses them away into a corner, before retaking his seat at the table. Eyes never leaving Mann, he picks up his coffee cup and takes a sip, only to find it has grown cold. With a faint look of displeasure, he puts the cup down and pushes it to one side.

Finally, some peace and quiet to talk properly, he says. Now, *tell me about those two kids, David. And don't give me any of that wishy-washy middle-class bullshit, either.*

Mann goggles back at him for a moment, before letting out a long defeated sigh, his body deflating like a withered balloon left over from a birthday party. Rubbing absently at his wrists, he gazes down at the formica tabletop, remembering. *Look, I just want you to know something,* he begins. *I tried to go home after it happened, I really did. I watched that truck go over the cliff, and no matter how crazy everything felt, no matter that the world didn't seem to make any sense any more, I told myself that I'd survived.* He sniffs. *But walking back into that house…I felt like I was drowning right where I stood. That bitch I married, the two kids…they didn't want me to be a* man, *you see? All they wanted was a doormat with a steady paycheck. But I wasn't gonna be that any more, not after everything I'd just gone through.*

His eyes look up at Ryder, suddenly defiant. *Watching that goddamn truck fall, I felt like a real man for the first time in years. Maybe ever. I didn't wanna lose that. So I left. Just got up early one morning and drove away. Didn't look back once.*

Good for you, Ryder says wryly. *What then?*

I just…drove. Didn't know where I was going or what I was doing. I was looking for something, I guess, but I still didn't know what it was. So I just drove. I'd stop at places like this when I got hungry or thirsty, and when I got tired I'd sleep in my car. That was all I did for a couple of weeks.

And how did that feel? the other man asks him.

Good, Mann says wistfully. *It felt good. I was free, understand? But… it wasn't enough. Something was still missing. It wasn't until that asshole tailgated me that night on I-10 that I finally figured it out. The rain was coming down hard, not as hard as this, but pretty bad. And of a sudden this prick in a muscle car was crawling right up my ass. Must have sat behind me for ten minutes just honking his horn.* He sarcastically mimes the action. *If I'd had to brake suddenly, we'd both have been roadkill.*

So what did you do?

Mann grins. *Once he finally overtook me, I waited till the next bend and ran him right off the fucking road, is what I did. It was a pretty steep drop, and there was no way he was walking away from that wreck. I pulled over and got out of my car to watch. The rain was still coming down in sheets but I didn't care. I felt it again, you see? The same thing I'd felt when that fucking truck went off the cliff. It was so simple. That was all I needed. His* eyes gleam. *When you've been denied something for your entire life, it's like a goddamn drug.*

Ryder leans thoughtfully back in his chair, a priest taking confession. *And so you just carried right on doing it.*

Mann fidgets uncomfortably. *Look, only every now and then, understand? I'm not some goddamn maniac or something. Mostly I don't bother people as long as they don't bother me. But sometimes I just get this itch.* He slams his hand on the tabletop. *And dammit, some of them deserve it! They drive like complete fucking lunatics. If it weren't for me, god knows how many other people they might end up killing.*

He stares over at Ryder, daring him to say otherwise. But the other man merely smiles, and averts his head to gaze around at the surrounding carnage. *So here we are,* he says quietly. *Two killers.*

What the hell do you want from me, anyway? Mann snorts impatiently.

Ryder turns to regard him for a moment before replying. *Oh, it's very simple, David,* he says, his eyes bright as fresh snowfall. *I want you…to stop me.*

Mann immediately looks alarmed. *Stop you?* he says incredulously. *Stop you how? Christ, you've got a fucking gun.*

Ryder gets to his feet. *We're going to play a game,* he tells his companion, walking away from the table and crossing the diner towards the sleeping trucker. Mann watches dumbly as Ryder leans in and deftly scoops the keys to the sleeping man's vehicle up off the table, before sauntering back over to rejoin him.

Ryder holds his prize aloft in the air. *You've got two minutes, David.* He mimes turning an ignition. *Then I'm coming after you.*

W-what? Mann's eyes bulge in disbelief. *You're crazy, I'm not doing it!*

Then I'll shoot you right where you sit, Ryder says calmly, his hand dropping to the butt of his pistol. *But this way you have a chance.* He gives

Mann an encouraging smile. *Come on, David. I just want you to show me what a Mann you are.*

Mann leaps to his feet. *F-fuck you!*

Clock's ticking. Tick, tick. Ryder glances over towards the window. *The roads must be pretty wet. How fast will you be able to drive, David? How much distance will you be able to put between us before I come after you?*

You rotten bastard, Mann hisses, before wheeling unsteadily around and lurching out of the diner.

Ryder waits until the other man has exited, then slowly walks over to the counter and pours himself a glass of what was once ice water. Drinking the tepid liquid, he watches as the headlights of Mann's Plymouth blaze into life and back hurriedly away from the window. Within moments, the car has sped away into the night.

Ryder finishes his glass of water. Humming to himself, he consults his wristwatch.

A few feet away, the trucker suddenly awakens and sits bolt upright. Eyes blinking, he gazes over at Ryder, completely disorientated. *What the hell time is it?* he asks groggily.

It's a little past the wolf's hour, Ryder tells him calmly, before striding from the diner. As he pushes open the door and walks into the waiting darkness, he hears a strangled cry from behind him.

Shoulders hunched against the driving rain, Ryder crosses to the trucker's rig and climbs inside. He is quite prepared to shoot the vehicle's owner if the man rushes out and attempts to stop him, but apparently the trucker is still too distracted by the grisly scene he has awoken to discover inside. Inserting the keys into the ignition, Ryder starts the engine and carefully reverses out onto the highway.

The dark road stretches before him like a long black river. Somewhere ahead, David Mann is waiting for him.

Ryder winds down his window and breathes deeply. The air smells of ozone and murder. It is a night for killers.

America's highways are filled with monsters, and he and Mann are but two of them.

Laughing, Death guns his engine and speeds away into the darkness, soon to be swallowed by the driving rain.

ARLETTY LONG

Marianna Hill in Messiah of Evil, 1973
written & directed by Willard Huyck & Gloria Katz

AFTER ESCAPING THE CURSED TOWN OF POINT DUME, ARLETTY LONG soon found herself committed to a California State mental hospital. No one would believe her crazed stories of the dark preacher who had returned from the sea, and the undead congregation he was amassing to help spread his profane gospel. Some said she'd suffered a complete mental breakdown after the death of her father, the painter Joseph Long. Others suggested that she'd simply been a paranoid schizophrenic all along; after all, one only had to glance at her father's unsettling canvases to recognise that mental illness probably ran in the family. But whatever the true cause of her illness, it was agreed that it seemed unlikely she would ever recover.

Arletty was a docile enough patient during daylight hours, when she would quietly sit in the wooded hospital gardens and paint disturbing, surrealistic images of a churning black sea, a blood red moon rising high in the sky above it. (Her doctors took great interest in these paintings, and were forced to admit Arletty had inherited some of her father's talent, while also concluding that her peculiar artistic obsession was yet further evidence of her incurable madness.) However, after the sun had set and the moon began to creep into the sky, Arletty would grow increasingly anxious. Resisting the call of sleep, she would roam the corridors of the hospital, recounting her insane story to anyone she encountered, patients and orderlies alike. Eventually she would work herself up into a shrieking frenzy, at which point it would be necessary to restrain and sedate her. Even then, it was apparent that unconsciousness offered no refuge from her hallucinatory fantasies; she would thrash and writhe in her restraints, shouting out in her sleep. *He put his death inside me!* she would cry. *I can feel it crawling up my throat, crouching on my tongue!*

This state of affairs continued for several weeks, until the patient's doctors finally decided that their patient was posing an increasing danger to herself and others, and it had therefore become necessary to place her in a more secure hospital. During her more lucid moments, Arletty herself would beg to be sent somewhere further away from the ocean, claiming that she was continually plagued by what she called the 'malevolent whispering of the black tide', despite the hospital being over a hundred miles inland.

And so, after some consideration, an official decision was taken to transfer her all the way across the country, to the Danvers State Hospital in Massachusetts.

After Danvers's closure in 1992, the derelict building quickly became a repository for all manner of folktales and urban legends, but in the mid-1970s, the hospital was merely another state-run mental institution, albeit a particularly gothic and imposing one. Indeed, Arletty's first thought upon glimpsing her new home was, *It's like some huge horned bat, squatting atop the hill. Wings spread in readiness to capture the unwary. A place of suffering and secrets.*

At that point in time, the hospital's many secrets were still kept tightly locked behind reinforced doors and barred windows; one such riddle being the story of exactly what happened to Arletty Long after her admission to Danvers. But secrets can become a cancer if they are left to fester in the dark, and it is long past time that the fates of Arletty and so many others were revealed.

Despite the stark contrast between the airy, sunlit atmosphere of her previous institution and the forbidding gloom of her current surroundings, Arletty's condition did initially seem to improve after she first arrived in Massachusetts. No longer did she complain of hearing voices, nor scream out in terror during the night. Instead, she entered into a kind of lulled daze, her eyes becoming hollow and vacant. It were as if her visions and nightmares had been the only thing filling her up, and that without them, she was little more than a broken, empty vessel. Now that her fits had subsided, the Danvers staff paid less and less attention to her, and Arletty quietly began to fade unobtrusively into the background, like a distant ship in the fog.

One grey October morning, when the patients on Arletty's ward were exercising in the grounds, a younger woman approached her. Arletty recognised her as the inmate occupying the cell next to hers. They had never previously spoken, but she often heard the girl talking to herself after lights out.

The girl fixed Arletty with her fierce dark eyes. *I'm Alice,* she said, in a broad New Jersey accent.

Arletty smiled hesitantly. She had grown unused to conversation. *And I'm Arletty,* she said softly.

I know, Alice replied, hurriedly glancing around to see if they were being watched. *Look, I gotta message for you.*

A message? Arletty's voice faltered. *Who from?*

Alice's voice dropped to a conspiratorial murmur. *My friend Simon wants to talk to you.*

Arletty did not remember ever knowing anyone called Simon, and that alone was enough to make her uneasy. *I…don't think I know him,* she said stumblingly.

The girl cackled. *Oh, but Simon knows you. He knows everyone here.*

Arletty looked around for an orderly. Her hand flew to her dark hair, twisting it frantically. She suddenly found she did not wish to have this conversation. *I…*

Alice grabbed her roughly by the shoulders, and Arletty's voice died instantly in her throat. *Listen to me, looneytunes,* the girl hissed. *Simon will come visit you in the night. You'll hear him whispering when you're alone in the dark. That's where he lives, see?*

Just then an orderly wandered into view, and Alice quickly released Arletty from her grip, before patting her encouragingly on the upper arm. *All you gotta do is let him in,* she told Arletty brightly. *It's that simple. Just let him in. He's in all of us here, see? But some he likes more than others.*

She pointed towards a blank-eyed woman standing on her own towards the edge of the field. *That whacko Mary Hobbes over there is his favourite. But he likes to come and go as he pleases. It really ain't so bad. Once he's inside you, he'll tell you stuff, real juicy like.* A smile spread across Alice's face like a slowly creeping stain. *Simon knows all kinds of good stuff.*

Later that night, just as Alice had promised, Simon came to Arletty. It was after lights out, and the sky outside her cell window was clouded and moonless. Arletty lay there alone in her cot, panic rising in her throat, feeling as though she might drown in all that darkness.

And then she heard it: a sly, serpentine voice, speaking to her from everywhere at once, both within her head and without. *Hello…Arletty.*

She did not answer. *If there is a Devil, this is what he sounds like,* Arletty thought.

Simon chuckled. *Oh, I'm no devil. I just like to have fun, don't you, Arletty? I have lots of fun with my friends. Won't you be my friend?*

Arletty clamped her hands over her ears, although it did nothing to drown out Simon's voice. *No! Leave me alone!* she cried.

Now, don't be like that, Simon coaxed. *Everyone at Danvers is my friend, Arletty. And do you know why? It's because bad things happen to people I don't like. Real…bad…things.*

She could feel him, squirming inside her mind like an scorpion, impossible to resist. So Arletty did the only thing she could think to do in that moment: she prayed. Not to God in Heaven, but to the only real power she understood, the same unholy master she had fled Point Dume to escape.

Please, she begged. *I am yours forever. I will faithfully spread your Word. Just protect me now.*

The next moment, her head was filled with the sound of the roaring ocean, rising up to drown out Simon's thwarted shrieks. Within seconds, the entity had been completely banished from the room.

Then came another voice, deep and ageless: *My child.*

The preacher.

Arletty flung herself out of bed, landing in a heap on the cold floor. Scrambling up to her knees, she began to pray, babbling her devotion to the darkness. As she prostrated herself before her new master, her skull was suddenly awash with visions; glimpses of past and future both, crashing through her mind in a black flood. She heard the preacher's voice describing the end of the world in words that were both terrible and beautiful in equal measure.

And where she had once been empty, she was now filled up.

When she saw Alice in the dining hall at breakfast the next morning, the girl scowled at her, then leant down and spat in her cereal. *You'll be sorry*, she spat, before scuttling away to another table.

Arletty pushed the bowl away untouched. She was no longer hungry anyway, not since she'd accepted the preacher's blessing. She wondered how long it would be before she began to feel the pangs of a very different hunger. When the preacher's flock took their unholy communion, there was no pretence of divine transubstantial miracles; only actual flesh and blood would suffice.

Once breakfast was over, an orderly appeared and told her she had a visitor: a writer named David Norliss wished to speak to her. The name was unfamiliar to Arletty, but she supposed it did not matter. All she had to offer anyone now was the Word of her dark master, and the more people that heard it, the better.

Norliss was waiting for her in a gazebo on the hospital grounds, a pile of smouldering cigarette butts already amassed at his feet. The sky overhead was black and thunderous, and such was the ferocity of the rainfall that the orderly had to escort Arletty to the gazebo underneath an umbrella. Once she was safely undercover, the orderly then retreated to a respectful distance, huddling miserably under his umbrella and keeping a watchful eye on his patient and her visitor.

Arletty looked warily at Norliss, saying nothing. There was something haunted-looking about the man, hardly alleviated by the welcoming smile he gave her.

Stubbing out his current cigarette, the writer dropped the butt to the floor, then offered her his hand in greeting. *Hi Arletty, I'm David Norliss.*

She did not take his hand, and eventually Norliss let it fall it back to his side. *You're probably wondering who the hell I am,* he said wryly. *Well, the thing is, I'm currently working on a new book. And a little while back, my research took me to the home of a man named James Cort. Does that ring any bells?*

Arletty thought she vaguely recognised the name, but it seemed very distant to her, a relic of another existence entirely. She remained silent, waiting to see where this was all leading.

Norliss smiled ruefully. *Well, let me see if I can help jog your memory. James Cort died recently, but while he was alive, he was an artist, much like your own father. They were friends, in fact. So it's probably no coincidence they shared some of the same interests. Very strange interests. Cort's widow showed me some of the letters your father sent to him. They were…intriguing, to say the least.*

My father is dead, Arletty told him, her gaze drifting out across the hospital grounds. *I hadn't seen him for a long time before he died.*

She'd piqued the writer's interest, she could tell. *I'm very sorry to hear that,* Norliss said quickly, not looking at all sorry. *Do you mind if I ask how he died?*

It was…an accident, Arletty replied, her voice growing distant.

In his letters to Cort, he talked of a town named Point Dume. The events he described there…well, they were very disturbing. Norliss lit another cigarette, huffing on it like it was his first one of the day. *To be perfectly honest with you, I'd be quite inclined to doubt your father's sanity, were it not for some of the events I've recently witnessed myself.*

Arletty turned and met his eye. *My father wasn't insane, Mr Norliss,* she told him flatly. *Any more than I am. Oh, I know it makes people more comfortable to think that we are. God, I thought my father was crazy too, until I saw and spoke to him again. Then I understood.*

Norliss's eyes narrowed. *I thought you said you didn't see your father before he died?*

I didn't, Arletty said. *This was after his death.*

He considered her silently. Arletty thought the man might now dismiss her as a lunatic, just throw his cigarette to the ground and abandon her to babble her nonsense to the rain.

But he didn't. He believed her, she could tell. As much as he hated to, he believed her.

Finally, Norliss spoke. *And the preacher?* he asked. *Is he coming back, like your father said?*

Arletty smiled. *He has already returned, Mr Norliss. He is there in Point Dume now, waiting. If you go there yourself, you may receive his blessing too. It is your only hope of surviving what is to come.*

And what is that?

The End Times, Arletty replied.

She saw Norliss struggling to disguise his obvious scepticism. Apparently he could accept the notion of the undead rising from their graves or of a malign preacher returning from the sea after a hundred-year exile, but Biblical prophecies of Armageddon were simply beyond the pale.

I…see, he said slowly, removing his cigarette from his mouth and examining it carefully between his fingers. *And how exactly does the world end, Arletty? Does the preacher bring it about?*

Arletty smiled and shook her head. *His return is only a harbinger of the times to come, Mr Norliss. He will lead us all to salvation after the world has fallen.*

So you don't know, is that what you're saying?

She thought back to the visions she'd glimpsed the previous night, and the ancient verses the preacher had recited to her. *The third angel blew his trumpet, and a great star fell from heaven, blazing like a torch, and it fell on a third of the rivers and on the springs of water,* she told Norliss, her voice trembling with awe. *The name of the star is Wormwood. A third of the waters became wormwood, and many people died from the water, because it had been made bitter.*

Repeating the preacher's words, Arletty knew their wisdom to be true, and understood that the rest of the world would come to know the same soon enough.

Norliss sighed and tossed his cigarette away. Whatever he had come here looking for, this was clearly not it.

Arletty called out towards the waiting orderly. *I'd like to go back inside now.*

As she waited for the man to collect her, she turned back to Norliss. *Go to Point Dume, Mr Norliss. The preacher will show you The Way. And then you will believe.*

She left the writer staring into the pouring rain and hurried back inside the hospital, where she spent the rest of the day sequestered in her cell, praying for guidance. Something was about to happen, that much was clear to her. The storm clouds lingered overhead until late that evening, the constant growl of the thunder seeming to mock and belittle her attempts at prayer. The air around Arletty grew thick and oppressive, her room choked by deep shadows. It was an ill portent, she knew.

At last, a whispered voice told her: *Do not be afraid, my child. I am here.*

Reassured, Arletty went to her cot and laid down. She closed her eyes and imagined that she was standing on the Point Dume shoreline, the wine-dark sea stretching out before her. All at once, her ears were filled with the sound of the rushing waves. Her breathing grew calm and steady. She did not notice when the lights in her ward were turned out, nor when the door to her cell was locked for the night.

Hours passed. The ward around her grew completely silent, save for the occasional patient crying out in the night.

Then the sound of approaching footsteps became audible, probably a passing orderly on their rounds. But if Arletty heard them, she did not react.

The footsteps moved closer, then paused outside the adjoining cell. There was the stealthy sound of a key turning in a lock, after which the footsteps continued towards Arletty's own door. Once again there was a pause, followed by the quiet jangle of keys and the thud of a bolt being drawn back. The task at hand accomplished, the footsteps slowly retreated away down the corridor.

It appeared that Simon's influence did not extend solely to the patients at Danvers.

Arletty did not move from the bed. A few more minutes passed without any incident, until she heard the door to Alice's cell creaking carefully open.

Moments later, the handle on Arletty's door turned with a plaintive squeak. Her visitor had arrived.

There was the sound of soft footsteps padding over towards the bed. Somewhere else in the room, Arletty could sense an unseen presence gathering itself in the darkness.

Then, she heard a familiar voice. *Hello again, Arletty.*

Opening her eyes, Arletty saw Alice staring down at her, her dark eyes glittering in the gloom.

Simon's here to play a little game with you, the voice sneered. *It's called 'How Long Can You Hold Your Breath?'*

Arletty did not move or speak as she watched Alice reach down and remove one of the pillows from behind her head.

Don't be boring, Arletty, Simon chided. *Say something.*

But instead, Arletty merely closed her eyes once more, willing herself back to the darkened beach, the night ocean. And moments later, when the soft pillow folded over her face, she hardly noticed it.

Leaving her cell at Danvers behind forever, Arletty imagined herself wading forward into the surf, feeling its cold fingers teasing at her legs and thighs. Above the sound of the encroaching tide, she heard the preacher's voice calling to her. *Come to me, child. Descend so that you may rise again.*

Arms outstretched to receive him, Arletty plunged into the black sea, sinking down, down, down. And if that fathomless dark had an end, she did not find it.

ERIC BINFORD

Dennis Christopher in Fade to Black, *1980*
written & directed by Vernon Zimmerman

Eric Binford had always dreamed of being in the movies. He worked as a gopher for the Los Angeles film distributor Continental Film Services, which, in truth, was about as close to a job in the real movie industry as he was ever likely to manage. When he could steal time away from making his deliveries, he liked to ride the company's battered old Vespa around the city, visiting landmarks from Hollywood's Golden Age. It made him feel as though he was a part of something, even if it was only the tiniest speck on the glorious canvas of the area's artistic history. As far as Eric was concerned, that history was in increasing danger of being forgotten or outright ignored, and so he saw it as his duty to cram his head full of as much Hollywood information, trivia and gossip as he could manage. His co-workers at Continental liked to joke – not a little unkindly – that the inside of Eric's skull must resemble their place of business: a large dusty warehouse filled to bursting with fading film prints and disposable movie ephemera. And at least, they would invariably add, *they* got to go home at the end of every working day.

On this particular afternoon, Eric was returning from making a delivery along Sunset Boulevard. As usual, he had been noting particular sites of interest as he drove; there was the old Warner Brothers studio where Jolson's *The Jazz Singer*, the first talking picture, had been shot; further on up the street was Jayne Mansfield's Pink Palace mansion, her home for the decade prior to her death in a car accident. So distracted was Eric by the constant buzz of movie trivia in his head that he failed to notice the Vespa's labouring engine beginning to cough and wheeze underneath him. Only when the moped finally came juddering to a halt did he come to realise his predicament.

Cursing, he tried to restart it, without success. A look of resignation on his face, Eric dismounted the Vespa, then wheeled it over to the side of the road. The bike was well past its prime, mostly held together with duct tape and hope, but he had little doubt that his boss at Continental would hold him entirely responsible for this latest malfunction. He could imagine the man's tirade now: *No one else here has these constant problems, Binford. Why don't you wake up and pull your head outta your ass? This is comin' outta your pay!*

With a sigh, Eric lit a cigarette and kneeled down to examine the bike, although he might as well have been staring at the inner workings of a moon rocket for all the hope he had of effecting a repair himself. Monastically devoting one's self to a lifelong obsession with the movies left little time for more practical concerns, after all. He stared dumbly at the Vespa's rusted mechanics for a few moments, before quickly giving up and climbing back to his feet. It looked at though he would be walking the rest of the way back to the warehouse.

The next instant, a small stone thudded into the side of his skull.

Eric stumbled backwards, more startled than injured. Judging by the size of the missile, it seemed as though the intent of the attack had been to annoy, rather than wound. Looking around, he quickly located the culprit: a small blond-headed boy standing at the foot of a nearby driveway.

Anachronistically dressed in a Buster Brown suit, the boy proceeded to dance a mocking jig, then stick his tongue out and blow a raspberry at his bewildered target.

Hey, you little creep! Eric yelled.

Snickering, the boy turned and hightailed it up the driveway.

Eric stood and pondered his next move. Probably just some spoiled child actor brat. This was L.A.; spit in the air and you'd hit a dozen of them. Still, part of him dearly wanted to chase after the kid and kick his ass a little, no matter that he couldn't have been more than ten years old. Perpetually bullied nerds like Eric don't get the chance to kick anyone's ass very often. But there was probably a doting mom waiting at the top of the driveway, and one thing you never did was fuck around with Hollywood moms and their meal ticket offspring; not unless you wanted to get hit by a lawsuit, you didn't.

Then he noticed the address at the foot of the driveway: 10086 Sunset Boulevard.

It had been three decades since the Gillis murder, and by now most people had probably forgotten what happened at that particular address. Los Angeles was a town where celebrity scandal ran more cheaply and plentifully than fresh water, and so a hack screenwriter being gunned down by his mistress was pretty B-grade gossip thirty years down the line, even if the mistress in question had been a reclusive silent movie actress twice the man's age. I mean, who the hell even cares about screenwriters anyway?

But Eric hadn't forgotten. Joe Gillis's body had been found floating in the house's swimming pool, shot dead by Norma Desmond, forgotten star of many of Cecil B. DeMille's early pictures. Theirs had been a doomed, twisted love affair: Gillis, the ambitious grifter on the make, playing gigolo to Desmond's deranged prima donna. At her trial, a battery of Beverly Hills doctors had lined up to pronounce the actress hopelessly and incurably insane, and so she had lived out the rest of her days in a sanitarium, until her death in the early 1970's. Her Sunset Boulevard mansion had never been sold; control of Desmond's estate had passed to her first husband, the director Max von Mayerling, who had continued to care for her during her years of madness and seclusion. But in the wake of the actress's death, he had steadfastly refused to place the old house on the market, telling the press that 'Even the dead need somewhere to live'. Instead, he had simply gone back to Europe, and abandoned 10086 Sunset Boulevard to its ghosts.

Eric had seen old crime photos of the house, but had never actually taken the time to look upon it with his own eyes. So now that he was stranded right outside its entrance, it would seem to be an opportune time for him to correct that oversight, never mind the added incentive of kicking the ass of a certain tousle-headed brat lurking somewhere inside the grounds. Leaving the Vespa parked by the exterior wall, Eric began to walk the length of the driveway.

Upon reaching the top, Eric then found he needed to climb a set of stone steps to reach the house itself. Winded by his exertions, he paused for a moment to take the sight in properly. Even in the bright sunlight of a Los Angeles afternoon, Norma Desmond's mansion looked dark and gloomy, its exterior gardens brown and unkempt. The property had a slightly crazed, unhappy air to it, as if it had been infected by its owner's burgeoning madness. Looking at it, Eric felt a deliciously morbid thrill; even the houses in Hollywood had backstories fit for the kinds of movies he loved. Imagine the darkly romantic *film noir* that could be made about the Desmond mansion and its storied history!

Finishing his cigarette, he was about to casually drop it to the concrete when he suddenly caught himself. Despite the house's evident state of decay, Eric could not bring himself to be disrespectful to a hallowed site of Hollywood royalty, and so stubbed out the butt on his heel and guiltily pocketed it instead, as if Norma's ghost might march outside and lecture him for littering. By now, the doom-haunted atmosphere of the mansion had him completely transfixed. All thoughts of his childish tormentor forgotten, he decided to explore the grounds further, in a bid to find the swimming pool that had provided Joe Gillis with his watery grave.

He discovered it on the far side of the mansion: a private, shaded enclosure bordered by clustered trees and bushes. The pool, obviously, had been drained, its bottom littered by a carpet of dead leaves and scattered pools of rust-coloured water that Eric could almost fool himself into thinking were blood. But despite the violence that had been perpetrated here, it was a peaceful, calming spot. Eric immediately found himself falling in love with its tranquil air of hushed privacy. Here was somewhere completely hidden away from the prying, sneering eyes of the world, from the scolds and the bullies and the people who would never, ever understand you, no matter how empathetic and open-minded they professed themselves to be. For this short time, here was somewhere that was *his*, and his alone.

Lighting another cigarette, he lay down in the shade of a tree and gazed up at the nearby house, imagining the old-time Hollywood parties that were once held there. Soothed by these borrowed memories, Eric closed his eyes and was soon asleep, his cigarette slipping from between his limp fingers and burning itself out upon the tiled walkway surrounding the pool.

He was awoken by the sound of a nasal, drawling voice. *Hey kid. What's your poison?*

With a start, Eric opened his eyes to find a man standing over him. The man was dressed in a white jacket and black shirt, and had dark, receding hair and a slight overbite. He regarded Eric with wry, detached amusement.

Eric sat up hurriedly. The sky overhead was now darkening, the pool area illuminated by a set of electric lights along one wall. He must have been asleep for hours. Not only that, but there were *people* here. He looked over to the other side of the pool to see another two men watching him. One was grey-haired with a moustache, wearing a dark suit and polka-dotted bow tie and appearing somewhat unsteady on his feet; the other was younger, with a naggingly familiar roguish look about him. Both held drinks in their hands, and stood next to a table filled with bottles of alcohol.

This must be some kind of cocktail party, meaning the house must still be in use. How could he have been so stupid? He was lucky these men weren't threatening to call the cops.

I-I'm s-sorry, Eric stammered, clambering to his feet. *I-I'll be g-going now.*

Going? the man standing at his side said. *You haven't even had a drink yet.* He glanced over at the older man. *Hey, Mayhew, pour the kid a martini. And go easy on the gin, he barely looks old enough to shave.*

The older man affected a look of offence. *Son, by the time I was that boy's age, I was partakin' of a bottle of the finest malt whiskey every night.* He raised his glass to the sky. *It put hellfire in my belly and calmed the gapin' wound in my soul, the gapin' wound that every wordsmith must possess in order to summon forth prose that is poetic and honest and true...*

Yeah, yeah, yeah. Spare us the sermon and just pour the kid the goddamn drink, willya? The man looked apologetically back at Eric. *You'll have to excuse Bill. He started early. Or maybe he finished late. Damned if I know.*

Eric stared over at the older man, agog. *Bill…Mayhew? You mean W.P. Mayhew, the writer?*

The man shrugged. *Sure. We're all writers here.* He shot Eric a suspicious look. *Why, aren't you?*

I, uh… His mind racing, Eric thought back to his script, the one he'd spent years shut away in his bedroom working on. *Y-yeah, I'm a writer. I got this script, 'Alabama and the Forty Thieves'. It's in…development at the moment.*

Sure, that was a lie, but when you thought about it, W.P. Mayhew had been dead and buried these past twenty years too, so him standing there blithely mixing Eric a martini could hardly be any less of an untruth.

Yeah, I feel your pain, kid. The man extended his hand. *My name's Dix. Glad to meet ya. Come on over here and I'll introduce you to the rest of the fellas.*

Dix started off around the pool, with Eric trotting along behind him. Eric's mind was still falling over itself with confusion, thought piling untidily upon thought, when something suddenly occurred to him.

Say, you wouldn't be Dixon Steele, would you? he asked the other man hesitantly.

Dix shrugged. *Well, if I'm not, I feel sorry for the poor bastard that is.*

You wrote 'Althea Bruce', Eric said excitedly, unable to help himself. *That's a great movie, a real all-timer.*

Dix stopped in his tracks and turned to stare at Eric. *What the hell do you know about 'Althea Bruce', kid?* he said quietly, an edge of menace creeping into his voice. *I never saw any such picture, not with my name on it.*

Too late, Eric remembered that the movie of *Althea Bruce*, although scripted by Dixon Steele, had been shot after the writer's suicide in 1950. The finished film had been dedicated to his memory. *I-I'm sorry, Mr Steele,* Eric said quickly. *I must've been…confused.*

Dix glared at him for a moment longer. *Yeah, I guess you must.* Then the cloud passed, and his face lightened. *But what the hell, happens to the best of us,* he told Eric. *By the time these goddamn scripts are run through the sausage-maker, who's to say whose name ends up on them? Could be you, me, or Jesus H. Christ Himself.*

They joined the others by the drinks table, where Dix finished making the necessary introductions. *As we've already established, this is Bill Mayhew...*

Mayhew presented Eric with his cocktail, and gently inclined his head in greeting. *Charmed,* he purred.

Dix gestured towards the final member of the party. *...and this no-good heel here is Joe Gillis.*

Eric gazed at the man in shock. It wasn't as though Joe Gillis was any deader than the other two writers standing at his side, but there was something about seeing him here, at the very site of his murder, and to all appearances alive and breathing, that quite discomfited Eric.

Gillis smiled. *What's the matter, kid? You look like you've seen a ghost.*

Eric gulped at his drink. *S-sorry, this is all just...a little new to me.*

Well, trust me, it gets old real quick, Gillis retorted.

We humble scriveners are little more than worker bees, Mayhew announced loudly. *Day after day we toil, our achin' fingers goin' buzz buzz buzz on our typewriter keys, workin' to bring the pollen of our words back to the Hollywood hive. And our dreary lifespans are measured in months, if not mere weeks.*

Perhaps a little overstated, but the man has a point, Dix said.

But you're all great writers! Eric insisted. Okay, so maybe that wasn't entirely true of Gillis, but he was hardly going to point *that* out.

And yet, here we are, exiled to the arid wilderness, much as our Lord and Saviour was exiled! Mayhew bellowed, staggering away to piss into the bushes. *Only Jesus resisted His temptation, whereas we poor souls already made our covenant with Lucifer, and so must suffer accordingly!*

What's he talking about? Eric murmured to Dix.

The party, Dix sighed. *In the main house.*

'Talent' only, Gillis said sourly. *Actors are only interested in what we have to say when we write it down on paper for them, so that they can pretend they made it up themselves.*

Oh, Eric said, casting an envious sidelong glance towards the mansion. All of a sudden he really didn't want to be stuck here with three deadbeat screenwriters complaining about their miserable lot. He had no clue as to what might be happening to him, but if there was the remotest opportunity of catching a glimpse of some real Hollywood stars – actual legends of the silver screen – he dearly wanted to seize it while he could.

You should go inside, Gillis suddenly prompted, as if gleaning his intentions. *I hear Norma wants to meet you.* He and Dix gave a nasty laugh.

Norma…Desmond? Eric said disbelievingly. *Wants to meet…me?*

Dinner is served, Gillis said, miming the action of pulling a bell cord. *Ding ding.*

Go on and join the fun, kid, Dix told him. *Bring us starving hacks back a canapé. If you make it out in one piece, that is.*

Hastily bidding the group of writers goodbye, Eric scurried away from the pool area and back towards the mansion's entrance. As he bustled past the front windows, he caught snatched glimpses of the laughing faces assembled inside, the partygoers no less beautiful or recognisable for the fact that he was seeing them in living colour for the first time, and not projected in black and white upon a screen.

All he had ever wanted, dreamt of, was here.

Was this all a dream? Eric tried pinching himself, looking down at his hands, all the things you were supposed to do to snap yourself out of sleep. But still the dream persisted. At least no one could accuse him of taking willing refuge inside a fantasy. He'd tried to wake himself up, and it hadn't worked. So, as far as Eric was concerned, that implied he was somehow meant to be here.

None of which prevented him from being seized by a sudden terror as he stood before the front door. Eric glanced down at himself, as if seeing his clothes for the very first time: the worn and faded jeans, the spray of pinhole burns that littered his sweater like blackheads. How could he even pretend he belonged in that house, mingling with people who were like gods to him? He was barely even fit to clean up after them. So appalled was Eric that he might have turned on his heels and fled down the driveway, had it not been for a sudden raspberry noise from behind him.

He wheeled around to see the bratty blond kid standing there, face contorted in a grotesque sneer, tongue extruding like a graveworm grown fat on the bodies of the dead. *Jeepers creepers, where'd you get those PEEPERS?* the child screeched, before sprinting away into the bushes with a cackle.

There was something quite unnerving about the kid, Eric decided. He seemed less like a young boy and more akin to some kind of infernal imp, sent here to startle and terrorise the unwary. Either way, he was more the stuff of nightmares than fantasies, and the impulse to be as far away from him as possible suddenly overrode all of Eric's other concerns. Seizing the handle to the front door, he thrust it open and boldly stepped across the threshold.

At first glance, the downstairs interior of the house resembled a crepuscular forest. The assemblage of stone pillars inside put Eric in mind of clustered tree trunks, and their arches overhanging boughs. A grand staircase curled off to the right, but Eric's attention was quickly seized by the array of famous faces he glimpsed slipping in and out of the darkness.

There, wasn't that Georgia Lorrison talking to Norman Maine? And over on the other side of the room, carefully checking her makeup in an antique mirror, Rita Shawn! God, and sitting on that chaise-longue, slyly slipping his arm around a beautiful sad-eyed blonde girl, was the screen idol and notorious ladykiller Neville Sinclair.

Enraptured, Eric moved through the room, briefly pausing to allow Blanche Hudson's wheelchair to pass in front of him. The crippled actress murmured her thanks, but Eric barely heard her. His attention was already being drawn elsewhere, his eyes greedily drinking in the fame and beauty surrounding him on all sides.

And if the other guests noticed him staring, they did not mind, for being admired and envied was surely their due.

Eventually, he reached the far edge of the room, to find the director Jake Hannaford and his legendary drinking companion, iconic tough guy actor Phil Duncan, working their way through a decanter of scotch. As he approached, he caught the tail end of their conversation, Hannaford quietly telling Duncan: *I hear* she *might be making an appearance tonight.*

Duncan looked visibly alarmed at this piece of information, but whomever they might have been discussing was of entirely no interest to Eric. He was standing before *Phil Duncan*, whose crooked, world-weary face had been posthumously emblazoned on a million book covers, T-shirts, and student dorm posters. Many were the nights Eric had mimicked Duncan's insouciant smile in front of his bedroom mirror. Too intimidated to speak, he simply stood there, mouth hanging open like a starving baby bird.

Eventually registering his presence, Hannaford turned and shot him an irritated look. *Well, kid, what the fuck is it?* he demanded.

After goggling mutely for a few more moments, Eric finally located his voice. *I'm sorry, Mr Hannaford. It's just that you…both of you, you and Mr Duncan both, well, you made some of my favourite movies of all time.*

Oh, is that all? Hannaford sneered. *I thought for a minute you were gonna tell me my cock was hanging out of my pants.*

W-what? Eric looked like he'd been slapped. *No, I just wanted…*

He'd probably like that, the little pansy, Duncan drawled. *Doesn't he look like a pansy to you, Jake?*

Hannaford took a swallow of scotch, eyeing Eric over the rim of his glass. *You a movie buff, kid?*

Eric smiled, suddenly on surer ground. *I sure am. I've seen all the movies you made together, several times. I know all the dialogue off by heart.*

Oh, fuck that, Hannaford spat. *Movies are just a means to an end. They're light and shadow, nothing more.* He thrust a clenched fist into the air. *There's no there there, you understand? They're not important. No, what's truly important, the one thing any man worth his ballsack should dedicate his life to the pursuit of…is pussy.*

Eric stared at him, dumbfounded. *I think movies…are important,* he mumbled.

I told you he was a pansy, Duncan said, looking bored.

N-no, I like girls, Eric replied in a small voice.

Oh yeah? Hannaford shot him a look. *When was the last time you got laid?*

Gentlemen, if I might interject? An sepulchral, instantly recognisable voice sounded from over Eric's shoulder. *There's someone I'd like this young man to meet.*

Startled, Eric turned and looked into the face of horror legend Byron Orlok. His eyes widened for a moment. Orlok's lined, cadaverous features were just as menacing as they appeared on the big screen, but up close, Eric saw only kindness in the old man's gaze.

Sure, get him the hell out of my sight, Hannaford growled, reaching for the whisky decanter.

Orlok placed a fatherly arm around Eric's shoulders and slowly led him away, tracing a path through the partygoers with the heavy wooden cane he carried. *Never mind those drunken bullies,* he murmured.

Oh, I don't mind, Eric shrugged. *I'm kinda used to it. And they* are *heroes of mine.*

Well, just remember that there's a very good reason they say never to meet your heroes.

Eric suddenly remembered exactly who he was talking to. *But I mean, you're my hero too, Mr Orlok. Your horror pictures are the best.*

Orlok gave a pained grimace. *Oh, that old junk…*

No, I really mean it! You're a legend. Eric's eyes scanned the room. *I guess…everyone here is a legend.*

Of a sort, I suppose, Orlok sighed. *But sometimes legends are better off staying dead and buried, don't you think?*

That's just what I don't understand, Eric told him. *Everyone in this room should be dead. But here they all are, laughing and drinking and having a good time. So am I just dreaming?*

The old man gave a bitter laugh. *Oh no, young man. This isn't* your *dream. You just stumbled into it. It's America's dream of itself.* His eyes grew sad. *That's all Hollywood has ever been, you see.*

Eric stared at him uncomprehendingly. *I don't understand.*

And it's much better that you don't, Orlok murmured gravely. *Just take my advice. The wisest thing you can do now is leave this place. You're not dreaming, and you can walk out any time you like. So do it. Get out, before* she *gets here. It will be much the worse for you if you stay.*

Eric was growing more and more confused. *But who is* she? *I heard them talking about her back there too. Do you mean Norma Desmond?*

Orlok's face was now pale. *No, not Miss Desmond,* he muttered, leaning heavily on his cane. *An outsider. But I dare not speak her name. To do so is to invoke her. She will arrive here in her own good time, and I will play no part in it.* He gripped Eric's shoulder with all the strength his arthritic fingers could muster, his eyes imploring. *Please, trust in an old man's word that you are far better off not knowing her name.*

But despite Orlok's warning, Eric found he couldn't bring himself to leave. All that awaited him outside the walls of the Desmond mansion was more of the same mockery and derision he had always known. For years he had sought refuge in celluloid fantasies, and now he had finally been offered a sanctuary, one suffused with the divine power of the movies that were Eric's only religion. Why, the day's events could hardly have been any more miraculous if he had simply stepped into a movie screen and entered the fantasy world of light and shadow that lay beyond.

Please, he begged Orlok. *I want to stay a little longer. You don't know how much this all means to me.*

The old man sighed again. *But it's all just an illusion, my boy.*

So what's the harm in illusions?

Orlok snorted. *If you stay a little while longer, you may learn that for yourself. But perhaps that would be no bad thing.* He motioned towards a nearby chair. *Please, help me over to that chair. My legs are not as strong as they used to be.*

Eric did as the old man asked, and assisted Orlok down into his seat. The horror icon's features had grown papery and grey, and Eric began to worry whether he might have caused the old man to become seriously ill, never mind that Byron Orlok was already ten years dead. Eric had visited his gravesite in the Hollywood Forever Cemetery himself.

But his mounting anxiety was quickly interrupted by the arrival of another party guest at their side, a middle-aged man with a haughty, aristocratic air about him. *Byron, my dear fellow!* he exclaimed. *How long has it been?*

Orlok smiled weakly. *Who can say, Tony, who can say?* He gestured towards Eric. *This young man was just helping me to take the load off my old bones. But I'm afraid I don't know your name, my boy.*

Eric offered the new arrival his hand. *I'm Eric. Eric Binford.*

The man shook it heartily. *Well, Eric, any friend of this ghoulish old warhorse is a friend of mine. I am Anthony John.*

Eric recognised the name, but had to think for a moment as to where from. He assumed the man was an actor – most people here were, and he certainly had that air about him – but his face didn't seen particularly familiar.

Then it came to him. Anthony John had been a famous Broadway star during the first half of the twentieth century, far better known for his great stage roles than his rather sporadic film appearances. But he was perhaps most famous now for losing his mind during an extended run of *Othello*. Consumed by the jealousy of the part, John had strangled the waitress he had been conducting a clandestine affair with, before wholly embracing his role as the doomed Moor and killing himself onstage, in full view of a packed house.

Still, Eric thought it best not to mention the scandal. Instead, he settled for telling the actor, *I hear your Othello was really great. People always say they wished you had played the part in a movie and not Welles.*

John's eyes bulged in disbelief. Orson *Welles?* he bellowed. *They let that overweight ham play Othello? In a movie?*

Umm…yeah.

My god! The actor's cheeks were flushed with rage. *That huckster should never be allowed anywhere near the Bard! He's nothing but a salesman, a pimp for his own vanity!* He let out a long, theatrical moan. *Come, my boy, I need a stiff drink after hearing of such a travesty.*

Before Eric could protest, John seized him by the arm and dragged him away, leaving Orlok alone. Upon arriving at the bar, the actor ordered a bottle of champagne, pouring himself and Eric a generous glass. Gulping it down in one, John peered closely at Eric. *Tell me, boy*, he said. *Are you one of us? A thespian?*

In truth, Eric was frightened to say no, lest he be denounced as an impostor and ejected from the party. *Well, a little*, he said finally, thinking back to those late-night sessions with mirror and make-up kit. *I've played a few small roles. But I'm still pretty new to it.*

Ah, I could tell, I could tell, John said sagely. *You have that same peculiar light in your eyes I know so well.* He leaned in closer, his voice dropping to a whisper. *Tell me, boy. Do you ever find that certain roles give you the willies?*

The…willies? Eric said blankly.

Yes. By which I mean to say that certain roles inhabit you, rather than you inhabiting them.

Well…I dunno. Eric recalled his Cody Jarrett impersonation, the way that channeling Cagney's madness had seemed to unlock something deep inside himself. *Maybe a little, yeah.*

Take my advice, boy. Don't fight it. Let it happen. Only then will you be truly great.

I'd like to be great, Eric whispered.

And so you shall, John assured him. *Just remember this: you must find that quality within yourself which the role requires. With Othello it was jealousy. Find it, hold it, live it. Do you see?*

Yes, Eric breathed.

They said I went too far, but what do they know? the actor scoffed. *They will never comprehend the alchemy of performance.*

There is a kind of magic to it, isn't there? Eric said.

Of course there is! an imperious voice interjected.

Eric turned to see none other than Norma Desmond herself, sweeping across the floor towards where he and Anthony John stood. For a moment, he was put in mind of the figurehead of some great war vessel, surging through the ocean to destroy them.

Now you've gone and done it, boy, John murmured.

Movies are *magic,* Norma announced as she arrived beside them. *Our picture houses are enchanted kingdoms, wherein still photographs are made to move, and ordinary men and women are transformed into gods.* She regarded Anthony John with undisguised disdain. *In comparison,the theatres on Broadway are mere kindergartens, filled with unruly children playing dress-up.*

The other actor bowed sardonically. *It is a pleasure to see you again too, Miss Desmond.*

What have I told you about sneaking in here, thespian? Norma snapped. *You are not fit to breathe the same Olympian air as we gods.*

I…? John's face darkened. *I am one of the most acclaimed actors of this century, equally at home with the poetry of O'Neill and Shakespeare! Whereas you, dear lady, were driven into enforced retirement the moment you had to speak so much as a single word aloud!*

Norma flashed him a cruel smirk. *What does mere acclaim amount to when placed next to the adoration of millions? Need I remind you that more people saw one of my pictures in its first week than attended your Othello over the entire two years of its run? My great performances are immortal, preserved forever.* She thrust her face into John's, purring, *Yours are as clouds in a brilliant summer sky, flitting and fleeting.*

Eric glanced down to see the male actor's hands twisting into vicious claws, possessing a mind and will of their own and but one purpose: to murder. *Gargoyle!* John spat. *Strumpet!*

Norma merely regarded him with contemptuous satisfaction. Eric thought that the male actor might be about to launch himself at her, when Norman Maine suddenly materialised at John's side and placed a warning hand on his arm. *Steady on, old man,* he said softly. *Let's go to the bar and get you another drink, shall we?*

Eric and Norma both watched in silence as Maine led the other actor away, John's hunched figure visibly trembling with rage.

Face etched with triumph, Norma turned towards Eric. *Now then, young man. What about you?*

Now that he was alone with Norma, Eric suddenly realised that she terrified him. *M-me?* he said.

Well, who else, she said impatiently. *I'm told you're an excellent screenwriter.*

Uh, well, I'm just a beginner, really…

That doesn't matter! Norma thundered. *Talent can be honed and shaped, if you have an experienced enough mentor.* Her eyes gleamed madly. *And you won't have had any time to learn all the bad habits so beloved of two-bit hack writers everywhere!*

Without even thinking, Eric spoke his name. *You mean like Joe Gillis?*

At the mere mention of Gillis's name, a graveyard chill crept into the air, as if they were both standing in the midst of some vast tomb and not a glamorous Hollywood party.

Norma drew herself up like a gorgon. *Never speak his name in this house!* she hissed. *He is a despicable liar, nothing but a vile Judas in a cheap suit. He used and betrayed me!*

Eric cringed. *I'm sorry, Miss Desmond,* he wailed. *I had no idea, honestly.*

The actress glared at him for a moment, then relented, her features softening. *Oh, I forgive you,* she cooed. *You have a great deal to learn, but you're still young. Just listen to everything I tell you, and never question my wisdom. I can't abide arrogant men who answer back.*

Uh, okay.

She looked him up and down critically. *But if we're going to work together, you're going to need a new wardrobe. You look like a bum.*

W-work together? Eric stammered.

Yes, on my 'Salome' script. I should never have let that Poverty Row hack anywhere near it. You and I will need to start over completely. Norma's face grew flirtatious. *But first, we need to get you out of these terrible clothes. I have some old suits in one of the bedrooms upstairs that should fit you. Come with me.* She linked her arm through his and began to pull him away.

Eric felt all but helpless in the face of Norma's implacable will, but something told him going upstairs with her would be a very bad idea. *What about your party?* he whined.

Oh, screw the party, the actress said dismissively. *Most of the people here are complete nobodies anyway. I only invite them because it gets so dreadfully tedious being cooped up here on my own. But now I have you!* She tugged at his arm again, dragging him across the floor. *We can play dress-up! It'll be such fun!*

She led Eric towards the staircase, pulling him along like a recalcitrant puppy. As they crossed the floor, he was uncomfortably aware of the partygoers whispering and tittering to each other behind raised hands as they passed by. What would happen if he went upstairs with Norma? Would she simply seduce him, or something worse? Eric wondered if he were about to be sacrificed to some rapacious god of celluloid. Would he end up floating facedown in Norma's swimming pool while Gillis and the other writers looked on and toasted his demise?

But as they reached the foot of the grand staircase, Norma glanced over towards the entrance to the house and immediately froze, an expression of the blackest hatred seeping into her features. Eric stared at her, horrified. The actress suddenly looked grotesquely old, as though a glamour had been torn away to reveal the fairytale witch lurking underneath. What could have wrought such a transformation?

Following Norma's gaze, Eric saw a young blonde woman standing outside the mansion's open doorway. She seemed to glow with some inner radiance, and to his eyes seemed almost beatific, impossibly lovely; the living embodiment of everything that the movies promised.

He recognised her, of course. Her tragic story was a fixture of every muckraking Hollywood history, every cautionary tale told by agents to their young female clients.

Lylah Clare, he whispered.

The next instant, Eric felt Norma's hand strike his cheek, her fingernails raking his flesh and drawing blood. *What have you* done? she spat.

Hand clutched to his injured face, Eric stumbled away and fell into a nearby chair. He watched as Lylah gave Norma a cold smile, and, very slowly and deliberately, stepped across the threshold.

Well, she purred, gazing around at her surroundings. *Doesn't this seem like a darling little party?*

Norma stepped forward to confront her unwanted guest. *Get out!* she shrieked. *Get out of this house!*

Lylah just giggled. *But Norma dear, I've only just got here.*

A terrible silence enshrouded the room. Glancing around, Eric saw the other party guests quietly moving to join Norma, gathering at her back like an army. Their eyes were all locked on Lylah, a palpable loathing oozing from their pores. Such was the potency of their collective hatred that Eric immediately began to feel nauseous.

But Lylah was unfazed. She scanned the assembled faces and smirked. *Oh, how lovely to see so many of my old friends here*, she said slyly. *Remind me, just how many of you have I fucked?*

No one spoke. *Probably most of you,* Lylah laughed, *although I can barely recall the details, you were all so unmemorable.* Her gaze sought out Neville Sinclair. *Yes, even you, you Nazi bastard. You're not as much of a swordsman as your movies make out, are you?*

Sinclair bristled, but did nothing. He glanced towards his hostess, waiting for his cue to act.

Norma continued to stare silently at Lylah, her eyes wide and unblinking, as if she were willing the younger woman to turn to stone. But as the seconds passed and Lylah stubbornly remained flesh and bone, Norma slowly turned to her guests and murmured, *Take her.*

A dreadful canine shriek erupted in the room as the partygoers swooped down upon their victim en masse. In the instant before she disappeared from view, Eric glimpsed Lylah standing firm, howling her defiant laughter in their faces. Then the rushing mob was upon her, dragging her down to the floor, submerging her in a tsunami of hatred and violence. All Eric could make out was a whirl of fists and feet, rising and falling, rising and falling, each descent punctuated by a wet thud or the cracking of bone. He barely recognised the faces of Lylah's attackers, even though he saw them every night, gazing down upon him from the walls of his bedroom. He knew those faces as well as he knew his own, only now they had become twisted mockeries of their own beauty.

As Eric looked on in horror, something wet splattered the front of his pullover. He glanced down to see a spray of blood soaking into the cheap material. The blood of one of the most beautiful screen goddesses who'd ever lived. Lylah Clare had already died once at the hands of Hollywood; could he really stand idly by and let it happen again?

Eric leapt to his feet. Lurching forward, he plunged into the heart of the mob, shoving Lylah's attackers aside with all the strength he could muster. *Leave her alone, you bastards!* he cried. Expecting to meet stiff resistance, he strangely found little or none; the tide of violence parting before him as if he were some Biblical prophet, and not merely a skinny movie nerd who'd never had a girlfriend.

Pushing his way through the huddled bodies, past Norma and Neville Sinclair, he finally came upon Lylah, a wretched broken thing lying at his feet like a hatchling fallen from its nest. Her white dress was by now almost completely scarlet, her once-perfect features a shattered ruin.

Eric knelt to her with an appalled moan, bending to cradle her limp head in his lap. *I'm sorry*, he whispered.

Lylah's eyes opened. Despite her grievous injuries, they shone bright and clear, gazing up at him with the sheerest spite. *Did you think you could save me, Eric?* she cackled. *Too many men have tried that, I'm afraid. Some girls just don't want to be saved. Some girls only want to be loved.*

Her hands suddenly snapped up, clamping around Eric's skull with an unearthly strength and forcing his face down towards her own.

Kiss me, my hero, Lylah crooned, opening her mouth wide to receive him.

As she pulled Eric to her, she began to laugh, an awful hollow sound that blossomed from her lungs like poison. Eric gazed down into Lylah's bloodied, splintered mouth, the shards of her shattered teeth like the fangs of some great predator, and thought that she might be about to swallow him whole. He struggled in her grip, and felt the starlet's hands slipping against his skin, so slick were they with her own blood. Redoubling his efforts, he at last managed to squirm free, pushing himself away from Lylah and crawling across the floor. But her hideous laughter still followed him, and so noxious was its sound that Eric barely got any further than a few yards before he could do nothing more than clamp his hands over his ears and curl up in agony.

The next thing he knew, a heavy weight had landed on his back. Before he could react, long limbs snaked around his own, and clawed fingernails dug into the meat of his shoulders. Eric turned his head in panic, only to see Lylah's ruined face gazing back at him. Tunelessly, she began to sing. *It looks like we two will never be one*, she caterwauled. *Something must be done!*

Eric screamed, and dragged himself to his feet, struggling under Lylah's weight. She began to howl with laughter, feet kicking against his ribs. Eric stumbled forward, careening drunkenly around the room, slamming into walls and furniture in a fruitless attempt to throw his tormentor off. And all the while, Lylah's laughter continued. The sound of it spread across the room, infecting the house with its bottomless madness and malignity. Everywhere Eric turned, he saw the party degenerating into an obscene orgy of delirious sex, brutality and death.

Phil Duncan and Jake Hannaford were beating each other bloody with whatever implements they had to hand. As Eric looked on, Hannaford knocked the actor to the floor with a glass ashtray, and as Duncan lay there, dazed and bleeding, Hannaford leaned in and began to kiss him passionately. Backing away from the two men, Eric staggered to the other side of the room, and nearly fell into Rita Shawn's lap. She gazed sightlessly back at him, her *décolletage* covered with vomit. She held a bottle of vodka in one lifeless hand, a vial of pills in the other. Sitting next to her, Norman Maine was brutally hacking at his wrists with an ice pick.

Moaning with horror, Eric span around, only to see Neville Sinclair forcing himself upon the same sad-eyed blonde he had been courting earlier in the party, his hands tearing at her underwear as she writhed and screamed beneath him. Eric desperately wanted to try and help her, but in the next instant he heard a terrified shriek, and his head snapped around to see Blanche Hudson's wheelchair being propelled at great speed towards the nearby French windows. Behind her, the impish blond-haired child giggled malevolently, his small pale legs moving like pistons. Horrified, Eric watched as the child sent the wheelchair crashing through the windows in a shower of broken glass, its passenger spilling like a rag doll to the stone patio beyond.

Still, as awful as those sights were, they were far from the worst of it. The very worst thing, Eric soon realised, were the hollow-eyed apparitions he saw creeping from the surrounding shadows, the jaws of their sallow, bloodless faces attenuated into paralysed screams. They capered through the room with glee, revelling in the vile bacchanal unfolding before them, their jerking, spastic bodies joining in a hideous *danse macabre*.

Eric felt Lylah's lips brush his earlobe. *How do you like the party, darling?* she murmured.

The dreadful enormity of what was taking place finally overwhelmed him. Eric's legs buckled, and he crashed heavily to the floor. In response, Lylah only tightened her grip, her long fingernails sinking ever deeper into his flesh.

With horror, Eric realised she was slowly beginning to *merge* with him, the meat of her body flowing into his, as if they were two mountain streams joining into one.

I think it's almost time we left, don't you? the actress whispered. *I'm so looking forward to seeing Los Angeles again.*

Eric screamed, a high, keening sound of utter despair.

Then a shadow fell upon them, cutting his cry short. Eric looked up to see Byron Orlok standing over them, his stout wooden cane raised above his head. *Get away from him, dybbuk!* the old man thundered.

Lylah shrieked in rage, but with her claws sunk so deeply into Eric, could not lift her arms to defend herself. Orlok's cane came smashing down onto her skull, snapping Lylah's head back and breaking her grip upon her intended victim. She flew backwards through the air, landing in a tangled senseless heap a few feet away.

Orlok helped Eric to his feet. *Quickly, boy,* he urged. *Before she recovers.*

The two men hobbled across the room. As they neared the front door, Eric began to sob helplessly. Overcome with grief and terror, all he could manage to say was *Why?* repeating the word over and over again.

Orlok said nothing until they arrived safely at the doorway. Then he turned to Eric, a great sorrow in his eyes, and quietly told him, *The dream cannot hold, my boy. It never does.*

Eric felt Orlok's hand at his elbow, gently urging him forwards. He stumbled across the threshold and out into the open air, and in the next moment, heard the mansion's door slam shut behind him.

It was now dawn, the sky overhead flushed with red, as though the violence inside the house had spilled out into the heavens. Eric turned to look back at the mansion, but it now appeared to be exactly what it was: a crumbling, deserted building, abandoned to time and the elements, inhabited by nothing more than fading memories.

He limped away down the drive, as quickly as his trembling legs could carry him.

Eric began to wonder how he would ever manage to live with what he had just witnessed. Surely the memories would inevitably return every time he attempted sleep, Lylah's grinning, bloodied face looming up from the depths of his nightmare to claim him once more.

But strangely enough, by the time he reached the bottom of the driveway, the night's events, unspeakable as they were, had already begun to fade from his mind. Despite what Orlok had told him, despite the lingering pain in his shoulders, it were as if the whole experience really had been nothing but a dream, and now, as dreams do, it was dissipating like smoke upon the breeze.

Pausing to light a cigarette, Eric let the last few jumbled memories of the night drift gradually from his mind, and did not mourn their passing when they were gone.

He collected the Vespa from where it still rested against the wall and began to walk away, leaving 10086 Sunset Boulevard behind him forever.

Or so he might have thought.

Because, given the terrible events that were to follow, one cannot help but wonder whether a splintered trace of that night continued to linger in Eric Binford's mind. Was the murderous rage that subsequently overtook Eric always there within him, or did he unknowingly carry it away from the Desmond mansion, buried deep inside the loam of his subconscious like a malignant seed? Were the ensuing killings – the series of murders referred to by the press as the 'Silver Screen Slayings' and Eric's own death at the hands of the Los Angeles police – the result of that same seed bearing a dreadful fruit?

And when he committed the five murders that finally gifted him with his own dark measure of Hollywood immortality, did he hear the distant sound of Lylah Clare's laughter?

WENDY TORRANCE

Shelley Duvall in The Shining, *1980*
written by Diane Johnson & Stanley Kubrick
based on the novel by Stephen King
directed by Stanley Kubrick

AS SHE STOOD ON THE CLIFF EDGE WATCHING THE BOAT VANISH INTO the fog, Wendy Torrance started to wonder – certainly not for the first time in her life – exactly what the hell she thought she was doing.

Aware that she was about to mercilessly rub her face in her own credulousness and stupidity, she began to mentally list any such previous occasions that sprang to mind. Those extra special missteps she liked to think of as her Big Mistakes.

Well, for starters, there was the day she'd first agreed to marry Jack Torrance, in the face of her mother's furious insistence that he was a no good Irish drunk who'd never amount to a damn thing. Then, a few years further down the line, the time she'd chosen to stay with Jack after he broke their infant son Danny's arm in a drunken rage. (Wendy subsequently told her mother Danny had broken it in a fall.)

And of course, to top it all off, agreeing to spend the winter with him in the Overlook Hotel *definitely* qualified. Christ, even if the place hadn't been haunted, what sort of a weak-willed doormat blindly follows a frustrated alcoholic with anger management issues to a snowbound hotel where they'll be trapped together for several months?

Oh, just Wendy Torrance, that's who.

After she and Danny had escaped Jack and the Overlook and she lay recovering in hospital, her mother had come to visit. Sitting at Wendy's bedside, she'd lit up a cigarette and pointed it at her daughter like a skeletal finger. *Didn't I tell you, Wendy?* she'd said. *I always said Jack was no good. Just like your damn father. But you had to go and marry him anyway. Well, they always say girls want to marry their fathers. I just hope you're satisfied with how that turned out.*

Afterwards, her mother had told Wendy that she and Danny could come and stay with her for a little while, until she'd figured out how the hell she was going to support them both. Truthfully, the idea filled Wendy with dread, but what else could she do? She'd never worked a day in her life; Jack had been the family breadwinner while she stayed home with Danny. Yes, there had been plenty of occasions where he'd stumbled home with nothing more than a pocketful of stale crumbs, but they'd always managed, just about. But how would she manage to raise a young child all on her own, never mind one as, well, *different* as Danny?

Then she'd received the phone call from Marcia Sindell. Marcia introduced herself as a New York literary agent, and was the sort of tough no-nonsense broad Wendy had always secretly dreamt of being.

Wendy, I'm not going to bullshit you, Marcia had told her. *You have a helluva story to tell, and one that I think could make us both a lot of money. It's got everything: hauntings, murders, and a desperate young family in peril. Fuck the American Dream; this is the American Nightmare. Of course, I don't know whether you'll have the first fucking idea about how to write a book, but that's okay. I'll help you through it, and it doesn't have to be Saul fucking Bellow, god forbid.*

Write a whole *book*? But *Jack* had been the writer, not her. The very thought of it had frightened Wendy so much that she'd almost slammed the phone down on Marcia then and there. Still, little by little, the agent had coaxed her into it, assuring Wendy that she'd be able to get her a large advance, more than enough for her and Danny to live on while she set about writing the book.

But while the thought of money was tempting, what had really sealed it for Wendy was learning that Marcia was also Paul Sheldon's agent; the man who wrote the Misery Chastain books Wendy loved so much.

When she'd admitted this to Marcia, the agent had cackled savagely. *Oh, poor Paul,* she howled. *He'd so desperately like to write something highbrow, something that would win him a few awards, but all people want is more Misery. Well, Wendy, you take my advice. I know that you and your little boy don't have so much as a pot to piss in, so just remember that no one ever went poor giving the great American public exactly what they want.*

Finally, Wendy had agreed, quickly realising that not agreeing with Marcia was akin to attempting to sail against an oncoming hurricane in a dinghy. And she had to admit the agent had been as good as her word; within a matter of weeks, she'd secured Wendy a very healthy advance from a major publishing house. After Wendy first left the hospital, she and Danny had had little option but to check into a fleabag motel for a few weeks, and despite her unexpected windfall, she began to fret to Marcia about where exactly they might live while she attempted to write the book.

The agent had briskly cut her off, like a gardener snipping a rose bush. *I'll make some calls,* she told Wendy. *We'll find you some kind of a writers' retreat, somewhere quiet and private.*

The next day she'd called Wendy back and told her about the lighthouse.

Located off the coast of New England, the building had been decommissioned for many years and was now operated by a historical trust, who ran it as a retreat for artists. Marcia knew someone on the board of the trust, and had arranged a three-month lease for Wendy and Danny. *That'll be enough time for you to get started,* she told Wendy. *And no one will bother you there. It's miles from anywhere. But you'll have a radio, and a boat will bring you everything you need once a week.*

On the face of it, the lighthouse sounded perfect; probably about as perfect as the Overlook Hotel had once sounded to Jack. Wendy began to feel the dull throb of dread in her bones, and told Marcia she would need to talk it over with Danny before accepting.

That same afternoon, she sat down with her son and explained the situation to him. She remembered when Jack had first got the position at the Overlook; Danny had had one of his episodes and passed out, a harbinger of the horrors to come. By now, Wendy had learned to her cost not to ignore such things, and pressed her son for his reaction.

So do you think we should go, Doc?

Danny shrugged. *I guess. If it's good for you, Mom.*

But what does Tony think? Tony was his so-called imaginary friend, the little boy in Danny's mouth who told him things no one could possibly know.

I don't hear Tony any more, he sighed disconsolately. *Not since the Overlook.*

So Wendy mulled it over, and eventually decided to accept the offer. Surely not *every* old building could be haunted, and a boat would be visiting them weekly if they should suddenly want to leave.

Besides, she reminded herself, she wasn't Jack.

Wendy knew now – had *always* known, in truth – that her deceased husband had carried a caged monster around inside him his entire life, forever scratching and clawing to get out. His alcoholism had occasionally enabled it to lash out through the bars and hurt her and Danny, but it had taken the power of the Overlook to finally unlock the door of its prison and set it free.

But *she* had no such creature inside her. She told Marcia they would go, and began to make preparations to leave the following week.

That night, she awoke to find Danny standing silently by her bed. When she turned the bedside lamp on, she thought she glimpsed – for the merest fraction of a second – the lunatic ghost of Jack's face lurking just behind Danny's impassive features, like a waiting spider concealed in its burrow. His crazed leer, his lascivious grin.

She gave a start, and then it was gone. Only her son remained, gazing blankly back at her.

Wendy sat up in bed and took Danny's hand. *Did you have a bad dream, Doc?*

He said nothing.

Did…did Tony visit you?

Danny slowly shook his head. *No…not Tony.*

Then he turned and shuffled back to his own bed.

A week had passed without any further incident, but a seed of doubt had been planted in Wendy's mind. Still, even if this did turn out to be yet another in the long line of Wendy's Big Mistakes, it was far too late to do anything about it now.

Standing on the shore of the tiny island that would be hers and Danny's home for the next three months, Wendy glanced down to see her son standing at her side. She reached down to take his hand, and mother and son silently watched the boat that had brought them here slowly vanish over the horizon.

Once it had finally disappeared from view, Wendy led Danny over towards the small cottage adjoining the lighthouse. The lighthouse itself was little more than an empty shell now, and she warned Danny not to try and go inside without her, fearing for his safety on the steep spiral staircase. But the cottage, although cramped by modern-day standards, had been carefully restored, and proved to be a cosy, welcoming space, filled with mahogany furnishings, maritime antiques, and shelves crammed with books. For the first time she could remember, Wendy considered the possibility that she might actually be happy here.

For the rest of that day, she and Danny did little more than unpack, explore what little there was of the island together, and eat a hearty supper. After the meal, they were both so exhausted that they went immediately to bed. There was only one bedroom in the cottage, a garret with two single beds, and after she'd tucked Danny in, Wendy crawled underneath her covers and lay there listening to the waves crashing against the rocks outside. Within minutes, she was asleep.

The sound of the ocean followed her into her dreams, where it slowly transformed into an indecipherable voice, whispering softly to her. In the dream, she was moving through the Overlook's vast garden maze. The closer she came to the centre, the louder the whispering became, and she found herself breaking into a run, desperate to solve the maze and discover exactly who was speaking to her.

At last, she rounded a corner and emerged into the heart of the labyrinth. There she saw Danny, standing with his eyes closed, as motionless as one of the various statues placed throughout the maze. The only part of him that was moving was his lips: the source of the whispering that had inexorably drawn her here.

But as Wendy moved closer to her son, close enough to finally discern what he was whispering, she realised that it was not Danny's own voice emanating from his mouth, but her dead husband's.

I wish we could stay here for ever and ever, Jack's voice hissed, the words gradually turning into a repetitive torrent. *And ever and ever andeverandeverandeverandeverandeverandeverand…*

Then Danny's eyes opened to look at her. They were still her son's eyes, the same eyes she'd spent hours lovingly gazing into while he was a baby, but now she could see Jack *inside* him, feel his poisonous, murderous rage spilling out of her son's pores. She wanted to run, to escape the maze, but when she looked around the hedge had sealed itself behind her, trapping her with Jack for eternity.

She awoke to discover Danny standing over her. Breathless from the shock of the nightmare, Wendy found herself unable to speak.

You dreamt about Daddy, didn't you? Danny asked her.

Her equilibrium gradually returning, Wendy reached across to her nightstand to take a drink of water. Swallowing a mouthful of the liquid, she turned back to her son. *I…I don't really remember, Danny,* she lied. *Isn't it funny how quickly you can forget a dream?*

You don't have to lie, Danny said flatly. *I dream about him too. All the time.*

Wendy slept very little for the remainder of the night. The next morning, she made them both breakfast, then decided it was finally time to try and begin work. She still had Jack's old Adler typewriter, and after some impassioned internal back-and-forth, had resolved to bring it along to the lighthouse with her. The machine certainly hadn't brought her husband any luck with his own writing, but part of her desperately hoped that she could manage to turn that jinx around, and make something good out of something bad.

She sent Danny off to play, then set the typewriter up at a small desk placed in front of a window, so that she could look out at the sea while she wrote. But Wendy soon became bogged down in her task. She understood how important beginnings were, but could not seem to find the right words to commence the book. Time and time again, she typed out an opening sentence, before ripping the page from the typewriter and screwing it up into a ball. She quickly decided that writing wasn't just like pulling teeth; it was like pulling an entire *mouthful* of teeth, over and over and over again. Tears of frustration prickling in her eyes, she lowered her forehead to the desk in defeat. *Jack would know what to write*, she thought.

The next moment, she heard Danny scampering into the room behind her. Wiping hurriedly at her eyes, she straightened up and turned to face him. *Hey, Doc*, she said, forcing a smile onto her face. *You having a good time?*

Look, Mom! he said, waving a small object in the air. *Look what I found in the rocks!*

He handed her the object, which turned out to be a soapstone carving of a mermaid. It felt oily and somehow unpleasant between her fingers, and Wendy wrinkled her nose in instinctive distaste.

You don't like it? Danny said in a small voice.

She'd disappointed him. *No, it's great,* Wendy said quickly, silently reprimanding herself. *You were clever to find it, I bet it's real old. But it's a little dirty. Be a good boy and go clean it up in the sink so that you don't catch any germs, okay?*

Danny's face brightened, and he ran off to the bathroom as instructed. Watching him go, Wendy told herself that she was being ridiculous; the carving was just some harmless old piece of flotsam. The unclean sensation she'd experienced while holding it was just her nerves acting up. She hadn't anticipated quite how distressing confronting old ghosts was going to be.

After many more days of fruitless struggle, Wendy at last found her way into the book, via Danny's voice. She'd wanted to avoid dredging up any painful memories for him, but when her son saw her repeatedly failing to make any headway with her writing, with typical childish directness he asked her why. Disarmed, Wendy confided in him about how insecure and frightened trying to write the book was making her. They began to talk about their experience at the Overlook, and Wendy started to realise that hearing her son's perspective helped unlock something for her. Finding an old reel-to-reel recorder in the cottage, she began to tape Danny's recollections, and weave them into the book alongside her own. After all, he'd always understood the hotel far better than she or Jack, and what was true then was still the case now. Wendy gradually began to understand that Danny was in fact helping to lead her through the maze of the book, and having her son beside her made her feel both more confident and less alone. The pages slowly began to pile up, and when she sent carbon copies of her efforts back to Marcia, the agent wrote her an encouraging letter in reply.

Jack continued to be a lurking presence in her dreams, but Wendy supposed that was only to be expected. Otherwise, she now felt more at peace than she had done for months. The pall of dread that had hung over her ever since their time at the hotel had finally started to lift. It had taken this long, but Wendy felt as though she had at last managed to escape the Overlook.

Then she awoke one night, Jack's sly whisper still lingering in her ear, to find Danny missing from his bed. A terrible drowning sensation swept over her, as though the sea outside her window had risen to engulf the cottage. Wendy sprang out of bed calling her son's name, but he was nowhere to be found: not in the bathroom, nor in any of the rooms downstairs.

Heedless of the chill ocean air, Wendy dashed from the cottage in her nightclothes, screaming for Danny. In her terror, she'd neglected to pick up a flashlight before leaving the house, but once she set foot outside, she found the island bathed in an unearthly white glow, as though the darkened heavens had parted to permit a divine illumination to shine down on her.

Looking up, Wendy saw that, unaccountably, the source of the glare was in fact the long-decommissioned lighthouse, its summit burning as clear and stark as phosphorus. But she had little time in which to ponder this mystery. In the next moment, her eyes instinctively followed the direction of the swirling light and saw it pick out Danny's distant figure down on the nearby shoreline, about to wander into the greedily clutching waves.

Danny! she screamed again, struggling to be heard over the crashing din of the sea. Her bare feet scraping tenderly against rock and shingle, Wendy sprinted after him, convinced that she would never reach her son in time. But Danny was still a young boy, his undeveloped body too weak to make much headway against the strength of the tide, and she managed to catch up to him before he waded too deep. Wendy gathered him up in her arms and ran for the shore, the sea hissing its displeasure behind her.

Collapsing down on the wet sand, she grabbed Danny by the shoulders, shaking him frantically. *What the hell do you think you were doing!?!* she shrieked. *You could have died!*

Danny gazed up at her, his terrified face streaked with tears, and suddenly in her mind's eye Wendy saw Jack shaking him by the arm; little baby Danny, no bigger than a child's doll, his cries turning to screams as his limb snapped under the force of Jack's drunken assault.

The image was so immediate, so horrifying, that she instantly stopped and pulled Danny tightly to her breast. *I'm so sorry, Doc, I didn't mean to hurt you,* she sobbed. *I was just scared, so scared…*

They both remained there for some time, crying and holding each other, until Wendy at last felt able to speak again. *What happened out there, Danny?* she whispered. *Why did you go in the water?*

It was the lady, he whispered back. *The lady who lives in the ocean. She was calling to me. And I knew I shouldn't go, but I couldn't make my legs stop walking.*

Wendy sat on the edge of Danny's bed for the rest of the night, watching him as he slept. Wanting the tactile reassurance of a weapon in her hand, she'd found an old axe lying discarded in a cupboard, but the blade was dulled and stained with rust, and besides, holding it summoned up unwelcome pictures in her mind, pictures she would much rather not think about.

In the end, she settled for a kitchen knife, just as she had done on that final dreadful night in the Overlook. Clutching it between her clammy, rigid fingers, Wendy sat there until dawn listening out for the smallest sound.

Listening for the siren call of the lady who lived in the ocean, yet hearing nothing but the waves.

TWILIGHT'S LAST SCREAMING

Sometime around 7AM, Danny had awoken, and lay there staring mutely up at her, waiting for Wendy to speak. She offered him a wan smile and reached down to stroke his tangled hair. Finally she asked him, *Are there bad things here, Doc? Like in the Overlook?*

I don't know, he replied eventually. *Maybe.*

Then we'll leave right away, she told him. *I'm not gonna let anything hurt you, okay? Not ever again.*

But when she'd radioed in to the mainland, they'd told her there was a storm brewing, and that the boat would be unlikely to be able to make it out to the island until it passed. *Just hang tight, Mrs Torrance,* they told her. *It'll all be over in a day or two, and then we'll be right out to you.*

How could she hope to make them understand it was all happening again?

Wendy assured Danny that the boat would be with them soon, and told him to stay in bed with his colouring books and rest until then. Leaving him alone in the garret room, she moved downstairs and forced herself to sit at her writing desk. Reliving those final, terrible days at the Overlook was just about the last thing she wanted to be doing right now, but even so, better that than simply sitting here staring out at the churning sea, wondering what dread things might be concealed within its black depths.

Her fingers began to move over the typewriter keys, and within minutes she was transported back to the hotel. The sound of the ocean faded away, and was replaced by the immaculate, ominous silence of the Overlook. She recalled moving through the hotel's vast lounge area, drawn irresistibly towards Jack's writing desk at the far end. He'd been sequestered away in here for weeks, flying into a rage at the slightest interruption to his work. Until then, Wendy had told herself that she needed to make allowances; her husband was an artist, after all. But it had grown increasingly apparent that things were very wrong – with Jack, with Danny, with the hotel itself – and the urge to see exactly what he'd been working on all this time had at last become overpowering.

She remembered gazing down at the sheet of paper in his typewriter, the exact same typewriter she was using to describe the scene now, and what she'd seen typed there:

```
All work and no play makes Jack a dull boy.
All work and no play makes Jack a dull boy.
```

The same deadly repetition, the entire page filled with it. She'd felt the world falling away underneath her, and had looked to Jack's manuscript, piled neatly besides the typewriter, desperate for some sign that the current page was just an aberration.

Any indication that her husband had not completely lost his mind.

But his work-in-progress was no different: just page upon page of the same phrase, varying only in the layout of the sentences and paragraphs. Wendy imagined the words spinning round and round in Jack's brain, a lunatic mantra whirling faster and faster, until…what? What would happen when her dull boy decided it was finally time to play?

It was at that moment Jack had discovered her: Bluebeard's wife caught in the act of uncovering her husband's most forbidden secret. But as Wendy steeled herself to try and describe the terror she'd felt at Jack's entrance, she heard a strangled cry from the bedroom upstairs.

She leapt out of her seat, ready to run to Danny's aid, but immediately froze when she saw who was waiting behind her, just as if he'd escaped from within the pages of her book.

Jack.

He looked exactly as he had on that last day in the Overlook, wearing a red jacket with a checkered shirt and blue jeans. Unshaven, his hair wild and unkempt. The crazed slash of his eyebrows, as though they'd been scored into his face by a madman.

He grinned. *Wendy, I'm home.*

Wendy slumped back into her seat, unable to breathe.

Jack gestured towards the desk. *That's* my *typewriter, Wendy,* he said. *What the hell are you doing with* my *goddamn typewriter?*

She felt the tears coming, as they had so often with Jack. *I'm…writing,* she whispered.

His face contorted in a vicious parody of her own. '*Ooh, I'm writing.*' he wailed. *And who the hell told you that you were a writer, you stupid bitch?*

No one…I just thought…

That's fucking right! Jack screamed. *No one! No one at all! That's because you can barely write a grocery list without a fucking dictionary! And it's not enough that you ruined my life, oh no. I'm barely cold in the ground and now you think you're gonna boil down my bones to make a few bucks!*

He stepped forward, looming over her. Wendy felt herself cowering. *Jack, please…*

Reaching down, Jack tore the page from the typewriter and began to read it, his eyes seething with contempt. *Jesus fucking Christ,* he spat, balling the page up and tossing it away. *You really think anyone's gonna publish this drivel? Wendy, you're even fucking dumber than I thought.*

Over the past few weeks, Wendy had been carefully erecting a wall in her mind, a defence against the tempest of self-doubt that threatened to engulf her every time she sat down to write. Each finished page was a single brick, and as her manuscript slowly grew, so did the wall. But now Jack was reaching into her mind and threatening to tear the entire edifice down with a single stroke. She could feel it starting to crumble, and knew that if it did, so would she. And then what would be left for her and Danny? After all, it was not just her story – it was *his,* too.

Jack grabbed her face, squashing her cheeks between his cold fingers. *I'm gonna enjoy making you pay for what you did to me,* he leered. *And not just at the Overlook. Every rotten year of our marriage, I'm gonna take it out of your miserable snivelling hide.*

Wendy gazed back at him, trying to force down the horror she felt rising in her belly. *Jack, please. There are things I should have said to you at the hotel, I know that now. But there just wasn't time. Please…*

He released her from his grip, relishing her terror. *Go on,* he purred. *I'm all fucking ears, oh light of my life.*

In that moment, she felt something erupt within her, like a hot spring bursting from the earth. *I…I want you to go fuck yourself, you stupid, vile pig.*

Jack stared at her in complete astonishment. *What did you say?*

Wendy sprang to her feet, thrusting her face into his. *You heard me, Jack Torrance. Go…fuck…yourself.* Raising her hands to his chest, she shoved him backwards. *You're dead, and you don't scare me anymore.*

His mouth hung open, giving him a dull, bovine expression. *I…*

Shut up, I'm the one talking here, she snapped. *You know what you are, Jack? A hopeless, talentless failure. I spent my whole life believing in you, when all you did was piss and moan and drink and whine about the great works you were going to write as soon as you found the precious time. And then, when you finally had it, what happened? You had nothing whatsoever to say!*

Rage bloomed in Jack's eyes, but Wendy recognised something else there too. A look of frightened inadequacy she'd glimpsed in her own eyes. *I'll…kill you for this,* he panted.

No, you won't. Because I've beaten you. I have all the things you wanted. A book deal, a big agent, money in the bank. I'm a writer, Jack. And you're nothing anymore. No, even worse than that. You never were anything.

As those words left her lips, Jack screamed, his hands bunching into fists. She could see he was about to launch himself at her, but in the next instant, she heard a plaintive voice from the staircase. *Mommy?*

Knowing that she was in immediate danger but unable to suppress her maternal instincts, Wendy glanced around to see Danny standing poised on the stairs. At any moment, she expected to feel Jack's weight crashing into her, sending her sprawling helplessly to the floor. There, she would be unable to defend herself against his assault, and Danny would have to stand and watch as his dead father unleashed the full extent of his terrible fury upon her, leaving her a broken, bloodied thing.

But the attack never came. When she looked around again, Jack had vanished.

She ran straight to Danny, gathering him up into her arms. *What is it, Doc? What happened?*

He clung to her tightly. *I was resting in bed, just like you told me,* he whispered. *But then I started to feel funny, like I used to when Tony came to visit. And I guess I fell asleep, because I dreamt of you and Daddy fighting. But then when I woke up again, I could still hear Daddy's voice. Was he here, Mommy? Has Daddy come back, like the people in the Overlook came back?*

No, of course not, Wendy said hurriedly, not knowing what else to tell him. *It was only a bad dream, Doc. And you know what you do with bad dreams? You just let them go.*

Her body was still vibrating, supercharged with the shock of Jack's appearance. She took Danny through to the kitchen, where she fixed them both hot chocolate with marshmallows. Mother and son sat together in silence, sipping their drinks and watching the heavy rain lash at the window. The cloying sweetness of the beverage helped cut through the fog in Wendy's mind, and she began to try desperately to think of a way to keep her and Danny safe.

The first thing was to flee from the island as soon as they were able, get away from whatever was trying to lure her son into the ocean's clutches. But what about *Jack?* Despite her small victory over him, Wendy was certain she had not managed to banish her husband for good. He would undoubtedly return, more enraged, more murderous, than ever. If his ghost had followed them here, then there would be no escaping him.

It suddenly occurred to her that Jack was probably using Danny as some kind of vessel; emerging from within his dreams and using the boy's psychic energies to manifest himself. How, then, could she ever hope to exorcise him?

She looked over towards her son. He was staring down into his hot chocolate, lost in a daydream. *You could just let him go into the sea*, a sly voice whispered in her mind. *Then it would all be over. No more ghosts, no more nightmares…*

In that instant, Danny looked up at her with wide, frightened eyes, as if sensing exactly what she was thinking, and a fist of nausea slammed Wendy in the gut. She immediately pushed such thoughts away. They were not hers; she would die before ever hurting Danny. It was this place and everything that lurked in it making her think such thoughts. Dark, malevolent things, trying to claw their way through the widening cracks in her mind. But she needed to be strong, for both their sakes. It had been so easy to be weak while married to Jack, but she was not that person anymore, could not allow herself to be.

She and Danny spent the rest of the day in the bedroom, huddled up in bed reading and listening to music. Outside, the tempest continued to grow in intensity, and although Wendy normally enjoyed storms, she prayed with all her heart for this one to be over soon. It frightened her terribly; not simply the sheer unbridled force of it, but also the knowledge of what might be lurking at its heart. As the sky overhead grew thick with gathering darkness, plunging their little room into shadow, Danny crawled into bed beside her, and the two of them curled up together and drifted into sleep, hoping that by the time they woke again, the storm would have faded away, along with their dreams.

It was not to be. A few hours later, Wendy was snatched from sleep by a huge thunderclap overhead. Disorientated, she looked around wildly, needing reassurance that she and Danny were safe, but could not see anything in the darkness. She fumbled for the bedside light, and although its glow was feebly ineffectual against the black void engulfing the island, it was enough to prove to her that they were still alone in the bedroom.

Danny shifted in her arms, making a dull moaning sound, and when Wendy glanced down at him, she saw that he was in the throes of a fit; his eyes rolling back in his skull, his lips flecked with foam. The sight of it made her gasp, but the sound of her distress was immediately drowned out by another bellow of thunder, accompanied by a fierce howl of wind that shook the entire frame of the cottage.

But wait. That howl had not *just* been the wind, had it? Wendy was suddenly convinced she'd heard something underneath it; another sound that might have been much less elemental in its power, but was far more terrifying in what it represented.

WENDY!

Wendy scrambled to the window and peered out into the storm. There, waiting at the front door below, stood Jack, hair plastered to his face, rain streaming down his contorted features. To look at, he reminded Wendy of a cathedral gargoyle, its face tilted up towards a storm.

Seeing her at the window, he grinned. In his hands, he held an axe. The same axe Wendy had found lying rusted and forgotten in the cupboard, but now somehow renewed; its blade bright and wickedly sharp.

I'll huff and I'll puff and I'll blow your house in! he screamed, before smashing the axe into the cottage door.

Past and present collided in Wendy's mind, and she slumped back down to the bed, struggling not to faint. Just as she'd feared, it was all happening again, like some dreadful spiralling nightmare that would forever repeat itself, again and again and again, until it finally claimed her. But what could she do? There was nowhere at all for them to run, and besides,

Danny was still lost to his delirium. If Wendy had to bear his weight, Jack would easily catch them both.

There was only one thing for it, as much as the idea of abandoning him horrified her. If she hid Danny and lured Jack away, then perhaps her son might survive the night. Jack could have her, and hopefully taking her life would be enough to sate his fury. It would be awful for Danny, but he would at least be alive, and all he would have to do was wait out the remainder of the storm before the boat came to rescue him.

At the thought of it, a huge wracking sob took hold of Wendy's body, but she gathered her strength and forced herself up from the bed. Downstairs, Jack was continuing his furious assault on the cottage door, which could not hope to keep him out for much longer. Bundling Danny up in a blanket, she kissed his forehead, then lay him on his side and pushed him under the bed.

In her heart, Wendy knew it was no sort of a hiding place, but she had no time left to seek out anything better. No time at all.

Another axe blow from downstairs brought her to her feet, and she dashed from the bedroom, hurtling down the cramped staircase to the floor below. Jack would be inside the cottage within moments.

A window in the wall opposite the front door looked out upon the nearby shore. Scrabbling frantically to open it, Wendy managed to clamber through and escape just as Jack burst into the room behind her.

WENDYYYYYYYY!

Almost instantly, she found herself soaked to the skin, drenched in rain and spray from the ocean. The force of the wind outside was staggering, driving the rainfall against her like thousands of tiny daggers. Wendy wondered how long she could survive in such conditions, but reminded herself it hardly mattered. Letting out a hysterical giggle, she turned and glanced back towards her husband, who was now peering after her through the open cottage window.

Fuck you, Jack! she screamed.

Lowering her head against the wind, she stumbled towards the nearby shoreline. Wendy knew she could not run from Jack, not for very long, but was determined that she would not make it easy for him. Teeth already chattering from the cold, she pushed onwards. She felt as though she was fighting her way through an army of banshees, swirling and shrieking in the air around her, collectively trying to drive her to her knees.

Wendy was dimly aware of Jack giving chase, the distant sound of his feet crunching against the shingle, but it was impossible to gauge his true distance from her in the midst of the storm. The noise of the wind distorted everything. One second he seemed to be several yards away, the next, his hot, ragged breath was on her neck. But the ocean was growing closer, the rushing waves rising up to greet her. Wendy considered simply throwing herself into its violent churn; she would sink down quickly, and drowning was surely a more peaceful death than whatever Jack had in mind for her.

But then she heard the axe singing, high and bright above the driving wind, and the next moment she felt its edge against her back, cleanly parting dermis, epidermis and cloth. The shock of the assault immediately drove her to her knees, before she even began to feel the pain. Wendy's hands clawed at the sodden grit of the sea shore, her back quickly growing warm with her own blood.

Slowly, she looked up at Jack. His figure was smeared and indistinct in the downpour, like a ink sketch blurred by a water spill. *I've been looking forward to this...for a very long time*, he panted, raising the blade above his head.

Wendy closed her eyes, anticipating his final strike.

Then, she thought she heard another song, one she initially took to be that of the descending axe. But no – it was higher and sweeter than that, far more alluring in its aspect. And the accompanying death blow she was expecting to arrive with it never came.

Opening her eyes, Wendy saw that Jack had frozen in mid-stroke, a confused smile upon his face, his greedy, baleful eyes fixed upon the ocean behind her.

She looked around to see a distant female figure perched upon a rocky outcrop some way out to sea. The figure was nude, its flesh sallow, and below its naked breasts its human torso gave way to the lower body and tail of a fish.

Jack took a hesitant step forward, and in response, the mermaid's song grew louder and ever more irresistible, calling him out into the sea, to her side.

Wendy scrambled out of her husband's path. He took one more step forward, then another, but she could see that he was straining with every sinew to resist his seductress's imprecation.

Mommy?

Wendy looked around to see Danny standing by the cottage, trying desperately to see her through the spray and storm. She was about to scream at him to stay where he was, but then something occurred to her.

Danny? she yelled. *I'm over here on the shore. Your Daddy is here too, can you see him?*

Yes. Mommy, I'm scared!

She looked back at Jack. He could not meet her eyes, his gaze drawn helplessly towards the waiting mermaid, but she could feel him hating her, desperate to throw off the siren's call and attend to the murderous duty first entrusted to him by the Overlook all those long months ago.

Danny! You need to let your Daddy go! Do you understand? Let him go!

Her son did not reply, and she wondered for a moment whether he hadn't heard her, or simply didn't understand. But in the next moment, Jack uttered a low snarl, and his dragging feet began to gouge a pathway through the sand. Wendy watched as he slowly inched forwards, the eager sea showering him with cold kisses. Before long he was waist-deep in the water, arms outstretched towards the waiting mermaid.

Soon, they were both swallowed up by the tempest. Wendy heard the mermaid's song build to a screeching crescendo above the wind, no longer seductive but terrifying in its malevolent triumph, and then, mercifully, it was cut short. All that was left was the howl of the elements, and the sound of her son's footsteps rushing across the shingle towards her.

Danny ran into her arms, and they held each other tightly against the storm. Safe in the knowledge that its fury would soon pass, leaving behind it the promise of a calmer, brighter day.

JIMMY QUINN

Michael Moriarty in Q, *1982*
written & directed by Larry Cohen

I AIN'T NEVER BEEN AFRAID OF HEIGHTS, YOU ASSHOLES! SCREAMED JIMMY Quinn, gazing down at the sidewalk, lying some ten storeys below.

In response, he heard Johnny Boy cackling from behind him. *It ain't the height ya need to be afraid of, ya dumb bastard! It's what happens to ya once ya hit the ground!*

It had turned out to be yet another in a long line of bad days for Jimmy, stretching all the way back to the morning of his birth, when he'd emerged from his mother's womb with the umbilical cord wound tightly around his neck. *And you've been trying to get yourself killed ever since,* she'd always been fond of telling him.

Currently, Jimmy was being dangled by his ankles out of his own apartment window. However, he would take extreme umbrage at the suggestion that this decidedly fraught situation was in any way of his own making. No, it was all the fault of the cheating goddamn New York City brass, and that goddamn monster bird too. If the bird had been there in its nest when he'd led the cops to the top of the Chrysler Building like it was meant to be, and if the mayor hadn't screwed him every which way to Sunday when it *wasn't*, then he would have been a millionaire, totally free and clear. Instead, he was still stuck here in this fucking apartment with Joanie, still stuck being the same two-bit loser he'd always been.

And then, because things can *always* get worse, Johnny Boy Civello and his goons had come to pay him a visit.

Where's the fuckin' money, Quinn? Johnny Boy demanded, signalling to his boys to lower Jimmy another few inches.

Word had spread quickly around the New York underworld that Quinn had made a big score; unfortunately for Jimmy, the news that the city had abruptly withdrawn its million dollar payment hadn't gotten around nearly as fast. So it had only been a matter of time before the vultures started trying to get their beaks wet. If anything, Quinn was mildly insulted the first carrion bird to descend upon him had been one as low on the pecking order as Johnny Boy; everyone knew he was dumb as a box of rocks, dumber than Jimmy even, and he wasn't even a made guy for Chrissake. Still, his cousin Charlie was, and that was more than enough for Johnny Boy. As far as he was concerned, that was a gold-plated license to steal.

Not that Johnny Boy saw any of this as *stealing*, mind you. *Be reasonable, Jimmy,* he cooed. *We only want our twenty-five percent. That way we can make sure no else comes round here botherin' ya. We're doin' youse a service here.*

Twenty-five percent. Two hundred and fifty grand. Even if Jimmy had the money, he knew giving it to Johnny Boy would be like offering dope to a junkie. Sooner or later he'd be back for more, most likely when the hood had a gambling debt of his own to settle. Which was, by all accounts, frequently.

Still, buying some time to think was preferable to trying to do a handstand on the sidewalk at one hundred miles an hour. *I don't got it here, Johnny,* Quinn babbled. *Money like that, you need to put it to work for you. I got it invested, see? That's the smart thing to do.*

There was silence behind him for a second, and Quinn closed his eyes, steeling himself for the sickening drop that would come next. But unexpectedly, he found himself being hauled back through the window and thrown to the floor.

Johnny Boy squatted down before him. Pushing his pork pie hat further back onto his head, he thrust his face aggressively into Quinn's. *Nah. The smart thing is for you to uninvest it as quickly as fuckin' possible, understand?*

Quinn nodded vigorously. *It'll take time, though,* he insisted. *It's, uh, all tied up in stocks and shares. That shit's like trying to get your leg outta a mantrap, ya know?*

He could see his tormentor's eyes glaze over. *Yeah, yeah, spare me the bullshit,* Johnny Boy said, reaching up to scratch distractedly at the old gunshot scar on the side of his neck.

If only the gunman's aim had been a little better, Quinn thought ruefully.

Okay, ya got until Friday, Jimmy, Johnny Boy said finally. *Otherwise out the window youse go again. And this time youse won't just be admiring the view, youse'll be splattered all over it.*

Rising to his feet, the hood gestured to his two goombahs and they all turned to leave, although not before one of the men had planted a boot between Jimmy's ribs for good measure. As Quinn groaned and curled up into a ball, he heard Johnny Boy shout from the hallway, *And maybe next time wear a fuckin' diaper if you're gonna piss yourself again!*

Quinn remained where he was for a short time, letting the pain in his ribs slowly subside. Eventually, he hauled himself upright, wincing at every step, and began the process of cleaning both himself and the place up. Luckily, the damage was only cosmetic, in both instances. Quinn knew full well that if Joanie came home and got wise to the fact that a bunch of gangsters had been beating down their door – *again* – she'd probably throw him out of the goddamn window herself. He'd had to grovel like a bum for her to take him back in the first place; this would undoubtedly be the straw that broke Quinn's back. Not to mention the rest of him.

But what the hell was he gonna do? Johnny Boy was convinced Jimmy was rolling in dough, and nothing Quinn could say was going to persuade him otherwise. You might as well stand directly in the path of an avalanche and plead with it not to hit you. That said, he had no earthly means of laying his hands on even a tenth of the sort of money the mobster was demanding. When the mayor stiffed him, Quinn had wanted to sue the city for breach of contract, but when he'd suggested to his lawyer – wait, *ex*-fuckin' lawyer – that he try the case on a contingency basis, the bastard had laughed in his face. *Yeah, right*, he'd scoffed. *To do that, I'd need to believe we were actually gonna win. And you, Jimmy, would come second in a game of solitaire. You're not even a born loser, you're some kinda karmic fuckin' reincarnation of one.*

Quinn crossed to the window and gazed out at the city. This was meant to be a country where little guys like him could make something of themselves. But it was all bullshit. The American Dream was like trying to climb a greasy pole, and if you ever managed to get close to the top, someone was always waiting there to kick you in the face and send you tumbling back down to the bottom. It was a rigged game, but there was still never any shortage of suckers like him waiting to try their luck. Even now, part of him believed that there might be something else around the next corner beyond another goddamn corner.

And what happens if you walk around enough corners? You end up right back where you fuckin' started.

All of a sudden Quinn felt very tired. He lay down on the couch and pulled a throw over himself. Maybe things would look better once he woke up. Maybe he could dream himself into a better place and stay there. Maybe.

The next thing he knew, Joanie was shaking him awake. *Jimmy, there's someone on the phone for you. It sounds important.*

He shoved her away. *Ain't I told you a million times that I'm not in, ever? Anyone who wants to talk to me is by definition someone I don't wanna talk to.*

Joanie angrily smacked him around the head. *Jimmy, he says he's a professor at some university. He wants to talk to you about the monster. Says he saw you on TV.*

Quinn considered this. Universities had money, right? Maybe the guy wanted him to do a lecture about the bird or something. They probably lapped up all that wacky Aztec shit. And he'd heard there was good money to be made in those things. Maybe he could put together some kinda lecture tour and rake in some decent dough. Hell, no one could say that Jimmy Quinn couldn't talk the ass off a brass monkey. Maybe he could even charge by the word, just like writers did. By the goddamn word! That always sounded like one helluva racket to Jimmy.

Okay, okay, he mumbled, getting up off the couch and slouching over towards the waiting phone.

Picking up the receiver, Quinn affected his best *I'm way too busy for this shit* tone of voice. *So who's this?* he demanded.

Mr Quinn? said a cultured but audibly nervous voice on the other end of the line. *My name is Professor Dexter Stanley. I'm on the faculty of Horlicks University, up in Maine.*

Congratulations, Quinn replied. *What's that gotta do with me?*

A pause. Finally, Stanley spoke again, his voice dropping to a choked whisper, as though he was deathly afraid of being overheard. *Monsters, Mr Quinn. I wanted to talk to you about monsters.*

The next morning, Quinn set out on the long drive up to Maine, in a car he'd borrowed from a nearby parking lot. The precise semantics of this transaction were quite important to him. Because, although he certainly hadn't asked anyone's permission to borrow it, Quinn fully intended to return the vehicle within a day or two, and would have reacted with indignant outrage at the slightest suggestion that he'd stolen it.

Other than running his mouth off, driving was the only other thing Quinn could do with any degree of competency. So, now that he was back behind the wheel of a car, Jimmy at last began to feel somewhat more in control. He always did his best thinking while he was driving, and started to mull over the details of the conversation he'd had with Professor Stanley the previous afternoon.

The man had told him a bizarre story concerning the discovery of an old crate at his university, dating back to an Arctic expedition mounted nearly fifty years earlier. Thinking that the crate would probably contain little more than dust by now, Stanley had blithely opened it – and unleashed a monster. Whatever the creature inside the box was, it had laid dormant for several decades, before awakening with a furious, insatiable hunger. So far it had devoured three people, including the wife of Stanley's best friend Henry. The two men thought they had managed to subsequently dispose of the monster, dumping the crate that served as its lair at the bottom of a nearby quarry, but now it had apparently returned.

It must know my scent, Stanley had gibbered. *It followed me all the way back home, and now it's holed up in my basement. I don't know what to do. Please – I saw your interview on the TV and you seem to have some expertise in these matters. You must help me. I can pay you, of course.*

Quinn had never been accused of having any expertise in anything much at all, and figured the professor was either clutching desperately at straws, or else had gone completely round the fucking bend. Jimmy's money would've been on the latter, had he but a single red cent to his name.

On the other hand, it sounded like Stanley probably had a few bucks stashed away.

Twenty G's, he'd told the man.

The professor gulped. *Twenty thousand dollars? That's rather a lot of money.*

Like you said, I got expertise. And experts don't come cheap. I bet you don't get outta bed for the price of a cuppa coffee neither.

Well, no…

Besides, what'll happen if the cops find out about alla them people it ate? Quinn might have been a dumbass, but his ass wasn't quite dumb enough to buy that Henry's wife had slipped and fallen straight into the monster's mouth by accident. After all, he had form in these sorts of matters himself. *You could get busted as an accessory, or worse,* he taunted Stanley. *Twenty grand and I don't breathe a word to anyone. Ten upfront.*

The professor had finally agreed to Jimmy's terms, so now Quinn was heading to Maine. Of course, he didn't have the faintest idea of what the hell he was gonna do when he got there, Jimmy being a devoted student of the school of making shit up as you went along, but even if he just took the ten grand and ran, it would still be a tidy little payday. With ten grand in his pocket, he could put some distance between himself and the city of

New York, not to mention the assorted scumbags that dwelt within it. He could start over, maybe go somewhere warm.

Alternatively, he was starting to get a few other ideas. What had worked once might yet work again. If it ain't broke, don't fuckin' fix it, right?

When Quinn pulled up outside Stanley's house several hours later, it was to find the professor sitting on his front porch, steadily working his way through a bottle of scotch and already three sheets to the wind. As Jimmy sauntered up the path to the house, Stanley attempted to rise to greet his visitor, before his legs gave way underneath him and sent his ass right back down to the floor.

Don't get up onna account of me, Prof, Quinn told him with a smirk.

You'll have to exchushhe me, Stanley slurred. *It'shh been rather a… trying day.*

Yeah, yeah, I know all about those. You got the dough?

Stanley groped amongst his various pockets, finally managing to extract a crumpled envelope. *It'shh all there.*

Quinn quickly counted it anyway, having learned over the course of his life to instinctively distrust anyone obviously smarter than him. Seeing as that applied to most of the population of America, it had been a rather hard-learnt lesson.

Satisfied, he tucked the envelope safely away in his jacket and turned his attention back to Stanley. *Okay, Prof. You said this thing is hiding out in your basement?*

The professor nodded. *There'shh an old chest freezer down there. Hashn't worked for years. It crawled inshide there. I managed to padlock the lid while it was asleep, but now I don't know what else to do! You have to help me kill it somehow!*

One thing at a time, Prof, Quinn told him. *How's about I just go down there and take a look-see first?*

Stanley directed him into the house, conspicuously not setting foot inside himself. Stepping across the threshold, Quinn began to creep through the rooms, scoping the place out like a thief. It seemed like every room was full of nothing but books. Books! What use were they? In Jimmy's world, you lived by your wits, not according to what some goddamn Poindexter wrote in a book. All this so-called learning hadn't done Stanley any good, had it?

The plain and simple truth of it was this, Quinn decided: not only were there plenty of things that couldn't be taught by books, there were plenty of things in the world that didn't even *exist* in them.

Things like the creature in Stanley's basement.

Quinn stood at the top of the cellar stairs, trying to find the courage to descend. He reached inside his pocket and touched the envelope of money stashed there. The feel of it reassured him. There was more where that came from, if he just held his nerve and saw this through.

Tiptoeing down the steps, Quinn emerged into the basement, crowded with boxes of yet more goddamn books. It made it difficult to manoeuvre down here, but he was starting to see how that might work to his advantage. In the corner sat the chest freezer, a padlock chain wrapped around its handle. The room was completely silent, but Jimmy could already tell he wasn't alone. Beneath the musty smell of old books, there lay another scent. The animal musk of something that had been locked up in a cage for far too long, a thick stew of wet fur and piss and shit and the purest aggression.

Placing a hand over his nose and mouth, Quinn took a couple of stealthy steps towards the freezer. In response, the lid of the creature's makeshift lair immediately slammed upwards. It only moved a few inches before catching on the padlock chain, but that was enough space to permit the claws of the freezer's inhabitant to peek through. They were long, curved, and exceedingly sharp.

Quinn stared at them for a moment, imagining them tearing into human flesh. Claws like that could tear through a person in seconds. Maybe more than one person. *Three* people, even.

He heard a vaguely simian chittering from inside the freezer, and then the claws slowly withdrew, allowing the lid to fall back into place.

Quinn's mind was racing. This was too fuckin' perfect. It could all work out for him, whatever happened. If he tricked Johnny Boy and his goons into coming down here, either they'd all get eaten and boom! Jimmy's problems would be solved and he'd be up ten grand into the bargain. Or, in the unlikely event those dumb goombahs managed to kill the thing before it killed them, he'd still be able to claim the rest of his twenty G's from the professor. And *maybe* that'd be enough to buy Johnny Boy off, for a little while at least.

He ran back upstairs and into Stanley's study, where he picked up the phone and called the operator. There was a bar in Little Italy where Johnny Boy spent most of his time; Quinn figured it was probably the best place to try and reach him. He got the number and dialled it, his heart thudding in his chest.

Could he pull this off? The tricky part was trying to get Johnny Boy up here to Maine in the first place. The fuckin' mook would probably get a nosebleed just by leaving Manhattan. But two hundred and fifty grand bought a lot of handkerchiefs.

He got through to the bar and asked for Johnny Boy. *Hold on a minute,* the sullen voice on the other end of the line said, before putting the receiver down with a thud. Quinn waited for so long that he thought the bartender had forgotten all about him, until suddenly the phone was picked up again.

Who's dis? Johnny Boy demanded. *I'm in the middle of a fuckin' pool game here.*

It's Jimmy, Quinn said. *I got your money.*

No shit? Johnny Boy tried to mask the elation in his voice, then grew suspicious. *That was pretty fuckin' quick. Youse'd better not be fuckin' with me, Jimmy.*

I'm not, I swear. But there's a small catch.

A catch? I'll catch your face with my fist, ya fuckin' asshole.

No, hear me out, Jimmy pleaded. *I got the money, but it's with my, uh, broker. And he's at his place in Maine right now.*

Will you listen to this guy? Johnny Boy bellowed incredulously. *Fuckin' Maine! I'd need a fuckin' passport to go up there. Bring it back to Manhattan, ya stupid fuckin' dipshit.*

Quinn began to pace the room. *Johnny, look. I'm on my way there now. I'm meeting him at his place later this afternoon. But I'm scared to bring this much bread back into the city. I owe a lotta money to a lotta people. They get one whiff of this dough and they'll be all over me like fleas on a fuckin' wino. And you know what a hard luck case I am. I'm scared I'll get robbed before I even get it to you.*

There was silence on the other end of the line. If he listened hard, Jimmy thought he might be able to hear the slow hiss of Johnny Boy's greed incinerating what few brain cells the mobster had left.

Then: *I guess youse gotta point, Quinn. You're the only guy I ever knew could lose an ass-kicking contest against a one-legged man.* The next instant, Jimmy heard him yell across the room. *Hey, Sally! How long's it take to drive to Maine from here?*

It was settled.

When Quinn returned to the front porch, he found Stanley passed out flat on his back. This was undoubtedly for the best, Jimmy decided. After retrieving the padlock key from the professor's pockets, he helped the unconscious man up to his bedroom, deposited him on the mattress, then securely locked the door to the room. With any luck, Stanley would be out cold for the rest of the day. No need for him and all his book-learning to get in the way and complicate matters. Whatever happened next was going to be all about street-smarts, pure and simple.

With the professor safely tucked away upstairs, Quinn fixed himself a little lunch. Given the typically parlous state of his own icebox at home, he was pleased to discover the professor maintained a more than generously stocked refrigerator. Jimmy loaded up on sandwiches, chips and beer, and settled down in front of the TV to wait for Johnny Boy to arrive.

Never one for properly managing his own worst instincts, Quinn sank one too many beers while he was waiting and promptly fell into a deep doze. He was awakened hours later by impatient voices outside and a loud banging at the front door. *Hey, Quinn! You in there, asshole?*

Quinn scrambled to his feet and ran to answer the door, opening it to reveal a pissed-off looking Johnny Boy and his two goons, all brandishing handguns.

For Chrissake, Johnny! Quinn hissed. *Put those fuckin' things away! This is a respectable neighbourhood!*

Ignoring him, the threesome trooped inside the house, carefully checking each of the downstairs rooms as they went. When they were finally satisfied that Quinn was alone, Johnny Boy flashed him a shark-like grin. *Just makin' sure, Jimmy. I know what a slippery motherfucker youse are.*

Quinn affected a wounded look. *Johnny. What the hell could I do to you in Maine, of all places? Set a fuckin' lobster on you?*

Johnny Boy scowled. *Yeah, well, the fuckin' drive up here nearly killed me, for starters. So I ain't in the mood for any of your bullshit. Where's this broker of yours?*

He's asleep upstairs, Quinn replied. *We sank a few while we were waiting.*

Johnny Boy signalled for one of his boys to go up and check, before turning back to Quinn. *And the money?*

It's downstairs, in the basement, Quinn told him. *He has an old chest freezer he uses for safekeeping. All you gotta do is go down there, open it on up and the bread's all yours.*

Johnny Boy cackled. *Yeah, right. What'd you take me for, a fuckin' dumbbell? You could have wired that freezer with a bomb or anything.*

Quinn felt his blood suddenly run cold. *Johnny! Do I look like I know how to rig a bomb?*

Before he could say anything else, Johnny Boy poked him viciously in the ribs with his pistol. *Not another fuckin' word outta youse, Quinn. You're comin' down there with us. And if the money ain't in the freezer like you said, your sorry ass is goin' straight in there instead.*

Moments later, Johnny Boy's goon returned from upstairs and gave him the all-clear. Johnny Boy immediately turned to Quinn and prodded him with the gun again. *You first.*

Sweat prickling on his brow, Quinn led them towards the basement steps. This wasn't how it was meant to go. If that thing in the freezer was as fast and as deadly as Stanley said, it'd chew him up with the rest of them before he had time to so much as draw a last breath. With all of those goddamn boxes jamming up the basement, he'd be trapped. And even if these idiots managed to kill the creature, Johnny Boy would know it had been a setup. So into the freezer Quinn would go, to do his best impersonation of a Sunday roast.

He was fucked.

Quinn slowly led them down the steps, fearful that his legs would buckle underneath him at any moment. When they emerged into the basement, he paused, pointing one trembling finger at the freezer in the corner. *That's it,* he said.

Johnny Boy swiftly planted a boot in Jimmy's ass. *I know what a fuckin' freezer looks like, asshole. Now open it the fuck up.*

Quinn felt like a condemned man being marched to the gallows. A lifelong atheist by temperament, he fought the urge to murmur a silent prayer. Even someone as opportunistic as Jimmy recognised that he'd left it a little late for a sudden Damascene conversion.

He heard one of Johnny Boy's goons mutter behind him, *Jesus, this place stinks like shit.*

Reaching the freezer, Quinn reached for the stout padlock and cradled it in his hand, testing its resolute weight. The professor sure hadn't been taking any chances. This thing could keep out a goddamn army.

Keep *out…*

Quinn suddenly had an idea. True, it wasn't *much* of an idea, but neither was getting eaten by that thing in the freezer.

Johnny Boy bellowed impatiently from behind him. *Yo, Jimmy! Havin' second thoughts over there?* He cocked his pistol to emphasise how much of a bad idea this was.

Quinn gave him a reassuring wave. *We're all good!* He took out the key and inserted it into the padlock. *This thing's just a little stiff, is all…*

Dropping to his knees, he pantomimed struggling with the lock. *Just gimme a second…*

It was now or never.

There! The padlock clicked open, and Quinn reached one hand up to push open the freezer lid, before frantically ducking back down.

The next instant he heard a loud roar, immediately followed by several terrified screams. He felt something leap out of the freezer, hurling itself right over him and in the direction of the other three men. Without even daring to look, Quinn immediately scrambled inside the freezer, taking the creature's place in its lair like a cuckoo invading a bird's nest. Frantically reaching out for the padlock, he fumbled to secure it around the chain once again, thus ensuring his safety.

Quinn kept his eyes focused on the lock, trying not to look at what was unfolding in the basement beyond. But he could not avoid catching blurred glimpses of white fur and flashing claws, and intermittent sprays of red. A lot of red.

When the padlock finally clicked back into place, Quinn withdrew inside the freezer and allowed the lid to close over him, enveloping him in darkness. Within his makeshift sanctuary, he could still make out the dying gurgles of Johnny Boy and the two men, but those soon died away, to be replaced by the moist sounds of the creature's feeding.

Listening to it, Jimmy wanted to sing Hallelujah and vomit at the same time.

Eventually, the creature finished its grisly meal. Quinn heard it chitter with satisfaction, and then the wet sounds of its approaching footsteps on the bloody basement floor. The next moment, it attempted to re-enter its lair, only to find its passage blocked by the padlock.

Quinn curled into a tight little ball as the creature's furious roars filled the basement. Again and again, it tried to tear open the freezer lid, but the lock continued to hold fast.

Finally, it gave up. Lying there in the shadows, Quinn could hear it growling and pacing the room. It seemed entirely unwilling to leave the darkness of the basement and abandon its new lair.

But surely it would give up and go away eventually, wouldn't it?

Outside the freezer, the creature continued to pace and prowl. He could hear its guttural breath, the rasping click of its claws on the basement floor.

And if it didn't, surely Jimmy would think of something, just like he always did.

Click…click…click…

Wouldn't he?

RHODA

Catherine Burns in Last Summer, *1969*
written by Eleanor Perry
based on the novel by Evan Hunter
directed by Frank Perry

IT'S FUNNY HOW QUICKLY THINGS CAN CHANGE, RHODA THOUGHT TO HERSELF. When she first got up this morning, it had seemed to be an entirely unremarkable day, just another in a lifetime of similar days, her past and future stretching off in two long unbroken lines. Unimaginative people, the sort of people she worked with every day, were fond of saying that life was like a river, but that wasn't true at all, at least not for her. Rhoda knew that her own existence resembled nothing more than a vast traffic jam, gridlocked in all directions. Perfect stasis, fixed and unmoving. And just as if she were trapped in a stalled car, the air around her had long ago grown stale and oppressive. Still, she had little choice but to keep on breathing it.

Because it was either that or stop living.

She'd seriously considered that option once, a long time ago now. At the end of that awful summer's day out on Fire Island, the late afternoon sun burning a hole in the watercolour sky, she'd thought about simply walking into the sea and drowning herself, following in her mother's doomed footsteps. That day was the last time her life had changed irrevocably, without any indication or warning. And although Rhoda had ultimately rejected the thought of suicide, unable to countenance leaving her father alone in the world, what she'd experienced that day caused her to forever flee from the possibility of change. No more would she admit the unexpected into her life, because with the unexpected arrived the possibility of threat and danger. She abandoned her cherished dreams of becoming a writer, because with the writing life came uncertainty, and that she could no longer tolerate.

Upon returning to the holiday cottage she and her father were renting for the summer, he'd taken one look at Rhoda's puffy, sunken face and asked her what was wrong. Unable to lie, she'd broken down and told him what the other kids had done to her. Her father's only response was to slap her across the face and berate her for having worn a bikini, which she'd only done in the first place because the others had browbeaten her into it. *I told you what would happen if you went around flaunting yourself*, he told her disgustedly. After he stormed from the room, Rhoda sat and stared out at the waves, wishing she'd surrendered herself to them after all. But that moment had passed, and all she could do now was go on living.

Still, her father's cruelty at least made it easier for her to finally abandon him. Desperate to lose herself in the anonymity of a large unfamiliar city, Rhoda left Cleveland and relocated to Chicago as soon as she turned twenty-one, the sole life change she ever permitted herself to make. She found a job in the secretarial pool at Thorn Industries, rented a small apartment, and turned her back on the world. She had no friends, and rarely ventured outside, except to go to work. The crowded city streets made her nervous, and although she attempted to eat out once or twice during her first few months in Chicago, Rhoda always felt as though everyone in the restaurant was watching her, causing her stomach to cramp with uncontrollable anxiety. That particular experiment was therefore quickly aborted, and from that day on she would only order takeout.

The other secretaries at Thorn made the expected social overtures at first, but Rhoda found it easy enough to rebuff them. She was naturally shy and awkward anyway, so it was simply a matter of embracing her natural instincts, rather than striving to overcome them. After all, it was nothing less than the desperate pursuit of friendship that had torn her life apart in the first place. Before long, the other girls began to leave her alone, restricting their pleasantries to the bare minimum, mumbled good mornings and hasty goodnights. The work itself was routine and monotonous, but Rhoda didn't care. There was always enough of it to fill her days, and that was all she required. After all, she reasoned, nature abhors a vacuum. So if a person had too much free time, then eventually something would rush in to fill it…and that unknown *something* was precisely what Rhoda wished to avoid.

At this, she proved quite successful. Beyond the minor inconveniences of everyday existence – delays on the L, say, or a leak in her bathroom – Rhoda soon found she had almost entirely managed to eliminate the unexpected from her life. Each day was now practically indistinguishable from the next, which meant that she had nothing whatsoever to worry about, or indeed look forward to. But with nothing to anticipate, Rhoda did not experience the usual quickening or slowing of time that occurs when a person is waiting for an particular event to take place. Her days simply…*passed*, one blurring into another. Without her noticing, weeks soon became months, and months became years. Before she even knew it, the seventies had become the eighties, and still very little had ever changed for her. She had the same job, the same apartment, even the same face, give or take a few more lines here and there. She was neither happy nor unhappy, but it hardly mattered to her. As Rhoda perceived it, any attempt to pursue the former state normally only resulted in one achieving the latter.

Far better to live one's life in a perfectly straight line, she told herself. It wasn't as though everyone wasn't going to arrive at the same fixed point sooner or later anyway. Just as her mother had found out.

But today, something had finally changed.

She'd been sipping at her (decaffeinated) morning latte and examining the contents of her in-tray when she saw him. He'd entered through the doors at the far side of the room, laughing and joking with Paul Buher, Thorn's deputy chairman.

That's the new executive, the girl to her left had whispered to someone. *I hear they headhunted him from New York.*

Whoever or whatever he was now, Rhoda had known him only as Dan. It had been more than twenty years since she'd last seen him – his tanned, handsome face bobbing rhythmically at her own, contorting in brutish ecstasy – but time hadn't changed him all that much either. He was paler now, thicker around the middle, but she could still sense the same lazily vicious arrogance about him. It was there in the way he blithely entered an unfamiliar room, continually pushing forwards like a shark. An apex predator poised to chase and devour.

As he and Buher passed the secretarial pool, Dan had glanced across at the assembled women and flashed them a smile, baring his perfect white teeth. His eyes had briefly met Rhoda's, and for one dreadful moment, she thought that he'd recognised her too.

Fearing she was going to be sick, she'd immediately dashed to the ladies' room. After she was safely sequestered in a cubicle, the nausea had gradually subsided, although her instinctive terror had not. It was hot and fiercely bright, piercing her insides like a laser. Rhoda's first impulse was to quit her job, just walk out now and never come back. She could go home, spend the rest of the day in bed, and worry about finding a new job tomorrow.

But the more she thought about it, the more that prospect sparked an even greater fear inside her. She was nearly thirty now, and had never made any attempt to better her situation at Thorn. Why would anyone else choose to employ her? Her experience and qualifications were little more than mediocre, not to mention that she was dumpy, unattractive and practically middle-aged. Rhoda knew what men really looked for in their secretaries, and it certainly wasn't how many words they could type per minute. There would always be someone younger and prettier than her. She would be an absolute fool to leave Thorn.

And perhaps Dan would never even recognise her. No one else ever gave her a second glance, why should he be any different? She would return to the anonymity of the secretarial pool and hide herself in its depths, like a startled minnow. It's not as if she'd ever meant anything to him, and doubtless there had been dozens of girls since that day on Fire Island. God, he'd probably long since convinced himself that she'd *wanted* what he'd done to her, that he'd done poor pathetic Rhoda a favour by ridding her of the wearisome millstone of her virginity.

Burying her terror deep inside, she'd returned to her desk and spent the rest of the day typing furiously, working until her fingers ached, never once looking up from her tasks or breaking to eat lunch or go to the bathroom or anything. She would pay no heed to the world, and hoped fervently that it would have the good grace to ignore her in return.

As the clock neared 5PM, it seemed as though her plan of concealment had worked. But as Rhoda allowed herself to relax for a moment, easing back into her seat and looking up at her surroundings for the first time in hours, she saw her supervisor approaching.

Dan wants to see you in his office, the woman said, giving Rhoda a curious look.

Rhoda felt the crackle of frost in her veins. *W-why?* she croaked.

Beats me, her supervisor shrugged, not even bothering to disguise her bafflement that Rhoda should be singled out for any particular attention. *But don't keep him waiting.*

She slowly got to her feet, her limbs sluggish and unresponsive. *I could still run*, she told herself. *Run and never come back.* But it were as though she were lost in the throes of a nightmare, her body stricken with sleep paralysis. Every single step she took required an excruciating effort, and as much as Rhoda might have willed it otherwise, each one only served to take her closer and closer to Dan's office.

Upon arriving at his door, she reached up and knocked, so gently that she hoped he might not even hear. But he'd been listening out for her, waiting in patient readiness, and in the next instant she heard his voice call out, casual and welcoming, *Come in!*

Her eyes never moving from the floor, Rhoda pushed the door open and approached Dan's desk, hands clasped protectively together against her belly, nervously writhing fingers entwined like a nest of worms. *You asked for me?* she mumbled.

Please, sit, he instructed.

Rhoda did so, and eventually found herself compelled to glance up at him. Looking into Dan's eyes, she felt like she was fifteen years old again, and immediately froze in her seat, entirely helpless.

He smiled. *Well,* he said. *Well, well, well. I guess the world really is as small as they say.*

Yes, Rhoda said faintly.

When I first saw you sitting there, I thought, hell, this is just meant to be. There's really no other explanation for it, is there? I mean, I come here all the way from Manhattan, and here you are, all these years later. He paused. *Where is it you were from again…?*

Cleveland, Ohio, she replied.

That's it! he exclaimed, jabbing his finger at her. *So for us both to find our way here to Chicago, after all this time…well. Well.* Dan gazed around his office in wonderment, as if seeing it for the first time. *As a stranger here, I can't tell you how good it feels to run into an old friend.*

Rhoda felt a sharp pain inside her. *B-but…* she stammered.

Dan's eyes were bright. *What is it?*

But…we b-barely knew each other, she finally managed. *Hardly at all, r-really.*

An insinuating smile. *Oh, I wouldn't say that, would you? I wouldn't say that at all, Rhoda.*

Her face burned. *I…suppose not.*

You know, I've never forgotten that summer, he said distantly. *It almost seems like a dream now, doesn't it? Everything was so perfect. Those long hot endless days. You know, Peter and I still see each other every year. And Sandy, well.* Dan laughed softly. *If I say that she was something of a solid gold bitch, I'm sure you won't disagree with me, will you?*

Rhoda gave a small shake of the head.

But Christ, how we adored her back then. And now here you are! Oh, wait until I tell Peter…

With an almost superhuman effort, Rhoda forced herself back to her feet. *Was…was there anything else?* she blurted out. *It's just that I have an appointment. At the, the dentist.*

Dan leapt up from his seat. *Oh, don't let me keep you, Rhoda! I just wanted to catch up and say hello. It's really made my day, seeing you again.*

Rhoda forced a small smile. *Well…hello.*

She was halfway to the door when his voice stopped her again. *Oh, there was just one more thing. Can't believe I didn't mention it before.*

Rhoda glanced back over her shoulder, to see Dan gazing out of his window at the cityscape beyond. *Yes?* she said quietly.

I'm going to need my own secretary, he replied, never once moving his eyes from the window. *So I've requested you. Seeing as we already have an existing relationship. You can start tomorrow morning.*

Rhoda looked over at the empty desk outside Dan's office, just a few short steps away from his own. There would be no hiding from him there, ever. He would be able to observe her always, little more than a rat in a lab, there to be poked and prodded and tortured at his leisure.

Me? was all she could manage by way of a reply.

Oh, I know it's a step up in responsibility, but I'm sure you can handle it, Dan responded. *I remember how clever you were back then. How you always thought you were smarter than the rest of us.*

Rhoda said nothing.

He laughed mirthlessly. *But that was a long time ago, am I right? And hey, you can look for a little something extra in your paycheck from now on. I mean, what else are old friends for?*

She did not sleep that night, adrift in her bed like a shipwreck survivor floating on a dark and turbulent sea. What could she do? To stay in the job was unthinkable, to quit was impossible. For the first time since that day on the beach, Rhoda began to consider taking her own life. But even in the depths of her despair, she retained her inherent practicality. She would not be rushed into such drastic measures, not without properly considering exactly how she would do it, and when and where the final act would be carried out. However much her life might be at the mercy of blind fate, the knowledge that she could still control the manner of her own death comforted her somewhat, and when Rhoda returned to work the next morning, she felt more at peace than she had done in years. She accepted that her entire existence lacked any real significance or meaning, and thus could be terminated without consequence. This cold-eyed acceptance of her own irrelevance freed her to go through the motions of the working day, for if *she* didn't matter, than surely nothing else that might happen to her mattered either.

She arrived to find a bouquet of flowers awaiting her at her new desk, and as she took her seat, Rhoda could feel her neck prickling under the jealous gaze of the other secretaries. She pushed the sensation away, determined that she should not feel anything while she was within these four walls. She would be nothing but a hollowed-out effigy of herself, emptied of all but the barest modicum of awareness and emotion.

Aside from the small gesture of the flowers, Dan was entirely preoccupied with his new job and hardly even seemed to notice Rhoda's presence outside his office door, save when he needed her to take dictation or bring him refreshments. Days went by without any meaningful interaction occurring between them both. Was it that he could not bear to face her, she wondered? Perhaps promoting her to this position had been Dan's misguided attempt at atonement, but now that Rhoda was an inescapable part of his working day, he preferred instead to try and ignore her?

Or perhaps he simply enjoyed the small humiliation of making Rhoda fetch coffee for the man who had raped her. Perhaps whenever she was safely out of the room with the door closed behind her, he would cackle with sadistic relish or make obscene gestures in her direction, as though he were once again the same vulgar adolescent she used to know. She had previously thought that by abandoning all feeling, she might be able to endure the torment of facing Dan day-in, day-out, but now that he seemed to be responding almost in kind, Rhoda's resolve felt as though it were on the verge of shattering. She thought she might have borne him being caring, or cruel, or even perversely flirtatious, but what she could *not* bear was being entirely ignorant of what he was thinking.

Then, after several weeks had passed, Dan called her into his office one morning. He told her that Damien Thorn, the young CEO of Thorn Industries, was visiting the Chicago offices the next day. *I've gotta give him a presentation, and I hear he's a real hard-ass*, Dan said ruefully. *So I'm gonna have to stay late in the office tonight to prepare, and I'll need you to stay too, okay?*

It wasn't okay, not nearly okay, but what could she possibly tell him? Even if she wished to risk Dan's opprobrium, she had no conceivable excuse not to stay late. Everyone in the office knew that she lived alone, had no friends or family in the city. She was trapped.

Of course, Rhoda said meekly.

Great! Dan said. *I'll order in, we'll make it fun. And listen – I know I've been kinda distant these past few weeks. It's just the pressure, you know? New job, I want to make a good impression. But I didn't want you to think it was anything to do with you. You've been doing a great job, Rhoda, just like I knew you would.*

For the rest of the day, the office was abuzz with the news of Damien Thorn's visit. The CEO rarely visited Chicago these days, having barely survived the freak explosion that had claimed the lives of his aunt and uncle here several years ago, and his occasional appearances in the building were always guaranteed to attract the attention of Thorn's female staff. Rich, powerful, and darkly handsome, Damien was by now one of America's most eligible bachelors, and although some snidely questioned the sexuality of a man who could have had practically any woman he desired and yet remained stubbornly single, none of the girls in the secretarial pool were going to let idle gossip get in the way of their fantasies of snaring the only surviving member of one of the country's wealthiest family dynasties.

But Rhoda paid the excited chatter little mind. After all, she was unlikely to meet Damien, and he would almost certainly be quite oblivious to her if she did. And she had no time for empty-headed romantic fantasies, no matter how improbable and harmless they might appear to be. Because, deep down, she knew that such things were never harmless. Rhoda had allowed herself to become the victim of such a fantasy once, back when she'd dared to believe that Peter might care for her, and had blindly stumbled into her own undoing as a result.

Ever since that day, she had been determined to never let such a thing happen again, but ultimately, where had that determination got her? Tonight, Rhoda would be left alone with the same man who'd callously raped her when they were both little more than children, and as blind as she might have been then, what good did perceiving him clearly do her now?

That evening, as the other employees on the floor began to depart for home, Rhoda joined Dan in his office. They worked on his presentation together for several hours, until the building had grown dark around them and the cleaners had been and gone.

Finally, Dan eased back in his chair with a yawn. *Right, how's about we order some dinner?* he asked her.

Rhoda nodded. In truth, she would rather have skipped dinner and kept on working, so that this might be over with all the more quickly, but she could hardly tell Dan that.

He grinned, his face reminding her of the capricious teenager he'd once been. *Tell you what. Before I order, let's have ourselves a little aperitif.* He jumped to his feet and walked towards the office's well-stocked drinks trolley. *What's your poison, Rhoda?*

She hesitated. *I…don't drink.*

Dan stared at her, incredulous. *Christ, are you serious? You're not fifteen anymore.*

I don't like the taste. She'd already told him this, all those years before. That rainy summer's afternoon, the four of them trapped in Sandy's living room. Rhoda had recounted the story of her mother's death: her parents' beach party; the drunken bet that her mother couldn't swim out to a nearby sand bar and back; the male party guest who'd kissed Rhoda full on the mouth and felt her up.

And finally, her mother's farewell before she ran down to the beach and disappeared into the waves forever, the sour taste of whisky on her lips as she kissed her daughter goodbye. Rhoda still dreamt of that night even now, and after she woke, always imagined the tang of alcohol lingering on her tongue. Ever since then, every time she tried to take a drink, it only served to remind Rhoda of her own inescapable loneliness. *This is what loss tastes like.*

But of course, Dan didn't remember her telling him any of this. Ignoring Rhoda's protestations, he poured them both a bourbon on the rocks. *Well, I'm not gonna drink alone. I'm your boss and you have to do what I tell you, right?*

When he handed Rhoda the drink, he stood over her until she took a sip, snorting with laughter when she coughed and grimaced. *It's an acquired taste,* he told her. *Just down it and the next one will be easier.*

Hoping that Dan might move away if she did as he instructed, Rhoda forced herself to gulp down the rest of the bourbon, barely managing not to retch. *Good girl!* he cried, reaching down to squeeze her shoulder. *We'll make a party animal out of you yet.*

Quickly downing his own bourbon, Dan took her glass and, to Rhoda's horror, poured them both another. At least this time he didn't stick around to watch her drink it, but instead returned to his seat. Cradling his glass against his chest, Dan threw his feet up onto the desk and leaned back in his chair, watching Rhoda as though she were an animal in a zoo.

Well, here we are, he said amiably. *Just like old times.*

Not knowing what to say, Rhoda took another sip of her drink. It tasted no fouler in her mouth than the curses she so dearly wanted to hurl at him.

Do you think about that summer very often? Dan suddenly asked her. *Seeing you again brought it all right back to me, I have to say.*

I remember it…very well, she said quietly.

A flash of white teeth. *Yeah, I'll bet you do,* he murmured. *Hell, I know we played a little rough occasionally, but kids will be kids, am I right? And we had some good times together, you must admit.*

The room around her suddenly grew indistinct, as though she were viewing it through a scrim of ice. A roaring noise filled her ears. Rhoda wobbled unsteadily to her feet, slopping bourbon onto the carpet. *I think I should leave,* she said faintly.

Dan stared at her. *Did I say you could go?* he said.

I…

Rhoda. His eyes moved to the ceiling. *Did I give you* permission?

N-no, but…

Then sit your fat ass down in that chair! he screamed.

Terrified, she immediately collapsed back into her seat.

That's much better, Dan said. Taking a long slow sip of his bourbon, his eyes studied her. *I'm sorry I said that about your ass, Rhoda. That was uncalled for. But you should really start taking better care of yourself. Attend some aerobics classes, maybe. All the girls are doing it now.*

I will, she gulped.

I mean, just look at yourself. You were plump back then, but now you've really let yourself go.

I'm sorry, I'm sorry, Rhoda whispered, hating herself.

Stand up a second, will you?

She did as Dan ordered. All of a sudden the room seemed very hot. As hot as that long ago day they'd taken her amongst the trees, the air arid and stifling, his naked body slick and eager against her own...

Dan placed his elbows on the desk and leaned forward. *Right, take off your dress.*

Instantly, she was jerked out of the past and back into the present. *W-what?*

You heard what I said, Rhoda.

No!

He laughed. *Oh, you don't need to worry. I'm not going to lay a finger on you. I mean, we're not kids any more, are we? If I want to get laid, I can go out to a bar and fuck any girl I choose. So no, I'm not going to touch you, Rhoda. Not ever again.*

I won't do it! she cried.

Finishing his bourbon, Dan got up from the desk and sauntered back to the drinks trolley. Pouring himself another, he leaned back against the wall, placing himself squarely between Rhoda and the office door. If she tried to run now, she would have to make it past him.

If you don't, I'll fire you, he said. *I'll fire you and make sure the only job you can get is cleaning fucking toilets. I can do that, you know. If you get a bad reference from Thorn...who else in Chicago is gonna hire you?*

Slowly, Rhoda turned her head to gaze out of the window. The lights of the city beckoned to her, beacons on a faraway shore. She could end it all now, rush over there and simply throw herself through the glass.

I'm waiting, Rhoda.

Rhoda rose to her feet and began to unbutton her dress, her fingers feeling fat and clumsy, numbed of all sensation. Finally, the garment slipped from her shoulders and slid to the floor, puddling around her feet like tears.

Turn around in a circle, Dan instructed.

Arms crossed tightly over her chest, she did so.

He sighed. *Do you know what I think, Rhoda?* When she didn't answer, he continued. *I think you don't love yourself enough. What do you have to say about that? Well?*

I don't love myself...at all, she whimpered.

You can sit down now, Dan told her. Gratefully, she sank back into her seat, but he had not finished with her yet. *Now, I want you to do one more thing for me*, he said.

What?

Simple. He took a long swallow of bourbon. *I want you to love yourself.*

I...I don't understand.

Oh, sure you do, he coaxed. *Just like you do when you're alone. When no one's watching.*

Suddenly, Rhoda couldn't hold back the nausea any longer. Craning her head to one side, she vomited onto the carpet. *Oh god*, she moaned.

It's okay, you can clean it up afterwards, Dan said. *First things first.*

I can't, I can't! she sobbed.

It's easy. Just slide your fingers down into your panties. Go on, gently does it. Just like a lover would.

Her hand shaking, Rhoda edged her fingers underneath the elastic waistband of her underwear. They felt cold and alien against her skin, nothing like a lover's at all.

Now, move them back and forth, he murmured. *You know how to do it, don't you, Rhoda? I bet you do it every night. Hell, I bet you think of me when you do it, don't you?*

Her mind seemed to float above the room, observing events from afar. Rhoda's body was no longer her own. It was merely a clumsy machine, a tool fit for but a single purpose.

As her hand began to move stiffly between her thighs, she only prayed that it would not take long, that the machine would not break down before its allotted task had been completed.

After it was all over, Dan left her huddled naked on the floor of the office. *I can trust you to get everything cleaned up, can't I?* he told her. *And don't take too long about it. I want you back here ready to start work first thing tomorrow morning.*

Once he'd gone, Rhoda just lay there weeping for awhile, watching as the sky outside the office windows gradually began to redden. She could not think coherently, nor imagine what on earth she might do once she finally escaped the building. All she had left to guide her were her most primal instincts, which were telling her to get up, get dressed, and get out of here.

Forcing herself upright, she began to gather her clothes together into a pile, then suddenly froze.

Someone was behind her.

Rhoda's head whipped around to see the figure of a young man standing in the doorway. She immediately let out a scream, pulling her discarded dress towards her chest to cover her nudity.

Motioning for her to be calm, the young man slowly stepped forward, the dawn light revealing his face as he moved into the room.

Horrified, Rhoda realised that it was Damien Thorn.

Ohmigod ohmigod, she moaned, burying her face in her hands. *I'm sorry, I'm so sorry...*

Shhhh now, he told her, pulling his jacket off and bending to drape it around her shoulders. *Are you alright? What happened to you?*

Rhoda started to weep again. *I can't tell you,* she babbled. *How can I possibly tell you? Please, Mr Thorn, just let me go home now and you'll never see me again, I promise.*

Damien fetched Rhoda a glass of water and sat with her until her sobs started to subside. *You work here, yes?* he asked her gently.

She gave a reluctant nod.

Then you're my responsibility. And I take my responsibilities very seriously, Rhoda. So I want you to tell me exactly what happened to you. Don't leave anything out, anything at all.

His clear blue eyes were like a cool sea washing over her, cleansing her despoiled flesh, and so Rhoda did not even think to ask how he knew her name. Instead, she began to tell Damien everything, starting with that dreadful summer's day of so many years ago.

He listened quietly, never interrupting or questioning her, and when she had finally finished, he reached over and took her hand delicately between his own. *Thank you for telling me everything,* he said. *I appreciate your honesty, Rhoda. And now I'm going to be completely honest in return, if that's okay with you. I'm going to tell you exactly who I am and what I'm going to do. And if, at the end of it, you decide to follow me, then you'll never have to worry about another thing in your entire life. Not Dan, not anything. Understand?*

Rhoda nodded, rapt. And when Damien told her who he truly was and what he was here on Earth to do, she realised she had at last found the certainty she'd craved for so many years. Even sitting with him now, she could feel Damien's unholy power coursing through his deceptively gentle hands. Rhoda had never worshipped God, not since her mother had been so cruelly taken from her, because she found it impossible to deny just how little God cared about her in return. But here was an entity, a divine being, comforting her, advising her, sitting here with her as though she *mattered*.

She would give herself completely to him, Rhoda decided. Whatever he wanted, she was ready to give. *I'm yours*, she whispered.

Good, he said, bending to gently kiss her forehead. *Now, I want you to get dressed, and take the rest of the day off. I'll get my driver to take you home.*

But Dan... she began worriedly, before Damien cut her off with a gesture.

I said you wouldn't have to worry about Dan, didn't I? Just go home, and I'll take care of everything.

He left Rhoda alone while she dressed, and then escorted her down to his limousine, drawing baffled but envious glances from the other secretaries they passed on their way. Once she was sat safely in the back of the vehicle, she found herself stricken at the thought of saying goodbye to Damien. *When will I see you again?* she implored him, suddenly fighting back tears.

I will always be with you, he murmured.

But I want to serve! How am I to serve?

When you are needed, I will call.

He closed the limousine door, abandoning her to the shadows that would be her home from this day forward.

After she arrived home, Rhoda pulled all the curtains closed, then ran a bath, as hot as she could bear. Soaking in the tub, she could feel exhaustion rapidly overtaking her. After she got out, she brushed her teeth in an attempt to banish the foul taste of bourbon that still lingered on her tongue, then went directly to bed, where she slept for a full twelve hours.

She awoke crying Damien's name.

Finding the room dark, she picked up the TV remote and turned on WGN-TV, the local news channel, craving some reassurance that the world around her had not changed, even if her own existence had altered irrevocably.

Surrounded by a crowd of onlookers, a news reporter was standing outside a building Rhoda knew as well as the exterior of her own home: the Chicago headquarters of Thorn Industries. The reporter was describing how, earlier that day, an executive at Thorn had opened the window to his thirtieth-floor office and thrown himself out onto the street below. Even before Dan's photograph flashed up on the screen – blond, smiling, apparently without a care in the world – she already knew who the reporter was talking about.

Her new master had kept his promise to her.

Turning off the TV, Rhoda settled back down in bed and went straight back to sleep. She slept without interruption, right through till morning, and even then, she was only awoken by the insistent summons of the ringing telephone. Groggily, she gave in and answered it, to find her old supervisor on the other end of the line. She asked if Rhoda had heard the terrible news, and when she said that she had, the woman said that while it was all just too bad, Dan's death now left Rhoda without a role at Thorn. It would take quite some time to replace him, she informed her, and they'd filled Rhoda's old spot in the secretarial pool weeks ago. So regretfully, the company were just going to have to let her go.

Rhoda hung up on the woman while she was still in mid-sentence, then giggled madly, her laughter sounding hollow and lifeless in the emptiness of her apartment.

She supposed this was what people meant when they warned against making deals with the Devil.

No matter. Her miserable charade of a life was over now anyway; the telephone call had only served to confirm what she already knew. No longer would she squirm and struggle within the unrelenting grip of anxiety, or fear the attentions of a cruel, uncaring world that had only ever meant her mockery and harm.

A new world was nigh; the Antichrist had promised her as much. A new world where all the forgotten, discarded people like her would at last rise up and claim that which they had been denied for so long.

So, until that day finally arrived, Rhoda would simply remain here in the dark and await his summons.

PAUL HACKETT

Griffin Dunne in After Hours, *1985*
written by Joseph Minion
directed by Martin Scorsese

WHEN PAUL HACKETT WAS A SMALL BOY, HIS MATERNAL GRANDMOTHER, a staunchly Catholic Irishwoman from the old country, held his hand over a naked flame and sternly told him, *That's what Hell feels like all the time. Be sure you don't take a wrong turn and end up there, now.*

And although Paul liked to believe that he'd left the old woman's dogmatic warnings far behind him, tossed into the dustbin of history alongside other such childhood relics as his pacifier and favourite comfort blanket, in truth the experience had never quite left him.

So during that awful, endless night in Manhattan's Soho district, the night that had begun with the promise of easy sex and ended in paranoia and looming violence, he had begun to hear his grandmother's voice berating him from across the years, reedy and insinuating. *This is it,*

Paul. You took a wrong turn, and now you're in Hell. Didn't I always warn you?

Something had been revealed to Paul that night. A veil had been ripped away, and he'd at last come to understand that the world was not the comfortably reassuring, even slightly dull place he had hitherto always believed it to be. No, the world was a living nightmare: an illogical shrieking horrorshow filled with people (mainly women, it seemed) who wanted to hurt you, perhaps even kill you.

Because he *had* nearly died, Paul was certain of that one fact. Finally driven to the edge of madness, he had fallen to his knees in the middle of the street and screamed up to the heavens, *What do you want from me? What have I done?*

All he'd wanted was to meet a nice girl. Did he have to die for it?

And the answer he had received was a divinely emphatic *yes*.

So, although he had in the end survived, stumbling into the blessed sanctuary of his workplace along with the coming of the dawn – battered and bloodied, half out of his mind, covered in plaster dust and looking like his own mournful ghost – as a result of that one impulsively lustful sojourn into Soho, Paul had lost everything. That same morning, his boss had taken one look at him and fired him on the spot. Unable to find similar employment, he'd fallen behind on the rent and been evicted from his apartment. His entire existence – once as safe and secure as that of a hamster in a cage – now lay in ruins. No nice normal girl, or even one as unstable as Marcy or Gail or Julie or the rest of them, would ever look at him twice now. He'd been forced to take a job as a lowly receptionist at Thorn Industries' New York offices, and lived in a tiny box room he sublet from a crazy cokehead wannabe actress named Holly. He was now prematurely greying, hollow-eyed and rapidly gaining weight. One night, he had drunk an entire bottle of vodka and attempted to take an overdose of sleeping pills, only to vomit the whole cocktail up over the bathroom floor. So powerless was he, so unable to resist the inexorable tide of misery sweeping through his existence, that he couldn't even manage to take his own life. He was driftwood; nothing but downwardly mobile detritus.

Six months later, the phone calls began.

Holly had wakened him one night to disapprovingly inform him there was a girl calling for him. Groggy with sleep, Paul had looked at his watch to discover it was nearly one in the morning. Who on earth could be calling him at such an hour? A *girl*? He didn't know any girls, not any more.

It sounds like a long distance call, his roommate told him curtly. *She sounds real faint, real far away. Tell her to check the goddamn time difference in future, I have to get up early for an audition tomorrow.*

Paul had stumbled to the telephone, certain that the call could only signify something terrible. Good news could always wait until morning. Only bad tidings ever arrived after dark.

He picked up the receiver, his hand trembling with apprehension. *Hello?*

Paul, is that you? The voice was faint as mist, shrouded in a haze of crackling distortion that reminded him of the sound of burning flames. But it was immediately recognisable for all that: the same breathy, alluring tones that had lured him to Soho all those months before.

Marcy.

Paul, I thought you were coming over?

Poor dead Marcy Franklin, who had taken her own life after Paul rejected her, repelled by her casual stories of rape and dark hints that her ripely desirable body might be marred by disfiguring scars. Whose half-naked corpse he'd callously abandoned in an empty artist's loft.

And she *had* been dead, he was sure of it. There had been no light left in those sleepily enigmatic eyes, no warmth remaining in her rapidly paling flesh (which, wouldn't you know it, turned out to be flawless after all). Dead, dead, dead.

But here she was, calling from some faraway place.

Paul, I miss you.

He slammed the phone down, hurried back into his room and took refuge underneath the bedclothes. His nightmare was not yet over, it seemed. He was still caught in the throes of the same bad dream that had come spilling out of his unconscious to consume his waking existence. The past six months, as miserable as they had been, were merely a brief respite from the horror that had now returned to claim him. He had thought that, once he'd escaped from the hellish environs of Soho, he might actually be safe. But nowhere was safe, not even this crappy little sublet room in Queens.

It's after hours. Different rules apply.

Someone in Soho had once told him that, and it turned out to be the truest thing Paul had ever heard.

He did not go into work the next morning, calling in sick and remaining in bed all day. But come nightfall, he was there, poised and ready by the telephone. He knew she would call again. So when the telephone began its shrieking summons sometime after midnight, Paul had plucked it from its cradle before it even completed its first ring.

Marcy? he said.

A hissing silence on the other end of the line, then a soft giggle.

Marcy, I'm sorry. About everything. I didn't know.

Another giggle.

But can you please make it stop? I'll do anything. Just please…stop.

Then, two simple whispered words. Meaningless to most, but not to Paul.

Surrender Dorothy.

A sudden terror gripped him, and he impulsively yanked the telephone cord from the wall. Wrapping the disconnected cable around the phone, he carried it back into his room, where he thrust it to the bottom of his laundry basket. Then he barricaded himself inside the room and went back to bed, where he remained for the next twenty-four hours, ignoring Holly's increasingly irate knocks on the door and vociferous demands to know where in the hell the goddamn telephone was.

The next night, Paul was lying in bed fruitlessly attempting to masturbate for the fourth time that day when he heard a muffled ringing coming from the laundry basket. He accepted this latest development with a fatalistic resignation. After all, there was a dead girl on the other end of the line. Why should it be any more difficult to accept that she was calling him on a disconnected phone?

Retrieving the telephone from the basket, he picked up the receiver. *Hello, Marcy.*

I miss you, Paul.

He suddenly realised he didn't care what else happened to him now. He had already taken that wrong turn his grandmother had always warned him about. He'd entered into a hell entirely of his own making, and would simply accept whatever punishment was due. *I'll come to you, Marcy. Just tell me where.*

She named a famous old restaurant in the Village, The Dante.

I'll be there in thirty minutes, he said.

Dressing quickly, Paul exited his room, only to encounter Holly waiting in the hallway outside. Before she could begin to berate him, he told her that he was leaving the apartment for good and that she could sell anything of value she found in his room. Then, leaving his dumbfounded roommate behind, he hurried down onto the street to hail a cab.

It was a chill fall evening, misty with rain, but he did not have to wait long. A taxi emerged from the gloom like a furtive, prowling animal and pulled up beside him. As Paul climbed into the back seat, he was briefly seized by the impression that he was climbing into his own coffin.

Inside, the cab was uncomfortably warm and stuffy, and Paul found he could barely breathe. *Excuse me* – he quickly checked the driver's registration – *Travis? Could you turn the heater down a little? It's really hot in here.*

The cabbie, a gaunt-faced man in his forties, gazed blankly back at him from the rearview mirror. *You get used to it,* he replied sullenly, making no move to grant Paul's request. *Where you headed?*

Accepting this small defeat as he had accepted so many others of late, Paul slumped back in his seat and told Travis his destination. *I'm going to meet a dead girl,* he added with a bitter laugh.

The cabbie shrugged. *Alive or dead, they're all the same to me. Women are like a goddamn union. They're only out for themselves, and you can't trust a single one of them.*

Paul nodded, finding the man's unabashed misogyny curiously comforting. He'd always considered himself one of life's nice guys, and where exactly had it got him? Shattered, destitute and alone. He suddenly wished he could just pick up a gun and blow away all of the women who had ever tormented him. Gazing at Travis's night-black eyes in the rearview mirror, something told him the cabbie entertained similar thoughts on a regular basis.

TWILIGHT'S LAST SCREAMING

When they arrived at The Dante, Paul gave the taxi driver a large tip, which he accepted with a wordless nod. As he stood hesitating outside the restaurant, Paul's body shivered like a cobweb in the wind, feeling as though it might fly apart at any moment. What would he discover when he stepped across the threshold? Something inexplicable, ineffable? Or merely a cosy family-run Village restaurant?

Inside, he found The Dante to be clean and brightly lit, unfussy in its décor save for the large murals adorning the walls. The dining room was mostly empty, and he could see no sign of Marcy. Not that he even knew exactly *what* he was expecting to see. A bodiless spectre, looming accusingly at his shoulder? Or a grinning, decaying corpse, propped up in a corner booth and beckoning to him in dreadful invitation?

Shuddering at the thought of it, Paul took a seat at the bar and ordered a drink, which he promptly downed. Ordering another, he did exactly the same.

Yeah, I've had a few nights like that myself, said a voice over to his left.

Paul shifted in his seat to see an older, darkly-featured man gazing back at him. His face had a cunning, almost diabolical cast to it, and Paul quickly realised that he recognised him from somewhere. Was he an actor…?

Yes! From what he could recall, the man had enjoyed some success on stage and screen early on in his career, but things had dwindled to the point where he was now a regular on a daytime soap opera, *Invitation to Love.* But what was his name again…?

Guy Woodhouse, the man said, getting up from his stool and extending a hand in greeting. *Let me get you another one of those.*

Paul shook Guy's hand, and gestured towards the adjacent stool. *Paul Hackett,* he replied. Signalling to the bartender for another round of drinks, Guy sat down and smirked apologetically. *Sorry if I'm interrupting anything,* he told Paul. *But you looked like you could maybe use some company. Rough night?*

You could say that, Paul told him. *I'm here to meet a girl. Someone I dated once.*

Doesn't sound too bad. Giving it another try?

The thing is, Paul began, far beyond the point of caring what the man thought of him. *She's dead. She's been dead for six months, but now she won't stop calling me.*

He expected Guy to immediately jump up from his seat and move back to the other end of the bar, but he didn't. Instead, the actor stared ruminatively into his drink, his eyes two dark pools. *That's pretty crazy*, he murmured finally. *You probably think I don't believe you, right?*

Paul sighed and nodded.

A humourless grin. *Well, I do. See, I've seen and done some pretty crazy stuff myself. Stuff I kinda regret now I'm older. So I know that sometimes guys like us need a friend. And it just so happens that I might be able to help you out.*

How? Paul asked wonderingly.

Guy knocked back his drink. *I know some people. They call themselves Palladists. They're into all sorts of crazy shit, so they might be able to help you. They have regular meetings just a couple of blocks from here. I could take you there right now.*

Had Paul made yet another terrible mistake coming here tonight? This man might take him anywhere, do anything to him. He looked at his watch, finding that it was now after eleven.

(*It's after hours. Different rules apply.*)

Was he doomed to chase Marcy in perpetuity, and stumble into nightmare after nightmare in the attempt? *I don't know…* he mumbled.

Guy clapped him encouragingly on the back. *What else have you got to lose, right? That's what I always tell myself, anyway.*

Shrinking from the man's touch, Paul looked worriedly around the restaurant. *But what about Marcy…?*

Hell, if she's been dead for six months already, I bet she can wait a little longer.

Tossing a few bills onto the bar, Guy led him outside. On the street, a steady rain had begun to fall, and the wet sidewalk gleamed redly with reflected neon. Gazing around, Paul noticed a priest concealed in the shadows of an alleyway on the opposite side of the street. The man seemed to be watching them, and Paul had to fight a sudden urge to dash over there and throw himself down at the priest's feet. He would confess everything, beg for divine forgiveness.

Instead, he allowed his newfound guide to lead him to a grand old townhouse a few blocks away. The structure had been painted a deep shade of crimson, and all of its windows were dark, save for a single light burning in the first floor window. It reminded Paul of a gigantic termite mound, filled with scuttling drones. But drones acting in the faithful service of what?

Guy took him by the elbow. *Now, these meetings can seem a little… eccentric to an outsider. But trust me, the people in there can help you. Hell, I wouldn't be where I am today without 'em.*

Perhaps it was just a trick of the streetlight overhead, but Paul thought he glimpsed a haunted look in Guy's eyes as he spoke those words.

The other man led him forward and knocked gently on the front door. Moments later, it was answered by a tall elderly gentleman, who Paul adjudged must be in his eighties.

Ah, the man said, in an impeccably clipped English accent. *We've been expecting you, Mr Hackett.*

Paul took a startled step backwards. *How do you know my name?*

The man flashed him a thin smile. *There are very few things we do not know, Mr Hackett. Ours is a faith founded on knowledge and discovery, rather than blind acceptance. But if it makes you feel on more of an equal footing, my name is Dr. Judd. I used to be like you, mortally afraid of what I did not know…but much like Guy here, I eventually had the truth revealed to me.*

Judd stood aside to let them enter the townhouse. Paul hesitated, but soon found himself propelled forwards by Guy's gentle but insistent hand.

Inside, he found himself in a darkened living room, filled with antique furniture and expensive-looking *objets d'art.* The space was lit only by a single standing lamp, and several sets of expectant eyes watched him from the shadows. As his vision gradually adjusted to the gloom, Paul could see that the room was populated by a number of well-dressed men and women, all in advanced middle-age or older.

The Palladists.

He began to feel like a naughty schoolboy, summoned before his elders on account of his delinquent behaviour. Oblivious to his disquiet, Guy led him to a wing-backed chair sitting empty in the centre of the room.

Hopelessly, Paul attempted to demur. *Please, can't I just sit and watch for a while?*

Judd's silkily persuasive voice at his ear: *Everyone is gathered here for you, Paul. Tonight is solely about you.*

Numbly, Paul took his place amongst the group. Once he was sitting down, a crystal glass, filled to the brim with red wine, was placed on a small table in front of him. Another man then stepped forward from the shadows, his face as cracked and lined as a parched river bed. *We know why you are here, Paul,* he said tonelessly. *You caused the death of an innocent girl, and now she cannot rest.*

Paul flinched. *It wasn't my fault!* he tried to insist. *I'd only just met her, how was I to know how screwed up she was?*

The man regarded him dispassionately. *No more evasions. You must learn to accept responsibility. Everyone here in this room willingly bears the responsibility of their own actions. We do not blame others for our personal failings, nor can we absolve them of their own sins. That is a burden each man must carry alone. It is the obligation of every right-thinking human being.*

Paul looked desperately around the room for Guy, who seemed to be staying well out of sight. *Guy said that you could help me!*

And we will. As soon as you accept what you did.

A familiar voice seemed to whisper in Paul's ear. *Surrender Dorothy…*

He nodded in defeat. *Alright, alright. Yes, it's my fault she's dead. You happy?*

The man gave a small shrug. *My own happiness has nothing to do with it. But I can help you, if you are willing to do as I say.*

Anything, Paul begged. *Please, just make it stop.*

Marcy Franklin has staked a claim on you. The dead are utterly single-minded; they pursue that which they lack with a terrible, all-consuming desire. She will never stop, or relinquish her hold on you. You must give her what she wants, Paul. It's the only way.

He didn't understand. *What?*

You must join her in death. The man leant down and pushed the wine glass towards him. *All you need do is drink this. It won't hurt.*

Paul stared at the glass, the dark crimson hue of the liquid inside suddenly taking on a sinister cast. Suicide? It wasn't like he hadn't already tried it. Maybe he should just drink it and be damned.

(That's what Hell feels like all the time…)

But something about the man's icy manner held him back. There was no concern for Paul's suffering there; merely a masked contempt, like that of a doctor towards a whining hypochondriac.

Flushed with a sudden anger, Paul leapt up from the chair. *You're nuts! I'm not gonna kill myself!*

The man did not react to his meagre display of defiance. Instead, he merely regarded Paul as though he were a species of rare insect. *You should want to,* he sighed. *It is your obligation.*

Get the hell outta my way! Paul shoved him aside and made for the door. He was almost at the exit when Guy appeared in his path, his face pleading. *Paul, you gotta do what they tell you. It'll be bad for you if you don't.*

Without thinking, Paul lashed out and slammed a fist into the side of Guy's skull, sending him sprawling sideways. He crashed into a small table, smashing the antique Tiffany lamp placed on top of it. Watching Guy fall filled Paul with a joy he'd not known in months. Letting out a manic bellow of triumph, he flung open the front door and fled from the house.

Outside, the rain was hitting the sidewalk like a deluge of falling shrapnel. Paul immediately found himself soaked to the skin. His first instinct was to get out of the downpour, but where could he go? He'd already told Holly he wasn't coming back, and nowhere else seemed remotely safe.

Unthinkingly, he stepped out into the road, realising too late that an approaching taxi was bearing down on him. Stumbling backwards, he tripped and fell sprawling into the gutter, grazing his scalp on the kerb. He lay there for a moment, dazed and bleeding, his blood mingling with the rainwater flowing into the storm drain, to nourish whatever dark things lurked in the sewers below.

He was dimly aware of a car door opening, and then a figure standing over him, rendered featureless by the glare of the streetlight at its back.

Paul?

Blinking water from his eyes, he gazed up mutely.

The figure leaned closer, extending a slender hand towards him. *Paul, it's me…*

Marcy.

Paul's first thought was that she looked the same as when he last saw her, but of course she'd been dead then, or so he'd believed.

Now, she appeared to be very much alive: eyes bright, lips pink and full.

Come with me, Paul.

Offering no resistance, he allowed her to pull him upright and help him into the waiting taxi that had ferried her to his side. Glancing around, Paul thought he glimpsed the same priest he had seen earlier rushing across the street towards them, but found himself bundled inside the vehicle before he could react.

Instructing the cab driver to take them to an address in Brooklyn, Marcy turned back towards Paul, her hand still clasped around his.

Oh, your poor head! she exclaimed. She offered him a tissue for his injured scalp, which he accepted. *I'm sorry you hurt yourself, but I'm very glad you came, Paul.*

He pressed the wadded tissue gingerly to his skull. *Marcy, I don't understand any of this.*

A giggle. *What's to understand?*

You were dead. I saw you.

How can I be dead, silly? I'm sitting right here with you.

The next moment, she leaned across and kissed him full on the mouth.

Despite everything, Paul found himself entirely unable to resist her. He felt as if some huge inner boil had been lanced, and all of the accumulated loneliness of the last six months was gushing out in a torrent. He took Marcy in his arms, his hands exploring her, clutching at her, needing her. They remained lost in each other for several minutes, until Marcy finally pulled away. *Wow,* she said.

Suddenly embarrassed by the force of his overwhelming desire, Paul looked away, staring out through the car window at the rain-blurred city. *Where exactly are we going?* he asked Marcy quietly.

Oh, I have an apartment in Brooklyn now. It's a new building, really nice. I had to get out of Soho, it was really killing me.

Paul looked at her sharply, and she giggled again. For an instant, the wash of coloured light spilling in through the taxi windows seemed to smear and dissolve her features, stripping away the false surface to reveal the leering skull underneath.

Paul's hand flew to his mouth, stifling an appalled moan, but then she was just Marcy again, pouting and innocently pretty.

The taxi pulled to a stop. *We're here!* Marcy said.

Emerging from the cab, Paul looked up to see a five-storey apartment block, impersonally modern in its design. A large 'NOW RENTING' banner was displayed on the exterior, but despite the invitation, all of the complex's windows were dark, save for a light burning in one of the uppermost apartments.

It looks almost empty, Paul said, as he allowed Marcy to lead him towards the building's entrance.

Oh, there are still a few vacant apartments left, Marcy replied. *But it's not empty, far from it. You'll probably meet my neighbours, they're really fun people!*

Once inside, they climbed the stairs to the fourth floor. Despite his earlier impression of the building being all but deserted, Paul could now hear the sounds of a party emanating from behind one of the apartment doors. Indeed, as they crossed the hallway to Marcy's own front door, the entrance to the adjacent apartment suddenly opened, revealing an impish-looking little man with a canary perched on one shoulder.

Marcy, my dear, he cooed in delight. *You're just in time for the party!* He peered at Paul with interest. *Your new friend is welcome too, of course…*

Thanks, Mr Chazen, Marcy replied, glancing sideways at Paul. *Maybe just a quick drink?*

Paul nodded half-heartedly, trying to mask his frustration. He was assailed by a familiar nausea, a sick sensation of *déjà vu*. Whenever he seemed to be on the verge of getting Marcy into bed, something always happened to prevent it…

They followed Chazen into his apartment, to find a motley gathering of mostly middle-aged men and women sitting around a dinner table wearing party hats and sipping champagne. Two other morose-looking men stood off to the side, drinking beers and studiedly eschewing the festivities.

Chazen introduced Paul to everyone at the table: Mrs Clark, the Clotkin sisters, Malcolm and Rebecca Stinnett – who didn't live here anymore but had just popped in for a visit – and two dancers, Gerda and Sandra.

Welcome to our celebration! Gerda purred.

Thanks, Paul said. *What are we celebrating, exactly?*

Beside him, Chazen cackled loudly. *And why do we need an excuse to celebrate, young man?*

Some of the group's faces seemed oddly familiar, but before Paul could give the matter any further thought, Marcy dragged him away to meet the rest of the partygoers. *Everyone here is lovely,* she whispered. *But they're all a bit...old. We're the new wave.*

They joined the other two men, who Marcy introduced as Frank and Reno. Frank was a heavyset man, his face perpetually covered with a sheen of perspiration. Reno was thinner, and possessed a jittery, livewire energy. In contrast to the other guests, they both glowered sullenly at Paul. He began to wonder whether they each had designs on Marcy, and resented his presence here.

And what is it you guys do? Paul asked, trying desperately to break the ice.

I'm an artist, Reno growled. *Who the fuck are you?*

Oh, Reno, Marcy twittered. *Don't mind him, Paul. He's a real grouch until you get to know him.*

Paul stared at the man. Again, he had the strange feeling he recognised him from somewhere. An artist named Reno...

Then it struck him, and he smiled.

What's so funny? Reno demanded.

Oh, it's nothing, Paul said hurriedly. *Something about you seemed familiar, and then I realised what it was. There was that crazy artist who killed a bunch of people with a power drill in the Village a few years back. I think his name was Reno, wasn't it?*

Yeah, Reno said flatly. *Reno Miller.*

But I heard he killed himself in jail. So I guess it can't be you after all. Paul laughed a little too loudly, hoping the others would join in on the joke. Marcy duly followed his lead, but the two men remained resolutely granite-faced.

Paul was saved from any further awkwardness when a loud cheer erupted in the room behind him. He looked around to see Mr Chazen ferrying a large cake through from the kitchen, its thickly-iced top ablaze with candles. The little man placed the cake on the dinner table, then turned and gestured for Paul to join him. *As our newest member, the honour goes to you, Paul.*

For the second time that evening, Paul began to feel stricken by claustrophobia, as though the room were closing around him like a fist. He forced a hesitant smile onto his face and moved to Chazen's side. The other man grinned broadly. *First, the candles.*

Taking a deep breath, Paul leaned down and blew out the candles. The assembled celebrants shrieked and applauded.

Chazen produced a gleaming kitchen knife and handed it to Paul. *And now…cut.*

Paul positioned the blade over the cake. *How big a piece would you like?*

His host cackled. *Oh no, not the cake, Paul! Yourself!*

Paul felt Marcy's presence at his side. He looked around to see her gesturing at her forearm with an outstretched finger. *Cut lengthways, like this*, she instructed. *You want it to be quick.*

She smiled, and her once perfect smile was now blackened and fetid. *Trust me, I know.*

Paul let out a moan and stumbled backwards, dropping the knife to the floor. Chazen quickly scooped it up and brandished it towards him. *Come on, Paul. Two quick cuts and it'll all be over. And then you and Marcy can be together forever.*

Marcy and the others fell in behind the old man, sweeping down on Paul like locusts. As he gazed upon them, he could see the flesh of their faces beginning to blister and peel, the collective facade falling away to reveal the black corruption festering underneath.

Dead, all of them. Marcy and Reno Miller and the rest, all dead and utterly damned.

As damned as him.

With a shrill cry of anguish, Paul collapsed to the floor and thrust his arms up before his eyes, trying to shield them from the appalling vision looming over him. He began to sob, long, wracking gasps of desolation.

Then he heard Marcy's voice, or a slithering, croaking mockery of it. It sounded all the more awful for the soothing tone it was attempting. *Be with me, Paul. It's the only way.*

Why fight it any more? He was tired of running, so very tired.

But before he could submit, Paul became dimly aware of a door crashing open somewhere nearby. A loud bellow of anger sounded through the room. *Back, devils! Leave this man be!*

The next moment, Paul felt a hand reaching under his armpit, helping him up to his feet. He looked up to see the same priest he had seen watching him on the street earlier that evening. The man brandished a large silver crucifix at the damned horde, who gibbered and hissed in response.

Come with me, Mr Hackett, he told Paul. *Hurry! We don't have much time.*

They backed out of the apartment, the priest holding the dead at bay. But when Paul instinctively turned towards the staircase leading back down to the building's exit, the priest roughly seized his arm.

No! he said sternly. *We must go up. That way only leads to damnation.*

But –

It was no use. The man propelled Paul up the stairs to the top floor, where they found an open apartment entrance waiting for them. The priest shoved Paul inside, then slammed the door closed.

Paul slumped against the wall, the burst of adrenaline that had enabled him to make the ascent quickly fading. *What the hell is happening to me?* he moaned.

The priest smiled grimly. *Hell is right, Mr Hackett. Satan's forces have been marshalled against you this evening, all in an attempt to keep you from arriving here and fulfilling your destiny.*

Paul pressed his face into the cool plaster of the wall and moaned again. He couldn't take any more of this. Everywhere he went, people were telling him impossible, awful things, things that couldn't possibly be true.

But he'd seen Marcy. Touched her, *kissed* her.

Kissed that beautiful, lying face, utterly oblivious to the horror that lay masked behind it…

Grabbing his arm, the priest span Paul around and slapped him across the cheek. *Listen to me, man! This building stands over a gateway to Hell. You must now make a choice. Either guard it and serve as its Sentinel…or be damned yourself. Do you understand me, Mr Hackett?*

Why me? Paul whined. *I'm just a word processor, for Chrissake!*

The priest frowned at his casual blasphemy. *You have been chosen. Sister Theresa, the woman who held this post before you…she lacked the necessary strength to carry out her task.*

Stepping aside, the priest gestured towards the nearby bathroom doorway. Paul hesitantly peered inside, to see the lifeless body of a nun sprawled upon the tiled floor. Sleeping pills lay scattered around her like fallen hailstones, her white, sightless eyes imploring him to take on her terrible burden.

You must assume her role, lest the denizens of Hell spill forth to corrupt the Earth. Those damned souls you saw down there are just the start of it. Thousands more would follow. Will you allow such a thing to happen?

Paul closed his eyes, unable to bear the sight of the dead woman any longer. *What would I have to do?*

Just sit…and watch, the priest told him. *You could never leave this building again. But the church would attend to all your needs. You would want for nothing. And for your sacrifice, you would be granted absolution for your sins.*

Sit and watch? Paul had to admit, it didn't sound too bad. Certainly no worse than word processing, or working as a goddamn receptionist. And this was a good apartment, certainly preferable to subletting from a crazy, strung-out actress. He would never have to venture out on the streets of New York again, to be chased and harried and tormented…

The choice was made. Wearily, he nodded in acceptance.

The priest began to turn out all the lights in the room, then moved back to Paul's side. They both stood silently in the dark for a few moments, before Paul became aware of a nearby glow, steadily increasing in intensity. He looked down to see the crucifix in the priest's hands humming with an unearthly, beatific light. Was this some parlour trick, or truly a genuine miracle?

Watch the cross, the priest instructed him. *Do not look away from it.*

In truth, Paul doubted he could have torn his eyes away from the crucifix even if he'd tried. Something in the light soothed him, spoke to him. He'd never felt such serenity. Even when the light continued to build in strength, its glare burning brighter than the heart of a thousand suns, he found he could not avert his gaze.

The brightness swelled to consume everything, extinguishing his eyes like two candles, and then he knew no more.

When he came to, he was sitting in a chair. Paul could feel the warmth of the early morning sun on his face, and yet the world around him was still in absolute darkness.

The next moment, he felt the priest's reassuring hand on his shoulder.

What happened to my eyes? Paul said.

No man can gaze into Hell and remain sane, the priest replied, with quiet regret. *This is the only way.*

Paul supposed he should have been horrified at the theft of his sight, but it hardly seemed to matter. It was the final sacrifice he'd been required to make, but in exchange for all that he'd lost, he had finally regained that which had value beyond measure.

As his grandmother warned him when he was a child, he had indeed taken the wrong path; but now, miraculously, he'd found his way back.

After a time, the priest left Paul alone, clutching the silver crucifix in his lap and gazing out over the city that he would never see again. Still, his solitude was to be short-lived. After dark, the devils would emerge from below and caper around his room, taunting him and murmuring sly temptations into his ears. But even when Marcy came to him, her moist tongue teasing his cheek, telling him of all the forbidden pleasures he could know if he would only relinquish his thankless post and join her in Hell, he did not flinch, nor doubt his divine calling.

Paul Hackett sat perched on the edge of a black abyss, in Hell but not of it, and at last felt at peace. He knew not lust nor want nor need. He now dwelt in a land of eternal shadow, inhabited only by ghosts and whispers, and thought to himself that he had never known such happiness.

PATRICK BATEMAN

Christian Bale in American Psycho, *2000*
written by Mary Harron & Guinevere Turner
based on the novel by Bret Easton Ellis
directed by Mary Harron

Limo

IT'S A LITTLE PAST 1 AM, AND I'M RIDING IN A LIMO WITH CRAIG MCDERMOTT and Timothy Bryce. We're drinking Cristal champagne and smoking Cuban cigars, and Bryce is telling us about some hardbody he fucked in the toilets at Tunnel last night.

'It was only after I slipped it in that she told me she was on her period, for Chrissake!' he complains.

McDermott pulls a disgusted face, and although the thought of a woman's blood on my stiffened cock doesn't repulse me – quite the opposite, in fact – I make a nauseated sound anyway and avert my head to gaze out of the limo window. We're driving through Long Island, on the way to some very exclusive private party Bryce got us invites to, and the absence of any city lights outside the window gives me the momentary impression that we are travelling through some fathomless, infinite void. Disturbed, I close my eyes and mentally recite the names of my current ten favourite Manhattan restaurants, in ascending order. This calms me enough to reopen my eyes and look back at McDermott.

The party we are attending tonight is a masquerade, and accordingly, we are all outfitted in cloaks and masks. Underneath my cloak, I am wearing a four-button double breasted wool and silk suit, a cotton shirt with a button-down collar by Valentino Couture, a patterned silk tie by Armani and cap-toed leather slip-ons by Allen-Edmonds. However, I have no idea what the others are wearing, which fills me with a nagging sense of discomfort.

The limo driver has the car radio playing softly in the background, and I hear the DJ announcing Phil Collins's 'Another Day in Paradise' as his next selection. It's the first single from Phil's new album *But Seriously...*, which, as the title suggests, is lyrically an altogether more thoughtful, mature record than the one which preceded it, *No Jacket Required*. While I've long been of the opinion that, despite his considerable commercial success as a solo artist, Collins's greatest work has resulted from his time as a member of the band Genesis, *But Seriously...* represents a concerted effort to marry the sophistication of Genesis's lyrics with the commercial pop approach of Phil's solo material, and as such, could win him an even wider audience. It isn't hard to imagine the intellectual college rock crowd, fans of such politically-orientated agit-rockers such as Springsteen and Elvis Costello, falling for Phil's impassioned plea for empathy and understanding. Rock critics like to praise Costello's ability for lyrical wordplay, but has he ever written a couplet as affecting as: *She's got blisters on the soles of her feet / She can't walk but she's trying* ? Collins previously addressed the problem of homelessness in the song 'Man on the Corner' from Genesis's 1981 record *Abacab*, and although that was my favourite track from the album, 'Another Day in Paradise' is a sadder, more reflective song, and far surpasses it. It's no exaggeration to say it's probably the most moving song to address the plight of the underclass since Elvis Presley's 'In the Ghetto', and has certainly made me reconsider my attitudes towards New York's homeless problem.

'Can you turn the radio up?' I ask the limo driver, who immediately reaches down and turns up the dial. The song's chorus fills the car, which causes Bryce and McDermott to jeer wildly.

'Christ, Phil *Collins?*' says Bryce. 'What's next, Bateman, Mike & the fucking Mechanics?'

Despite featuring another member of Genesis, Tony Banks, Mike & the Mechanics's music is entirely inferior to that of Phil Collins, but I resist the urge to argue the point.

The song ends, prompting McDermott to lean forward. 'Hey, did you guys hear they're making a movie about Sherman McCoy?'

McCoy had been a bond trader at the same Wall Street firm I work at, Pierce & Pierce. Driving back from Kennedy Airport one night, he'd gotten lost and ended up in the Bronx, where he'd accidentally collided with a young black mugger. Despite McCoy's obvious innocence, the prejudice of the New York liberal establishment had caused him to lose his family, his job, everything, and he was now awaiting trial for vehicular manslaughter. A tragic, sobering affair, and one that had been making news headlines all year.

'They're letting some greasy wop bastard direct it,' Bryce groans. 'He'll just fuck it all up. You need a WASP to tell that story properly.'

The director assigned to the film is Brian De Palma, who previously made one of my favourite movies, *Body Double*. I think to myself that De Palma would actually be a perfect choice to make a film of *my* life, given his undoubted skill at choreographing visceral set-pieces of sexuality, violence and murder. But the evident thrill De Palma gets from such subject matter tends to offend many mainstream critics, which leads me to suspect he'd never even be offered the job, and it would instead go to someone who'd probably water down the subject matter to make it more palatable for a wider audience and thereby turn it into a rather lame satire; perhaps even a *female* director.

I find the thought so depressing that an overpowering wave of anxiety washes over me and I begin to wonder what my life even *means*, if its essence can be trivialised and wiped away so easily and so utterly. My hands begin to tremble and I gulp down the rest of my champagne, wondering how much longer I'm going to be trapped in this car.

'Does anyone have a Xanax?' I ask.

Party

I'm sitting in the library of a large mansion house watching two hardbodies get it on in front of me. The party Bryce has brought us to is some kind of ritualised orgy (Satanic, perhaps?), and after an opening ceremony where we watched a bunch of girls strip down to G-strings and high-heels, everyone is now free to wander through the house and fuck whomever they please. McDermott is sat next to me on the chaise-longue, watching the girls and fondling himself underneath his cloak. Bryce, meanwhile, is off in the corner of the library vigorously fucking another hardbody while several other masked men look on. I note with quiet satisfaction that his ass lacks the muscle definition of my own.

'Isn't this fucking *hot*, Bateman?' McDermott pants.

'It'd be way hotter if *that* girl was fucking the other one with a razor-lined strap-on,' I point out. But either McDermott isn't listening or he can't hear me over the monotonous organ music playing somewhere else in the house, and he just nods and smiles.

Growing bored, I get up and move over to Bryce, in time to see him withdraw his cock from the hardbody's cunt and come all over her toned stomach. Seeing me approach, he gives me a thumbs-up and asks if I want to do a line.

Beneath him, the hardbody is trying to get up off the coffee table she's lying on, but Bryce quickly pushes her back down onto her back. 'Uh-uh. Stay right where you are, honey,' he tells her. Obediently, she complies with his instruction, and he turns back to me. '*Well*, Bateman?'

I nod. Bryce produces a vial of cocaine and chops out two lines on the girl's well-shaped tits. She lies there motionless as, in turn, we each push our masks up onto our foreheads, bend down and snort the coke. Luckily it's good, and as the rush hits me, I fantasise for an instant about cutting both of the hardbody's breasts off and making her eat them.

'Don't *stare*, Bateman,' Bryce chides me. 'The poor girl isn't just some *object*. If you want to fuck her, fuck her.'

'Uh, maybe later,' I mumble.

The girl looks up at us. 'Can I have some of that?' she asks Bryce.

He tucks the vial back into his pocket and shakes his head. 'Sorry, sweetheart. Far too good to share.'

Bryce and I move away from the girl. McDermott is now on his knees masturbating in front of the two hardbodies, so we leave him to finish and exit the library. But every room we enter is the same: masked men and women robotically engaging in various sex acts. No one seems to really be enjoying themselves, and all of a sudden I wish I could run screaming through the mansion with a chainsaw, carving up the participants as I go and spraying the walls with their thick red blood, to match the lengths of crimson carpet that have been laid throughout the house.

'Great party, huh Bateman?' Bryce says.

'Uh-huh,' I reply non-committally.

'You haven't fucked anyone yet, have you?'

'I'm just…waiting for the right girl,' I tell him.

He laughs hysterically and claps me on the back. 'Oh, by the way,' he says. 'I hear Donald Trump is here.'

'What?' I reply, excited and confused all at once. 'But…how would anyone even *know*?'

Bryce cackles and makes an insinuating gesture with his right pinky. 'Hung like a Chinese mouse.'

Offended, I shove him away. 'You don't know what you're talking about, Bryce. As if you could keep a woman like Ivana happy with a small cock.'

'Well, I hear she's *not* happy.'

All this talk about the state of Donald Trump's marriage is beginning to make me anxious again, so I ignore Bryce and stride off into a nearby hallway, heading nowhere in particular, nowhere at all. The cocaine is giving me the jitters and I can feel an animal stirring in my stomach, rousing itself from hibernation, demanding to be fed. I just need a few minutes of quiet and perhaps a Valium, but everywhere I look there are naked people fucking and that goddamn music playing endlessly. I suddenly remember an episode of *The Patty Winters Show* I watched recently. It was on Satanic Cults and she interviewed a number of people who had participated in human sacrifices. I begin to wonder whether that could happen here, tonight, at this very party, and I can feel my panic mounting.

I lean against a pillar and attempt to bring my breathing under control, but the next moment, a girl approaches me out of the shadows. Like all the women here, she is tall and slim, with long legs and high breasts.

'Hello,' she purrs. 'You look as though you might be lonely.'

I don't know how to respond to this, so I say the first thing that comes into my head. 'The fresh-grilled *foie gras* at Le Cirque is excellent,' I tell her.

'Uh, okay,' she says, after a confused pause. 'Look, would you like to go somewhere more private?'

Although I know she's only inviting me to have sex, for an instant it's as though she has peered into my soul and understood me completely, and I find myself overwhelmingly moved. Nodding dumbly, I allow her to escort me away.

The girl takes me upstairs, leading me down a long corridor past countless bedrooms until she finds the one she's looking for. 'I think here will be perfect,' she says.

Up here away from the party, the house is quiet and deserted, and I have no reason to disagree with her assessment. She takes my hand and we move inside the bedroom. An antique four-poster bed dominates the space, and the girl tries to lead me towards it.

I resist. 'In there,' I say, motioning towards the en-suite bathroom.

The girl shrugs, and we move into the adjacent room. Once we are inside, I close the door behind us and lock it. 'I want us to take a shower together and don't want to be disturbed,' I explain.

'Whatever you'd like.' The girl bends over the bathtub and turns on the shower. 'Why don't you get undressed?'

'You first,' I instruct, sitting down on the toilet to watch her.

Languidly, she kicks off her high heels, then begins to remove her G-string, until I tell her to stop. 'Turn around,' I say. 'Show me your ass.'

She does as she's told, sliding down her underwear and bending over to display her ass for me. It's tanned, well-muscled and almost perfect-looking, save for a small birthmark under her right buttock.

Admiring the view, I reach inside my right trouser pocket, my hand closing around the hard object it finds there.

Eventually, she straightens up and turns around to face me. 'Now you,' she murmurs.

'Wait,' I say. 'Take your mask off too. I want to see what you look like.'

Her tone instantly shifts from flirtatious to stern. 'I can't do that,' she insists.

'Oh, I think you can,' I say.

'No, listen. It's against the rules.'

I spring to my feet, pulling out the flick knife I had concealed in my pocket. Popping the blade, I wave it in the air. 'Do I look like I care about the fucking *rules?*' I shriek.

She freezes for a second, then lunges towards the locked door. But what she doesn't notice in her panic is that the water spray from the shower has created a small puddle on the bathroom floor. Her foot lands squarely in the water and immediately skids out from underneath her, sending her crashing face-first into the door.

Dazed, the girl can do nothing to resist as I reach down and grab her by the hair, yanking her away from the doorway. I lean down and scream into her face. 'I *said*, I want to see what you look like!'

She is only semi-conscious right now, but I hear her mutter, 'Please… I'll do…whatever…'

Putting my knife away for now, I rip away the mask to reveal her face. She has the looks of a model: sea-green eyes, a pert, upturned nose, and even white teeth. But now that I've seen her, it isn't enough. Regardless of how beautiful she is, I find myself disappointed.

'Please…' she moans.

Irritated, I lift her up by her hair again and begin to methodically beat her face against the porcelain rim of the bathtub, not stopping until all of her front teeth lie on the bathroom floor in a bloodied pile of fragments.

By now the girl has begun to scream, and so I reach around for her discarded G-string and stuff it into her ruined mouth, which helps dull the noise somewhat.

'You know,' I say. 'I still don't think we've seen what you *really* look like.'

Taking my flick knife, I place the tip of the blade underneath her chin and very carefully begin to cut into the meat of her face, slicing upwards and around her hairline. Luckily the girl has fainted by now, so I am able to work quickly and make a fairly neat job of the operation. Within a few more seconds, I have cut my way around her face and along the other side of her jaw. When my knife blade arrives back at its original starting point, I put the weapon to one side, then insert my fingers underneath the opened flap of flesh and pull. With a little effort, I am able to tear away the skin of her entire face.

'There,' I say, tossing the bloodied scrap of tissue into the tub. 'Now I can see you properly.'

The agony of having her face removed has shocked the girl back into consciousness, and she immediately begins to scream again. The G-string is too insubstantial to fully choke her cries, and within moments there is a banging at the bathroom door. 'What's going on in there?' a male voice shouts.

Waves of adrenaline course through my body, but without sufficient time alone with the girl to work the rush off, I am locked in a helpless mania. The door judders in its frame again, and I wonder how much longer it can hold.

'Just a second,' I cry, quickly stuffing my knife back into my pocket. I grab the stricken girl and throw her into the bathtub, then unlock the door and open it a crack, keeping my shoulder pressed firmly against the woodwork.

A masked face peers in at me. 'People heard screaming from up here,' it informs me.

'Just an accident,' I gibber. 'She slipped getting out of the bathtub and hit her head. She may need medical attention.'

I avert my head slightly, allowing my inquisitor a view of the girl lying in the tub. Then, when he attempts to push his way inside, I suddenly step backwards and wrench open the door, sending him sprawling forwards into the bathroom.

I burst through the doorway and dash out through the bedroom, hurtling along the corridor towards the staircase. From behind me, I hear a distant cry of dismay.

People from the party have begun to move in this direction, attracted by the commotion, and I am forced to pull my knife to prevent anyone getting too close. 'Stay away from me!' I scream. 'I'll fucking cut you!'

I half-run, half-fall down the staircase, and land in a heap at the bottom. As I begin to drag myself upright, I am confronted by the figure of McDermott. '*Bateman?*' he says incredulously. 'You're covered in *blood*. What the *fuck?*'

Slowly, I get to my feet. Around us, time seems to have stopped. A crowd of people has gathered to watch and stand there in the background, silent and unmoving. Their frozen figures seem to judder and sway before my eyes, as though this is all a paused video image I am observing on a TV screen.

My hand tightens around my knife. 'You know, McDermott,' I say in a monotone. 'I always thought you were a shitty dresser.'

There is a flash of steel as my knife plunges into his belly. McDermott sinks to his knees with a groan. Before I start running again, I note with satisfaction the puddle of urine pooling around his legs.

Shoving my way past various masked attendants, I fight my way to the front door, still brandishing my bloody knife. When I arrive at the doorway, I find it open to the night air, like a mouth readying itself to spit out an unwanted morsel. I sprint out into the darkness in search of Bryce's hired limo, my feet crunching on the gravel driveway. I am suddenly reminded of the crunch of the girl's teeth shattering against the rim of the bathtub and I cackle wildly.

But when I find the parking area, all of the fucking limousines look the same and I am forced to stop at each one in turn, opening the doors and yelling at the started drivers, *'Bryce? Timothy Bryce?'* The whole process takes so long that I'm certain I will be caught at any moment, but eventually I come to a limo where the driver responds to the mention of Bryce's name.

'Mr Bryce?' he says, looking at me curiously.

'Uh, yes,' I say breathlessly, throwing myself into the back of the vehicle. 'Now let's get the fuck out of here.'

Does he realise I'm not Bryce, or is he looking at the bloodstains on my cloak? Either way, he isn't moving fast enough. 'But what about your two friends?' he says finally.

'They'll, uh, be taking a cab,' I offer lamely. 'Now, please. I'm in rather a hurry.'

At last, he starts the engine and begins to manoeuvre the limo back along the driveway. A crowd of people have gathered outside the mansion and I duck instinctively, forgetting the car has black tinted windows. 'Stop him!' someone yells, but no one moves.

When we reach the end of the driveway, something occurs to me, and I lean forward to the driver. 'Where are you taking me?' I ask.

He gives me that curious look again. 'Back to Manhattan, of course,' he replies carefully.

'No,' I say.

'No?'

There's no way I can go back to New York now. Even if McDermott survived my attack and I somehow convince him not to press charges, everyone will know I killed that girl. And judging by what Bryce told me about the sort of people who run that party, it's entirely possible my life might be in danger as a result.

Whether I wanted it or not, perhaps this is the exit I've always been looking for.

'No,' I insist to the driver. 'I want you to head…I don't know, *south.*' I fumble for my wallet and fling several hundred dollar bills down onto the front seat, all the cash I have on me. 'Take it, all of it. Just…keep…*driving.*'

He looks down at the money, mentally counting it, then nods. Relieved, I slump back into my seat and search around for booze, eventually finding an unopened bottle of Stoli vodka. My mind is being buffeted by alternating waves of euphoria and despair, and if I don't level myself out soon I may end up simply throwing myself out into the road. I twist the cap off the vodka bottle and raise it to my lips, gulping at the contents like a hungry baby. It helps a little, but it isn't enough.

I signal to the driver. 'Do you have any Xanax? Valium? Even a fucking Halcion?'

He shakes his head. A black pit yawns beneath me, and I feel as though I might start to scream and never stop screaming.

Then I notice something lying on the floor of the limo: a small white pill that one of the others must have dropped earlier. In my delirium, I don't recognise what kind of pill it is, it could be Valium or Tylenol or Ecstasy or anything, but I pick it up and swallow it anyway and maybe it works or maybe it's just a placebo or maybe it's the fact that I drink most of the vodka in the bottle but eventually I pass out.

Witch

I awake to daylight, a wash of grey morning light that makes everything appear to be the colour of dirty dishwater. My skull throbs and my tongue is like a slab of cold dead meat in my mouth. Struggling upright in my seat, I notice the driver watching me in the rearview mirror.

'Where are we?' I ask him.

'Somewhere in Maryland,' he replies.

'*Maryland?*' I say incredulously.

He shrugs. 'You told me to drive. I drove.'

I turn and look out of the limo window. We are travelling along a deserted highway bisecting a thick forest. The woodland looks as though it might stretch for miles in either direction.

I could lose myself in there, I think to myself.

And then I think, *Would anyone even notice I was gone?*

The driver looks back at me again. 'Listen, Mr…Bryce.'

By now, I have removed my mask and it is obvious that I am *not* Bryce, but he chooses to continue with the charade.

'I gotta get the limo back to Manhattan,' he continues. 'It's booked out on another job this evening, and I haven't slept all night. So you can either ride back with me, or…?'

'Stop the car,' I tell him.

'But we're in the middle of a forest,' he says.

'Stop the fucking car,' I say.

He sighs, but pulls over to the side of the highway. I open the door, then glance back at him.

'You never saw me,' I say.

I get out of the car and stumble into the trees. My cloak immediately begins to snag on their protruding branches, so I quickly discard it. Thus unimpaired, I am free to plunge deeper into the forest. I cannot actually remember the last time I was even *in* a forest and so by any rational measure should find myself seized by uncontrollable anxiety at the prospect of being surrounded by this much *nature*, but instead a wave of preternatural calm washes over me. Although I have absolutely no idea why, a part of me is entirely certain I am somehow meant to be here.

I press on for hours, stopping only to drink some water from a stream. My stomach eventually begins to cramp with hunger, but then I come across a dead bird lying at the base of a tree. It appears to have died fairly recently and so I decide to eat it raw. Although its flesh tastes gamey and unappetising, I remind myself that I have eaten much worse things. After finishing my meal, I carefully wipe my bloodied fingers on my Armani tie. My suit is muddied and torn, my leather slip-ons ruined, but I console myself with the thought that I am still undoubtedly the best-dressed man within a hundred mile radius. Laughing madly, I continue onwards, searching for whatever awaits me at the heart of the forest.

Night falls in the woods with surprising speed, and before long the dark closes around me like a burial shroud. It is so thick I can almost taste it, oily and bitter in my mouth. Now that I am rendered practically blind, my hearing seems to grow more acute in a bid to compensate, and suddenly all I can hear is my own ragged breathing, the incessant hammer of my pounding heart. Panicking, I collide with a tree in the darkness and fall heavily to the earth. I should stay here, I realise; try to get some sleep and carry on my way once dawn arrives. But the thought of sitting here marooned in the pitch dark fills me with an indescribable horror, and although all energy seems to have suddenly fled my body, I consider trying to continue on my hands and knees, anything to keep moving.

Then I remember something: the book of matches I keep in my jacket pocket for lighting cigars. Fumbling for them in the blackness, I count the remaining matches with my fingers; there are only a few left, but at least they will allow me to get my bearings.

My hands trembling, I clumsily attempt to strike the match. It takes me a few tries to get it to ignite, but finally there is a flare of phosphorus and I find myself blinded by light instead of dark.

It takes a few seconds for my vision to clear but eventually it does, and it is now that I look around at my surroundings and see it.

A house.

The sight of something manmade fills me with a kind of elation, which lends me enough strength to climb back to my feet. The next instant the match goes out, and I frantically fumble to light another, wondering whether the house will still be there once I can see again, or if it was simply a hallucination.

But no, the house is real. It is old, and derelict, but none of that matters. It will provide me with some measure of shelter and safety during the long night ahead, and that is all I care about right now. I hurry over towards its entrance, making it most of the way before my match expires again. Not wishing to waste what few matches I have left, I blindly grope my way along the few remaining yards to the house, eventually managing to stumble across the threshold.

It feels slightly warmer inside, almost as though the space is inhabited by another living, breathing being, but of course that is impossible and I tell myself that it's simply due to the thick old walls retaining some of the heat of the day. I light another match so that I might better examine my surroundings and find somewhere to hunker down. Unsurprisingly, much of the house's roof has rotted away or fallen in, and I can feel a light rain beginning to fall from the sky. Seeking some kind of shelter, I move through the downstairs rooms, eventually coming to a basement staircase. The darkness below reminds me of a set of gaping jaws, and the thought of willingly descending into that black void makes me freeze in my tracks for a moment.

But I have a weapon, I remind myself. And besides, what can possibly be down there that would be more monstrous than me?

Lighting another match, I hold it in one hand while taking out my knife with the other, then slowly begin to move down the stairs. The smell of mould and rot is pervasive, but the deeper I descend into the house's underbelly, the more I become aware of another scent lurking underneath them, a scent I quickly recognise.

It is the smell of corruption, of dead things.

Looking around, I begin to notice something else. There are clusters of small handprints daubed all over the walls of the staircase, undoubtedly put there by children. The marks are a faded brownish colour, most likely just mud and dirt. Nothing more than kids playing out in the forest, filthy from their games.

But I also know that it's quite possible the handprints were made by fresh blood.

What happened in this house?

I reach the bottom of the steps, and holding the match up in the air, check my surroundings. Aside from more of the handprints scattered across each of the four walls, there is nothing remarkable about the cellar. It is entirely empty, with a hard-packed dirt floor. And although there is a chill in the basement air, it is quite dry down here. I tell myself it will be an acceptable place to spend the next few hours.

Just then my match goes out, and I suddenly realise I am not alone.

I hear a hoarse, tortured breathing behind me, the sound of something very old that has forgotten how to die. But then the breathing swells to fill the space and it is all around me, everywhere at once, as though I am trapped *inside* whatever is making this dreadful sound, as though the basement staircase was indeed a ravenous mouth and I have walked straight into the thing's belly.

I scream.

There is a dry chuckle from the darkness. *Your fear is a coarse, animal thing*, an ancient voice says. I cannot tell if the voice is male or female. *It is not what I seek.*

I am vaguely aware of my bladder letting go, of a wet stain spreading across the crotch of my wool and silk trousers.

Step forward, into the corner, the voice instructs me.

I shuffle forward, unable to resist its imprecation. I cannot see anything in the darkness and am seized by a terror that I might simply step forwards into absolute nothingness, tumbling down into emptiness for all eternity.

But then my searching hands encounter the cool stone of the basement wall and I slump gratefully against it, pressing my cheek upon the brickwork. Slowly, I slide down to my knees, fear and exhaustion claiming me. I start to cry, and suddenly wish that I could burrow down into the earth of the cellar and sleep there for a century, senseless, lifeless.

There was another like you once, says the voice. *His name was Parr. He was a pathetic murdering wretch, just as you are. He brought the little ones to me, as will you. It is their fear I crave.*

'Yes,' I gibber. I'd gladly agree to anything, just to make that terrible voice stop talking.

You belong to me now.

'Yes, yes!' I shriek, with the dawning awareness that I no longer exist as a person, and perhaps never did. Everything I *was* was only a means to bring me here, now, in this place, and beyond that, everything I *am* is hers.

I feel her cold hands caressing my skull, cradling me to her.

There is no Patrick Bateman.

His shattered remains recede into the distance behind me, like a crumbling statue on a shore. There are no such things as names on the black ocean I travel now, and my destination does not lie on any map.

This is an ending, but not an exit.

THE NARRATOR

Rod Serling in The Twilight Zone, *1959-1964*
created by Rod Serling

PICTURE A MAN: DARK HAIR, THICK EYEBROWS, TIGHTLY CLENCHED JAW. HE wears a black suit, and always carries a lit cigarette in his hand. To look at, he could be any man: perhaps a Madison Avenue ad executive, a travelling salesman, or even a lay preacher. But he is none of those things. This man has no name, and no occupation…in the accepted sense of the word. His sole task on this earth is simply to bear witness; to watch, record, and understand. Some might call him a scribe, or a storyteller. But to us, he is only the Narrator. The man entrusted with monitoring the shadow history of the world. A history you won't find in any textbook or library – at least, not this side of…the Twilight Zone.

Stepping from the shaded interior of his tiny shack, the Narrator stared out at the barren expanse of the Mojave and lit another cigarette. It was barely noon and he was already halfway through his first pack. The Narrator owned no watch or clock – he understood only too well how unpredictably treacherous such devices could be – and so measured the passing hours and minutes only by the movement of the sun and the amount of cigarettes he'd smoked that day.

As he inhaled, the arid combination of tobacco smoke and the dry desert air caused him to start to cough uncontrollably. Doubling over, the Narrator spat onto the sand, spotting it with crimson.

How much longer did he have, he wondered?

He pushed the thought away. The only story he could not properly foresee was his own, and yet he was almost certain he would be dead before the cancer finally took him. For he could now sense the insidious forces gathering around him, rising to envelop him like a black tide. The Narrator knew all their hidden stories, the dread narratives they were weaving across the span of the globe, and therefore understood that he could not be permitted to live.

The merciless heat of the sun had already turned his bloody spittle brown, and he quickly kicked sand over it. Looking up, he scanned the desert vista, searching for what he knew he would find there.

And there it was: off in the middle distance perched atop a cactus.

The raven, watching him.

He knew how insane that sounded. *That crazy old dude, living all by himself out in the middle of the desert. The sun boiled his brain, did a real number on him. He even thought the fuckin' birds were watching him.*

But no – he had only moved out here in order to *preserve* his sanity, because otherwise the weight of the world's stories unceasingly pressing down on him had been far too much for any man to bear. Out here in the desert, the solitude and the quiet helped keep the flow of information tolerable, just about.

And out here, where the Narrator might not see another living soul for weeks on end, he *knew* when he was being watched. Even if it was by a fucking bird.

Finishing his cigarette, he flicked the butt away into the brush.

There was no way of knowing precisely how much time he had left, but it needed to be enough, *had* to be. There were still so many stories left to tell, and the future of the world – such as it was – might depend on it.

The Narrator's daily routine was always the same: rise early, smoke a cigarette, drink a pot of strong black coffee (accompanied by more cigarettes), then sit down to begin work (interspersed with regular tobacco breaks). His needs were simple, and the shack in which he lived was furnished accordingly. A cot, a stove and refrigerator, a small desk and chair. The only exceptions to the spartan nature of his living arrangement were a portable television set and the rickety bookcases that lined the entirety of two walls, each shelf filled with a collection of identical black notebooks. Every one of those books was, in turn, filled with page upon page of stories. Together, they comprised the secret history of the world. A history the Narrator had devoted his entire adult life to recording.

But why secret?

Because powerful forces had worked assiduously to make sure it remained so.

Because of the very few people that knew anything of this history, most of those that did would eventually learn to their cost that it was far preferable to live in ignorance.

The narratives that unfolded across those pages, set down in the Narrator's cramped, densely stitched handwriting (he wrote like he talked, through gritted teeth), detailed arcane, unspeakable things: dark tales of conspiracies and corruption and murder; of aliens and ghosts and monsters; of liminal spaces and other dimensions; of angels and devils and damned things; of life and death and whatever else lies in-between.

These were the stories the Narrator dreamt of every night, the stories that had been entrusted to him and him alone.

Once upon a time, when the stories had first begun revealing themselves to him, they had been far easier to take. Oh, they had still been nebulous, unpleasant things, disquieting tales retrieved from the shadow realm the Narrator had privately christened *The Twilight Zone*, but there had nevertheless been a certain sense of *order* to them, a discernible feeling that, while the moral compass of the world might waver at times, it would usually end up pointing in the right direction.

But over the years, all that had changed. Now, any belief he had once possessed in a moral order was rapidly dissipating. The stories that came to him every night were no longer parables of the guilty being punished, or good triumphing over evil. Instead, they spoke of a collapsing world where to be decent was to be damned, and evil was permitted, even encouraged, to flourish; of a pervasive spiritual rot infesting the universe; of a looming apocalypse slowly and patiently being willed into being. It was as if the Earth had somehow switched places, and what was once the Twilight Zone – a half-glimpsed, inexplicable dimension only ever experienced by an unfortunate few – was now the limbo occupied by all of humanity.

Previously, the Narrator had never really thought too much about whether he believed in any sort of a God, but – given that he certainly had sufficient knowledge of the Devil and many of His works – he supposed he must.

Which could only lead him to subsequently conclude that God had finally turned His back upon the world he'd created.

So, when the overwhelming flood of apathy and decay had become too much, the Narrator had fled from humanity, fled from existence, out into the wasteland of the Mojave Desert. He was still visited by the dreams every night, but stripping everything else away had at least allowed him to focus, to conserve his remaining strength for the one task that had been allotted to him. Now, all he did was dream, then wake to dutifully set the dreams down on paper. Other than occasional breaks for nourishment and cigarettes, that was his life. He saw no one, save for on the monthly supply runs he would make into the nearest town.

Once, when he had first arrived here, there had been others. The vampire woman, who lived out in Joshua Tree, and Papa Jupiter's cannibal tribe, who dwelt up in the surrounding hills. But they'd all mostly left him alone, perhaps due to some ineffable sense that he should not be touched, or simply because they could smell the incipient black rot blossoming inside him. Papa Jupiter's daughter Ruby had visited him occasionally; she would trade small scavenged items for cigarettes, and every now and then they would sleep together, but the Narrator had not seen her or any of the others for years. But in the meantime, he had dreamt their stories, recorded them in his notebooks, and thus understood that they had all ended in the same way that every story must eventually end.

Just as his own soon would.

The previous night, the Narrator had dreamt of a cold-eyed stranger – A man? A ghost? – who had strode out of America's past and carried his implacable sense of frontier vengeance into the modern world, seeding it there like knotweed. Picturing the man's face in his thoughts unnerved him somehow, and he was not used to feeling unnerved. But try as he might, the Narrator could not manage to shake the impression that he had been made privy to something of particular import, although relating to exactly what he did not know. The Stranger's lined, emotionless features haunted him, as though he had accidentally glimpsed some blasphemous idol unfit for human eyes.

Still, he wrote down what he knew of the Stranger's story nonetheless; he could not yet see where the tale ended, but felt compelled to record the information that had been imparted to him.

Upon finishing the account, the Narrator smoked another cigarette, then ate a small lunch of bread and cheese. There were yet more stories to be written – there were *always* more stories – but he could not get the Stranger's face out of his mind, and given that he was now down to his last carton of cigarettes, he decided to drive into town for supplies. Perhaps the long drive would help clear his head.

The journey passed without incident; although the Narrator usually found the drive tedious, on this occasion the monotonous stretches of deserted highway actually served to quell his nagging paranoia. When he finally arrived at his destination, he felt sanguine enough to decide to treat himself to a cold beer. The town's bar wasn't much – the town itself wasn't much – but it was dark and cool and no one bothered you there. The first rule of life out here in the desert was to mind your own damn business.

Taking a seat at the bar, the Narrator lit a cigarette and ordered his beer. As he waited, he found his eyes unavoidably drawn to the television set affixed to the nearby wall. Currently, a talk show was playing: *The Rupert Pupkin Show*. The titular host, as unbearably insistent as a toothache, finished talking to his first guest, an actress named Chris MacNeil, and effusively introduced his second. The Narrator recognised the man's name, a disgraced former politician, now in the process of being rehabilitated as a current affairs pundit on the cable channel Thorn TV.

Greg Stillson.

Stillson sauntered on camera, a creature resplendent in his natural habitat. Quickly ticking off the expected boxes, he offered up a shit-eating grin for the audience, a kiss on both cheeks for the actress, and an enthusiastic handshake for the host. He might have been a figure on a zoetrope, repeating the same rote gestures over and over again. As the two men shook hands, the Narrator found himself musing how much they both symbolised the state of modern America, the steady slide towards apathy and nihilism he had been documenting for all these years. Both were seemingly unrepentant former criminals, now rewarded for their infamy. In a better world they would be shamed and hounded, not lauded. Once upon a time, that would undoubtedly have been the outcome of their stories. But now, nothing mattered anymore. No one cared.

If anything, both men were admired for having gotten away with it. And what sort of a goddamn story was that to tell people?

The Narrator's drink was placed in front of him, and he hurriedly raised the bottle to his lips. The beer tasted bland, metallic, but he gulped it down nonetheless, hoping it would soothe his rising nausea. He could not tear his gaze away from Stillson's face; the pantomime insincerity of his body language masking the absence of feeling in his rattlesnake eyes. Why couldn't people *see*?

Abruptly, the picture on the television disintegrated into a burst of white noise. When it flickered back into life a second later, a close-up of Pupkin's face now filled the screen.

Slowly, the host turned to stare directly at camera, directly out at the Narrator. A wide, idiot grin spread across his face as he began to intone : *The third angel blew his trumpet, and a great star fell from heaven, blazing like a torch, and it fell on a third of the rivers and on the springs of water. The name of the star is Wormwood. A third of the waters became wormwood, and many people died from the water, because it had been made bitter.*

As Pupkin finished speaking, the image once again dissolved to static, before returning to the regular show. Stillson was still talking away like nothing had happened.

But the Narrator barely even noticed. A flurry of images began to flash through his skull, dreadful tableaus of Greg Stillson's future, *America's* future. And in that instant, he saw it all. He saw where all his stories had been leading, glimpsed the true face of the being whose plans were now so close to fruition.

The Great Beast. The Antichrist.

Buy you another?

The unexpected voice at his side caused the Narrator to spin around in his seat, and he found himself staring into a familiar set of eyes. Eyes colder than the bottom of the ocean, colder than death itself.

A stranger's eyes.

You look like you could use one, the Stranger said.

Letting out a low moan, the Narrator stumbled backwards off his stool, almost falling to the floor. The Stranger sat unmoving as a corpse, making no move to stop him. Flinging whatever banknotes he found in his pocket down onto the bar, the Narrator turned and fled.

Outside, he got straight into his truck and headed directly out of town, all thoughts of supplies disregarded. He told himself he would not need them now.

His story was almost at an end.

He drove back to his shack as fast as the engine of his old pickup could manage. By the time he arrived, the moon was high in the sky, the chill of the nocturnal desert air nipping at his skin. Still, it was nothing compared to the bone-numbing cold he'd felt when those eyes looked upon him.

There was very little time left. The Narrator began to load up his truck with the contents of his bookshelves, staggering back and forth between shack and vehicle with as many journals as he could carry in his arms at one time. His breath began to scorch in his lungs, and he could taste blood on his tongue. Cursing the stupidity of his decades-long cigarette habit, he forced himself onwards.

Finally, the task was finished, but the night's work was still far from over. Tossing a shovel and tarpaulin in with the piles of notebooks, the Narrator got back into the truck and drove out into the middle of the desert, close to the base of the hills.

There, he began to dig. He dug deep and wide, a pit large enough to accommodate a lifetime's worth of stories. Like all those who dedicate their lives to the written word, the Narrator was a sedentary creature, and the strain of his desperate task was almost too much for him. His bones and sinews shrieked; his lungs felt as though they might combust. But he would not stop. Otherwise it would all have been for naught, and now that he was so close to the end of his life, the Narrator could at last admit to himself that all he'd ever wanted was for his stories to make a small difference in the world.

When the hole was finished, he spread the tarpaulin inside, and then began to hurriedly fill the pit with his notebooks. He had always kept his library in careful order until now, but let whoever found the journals try and make sense of them. The sky above was beginning to redden, and the Narrator felt sure his *denouement* was almost upon him.

Once all the notebooks were in place, he covered them with earth, feeling on the verge of collapse. But still his task was not quite complete; one last finishing touch remained.

A large boulder stood next to the final resting place of the Narrator's stories, and taking out a penknife, he carefully carved a memoriam into its surface:

'Submitted for your consideration'

By now, it was dawn. The Narrator considered lying down on the ground and simply letting the desert sun burn him away to nothing, but understood that his own story would not be permitted to end on such a note of anticlimax. Instead, he clambered wearily back into his truck and drove home.

Arriving back at the shack, he immediately sensed something had changed. It was not simply that the vacant structure seemed hollowed out, entirely devoid of purpose now that it had been emptied of his stories; no, something else was here. The shadows inside the shack seemed to spill out into the surrounding desert, tainting the dry air with a clammy chill.

Lighting a cigarette, the Narrator stepped inside, to find the Stranger waiting for him. The man sat at the Narrator's desk, his feet planted on its surface. Even now, the Narrator found himself offended by the boorish contemptuousness of the act.

Get your damn feet off my desk, he whispered.

The Stranger's eyes narrowed, but he silently did as he was instructed.

Who the hell are you? the Narrator demanded.

It doesn't matter, said the Stranger. *I have a job to do, and I'm here to do it.*

And who would employ a man like you?

I work for a company named Parallax. Maybe you've heard of them.

The Narrator had, of course. He'd written down a great many stories concerning Parallax, and they had all ended exactly the same way.

Can I finish my cigarette first? he asked the Stranger, who nodded in wordless assent.

The Narrator crossed to his cot and sat down heavily. Raising the cigarette to his mouth, he inhaled deeply, then held the slim tube up in the air for a moment, inspecting it. Suddenly, he began to laugh.

You want to hear something funny? he asked the Stranger.

The other man said nothing, merely sat and stared at him.

I have lung cancer.

The Stranger removed a large handgun from his shoulder holster and put it down on the desk. The metal of the weapon gleamed dully in the half-light of the shack.

So the thing of it is, you're really doing me a favour.

The other man's face registered no visible response, no emotion. Returning the cigarette to his lips, the Narrator closed his eyes and inhaled again, letting the tobacco smoke fill his lungs, relishing its sweetly toxic taste. Unwilling to part with it, he held the smoke inside himself for several long seconds, a miser greedily hoarding precious jewels. He began to fantasise that if he held it there long enough, his lung capillaries would eventually start to wither and blacken, setting off a chain reaction that would ultimately cause his whole body to crumple into ash, as though it were nothing more than the residue of the untold thousands of cigarettes it had consumed over his lifetime.

But in the end, he simply let the smoke go, allowing it to slowly hiss out through his gritted teeth like a steam from a vent.

This was how his story ended, the Narrator thought. Not with a well-timed fade out, or a final monologue. Just with a breath.

He heard the click of a revolver. Then, a distant voice echoing in his mind.

And now, a word from our sponsor!

INTERLUDE

NIKKI BRAND

Debbie Harry in Videodrome, *1983*
written & directed by David Cronenberg

SETTING: *A darkened three-walled red set, the rear wall constructed out of moist clay. A black iron grille has been built into the floor. The set has been arranged in a classic talkshow format: three chairs on the right-hand side for the guests, with a coffee table in front of them, and the interviewer's chair facing them on the left.*

ANNOUNCER: And now here it is, *Videodrome* with Nikki Brand! This evening Nikki's guests are legendary black magician Dr. Julian Karswell, the former United States Ambassador to the United Kingdom Robert Thorn, and controversial cult author John Morlar! Take it away, Nikki!

NIKKI BRAND: Our subject on tonight's show is Damien Thorn, the one and only Antichrist. Who is he? What does he want? What's his favourite leisure activity? This evening, we're going to try and find out exactly what makes him tick. Dr. Julian Karswell, you're the man who first introduced the Antichrist to the world. Are you proud of your accomplishment?

JULIAN KARSWELL: Very much so, Ms Brand. It's a matter of great regret to me that I wasn't around to mentor Damien and watch him come of age, but I've been keeping an eye on proceedings from beyond the veil, as it were, and overall, I would have to say things seem to be working out quite satisfactorily. There have undoubtedly been a few bumps in the road along the way, but Damien seems to have navigated them quite successfully. So yes: without a doubt, bringing about the birth of the Antichrist would have to count as my finest achievement.

BRAND: And what about you, Robert Thorn? You gave the Antichrist his first start in life, and failed to kill him when you had the chance. How do *you* feel?

ROBERT THORN [*turns to stare at Karswell*]: You? *You* were responsible for that…abomination?

KARSWELL [*preening*]: Why, yes.

THORN: Bastard! I'll kill you!

KARSWELL: Oh dear…

Thorn erupts from his seat, hands outstretched towards Karswell, as if to throttle him. But before he can seize the other man, Karswell makes a quick gesture with his left hand, causing Thorn to abruptly stop in his tracks and look around wildly, his unseeing eyes gazing out blankly at the studio audience.

THORN: I…I'm blind! What the hell have you done to me?

Knocking his chair over, Thorn blunders off towards the side of the set, waving his arms helplessly in the air. In response, two Videodrome stagehands, both wearing black hoods and chainmail aprons, emerge and roughly manhandle Thorn back to his seat.

BRAND: Dr. Karswell, if you wouldn't mind…?

KARSWELL: Of course, my dear.

Karswell gestures again, and Thorn's eyes slowly clear. He gazes across at Karswell with visceral loathing.

BRAND [*tuts*]: We can't have that sort of threatening behaviour on my show, you naughty boy. What if any children are watching? Gentlemen, please show Robert here the error of his ways.

The two stagehands take it in turns to punch Thorn in the face, until he slumps back into his seat, bloodied and semi-conscious.

BRAND: There. I don't think you'll misbehave again, will you, lover?

THORN: (*Unintelligible*)

BRAND: Now, if we could return to my original question…

THORN [*sobs*]: I'm sorry. (*Pause*) I should have killed him in the church. I had him there, in my hands, helpless. But I couldn't do it. He was just a little boy. I was weak, too weak. I'm so, so, sorry. He's going to destroy everything, isn't he?

KARSWELL [*pleased*]: Oh yes, most certainly.

THORN: May God forgive me.

KARSWELL: And why should he? Answer me that, Mr Thorn. After all, he didn't forgive *my* Master. Time and time again, we are told that God is merciful above all others, but where's the proof of it? One minor show of defiance, and my Master was condemned to an eternity of desolation. I tell you, when I hear about God's mercy, it makes me want to vomit at the sheer hypocrisy of it. Well, He's going to pay for it now. Him, and all his so-called children. And I'm going to relish every second.

JOHN MORLAR: My, but you're a smug little bastard, aren't you?

BRAND: John Morlar, what about you? You didn't encounter Damien Thorn until well after he'd reached maturity. What were your impressions of him as a grown man?

MORLAR: Impressions? Very well, I'll tell you. A feeble cripple in a wheelchair, hiding behind an old man and a whore. Antichrist! He probably couldn't even wipe his own backside. Like all so-called powerful men, he's really nothing but a coward. He seeks to control the world because he's terrified of it. He loathes humanity because, despite all his infernal power, at heart he knows he's no better than us. He's as weak and despicable as any other man or woman. The foundations of His Father's vile kingdom were constructed on everything that is odious and contemptible in the world, and like so many other privileged scions before him, Damien Thorn now believes it is his birthright to lord it over the rest of us. I despise him, and everything he stands for. If I could tear open the ground and piss on the flames of Hell right now, I would do it gladly.

BRAND: Such hostility, lover. You should try yoga, it can work wonders.

KARSWELL: And yet, Morlar…that 'feeble cripple' beat you.

MORLAR: Only because, much like his Father, he's a worthless little cheat. I had him on his knees. If it hadn't been for the treachery of my own government, implanting that fucking explosive in my spine…

KARSWELL: Well, what you call *cheating*, I prefer to think of as outsmarting one's opponent. But don't be too upset, Morlar. You are simply one of many who fell to the divine supremacy of The Great Beast. I know you liked to believe you were somehow better than all the rest, but sadly it was not the case. Still, you were surely no worse. Please, take some comfort in the fact that Heaven and all its armies cannot stand against Him now.

With a look of satisfaction, Karswell picks up a water glass and takes a sip.

MORLAR: Christ, it's like arguing with a garden slug. One day you're going to choke on your own self-satisfaction, Dr. Karswell.

Karswell waves Morlar away contemptuously.

MORLAR: In fact, why not today? Choke on it, Karswell, do you hear me? I want you to *choke.*

Karswell immediately tips the water glass up in the air until it is almost vertical to his mouth, helplessly gulping at the contents until liquid begins to spill from his lips. His other hand gesticulates frantically, but he is powerless to resist Morlar. Soon, the glass is empty, and Karswell slumps back in his seat, gasping and coughing.

MORLAR: No, that won't do at all. Why don't you choke on the glass instead, doctor? Go on, now, you can do it. Piece by piece, careful as you go.

A look of horror on his face, Karswell raises the receptacle to his mouth and begins to bite savagely at it, snapping off shards of glass with his teeth and quickly swallowing them down.

BRAND: What are you doing, Morlar? Stop it at once!

Too late. Karswell topples to the floor, limbs spasming, hacking up blood and splinters of broken glass. Within moments, he is still. Morlar smiles and raises his own glass in the air.

MORLAR: Cheers.

Nikki signals towards the wings. Instantly, the two stagehands reappear, this time armed with electric cattle-prods.

BRAND: Please teach Mr Morlar to show some respect for his fellow guests.

The stagehands advance on Morlar, who merely turns and glances contemptuously at them over his shoulder. Immediately, they begin to attack each other with the prods, rapidly stunning themselves into submission.

MORLAR [*to Nikki*]: You vacuous little bitch.

Morlar gets to his feet and begins to advance on Nikki.

BRAND: Now then, lover…let's not get upset. We're only giving the viewers what they want.

MORLAR: You think you can bring me here and make me dance for his amusement? Like I'm some flea-bitten monkey? This particular monkey has teeth, *lover*. And it bites.

BRAND: Don't forget where you are, Morlar!

MORLAR: He may have destroyed my body but my power remains. Damien Thorn can buy himself all the corrupt politicians he wants, he can buy himself the U.S. Presidency, the entire stinking planet, it won't save him from me.

BRAND: What are you going to do? You're just a brain in a fucking jar. He keeps you locked in a bunker deep underground, far away from anyone. You're nothing but a trophy, a useless lump of flesh. He destroyed you!

MORLAR: No. He *freed* me. And now I'm going to tear it all down. Starting with this miserable little freakshow.

Morlar looks towards camera. There is an immediate electronic shriek, and the camera cuts to Nikki Brand. She begins to scream, the television image of her face warping and distorting into a frozen cry of anguish. There is a deafening burst of static, and then the screen goes dark for a second, before a title card appears:

SORRY! WE ARE EXPERIENCING TECHNICAL DIFFICULTIES

DAVID

Will McMillan in The Crazies, *1973*
written by Paul McCollough and George A. Romero
directed by George A. Romero

At this point, Norliss had spent three straight hours within the confines of Danvers State Hospital, and was starting to feel a distinct urge to book himself into his own private room. Arletty Long and her babbling about the looming apocalypse hadn't gotten the day off to a particularly encouraging start, and now he'd been left sitting in a corridor for well over an hour while they readied the next patient on his list, with nothing to do but chain smoke and count the droplets of rain striking the window opposite. It was like Danvers had been deliberately designed to give you the goddamn spooks anyway, some kind of Edgar Allan Poe wet dream, but it wasn't just the look of the place that was getting to him. Maybe it was that the persistent smell of disinfectant in his nostrils was starting to give Norliss a headache, but underneath the slow aching throb in his skull, he'd swear he could hear a distant voice whispering to him, like a nebulous figure murmuring from the end of a long dark tunnel…

Mr Norliss?

Startled, he glanced up to see a blank-faced orderly standing over him. *David is ready for you now.*

The man led him along a seemingly endless tangle of corridors towards Danvers's maximum security wing. Given the constant unruly din in the rest of the hospital, Norliss had half-expected the atmosphere in the wing to be an unbearable cacophony of shrieking and jabbering, but instead he found it suffused with an eerie hush; an all-encompassing quiet that put him in mind of the silence at the bottom of a deep dark ocean, heavy enough to crush the last vestiges of air from your agonised lungs.

Norliss supposed it was because they kept the patients here well sedated, but it was disquieting nonetheless. Not to mention irritating; how in the hell was he going to get any useful information out of a patient who was too doped up to speak coherently?

David was one of the last remaining survivors of Evans City, a small Pennsylvania town that had, for all intents and purposes, simply been wiped off the map a year or two back. The whole area was now an officially designated No Man's Land, sealed off from the outside world by perimeter walls of concrete and barbed wire and kept under twenty-four hour guard by the military. So, as far as said outside world was concerned, Evans City no longer existed, and if you valued a quiet, untroubled existence, it was better not to ask too many questions as to exactly why.

But asking questions was precisely what Norliss did, and after spending months resolutely poking around in the dark, he'd managed to discover that Evans City had been the site of a bioweapons accident. An experimental chemical codenamed Trixie had somehow ended up in the town's water supply, resulting in the entire population going homicidally insane and attacking anyone within sight. As you might expect, an awful lot of people had died as a result. And from what Norliss had been able to uncover, the longer-term effects of Trixie had eventually killed most of the survivors to boot. The few that were left were all stark raving bananas, and so far, had been entirely unable to tell Norliss anything of use about the incident.

So, on the face of it, he had little reason to think that David would really be any different. Except that something *was* seemingly different about the man. The other survivors were all hidden in plain sight, left to languish in various out-of-the-way county hospitals until they eventually did the powers that be a favour and quietly died. Hopelessly, incurably insane, they were un-people; societal detritus that had been coldly and quietly swept under the carpet, by governmental authorities who were quietly confident that said detritus could offer little or no insight or assistance to anyone who happened to peer under the carpet and discover them.

Which, as far as Norliss was concerned, was pretty much exactly how things had played out so far.

But David? Well, for starters, he didn't even *exist*; not as a registered inmate of Danvers State Hospital, anyway. It had taken an anonymous tip-off to lead Norliss here in the first place, and a lot of greased palms and *sotto voce* coaxing to get him twenty minutes alone with the man. No, someone had gone to quite significant lengths to hide David away. And while Norliss had never claimed to be any sort of a genius, it didn't take a smartass to know that the things people hide away are usually the same things that reward the extra effort it takes to find them.

That said, matters didn't look overly encouraging when the orderly first let him into David's cell. Norliss found the man sitting on the edge of his cot, staring dully into space, arms hanging limply by his sides. He had a heavy-browed face, and that aspect of his physiognomy, combined with the harsh top-light in the room, had the effect of casting his eyes into deep shadow.

Norliss doubted that was the sole reason he could discern no light in them at all, however.

I'll be right outside, the orderly said quietly. *Just knock if you need me.*

Norliss nodded, and waited for the man to leave. As the cell door closed behind the orderly, the writer pulled up a chair and sat down in front of David, careful not to crowd him. *Good afternoon, David*, Norliss said. *My name is Norliss. I'm a writer, and I'd just like to ask you a few questions, if I may.*

Nothing. David continued staring into space, at a point somewhere over his visitor's left shoulder. Peering closer, Norliss could see a bubble of saliva forming at the corner of the man's half-open mouth.

It seemed hopeless. But Norliss told himself there had to be a good reason he'd been led here, and stubbornly persisted.

David, I'd like to speak to you about what happened in Evans City.

There was a pause, and then Norliss felt the atmosphere in the room suddenly shift, as if a flashlight had just been turned on in a dark cave.

David was looking directly at him.

Norliss inched closer. *Do you remember Evans City, David?*

Another pause. He saw David glance quickly at the cell door, then back at him. Unexpectedly, the man then leaned in towards him, his face growing suddenly animated. *Of course I do,* he hissed. *I'm not crazy, not like the rest of these fucking whackos. They just keep me here to shut me the fuck up!*

Norliss had already been warned that David suffered from acute paranoia and delusions of persecution, but he was happy enough for now to see how this played out and make that judgement call for himself later. After all, he reminded himself, these were increasingly paranoid times; at least for anyone in possession of the right information.

Why do they want to shut you up, David? he asked.

The patient stared back at him, suspicion creeping into his gaze. *Who the hell are you, anyway?* David muttered. *Anyone could walk in here and say they're a goddamn writer.*

Norliss tried to lighten the mood. *That's true, but I do have the ulcer and the therapist's bills to prove it.*

David said nothing. Perhaps making jokes about mental health was not really the correct approach. Norliss tried again. *Believe me, David, I'm a friend. I know about Evans City. I know about Trixie.*

At the mention of Trixie, David gave a small start. *I'm here to find out the truth,* Norliss continued. *Why are they hiding you away in Danvers? Because of what you know?*

I don't know shit, David said flatly.

Then why? David, as far as this country is concerned, you don't even exist. *I had to bribe a doctor to get in to see you today.*

David laughed bitterly. *I knew there was something going on. Normally they keep me drugged to the goddamn eyeballs, but no one came round to give me my meds this morning.* He let out a defeated sigh and laid back on his cot. *Look, Norliss. It's not what I know, but what I am.*

And what's that?

I'm immune, David replied. Everyone in Evans City caught that fucking bug. I lost my girlfriend, my unborn baby. My oldest friend. Everyone caught it but me. I'm the medical wonder of the goddamn world, as sane as Sigmund fucking Freud. He averted his head and spat at the wall. *So here I am, locked away in the nut hatch.*

Norliss gazed at him, baffled. *I don't understand, David.*

A scowl. *Of course you don't.*

But I want to, the writer pleaded. *And I want to help you, if I can. So please, tell me. What happened after Evans City?*

You know they're listening, don't you? Do you know what they'll do to you, Norliss?

The writer concentrated hard on not glancing back over his shoulder. More and more often lately, he'd started to get the jitters, the creeping sensation that he was being watched crawling up his spine like a poisonous centipede. *You're not the one in the looney bin,* he silently reminded himself.

Fixing what he hoped was a reassuring smile upon his face, Norliss shrugged. *Occupational hazard,* he told the other man blithely. *You let me worry about that. All I need from you is the truth.*

David stared at him. *You really think you can help me?* Norliss could see the man struggling to repress a forlorn sense of hope.

Not right away, the writer admitted. *But if there's a story being covered up here, and I can make people listen…I'd like to think so.*

David ran his hands through his greasy hair. *I don't know how much use any of this is,* he muttered, *or even what the fuck it all means. But it's what happened, anyway.* He sat back up. *After I got rounded up, they stuck me in a cage with all the other crazies. But after a while, they noticed I wasn't getting sick. So they pulled me straight out again and put me in solitary instead. I figured they'd start doing all sorts of tests, trying to figure out what made me immune.*

But they didn't?

No, not at first. They just left me sitting there for a day or two. They took good care of me, brought me food, even some beer, but I couldn't get anyone to tell me what the hell was going on. Christ, the whole of Evans City was going down the fucking toilet and I was just sitting there getting shitfaced.

Making a fist, the patient smashed it into his open palm. *It was too late to save Clank, or Judy, but I coulda been doing something! he cried.*

Norliss remained silent as David composed himself. Eventually, the other man took a deep breath and continued. *Then two soldiers took me outta there and put me on a chopper, a big black Huey. No markings or anything. It took me to some kind of institute, Christ knows where. Nothing but corn fields in every direction, and this featureless white building smack in the middle of them. It looked like a weird monument or something, but God only knows what to. Anyway, some orderlies took me inside, and put me in another cell. Then, the tests started. They'd stick all sorts of shit into my body, and take all sorts of shit out. That went on for days, no one saying one single goddamn word to me beyond 'Roll up your sleeve' or 'Drop your pants and bend over'. Well, finally I got sick of it and took a swing at one of the doctors. Next thing, they sent in a couple of goons who zapped me with a cattle prod.* A sour grin. *So I didn't try that again.*

Norliss rubbed at his dry lips, wishing he had a glass of water. *And how long were you there for?*

Probably a couple of weeks. Once they were finished with me, they slipped a mickey into my morning OJ. Next thing I knew I woke up here, and down had turned into up.

What do you mean?

David glanced up at the ceiling. *Let me tell you how it is at Danvers, Norliss. You try and tell the doctors the truth about why you're here, and in return they up your meds. And why is that? Because the truth is fucking crazy.*

Norliss could feel a nervous energy taking hold of him. Jumping to his feet, he started to pace the narrow confines of the cell. *Do you know if they found an antidote for Trixie while you were there?*

A hollow laugh. *That's just it, Norliss. From what I could make out, they weren't even looking for one. I'd swear to it.*

Oh, come on, David. That doesn't make any sense. Admittedly, the other man seemed reasonably sane to Norliss, but there was only so much nonsensical black helicopters bullshit the writer could take. *What else would they need the only immune survivor for if not to create an antidote?*

David's voice dropped to a whisper. *Don't you get it, Norliss? They were trying to make Trixie better. They didn't want any survivors next time.*

Norliss felt his stomach slowly falling away. *This was a government installation?* he asked David weakly.

The inmate shook his head emphatically. *Not if you ask me. There wasn't a single government insignia anywhere that I saw. No one had a rank, and no one wore ID. No, this place was strictly a private operation.*

Project Trixie was black ops, they wouldn't have wanted you to know…

Suddenly, David leapt up from his mattress and grabbed Norliss by the lapels. The writer found himself being shoved backwards into the cell wall. *Goddamnit, listen to what I'm saying!* David yelled into his face. *This wasn't Project Trixie! They called it –*

In the next instant, the door to David's cell flew open and two orderlies burst in. Quickly flanking their patient, they grabbed him by the arms and forced him to release Norliss, before pinning David facedown onto his cot.

One of the orderlies, the same man who'd first escorted him to the cell, turned towards Norliss. *You'd better leave now, sir,* he instructed the writer.

Norliss stumbled towards the door, cursing his own stupidity. He knew there was more to David's story, a vital piece of the jigsaw still missing, and now he would never get to hear what it was.

Reaching the cell doorway, he paused and glanced back, his eyes momentarily meeting David's.

Struggling against his captors's grip, the inmate managed to raise his head up from the mattress, just long enough to scream, *Wormwood! They called it Wormwood!*

Norliss fled.

But that one word continued to follow him, along the hospital's twisting corridors and all the way out of the building. Even after he was safely in the parking lot, still it dogged him, like a spoken curse or magical incantation.

Wormwood.

The very same word Arletty Long had used during her babble about the coming apocalypse. She'd quoted some kind of Biblical verse at him, something about an angel blowing his trumpet. The usual religious bullshit. He hadn't paid it any mind at the time.

But now, here it was again. And while Norliss didn't know or indeed care much about religion, he did understand that there was no such thing as a bad coincidence.

He glanced up at the sky overhead. The rain had now stopped, but dark clouds still lingered above, pregnant with foreboding. For a moment, it was like Arletty was stood right next to him, her voice whispering into his ear.

A great star, blazing like a torch, fell from the sky…

Norliss climbed into his car. Glancing across at the passenger seat, he saw the roadmap he'd consulted on his drive up to Danvers. Picking it up, the writer tossed it away into the backseat.

The road he had to travel now would not be charted on any map.

Starting the engine, Norliss pulled out of the parking lot and drove away in search of Wormwood.

In search of the end of the world.

BOOK TWO

WORMWOOD

Bloody moon rising with a plague and a flood,
Join the mob, join the mob

– Tom Waits, "God's Away on Business"

KATHERINE

Kiernan Shipka & Emma Roberts in February, 2015
written & directed by Osgood Perkins

F EBRUARY IS A SUITABLE MONTH FOR DYING.
Katherine had read that somewhere once, back when she was in school. She couldn't remember exactly where, but the quote had stayed with her all the same. Because sometimes Katherine thought that it had *always* been February, ever since that black winter of a decade ago. That dreadful season which had taken her parents, her sanity, and finally, her first and only love, the dark thing that had crept out of the woods surrounding the Bramford School and claimed her for his virgin bride.

The entity she knew only as Black Philip.

But now, she was alone. Now, Katherine inhabited a realm of endless night, endless cold, where it was forever winter and she was forever alone. After the murders, she had been committed to an institution, despite Father

Brian's pleas that Katherine had not been responsible for her actions; that she had only acted under the influence of something wicked and ageless, something *other*. There, she had spent nine years becalmed in a desolate fog of pills and loneliness, always dreaming of him. The only thing that kept her from beating her brains out against her cell wall or attempting to swallow her own tongue was the dim hope that she might yet be reunited with her lost love, a hope that glowed as faintly as a distant beacon on a mist-shrouded shore.

Katherine nurtured that hope for all those long years, and then finally, her chance came. She'd escaped the institution and begun to make her way back to Bramford, posing under the name Joan. When she encountered the grieving parents of her last victim en route to the school, Katherine became certain that her return there was nothing short of preordained destiny, the result of some diabolic providence. Bill and Linda were driving to Bramford to lay flowers, a yearly pilgrimage they made to commemorate their daughter Rose's death, and offered to take Katherine along with them. How could this *not* be fate? After all, Black Philip was a demanding paramour, and his love came at a steep price.

So when she slaughtered Bill and Linda outside the school as her offering to him, carrying their severed heads inside the darkened building and down to the boiler room where her lover had previously made his lair, Katherine had barely been able to contain her joy. Her head was so full of feverish thoughts of him – his ragged claws raking her flesh, his cold tongue tracing the pathways of his desire across her body – that she'd almost tripped and fallen on the stairwell. Imagine that, if she'd broken her neck scant moments before their reunion!

And then she'd arrived at the boiler room, to find as it dark and empty and desolate as the rest of the world she inhabited. Of Black Philip, there was no sign. He had not waited for her, nor conspired to bring her back here to Bramford. *Of course*, Katherine realised. She was an anathema to him now, rendered vile and barren by Father Brian's exorcism. So instead, he had either crept back into those dark woods, patiently watching and waiting, or perhaps, taken another lover, another adoring bride to do his bidding…

No. She would not, *could* not, think of it. Stricken by her loss, Katherine had fled Bramford and set back out on the road, hardly caring what happened to her next. She'd fully expected to be recaptured and sent back to the institution before long. Perhaps that would even be for the best; there, she could simply sink back into a narcotic haze of numbed forgetting.

But to her surprise, no one came for her. So little did Katherine matter to anyone that she was left entirely free to drift, like a shipwrecked man's message that no one cared to read. In time, the freezing tide of her alienation washed her up on the shores of New York City, where she joined the ranks of the city's homeless, left to forage for food and warmth. Abandoned to their unknowable pain.

Now, she lies asleep in a urine-splattered alleyway, huddled under blankets and torn cardboard, lost in a dream of blood and snow. She sleeps fitfully, tossing underneath her covers and making small whimpering sounds. The sort of uneasy sleep a concerned lover might wake you from, if only you had someone to love you. If only you weren't all alone.

But when Katherine awakens with a start a few moments later, it is to discover that she is no longer alone. That someone is looking *at* her, not through her, nor away from her, for the first time in months.

The young woman squatting opposite her has the wide, unblinking eyes of a doll, if not the attire of one, being dressed in a similarly random array of worn and dirty scavenged clothes as Katherine. She is perhaps a few years older – the ravages of living rough make it difficult to tell – but in another life, they could have been friends, or even sisters. Both women bear an unmistakeable trace of vanished purity about them, like fresh cream gone sour. To look at them, it is clear that no one would ever have envisaged either woman ending up like this, cold and hungry in a filthy Manhattan alleyway.

Startled by the presence of another person, Katherine scrambles backwards against the brick wall, fumbling in her jeans for the dulled pocket knife that is her only protection.

But her new companion merely smiles, and tells her, *You're just like me.*

What do you mean? Katherine asks warily, her voice still groggy with sleep.

You've been touched. By one of Them. The young woman rolls up her sleeve to show Katherine a vicious-looking bite mark, reddened and seeping. *I got this nearly ten years ago. It's never healed. But now I can see things, sense things. That's how I found you.*

This girl is clearly crazy, thinks Katherine, who knows a thing or two about crazy herself. But something about those wide green eyes draws her in, soothes her, and instead of attacking her with the knife or simply running, Katherine waits to see what the young woman will say next.

In the end, all she does is introduce herself. *I'm Anita*, she tells Katherine. *But people always call me Needy.*

This at least prompts a hesitant smile from Katherine. *I'm…Joan*, she says instinctively, even though this is the first time she's been asked her name in the twelve months since she first escaped the institution.

No, it's not, Needy replies airily. *But that doesn't matter. You can call yourself whatever you like, I don't care.*

Katherine says nothing, her tongue stilled by how easily this odd young woman seems to read her. Needy studies her for a moment, then continues: *So listen. There's a place I know. It's warm, and they have coffee and donuts. Okay, so the donuts are a little stale, but beggars can't be choosers, right?*

Some kind of Christian homeless shelter, Katherine thinks, and her mind instinctively recoils. People. Looking at her, prying at her with their incessant questions. Asking her to accept the Lord into her heart. She shakes her head forcefully.

Wait, hear me out, Needy says quickly. *No one wants anything from you there. It's only for people like us. People who've been touched. We all share stories. But if you don't wanna talk, you don't have to. The lady who runs it, she's really nice. I know she'd like to meet you.*

People just like *her?* Katherine's mind begins to race. Perhaps there might be someone there who knew of Black Phillip. Who might even be able to help her find him again…

She gazes into Needy's wide eyes once more, immersing herself, as though she were diving for pearls in their emerald depths. As their eyes meet, the other woman smiles broadly. *It's really helped me, Kat, and I just know it'll help you too.*

And as Katherine meekly allows Needy to pull her upright and lead her from the stinking alleyway, so perplexed is she by this apparently fateful meeting, so beguiled by this strange young woman now taking her to who-knows-where, that she does not even think to question how on earth Needy knows her real name.

Needy escorts her uptown, to a synagogue basement in the Bronx. They descend a stairwell into the sort of anonymously communal space Katherine remembers vividly from the years she spent in the institution: the ever-present smell of bleach; neglected, eczematous paintwork; aged fluorescent tubes flickering overhead. A ring of folding plastic chairs has been arranged in the centre of the room, with a lectern placed down front. On the far side of the basement, an urn of coffee and the promised tray of donuts awaits them, and Needy wastes little time in leading her new friend there. Katherine stands shyly to one side as the other woman pours a styrofoam cup of coffee and picks out a donut, and when Needy turns and presents them to her, Katherine glances worriedly around the room, as if she might be breaching some social contract by accepting the treats.

It's okay, Needy assures her. *They're for us. And you're one of us too now, aren't you?*

Katherine nods hesitantly and takes a sip of the coffee. It is hot and bitter, and while it could never hope to warm the cold places nestled deep inside her, the sensation of heat on her tongue is so welcome, so unfamiliar, that she almost laughs at the feel of it and spits the liquid over Needy. Forcing herself to swallow, she takes another gulp of coffee, then turns her attention to the donut. As Needy warned her, the pastry is a day old, but it hardly matters to Katherine. The joy of the sugar rush startles her with its force, her teeth immediately beginning to ache with it. But it is a good pain, she decides – the sort of pain that reminds her she is alive, rather than making her want to die.

Continuing to bite greedily into the donut, she begins to look around the room, turning her attention to the other people gathered in the basement. The demographic of the group is a racially diverse one, and seems to be split fairly evenly between men and women. However, Katherine soon realises that she and Needy are easily the youngest attendees in the room; most of the others are middle-aged or older, and seem comfortable with themselves in a way that Katherine cannot begin to imagine. She watches as a black couple bicker animatedly nearby, and all of a sudden, she starts to feel self-conscious again. She has nothing in common with these people, whoever they are. She should leave, immediately.

The next instant she feels Needy's hand on her arm. *Regan! There's someone I want you to meet.*

Katherine glances up to see an energetic little woman bustling towards them. Snub-nosed and apple-cheeked, Katherine guesses her to be around sixty, but is immediately struck by her youthful, almost adolescent energy.

As their eyes meet, the woman flashes Katherine a broad smile. *Hello, sweetheart, I'm Regan MacNeil. Welcome to our little group!* Darting forward, she gives Katherine an impulsive hug.

Katherine imagines herself as a mouse wriggling in a trap, and tries not to squirm. Sensing her discomfort, Regan releases Katherine from the embrace, and gives her a sympathetic look.

Oh dear. What's wrong?

Katherine's eyes dart from side to side, and her voice emerges as a frightened whisper. *I don't know why I'm here. I don't know who you people are.*

Why, we're just like you! Regan assures her. *Everyone you see here –* she begins to point at the various group members in turn *– Mr Lutz, Isaac and Abby over there, Nancy, Needy and me…we've all been touched by something other. Inhabited. Our stories are all different, but at heart they're all the same. You'll hear some of those stories tonight.* She offers Katherine a warm smile. *And in time – whenever you're ready – you can tell us yours.*

Giving the younger woman's hand a squeeze, Regan turns to address the room. *Okay, everyone! Let's get started! We have a new addition to our little group tonight, so please do make her feel welcome. Isaac, why don't you kick things off?*

While everyone else joins the circle and picks a chair, the black man Katherine noticed earlier takes up a position at the lectern. He waits a few moments for the group's chatter to subside, and when it fails to do so, he glances over at Abby, the woman accompanying him to the meeting. Immediately, she stamps her foot impatiently against the wooden floor. *Shaddap,* she bellows. *Isaac's trying to talk here!*

Abby's annoyed outburst provokes a few muffled giggles, but the room quietens. Clearing his throat, Isaac steps forward and begins to address the group. *Evening, y'all. For anyone that don't know me, my name is Isaac Hendrix. So, must be about thirty years ago now. I was in college, and driving a cab to make ends meet. Had a beautiful wife – not as beautiful as you, Abby – and things were pretty good. Until all of a sudden, they weren't. I started seeing another man's face in the mirror, see? Dressing like him, acting like him. Didn't know who the hell he was, but it didn't matter. He was a part of me, like a cancer deep inside. And sometimes he'd just take over. I don't like to think about the things he made me do. I hurt people, cut people. I even attacked my baby. All these years later I'm still ashamed. It's like a stain on my soul.*

Then, a shrill voice sounds from the other side of the room. *Because the man who possessed you was a criminal! A psychopath!*

Katherine looks around to see an elderly woman tottering down the stairs into the basement. She is swathed in expensive furs, her face powdered a stark white. It puts Katherine in mind of a cracked sidewalk on a frosty January morning.

The old woman continues. *A no-good lowlife, just like the creature that took me!*

Isaac shrugs helplessly, prompting another interjection from Abby. *Isaac's already speaking! You tell her, Ms MacNeil!*

Regan motions for calm. *Mrs Benson, please wait your turn. You know how this works.*

I have something to say right now! the old woman retorts. *There's a larger issue here we're not addressing.*

And what might that be, ma'am? Isaac asks her with studied politeness.

Well, I'm very glad you asked, Mrs Benson replies. *Tell me, the man who inhabited your body was a pimp, was he not? A coloured pimp.*

In the background, Abby makes a disgusted noise, but Isaac merely nods. *Yes. His name was J.D. Walker.*

The old woman nods. *The filthy degenerate who possessed me was named Tonio Pérez. Before me, he inhabited my beloved brother Joel, and it's his fault my brother is dead. He was a monster, a Puerto Rican murderer.*

And what the fuck does where he came from have to do with anything, lady? Abby clambers to her feet, jabbing in the air with an outstretched finger.

Slowly, Mrs Benson turns to regard Abby, peering at her like an exhibit under glass. *These things, they don't belong here,* she tells Abby. *They're not like us.*

Regan gets to her feet and places a cautionary hand on Abby's elbow, attempting to defuse the situation. *Mrs Benson, perhaps you should sit down...*

Abby shrugs her off impatiently, her eyes never leaving the old woman. *And who the hell is 'us'?* she spits. *Does 'us' mean my black ass too, or just your pasty old white one?*

Mrs Benson looks around the room, appealing for support. *These are things from outside our culture, outside our country!* she cries. *We need to stop them coming in...*

Mr Lutz, a burly, bearded man who until now has mostly been staring at the floor, looks up and makes a growl of approval.

His voice sounding increasingly frayed, Isaac appeals for calm. *Please, Mrs Benson, this isn't helping...*

Ignoring him, Abby advances on her opponent. *You just an old racist, is all.*

Mrs Benson's eyes gleam. *Racist? Is it racist to point out that the demon who took you originated from a foreign country? From Africa?*

Abby makes a rude noise. *So what? Ain't like he needed no green card to possess my ass.*

If Tonio Pérez had never met my brother, Joel would still be alive now, Mrs Benson says firmly.

Say it, lady, Abby taunts her. *Say what you wanna say.*

Oh, it isn't just about what I want to say, the old woman tells her. *I've just come from a fundraiser for Greg Stillson, and he had some very interesting things to say about immigration in this country.*

That sorry cracker asshole? Abby scoffs. *He gonna send us all back where we came from when he's president, that right?*

Mrs Benson glances back towards Mr Lutz, seeking reinforcements. *I think we can all agree something needs to be done...*

Yeah, to make the good old US of A safe again for whitey, right? Eyes flaring with anger, Abby roughly shoves her opponent in the shoulder, causing her to stumble backwards.

Now it is Mr Lutz's turn to spring to his feet. He rushes to the old woman's side, placing a steadying arm around her shoulders.

But Mrs Benson is barely even aware of his presence. Her hands curling into arthritic claws, she lunges at Abby. *Yes!* the old woman hisses. *Because you know what? I'm sick of all you niggers! I know we're all supposed to be ever so liberal and understanding these days, but I'm fucking sick of it!* Her voice rises to a screech. *All the fucking coons and spics and chinks and the rest of you, you ruined my life! This used to be a good country, and now look at it! Well, I want to be safe again, and if voting for a cracker asshole is what it takes, then I'll damn well do it!*

Immediately, the basement is in uproar. Isaac is restraining Abby from launching herself at Mrs Benson, while Mr Lutz inserts himself between the two women. The rest of the group have leapt to their feet and clustered round the fracas, alternatively yelling angry epithets and fevered encouragement. Katherine glances around to see that even Needy has joined in, shrieking from the periphery and gesturing angrily towards Mrs Benson.

She might be back at Bramford. Fourteen years old again, listening to the other girls bitch and gossip and argue. Always on the outside staring in.

Katherine realises she cannot bear it any more, and before she knows it she is up on her feet and running towards the stairwell, without a word or a look back for Needy or Regan or anyone.

Her feet clatter up the steps and then she is outside again, her breath misting in the cold air. A freezing rain is falling from the sky, and all of a sudden, the comforting warmth of the synagogue basement, the coffee and the donuts and the rest of it, everything that was good just a few short moments ago, seems half a world away.

Katherine pulls her thin jacket around her, and wonders where a person goes next when they have absolutely nowhere left to go.

Hey.

A soft voice from behind her causes Katherine to spin around. Regan stands in the stairwell doorway, backlit by the single bulb illuminating the basement entrance. Despite her diminutive stature, for a moment she seems to tower over Katherine; an unknowable black shadow, so like the one that had appeared to her at school all those years ago.

Katherine's breath dies in her throat, but then Regan steps forward, the glow from a nearby streetlight catching her face, and Katherine can see that she is smiling.

I'm sorry about before, Regan says. *It isn't normally like that. People just seem to get so damn angry these days.*

It's okay, Katherine mumbles.

Regan shakes her head firmly. *It really isn't, Katherine. You came here looking for help, and you got a civil war instead. Please…let me make it up to you.*

You don't have to do that.

I know I don't. And I can't do much. But I can at least offer you a bath and a home-cooked meal. A place to stay for a night or two. Sound good?

Katherine considers the proposal for a moment, her eyes drifting up to the sky. The rain is still falling, and she spots a throb of lightning amongst the distant clouds. No one should be outside on a night like this, even someone as damned as her.

I'll even throw in a cup of hot chocolate. With marshmallows, of course.

Despite herself, Katherine smiles at the thought of it. And then, before she can even think to resist, Regan has linked arms with her and is leading Katherine towards her waiting car.

Regan lives alone in a cosy rent-controlled apartment in the East Village. Sitting Katherine down at the kitchen table, she proceeds to set about preparing a meal of pasta and salad, humming brightly to herself as she cooks. Katherine says nothing, content to watch her host work, soothed by the unfamiliar domesticity of it.

When the food is ready, Regan joins her at the table to eat, pouring them both a glass of red wine to accompany the meal. Katherine is too embarrassed to admit she has never drunk wine, and hesitantly sips at the ruby liquid. She does not honestly know if she likes the taste, but finds herself picking up the glass with increasing frequency anyway, relishing the soothing warmth that is seeping outwards from her belly.

So when Regan reaches over to top up her glass, Katherine does not demur. Her tongue freed by the alcohol, she at last feels liberated to speak.

So you're like me too? she asks Regan.

The other woman's eyes immediately drift to some faraway place. She nods distantly, putting down her fork. *It was a long time ago,* she murmurs. *I was just a kid. I don't even know why it chose me.*

As Regan continues to recount her story, Katherine finds herself astonished by the similarities between them. Two lonely adolescent girls with oft-absent or missing parents, seduced by dark entities posing as friends and playmates. Girls who were then subjected to appalling abuse and violence, and forced to kill in their malefic master's name. Two priests had died saving Regan from her demon, and despite the aching hole he left inside her, Katherine suddenly finds herself glad that Father Brian did not suffer a similar fate.

Still, Regan seems happy enough now, whereas Katherine cannot imagine ever being happy again. She is wondering how to admit this to her new friend, when Regan asks her, *What was its name? The demon that took you?*

He called himself Black Philip. Katherine's voice dropped to an awed whisper. *But I think he might have been the Devil.*

Ah, they all say that, laughs Regan. *Mine did too. Turned out he was just some old wind demon called Pazuzu.*

Oh, says Katherine, somewhat disappointed. She didn't like to admit that being chosen by the Devil had made her feel important, for the first and only time in her life.

It's okay, honey, Regan says, giving Katherine's hand a reassuring squeeze.

Katherine's eyes meet hers. *Do you ever…miss him?*

She expects Regan to react with shock and disdain, or simply laugh in her face. But instead, the other woman grows pensive. *Not any more,* she says finally. *But I know what you mean. It's so intimate, isn't it? Having someone that knows you so well. And despite how they treat you, the terrible things they make you do…when they're gone, it feels as though part of you has gone too.*

Katherine begins to sob helplessly. *I miss him. I'm so alone and I've got no one. I miss him so much.*

Regan leaps up from her chair and goes to Katherine, taking the sobbing girl into her arms. *Shhhh, sweetheart. I know, I know. But it does get easier,*

I promise. She reaches up and strokes Katherine's hair. *Do you want me to tell you what makes it easier?*

W-what?

Having friends to take care of you.

But I don't h-have any friends! I don't know anyone!

You know me.

Yeah, but –

Listen to me, Katherine. You're a sweet, lovely girl who's been through an awful lot. Well, I'm here to help you, and to be your friend. And sometimes, one friend is all you need to get you started. Why, I'm pretty sure that you'll have all the friends you can handle before you know it.

Regan reaches down to wipe the tears from Katherine's eyes. *And that, my girl, is a solemn promise.*

Katherine nods. *Okay.*

Now, how about that hot bath?

Regan runs her a bath filled with bubbles, and pours her another glass of wine to take into the tub with her. By now, Katherine is quite sleepy with all the food and alcohol, and lies drowsily in the bathtub, drifting in and out of wakefulness. For a time, the only sounds she is aware of are the soft crackle of the dissipating soap bubbles and her own shallow breathing, but eventually she begins to hear a voice talking somewhere else in the apartment: Regan, seemingly deep in conversation with someone.

She must be on the telephone, Katherine realises, and allows herself to drift away again. The distant chatter continues for some time, and although Katherine's sleep-fogged mind can only discern about one word out of five, she eventually decides that Regan must be talking to an acquaintance in the military, one she keeps addressing as 'Captain'.

Eventually, there is a gentle knock at the door. *You okay in there?* Regan asks softly.

Katherine sits up. *I'm fine.*

I don't wanna drag you out or anything, but I'm going to hit the sack soon, if that's alright? It's been a helluva long day.

Katherine murmurs her assent, and quickly clambers out of the tub and dries herself. Donning a bathrobe Regan gave her, she opens the bathroom door to find the other woman waiting in the hallway.

Wow, Regan tells her. *There was a real live girl under there. A pretty one, too.*

Thanks, Katherine says shyly.

Come on, Katherine, Regan says. *The rest of your life awaits.*

She leads Katherine to the guest bedroom, an unfussy but comfortable room whose only adornment is the array of stuffed toys piled upon the bed. Clearing most of them to a nearby shelf, Regan pulls back the bedclothes for Katherine.

I'm sure you'll be comfortable here, she says. *I'm just down the hall if you need anything. Now, you get a good night's sleep. Everything's gonna look real different in the morning, I promise.*

She gives Katherine a hug and exits the room, pulling the door closed behind her.

Her exhaustion mounting with every second, Katherine throws off the bathrobe and climbs into bed. She barely has time to pull an old teddy bear to her chest before sleep claims her.

The next thing she knows, the room around her is completely dark. Katherine attempts to sit up, but, try as she might, she cannot move. Despite Regan's apartment being situated in the very heart of the city, there is no light pollution spilling through the bedroom curtains, and she cannot hear a single sound – somehow, there is not merely silence in the room, but a total *absence* of noise, as though she has awoken into a vacuum, a bottomless, infinite abyss.

Still, she understands that she is not alone. Katherine thinks she can smell some form of exotic incense, and masked underneath that, something lingering and acrid, a vaguely uriniferous smell, but emitted by no manner of creature she can identify.

Something is here with her. Something inexpressibly old, and malevolent.

He's never left me.

Regan's disembodied voice, whispering in her ear.

He can't ever get back in, but all these years, he's been here by my side. I can't take it any more. I need someone else to take him from me. I've been searching all this time, you see. Most of the others from the group, they're too old. I thought Needy might be the one for a little while, but it's you, Katherine. You're just what Captain Howdy wants.

The next thing Katherine knows, the room is filled with the sound of whirring locusts, and a bloodless, black-lipped face grins horribly at her out of the darkness. She closes her eyes and tries to scream, but feels a great set of wings closing around her, crushing the breath from her lungs, pulling her into the entity's embrace.

She can do nothing to resist him. Her mind cries out for her lost love, but of course Black Philip is far from here, back in the dark New England woods he calls home.

Now, there is only Pazuzu.

Katherine's new paramour is alien, insectile. He speaks with the chitinous buzz of a thousand insects, not the alluring purr of a demon lover. Instead of seducing her, he merely takes what he desires by force.

She belongs to him now.

But lying there helpless at the centre of that great black void, Katherine tells herself that at least she won't be alone anymore.

R. J. MacREADY

Kurt Russell in The Thing, *1982*
written by Bill Lancaster
based on the story by John W. Campbell Jr.
directed by John Carpenter

T HE TWO MEN SIT HUDDLED AMONGST THE BURNING REMAINS OF THEIR camp, the scattered fires casting an infernal glow over the vast white silence surrounding them. They pass a bottle of whisky back and forth, each watching the flames slowly dwindle, saying nothing. They know that when the fire eventually dies, so will they.

Above the crackling of the flames, a hollow, desolate howl can be heard. It is only the Antarctic wind gusting through the wreckage of what was once Outpost 31, but to their ears it sounds like the cry of some great unearthly beast.

One of the pair, a black man named Childs, shivers. Perhaps in fear, perhaps only because of the cold. Either way, he takes another slug of whisky in an attempt to steady himself.

His companion, a heavily-bearded man who goes by the name of MacReady, smiles wearily.

Childs gazes over at him, the reflected flames flickering in his eyes. *What's so funny, MacReady?*

MacReady reaches gingerly for the bottle, careful not to aggravate his cracked ribs. Eventually, Childs relinquishes it to him. *I was just thinking of a story my grandaddy used to tell me*, the other man explains. *About the Wendigo.*

And just what the fuck is a Wendigo?

MacReady gazes out across the snow. *It's some kinda ancient demon that lives in the wind.*

Fuck that shit, Childs growls. *Ain't we got enough to worry about without you bringing up goddamn demons too?*

A resigned shrug. *I suppose, yeah.*

They sit in silence for a few more moments before Childs speaks again, as much to drown out the persistent moan of the wind as anything else. *How'd you end up in this frozen shithole anyway, MacReady?*

That is a very long story, Childs.

Childs scoffs. *Not too damn long, I hope. Cause I don't know exactly how much time we have left.*

MacReady takes a pull on the bottle. *I've never told anyone this story.*

You never tell shit to anyone, Childs replies impatiently. *Just sit up there in your cabin drinking all goddamn day.*

A sigh. *You really wanna know?*

Well, this could kinda be your last chance to get it off your chest, don't ya think?

MacReady considers this, then nods. *Fuck it*, he mutters. *Well, for starters, MacReady isn't my name, my real name. The R.J. doesn't even stand for anything, I just liked the way it sounded. Back when I was a kid, my name was Paul Hasleman.*

The other man snorts. *Well, 'Paul', I'm gonna keep right on calling you MacReady, if that's okay with you.*

A shrug. *That's all anyone's called me for the last fifteen years or so.* Another swallow of whisky. *But before that, back when I was still Paul, couldn't have been more than thirteen or so, the snow started talking to me.*

Childs goggles at him for a moment, then bursts into uproarious laughter. The frozen darkness surrounding them immediately transforms the sound of his amusement into something bleak and pitiful, and perhaps realising this, he stops. *Christ,* he says. *I knew you were nuts, MacReady, but don't that take it all.*

MacReady traces a line in the snow with one gloved finger. *Yeah, that's what they all said.*

Okay, shoot. What did the snow tell you?

Nothing, really, A scowl flashes across his face. *Look, it wasn't about that, see? The snow was a whole other world I could escape into. Somewhere quiet and peaceful, somewhere no one could bother me.*

Childs turns to look at the wreckage of the destroyed outpost, the airless whiteness of the landscape gradually reasserting itself as the flames begin to die away. He grins, the smile never reaching his eyes. *Well, hell. I guess wishes really can come true, right?*

MacReady cranes his head back and gazes up at the dark emptiness of the night sky, the cold bright stars like a thousand eyes studying him from on high. How many more of those Things were out there? How many other worlds had they assimilated? Maybe all of them. Maybe Earth was the last place left in the universe, and it was all Things out there now, gazing back at him and silently waiting for their victory to be complete.

He spits into a fire burning nearby, as if to try and hasten its dissolution, however minutely. *My parents called in a doctor, but he didn't know what the hell to do with me. Eventually I told my mom I hated her and stopped speaking altogether. A few weeks later they gave up trying to reach me and threw me in the nut hatch.*

Childs reaches over to take the bottle. *That's pretty rough.*

It wasn't so bad at first. The other kids mostly left me alone, so I could just sit there and listen to the snow. He laughs sourly. *Of course, by then it was about eighty degrees outside. But the doctors there made me take all these pills, and after a while I stopped hearing it.*

You got better.

No, I got worse. MacReady's eyes grow distant. *See, now that I couldn't hear the snow, I got angry. I started having these violent fits. One time, my folks came to visit and I hit my dad with a chair.*

The other man hoots. *Shit, what I wouldn't have given to bust a chair over my old man's head!*

Course, they called it all sorts of fancy names, tried to make out like I was schizo or something, but I knew that wasn't it. There wasn't anything wrong with me that I could tell. I just wanted to be left the fuck alone. I'd already seen enough of the world to know that it was a dirty, shitty place, and I didn't want a damn thing to do with it.

Childs takes a ruminative sip of whisky. *That's one way of looking at it, I guess.*

So eventually they gave up on me. Figured I was a hopeless case. MacReady's eyes gleam in the firelight. *Doctors don't like that, you know. They figure it makes them look bad, like people might wise up and start asking whether those big medical bills are really worth it.*

So what happened?

I busted out. No one was paying much attention by that point, so it was easy, really. The hard part was deciding what to do next. I lived rough for a while, rode the rails, stuff like that. All I wanted was to hear the snow again. But I never did. I figured it had just found some other kid to talk to. And without it, I was lost.

That's a real sad story, MacReady. Childs winks, then leans over and offers him the bottle. *Never thought I'd end up feeling sorry for your crazy ass.*

MacReady accepts the whisky, then flips him the bird. *Fuck you, Childs.*

So what then, little lost boy?

A shrug. *One day this chickenhawk tried to pick me up in the bus terminal. I followed him into the bathroom, and then I just fuckin' lost it, and hit him real hard. He fell down and hit his head on the bowl, there was fuckin' blood everywhere. I thought I'd killed him. Hell, maybe I did. I'll never know.*

MacReady exhales slowly, the ghost of his confession hovering in the air between them. *So I grabbed his wallet, then panicked and ran. When I looked inside the wallet, there wasn't much more than a few bucks and a picture of the guy's kids. Next thing I knew I was passing an army recruitment centre. Do your patriotic duty and come and kill godless commies in Vietnam. Well, I was so scared they were gonna nail me for killing that guy I went straight inside and joined up. I used his name, MacReady.*

Childs raises an eyebrow. *Guess they weren't too fussy who they took, huh?*

They asked me what I wanted to do, so I said I wanted to fly. I figured if I got up high enough, I might hear the voice of the snow again. A wry cackle. *Course, I didn't tell them that. Anyway, I aced all the tests, I was a smart kid back then. I must've been, because I didn't have any of the right background paperwork to apply to flight school. But they needed chopper pilots badly, and I guess someone somewhere looked the other way, because next thing I knew I was off to boot camp, followed by another nine months training to get my wings.*

How many tours?

MacReady holds up four fingers, and Childs whistles. *Shit. You really are nuts. Surprised you didn't get your lily-white ass shot off.*

I didn't know what the hell else to do, MacReady admits. *But yeah, that last tour was rough. I remember this one evac. A whole platoon, almost wiped out. But it was the damnedest thing, it looked like they'd attacked themselves. There was no trace of any Cong anywhere. Fuckin' fugazi. There was this one guy we picked up, his guts were hanging out of his belly. But he clung on for the whole ride back to base. The medic said he'd never seen anyone who wanted to live so bad. We figured he must have unfinished business somewhere.*

He holds the bottle of whisky up to the dim light, checking the volume of liquid inside, then takes a drink. *That's when I knew I was done. I had unfinished business too, see? I wanted to hear the snow again before I bought it for good. So I finished the tour, got my discharge and came home. A couple years later, I answered an advertisement for chopper pilots. 'Come see the frozen asshole of the world', I think it said. So I figured this was my big chance.* The pilot takes another gulp, then slumps wearily against the shattered wall to his right. *Shit, I always wanted to be an explorer when I was a kid.*

Guess you came to the right place to hear snow, Childs replies, looking around him.

Yeah, you'd think.

Childs scowls. *Shit, MacReady, I don't hear nothing but goddamn snow out here! You mean to tell me it still won't speak to you?*

MacReady offers him the remaining whisky. *Looks like we're almost done*, he says quietly. After Childs accepts the bottle, the pilot turns and stares off into the encroaching darkness. *Nothing, the whole time I was here*, he murmurs. *I started to think that maybe the doctors were right all along, that I was crazy after all.*

Hell, I don't need a doctor to tell you that.

But then, recently…I don't know. MacReady rubs at the frost gathering on his beard. *Maybe. I felt like there was something. Very faint, like a radio signal drifting out of range. But I thought if I sat up there in my shack and concentrated, I might be able to tune into it.* His eyes drill into Childs. *And then all this shit started.*

Seemingly oblivious to MacReady's gaze, the other man drains the whisky bottle, then flips it upside down and stabs the neck into the snow. *That's all she wrote*, he announces, then glances around at the camp. *Fire's almost out.*

MacReady stares at him, unblinking. *So what happens now?*

Childs meets his gaze. His eyes are suddenly empty, almost lifeless. *I think you know, MacReady.*

Yeah. A pause. *So when did you take him?*

There is a moment of silence, then Childs's face seems to stretch and shift for an instant, as though it were an ill-fitting Halloween mask in need of adjustment. *We found him wandering outside in the snow*, he says, in a voice that is simultaneously Childs and yet not-Childs. *He would have died if we had not taken him.*

He is dead, MacReady spits. *Don't try and pretend he isn't.*

He is in here, with us, the Childs-thing says. *It is simply a matter of perspective. Our consciousness is very different from yours, MacReady.*

I gotta hand it to you, the pilot says ruefully. *You get better at this every time. I mean, Palmer was a fuckin' freak anyway, and Norris – well, they always say you should watch the quiet ones. As for Blair, he'd already lost the plot before you took him. But it took me a while with Childs. He was the same surly motherfucker I'd always known.*

The Childs-thing stares blankly back at him. *Tell me, MacReady. Did the snow really talk to you? Or was this some attempt at humour?*

Macready lets out a bitter laugh. *I guess that doesn't make much sense to you. Well, human beings don't make a hell of lotta sense. Someone maybe should've warned you about that.* Idly, the pilot plucks the empty whisky bottle out of the snow and begins to turn it over in his hands. *So here's my question: what happens to your fancy fuckin' extraterrestrial consciousness if you assimilate someone as crazy as me?*

In a flash, the Thing slips back into its Childs persona. *I guess we won't know till we try, will we?* Laughter rumbling in its chest, it raises one hand, Child's thick fingers already starting to twist and lengthen like taffy, long enough to reach all the way out from the depths of a nightmare and grab you.

Immediately, MacReady lashes out and smashes the whisky bottle against the nearby wall, raising the jagged remains to his throat. *What about if you take someone who's already dying?*

The Childs-thing freezes, its fingers slowly retracting. *Why resist?* it asks him. *You're going to die anyway. At least this way, a part of you will live on with us forever.*

MacReady snorts. *Yeah? Well, I've never been much of a people person. So that doesn't sound like any sort of party I'd want to attend.*

What do you want?

Here's what I propose. You go your way, I go mine. We're both gonna lie down and go to sleep in the ice anyway. Only difference is that one day, you might get to wake up again.

And you?

The pilot gazes up into the black sky, where the snow is starting to fall once more. *Maybe...maybe I'll get to hear it one more time before I go,* he murmurs.

That's all? You don't want to try and stop us?

MacReady slumps exhaustedly. *What the fuck do I care any more? If you want the damn planet so bad, take it. It's not like I'll be around to see it.*

The Childs-thing is silent for several long seconds. Finally, it nods. *You're a strange man, MacReady.*

Yeah, that's what they tell me. Wincing at his injuries, the pilot hauls himself unsteadily to his feet. *Well, I guess I'll say goodnight. Enjoy the rest of your party.*

MacReady staggers away into the darkness, occasionally glancing back over his shoulder at the imitation of the man he once knew as Childs. The

Thing does not move, remaining in place amongst the wreckage, like a watchful mantis poised motionless upon a plant stem.

Eventually, as the pilot reaches the periphery of the campsite, he gives one final look back, but can see nothing but a blur. The Childs-thing has been swallowed by the night.

MacReady turns and stumbles on through the snow, through the freezing dark. He can feel the indelible stain of the Antarctic cold settling into his bones, spreading throughout his body. It won't be long now.

But he resists and forces himself onwards, because there's something else out here now. Maybe it's the Wendigo, just like his grandaddy always said, lying in wait to tear him limb from limb and greedily devour his flesh.

But maybe it's something else: a distant voice speaking to him, growing clearer and clearer with every ragged step he takes away from the ruins of Outpost 31.

I'm coming, MacReady bellows into the howling wind. *Wait for me, I'm coming!*

And finally, after so many long, silent years, the snow replies, in that same seamless hiss he remembers from his childhood. *Listen, Paul! Are you ready to hear our story now? The same story we began when you were a boy?*

Yes, yes! he cries.

You haven't forgotten how it goes?

No, I still remember! I do!

Shrieking his gleeful affirmation to the skies, MacReady collapses to his knees, his tears of joy freezing instantly to gleaming diamonds on his cheeks.

The little lost boy has at last found his way home.

> *"The hiss was now becoming a roar – the whole world was*
> *a vast moving screen of snow – but even now it said peace, it*
> *said remoteness, it said cold, it said sleep."*

Silent Snow, Secret Snow, by Conrad Aiken

DAVID NORLISS

Roy Thinnes in The Norliss Tapes, *1973*
written by William F. Nolan
directed by Dan Curtis

(Note: the following passages have been transcribed from tape #18 of the so-called 'Norliss Tapes', a collection of recorded notes the writer David Norliss was compiling for his work-in-progress, a book originally intended to debunk the supernatural. But, according to his publisher Sanford Evans, events had taken an unexpected turn while Norliss was in the process of researching the book, and the writer subsequently insisted he would not be able to write it, at least not as initially planned. Norliss then disappeared under somewhat mysterious circumstances, but Evans continued to receive further instalments of the tapes in the mail for several months afterwards. Tape #18, however, was the last known recording sent to him. David Norliss has never been found.)

NORLISS: Chapter 18.

Today is July 12th. Forgive me, Sanford, if the following is a little scattershot. I've been up all night drinking, and my mental health is in pretty lousy shape these days anyway. I've gone deeper on this than I ever intended to, and I think I might finally have gone too deep. I don't believe there's any way back for me now, and my only hope is that these tapes might somehow do some good.

I don't mean as a book, mind – we're way beyond that. No. Sorry, old friend, but you're gonna have to write off that rather sizeable advance of yours. This is no longer a book, certainly not one you could ever publish.

This is a warning.

Christ, where does one start, when you've arrived at the very end without even realising it?

I guess you start at the beginning – the beginning of the end, that is.

I guess you start with Joe Frady.

I can imagine what you're thinking right now. That Joe Frady? The nut who gunned down Senator George Hammond?

Well, hear me out, Sanford. I don't believe Frady killed Hammond, any more than you or I did, but that isn't even my point. It's too late for Joe now, just as it's too late for me.

Anyway. In case you didn't know, Frady used to be a hell of a reporter back in the day. But in the end, he ruffled too many feathers, drank too much, pissed on too many of the wrong doorsteps, and wound up at some backwater local paper trying to hustle up stories where there weren't any to be hustled. I've known Joe a long time, and I think it was killing him. We didn't see each other that much any more, but we spoke on the phone a few times a year, usually just to bitch about our editors or whatever, and I could hear it in his voice. Like he was gonna start drinking again, or shoot someone, or some other goddamn thing.

Yeah, I know how that sounds. I still don't think he did it, and maybe once you finish listening to this you'll understand why.

But I digress. The important thing is, the last time Frady called me, he sounded different. He was onto something big, he said. So big it would rattle the foundations of the entire fucking country.

That's pretty big, I said, my tongue firmly wedged in my cheek.

But Joe wasn't joking. He asked me if I'd ever heard of a company named Parallax. I hadn't, just sounded like a camera manufacturer or something to me. But no. According to him, they were in the business of recruiting assassins. You know, the kind of guys who end up in the headlines for shooting Jack, or Bobby… or Senator George Hammond.

I wasn't sure how to take this at first – it sounded pretty far out – but I trusted Joe, and he <u>seemed</u> sober, so I let him talk. He didn't know too much else yet, but he had some leads that he was gonna chase down. And he sounded excited, you know? Just like the old Frady. He was convinced this was a major story.

Anyway, before he hung up, Joe said one more thing to me. He asked me if I was still working on my book – 'that mumbo-jumbo book', he called it and when I said I was, he told me I might want to look into Thorn Industries. You know them, right, Sanford? They make everything from soda pop to Agent Orange. Just another good old-fashioned American corporation.

So I was like, what the hell do Thorn have to do with anything? If this is about the goddamn 'Thorn Curse', that story's old enough to draw flies.

Nothing like that, he insisted. He told me he'd turned up a few interesting connections between Parallax and Thorn, which was what had got him started on this. But Thorn itself was outside the scope of what he was working on, so he hadn't paid the whole thing too much attention…until he started to notice a pattern. A very particular pattern, and one he thought might interest me.

'It's all connected,' he told me. 'I don't know exactly <u>how</u> yet, but it is.'

He told me he was gonna send me some documents in the mail, and that he didn't know when I might hear from him again. Then he said he was afraid he was being watched, and that we should only communicate with each other from now on by using the classifieds in the San Francisco Chronicle.

By now this was all getting pretty out to lunch, but like I said, I've known Frady a long time. So I said sure Joe, whatever you think's best.

A day or two later, I got his package in the mail. I didn't pay it too much mind at first, don't think I'd even looked at it when I saw on the news that Frady was missing at sea, presumed dead after a freak explosion on a yacht. Of course, we all know now he wasn't dead, not <u>then</u> anyway, but at the time it shook me up pretty badly. Not only because he was an old friend, but after everything he'd said to me…

'It's all connected.'

That afternoon I sat down and went through the research materials he'd sent. A pattern, he'd said.

I was half-expecting there to be nothing, that maybe Joe had been losing it after all.

But no, there it was. Clear as day. Clear as fucking Thallium. You know what they call Thallium, Sanford? The 'poisoner's poison'. Because it's odourless, tasteless and colourless.

I'm digressing again. Or maybe I'm not. Fuck it.

Frady had sent me documentation relating to a whole mess of seemingly unrelated incidents, the sorts of incidents he thought might pertain to the book I was currently researching. All well and good, one writer helping out another, yadda yadda.

But then I looked a little closer, and it turned out that maybe these incidents weren't all that unrelated after all.

For starters, there was that rash of so-called 'monster babies' being born around the country. You remember <u>that</u> one, right, Sanford? Who could forget? The Davis kid in LA, the Mallory baby in Seattle, then another one in LA... All horribly mutated and deformed, all killers. Now, what the hell could do that to a baby, right? That's what everyone wanted to know at the time. But all we got was a helluva lot of scientific hemming and hawing, a lot of frantic covering-up, and a distinct lack of fingers being pointed in any particular direction.

Only the files Frady sent me suggested that the mothers of the monster children had all been prescribed exactly the same brand of contraceptive pills: a brand which had now quietly been taken off the market.

A brand manufactured by a subsidiary of Thorn Industries.

Sure, these things happen. More often than you'd like to think. Wouldn't be the first time a big corporation grievously fucked up and was allowed to quietly sweep the mess underneath the carpet, right?

But there were more documents, a _lot_ more. The next file I came to concerned the strange case of Andy Brooks, a young GI who had supposedly been K.I.A in Vietnam, but had shown up at his parent's home in Florida a few days later, seemingly unharmed. I say 'seemingly' because, as the official narrative has it, the kid had completely lost his marbles while in-country and murdered four people 'in a bizarre fashion' after coming home, before finally being gunned down by police in the local cemetery.

Well, I say 'finally'. The funny thing is, his supposedly dead body went missing from the morgue shortly afterwards, but even that odd little detail isn't what concerns us here.

No, what's of most interest us is the anonymous letter sent shortly after Andy's death to his local newspaper, the Hernando Sun. I have a Xerox of it in front of me. It reads:

Dear Sir,

They are not telling you the Truth about Andy Brooks nor any of the other Patriots from his unit who died in Vietnam. They were not killed by the Viet Cong, nor did Andy just go crazy.

The Truth of it is, the rest of the men from his unit _killed_ _themselves_, while under the influence of a secret psychotropic drug codenamed 'The Ladder'. The drug was designed to heighten aggression in US soldiers and was tested on our men without their knowledge. I helped develop

it during my time with the Chemical Corps,
with funding and personnel supplied by Thorn
Industries.

Ask Richard Nixon and Damien Thorn.
<u>THEY KNOW THE TRUTH</u>.

Poor Andy Brooks never had a chance.

    ANON

Similar letters were sent to newspapers across the
country, but the only ones that ever saw print were
in a handful of the underground rags. The above
letter was apparently retrieved from the Hernando
Sun's crackpot file. The best place for it, you
might say, and you might even be right.

But the thing is, Frady had also managed to
source some classified Thorn company memos, which
<u>all made reference</u> to an unspecified secret project
called 'The Ladder'.

Which casts a whole different light on our
anonymous letter writer, no?

(Damien Thorn, btw, inherited the family company
after the deaths of his uncle Richard Thorn and aunt
Ann in that mysterious fire at the Thorn Museum a
few years back. I'm sure you remember, Sanford. The
Thorn Curse strikes again! Damien himself seems to
be unaffected so far, though – he's currently away
studying in England, with Paul Buher running Thorn
in his place. Interesting that he and not Buher is
the one namechecked in the letter, however.)

And there was more. Plenty more. Frady had done
his legwork, alright. Like I said, he used to be a
hell of a reporter. Maybe he was a little cuckoo

now, but looking at some of this stuff, who wouldn't be?

I mean, just to give you a taste, Thorn's involvement with the Vietnam War went a whole lot further than just dosing our troops with Christ knows what. I have other documents pertaining to a secret bioweapon codenamed 'Trixie', which Thorn also helped develop. Sounds similar to 'The Ladder', in that it drives people homicidally insane. I hope you're as relieved to see that your tax dollars are being well-spent as I am. Anyway, turns out a shitload of this Trixie stuff was accidentally dumped in a Pennsylvania town's water supply not too long ago, with predictable results. Still, you might wonder how they managed to hush that one up. I certainly did. It's a long story, one I won't get into now. But one small detail might interest you – when I went to look up the town in question on a map, it wasn't there any more. Like it had never even existed. Make of _that_ what you will.

Or there was 'Operation Razorteeth', tasked with developing a mutant strain of piranha that could survive in the rivers of North Vietnam. A little something to give Charlie a scare next time he goes for a paddle. I know, I know, it all sounds like a bad B-movie, Sanford, but I've seen the fucking files. And of course the piranhas got loose in American waters and chewed up a whole bunch of people. Oops-a-fucking-daisy, right?

But at what point do you start asking yourself this: how long can a string of so-called accidents get before you can start to tie a noose with it? When does coincidence turn into conspiracy? What I'm saying is, Sanford, when you sit down and go through all this stuff, it starts to look a lot less like bad luck and more like someone is laying the groundwork for something.

And no, don't ask me precisely what. I'm not crazy enough to go there.

Yet.

By the time I got to accounts of the dead coming back to life, even I was ready to call it a night. (Of course, this was before my own little encounter with a certain James Cort.) But there it was. A space probe – built by, you guessed it, Thorn – crashing down to Earth and infecting corpses with radiation that somehow caused them to come back to life as cannibalistic zombies. Or, shortly afterwards, an experiment with ultra-sonic radiation carried out by Thorn's UK operation on behalf of the British government. Now, this was supposedly all good, benign stuff, designed only to keep insects away from crops. Only – oops again! – same result. The dead rising from the grave to devour the living.

Both small-scale incidents, both hushed up. Still, you surely have to ask yourself: it must be fucking hard enough to accidentally resurrect the dead once. But <u>twice</u>?

And still there's more. But, Sanford, this whisky bottle is now empty and I'm sure you're as sick of listening to this horrorshow as I am. Hopefully I've made my point. So let me skip forward a ways and see if I can make it through to the end.

So, as far as I knew at this point, Frady was dead. Still, part of me kept one eye on the Chronicle classified section like we'd agreed. I just couldn't believe Joe was gone, I guess. He was always such a slippery bastard.

Then one day I saw the ad. It read:

    DN - I'm alive, but not feeling quite myself
    these days. Been deep sea fishing and I have
    a big catch for you. Mount Davidson, noon
    tomorrow. Make sure you come alone. JF

So he <u>was</u> alive. And deep undercover, that much was
obvious. By this point, as you'll remember, I'd
pulled my own little vanishing act, and I figured we
both probably had a lot to tell each other. So I
rose early the next morning and got a head start.
'Make sure you come alone' - to me, that meant he
thought I might be followed. Now, he wasn't to know
that no one knew where the hell I was either, but
what the hell. I changed cabs three times just in
case. I guess paranoia really is contagious.
    I got to Mount Davidson a little before eleven.
I guessed he meant for me to meet him by the cross
on the mount, so I walked up there, coughing my
lungs out and cursing Frady the whole goddamn way.
Trust a non-smoker to make a smoker walk up to the
highest natural point in the city. Anyway, I finally
made it up there, and the place seemed deserted
enough. But I hung back in the trees anyway. No
sense in advertising myself.
    I saw a few people wander by, just locals out for
a walk. But nothing suspicious. The only remotely
odd thing I saw was this big black bird, perched on
a tree nearby. It was too big to be a crow, but they
say ravens don't tend to come into cities. Anyway,
I swear this goddamn bird seemed to be watching me.
I was letting the whole thing get to me, I guess.
In the end I threw a rock at it and it flew off.
    Frady showed up a short time later. I hadn't seen
him for a few years, and he looked well - tanned
and healthy. Certainly not like he was hitting the

bottle again. But squirrelly. You could see it in his eyes. When I walked over to him he spent the whole time looking over my shoulder, as if there was someone stood right behind me. And when I greeted him, he raised a finger to his lips. 'It's <u>Richard</u>. Joe is lying dead at the bottom of the ocean, remember?'

I don't know how long we spoke for. He told me he'd infiltrated Parallax, posing as some kind of crazed sex offender. We had a good laugh over that, despite everything. He thought that they were lining him up to carry out their next assassination, and as soon as he had enough evidence, he was gonna blow the roof off the whole thing. It still sounded completely crazy to me, but hell, these are crazy times. And I could see Joe had the bit between his teeth. He thought this one was gonna win him the Pulitzer.

'Be careful,' I said. 'If these people are killers like you say, they won't think twice about offing some local reporter no one particularly gives a damn about.'

'You sure know how to hurt a guy, Dave,' he said with a grin, shrugging it off. But that was Joe. It wasn't like he ever gave much of a damn about anything himself. Then his grin faded. 'Did you read through those files I sent?'

I told him I had, and that while a year ago I might have laughed the whole thing off, no matter how much paperwork he waved in my face, recently I've been having a lot more trouble pretending that there's nothing lurking in the dark that wants to hurt us.

'I know what you mean,' he said quietly. 'These days I always check under the bed before I go to sleep at night. Guess I'm really starting to lose it, huh?'

But I didn't think so, and told him that. Joe sighed, and looked up at that big concrete cross towering over us. He took a step closer, and reached out a hand to touch it. It seemed to comfort him somehow.

Then he told me that he was sure Parallax were being financed by Thorn, even though maybe only two or three people at the very top of the company were privy to it. Think about it: on the one hand they're sweeping up all these juicy military-industrial government contracts, and then on the other, taking dark money to knock off senators and presidential candidates! He didn't know what sort of game they were playing, but was certain who was holding the cards: 'Paul Buher, the acting CEO. Possibly one or two others. And Damien Thorn for sure.'

'But he's still a kid,' I said. 'He's not even in the goddamn country.'

'I'm telling you, it all comes back to Damien Thorn. I don't know how or why yet. But his name on keeps cropping up, and people around him keep on dying. The Thorn Curse, right?'

'You think that has something to do with Parallax?'

'No, it isn't their style.' He suddenly looked very tired. 'Hell, I don't fucking know. I'm in way too deep on this, I can't see the goddamn Thorns for the trees. But maybe <u>you</u> can, Dave.'

We didn't speak for too much longer after that, and when we said our goodbyes, there was an air of finality about it. It felt like Frady knew he wasn't coming back from this. I think even Joe would admit he was always a car crash waiting to happen, but in his mind, he always figured that at least he'd be the one driving the car when it did.

Turned out that wasn't quite the case.

A few days later I saw it on the news: the senatorial candidate George Hammond had been gunned down at a rally dress rehearsal in Los Angeles. A disaffected journalist named Joe Frady had been shot trying to escape from the scene, and was believed to be the lone assassin responsible for Hammond's murder.

Something just snapped inside me, I guess. Christ, Frady and I weren't even all that close, but hearing that report just brought it all home to me. Everything he'd told me had been true. It wasn't as if I hadn't believed him before, exactly; more that part of me just didn't <u>want</u> to. The coward inside me hoped it would all just go away. Only now he'd been dragged kicking and screaming out into the daylight.

And so what the hell was he gonna do about it?

The first thing I did was jump on a plane to Chicago. I took a hotel room and started calling the head offices of Thorn Industries. I'm a writer, I'd like to interview Paul Buher for a book I'm writing yadda yadda. Got the brush-off every time: Mr Buher isn't in the office today, Mr Buher's diary is full, Mr Buher doesn't give interviews.

Eventually I managed to get through to his personal secretary, and when she started to give me the same old routine, I laid it on the line for her. I said, listen honey, all you need to do is give Mr Buher my message, and I guarantee you once he hears it, he is really gonna want to talk to me. And then I just reeled off a list of codenames: 'The Ladder', 'Operation Razorteeth' etc etc. She asked if that was the message, and I said it was and hung up.

Five minutes later I get the call from Buher. 'Mr Norliss. What time is good for you to meet tomorrow?'

I was at the Thorn offices bright and early the next morning, 8:30AM sharp. I was shown through to a private waiting area, given a fresh cup of coffee and a danish, the whole bit. Only then this secretary comes out and apologetically tells me that Mr Buher has unexpectedly been called away on business.

Well, I was just about to completely lose my shit with her when she suddenly says: 'But would you be interested in speaking to Mr Thorn instead?'

'Damien Thorn?' I said.

'Of course,' she replied.

'Excuse me, I was under the impression Mr Thorn was away studying in England.'

'Oh, he is, but he makes regular trips back over here whenever he's able. You're very lucky to have caught him, Mr Norliss.'

'Very lucky,' I agreed.

So without further ado, I was shown into the office of Damien Thorn himself. Now, I guess you don't have to subscribe to Forbes or the Wall Street Journal to know his story. It's tabloid fodder by now. Kid is born into a rich and powerful family, his father Robert Thorn often spoken of as a prospective future president, that and all the rest of it. Only people close to the family keep dying in weird accidents. Then the kid's mother goes crazy and kills herself, and as a result Robert loses his shit and is shot by police just as he's about to murder the kid. In a church, no less. After that, Damien is adopted by his father's brother Richard in the U.S. and everything goes quiet for a while.

But soon enough, accidents start happening again, and before you know it, Richard and a whole lot of other people are dead too.

So, perhaps understandably, Damien Thorn has always been a little press-shy. But here I am, sitting in his office. And this is after I have, in no uncertain terms, made it clear that I intend to make something of a nuisance of myself. Maybe he thinks he can buy me off. Thorn can certainly afford it, and I'm sure there's a company slush fund intended solely for persistent annoyances like me.

Or maybe he just thinks he can have his buddies at Parallax quietly take care of me. At this point, I was thinking it was probably a 50/50 proposition.

Either way, he's sitting there sipping at a freshly-squeezed grapefruit juice like he doesn't have a goddamn care in the world, like I'm just there to shine his shoes. If you asked me to define 'contempt', I'd show you a picture of his face in that moment.

But it was more than that, like what I was looking at was just a mask on top of a mask on top of a mask. As though the contempt was just an act too, disguising whatever really lay underneath.

And more than anything else, part of me knew I never ever wanted to see whatever that was.

I recorded our conversation that day, Sanford, and I've enclosed a copy along with this tape. I think it's better that you hear it yourself.

TWILIGHT'S LAST SCREAMING

<u>TRANSCRIPT OF CONVERSATION BETWEEN DAVID NORLISS &
DAMIEN THORN, RECORDED MORNING OF 16TH OCTOBER 1974</u>

NORLISS: Do you mind if I record this?

THORN: Go ahead. (PAUSE) You seem surprised, Mr
Norliss.

NORLISS: I'd have thought you might want to keep
our conversation off the record.

THORN: (LAUGHS) Very soon there'll come a day when
I'll no longer have anything to hide.

NORLISS: Could be sooner than you think.

THORN: Perhaps.

NORLISS: Brass tacks. Did Mr Buher's secretary pass
the message I left for him onto you?

THORN: She did, yes.

NORLISS: Do you have any comment?

THORN: Mr Norliss, I'm sure you're aware than I
can't speak about top secret work conducted on
behalf of the U.S. Government.

NORLISS: But you do admit that work was carried
out?

THORN: Of course. Thorn has always been proud of
the part we've played in helping to keep this great
country safe, healthy and prosperous.

NORLISS: So, is dosing U.S. soldiers with an untested hallucinogenic what you'd call safe? What about the dangerous virus that was let loose in our own country, or the experiments with radiation that led to some extremely bizarre and frightening side-effects? I mean, these experiments could hardly have gone any worse if you'd planned them that way, could they?

THORN: I'm sure I don't have to explain to you that it is in the nature of experiments to sometimes go wrong.

NORLISS: Quite often, in Thorn's case.

THORN: Squarely within what we would define as an acceptable margin of error.

NORLISS: An acceptable…? People <u>died</u>, Mr Thorn!

THORN: People die every day, don't they? Some of them close to you, I'm sure.

(PAUSE)

NORLISS: And what's that supposed to mean?

THORN: Only that we've all known people who died.

NORLISS: <u>You</u> certainly have.

THORN: You see what I mean, Mr Norliss? None of us are strangers to tragedy. It's the nature of the world, unfortunately.

NORLISS: That much is true, I suppose. (PAUSE) As it happens, a friend of mine did lose his life under tragic circumstances recently.

THORN: My condolences.

NORLISS: He was a journalist, investigating a company called Parallax.

THORN: You and your friends seem to spend an awful lot of time investigating companies, Mr Norliss. Aren't there any actual stories in the world anymore?

NORLISS: He seemed to believe this <u>was</u> a story. I think other people might do too, especially when they learn of Thorn's involvement with Parallax.

THORN: I'm afraid I'm not familiar with them personally. What is it they do?

NORLISS: Quietly, unobtrusively, leaving no trace of their involvement...they arrange to have important people killed.

THORN: (LAUGHS) And I'm sure their services would be very popular in modern day America. I almost wish I'd thought of the idea myself, I'm sure I could make a fortune.

NORLISS: Didn't you?

THORN: Come now, Mr Norliss. You shouldn't let your deceased friend's paranoid fantasies run away with you, no matter how much you miss him.

NORLISS: He had evidence that linked you and other Thorn board members to Parallax. He infiltrated them, you see. And then they killed him.

THORN: Which rather suggests they saw him coming, don't you think?

NORLISS: Just like you saw me coming.

THORN: I'm not sure what you mean.

NORLISS: It wasn't a coincidence you being here today, was it?

THORN: Oh, I'll admit I wanted to meet you.

NORLISS: Why? To see if I could be bought?

THORN: Anything can be bought, Mr Norliss, assuming it has any value as a commodity in the first place. Writers rarely do, alas.

NORLISS: Then <u>what</u>?

THORN: You interested me. I wanted to see what drove you. So many of the people that try to threaten me are nothing but tiresome ideologues.

NORLISS: And me?

THORN: Oh, I don't think you believe in very much at all, do you?
(SILENCE)
I can always use men like that. Empty men, who are waiting to be filled up.

NORLISS: Is this an extremely roundabout way of offering me a job?

THORN: (LAUGHS) You can call it that, if you like. You see, Mr Norliss, you were more correct than you knew. The experiments and their various outcomes were planned, all of them. Oh, certainly they were government contracts, but Thorn had its own particular agenda, quite separate and distinct from Uncle Sam's. It isn't even really accurate to call them 'experiments'. They were, in fact, <u>preparations</u>. We're readying America for the future, you see. We're planning for something far beyond whatever trumped-up little backwater war the US government decides to embark on next, no matter how profitable those wars may have been for Thorn. Something quite far beyond that indeed.

NORLISS: (PAUSE) And what would that be, Mr Thorn?

THORN: There is a great storm coming. A great revelation. This storm will wipe the Earth clean. Baptise it, if you like. Ready to be remade in my Father's image.

NORLISS: Your father? Robert Thorn is dead.

THORN: (LAUGHS) Only the select will survive to populate this brand new world. You could take your place amongst them, Mr Norliss.

NORLISS: You're crazy.

THORN: Am I? Ask yourself, is this any more crazy than infecting American citizens with a virus that drives them homicidally insane, or bringing the dead back to life? Or creating a company that assassinates public figures for profit?

NORLISS: I...I have to leave now.

THORN: You are quite free to go at any time, Mr Norliss. But let us be clear on one thing: the moment you set foot outside this office, my offer to you no longer stands.

NORLISS: I don't even know what you're offering me!

THORN: It is the greatest gift a man can be offered, but only by accepting it will you ever understand its true nature.

NORLISS: And if I just walk out?

THORN: It's a one-time only offer, Mr Norliss. There are no second chances, least of all for you.

(TAPE ENDS)

I left the office shortly after that, Sanford. Even though I was pretty sure I was signing my own death warrant by doing so. That was a week or so ago, and I've been moving from place to place ever since, trying to keep one step ahead of whatever's behind me. I haven't seen anything, you understand, but it's there all the same. Whether it's a flesh and blood assassin, or some amorphous curse, I know it's coming for me. Soon.

So this is my lousy attempt at a warning. I'm sorry if it doesn't make much sense or the loose ends don't tie up, but we've known each other a long time and I've never bullshitted you before, have I? Plus you have the files, and the Damien Thorn tape. Hopefully that will be enough to convince you. I'm sorry to have to drag you into this, but you're about the only person I trust right now. Spread the warning, Sanford. Shout it from the fucking rooftops if you have to, so that poor bastards like me and Joe Frady didn't die in vain.

Because there's a storm coming, my friend. The sky overhead is going dark, and I can hear the sound of distant thunder. I can feel the force of it gathering in the air, taste it on my tongue.

It tastes very much like blood.

(TAPE ENDS)

JAY HEIGHT

Maika Monroe in It Follows, *2014*
written & directed by David Robert Mitchell

BACK WHEN SHE WAS A LITTLE GIRL, JAY'S PARENTS ALWAYS USED TO TELL her how lucky she was to live in a place like Lumberton. And it was true; to a child's eyes, it appeared to be a bright and happy town. The sky overhead appeared fathomless, perpetually, dazzlingly blue; the picket fences whiter than white and neat and orderly as a fashion model's smile. It was a place out of time, where the kids still called their elders *sir* and *ma'am*, and old movies showed on TV all day long. An almost magical realm, representing the very best of America. A town where neighbours looked out for each other, and an apple pie would always be cooling on the windowsill.

But then it was as if a darkness had begun to creep in around the edges. Jay's father had died in a freak accident – although there were persistent rumours he'd been involved with some questionable business acquaintances and that his death had been far from accidental – and all at once, Jay and her mother and younger sister Kelly were left utterly alone in the world.

Suddenly, the sky didn't look quite so blue any more. Suddenly, neighbours began to lock their doors against neighbours.

And as though afflicted with a incurable wasting disease, Lumberton slowly began to decay. Its streets were atrophied limbs, devoid of energy or life, deserted houses multiplying along their lengths like rotting lesions. Poverty and crime took inexorable hold of the town, aggressive cancers devouring it from within. If you stood on your porch in the morning and inhaled, you could almost smell the stench of corruption on the air. Lumberton was sick, dying.

Then, like some dreadful avatar, representing everything that was rotten and shameful about the town, *it* had come.

No one knew what *it* really was. Whispered stories had begun circulating amongst the town's high school students of an entity – a ghost, a demon? – that would kill you if you had sex. But they were the sort of campfire anecdotes that were easily dismissed at first, especially because they all seemed to concern a friend of a friend of a friend. *I knew this guy whose brother's buddy slept with this girl, a real skank, and she passed it onto him.* The story seemed to be little more than a puritanical urban legend, designed to scare adolescents into fearful abstinence.

But then kids had started dying. Not friends of friends any more, but kids everyone knew. The football team's star quarterback, or that cute senior Annie. *You know, the one who was a total fucking bitch but no one deserves that. Did you hear her leg was bent right back, like totally snapped apart?*

Jay had never paid much attention to the stories. She was nineteen and in college now, and sleeping with a guy was no longer the big deal it had seemed to be back in high school, the way it still was to Kelly. She'd recently started dating this guy Hugh and liked him well enough, and knew that before much longer they'd drive out to some private place one evening and curl up together on the backseat of his car, where the only thing to fear would be failing to live up to your new lover's expectations, not some freaky sexually-transmitted monster.

But when that intimate moment finally came, Hugh had drugged her and tied her up, and told Jay that the thing from the stories was real, that it had been following him but would now come for her, unless she passed it onto someone else. Helpless, she'd sat there and watched in horror as this naked woman appeared out of nowhere, bearing down on her like a hungry shark.

Jay had looked into the woman's – *it's* – eyes and seen nothing there, just an empty void, as though she was peering through a powerful telescope into the furthermost reaches of deep space, cold and black and abyssal.

And finally, she'd believed.

They'd escaped from it that night, but Jay soon learned that it was hopeless, that you could never run far enough or fast enough. It was tireless, remorseless, and in the end it would always catch up with you. The thing had killed her friend Greg, and had come very close to killing her. And still, no one knew what it was or how to stop it. Out of desperation, Jay and her friends had devised some ludicrous plan to electrocute it in a swimming pool, the sort of thing that might only have worked in some kind of dream.

Jay reasoned to herself that this *could* all be a dream, that perhaps she was still lying unconscious on the backseat of Hugh's car, lost in a drugged-out haze. It made about as much sense as any other explanation.

But their plan had failed. They'd shot the thing in the head several times, which stopped it temporarily, but Jay knew that it would come back. It always did.

Afterwards, she'd slept with her childhood friend Paul, who'd then driven out to the wasteland on the edge of Lumberton and paid twenty bucks to fuck a hooker, rationalising that the woman would quickly transmit it to someone else, and maybe that way the chain could be safely prolonged for a time. Privately, Jay understood that the plan was little better than the last one. Without the benefit of a warning, the recipients of the infection would inevitably succumb to the creature, and before too long it would return to stalk Jay again, wearing the face of a friend or a lover or even her deceased father.

Jay withdrew inside her bedroom, barricading the door and refusing to speak to anyone. She barely ate or slept, just kept up a blank-eyed vigil at the bedroom window, fingers tightening on the sill every time someone passed by on the street outside. Even Jay's mother, who rarely paid any attention to her children these days, eventually began to notice something was amiss with her eldest daughter. But when she tried to ask Kelly what was wrong with her older sister, the girl just mumbled some excuse about Jay having boyfriend problems. What else could she say?

The next day, Kelly heard that Paul had been found dead in his shower; neck snapped grotesquely backwards, his open mouth filling with water. And she knew that Jay was right to be afraid; that very soon *it* would be arriving for her sister.

She begged her mom to do something. So when Jay still refused to open the door to her, Mrs Height decided that perhaps a male influence might help matters. Her two daughters were good girls, by and large, but she was worried that the long-term lack of a father figure had damaged them in some way. Perhaps it might help if a man spoke to Jay; someone strong and sensible, someone she could respect…?

For some time now, Mrs Height had been conducting a casual relationship with a man named Jeffrey Beaumont, the proprietor of Lumberton's oldest hardware store. Everyone in town saw Jeffrey as a decent, upstanding sort, a trusted pillar of the local community. And while it was true that some of the older folk secretly liked to gossip about the trouble Jeffrey had gotten himself into as a young man, all sorts of scandal involving an older woman and drugs and gangsters and sex and murder, it had been thirty years since the whole sordid business and by now, most of the townspeople were simply unaware it had ever taken place. These days, Lumberton only knew Jeffrey as the smiling, ever-present face behind the counter of the hardware store, the man who could tell you exactly how to hang a door or the difference between a common nail and a smooth box nail.

And even if Mrs Height knew him better than most, knew the forbidden things her lover liked to whisper to her when they lay together in bed at night; recognised the furtive look that crept into his eyes whenever he glanced out of the window and saw Jay sunning herself on the lawn, damp bathing suit clinging to her lithe young body, these were things you didn't speak of in polite company. Besides, they had nothing to do with Jeffrey's ability to offer firm and sensible masculine guidance to her increasingly troubled daughter.

So it was that one afternoon, Mrs Height having spirited Kelly away to the local mall, Jeffrey crept into the Height house and made his way upstairs to Jay's bedroom. Although he had every right to be in the house, had even been given his own front door key by Jay's mother, Jeffrey still got a thrill from sneaking through people's empty homes, peeking in drawers and cupboards as he went. One of the other things Lumberton did not know about him, that even his lover did not know, was that when the townspeople came into his hardware store to get their keys cut, Jeffrey always liked to secretly take an extra copy. That way, he was free to gain access to a property whenever the owners were safely out of town.

Of course, the people of Lumberton would have been appalled if they'd known what he was doing, but Jeffrey told himself that he wasn't hurting anyone. He never took anything, nor caused any sort of damage. No one would ever have known he'd been there; that was the entire point. He just liked to take a look around, to sit in the dark listening to the sounds of the empty house for awhile, and maybe to occasionally steal into a bedroom closet. There, he would peek out through the crack in the door, imagining the homeowners returning, undressing for bed, making love…

He knocked gently on Jay's door. *Jay? It's your mom's friend Jeffrey.*

A frightened voice from inside. *What do you want?*

Jeffrey kept his voice low and calm. He prided himself on his powers of persuasion. *I hear you've been having troubles. Your mom and your sister are very worried. I thought maybe I could help.*

You can't. No one can.

Jay, please listen, he told her. *I know there are things you can't talk to your mom about. And if you know anything about me, you'll know I've seen a few things in my time. There isn't much that can shock me. So if you need a friend, or just someone to talk to, I'm here for you.*

There was silence inside the room for a moment, before he heard the sound of a chest of drawers being dragged away from the door. The next moment, the door opened to reveal Jay, peering out at him like a condemned prisoner. Jeffrey tried to mask his shock at the change in her. Pretty, sleepy-eyed Jay, as sweetly alluring as a strawberry sundae, had become wan and skinny, her once-perfect skin blemished with acne. She reminded him of a piece of fruit left to rot, its flesh turning brown and withered.

Jay gazed at Jeffrey with reddened, weary eyes, the eyes of someone much older than nineteen, and told him, simply, *I'm going to die soon.*

Upon finally coaxing her out of the bedroom, Jeffrey drove her across town to Arlene's Diner. It had been a popular hangout amongst the local kids when he was younger, but much like the rest of the town, the passing years had not been kind to the restaurant, and now Arlene's was an increasingly dingy shadow of the place he had once known. Still, nostalgia or force of habit kept him coming back, and he strongly doubted Jay would care very much where they went.

They selected a corner booth, Jay insisting on sitting with her back to the wall, allowing her a clear view of anyone coming through the door. Jeffrey attempted to crack a joke about her training to be a cop, but Jay's only response was to begin picking at a splinter in the tabletop, and his attempt at humour dissipated in the air as soon as he uttered it. So instead, he hurriedly ordered them both coffee and apple pie and waited for the girl to speak.

Once the waitress had delivered their order, Jay sipped warily at her greasy coffee, then sat back in her seat and began to stare at him. Convinced this was some sort of test, Jeffrey assiduously held her gaze.

Her voice monotone, she finally asked him, *Do you believe there are things in this world we can't ever explain?*

Jeffrey thought about it. *I'll tell you one thing I do know,* he replied. *It's a strange world. Maybe stranger than most people ever realise.*

Jay seemed to accept this, and lapsed back into silence for a moment. Jeffrey did not press her, and when she spoke again, it was to confess everything that had happened to her over the preceding weeks. She left nothing out, telling him every last intimate detail.

As he listened, Jeffrey found himself shifting uncomfortably in his seat, and growing discreetly aroused at certain points in her story.

Jay recounted her bizarre tale with conviction and a hushed but fierce directness, and while no one could conceivably have blamed Jeffrey for scoffing at the horrifically surreal tale, he nevertheless found that he believed her. Listening to Jay speak, he had come to a dreadful understanding about their hometown that had previously eluded him for decades.

When she finally finished, Jeffrey reached across the table and gently took Jay's hand. *And now you think it's coming back for you?*

I know it is, she said. *I can feel it, getting closer.*

He smiled. *Then we'll just have to do something about that, won't we?*

But how? You can't stop it! We tried to kill it, and you can't!

Let me tell you something, Jay, Jeffrey said quietly. *There's a disease in Lumberton. I think there has been, ever since I was your age. All those years ago, something went bad here. Back then, the disease was a man named Frank Booth. A very bad man. Now, I killed Frank, and I thought for a time the disease had gone away. But a disease that bad, that evil…maybe you can't ever stop it. Maybe it just keeps on coming back.*

I don't understand, Jay said.

I think…that this thing might be Frank. A part of him anyway. The part of him that just wanted to fuck and kill. The part of him that couldn't die.

The instant Jeffrey spoke the words, he knew them to be true. And he finally understood what he had to do.

I knew a woman back then, he continued. *Dorothy Vallens. The Blue Lady. She was very beautiful, and very sad. Frank had kidnapped her family, and to save them, Dorothy would let him do things to her. Terrible things. After I killed Frank, Dorothy took her little boy and moved far away from here. I never saw her again after that. But a couple of years ago, I heard that she'd been horribly murdered. Assaulted, and mutilated. I…*

Jay leapt in to finish his sentence. *You think it…Frank…did that to her?*

Jeffrey nodded. *And I think he's been working his way back here ever since. Working his way back to me. I'm what he wants, Jay. He took Dorothy, and now I'm all that's left.*

He closed his eyes, remembering. *I think…he has an overdue love letter he wants to deliver.*

Jay pushed her coffee away, unfinished. Her pale cheeks grew flushed, and she would not meet Jeffrey's eye.

Eventually, she murmured, *But to pass it onto you, we'd have to…*

I know. He banished the thought of it from his mind, telling himself he was only doing what was necessary to save her. *Are you willing to do that, Jay?*

Jay stared out of the diner window, watching the clouds drift across the sky. Then, she gave an almost imperceptible nod.

TWILIGHT'S LAST SCREAMING

There was nothing more for either of them to say. Jeffrey paid the check, and they walked back to his car in mutual silence. He drove them out to the old automotive plant on the outskirts of town, the same place where Jay had originally been infected. Jeffrey knew that the local teenagers liked to come here, to drink and smoke dope and fool around.

As he parked the car, edging it into the lengthening evening shadow cast by the derelict building, he could almost fool himself into thinking that he was one of them again. Young, good-looking, a life full of possibility stretching away in front of him. A beautiful, willing girl sitting in the next seat.

But it was all a lie, wasn't it?

He and Jay sat there together for a few minutes, neither of them speaking, until Jay finally leaned over towards him and hesitantly pulled his lips to hers. As they kissed, part of her wondered whether Jeffrey had even believed a single word she had told him, or whether he was just the old perv she and Kelly had always said he was, merely using her paranoia as a means of forcing her to fuck him. She supposed she would never really know the truth, but felt as though she had little choice but to go along with it anyway.

So Jay lay there unresisting and let the older man do whatever he wanted to her. She didn't even flinch when Jeffrey paused in mid-coitus and, looking down at Jay with haunted eyes that seemed to be staring right through her, gazing back across decades, raised a hand and hit her twice, once across each cheek.

Shortly afterwards, when he came, Jeffrey began to sob and clutched Jay tightly to his chest, calling her *Sandy* over and over again. She didn't know who Sandy was and figured it didn't matter. So she just reached up and stroked his hair and told him it was okay.

When he stopped crying, they both dressed, neither looking at the other.

Jeffrey's gaze moved to the night sky overhead. *Now it's dark*, he whispered.

He took Jay straight home, dropping her on the corner so as to avoid seeing her mother. When she climbed out of the car, Jay turned back and quietly asked him, *Do you really think it'll be alright now?*

Jeffrey looked at her blankly. *Things haven't been alright for a very long time*, he said finally. *But I started something thirty years ago, and now I'm gonna try and finish it.*

Then he drove away, leaving Jay to the darkness.

When Jeffrey arrived home, he grabbed a beer from the refrigerator and went upstairs to his bedroom. There, he opened the closet and crept inside, closing the door behind him.

Settling down in the shadows, he popped open the beer and sipped at it, the melody of an old song replaying over and over in his mind.

In dreams, I walk with you…

Jeffrey felt comfortable and secure in the darkness of his hiding place. He didn't know how much time it would take for *it* to find him, but decided he could wait for as long as necessary. After all, he had been trying to find his way back to this place for years.

So he simply remained there in the closet, sipping at his beer and wondering what it would look like when it came for him. Would it wear Jay's face, or Dorothy's, or Sandy's?

Or perhaps the closet door would fly open to once again reveal Frank, crazed and feral, poised to deliver his final love letter to Jeffrey.

In dreams you're mine…

Pulling the darkness around him like a blanket, Jeffrey waited.

Waited for the candy-coloured clown they called the Sandman to come home to him again.

DR. JOHN MARKWAY

Richard Johnson in The Haunting, 1963
written by Nelson Gidding
based on the novel by Shirley Jackson
directed by Robert Wise

<u>Extracts from the journal of Dr. John Markway</u>

<u>Sept 12th 2013</u>

Call this what you will: the last foolish indulgence of an old crank who has spent his entire life attempting to explain the inexplicable, or merely a symptom of encroaching senility. But now that I am confined to this godforsaken wheelchair and mostly to the inside of this house, I find that the unshakeable urge to <u>understand</u> still drives me.

And yes, I am entirely aware that the inescapable fact of my own looming demise might play a not entirely insignificant role in this desire. Nevertheless, the unavoidable truth of it is that while I have dedicated (some might say wasted) my entire life to the study of the supernatural, I find I am hardly any closer to comprehending it. (I hate to even contemplate what the ratio of years expended vs volume of knowledge gained might be!) And despite the indisputable fact that these studies have, whether directly or indirectly, resulted in the deaths of several dear friends and loved ones, I still find myself driven to try and peer beyond the veil. (Would my darling Grace have wanted me to abandon my studies after her untimely death? Or poor Eleanor? I tell myself that they would not.)

The small modicum of fame accorded me by the dreadful events at Hill House meant I could take my research further afield, enabling me to travel the world in pursuit of the understanding I have always sought. The Overlook Hotel, the Carmichael mansion, the house at 112 Ocean Avenue in Amityville, Bly Manor, Taskerlands, the old boarding school in Saint-Cloud, the infamous 'death house' in Nerima, Tokyo; I have visited them all, and more. In some locations, my findings were inconclusive; in others, I can say with absolute certainty that they were 'inhabited', although by whom or by what was often less clear to me. But with every study I conducted, I could feel myself inching towards a gradual understanding. One day, I was certain, the entirety of the truth would be revealed to me.

But alas! The span of one man's earthly life is sadly finite. If only I'd had fifty more years, or a hundred!

Eventually, my increasing age and the attendant infirmity that comes with it meant I was no longer able to travel. As my old friend and colleague Theodora teasingly likes to tell me, the foremost prerequisite for this sort of research is not, in fact, a scientific background, nor indeed a mind that is open and objective, but rather, the plain and simple ability to run like hell when one's life is placed in mortal danger. It pains me to admit that there may be some truth in what she says; it pains me even more to concede that I am longer capable of that simple act of self-preservation.

So here I sit, quite alone in the world, awaiting my final moment of revelation. (I have of course promised Theo that I will communicate my findings from the other side, if it is at all within my power to do so.) I never remarried after Grace's death, and have no children, nor any extended family. I have my carer Lucia, who visits once a day, but she is Latina and highly superstitious, and I have learned from bitter experience not to ever speak to her of my interest in matters paranormal. My only meaningful contact with the outside world is now only by letter, telephone, or email.

Yes, even a doddering old fool like me has managed to educate myself as to the wonders of the internet! Indeed, I can hardly dare to imagine life without it; how else would a man in my constrained position be able to ensure they had an inexhaustible supply of good books, or fine whisky?

Or even one last opportunity to study (albeit from afar) the sort of bizarre phenomena I have devoted a lifetime to?

Once upon a time I would never have believed such a thing would be possible, but modern technology being what it is, and people being what they are, it seems that very little can go undocumented these days. Hour upon hour can be wasted online watching the minutiae of humanity's tedious little hobbies, their randomly-captured moments of embarrassment or humiliation, and even what they choose to get up to in the bedroom (or the living room, or the garden, or indeed in any public place you might care to imagine).

Inevitably then, we have finally arrived at a moment in time where evidence of the supernatural – some might say the _impossible_ – has also been captured on camera for the entire world to see. I speak, of course, of the recordings that have now popularly become known as the 'Meus Tapes'.

As far as I can make out, these recordings started leaking onto the internet sometime in 2007. No one knows where they came from or who might be responsible for editing the footage and uploading it. Regardless, it seems as though the material is documentary in nature, inasmuch as the occurrences portrayed within do not appear to be faked, and have been confirmed by the relevant authorities to feature both real people (some of whom are still alive, while many others are currently missing or dead) and actual, verifiable events.

Many of them tragic and, on the face of it, entirely inexplicable.

Now, there have been cases where putatively similar 'found-footage' recordings have been made public before. I myself have seen many of them, and can say without a shred of doubt that most of them are witless fakes: entirely tedious in form and content, conceived and performed by amateurs, and featuring the sort of phenomena that can be conjured up with the use of some fishing line and some cheap sound effects.

NB: Obviously I do not include the notorious 1992 'Ghostwatch' BBC broadcast amongst their number. Despite the fact that the footage has long been suppressed by the UK authorities, bootleg copies immediately began circulating amongst collectors and experts after the programme's first (and only) transmission. In my view, the broadcast serves as not only the most convincing visual documentation of supernatural activity on record, but also as an effectively dire warning against the dangers of trivialising such phenomena. One other possible exception is the assembly of filmed material popularly known as 'The Blair Witch Project'. Although I was not altogether convinced by the footage itself, its makers' unsolved disappearance and the fact that the film material was excavated during an archaeological dig, buried deep in the hitherto undisturbed foundations of an old building, where no modern-day artefact would or could ever possibly have been found, suggests some supernatural agency was indeed at work. However, the subject of witchcraft is rather outside my purview, having far more relevance to those amongst my academic colleagues who specialise in folkloric studies.

I admit, the first Meus Tape (long before they had even acquired that particular sobriquet) initially struck me as little more than a fascinating anomaly. It was passed onto me by a professor of my acquaintance who thought that it might prove to be of some interest, and I may have watched it once or twice before filing it away. It certainly raised some questions, but nevertheless seemed to be something of a (literal) dead end. One of the main subjects of the footage was deceased, while the other had disappeared. Irrespective of one's feelings about the veracity of the various supernatural events captured on-camera, my feeling was that it was a matter better dealt with by the police, rather than an ageing devotee of the paranormal.

Three years later, a second Meus Tape appeared online, followed by a third this very year. (Is there any meaning or motive to this seemingly regulated release pattern, I wonder?) And over that time, I will confess, my feelings about the matter have intensified, moving from an initial wary fascination to what is fast becoming an abiding obsession. Having recently concluded a close study of the third tape (temporally speaking the first, but I will deal with them in order of release, as it seems likely there may be some hidden significance in the manner in which the story has been revealed to us) and additional examination of the preceding two, I shall attempt to set down some random thoughts and analysis here. Perhaps these musings might be of use to future scholars; quite possibly they are nothing more than the attempts of an old eccentric to fend off the gradual dying of the light. That is not for me to decide. It will suffice for me to simply put some thoughts down on paper, in the hope it will help clear an increasingly fogged and cluttered mind.

But not tonight! Even the effort expended in typing these few short pages has set my arthritic finger joints to aching. Well, I shall doubtless return to the subject tomorrow. For now, I have an appointment with my old friend Glenfiddich.

Later

I fear that my earlier mention of Grace has stirred up old memories, and unwelcome ones at that. I have long maintained that a closed mind is no defence against the supernatural, and whatever my deceased wife's other superlative qualities may have been, it is fair to say that she lacked a certain degree of objectivity when it came to my particular academic speciality. Therefore her decision to join me unannounced at Hill House during our ill-fated field study there sadly proved to be a serious error of judgement on her part, one that was eventually to cost Grace her life.

Although she always insisted that she could not remember any details of the time she spent 'lost' within Hill House, she still never quite recovered from the trauma of it. She suffered from recurring nightmares about being trapped there; many were the nights I would be awakened by her feverish cries of 'Don't let it in!' or "Her hand, so cold, so cold!'. Over time, she became ever more withdrawn and depressed, quite unlike the vivacious soul I originally married. I tried to get her to speak to a doctor but she consistently refused. (I suspect because she was too embarrassed by the prospect of having to admit the truth of that which she had always scoffed at.)

For my part, I confess that, during my wife's slow decline, I increasingly took refuge in my work. I'll admit I did not know how to best help Grace with her trauma – I _had_ tried to warn her of the dangers, after all – and certainly experienced a degree of guilt as a result. Consequently, I spent more and more time at my office, or travelling to sites of interest further afield. Eventually, I am sorry to say, Grace succumbed to her terrors. If memory serves, I was away in England investigating Bly Manor (a wasted trip; if any entities had ever walked there, they appeared to have long since vacated the premises) when I received the news that my wife had taken a fatal overdose of barbiturates.

I am not certain why I suddenly feel the need to write this here. A touch of melancholy brought on by one too many glasses of 'the malt that wounds', perhaps. I fear I shall not sleep tonight, and Grace always seems closer to me at such times, when I lie there alone in the night, in the dark. How I wish I could hold her one last time. My poor darling!

Sept 13th 2013

Back to business. As I predicted, my sleep was fitful, but to hell with it. I must make good use of whatever waking hours are left to me! So let us turn now to the first of the Meus Tapes, apparently recorded during late 2006.

Tape 1: Sept 18th 2006 – Oct 8th 2006

As I stated earlier, when the first tape came into my possession, I was not entirely convinced by it, despite the storm of online notoriety that accompanied its release. I felt as though much of the phenomena contained within – the igniting ouija board, for example, or the woman being dragged from her bed – could have been easily faked with the judicious use of practical illusions. Even when the Los Angeles police confirmed the truth of the unsolved murder of Micah Sloat and subsequent disappearance of his girlfriend Katie, I maintained some doubts. Perhaps the tape was merely a hoax gone wrong? For instance, possibly the couple planned to exploit the footage for financial gain but had fallen out in the process of making it (the scenes of domestic dysfunction are quite convincing!), resulting in a bizarre crime of passion: Katie murdering Micah and cunningly incorporating the death into the tape. (Possibly she even intended to use her alleged possession as a form of exoneration!)

Still, there were admittedly other moments that gave me pause: the stealthy creep of demonic footprints, or the final grisly display of preternatural strength as Katie hurls her dead lover's body at the camera lens. And if nothing else, the footage accurately captured the often-humdrum nature of parapsychological study: long hours spent sitting around with nothing happening, waiting for the smallest sign of activity to occur. I was actually quite heartened by the fact that the tape provoked such an intense reaction from those who saw it; perhaps devoting my life to such supposedly far-fetched pursuits had not been a waste after all!

However, the identity of who had organised and released this footage remained unknown. Was it the accused murderer Katie? (The question of why the entity supposedly possessing her would want to do such a thing remains a mystery.) Or alternatively, was it someone connected with the L.A.P.D. (who adamantly denied any responsibility)? No one knew, although of course any number of internet conspiracy theories erupted in the wake of the recording's release.

I myself attempted my own small piece of detective work, by reaching out to Dr. Fredrichs, the psychic who can be seen consulting on the Sloat haunting in the tape. Although he tried to avoid the resulting attention once the tape was made public, it turned out he and I had several professional colleagues in common, and so he agreed (somewhat reluctantly) to talk with me about his experience. The following is a transcript of our conversation:

01/31/08

MARKWAY: Thank you for agreeing to speak to me, Doctor. I hope you don't mind if I record our conversation for my files.

FREDRICHS: Okay. I don't have too much to say, though. You've seen the tape. I really didn't spend that much time there.

MARKWAY: What was your first impression upon visiting the house?

FREDRICHS: Well, I knew <u>something</u> was there. I could sense it as soon as I entered the room. I'm sure you've had similar experiences.

MARKWAY: Well, I don't profess to be psychic. But yes.

FREDRICHS: It's funny, I knew there was a presence. But I felt as though it was trying to mask itself from me. At that stage no one really knew what it was and I think it was trying to avoid exposure. But I'll tell you what I felt like as soon as I crossed the threshold. I felt like a soldier in enemy territory. Exposed and alone. Instinctively,

I knew there was a sniper lurking somewhere, and he wanted to hurt me.

MARKWAY: So you realised fairly early on that the entity inhabiting the house was what you would define as a 'demon'?

FREDRICHS: Yes, although I understand some people view that as a loaded term. I don't mean to attach any particular religious significance to it. It's simply used to differentiate these entities from ghosts. Ordinary people experiencing an inhabitation don't always grasp the distinction. But they very quickly understand that a demon is an actively malign presence which can and will hurt them, whereas the same is not generally true of unquiet spirits.

MARKWAY: Not always the case in my experience. Anyway.

FREDRICHS: So I spent some time talking to the young woman…

MARKWAY: Katie.

FREDRICHS: (LONG PAUSE) Uh, yes. We established that the subject remembered certain paranormal occurrences in her parent's house when she was a small child. Lights flickering, banging, whispered voices, the usual kind of thing.

MARKWAY: Did she tell you then that her parents were dead?

FREDRICHS: No, she did not.

MARKWAY: Unusual for her not to mention it, don't you think?

FREDRICHS: As you can imagine, Dr. Markway, I now look back on my visit to that house and my interactions with Micah Sloat and…well, the entire subject in a whole new light.

MARKWAY: You seem very reluctant to speak Katie's name aloud.

FREDRICHS: (LONG PAUSE) It makes me uncomfortable.

MARKWAY: How so?

FREDRICHS: Names have power, Doctor. If you speak something's name aloud, it stands to reason you might attract its attention.

MARKWAY: Oh, come now. That's just superstition, surely?

FREDRICHS: If that's what you want to believe. (PAUSE) Please, can we hurry this up? I have a lunch appointment with a friend.

MARKWAY: Of course. I do appreciate you giving me your time. So, you quickly decided that a so-called demon was inhabiting the house?

FREDRICHS: Yes. Upon talking to the subject, the pattern was obvious. The house itself was not haunted; rather, the demon had been following her ever since childhood. I quickly realised that I could not offer either of them any real assistance with their problem, and was in fact placing myself in danger simply being in the house. So I recommended they speak instead to my colleague Dr. Johann Averies and left.

MARKWAY: The demonologist. He never returned their calls, did he?

FREDRICHS: He was out of the country, I believe.

MARKWAY: Unfortunate. There was no one else you could recommend to them? Katie was clearly in some distress.

FREDRICHS: (VISIBLY FLINCHES AT THE MENTION OF KATIE'S NAME) You really shouldn't… (PAUSE) Look, I'll be completely honest with you. I was really hoping they'd just leave me alone. I was very disturbed by what I felt in that house. As a firm rule, I don't mess around with demons or anything like that. Sometimes I'm able to communicate with those who have passed on and help bring the living a little comfort. That's really all I do.

MARKWAY: But you did go back.

FREDRICHS: Very briefly. I didn't want to, but she begged me. She sounded so convincing. Do you think it was inside her even then?

MARKWAY: I'm sure I can't say.

FREDRICHS: God. Women lie so well, don't they?

MARKWAY: You went back to the house…

FREDRICHS: Well, you've seen the footage. The moment I set foot on the threshold, I could feel it. It wasn't hiding any longer. The sheer level of malevolence…

MARKWAY: So you abandoned them?

FREDRICHS: And what in god's name would you have had me do? Die in that house alongside Micah Sloat?

MARKWAY: As trained experts, we do have a certain responsibility…

FREDRICHS: Oh, bullshit. How much responsibility do <u>you</u> take, Dr. Markway? How many people have died because of <u>you</u>? Maybe I should call upon Eleanor Vance and ask her for her opinion.

MARKWAY: Now, look here. I warned Eleanor. I told her to leave Hill House.

FREDRICHS: And I warned <u>them</u>. But people only listen to trained experts when it suits them, don't you think?

MARKWAY: Perhaps.

FREDRICHS: I'm done here.

MARKWAY: Please, just one or two more questions.

FREDRICHS: No, I've had enough of your questions. (UNINTELLIGIBLE)

MARKWAY: I'm sorry, what did you say?

FREDRICHS: I said you should be careful. Your questions might get you into trouble.

MARKWAY: Is that a threat?

FREDRICHS: (LAUGHS) A threat? Not from me.
(PAUSE)
I've seen her, you know. Only glimpses at first. I'd be out on the street, and I'd sense someone following me. So I'd turn around and look, and catch sight of her watching me from a crowd. Only for a second. Blink and you'd miss it. Just like a ghost. But she's real, Doctor. Very real. That was just the start of it.
(PAUSE)
The other night I looked out of the window and I saw her standing in the middle of the street. Not moving. Just staring up at me.
(PAUSE)
I don't think I have much time left.

(CONVERSATION ENDS)

In that, Dr. Fredrichs was unfortunately correct. He was found dead in his house some weeks later, killed by severe trauma to the skull. No one has ever been charged for his murder. The police verdict was that he had interrupted a burglary in progress.

Do I believe that? At the time, I told myself it was merely an unsettling coincidence. Correlation does not equal causation, after all. And Fredrichs did strike me as somewhat unstable, probably due to unresolved guilt over his failure to prevent Micah Sloat's death. So his claim that the possessed

Katie was stalking him seemed to me to be little more than a paranoid fantasy.

Several months later, the second Meus Tape appeared online, and matters suddenly started to take on a whole new complexion. But that will have to wait for tomorrow. Lucia is due to arrive soon and she does not approve of me spending too much time hunched over this computer. For a man who now spends most of his life sitting down, apparently I have terrible posture!

Later

Just awoke from a dream of Grace. A nightmare, in truth. It seems this little project of mine has stirred up some old ghosts, although I'm not at all certain what the subconscious connection between my beloved wife and the Meus Tapes might be.

I dreamt I was back in Hill House. The building was completely dark, and I could hear Grace's voice in the distance, calling for me. 'Come home, John!' she was crying. 'Please come home to me!'

I set out to find her, groping blindly through the seemingly endless gloom that surrounded me. But Hill House could never be trusted, even in broad daylight, and although I thought I recalled its layout very well, even in the depths of my dream, the doors were never quite where I remembered them being, and never led to the right rooms. I grew increasingly disorientated and frightened, and all the time Grace's cries became ever more desperate.

But suddenly, her voice seemed closer. All at once it seemed as though she were only in the next room. My despair immediately began to lift. 'I'm here, Grace!' I shouted.

The next moment I felt someone standing next to me. Not Grace, but a distinctive feminine presence I recalled almost as well. Eleanor always did have the uncanny knack of putting everyone's nerves on edge the moment she entered a room.

'That is not Grace,' she whispered to me. 'Always remember, this house wears many masks.'

And then she was gone.

Nevertheless, I was not alone. The creak of a nearby floorboard signalled Grace's arrival in the room. 'I'm here, John,' she breathed. 'I've found you at last.'

Then, I felt a hand close around my own. But not Grace's. Even now, I can remember the touch of her soft fingers, gentle as a summer rain. And regardless of whatever deprivations she may have suffered after death, this was not – could not ever be – her. The hand was cold, and unpleasantly dry. Touching it caused my skin to start tingling, as though it had come into contact with something noxious. It put me in mind of how it might feel to shake hands with a deadly serpent, knowing that as soon as it had you close, its venomous fangs would sink into your neck. I was certain of only one thing – that I did not want to see the face of whatever possessed such a hand.

I attempted to pull away, but it held me fast. A dreadful, enervating cold began to seep through my body, rooting me to the spot.

'Hold me,' the Grace-thing said.

Then I felt its bloodless lips brush my own, and at their touch I woke up screaming. Much to my shame, I found that I had wet myself in my sleep. For all the myriad indignities of old age, I have hitherto always managed to remain continent.

I cleaned myself up as best I could, then came straight to my desk. I surely shall not sleep again tonight, nor do I much wish to. Perhaps once the sun has risen, I will allow myself to rest further. But for now, a small drop of whisky to calm my nerves…

Sept 14th 2013

It seems my nerves needed more calming than I thought. I awoke to find myself still at my desk, head atop a pile of books, half-empty whisky bottle at my elbow. Damned fool that I am! Now my skull feels as though two tectonic plates are grinding together inside it. I shouldn't let myself get so upset by what are, after all, nothing but dreams. No matter how real they might seem at the time.

I shall fix myself a pot of coffee and then proceed. Work is always the best remedy.

Tape 2: March 2005 – October 9th 2007

The second Meus Tape appeared online some three years after the first, and changed everything. No longer was the first tape an isolated anomaly; for the first time, there seemed to be a distinct purpose to the release of this material, even if the world could not yet fully discern it. Moreover, there was now an attendant sense of revelation. A larger story was being told to us – although by exactly whom was still open to debate.

The footage begins over two years before Micah Sloat's death. Why does our unknown 'narrator' choose to reveal their story to the world in such a disjointed fashion? I cannot rightly say, but it seems as though it is part of the lesson that is to be imparted. For all the questions raised by the first Meus Tape, perhaps the answers lie further back, in the distant past.

We now learn that Katie has a younger sister, Kristi. She is married to one Daniel Rey, and together they have two children: Ali (from Daniel's previous marriage) and their own newborn child Hunter. However, recall that there was no mention whatsoever of Kristi in the earlier footage, even when Katie spoke about her childhood. So what are we to make of this omission? It is certainly clumsy storytelling, which might lead us to believe the tale is being made up on the fly. Are we in the hands of a particularly unreliable narrator? Or is there something else at work? Perhaps there are two separate forces guiding the material, vying for overall control. One seeking to reveal, the other to conceal.

Still, one thing is certain. The first Meus Tape was a rather primitive, *cinema verité* affair. This is far more elaborate. The film has been assembled out of the footage captured by a number of security cameras, installed in the house after an apparent burglary – although nothing of value was stolen save for a single item of jewellery. (Time and time again, we see the symbolism of these supposedly safe middle-class homes being abruptly entered from outside.) The result of this somewhat Orwellian state of affairs is that instead of only ever seeing the aftermath, we now witness several instances of full-blown supernatural phenomena. An explosion of psychokinetic force in Kristi's kitchen. A baby being taken from its crib by an invisible entity and floating in mid-air. Kristi being dragged out of the baby's nursery and down the stairs, struggling against her unseen attacker the whole time. It is almost as though the demonic presence in the Meus Tapes is gradually revealing itself to us. The rather coy display of the first tape has now become a far more blatant come-on, rather like a striptease routine. The main question in the audience's mind is now this: how much more will we be permitted to see/know?

There are also hints as to the presence's origin: more references to the supernatural trauma suffered during childhood by Katie <u>and</u> Kristi (contrary to the impression given by the earlier tape, it now seems as though Kristi was in fact the original locus of the haunting, and not her older sister; the discovery of the Latin word that gave these tapes their name – 'meus' meaning 'mine' – scratched into a door would seem to bear this out), and a studiedly throwaway mention of a black magic ritual involving a first-born male child being pledged to the demon. Should there be no son born to that particular generation, the demon will continue to plague the family until one is produced and the debt can finally be collected. At last we can begin to discern the full picture being painted for us. The unexplained disappearance of a box of home videos shot while the sisters were young children hints at future revelations to come. See how carefully we are being coaxed further and further into the labyrinth?

A pattern also begins to emerge: the representation of the male figures in these tapes (Micah, Dr. Fredrichs, Kristi's husband Daniel) is a distinctly ambivalent one. Time and time again, they are seen to be blinkered and often callous, closed off to the truth of what is happening until it is far too late. Even Dr. Fredrichs, who is far more sensitive (i.e. feminine) and thus aware of the danger posed by the entity, is nevertheless entirely self-interested and coldly abandons Micah and Katie to their fate. This construction seems to be entirely deliberate, and perhaps suggests a controlling female perspective is overseeing the production of the tapes.

This ambivalence pays off with a final revelation: we learn that Kristi's husband was in fact responsible for the events detailed in the first Meus Tape. In a desperate bid to save his wife from the demon, he conducted a blood ritual wherein Katie was offered up in her place. Still, as the very end of the tape affirms, this was not sufficient to save his family. We skip ahead several weeks to October 9th, 2007 (one day after Micah Sloat's death, remember) to witness the still-possessed Katie murdering Daniel and Kristi and abducting their young son Hunter.

By now it should be obvious that we are being invited to see Katie as something other than the antagonist of these tapes. Although her actions are certainly monstrous, it is also evident that she is being portrayed as the victim of several patriarchal oppressors (Micah, Daniel, et al). So, while the tapes serve to incriminate her as a murderer responsible for several deaths, they simultaneously function as a form of exoneration too. After all, viewed through this particular lens, how can any of these dreadful events be seen as her fault?

With this in mind, even before the release of the third Meus Tape, the identity of the person responsible for producing them was gradually becoming clear to me. But what purpose were they intended to serve? Were they meant as a confession? A cruel taunt?

Or a desperate cry for help?

Later

> From: <u>KT1982@AOL.COM</u> 11.29PM (1 hour ago)
> to me
>
> **pls help**
> **only u can understand**
> **help me us**

I received the above email a short time ago.

Let us get the blindingly obvious out of the way first. I do not know anyone with the email 'KT1982@ AOL.COM'. The address is not in my contacts list, and I have never previously received a single email from the sender.

All of this is to say: I think it's entirely clear who the email is from, or at least who I am <u>intended to believe</u> it is from. So, is it a hoax? Or am I expected to believe that 'KT' is somehow aware of my interest in her story, knows I am currently collating my notes on her, and therefore decided to send a cry for help to a man she has never met?

Admittedly, the former explanation seems far more likely. However, I am forced to wonder who could be responsible if so. While my interest in the Meus Tapes is certainly no secret in certain professional circles, my roster of colleagues and acquaintances has been rapidly thinned out with age, and I cannot imagine any of their remaining number would stoop to such an immature trick. I suppose it's possible that someone somewhere might bear a long-standing grudge against me (academic feuds being what they are!), but I am hard pressed to think of exactly who.

Beyond that, I can think of no possible culprit. The only person who visits me here at home is Lucia, and while she could certainly gain access to my notes/emails if she so desired (I tend to leave the computer on when I'm not at my desk), I cannot for the life of me imagine why she would want to do such a thing. I suppose I could ask her, but I fully expect to be met by the same blank look of incomprehension I get when I try and engage her in any sort of conversation that doesn't involve either God or her paycheck.

Which only leaves the alternative: that 'KT' is real. (I am suddenly reminded of the old saw about eliminating the impossible, etcetera etcetera.) The cryptically garbled reference to 'me us' was tantalising, I admit. Was it intended to read as 'meus', or was the 'us' a suggestion that there are also others who need help? Does this mean that Hunter Rey is still in Katie's custody?

Not knowing what else to do, I sent the following reply:

To: KT1982@AOL.COM

Who is this? How did you get my email?
I do not know how it is you think I can help you, but I am an old man, confined to a wheelchair. If this is intended as some sort of hoax, please do not contact me again.
Yours, Dr. John Markway

As yet, I have received no reply, no matter how long I sit here staring idiotically at my monitor. Regardless, I shall sit a little longer. Sleep still seems a very long way away.

Under the circumstances, I suppose it won't do any harm to resort to the whisky bottle for a little company as the night eases slowly into the wee hours…

Sept 14th 2013

Damnation!

Stupidly, I once again fell asleep in front of the computer. That accursed email had set my mind racing, and I believed a glass of whisky would help relax me. Well, one inevitably led to another, and like the old fool I am, I ended up dozing off. Thankfully there were no more Grace-related nightmares, although I did suffer a brief anxiety dream in which I woke up to find the house had been broken into while I slept.

On the other hand, when I subsequently awoke for real, it was to find a furious Lucia standing over me. There was no hiding the empty whisky bottle and my dishevelled state, and she immediately began to berate me in rapidfire Spanish. And while I know her tirade was only motivated by concern, I simply cannot abide being shouted at first thing in the morning, especially after a night of overindulgence. So yes, I freely admit I did not react particularly well.

Matters quickly grew worse. Although Lucia's display of temper eventually began to subside, it was quickly replaced by a show of anxiety that bordered on the hysterical. She began to insist that something was very wrong in the house, claiming that she could feel evil forces massing around me. She told me she wanted to perform some kind of harebrained cleansing ritual to protect me.

Well, I know I always preach the virtues of keeping an open mind, but quite frankly, there is a universe of difference between using scientific methodology to document and study the unexplained, and surrounding oneself with superstitious poppycock. When I told her I would permit no such thing, she said that the house was becoming unsafe for both of us, and that she could not possibly remain here unless I allowed her to take protective steps.

Under the circumstances, I felt as though I had little choice but to tell her to go. Of course, I regret it now. I was tired and ill-tempered, and doubtless I acted rashly. But dammit, she knows how I feel about such things!

Needless to say, she took it very badly. I don't think I have ever seen Lucia look so pale. She said very little more to me, just packed up the few things she had around the house and left.

I suppose I shall have to call her in a day or two and apologise. But I'm quite sure I can bumble along without her until then. Only my legs are weak, my brain is still as sharp as a scalpel! Still, she has to understand I will only allow her back if she agrees not to cross certain boundaries. I have observed old age causing certain peers and colleagues of mine to become increasingly soft-headed in their dotage, and am quite determined to ensure such a thing never happens to me.

One simple remedy for that is to keep on working, of course. So I shall put the distractions of this morning aside and endeavour to put down some coherent thoughts about the third and final (to date) Meus

Tape. (Admittedly, it does seem as though events in real life might now have overtaken my little project somewhat – assuming 'KT' is who she appears to be, anyway – but I do have an abiding hatred of leaving things unfinished.)

<u>*Tape 3: Sept 3rd 1988 – Nov 14th 1988*</u>

As one might have predicted, the third Meus Tape was comprised of material from the family home videos that went missing from the Rey household in 2007. There was a far shorter gap between the release of the second and third tapes than the first and second; only a year. Almost as though their anonymous creator was becoming increasingly desperate to see Katie and Kristi's full story revealed to the world.

I say anonymous, but really, by this point there can be little doubt that the tapes are being assembled and released by the missing Katie herself. While it's certainly possible that the first two tapes could have been created by other parties, she is far and away the most plausible suspect behind the theft of the home videos, and therefore must be considered as the author of all three Meus Tapes.

Up until now at least, the main question was <u>why</u>. Did Katie create them under her own agency, or was all this being done under the influence of the demonic force controlling her? Although I must reserve final judgement on the matter, the email I received yesterday would seem to point to the former. The tapes appear to be nothing less than a cry for help.

Events in the third Meus narrative unfold much as before: a steady accretion of supernatural activity within a household; an ineffectual paterfamilias who can do little to protect the family; increasing dysfunction between the mother and father figures; and a climactic paranormal eruption that claims the lives of several victims. A recurring pattern, repeating itself over generations. Can there be any doubt that our unseen narrator is trying to tell us that this will keep on happening until someone finally acts to stop it?

The significant difference in this tape is the revelation of direct human involvement in the demonic curse that has dogged the two sisters ever since childhood. Specifically, the confirmation (hinted at in the second tape) that the children's grandmother Lois is a senior member of a witches' coven. It was _she_ who made the pact with the demon; _she_ who inflicted it upon her own daughter Julie and subsequently (after Julie also failed to produce the male heir demanded by the demon) her granddaughters Kristi and Katie. The demon (given the childish nickname of 'Toby' by Kristi) was not the random intrusion suggested by the first Meus Tape, but a deliberate, targeted one.

However, some unanswered questions still remain. For instance, one is left to wonder how it is that, in adulthood, the sisters apparently have no clear memory of the events shown in this final tape. Not only do they witness the climactic deaths of their mother and her boyfriend, they are actively involved in them. Are we to infer some form of traumatic amnesia has taken place? Or that Lois or the demon magically wiped their memories? Given that the adult sisters still seem to possess _some_ recollection of the supernatural phenomena that was a feature of their early childhood (at one point in the second tape, Katie asks Kristi, 'Do you want to end up like Mom?', which makes one wonder to what degree her memory of events aligns with the truth of what we witness happen in tape three) it seems unlikely that such a violent and distressing memory would never have surfaced if so.

But what is the alternative explanation? That they in fact retained all memories of their childhood and everything in their adult lives – partners, children and the rest of it – were little more than props in a malign charade? The implications of that are disturbing, to say the least.

I suppose the only way for me to ever know more is to continue my dialogue with the mysterious 'KT'. But as this third tape clearly demonstrates, there is a very high degree of risk involved. Not only is there the question of whether Katie is still acting under the influence of the demon, but also to what degree the coven continue to be present in her life. Might she be their prisoner, or even their catspaw?

I tell myself that the wisest thing to do would be not to get involved. Ignore any further emails, delete the Meus Tapes from my hard drive and forget about the whole thing. Beg Lucia to come back and care for me while I descend into forgetful senility.

But I can't. You see, I cannot shake the impression that, in the course of my life's work, I have never managed to make a single jot of difference. That, despite all my efforts, I have merely added to the sum total of humanity's incomprehension, rather than subtracted from it. And that, for all my good intentions, I have only ever succeeded in hurting those around me. Or worse still, costing them their very lives.

As I sit here typing this, I look over at the framed photograph of Grace I keep on my desk and ask myself if I could have done more to save her, or Eleanor, or any of the others.

And the dreadful, unavoidable answer is <u>yes</u>.

Surely then, I must try to account for my failure? Attempt to save one life, even if it costs me my own?

<u>*Later*</u>

I just now received a reply from 'KT'. It read as follows:

> From: <u>KT1982@AOL.COM</u> 3.03PM (0 hours ago)
> to me
>
> i can only write u when toby is asleep if he finds out hell hurt me
> i want people to know the truth i made the tapes so they could see
> i would never hurt kristi or the others i am so sorry i dont care if I die now but please help hunter
> there is one more tape no one else has seen it will show you everything
>
>
> To: <u>KT1982@AOL.COM</u>
>
> Dear KT
> I want to help you if I can. Tell me exactly what I can do.
> There is another tape? Can you send it to me? It would help matters if I could understand everything properly.
> Yours, John

A reply from KT arrived a short time ago. There was no message, just a download link to an MP4 video file.

Tape 4: Sept 15th 2013

firstly let me state that the above date is correct

according to the time stamp, the tape was shot on the very same day I write this

not only that, but

no i'm getting ahead of myself. i have to do this properly so that people will know I'm not mad

god i don't know how much time i have

i'm sorry, im not thinking straight and my hands are shaking very badly. i shall have to stop and take a drink before I continue I think

the whisky helped, a little. i'm going to do my best to describe the tape now. forgive me, this is very hard. i'm rushing to put things down so cant type properly

how do you explain the inexplicable?

the tape starts in a car, driving through a residential neighbourhood. we cannot see the driver. the time is 437pm.

the car parks outside a house and the driver gets out and walks to the front door.

it is my house, my front door.

there is a long wait for the door to be answered. eventually it opens to reveal me, dr john markway. i say nothing, just stare up at the camera as though i was expecting the caller.

i look very old and frightened

the next moment there is some kind of explosion of unseen energy, and the video picture becomes distorted for a couple of seconds

when it clears you can see that my wheelchair has been thrown back against the far wall

i am on the ground i am not moving

the camera comes inside and approaches me. it holds on my face for a few seconds.

then the picture abruptly cuts and we are back in the car. it is dark now, an empty country road at night

the camera pans around to the back seat. i am lying there unconscious. my hands and feet are tied

then a hand comes into frame and shakes me awake

a woman's hand

i open my eyes and look around eventually i say where are we where are you taking me?

a voice says nowhere you brought yourself here doctor

i say nothing

the camera pans back around and we carry on driving for a short time

then the car turns off the road and arrives at a driveway, guarded by a familiar-looking set of rusted iron gates

the camera moves to me again, i struggle upright and peer to see where we have stopped

then I start screaming

there is another cut and then we are driving up to a large old house. it was once very grand but is now derelict and empty

no not empty

whatever walks there walks alone

i am still screaming when the car stops. the driver gets out of the car then moves round to the rear and pulls me out she throws me over her shoulder like i weigh nothing

please katie i beg

she does not answer and carries me over to the front porch

the doors are chained shut but then there is another burst of invisible force and the chain shatters and falls to the ground

the doors open and then we are inside hill house it is dark and cold and there are eyes everywhere

katie carries me up the staircase and along the hallway

i know where she is taking me

to the very heart of the house

we arrive at the nursery and she takes me inside

she places me on the floor and i begin to sob pleasepleaseplease

the camera moves to katies face its the first time we have seen her

there is nothing human there she is terrible yet somehow beautiful

i say was it ever really her

she says no

then she says it wont be long now and walks away

the camera holds on me as she leaves the room i get smaller and smaller until I am swallowed by the dark

the camera moves back through hill house down the staircase and through the entrance hall to the front door

she is of the dark nothing will touch her here

somewhere in the distance you can hear a scream

then nothing john is gone

john is part of the house now

tape ends

it is 436pm now i expect she will be here at any moment

i wonder whether it would always have turned out this way or did I make it happen by watching the tape?

was this always my future or did i choose it?

there's the doorbell now
grace i am coming back to you

CANDICE CARVETH

Cindy Hinds in The Brood, *1979*
written & directed by David Cronenberg

As Candice Carveth watched her father's casket being slowly lowered into the cold earth, she felt no grief, or sense of loss. All she felt was anger, anger that yet another life had been claimed by her mother's rage. A rage that still pursued Candice and her family down through the years like an unpaid debt; a debt that could never be settled or bartered away.

Nola Carveth had been dead for over a decade now, but she'd killed Frank just as sure as she'd killed her own parents and Candice's kindergarten teacher Ruth Mayer some thirteen years before. It made no difference whatsoever to Candice that they had all fallen prey to the murderous creatures borne of Nola's raging id, while her father had died from something as commonplace as a heart attack. Frank Carveth had been a decent, if limited, man, and had never entirely recovered from the horrors visited upon his family. Although he'd managed to save his daughter from Nola's uncontrollable anger, Candice had watched as her father slowly faded away over the ensuing years, all life and vitality ebbing from his body. It were as though her father had been some blind, defenceless subterranean animal, hitherto accustomed to a peaceful, shadowed existence but suddenly dragged squealing into the sunlight. Unable to face the full unadorned terror of the world he now dwelt in, Frank had ultimately died of shock.

Still, Nola could not be held solely accountable for his passing. Responsibility for the deaths of Frank and all the others could also be laid at Hal Raglan's door. Raglan, the doctor whose experimental psychoplasmics treatment first caused Nola to spawn her vengeful brood, had been the final victim of their fury. Candice supposed there was a kind of vicious justice in that, but it was not one that brought her any succour. How could it, when her mother's only legacy to her had not merely been the same bottomless anger that consumed Nola, but also its dreadful expression? The psychoplasmics process allowed patients to vent suppressed emotions by way of physiological changes to their bodies, but whereas in some cases the manifestations were unsightly but relatively cosmetic, it had also given rise to chronic diseases and inoperable cancers. In a perverse sense, Nola's children of rage had been psychoplasmics' ultimate validation; her body mutating to cathartically expel and act out her anger. As one of Raglan's other subjects had put it, she had been the doctor's queen bee.

While she had blocked out several of her more traumatic memories of her mother, Candice had since seen Raglan's medical files on Nola, and knew precisely what sort of monstrosity psychoplasmics had turned her into. And while she was Nola's only naturally conceived offspring, Candice was nevertheless just as much a product of her mother's rage as the brood. So, while she counted herself relatively fortunate that her body had not been affected to the same extent as Nola's, still she suffered long-term physiological effects from her emotional disorders. At periods of extreme stress and anger, Candice's body would break out in pustules and wart-like growths, both painful and disfiguring in nature. And although she was able to partially mitigate the attacks by the use of pharmaceutical remedies and meditation, they had still caused permanent scarring to her skin. As a result, Candice disliked going out in public even during the periods that her condition was dormant, and would frequently shut herself away for days on end when it was not.

Her father had always tended to her during such times, but now Frank was gone. And so Candice had had little choice but to emerge from the protective cocoon of the house they'd shared together, dressed protectively in a mourning veil, hooded shawl and dark glasses. Beneath her apparel, Candice could feel her skin itching with the sheer anxiety of being outside, not to mention her suppressed fury at the world that had taken her loving father away. Once she returned home she would have to apply emollient to her whole body and meditate for at least an hour, in the hope that she might be able to allay the worst of the coming attack.

As soon as the funeral service was over, Candice immediately left the graveside, ignoring the comforting blandishments of her father's friends and business partners. She'd made sure to have a taxi waiting for her, and hurriedly flung herself inside, desperate to be alone. Her grief was her own, just as her anger was; she would share them with no one.

But later that night, the storm of her repressed emotions was such that Candice found herself quite unable to focus, and instead she found herself aimlessly wandering the empty rooms of the house, finding it transformed into a strange, unfamiliar place now that Frank was gone. She felt like she was seeing her home for the first time, as though a magical glamour had been stripped away. What had previously been a sanctuary was now a prison, its walls permeated with years of accumulated sorrow and regret. Candice began to wonder how on earth she could continue to live here. The notion seemed almost unthinkable, were it not for the fact that the prospect of leaving was so much worse.

In desperation, she went to her father's liquor cabinet and opened a bottle of vodka. Given her almost total withdrawal from the world and its attendant social rituals, Candice was unused to alcohol, her only experience of it being an occasional glass of wine with dinner. The taste of the vodka made her gag, but once she mixed it with orange juice it became more tolerable, and she gradually came to appreciate the way it warmed the cold places inside her.

Nursing the drink to her chest, she wandered into her father's office, finding its impersonal clutter comforting. Very little in the room served to remind her of Frank. And yet it smelt of him; a trace of his warmth and presence still lingered.

Candice sat down at his desk and idly began to inspect the papers piled there. Mostly contracts and invoices; she knew she would have to attend to her father's outstanding business concerns at some point, but that could wait until another time. She knew exactly where the files she wanted were stored. Frank had kept them securely locked away in his desk ever since he had returned home one afternoon to find Candice pouring over them.

Copies of Dr. Raglan's patient files.

After Raglan's death, Frank and a number of other aggrieved parties filed a class action lawsuit against the doctor's Somafree Institute. With the original founder dead, there was little appetite on the behalf of any of the institute's remaining partners for a drawn-out legal battle, and the case was quickly settled. As part of the settlement, Raglan's private files were made available to the plaintiffs. Frank had brought copies home and spent weeks examining them, to little avail. If he'd hoped to find some kind of understanding about what had happened to his wife and family concealed within their pages, then that hope had proven to be an utterly forlorn one.

Frank never spoke to Candice about what he'd found in the files until several years later, on the day he arrived home to discover her reading them. And even then, after locking them safely away, all he said to her was, *There's nothing there, Candice. Raglan didn't know what he was doing. He didn't fucking know. He just let the genie out of the bottle and couldn't get it back inside. There's nothing there to help you or me or anyone. So just let the dead rest, honey.*

But what Candice understood all too well now was that the dead never rest. She carried them all around inside her, Grandma and Grandpa and Miss Mayer and Dr Hal and Nola and now her father too; each of them clamouring for their own personal restitution, a cacophony of dead voices singing a ceaseless song of anguish and despair. Candice knew that they would never let her rest, not for as long as she lived. How long could she hope to bear it?

There had to be a way to calm the voices, perhaps even silence them forever. How many other lives had Raglan destroyed? Where had this insanity first started?

Candice remembered reading Raglan's book, *The Shape of Rage*, sneaking it off the shelf when her father wasn't looking. In the early chapters he'd detailed his early psychiatric sessions with a particular subject, Patient P, whose bizarre physiological reactions to her course of therapy had provided Raglan with his initial breakthrough; one that ultimately led to the development of psychoplasmics.

She began to carefully go through the doctor's files, looking for some kind of possible match to the anonymous patient. An hour passed, then two. Candice was barely aware of the passage of time, save for the occasional need to refresh her drink. She started to suspect that Frank had deliberately limited her access to alcohol, fearing that it would only serve to inflame her anger and thereby worsen her condition. But all the vodka did was make her feel numb, and for Candice, banishing all feeling was something akin to a state of ecstasy.

Then, just as the words on the pages of the records were beginning to dance before her eyes and rearrange themselves into meaningless gibberish, she found what she was looking for: a collection of typewritten notes concerning one of Raglan's first patients, a woman named Pamela. Candice eagerly began to scan the xeroxed pages, searching for the answer to a question she had not yet properly managed to formulate.

Nov 17th

It is becoming apparent that Pamela is repressing a great deal of anger. Although on the surface she appears to be a cheerful, vivacious young woman, it only requires me to guide the conversation towards certain topics — her abusive, neglectful parents, or the various men who regularly attempt to court and seduce her, much to her consternation — for her discomfort to manifest itself. 'I don't want to talk about that,' she will tell me. 'It makes me feel bad inside.' Pamela possesses a strong, almost obsessive faith in God, and seems to believe that merely talking about such matters is a sin in and of itself.

So, as much I try and convince her that she NEEDS to discuss these feelings in order to properly release them, she adamantly refuses to even contemplate doing so.

For such a seemingly normal girl, there is something quite unsettling about that which I sense lurking behind her eyes.

<u>Jan 31st</u>

A fascinating session with Pamela today. I had thought I'd noticed her gaining a little weight recently, and it finally dawned on me that she was in fact pregnant. But when I attempted to raise the subject, she became quite vehement, insisting that such a thing was quite impossible. 'I'm sorry, Dr Raglan, but that's ridiculous,' she told me. 'You know what sort of girl I am, and there's just no way. I find the very idea offensive. I've put a few pounds on, is all. I just need to lay off the french fries at lunch.'

Regardless, I know what I see. So perhaps her fervent religious beliefs and strict personal morality are causing her to be in complete denial about the situation? It certainly wouldn't be the first time such a thing has occurred with a young female patient. But if the pregnancy – assuming it <u>is</u> one – continues to develop, how much longer will she be able to deny what is happening with her own body?

And yet…I feel as though I understand Pamela quite well now, and the look of horror in her eyes when I implied that she might have engaged in sexual intercourse was entirely genuine. So, if I am to take her at her word and she is indeed still _virgo intacta_, what other possibilities are we left with?

A phantom pregnancy? Could her repressed hysteria have reached a sufficient level to cause such a dramatic physiological reaction?

I shall have to monitor the situation carefully.

<u>March 7th</u>

Further developments with Pamela. Simply put, the matter of her visibly burgeoning pregnancy could no longer be ignored, despite her continued protestations. Eventually, when I persisted in my attempts to discuss her condition, she became quite upset, a rare display of the rage I have always suspected lurked beneath her placid exterior. She began to pace angrily around the office, throwing various ornaments and knick-knacks to the floor. I finally managed to calm her by describing the phenomenon of phantom pregnancies, and suggesting that this could offer a possible explanation for her current state. While many patients might be quite disturbed by the idea that their body had manifested a fictitious pregnancy as a consequence of psychological distress, Pamela actually seemed reassured by the notion. Her loathing of immorality apparently quite outweighs any fear she might have of her own disordered mind. In the end, I managed to persuade her to see an eminent New York gynaecologist of my acquaintance by agreeing to accompany her on the visit (and, at her insistence, vouching to my colleague in regards to Pamela's impeccable personal morality). The appointment is next week.

TWILIGHT'S LAST SCREAMING

<u>March 12th</u>

Unusually, I find myself almost at a loss for words. How best to describe the events of today?

As agreed, I accompanied Pamela to her gynaecological exam with Dr Sapirstein. She was obviously nervous, but seemed to take comfort in my presence. When the time came for her appointment, I assured her I would be right outside in the waiting room, and with her full agreement, would consult with the doctor as to his conclusions afterwards.

I waited for some twenty minutes, until Sapirstein asked to speak privately with me in his office. Fully expecting his diagnosis to confirm one possibility or the other – that is, either Pamela had been lying about her condition and was indeed pregnant, or she had not and the pregnancy was a hysterical one – I was astonished to discover that the answer was that <u>both</u> were seemingly true.

'It's the damndest thing, Hal,' he told me. 'There's no question that the girl is pregnant. There's nothing phantom about it. There's a baby in there, all right. A big one. But…' He paused to light his pipe, and puffed on it thoughtfully. 'She's completely intact. There's no doubt in my mind that your patient is indeed a virgin, just like she says. So how the hell do we explain this?'

'I know exactly what Pamela will say,' I told him. 'She'll think it was God's work. I'll have to work very hard to persuade her she's not carrying around the Second Coming in there.'

Sapirstein, never being much of a one for religion, snorted contemptuously at this. But I could tell he was desperately keen to find any sort of an explanation. Finally, he told me he would continue to act as her gynaecologist – pro bono – for the duration of the pregnancy, hoping that he and I might eventually get to the bottom of the matter.

As expected, when I broke the news to Pamela, she took it only as confirmation of her faith. 'My baby's a miracle,' she whispered.

'We don't know that, Pamela,' I warned her. 'The fact of the matter is, we don't know quite <u>what</u> your baby is.'

Her eyes flared. '<u>I</u> know what it is! A gift from God!'

That was the last she had to say about the subject. We made the rest of the drive back to New Jersey in silence, Pamela gently caressing her swollen belly.

A gift from God. I suppose it would be one explanation, but it is hardly the one I am rapidly coming to prefer. Not that my own explanation is scarcely any less unbelievable.

But let us suppose that, instead of a false pregnancy, Pamela's body actually managed to somehow conceive a <u>real child</u> as a result of her psychosis: an extraordinary physiological manifestation of her deep psychological trauma?

And then, if we do accept such a thing might be possible, then the next question must therefore be: what on earth would such a child be like?

<u>June 13th</u>

Pamela Voorhees gave birth to a baby boy today.

Although otherwise physically healthy, the child is terribly deformed. I know that, as a qualified medical professional, I should resist using such archaic, pejorative terms, but I will hereby admit in these pages that the first word that sprang to my mind was <u>monster</u>.

If the boy is indeed a child of his mother's rage, then I suppose we can now see what rage looks like when incarnated in the flesh. Privately, Sapirstein told me afterward the delivery that if it were up to him, he would quietly smother the baby. 'What sort of a life will that poor little bastard have?' he murmured.

Pamela, of course, is utterly blind to her child's abnormalities, seeing only a perfect, divine being. She already insists that she shares an uncanny bond with her baby, and can hear his every thought.

She has named him Jason.

Candice awoke the next morning to find herself still sitting at Frank's desk, a sour taste in her mouth and a sharp pain behind her right eye, as though a knitting needle were being continually jabbed into the socket. But even the nagging discomfort of her hangover did not mask the throbbing agony she could feel in her flesh. Glancing down at her arms, she could see that the skin had erupted in a storm of welts and blisters, and as her face contorted in dismay, the resultant pain left her in no doubt that her facial features had been similarly afflicted.

Stumbling through to the kitchen, Candice fixed herself a pot of coffee, the slow drip-feed of her own distress building in time with the hiss and rumble of the percolator. As she waited, she realised she could not stand to spend another day in this house. For her whole life, she had been as passive as a rag doll, a helpless victim of the trauma visited upon her by her parents. Now, Candice was seized by the irresistible compulsion to seize control of her own existence, to do *something*. Quite what that something might be, however, was still an unknowable mystery.

Pouring her coffee, she thought back to Raglan's account of his sessions with Patient P. Candice had never heard the name Pamela Voorhees before reading it in the files last night, and was certain the woman had not been a part of the class action lawsuit brought against the Somafree Institute.

Given that her child's birth long predated Raglan's development of his psychoplasmics treatment, she supposed that was hardly a surprise. Quite possibly the woman knew nothing at all about it, or of the unfortunate kinship she shared with Candice and so many others. Pamela's child would be a middle-aged man now. What sort of life had *he* had, lacking any sort of clinical support or understanding as to the truth of his condition?

Perhaps Candice could help them. Offer them advice, or even money, if they needed it. Better that than sitting around in this grave of a house fighting the urge to tear her seething skin from her bones.

All she had to go on were the contact details Raglan had listed for Pamela: an address in a small New Jersey town named Crystal Lake. Of course, the doctor's sessions with her had taken place nearly half a century before. By now she could very well have moved away, or even died. But even the slim hope that Pamela could still be found gave Candice an unexpected purpose, one she clung to fiercely.

Looking Crystal Lake up on a map, she estimated she could drive there in about seven hours. With the return journey thrown in, it would only mean about a day wasted if the trip came to naught. A day she would otherwise spend trapped here, as condemned to her solitude as any death row convict.

Still, Candice had never driven for so far, or for so long. Frank had taught her to drive some years before, but, given her abiding neurosis about social interaction, Candice had never officially qualified for a license. Could she make the long drive to New Jersey? Moreover, could she make it without being pulled over by the cops? She thought she could. Her father had been a careful, methodical man, and had been sure to pass on these small virtues to his daughter.

Candice decided she would leave first thing the next morning. She would spend the rest of that day recovering from her hangover and meditating, in a bid to suppress her gnawing anxiety over the coming trip. She supposed her search would doubtlessly involve speaking to other people once she arrived in Crystal Lake, but did her best to ignore the prospect for now. If she dwelled too much on the implications of her journey, her condition would only worsen, and she would never succeed in escaping the house.

She awoke early the following morning feeling refreshed, and although her skin still bore the marks of her psychological turmoil, the attendant discomfort had largely subsided. Nevertheless, Candice was always keen to avoid the prying eyes of others, and dressed in a baggy hooded top, wrapping a scarf around her lower face for good measure.

The drive itself passed mostly without incident. Although Candice could never quite rid herself of the irrational fear that every other driver on the road would somehow intuit that she had no legal right to be behind the wheel of a car, she drove cautiously and encountered no real problems, at least until she arrived in New Jersey and became lost trying to navigate the tangle of backwood roads leading to her destination. This mishap added a couple of hours to her journey, and so it was already late afternoon by the time she finally pulled into Crystal Lake.

The lengthening shadows on the ground only served to heighten the pall of despair that hung over the little town. As Candice drove through its streets, all she saw were closed-up businesses and neglected-looking houses. Certainly a town like this would be largely dependent upon its summer income, but it was now August and Crystal Lake looked for all the world like it was marooned in the depths of winter. What had happened here to drive the tourist trade away?

Finally, she came across a small diner that was still open for business. Much like the rest of the town, it had obviously seen far better days, but Candice could see signs of activity within. Parking up outside, she lingered on the sidewalk for a moment, summoning up the courage to enter the diner.

Once she did so, Candice felt as though she had, in the space of a few short steps, crossed into another era entirely. The diner had clearly not been renovated for many years, and the dim lighting and peeling paint of the décor made it an unappetising prospect as a place to order a meal. One side of the room was dominated by racks of dog-eared paperbacks and yellowed magazines, while a long wooden dinner counter ran the length of the other.

The only customer currently sitting at the counter was a middle-aged man dressed in work overalls and a dirty cap, and both he and the diner's only waitress turned to stare at Candice as she entered. The apprehensive expressions on their faces suggested that they thought she might be an extraterrestrial, or something worse.

Hello, Candice said quietly, glancing over at the waitress. *Are you open?*

The woman considered the question for a moment, then gave a curt nod, gesturing at one of the empty stools. As Candice warily took her seat, the waitress continued to peer at her in evident suspicion, before finally uttering a single word: *Getcha?*

Ordering a coffee and a burger, Candice stared down at the countertop, suddenly regretting the impulsive fool's errand that had brought her to this place. It was all too obvious that her presence in Crystal Lake was entirely unwelcome. Whatever had happened to the town had caused it to curl up into a defensive ball, brandishing its spines at the world like a porcupine. She began to fumble for her purse. Best to just pay what she owed and leave now. Travelling back to Toronto so soon after she had arrived here would be exhausting, but better that than spend another minute in this damned little town.

A voice at her side stopped her. *Are you lost, miss?*

Candice turned to see the older man gazing across at her. He seemed to have lowered his guard somewhat, and she thought she glimpsed a trace of sympathy in his eyes.

Uh, no, not really, she mumbled in reply. *At least, I don't think so.*

I just wondered, he said. *We don't get many young folks around here. Not these days, anyway.*

The waitress placed a steaming cup of coffee in front of Candice. Thanking the woman, she decided to confess the real reason for her visit. *Actually, I came here looking for someone,* she told the man. *It's stupid, really. I don't even know if she lives here any more.*

Well, everybody here knows just about everybody, the man said with a smile. *So why don't you shoot me her name and I'll tell you?*

Pamela Voorhees, Candice replied.

The first reply she received to this statement was a loud crash from behind the counter. Startled, Candice glanced around to see that the waitress had dropped a dinner plate to the floor. And when she looked back at the man, it was to discover his friendly smile had vanished.

And what's your business with that woman? he asked, his voice suddenly monotone.

It's kind of a long story, Candice said hesitantly. *But I was thinking I might be able to help her.*

Ain't no one that can help Pamela Voorhees, the man replied. *Certainly not now, and most probably they never could.*

Perhaps he hoped that might be the end of it, but Candice's blank expression finally prompted him to continue, although not before he gave a long, defeated sigh. *She's dead, miss,* he said, by way of explanation. *Has been for more'n ten years now. So whatever business you had with her is already done. And if there's one thing I do know, it's that you're a damn sight better off that way.*

The man grimaced, as though tasting something bitter. Turning away from Candice, he resumed drinking his coffee, his eyes staring emptily into space.

But she still had one final question. *And her son?* she asked the man softly. *What happened to Jason Voorhees?*

At the mention of the name, the waitress let out a strangled gasp, closer to a hiss. The man himself did not reply. Instead, he simply closed his eyes and shook his head sorrowfully.

I'm sorry, Candice said. *I don't understand—*

Better you just leave now, the waitress snapped, cutting her off. *There's no charge. Just go.*

Her face burning, Candice half-jumped, half-fell, from her seat and dashed from the diner. She'd been stupid to come here, so very stupid. She knew less than nothing about the world, or of the people dwelling in it. Her coming here had somehow caused others pain, and as someone who'd spent a great deal of her life being hurt, that was the absolute last thing Candice had ever wanted to do. She would return directly home and stay there for good, with only her own ghosts for company. Better that than stirring up other people's ghosts, ghosts she should have left well enough alone.

Her hands shaking, she fumbled clumsily with her car keys, and dropped them to the ground. Cursing, Candice bent to retrieve them, until they were lost to a shadow that suddenly loomed up in front of her.

Miss?

She glanced up to see the man from the diner. A sudden terror filled her. *I'm going now, honest I am,* Candice gabbled. *I won't bother you any more, I swear.*

The man reached down and plucked up the keys, gently placing them into the palm of her hand. *You can go whenever you like,* he said. *But I figured you were owed some kind of an explanation. You seem like a nice kid, and I'm guessing you don't got the first idea about what you just stumbled into, do you?*

I don't, I really don't, she pleaded.

The man sighed again, a mournful, bearlike sound. *I'm not sure where you ever heard the name Voorhees or what the hell you might want with them, but I'll tell you what I know. Don't know if it'll help, but it's all I can do for you.* He took off his cap and scratched at his scalp. *You were right, Pamela Voorhees spent most of her life here in Crystal Lake. Raised her boy Jason here too. She worked out at the summer camp on the lake, just a few miles from here.*

What happened?

Her boy drowned, right there in the lake. Must have been back in '57 or thereabouts. The kids working at the camp were meant to be watching him, but they were off fooling around or somesuch. Hell, it wasn't fair to expect them to mind him. That boy wasn't right in the head.

Candice's mind flashed back to Raglan's file. A monster, that's what he'd called Jason.

Pamela was never the same after that, the man continued. *Mind you, there were plenty said she wasn't quite right in the first place neither. The next year, two of the counsellors were murdered out there, stabbed to death. Back then, no one knew who'd done it, they thought it was some escaped lunatic or something. After that, there were all sorts of accidents at the camp. Word spread around quickly, and the place got a bad reputation. Folks around here started to call it Camp Blood. So wasn't long before the owners closed it down for good. And that was how it stayed, till their own son got the damn fool idea to reopen it himself some twenty years later.*

Candice gazed off into the distance. She knew exactly how these sorts of stories went. *And so it all started up again?* she asked.

Right enough. Once a place turns bad, it stays bad. And that's how it was with Camp Blood. Bunch of kids moved in to fix the old campsite up, and one day that June, Friday the 13th it was, all but one of them died. Murdered, they were, same as the kids twenty years before. Murdered by Pamela Voorhees.

Feeling unsteady, Candice sat down on the nearby kerb. *Because of Jason?*

The man spat onto the ground. *She never got over it. Folks said she claimed he still spoke to her.* He tapped his skull insinuatingly. *You know, voices in her head. Anyway, the moment they announced they were reopening the place, she just snapped, I guess. Butchered the whole lot of them, save for this one girl. Brave kid, she was. She managed to kill that crazy bitch all by herself. Cut Pamela's head clean off, she did.*

So much violence. This was Hal Raglan's legacy. Candice suddenly wished she'd brought the bottle of vodka with her, anything to help numb the sickness she felt right now. *And that was the end of it?*

The man did not reply. Instead, he took out a pouch of tobacco and began to methodically roll a cigarette. The whole process took so long that Candice became certain he was deliberately ignoring her, signalling his blunt contempt for the question.

Then he said, simply and softly, *No.*

Candice stared back at him. He seemed deeply reluctant to say any more, but eventually the relentlessness of her gaze forced a response.

Like I said, Camp Blood stayed bad, the man mumbled. *Every year, there's more killings up there. Folks round here, they mostly know to stay away, but outsiders? All they can see is a pretty-looking lake. They can't smell the blood in the air. They don't know that place is death.*

But why? Candice said. *If Pamela and her son are both dead and gone?*

I said Jason Voorhees was dead, the man said in a low voice. *I didn't say he was gone.*

That's crazy.

Maybe it is, the man replied sourly. *But someone killed all those people. Dozens of 'em by now. Everyone says it's Jason's ghost that's doing it, and I don't know enough to say any different. All I know is that place is cursed, and now here you come asking about it and stirring up more trouble.*

Candice climbed to her feet. *I'm sorry,* she told the man. *I didn't mean to cause you trouble. That was honestly the last thing I wanted to do.*

Well, you weren't to know any different, he replied. *But now you do. So take my advice. Leave here and forget all about Pamela Voorhees and Crystal Lake.*

I don't know if I can do that, Candice said, surprising herself with her own directness. *I think I need to see it for myself.*

His face paled. *You're not thinking about going up there?*

Candice unlocked the door to her car. *Thanks for telling me the whole story,* she said politely.

The man slammed his hand down on the vehicle's hood. *You're crazy!*

She looked at him levelly. *Sir? This is my father's car. I'd appreciate it if you didn't damage it in any way.*

He took a step back, his eyes beseeching her. *Miss, please. Don't you understand what I'm telling you? You'll never come back from there.*

Maybe I won't, at that, Candice said calmly, before climbing into the car and driving away.

It took her some time to locate the remains of the old campsite. There were no signs for it along the neighbouring roads any more, and the local residents were clearly determined to let it be swallowed by the surrounding woods, so that they might finally be allowed to pretend it had never even existed. But she was resolute in her search, and eventually found herself driving down an overgrown trail towards the lakeside. She could see a number of dilapidated shacks huddled there, haunted by shades of dreadful summers past.

Eventually the trail grew impassable for her car, forcing Candice to get out and continue the rest of the way on foot. As she walked, she gazed up at the evening sky, noting that it seemed to echo the camp's macabre nickname in its crimson hue. Perhaps, she thought, all of the blood spilt here had seeped up into the air above, instead of the ground below.

Ignoring the empty huts, she strode through the camp and made straight for the lake's edge, drawn by the gentle lapping of the water and the alluring crystalline glitter of its surface. Upon reaching the shore, she kicked off her shoes, relishing the feel of the warm sand between her toes. Gazing out at the lake, Candice realised she felt more at peace here than at any time she could remember. Was that wrong? So many people had died here, after all. Crystal Lake was a cursed place, shunned by everyone who knew its name. But *she* was cursed too, wasn't she? Perhaps such places only required the right kind of people to inhabit them. What was damned to others might be a blessed sanctuary for such as she.

Gripped by an impulsive, nameless urge, Candice stripped off her clothes and waded into the water. Normally so terrified of revealing her scarred flesh to the world, here she felt completely freed from her fear. After all, who would see her? Only ghosts, and she was accustomed enough to their presence by now.

She swam out into the lake until her feet could no longer touch the bottom. Although Candice was not a particularly strong swimmer, she felt no apprehension. Whatever happened to her now, she was certain that she'd somehow been meant to come here, and that certainty granted her a blissful sense of release she had never previously known. Candice had spent so much of her life imprisoned – in her father's house, within her own tortured flesh – that such bliss overrode all other possible concerns. She closed her eyes and turned over onto her back, revelling in the feeling of the cool water on her swollen skin.

Then, the voice of the man from the diner crept into her mind like a burglar.

Her boy drowned, right there in the lake.

Candice's eyes snapped open.

Jason.

Lifting her head, she began to scan the shoreline, unsure of exactly what she expected to see there. A revenant or a monster? A vengeful ghost or merely an anguished, raging man-child? Was Jason Voorhees out there somewhere now, watching her? Or did he lurk beneath the surface of the lake itself? Were his lifeless hands reaching out for her right at this very moment, eager to pull her down into the black depths so that she might share in his eternal loneliness?

The pleasant coolness of the water suddenly intensified into a sharp chill, and Candice shuddered. Cursing the loss of the peace she had felt, she began to swim back to shore, growing angrier at herself with every stroke. She'd let the man's ghost stories get to her, and now her annoyance was threatening to blossom into the sort of black rage Candice spent her whole life trying to suppress, the exact same rage that had eventually claimed her mother.

As soon as her feet touched bottom again, Candice ran from the water, her body trembling with the cold. She began to hurriedly gather up her clothes, wanting only to be dressed and safely back in the car.

In the next instant, she realised she was no longer alone.

She glanced up to see a towering silhouette blocking out the evening sky. The shape stank of filth and rot and, above all else, an almost palpable hatred that seemed to poison the very air around it.

Jason, Candice whispered.

Somewhere at the back of her mind, it occurred to her that it was as though he had sensed her anger and been summoned here by it, drawn to a kindred soul.

Jason Voorhees lumbered forward, the light of the setting sun catching the battered hockey mask he wore over his disfigured face.

He hides his face too, Candice thought, and felt a sudden sympathy for the creature, a sympathy that was just as quickly banished by the sight of the woodman's axe Jason carried in one hand.

A flood of thoughts swept through her mind in a deluge: should she run screaming back into the water? Fall to her knees and beg?

But she did none of those things. Instead, Candice threw her clothes down to the sand and stood naked before Jason, throwing her arms open and displaying her own disfigurement to him. She gazed into the two black pits of his mask, searching for the eyes concealed somewhere behind it.

You see? she told him. *I'm just like you. My mother made me like this. I didn't have a choice either.*

The creature paused where it stood, axe suspended in the air. Slowly, Jason's head cocked to one side, considering her.

We're the same, Candice continued. *That anger you feel? I feel it too. I felt it my whole life. My mother passed it onto me, just like yours did to you. But maybe we don't need to be this way any more.*

She took a single step towards Jason. He recoiled for an instant, and Candice thought he might be about to raise the axe and bury it in her skull.

But he didn't. Instead, he continued to watch her intently, head still cocked like an inquisitive dog.

Candice placed one hand on her chest, then carefully gestured across to Jason, signalling to him that they were the same. *I used to know a man called Dr. Raglan. He treated my mother, and yours too. He was the one who made us like this.* She raised her fingers to her face and body, tracing the knotted lines of her scars. *But he died a long time ago now. So did my mom.*

They hurt me really badly, but I think it's time to let go of that. I don't want all that rage inside me. It's made me too sick for far too long.

When Jason remained motionless, she took another step towards him, then gingerly reached out and placed her hand on the haft of his axe. Candice felt him tense for a instant, then relax. Encouraged, she curled her fingers around the weapon and pulled at it gently. After a moment's hesitation, he allowed her to take it from his grip and toss it to the sand.

They now faced each other unarmed. Although Candice knew Jason could easily crush her between his bare hands, this was as close to an equal footing as she could ask for. If she was quick, she could still snatch up the axe and attack him with it. That might buy her enough time to escape.

Instead, she asked, *Will you let me help you?*

Another slight movement of the head, signalling his curiosity. Slowly, Jason extended one massive hand towards Candice.

Taking it, she pulled him closer, reaching up to embrace him. The carrion stench of his body was almost overwhelming; her eyes immediately began to stream with tears, and Candice thought for a second that she might faint. But she told herself that she had borne worse, and would bear this.

Her arms closed around him. At first, she might have been holding a marble statue, stiff and unyielding, and Candice's breath caught in her throat. Had she made a terrible, naive mistake?

Then she felt Jason's arms, like two heavy chains, enfold her.

They stood there silently embracing, the only sound that of the tide's soft lullaby.

There, Candice said.

Jason's only response was to let out a long hollow sigh, like the sound of trapped air rushing from a tomb deep in the earth. It was a sigh that emanated from within his very bones, from the depths of the black absence he had carried inside him ever since the day of his birth.

The next moment, Candice felt his flesh starting to give way underneath her fingers. The creature's body, once so monolithic, now began to crumble and diminish. Candice continued to hold him as he slowly dwindled, the dust of his disintegrating flesh trickling through her hands, its steady passage marking the long years of Jason's agony.

Soon, there was nothing left of him but ashes, a pile of old rags and his mask.

Candice bent down to pick the mask up, turning it over in her hands and thinking.

The next moment, she drew her arm back and threw it out into the lake, as far as she could manage.

Candice watched as the mask landed on the surface of the water, bobbed there for a few seconds, then sank down into darkness.

The time for disguises was past.

Candice quickly dressed herself, then turned around and set out for her car. Her retreating figure was soon absorbed by the gloaming, and within moments it was as if no one had ever been there at all. That which she had left behind her hung in the air for a time, and was then carried out across the lake by the breeze, there to be scattered into nothingness.

ADAM CRAMER

William Shatner in
The Intruder, 1962
written by Charles Beaumont,
based on his novel
directed by Roger Corman

LIZ WETHERLY

Leslie Uggams in
Poor Pretty Eddie, 1975
written by B. W. Sandefur
directed by Richard Robinson

UPON BOARDING HIS FLIGHT FROM NEW ORLEANS TO ATLANTA, ADAM Cramer discovered he had been allocated a seat next to an elderly black lady. Summoning the stewardess, he insisted that he be allowed to change seats, and when asked why, smiled politely at the young woman and said, *You don't seriously expect me to sit next to a negro, do you?*

The flustered stewardess duly found another seat for him, and the rest of the flight passed without any further incident.

Such altercations were not altogether uncommon in Cramer's everyday life. Although he had eventually been forced to abandon his doomed battle against the repeal of the Jim Crow laws, as far as he was concerned, the so-called progressives behind such reforms did not represent either his views or those of the millions of ordinary decent people like him, and had absolutely no right to impose their ideology on large swathes of the population that they could in no way be said to speak for. And while he might have retired from propagating his own warped brand of grass-roots social activism, Cramer had now found employment as a DJ on the Louisiana talk radio station WUSA, whose conservative owners were more than happy to encourage his continual on-air screeds against desegregation, miscegenation, and the creeping liberalism that was rotting the country they so fervently loved from within.

His extremist views were therefore well-known in New Orleans, and consequently, Cramer enjoyed a certain level of minor but notorious celebrity in the city. So, more often than not, whenever he provoked incidents of this ilk, his actions would either go unopposed, or else were quietly applauded by those who tacitly approved of his beliefs.

Many of those who counted themselves amongst the latter group could be found at the regular fundraising soirées held by the WUSA owners, who, in addition to their mainstream media operations, had covert ties to several underground right-wing organisations, and made it their business to help facilitate the flow of dark money that kept such groups afloat. It was, in fact, one of these very evenings that had prompted Cramer's current trip. He'd been introduced to a man named Paul Buher, the acting CEO of Thorn Industries, who'd wasted no time in proclaiming himself a fan of Cramer's no-holds-barred approach. *Thorn are looking to expand into television and radio,* he'd informed the DJ. *You should come and look us up next time you're in Chicago. We can always use people with your sort of passion.*

Although he would always insist that any personal ambition came a distant second to his ongoing struggle against the liberal status quo, Cramer was not blind to the opportunities a multi-national conglomerate like Thorn could offer him. A nationally syndicated radio show for one, not to mention a chance to expand into television. And beyond that, who knew? If his brand proved successful enough, perhaps he could even leverage it into a political career, and the possibility of enacting real systemic reform.

At the first available opportunity, Cramer took some vacation time from WUSA and made plans for his trip to Chicago, allowing himself time for one small personal diversion along the way. His older sister Bertha lived near Athens, Georgia, and it had been some years since he'd seen her last. This was not entirely happenstance; Bertha's living circumstances were both rural and secluded, and in her brother's opinion, almost wildly dysfunctional. The same went for Bertha herself, whose once semi-successful light entertainment career had now given way to obesity, alcoholism and psychological instability. Regardless, she was all the family that Cramer had left.

He wrote to tell her of his intention to visit, and she immediately sent him back a postcard, written in her unruly, looping script: 'Can't WAIT to see you!!! You will meet my EDDIE he is THE BEST so GORGEOUS and TALENTED!!! XXXX'

Cramer assumed Eddie was Bertha's new lover. She'd enjoyed a succession of them over the years, and had a particular weakness for deeply mediocre musicians, whom she would always proclaim to be the next Elvis/Liberace/Swan. He would undoubtedly have to sit through a musical performance put on for his benefit and be expected to both applaud enthusiastically and extend an offer to pass on said mediocrity's demo tape to other DJs of his acquaintance.

The thought of it already giving him a tension headache, Cramer had booked his flight to Atlanta and another flight leaving for Chicago the very next morning.

Now the trip was underway, and had begun inauspiciously with the contretemps over the airline's seating arrangements. Cramer's mood was not improved when he landed in Atlanta and went to pick up his rental car, only to be welcomed onto the parking lot by a black attendant. Quietly simmering, he followed the man to his assigned vehicle, which appeared to be parked on the farthest possible point on the other side of the lot.

When they eventually arrived at the car, the attendant gave his customer a friendly smile and asked if there was anything else he could do for him.

Cramer slowly put on his sunglasses. *You can get the hell out of my way, boy,* he said.

The attendant's smile immediately vanished. He stared at Cramer for a moment, then stepped aside. *Yes...sir,* he replied, his face tight.

Satisfied, Cramer climbed into the car and drove away, giving the attendant a parting honk of the horn as he exited the lot. He made good time on the drive to Athens, and soon found himself navigating the gravel road leading down to 'Bertha's Oasis', the woodland lodge owned by his sister. Much like its proprietor, the Oasis had seen much better days, and from what Cramer had seen, now mainly served as a watering hole for a dubious array of local cretins and malcontents.

He pulled up outside, noting with distaste the rusted vehicles and junked auto parts stacked around the yard, the fly-strewn piles of dog excrement lurking treacherously underfoot. To think that his own sister lived in such squalor when all over the country, delinquent negro families were being showered with financial aid and social housing!

Now more than ever, something needed to be done. Cramer only hoped that this trip would provide him with the opportunity and means to do so.

He eased himself stiffly out of the car and gazed around. The yard was deserted and almost entirely silent, the only sound the rhythmic creak and splash of the nearby water wheel. Cramer's neck prickled with unease. The Oasis might have been secluded, but in his experience, it was rarely this quiet. Normally the air would be filled with the sound of barking dogs, unruly drunks, and, rising above it all, Bertha's insistent, incessant, whine.

Crossing to the building housing the lodge's bar, Cramer pushed the door open and peered inside. The interior was dark, the neon beer signs on the walls providing the only source of illumination. A unpleasant mixture of scents assailed his nostrils: beer and piss, which was only to be expected, but mingling with them, the stench of shit and scorched gunpowder.

And something else, too. A thick coppery smell, reeking of violence and death.

Removing his sunglasses, Cramer gingerly stepped across the threshold. Now that he'd left the eerie silence of the yard behind him, he could make out the hoarse, desolate sound of a woman sobbing.

Bertha.

Following the sound, Cramer moved through the bar, his eyes gradually adjusting to the gloom. Everywhere he looked, there were signs of violence: smashed glass, bullet holes, splashes of dried brown blood.

Eventually, he came upon his sister. Bertha sat sprawled on the floor next to a long trestle table, her face blurred with tears and thick make-up, reminding Cramer of a toddler's smeared finger-painting. A corpse was laid out atop the table: a young, good-looking man dressed in what had once been a yellow rhinestone shirt, before it was torn apart by multiple gunshots and stained crimson with the unfortunate victim's blood.

Bertha clutched one of the dead man's hands in her own, so tightly that Cramer thought she might be attempting to pull him back from the underworld through sheer force of will alone. He wasn't even sure he would put such a feat past her.

He crouched down in front of her. *Bertha?* he said gently.

Slowly, she raised her eyes to look at Cramer. The two siblings gazed at each other for a several, before Bertha opened her mouth, as if to reply. But instead, all that emerged was a long keening sound.

Cramer waited for the noise to finish, then raised a hand and slapped his sister across the face. *Bertha, now you quit that racket and just tell me what the hell happened here,* he demanded.

His sister stared dumbly back at him, her jaw hanging open, eyes sodden with grief. Cramer thought for a moment he was going to have to hit her again, but then Bertha spoke at last.

It was only three words, but it was enough to set in motion everything else that followed.

That nigger bitch, she said.

——

Cabrini-Green.

The way Liz Wetherly saw it, when she'd fled here she'd simply exchanged one living hell for another: Bertha's Oasis for a Chicago inner-city ghetto. These projects were once held up as an emblem of what could be achieved by the public housing system at its best, but, in the space of only a few short decades, had degenerated into a crime-ridden slum, a social embarrassment carefully sectioned off from the rest of the city. Racially-motivated urban planning and redlining had successfully isolated Cabrini-Green within Chicago, and the federal government's stranglehold on much-needed funds and amenities then worked to finish the job. The housing projects were by now little more than the city's dumping ground; the place black people were sent when they had nowhere else to go.

Just ask Liz's sister Ruthie-Jean. She'd lived on Chicago's West Side until 1968, but the riots that ensued after the death of Martin Luther King had left over a thousand people homeless. The city's solution? Send them to Cabrini-Green, where there were scores of vacancies caused by tenants fleeing the ailing projects. The influx of homeless, destitute people only worsened Cabrini's problems, which were further exacerbated by increasing gang violence and the economic downturn of the early 1970's. The area's manufacturing industry had recently been decimated, leaving many of the tenants in the projects out of work. In Ruthie-Jean's case, she'd worked in a local manufacturing plant owned by Thorn Industries, who had eventually elected to close the site and move the operation overseas.

Liz's success as a singer meant she always tried to help out Ruthie-Jean where she could, but her sister was a proud woman and there was only so much charity she could bear to accept. Normally when Liz came to the city to visit, she would book a hotel in Chicago's Gold Coast neighbourhood, which, although only a short distance from the projects, might as well have been on another planet entirely. She and Ruthie-Jean could thereby meet easily and conveniently without Liz having to endure the distressing squalor of her sister's living circumstances.

But nothing was remotely normal any more. The degradation Liz had endured at the hands of Eddie Collins, Bertha Cramer's psychotic and now-deceased lover, had left her teetering on the verge of a breakdown, and therefore the prospect of her staying in a hotel – or anywhere else – on her own was unthinkable. After her escape from the Oasis, Liz had barely even held it together long enough to get herself on a flight from Atlanta to Chicago. She'd called Ruthie-Jean from the airport, begging her sister to come and collect her when she landed.

Now, Liz lay huddled in the darkness of her sister's guest bedroom, in reality not much more than a large walk-in closet, piled high with crates of the belongings Ruthie-Jean no longer had space for in the rest of her cramped apartment. Like her sister, Liz had once been a proud woman, even bordering on arrogant at times (it was no secret to her that the white promoters she dealt with often called her *uppity* behind her back), but the horrors she'd just experienced had sent her plummeting back down to earth, her wings in tatters. For people like her, America was a land full of wrong turns, roads that seemed to be full of promise one minute but could lead you to outright catastrophe the next. She'd unwittingly stumbled upon such a road and had barely survived. Assailed by nightmares while she slept and panic attacks when she awoke, it was all Liz could do to simply lie here and await whatever disaster might come next.

And if there was one thing she was now sure of, it was that something would *always* come next. The worst part was simply waiting for it to happen.

Gazing into the shadows, Liz told herself that at least bad news travelled fast, meaning she probably wouldn't have too much longer to wait.

There was a gentle knock at the door, and Ruthie-Jean's head appeared. *Hey, you awake?* she whispered.

Liz did not reply, hoping that her sister would take the hint and withdraw.

No such luck. *I can see you are, girl. Don't be giving me no silent treatment, now.*

What is it? Liz mumbled.

I made some fresh coffee. Come sit out here with me and have a cup. The sun's shining and it's real pretty. Ruthie-Jean laughed. *Long as you don't look outside the window, anyway.*

I'm sick.

Her sister was resolute. *Then some sunshine will do you good.*

Liz sighed and rolled over in bed. *Please, Ruthie-Jean. I just want to be left alone.*

I left you alone for two whole days. You think you the only one bad shit happens to? Go take a walk outside and tell me that.

This is different.

An edge crept into Ruthie-Jean's voice. *Yeah, it's always different for you, ain't it? Just cause you can carry a damn tune. You reckon that makes you better, that you shouldn't have to suffer like the rest of us.*

Liz said nothing.

Undeterred, her sister continued. *And I tell you something else. It's like you just waiting for trouble to come calling. Well, I don't need that in my house. I don't need you bringing down any more trouble on me than I already got. So you just lie there and think about that awhile, and be sure you get your ass outta that bed before I throw it out.*

The door closed with an abrupt thud, the bedroom's thin walls trembling at Ruthie-Jean's angry exit.

Liz pulled the bedclothes over her head and retreated into the darkness to continue her forlorn vigil.

It wouldn't be much longer now, she was certain of it.

———

If there was one thing Adam Cramer knew, it was people. After all, a man in his particular line of work could hardly afford not to. People were his lifeblood, the fuel that kept his motor on the road. Like-minded people, everyday folks who shared his passions and beliefs. He had a little red address book he carried with him everywhere, and he prided himself on having friends in every major American city, even the ones he could hardly bear to set foot in; those that had allowed the niggers and degenerates to take hold and were now suffering the inevitable consequences.

So he made a few calls, caught up with a few old friends, pulled in a few favours, and within two hours had confirmation of the fact that, after fleeing the carnage she'd instigated at Bertha's place, Liz Wetherly had escaped to Chicago. Not only that, but he even had an address for her. That was the only problem with having your big black face plastered all over the covers of glossy magazines; it meant people tended to notice your comings and goings.

Cramer rubbed his hands together in satisfaction. He could now take care of both sets of business without having to go out of his way. As much as he resented his obligations to Bertha, there was never any question in his mind that he had a duty to track down Liz Wetherly and avenge his sister's loss. When all was said and done, family was family. And besides, no good ever came of letting a negro do exactly as they pleased. From what Bertha had told him, Wetherly had strutted into the Oasis like she owned the place, used her celebrity to turn poor simple Eddie's head, and then tossed him aside like a spent tissue after she was done. And all the while, his sister had been forced to look on from the sidelines, betrayed and humiliated by an uppity black bitch. How could he *not* take action?

Fortuitously, it also meant he had a good excuse for not staying here and being saddled with the burden of caring for his grief-stricken sister. *You want me to make her pay, don't you, sweetheart?* he gently reminded Bertha. *If I wait around here too long I might miss my chance. Better I be on that flight tomorrow morning just like I planned.*

After making some more calls, Cramer had arranged both to have Eddie Collins swiftly buried and to hire some local protection for his outing to the Cabrini-Green projects. His work done for the day, he retired early, and when he rose the next morning, Cramer was not surprised to find Bertha still sitting alone in the Oasis bar the next morning, deep into her cups. Wincing at the pervasive reek of stale bourbon on her breath, he gingerly kissed her goodbye and beat a hasty retreat to his hire car.

Several hours later, Cramer was picked up from Chicago O'Hare by a Thorn limousine. During the drive to his hotel, the DJ received a call on the car phone from Chuck Dietz, the company's Head of Media Development, who invited him to dinner that night. By Cramer's reckoning, that still gave him plenty of time to check into his hotel, freshen up, and take care of his business in Cabrini-Green beforehand. This satisfied him. Adam Cramer was a man who liked to do things properly, and having to rush a given task would inevitably leave him out of sorts for the rest of the day, which would not do at all when he still had an important business dinner ahead of him.

Once he'd finished at his hotel, Cramer left the building and walked to a parking lot a few blocks away, where two hired men were waiting for him in a tan sedan. The men introduced themselves as Otis and Mike, and their imposing bulk was such that they made the car they were driving seem like an undersized child's toy. It appeared his friends in Chicago had understood his particular needs perfectly.

They drove to Cabrini, Cramer's mood darkening further with every mile of their journey. Everywhere he looked, the streets were awash with trash and subhuman animals. It made him sick to see a great American city turned into a open air toilet. How could people look at ghettos like this and argue for racial equality? You put animals in cages where they belonged, you didn't let them run wild in the goddamn streets.

As they arrived outside Ruthie-Jean's apartment building, Cramer gazed up at the nearby cluster of tower blocks. The bright sunshine of the day only served to emphasise their drab dilapidation, the only colour on their walls coming from the gang tags sprayed across every available surface.

The towers put him in mind of long decaying fingers, grasping for a heaven that shrank from their touch, forever remaining just out of reach.

Cramer climbed out of the car and noticed a gang of black teenagers eyeballing them from across the lot. He glanced over at Mike, who motioned to the nearest member of the group. Warily, the kid moved closer, ready to bolt at the first sign of trouble.

Anything happens to this car, I'll repaint it in your fuckin' blood, understand? Mike informed him.

The kid pulled a face and sloped back to his friends, but the point had been made. The preliminaries taken care of, the two men escorted Cramer over to the block and up the dingy, graffiti-daubed stairwell. His eyes scanned the colourful array of gibberish and obscenities sprayed across the walls. *Sweets to the sweet*, he read as they climbed the final set of stairs, no doubt some sort of drug reference.

They continued along the dimly-lit corridor towards Ruthie-Jean's apartment door, the last one on the floor. Cramer could hear the distant hoots of the gang below, jeering disdainfully at the white intruders now that they were a safe distance away. How he wished he could just drop bombs on Cabrini-Green and everywhere else like it, expunging such places from existence and wiping the slate clean, so that ordinary decent folks might feel safe in their homes again.

Upon arriving at the door, Cramer made as if to knock and announce their visit, then caught himself.

Otis gave him a sour, tobacco-browned grin. *You just gonna knock politely and expect 'em to let you in, is that it?* he said.

You might have a point, Cramer admitted, and moved safely back.

The two men stepped forward and unleashed a furious volley of kicks upon the flimsy door, which quickly caved in and gave way. Cramer heard an alarmed shriek from somewhere inside. Wasting no time, the two goons advanced into the apartment, their hulking frames jostling for position in the narrow entrance hallway.

After a discreet pause, Cramer followed them, finding himself in a small but cosily-furnished living room. Otis held a struggling black woman by her hair. *This her?* he asked Cramer, yanking vigorously at his hostage's hair in a bid to quieten her.

Cramer peered closer at the woman and shrugged. *I have no idea,* he said. *Their monkey faces all look the damn same to me.*

The next moment, there was a crash from the other side of the room, and Mike entered. He held another woman captive, twisting one of her arms painfully behind her back. *What about this one?* he demanded.

Cramer turned to see the prisoner glaring fiercely at him, terrified but still defiant. *Oh yeah,* he said, taking a step towards the woman he now recognised as Liz Wetherly. *That's the one. I saw her on the TV singing a pretty nigger tune one time.*

And who the hell are you? Liz spat.

The DJ smiled. *Well, there's something of a story there, if you'd care to hear it,* he drawled. Pulling up a chair, he sat down in front of Liz. *So, as it happens, I was passing through Georgia yesterday and figured I'd pay my big sister Bertha a little visit.*

Cramer leaned forward in the chair, his voice dropping to a conspiratorial murmur. *Only she wasn't doing too well, no ma'am. Turned out she'd had another visitor before me. Some spiteful little black bitch, she said. A black bitch in heat, in fact. And what did this horny little nigger bitch do? Why, she only seduced the love of Bertha's life, stole him right away from her without a care in the world.*

Liz lunged forward, before being viciously jerked back by her captor. *I didn't seduce shit! That cracker asshole raped me, and that drunk bitch sister of yours stood by and let it happen!*

Shaking his head sadly, Cramer climbed back to his feet. *That's... impolite,* he said, before slapping Liz across the face. *You'd do well not to speak of my sister that way.*

It's the goddamn truth! Liz shrieked, her eyes filling with tears.

Well now, if I was looking for the truth, I'd hardly be asking a nigger for it, would I? Cramer chuckled, before turning to stare at Liz's sister. *Anyway, as you might imagine, I was quite beside myself when I heard Bertha's sad little story. What is to be done about this, I wondered? How can I possibly make things right again? A smile. And then I found out that a certain horny little nigger bitch had run away from the mess she'd made to go and hide out with her very own sister. And I thought to myself, it's true what they say after all. What goes around, comes around.*

Liz slumped. *What are you gonna do?* she whispered.

There's a lesson to be learned here, Cramer told her. *But I get the feeling you're too damn stupid and uppity to be taught it. So I thought maybe the thing to do was to teach Ruthie-Jean here instead. And maybe that way, you'll learn.*

No! Liz shrieked, trying again to break free from her captor's grip. Grunting, Mike raised one meaty fist and punched her in the back of the skull, sending Liz collapsing to her knees. Dazed, she began to pitch forward, only for her captor to grab her by the hair and jerk her head upright. *I think you're gonna wanna watch this,* missy, Mike growled.

Cramer nodded towards Otis, who released Ruthie-Jean from his grip, only to instantly wheel around and punch her savagely in the belly. Letting out a long, guttural moan, Liz's sister crashed to the floor.

Her attacker shot Cramer a glance. *You want any part of this yourself?*

The DJ gave a scowl of fastidious distaste. *No, I'd rather not get my hands dirty.* He sauntered over to the couch and made himself comfortable. *You gentlemen can do whatever you like to her, as long as she's still alive at the end of it. Feel free to take your time, we have all afternoon.*

So they did.

And when it was finally over, as Liz crouched weeping over her sister's senseless, crumpled body, Cramer turned to her and said, *You may think you're some kind of big shot, Miss Wetherly, but never forget whose damn country this really is.*

———

After the men had finally left, it had taken the paramedics nearly an hour to arrive. A rash of recent sniper attacks had left the authorities reluctant to set foot in Cabrini-Green, and for a time, Liz thought her call had been ignored entirely. She paced the apartment like a restless panther, certain that Ruthie-Jean would die before help ever arrived.

Now, her sister lay motionless in a hospital bed, her body swathed in bandages. As she sat watching Ruthie-Jean, Liz was suddenly gripped by a distant childhood memory. She recalled snapping the arms off her sister's favourite doll, after she had refused to let Liz play with it. The two events now seemed inextricably linked in her mind, as if there was a direct line of causation stretching across the decades that separated them.

It was her fault, all of it.

And all she could do to make amends was cover Ruthie-Jean's medical bills, pay the doctors to stitch the poor broken doll back together. But she couldn't take any of it back, or make the hurt and the terror go away. As Liz knew herself, that would stay with Ruthie-Jean, maybe forever.

I'm so, so sorry, she whispered, reaching across to take her sister's hand.

She felt the muscles in Ruthie-Jean's hand flex weakly, and her sister's one visible eye fluttered open, swollen and bloodshot. *Ain't…your fault*, she mumbled thickly, before her eye closed again. *Hurts…to talk*, she lisped through broken teeth.

Then don't, Liz told her. *The cops still want to speak to you, but I'll hold them off for as long as I can.*

The eye opened again. *What…you tell them?*

Nothing. I said we didn't know who the men were. They just burst in and tried to rob us.

Ruthie-Jean's hand squeezed Liz's, signalling her her wordless approval. Both sisters knew there was no sense in trying to get the police involved. It would undoubtedly lead to further reprisals, and it wasn't as if the Chicago P.D. gave a good goddamn about anything that happened to black folks at Cabrini-Green anyway.

Still, a wild beast had been awakened within Liz's belly; a seething, rabid thing, thirsting for vengeance. She knew she would not be able to rest until someone had been made to pay for what had been done to her and Ruthie-Jean.

Hot tears seared at the corners of her eyes. *I got to do something, Ruthie-Jean. It's not right.*

Her sister breathed deep. *It's how…the world is. You know that.*

Not my world! Liz cried. *I won't live in it, I damn well won't!*

Ruthie-Jean gazed back at her from the bed. There was something unreadable in her look, and Liz was suddenly convinced her sister was holding back some dreadful, forbidden knowledge from her. *What is it, Ruthie-Jean?* she murmured, leaning in. *Tell me.*

Her sister closed her eye again, letting out a soft sigh. Liz thought for a moment that she might have lapsed back into unconsciousness, but then Ruthie-Jean spoke again, the effort of speaking the words – or perhaps just the bitter taste of their meaning – visibly painful on her ruined lips.

Go speak to…the Candyman, she said.

———

Liz stood before the bathroom mirror, her reflection staring idiotically back at her. After the dreadful events of the last few days, she wouldn't have thought she still had it in her to feel ridiculous – there were far worse things in life than mere embarrassment, after all – but apparently she did.

Candyman… she began, before immediately stopping herself.

It wasn't as though she hadn't previously been familiar with the Candyman's legend. Anyone who'd spent any time at all in Cabrini-Green could hardly have failed to notice the graffitied tributes to him everywhere. *Sweets to the sweet*, they read. *Be my victim*. An urban folktale, intended to keep children safely inside after dark. And in a place like Cabrini-Green, who could blame worried parents for perpetuating such a story? When Ruthie-Jean had first moved to the projects, she and Liz had laughed about it together. God knows her sister had needed something to laugh about back then. *At least you've got your very own boogeyman here*, Liz had told her. *And he's even a brother! Hell, maybe he's single, too.*

But Ruthie-Jean had gradually stopped laughing at the stories. *It ain't funny*, she would insist whenever Liz tried to crack a Candyman joke. *Not to us folks that live here.*

So after a while, Liz had stopped raising the subject. Candyman was just added to the long list of things that they didn't talk about.

And now Ruthie-Jean expected her to conjure the local boogeyman up and beg for his aid. Liz supposed it was understandable enough, really. Her sister was in severe pain, terrified and alone, and, unable to turn to the police for help, had seized upon the first possible solution her poor scrambled brain had come up with. A mythical, hook-handed monster.

So what am I supposed to say to him when he comes? she'd asked Ruthie-Jean, trying not to sound impatient. *I mean, won't he just rip my guts out with that big ole hook of his?*

You have to…offer him something, her sister had told her. *Pay tribute. And then…he might perform a service in return.*

So here she was, standing in front of the mirror like some dumb kid. Of course Liz had promised Ruthie-Jean she'd do it, secure in the knowledge that she never would. But the more she'd thought about it, the less able she felt to refuse her sister's request, ridiculous as it was. Ruthie-Jean hadn't asked for any of this. Liz had summoned plenty of trouble down upon them both without any need for campfire stories or hoodoo bullshit. So she figured the least she could do now was try and summon up a little payback too.

Because if she didn't at least make the attempt, she wasn't sure she'd ever be able to look her sister square in the eye again.

Candyman, Liz said, squeezing her hands into tight fists. *Candyman, Candyman.* She closed her eyes. *Come on, you motherfucker…Candyman!*

Nothing happened. Liz opened her eyes, to find herself alone in the bathroom. No monsters lurked over her shoulder, no boogeymen poised to tear out her insides.

She felt a sudden sadness. For a split second, she'd almost managed to make herself believe. But it was just a story, like so many other things she'd been told in her life.

I'm sorry, Ruthie-Jean, she murmured to the mirror. Turning off the light, she exited the bathroom.

Stopping off in the kitchen to pour herself a glass of water, she continued on to the guest bedroom. Every bone in her body ached, and those bastards had barely even laid a finger on her. All she wanted to do now was to sleep for twelve hours straight. And then, once she could start to think clearly again, she could maybe come up with a way of making all of this up to Ruthie-Jean.

Entering the darkened room, Liz reached down to turn the bedclothes back.

But something was wrong. The surface of the bed appeared to be… moving?

Certain that the shadows were playing tricks on her, Liz turned the bedside lamp on, only to see that the bed was crawling with hundreds of plump swarming bees.

She shrieked.

A roaring sound filled Liz's ears, drowning out the sound of her own terror. And then, rising above it all, a deep baritone voice, richly melodic and yet somehow terrible.

Elizabeth, the voice said.

She whirled around to see a dark figure stepping out of the shadows. A tall black man, incongruously dressed in a long fur-trimmed coat. *He looks like he just walked in off 42nd Street,* she thought crazily.

Then Liz glanced down to see a sharpened hook hammered into the bloodied stump at the end of his right arm.

She fell to her knees. *Ohmigod,* she moaned. *You're real.*

The Candyman loomed over her. *All stories are real, if only enough people believe in them,* he purred, raising his hook in the air. *And now, Elizabeth, you will become a part of my story. You will die, only to live forever in painted slogans and frightened whispers.*

She shrank from him, holding up her hands in terrified supplication. *Wait!* she begged. *Please…*

Always the politest of monsters, the Candyman stayed his hand, if only for a few more seconds. *Well?* he said.

Unsteadily, Liz got to her feet and forced herself to look him in the eye. *I…I h-have something for you,* she stammered.

You would bargain with me?

Her voice catching in her throat, Liz began to sing. Somewhat uncertainly at first, but as the song went on and she noticed the Candyman's eyes begin to gleam, with increasing power and assurance.

> *Oh freedom*
> *Oh freedom*
> *Oh freedom over me!*
> *And before I'd be a slave*
> *I'll be buried in my grave*
> *And go home to my Lord and be free*

Ah, the Candyman sighed, his hook dropping harmlessly to his side. And Liz continued to sing.

> *No more moaning*
> *No more moaning*
> *No more moaning over me!*

Finally, he motioned for her to stop. And perhaps she was only imagining it, but Liz thought she glimpsed the beginnings of a tear in the monster's eye.

There was silence in the bedroom for a moment.

What would you have me do? the Candyman asked her.

———

Just as he'd planned, Cramer had finished his business in Cabrini in plenty of time to return to his hotel and change before dinner. He'd stood under a scalding hot shower for a good half an hour, making sure to eradicate the stink of the slums from his skin. The afternoon's events had been an unpleasant distraction, but that was all over with now. The scales had been balanced, and now he could attend to the real reason for his visit to Chicago.

Dietz had reserved them both a table in Gene & Georgetti, which he assured his dinner guest was the best steakhouse in the city. Cramer arrived there at 8PM sharp to find Dietz already waiting for him, a sharply-dressed man with small, rodential eyes. As the DJ had expected, he found the Thorn employee to be little more than an unctuous cynic. Unlike Cramer, Dietz was no ideologue. He was only interested in ratings and money, which a controversial show like Cramer's was certain to generate.

We think you're gonna be big, he told his guest. *Our boss has a nose for these things, and he reckons there's a huge audience out there who think just like you.*

Yes, Mr Buher and I had a good talk about this back in New Orleans, Cramer said.

Oh no, I don't mean Paul, Dietz replied. A crafty look crept across his face. *Between you and me, Buher's a good guy, but strictly a yes-man. No,*

I mean the real *boss. Mister Numero Uno. Me and him, we're pretty tight, see.*

Like many Americans, Cramer was quite familiar with both the Thorn dynasty's eventful history and the swirl of fevered gossip surrounding it. *You mean Damien Thorn?*

Dietz nodded smugly. *Matter of fact, he's coming here tonight. He happened to be over from England and wanted to meet you in person. That's a pretty big deal, lemme tell you.*

Cramer didn't doubt it. He allowed himself a small smile of satisfaction. Damien Thorn struck him as precisely the sort of man he wished to do business with; someone with *real* power and vision, not this oily little corporate lickspittle. *Well, it sounds like we have quite a lot to celebrate,* he told Dietz.

The other man slammed his palm on the table. *Damn straight we do!* He got to his feet. *Tell you what. I gotta take a piss, but why don't you order us a bottle of Cristal while I'm gone? That way we can have it here waiting when Damien arrives.*

Cramer agreed, and Dietz hurried off towards the bathroom. Several minutes passed, during which the bottle of champagne was both ordered and delivered to the table, but there was no sign of the Thorn employee's return. Cramer quickly grew annoyed. What sort of way was this to treat an important dinner guest? No doubt Dietz was locked away in a cubicle busily chopping up lines of cocaine with his platinum Amex card – he certainly struck Cramer as the type. Such a flagrant show of disrespect rankled with the DJ. The sooner Damien Thorn got here, the better.

When yet more time went by and still Dietz had not returned, Cramer finally decided to see what the hell was keeping the man. He marched to the restaurant bathroom and brusquely shoved open the door, loudly announcing his arrival. *Dietz, are you in here?* he called out impatiently.

There was a low whine from over by the row of urinals. Cramer looked around to see Dietz lying sprawled on the floor, pants down around his ankles, a pool of urine puddling around him. His eyes were glazed and unseeing, his mouth hanging open like a discarded ventriloquist's dummy.

Cramer moved towards him, bewildered. *Dietz, what –?*

In the next instant, he heard a loud crash behind him. Cramer's head snapped around to see one of the cubicle doors flying open, and what appeared to be a cloud of angry bees swarming out of the stall. Before he could even react, the insects had quickly filled the bathroom, the sound of their collective fury like a wall of white noise, rising to engulf everything.

Too stunned to move, Cramer began to cower and flap ineffectually at the air. His entire field of vision was swamped by a blur of tiny whirring bodies, and he quickly lost all sense of his surroundings. His mind on the verge of collapse, he looked up to dimly see a large figure floating through the air towards him.

The Candyman roared, raising his arm to deliver the killing blow.

Stumbling backwards, Cramer stepped into the puddle of Dietz's urine. This one accidental act saved his life. His foot slipped out from underneath him, sending Cramer crashing to the tiled floor. The Candyman's hook passed harmlessly over his head, missing him by mere inches.

From his position on the floor, Cramer's view of the bathroom was no longer obscured by the swarming bees, and his panic-stricken mind quickly regained its bearings. Scuttling beetle-like across the bathroom, he managed to reach the doorway before the Candyman could attack again, and frantically pushed his way through into the restaurant.

Thus reprieved, the DJ immediately clambered to his feet and proceeded to run the entire length of the room shrieking and yelling at the top of his lungs, weaving unsteadily through the rows of tables and violently knocking one waiter to the floor. Upon reaching the restaurant exit, he burst through the doors and out onto the street, where his panicked momentum sent him stumbling into a waiting pair of arms.

Cramer's hands clawed madly at the empty air. *Oh god, oh fuck! Keep them away from me!* he screamed.

Calm down, you're safe now, a quiet voice told him. *Tell me exactly what happened.*

Bees! Cramer cried. *The whole room was full of bees! And then this huge fucking nigger tried to kill me!*

That's quite a story, Mr Cramer, Damien Thorn said calmly. He gestured towards a waiting limousine. *Why don't we get back into my car and discuss it?*

The limousine crept through the deserted streets towards the waiting towers of Cabrini-Green. It was now well past three in the morning, and the sight of such a vehicle in such a neighbourhood, which would be incongruous enough even in the middle of the afternoon, might at this hour be considered as little more than an outright provocation. Anyone still present on the streets to witness the passage of the limousine was, it's safe to assume, perhaps not the type of person whose attention one would envisage its owner wishing to attract, and yet, the vehicle proceeded to pull up outside the front of the housing project with such quiet authority that one could easily imagine it was simply arriving at a luxury hotel.

Moments later, the rear passenger door opened and Damien Thorn climbed out. He turned to signal to the driver, who promptly drove away into the night, not wishing to tarry here any longer than necessary.

It's hard to imagine many rich white men finding themselves stranded alone on the streets of Cabrini-Green at 3AM without instantly commencing a frantic attempt to run and hide, but Damien did nothing of the sort. He knew that several of sets of eyes were watching him from the darkness nearby, and yet he remained in place, standing unmoving in the parking lot.

No one emerged from the shadows to challenge or confront him.

Gazing up at the nearby tower blocks, Damien smiled. Taking his time, he began to walk deeper into the projects, as casually as if he were out for a Sunday stroll in the park. And still he was left to proceed unmolested. The lurking predators of Cabrini-Green instinctively recognised a beast far deadlier than themselves when they saw it.

He continued to the rear of the blocks, seeking out a row of garages situated there. Out back, the air was thick with the stench of urine, and Damien could feel the constant crunch of discarded hypodermic syringes underfoot. There was no illumination this far away from the street, and yet he moved through the darkness as easily and assuredly as an alleycat.

Eventually, he arrived at the last garage on the row. The rusted roller door was already open to about waist height, and Damien reached down to hoist it up the rest of the way. The door gave a piercing shriek of protest, but eventually yielded to reveal the hungry dark maw of the space beyond.

As the shadows gradually parted, he was able to discern a huddled, motionless shape in the middle of the garage. Moving forward, Damien found a battered old shopping cart missing two of its wheels. Inside the cart sat a featureless dummy wearing an old raincoat, a papier maché hook attached to one of its arms. A small pile of candies lay in the dummy's lap, and a sign hung around its neck read: 'SweeTs to The SweeT'

Damien waited.

As the seconds passed, he became aware of a growing heaviness in the atmosphere of the garage, as though the darkness itself was taking on form. A faint buzzing sound lingered in his ears.

Show yourself, Damien ordered.

There was a heavy sigh from the shadows, then a slow rustling sound. Damien looked down to see the dummy's form beginning to stiffen and twitch, its floppy limbs gradually assuming the fleshy solidity of meat and bone.

Within moments, the figure of the Candyman had materialised before him.

The shopping cart promptly collapsed beneath the apparition, who stepped from the wreckage with his hook raised, ready to greet his visitor with the sort of welcome such impertinence demanded.

Stay your hand, little ghost, Damien told him.

The Candyman paused. *Who are you, to come to this place and command me?* he said in wonder.

In response, Damien revealed his true face to the Candyman, the sight of which caused even as terrible a being as he to shrink back in sudden alarm.

What does the Great Beast want with such as I? the Candyman whispered.

You have threatened a man under my protection, little ghost, the Beast replied. *I will not permit him to come to any harm. I have a use for him, and I will not see my plans interfered with.*

And if I defy you?

Damien opened his arms. *My Father's kingdom stands ready to admit you, where you can join all the other unquiet spirits who have been sent onto their ultimate reward, such as it is.*

The Candyman absorbed this. *I made a bargain. My word means much to me.*

I will make things right with the woman and see that she is not troubled again, Damien promised him. *In return, you will withdraw to the shadows and abandon all claims to Adam Cramer. And if you feel as though you are still owed something, remember that your legend has been well burnished this day. Your power and influence will only increase as these stories are handed down through the years.*

The Candyman bridled at the settlement that was being forced upon him, but knew he could do little to stand against the Beast's will.

Finally, he inclined his head in agreement. *Very well.*

Damien nodded. *You have my gratitude, little ghost.* He turned to leave. *I hope that we do not have cause to speak again.*

The Candyman watched silently as Damien exited the garage and vanished into the darkness of Cabrini-Green. He had given the Beast his word and did not mean to go back on it, but the matter still rankled with him. The woman had knowingly summoned him, and his legend insisted that there was always a price to be paid for that. The Candyman was not at all accustomed to being denied his due.

After all, what's blood if not for shedding?

Then and there, the Candyman vowed that, one day, there would come a reckoning with Liz and Ruthie-Jean Wetherly.

———

Later that same morning, Ruthie-Jean received an unexpected visitor in her hospital room. Hearing a knock on the door, she glanced up from her pillow, expecting to see Liz standing in the doorway (although it was not usually her sister's custom to announce herself before entering).

But instead of Liz Wetherly, she saw a well-dressed young man standing before her. A well-dressed young *white* man, saturnine-eyed and carrying a large bouquet of flowers.

Instantly recognising the visitor, Ruthie-Jean's breath caught in her throat. She immediately tried to struggle upright in her bed, gasping at the sudden pain in her ribs.

Please don't try and sit up on my account, Ruthie-Jean, Damien Thorn said, motioning for her to stay put. *I heard about your recent troubles, and thought I should come and check that you were okay.* He stepped forward, then paused politely. *May I come in?*

Y-yes sir, Mister Thorn, Ruthie-Jean stammered, completely bewildered as to what the young owner of Thorn Industries could possibly be doing in her hospital room.

Please, call me Damien, her visitor murmured. *After all, I understand that you don't work for me any longer. So there's hardly any need for formalities, is there? All we are is two friends, or at least I hope we soon shall be.*

He crossed to her bed and gently laid the flowers down before her. *A small token of my concern.*

Ruthie-Jean's nostrils were immediately filled with the scent of the bouquet. The flowers smelled wild and intoxicating, impossibly fragrant, as though she were lying in a country meadow rather than a sterile hospital room. She closed her eyes and lay back on her pillow, inhaling deeply. *They're beautiful,* she sighed.

Damien pulled up a chair and sat down next to the bed. *I was very sorry to hear about the attack. It's a terrible thing, when people can't even feel safe in their own homes.*

A small part of Ruthie-Jean wanted to tell him that she might never have ended up somewhere she couldn't feel safe had she not lost her job working for Thorn. But she was tired and in a great deal of pain, and all her problems seemed far too big to talk about. So instead, she simply nodded quietly.

Damien studied her carefully. *I visited Cabrini-Green myself last night.*

She opened her eyes and gazed at him in complete astonishment. *You--?*

I don't think a young woman should be forced to live on her own in such a terrible place. Do you?

Well, no, o-of course not, but w-what can I--?

Ruthie-Jean found herself cut off by the entrance of another voice into the conversation. *Excuse me, but who's this?*

She looked up to see Liz stood framed in the doorway, glaring at Damien.

In response, the young man flashed Liz a broad smile and got to his feet, extending a hand in greeting. *You must be Liz Wetherly,* he said smoothly. *My name is Damien Thorn.*

She did not accept the gesture. *Thorn? Then you're the one who fired my sister, right?*

Unperturbed, Damien withdrew his hand. *That isn't quite the way things happened, Ms Wetherly,* he replied, not missing a beat. *But it is one of the matters I came here to discuss.*

My job? Ruthie-Jean said.

Damien turned back to her. *As you know, that particular plant was moved overseas. But Thorn never should have let an employee of your quality and experience go, Ruthie-Jean. That was a terrible oversight, for which I must apologise.* Another smile. *But if you're at all interested, I'd like to offer you a position in our chemical plant, which I can assure you will be staying in Chicago for many years to come.*

Ruthie-Jean eased herself upright. *You're offering me a new job?*

On an increased salary and benefits, of course.

Unable to believe her good fortune, Ruthie-Jean started to laugh, before her broken ribs quickly turned her unexpected joy to discomfort. She gazed over at her sister, managing a weak smile despite the pain. *Can you believe it, Liz? They're gonna give me my job back.*

Liz remained stony-faced. *That right? So what's the catch, Mister Thorn?*

Damien's head slowly turned towards her. For a moment, Liz was reminded of a cobra rising from its basket. She thought she glimpsed a level of malevolence in his eyes of such a magnitude as to make Eddie Collins seem like a spiteful child. *The catch?* he said softly.

Ain't there always a catch? Liz shot back.

A shrug. *No, no catch. Merely a small…unpleasantness I wanted to clear up.* He paused. *The two men who attacked you are both known to the Chicago police. They will be apprehended and punished, you have my word on that. However, their accomplice is a valued Thorn employee, or very soon will be. Now, he has of course been severely reprimanded over this matter.* Damien's eyes moved to Ruthie-Jean. *But I would ask that you keep his involvement to yourself. And I promise you that your paths will never cross again.*

Ruthie-Jean looked helplessly at her sister, who duly erupted at Damien. *You're bribing her! Just to keep that sonofabitch safe! Do you know what his sister did to me, her and her cracker boyfriend?*

Damien's eyes were unwavering. *It's not a bribe, Ms Wetherly. I'm merely trying to see that everyone's best interests are looked after. And yes, I heard about your terrible ordeal. If there's anything my company can do to make it up to you, I assure you we will.* He cocked his head thoughtfully. *Perhaps you would like to perform at our annual Thorn summer ball? We would of course offer you a generous fee.*

Shove it up your ass! Liz glared down at Ruthie-Jean. *You gonna take his bribe and let them all get away with what they did?*

Her sister gestured mutely and slumped back against her pillows. *And what the hell else am I supposed to do?* she moaned. *It ain't you that has to live in that damn awful place, it's me! This could be my ticket out of there, Lizzie!*

Liz looked between them, appalled. She'd never expected justice for anything that had happened to her, but this was altogether too much to bear. *You can both go to hell, the pair of you,* she muttered, before storming out of the room.

Damien and Ruthie-Jean watched her go, saying nothing. Finally, Ruthie-Jean broke the silence. *I'm real sorry about that, Mr Thorn,* she told her visitor, squirming with embarrassment. *Lizzie always had a bitch of a temper on her. But she'll get over it. She didn't mean what she said.*

Damien laughed. *Oh, she meant every word, Ruthie-Jean,* he said with evident amusement. *And what's more, she was quite right.* A wry pause. *But we hardly need that let us concern us now. I'll tell my team to get in touch with you about that position. Shall we say you'll come back to work in a month from now?*

Ruthie-Jean thanked him, and shook his hand before he left. As she watched him exit the room, she thought about what a nice young man Damien Thorn was, especially for a rich white businessman. And handsome too; it was no surprise that all the girls at Thorn were attracted to him. It was too bad about Lizzie, but her sister had always thought she could bully the world into being exactly what she wanted it to be, instead of just accepting the way things were and trying to do the best you could. For better or for worse, folks like Damien would always run things, and frankly, if they were as nice and polite as him, then matters could definitely be a hell of a lot worse.

On his way out of the hospital, Damien passed Liz Wetherly in the corridor, their eyes meeting as he walked by. Neither of them spoke a word, but he offered her a smile of such fearful malignity that she had to lock herself in a toilet stall for half an hour afterwards until she finally stopped trembling.

Liz left Chicago the next day.

Some months later, when she was back home in New York, Liz left her apartment one afternoon intending to catch a cab downtown. It was already raining heavily, and as she waited on the sidewalk, the downpour began to further intensify, causing her to despair of ever finding a taxi.

However, her luck was apparently in. Moments later, a cab drove into view, its flag up. Liz hurriedly hailed it down and clambered inside. The driver, an intense-looking young man with dark hair and even darker eyes, nodded wordlessly when she told him her destination. Pulling away from the kerb, he reached down and turned on the car radio.

It took Liz a few seconds to recognise the voice of the man speaking on the airwaves.

Why do we tolerate it, friends? Why do we sit back and allow these cesspits to infect our cities, their rancid corruption spreading further and further by the day? Rest assured, I speak from personal experience, as someone who has visited one of these negro ghettos and beheld their savagery and squalor with my own two eyes. And I'm telling you now, we should send in the National Guard to each and every one of these neighbourhoods and just clean them out...

Adam Cramer.

Her stomach turning over, Liz leaned forward to speak to the driver. *Excuse me* – she glanced down at the cabbie's identification – *Travis, but would you mind changing the channel?*

The taxi driver's eyes gazed back at her from the rear view mirror. He said nothing for several moments, then turned to look Liz squarely in the face. A wide, humourless grin spread across his features. *Yeah, as a matter of fact, I would,* he told her.

Angered, Liz initially held his gaze, but the more she looked, the more she saw nothing but a void behind the cabbie's eyes, a black emptiness so vast that she felt as though she might drown in its depths.

She quickly glanced away, slumping back in her seat. Satisfied, the taxi driver turned his attention back to the road ahead.

For the rest of the journey, Liz sat staring out of the rain-streaked window, trying to tune out the hectoring voice on the radio. The city she perceived beyond the window was little more than a blur, an amorphous mass of movement and colour bleeding together into shapeless chaos, and she soon realised she did not recognise it at all.

FRED MADISON

Bull Pullman in Lost Highway, *1997*
written by Barry Gifford & David Lynch
directed by David Lynch

IT IS NIGHT, AND FRED MADISON IS RIDING THE LOST HIGHWAY AGAIN. The yellow lines of the road streak towards him through the darkness, leading him onwards. Surely all he need do is follow them, and eventually they will help him get away, escape the dreadful labyrinth which has ensnared him.

But this is a lie, a hopeless fantasy. The lost highway has no entrance and no exit. It loops endlessly in upon itself, spiralling around forever, leading Fred Madison inexorably back to the same destination, time and time again.

Himself.

How long has he been driving now? How many miles has he travelled?

Instinctively, Fred glances down at the odometer, then catches himself and looks away again. It doesn't matter what the clock tells him, the same way it didn't matter what those freaky videotapes had showed him doing or what crimes the cops insisted he'd committed. None of it was the way Fred remembered it, and that was all that counted. Odometers can be rolled back and police evidence can be tampered with, but you can't fuck with a man's memories. As Fred always told people, he liked to remember things his own way. He knows exactly who he is and what he's done, and all he needs now is a little time to get his head straightened out.

Christ, but he's tired. He just needs to get the hell off this road and rest awhile, somewhere quiet and secluded where no one can find him. *No one*. Not his wife Renee, not Alice Wakefield, not Mr Eddy or Dick Laurent or whatever the fuck his name was.

And not…

Too late, Fred reminds himself not to think of him; the nameless sallow-faced homunculus that has followed him like a muttered curse all the way from Los Angeles.

The Mystery Man.

Fred recalls old monster stories from his childhood, the way you have to invite vampires across the threshold before they can get you. He knows better now. That isn't the way it really works at all.

All you have to do is think of them, and then they're inside you, and they never, ever let go.

Fred tries to push all thoughts of the Mystery Man from his mind, but in the next instant he glances up at the rearview mirror and his tormentor is there once again, grinning back at him from the backseat, rubbing his hands in gleeful expectation of where this endless road will take them next. In anticipation of just how many more lives Fred will take in pursuit of the one woman that he can never have.

Upon seeing the man's face reflected in the mirror, Fred's instinctive shock is such that he nearly loses control of his vehicle and spins off the road, but he manages to stamp his foot down on the brake just in time.

Screeching to a halt in the middle of the highway, Fred pulls out his revolver, spins around and blindly fires three shots into the rear of the car.

Of course, there is no one behind him, and the slugs tear harmlessly into the fabric of the backseat.

Breath shuddering from his lungs, Fred's head slumps against the car window. Closing his eyes, he thinks for a moment, then fumbles in his jacket for a cigarette. Lights it, takes a drag, then presses the burning tip against the flesh of his forearm.

He hisses with the pain, but it helps make things clearer, for a minute anyway. Still, he desperately needs to sleep, although not until he's swallowed enough bourbon to drown any nascent dreams of her, before he even has a chance to dream them.

Then, as Fred sits up and makes to restart the engine, he sees it, glowing faintly in the distance. An old neon sign, or at least the burnt-out remnants of one, spelling out the half-forgotten memory of a motel like a child's magnetic letters scattered randomly across a refrigerator door.

B   E
M   E
Vacancy

A shithole, no doubt. Probably a whorehouse, or some kind of mob hideout. But gangsters and whores don't scare Fred anymore, not after everything he's seen and done, and so he turns the ignition key and drives the short distance to the exit leading off to the motel.

As he pulls into the parking lot, Fred scans his surroundings, looking for entrances and exits, places to hide. *That's just how a guilty man thinks,* he reminds himself.

Still, you can never be too careful.

The motel itself is a featureless, nondescript-looking building, probably built back in the fifties or thereabouts. But Fred's eyes are immediately drawn to the house looming over it from the hillside behind: an old Victorian mansion, beaten and weathered with the passing of the years, but still the sort of house that dominates everything around it, like some great unholy effigy.

If its windows were eyes, they would be bright with incipient madness, Fred thinks. And if ever a house could be said to be haunted just by looking at it, it would be this one.

But haunted by what, he wonders?

Fred parks up in front of the motel office, and upon climbing out of the car is immediately accosted by another resident of the motel, a man waving a crumpled-looking cigarette at him.

Hey buddy, you gotta light?

The man is dressed like he just stepped out of an old movie: threadbare grey clothes and matching fedora. He is unshaven, eyes rimmed with red, and as he approaches, Fred catches a strong smell of body odour. Not to put too fine a point on it, but the guy looks like a stack of shit dressed in a cheap suit.

Fred produces his lighter and hands it to the man, who gratefully sparks up his cigarette. *Thanks pal. Say, you new around here?*

Fred nods.

Pleased to meetya. I'm Al. Al Roberts.

The man grabs Fred's hand and shakes it enthusiastically. Fred does not reciprocate his introduction, but Al barely seems to notice.

Well, it ain't such a bad place to hole up, he continues, before his voice drops to a confidential whisper. *The guy who runs it – well, he's a bit of a funny customer. I think he might be a pansy or something. But he minds his own business, if you know what I mean. No one bothers you here.*

Thanks for the tip, Fred tells him, and begins to walk away towards the office. But he only gets a few steps before he is stopped by Al's voice calling out to him.

Say! Whereabouts you from, buddy?

Fred sighs inwardly. *Originally Los Angeles,* he tells the man. *But I get around.*

Been driving awhile, huh?

Fred agrees that this is the case.

Don't suppose you bumped into a girl named Vera on your travels, did ya? We parted ways awhile back and I've been looking for her ever since.

Sorry, no.

Al looks stricken. *Only we had a bit of a bust-up, ya see. And I really want to make it up to her.*

He looks so pathetic that Fred feels a sudden unexpected kinship with him. *Yeah, they really stick it to you, don't they?* he tells Al. *My advice to you is, don't ever look back.*

Leaving Al to finish his cigarette, Fred continues on to the motel office. Finding it empty, he rings the bell on the counter, and a few moments later a nervous-looking older man emerges from the back parlour. He is tall and skinny, and puts Fred in mind of a gawky wading bird, his long throat habitually gulping like a blocked drain. Upon seeing Fred, he smiles hesitantly, wearing the expression as if it were a shoe that didn't fit.

Looking for a room? he asks.

Read my mind, Fred replies.

He pays for one night in advance, and is waiting expectantly for his room key when the man pushes the motel register towards him. *If you can just sign your John Hancock here…*

Fred stares dumbly down at the register, mind racing. Who is he now? Fred Madison, or someone else entirely? Pete Dayton, maybe? His hands fly up to his face, exploring its contours, trying to decide if he recognises what he finds there.

The motel manager looks faintly alarmed. *Oh, you don't have to sign if you don't want. It's just a formality, really.*

No, no, it's fine. Fred says hurriedly. He bends down over the register, eyes scanning the list of guests, past and present. A succession of seemingly random names leap out at him: *Tony Wilson, John Ryder, Richard Paley, Charles Haskell Jr, Jerry Blake…*

All men, travelling alone. Fred isn't sure why, but he is suddenly struck by the realisation that all of the names are simply aliases, smokescreens conjured up by a procession of fugitives, desperate to stay one step ahead of whoever or whatever is pursuing them.

No one real stays here, Fred thinks.

And what about *him*? Is Fred Madison real any more? Was he ever?

On the other side of the counter, the man shifts uncomfortably and coughs.

Quickly, Fred lowers the pen to the register. A name suddenly bubbles up out of his subconscious: *Clay Gregory.*

Someone he once was, or might yet be? It doesn't matter. He signs and pushes the register away.

The motel manager checks the signature and closes the book with a snap. *Thank you, Mr Gregory. And welcome to the Bates Motel.*

Fred exits the office and returns to his car, where he takes out his overnight bag and a fifth of bourbon. But as he slams the trunk closed, he is once again confronted by Al, this time with a second man in tow.

Hi fellas, Fred says warily.

Al's eyes instantly fix upon the bourbon Fred is holding. *I told ya Fred looked like a man who was holding! Fred, I want you to meet a good friend of mine, Jerry Blake.*

Fred dutifully turns to shake hands with the man. Looking into Jerry's eyes, he is immediately put in mind of a dog that has bitten down and won't let go.

Pleased to meet you, Fred, says Jerry. *You travelling alone?*

I guess so, Fred replies.

Got a family?

Guess not.

A man should have a family, Jerry tells him. *Don't you think?*

I'm working on it, Jerry, Fred says. *Now if you'll just excuse me…*

But before he can slip away, Al is placing a too-friendly arm around his shoulder. *Funny thing is, me and Jerry were just saying how much we could use a nightcap, stuck all the way out here without so much as a bar or a beer in sight. And now here you are, with your very own bottle!*

Fred holds up his hands. *Fellas, I was just gonna have a quick drink and then hit the sack.*

Well, we'll just have that quick drink with you! Al cries. *A man should never have to drink alone. It's practically a goddamn sin.*

The next moment, Fred finds himself flanked by the two men, who accompany him to his room like prison guards escorting a convict.

As they walk, Fred can't help thinking of his death row cell back in Los Angeles: the walls closing in like a vice, the overhead bulb burning bright, so bright he thought his eyes might burst. He can feel a headache coming on.

Inside the room, Al takes charge of pouring the drinks, and Fred downs his quickly, hoping his two uninvited guests might get the message and leave. But whenever he looks down his glass has been refilled, and no matter how much he drinks, his head keeps on getting worse, the pain getting so bad he can't even speak, and the whole time Al and Jerry just won't stop talking. Maybe it's the booze, maybe it's the headache, but Fred could swear Jerry's family is different every time he talks about them. Like one minute he has a teenage daughter, the next three boys.

Eventually, Fred just gives up, crawls onto the bed and passes out.

When he awakes again, the room is dark and empty. Fred isn't sure whether he needs to piss or puke first, but either way he needs to do it quick. He stumbles up off the bed and into the bathroom, but the moment he hits the light switch all thoughts of his bodily discomfort are swiftly banished from his mind.

The Mystery Man lies stretched out in the bathtub before him, his naked body white as a dead albino rat. The bathwater is stained crimson, and fresh gore is slathered all over the man's hands.

Raising one arm, he points a bloody finger at Fred and hisses, *No one ever runs, Fred. You'll always be caught in your own private trap, and I'll always be right here with you.*

And then Fred is screaming. He flails around, his arm knocking the lamp from the nightstand, and he suddenly realises he is back on the bed. The motel room is silent, and when Fred finally summons up the courage to get up and peer into the bathroom, he finds it deserted, the bathtub pristine and unused.

He checks his watch: just gone 4AM. Fred knows he won't sleep again tonight, so elects to step out into the dawn air and have a cigarette instead.

The sky overhead is bruised the colour of a junkie's arm and Fred stares up at it as he smokes, watching it shift and change, wishing it would just turn blue and help soothe the snarling animal inside his skull.

The next moment he is startled by a low growl nearby, and thinks, *It's escaped.* But of course the sound is only that of a car entering the motel parking lot, another refugee from the lost highway. Fred watches as the vehicle pulls up in the spot next to his own, but, conscious of minding his own business, is about to look away again when the female driver eases herself from the car.

And then he can't look anywhere else, the sight of the woman filling his peripheral vision like a Cinerama screen; there is nothing else to see but her.

Renee.

Of course, Fred knows that won't be her name, the same way she was Alice the last time they met. This time she looks like a cheap hooker, all dayglo clothes and peroxide hair, furiously chewing gum like it's the only way she can rid herself of her own bad taste.

But the face is always the same, the face that has haunted him all the way down that endless black highway.

She glances over at Fred, sees him watching her. *Hey, mister. I grow an extra titty or something?*

He can barely speak. *Not that I can see.*

So what the hell is it? She moves closer, peering back at him. *Lemme guess, I remind you of someone.*

Fred grins weakly. *Something like that.*

She sniffs. *Gimme one of those, willya?*

Fred gives her a cigarette and lights it for her. He waits silently as she looks critically at their surroundings. *Kind of a shithole, huh?*

He shrugs. *It's quiet. The sheets are clean.*

Yeah, I just need a hot shower and a soft bed before I get back on the road.

She's running from something, Fred can tell. She has the same furtive look in her eyes as he does when he stands before the bathroom mirror.

What's your name? she suddenly asks.

Don't you know? Fred whispers.

She flashes him a look. *How the hell would I know? Do you really think we know each other? Wait, did we…? Back in Detroit?* Her face scrunches up, trying to think. *Honey, I slept with a lotta johns back then. You can't expect me to remember a face.*

I've never been to Detroit, he admits. *My name's Fred. Fred Madison.*

She gives no sign of recognition. *Huh. Well, I'm Alabama Whitman. Guess I've just got one of those faces, huh?*

Guess so, Fred says quietly.

Listen, do you think there's a night manager around? I could really use that shower.

I've only seen one guy, Fred tells her. *His name's Bates. He normally hides out in the parlour behind the office.*

Great, thanks. Alabama drops her cigarette to the floor and grinds it out with her heel. *See you around, Fred,* she says with a sly wink.

He watches her as she pivots and walks away, knowing that Alabama knows he is watching her. When she turns into the office, she gives a little wiggle; purely for his benefit, Fred assumes.

His stomach twists, and he can feel the headache creeping back again. Unsure exactly what else to do, he lights another cigarette and waits.

A few minutes later, Alabama emerges from the office and heads directly for the cabin directly adjacent to the office: number one. She does not look at Fred, simply unlocks the door and steps inside.

Fred's skin begins to prickle. Something is happening.

A short time later, he hears the distant hiss of running water from Alabama's room. He imagines her, disrobing, stepping into the shower. He squeezes his eyes shut, fireworks of dread exploding inside his skull.

Hearing a door slam nearby, Fred opens his eyes and looks up, to see Bates emerging from the office. He seems flustered, first glancing over at Fred, then back at Alabama's cabin. Fred is about to offer a greeting when the man turns and runs, scurrying away from the motel building and up the hillside to the nearby mansion.

A nameless urge compels Fred to follow him. Hanging back until Bates vanishes inside the house, he gives chase, hurrying up the steps cut into the steep hillside.

He must be quick now. Fred can already feel his body starting to change, blooming with the promise of a new identity, another new beginning.

Mounting the porch, he tries the front door, finding it open. Letting himself into the house, Fred peers around the dingy interior, flocks of stuffed birds staring back at him from every shelf, every corner, as if they'd all migrated here when they died.

He hears a sound from upstairs and slowly climbs the staircase. His head swells and throbs, rolling like a ship on a stormy ocean.

Not much time left now.

At the top of the stairs, there is a doorway on the left. Fred hears a soft giggle from inside, then an old woman's voice, venomous as a spider: *You disgust me, boy. You spy on these naked girls through your little peephole, lust seeping from your filthy pores, and then what? You have the nerve to blame me for what happens next! Well, no more! You won't hide behind my skirts any longer!*

Then Bates: *Shut up, Mother! Shut up!*

Fred bursts into the room, to find Bates completely alone. He stands before the bed dressed only in his underwear, an old dress laid out on the mattress in front of him. Upon seeing Fred, his eyes bulge madly and he lets out a high-pitched shriek, launching himself at the intruder. But despite his lunatic rage, Bates is old, growing frailer by the day. Fred easily overpowers him and knocks him to the floor. There, he fastens his hands around the motel manager's skinny throat and begins to squeeze. Bates stares back at him in horror, his face turning purple.

But as the life gradually ebbs from his body, something odd happens. The look of terror in Bates's eyes fades away, to be replaced by one of recognition, possibly even love.

He manages to gurgle one last word before he dies: *Mother.*

Fred reaches down and tenderly strokes the man's cheek. *I'm here*, he murmurs.

Then a tempest of agony erupts inside his skull, sending him sprawling to the threadbare carpet. Fred's body twists and spasms, contorting itself into new shapes, new forms. He can feel his breasts swelling, growing heavy; his sex retreating inside him. Steadily, his screams of pain grow higher and higher in pitch.

And when it is all over, when this latest transformation is complete, Fred no longer exists. For all those years, all poor pitiful Norman Bates could do was pretend to be the mother he so desperately longed for, but now that sly chameleon Fred Madison, so practised in the ways of assuming other people's lives for his own, has *become* her.

Picking herself up from the floor, Mrs Bates quickly removes Fred's uncomfortable clothes and dons her old dress, the one her son Norman has looked after so carefully all these years. It was a good dress, one of her favourites; it smells faintly of mothballs, but some fresh air will take care of that soon enough.

One she is dressed, she heads down to the kitchen to collect the last item she requires. Pulling open a drawer, Mrs Bates takes out a heavy kitchen knife, testing its edge with her finger.

Sharp as a broken promise, she thinks. As much as she used to lose her temper with Norman, he was a good boy really. Her son could always be relied on to take care of the little things around the house, and did any boy ever love their mother more than he?

But still, Norman is gone.

Now, there is only the girl. There is *always* the girl.

It doesn't matter what she calls herself, Alabama Whitman or Alice Wakefield or Renee Madison, she is always the same. Unfaithful, deceitful, duplicitous. Mrs Bates always warned her son about those sorts of girls and can only assume Fred Madison's mother didn't do the same for him. All they know how to do is lie, lie, lie, and what else can you do with a girl like that other than simply cut the truth out of them?

But when Fred tried to cut it out of Renee, he was too clumsy, too brutish. He tore her flesh apart looking for it, but in the end the truth got away from him, only to return in the form of Alice Wakefield, and now Alabama Whitman.

But Mother? Ah, doesn't Mother always know best?

Mother knows the delicate places on a woman's body; knows precisely where to cut.

Running her finger along the knife blade, she imagines Alabama standing naked in the shower, pink and pert and unsuspecting and helpless.

Imagines the flashing knife, the screams, the dark blood swirling away down the plughole.

And imagining it all, she smiles a dreadful smile, a smile birthed from a graveyard.

Even by Fred Madison's standards, it should be something to remember.

DEAN CORSO

Johnny Depp in The Ninth Gate, *1999*
written by John Brownjohn, Enrique Urbizu and Roman Polanski
based on the novel by Arturo Pérez-Reverte
directed by Roman Polanski

DEAN CORSO ROLLED HIS EYES AND LIT ANOTHER CIGARETTE, BY HIS reckoning the third of this telephone conversation.

Walter, Walter, listen, he implored. *I'm on vacation. I just got back from… Christ knows where, and now I need a break. A long one. I'm certainly not in the mood to go chasing around the fucking woods. In Tennessee, of all places.*

The voice on the other end of the line belonged to a man named Walter Paisley, the owner of an occult bookstore in Los Angeles, and one of Corso's oldest clients.

But this is the goddamn Necronomicon we're talking about here! Walter exclaimed. *It's like the Holy Grail of grimoires. And all you gotta do is find the cabin and take it. There's no one living there, Corso. It'll be easier than stealing Helen Keller's wallet.*

No, Corso insisted flatly.

Don't I always pay you well? Didn't you come up trumps when you tracked down that Torrance manuscript for me?

The last job Corso had taken on for Walter had involved acquiring the last work of one Jack Torrance, an unknown writer who had gone berserk while working as the winter caretaker at a hotel in the Colorado mountains.

The money was fine, Walter. But it was an easy job. All I had to do was convince his widow. And frankly, she seemed quite glad to be rid of it.

In truth, Corso had been plagued by bad dreams ever since he'd first touched the manuscript, nightmares of being chased through an endless, frozen maze. But he wasn't about to tell Walter that.

Did you read it, by the way? Walter suddenly asked him. *Pretty interesting stuff, huh?*

Corso exhaled a lungful of smoke. *I glanced through it. The plot didn't really grab me.*

Walter sniffed. *Anyway, the Necronomicon…*

Walter, I said no before, and I'll keep on saying no until we're both very old men. Call me again in a month, or six. And with that, Corso hung up.

What he hadn't told Walter was that the mere thought of tangling with another cursed book made his flesh creep uncontrollably, and left him scrabbling for the nearest whisky bottle. It was twice now that Corso had set off in pursuit of fabulously rare grimoires – *The Nine Gates of the Kingdom of Shadows* and *The Three Mothers*, respectively – and twice that he'd barely avoided mortal damnation as a result. Not only that, but he was fairly certain that he was currently very near the top of a certain Satanic personage's shit list. So no, he was done with black magic. From now on, Corso was sticking to what he knew – which generally meant bilking ignorant families out of any antique books that they happened to inherit.

The next moment, the doorbell to his apartment rang.

Not being a man particularly overburdened with friends, Corso was unaccustomed to being visited at home, and as such, did not welcome the intrusion. Besides, it was only 11AM, and he was a firm believer in the maxim that good news always slept until noon. He decided to ignore the summons.

A few seconds passed, and then the bell rang again, trilling its insistence that Corso respond. When he persisted in his refusal to do so, the caller began to bang upon the door with their fist. The constant din was starting to grate on Corso's already-fragile nerves, and, finally admitting defeat, he viciously stabbed out his cigarette.

Striding angrily to the front door, Corso threw it open, and, without waiting to see exactly who his caller was, snarled, *What the hell?*

An elderly Catholic priest stood before him, smiling indulgently at Corso's casual blasphemy. *And a very good morning to you, Mr Corso,* he said softly, inclining his head in greeting. *My name is Monsignor Franchino.*

Given his somewhat low character, not to mention his recent forays into the realm of the malign, the book dealer might have been less surprised to find the Devil Himself waiting outside his front door. Corso gazed dumbly at the monsignor for several long seconds.

I wonder…could I perhaps step inside for a few moments? said Franchino, undeterred by the dealer's silence. *There's rather a brisk wind out this morning, and my old bones are singing an almighty hosanna.*

Still bewildered, Corso stood aside and allowed the monsignor to enter his apartment. The old man eased himself down onto the nearby couch, and waited patiently while his host decided exactly what to do with himself. Corso considered remaining on his feet, in the hope that it would signal to the priest not to get too comfortable, but ultimately decided there was very little point. He could already tell that his holy visitor did not intend to be dissuaded from whatever the purpose of his visit was.

Lighting another cigarette to calm his nerves, Corso slumped down into an easy chair. Random priests showing up on your doorstep unannounced was never a good sign, he decided.

Okay, Father, the dealer sighed. *What's this about?*

The monsignor laughed. *Books, Mr Corso, what else? One very special book in particular.*

Corso made an apologetic gesture. *Father, I'm afraid you've caught me at a bad time. I'm not accepting any commissions right now. But if you like, I can recommend some other dealers…*

Ah no, it is I who must apologise to you, Franchino interjected. *You see, you are the only possible man for this job.*

And why is that?

The old man's eyes studied him, twinkling with amusement. Corso felt as though he were laid out on a marble slab for inspection. *Well, how exactly shall I put it?* the monsignor eventually replied. *Perhaps that…you know the territory in question better than anyone else?*

Something about Franchino's manner was beginning to make Corso feel decidedly queasy. *That…doesn't sound like the sort of work I'm interested in right now,* he stammered.

No? Franchino reached inside his coat and produced a cheque, which he presented to the dealer. *Perhaps this will help persuade you. I think you'll find the Vatican has very deep pockets.*

Corso gazed at the slip of paper. He had to admit that the number of zeroes printed upon it was indeed very persuasive. Nevertheless, he still didn't like where this was going, not one bit.

It's…it's not about the money, Corso said reluctantly, carefully enunciating the unfamiliar words as though they were a language entirely foreign to him, which, in most respects, they were.

Oh, really? Franchino said. *Well, then. What if I were to tell you that the Church was in a position to help resolve certain other…predicaments of yours?*

Predicaments? The dealer chewed at the butt of his cigarette. *I don't know what you mean.*

Come now, Mr Corso, the monsignor said. *Given your recent experiences, you can hardly claim to be a non-believer any more. In which case, has it not occurred to you where a man of your somewhat dubious moral standing might end up after death? Or what sort of treatment might await you there, given your rather…complex relationship with its presiding deity?*

Suddenly tasting sulphur on his tongue, Corso coughed and rapidly extinguished his cigarette. *What are you offering me, Monsignor?*

The priest leaned forward, his eyes bright. *A reward beyond price, Mr Corso,* he said. *I am offering you absolution.*

Franchino had a limousine waiting in readiness outside, and he and Corso rode uptown to an apartment block in Brooklyn. Little was said between them on the journey; all the monsignor would tell Corso was that there was someone he needed the dealer to meet before they could proceed.

Once inside the building, they climbed to the top floor, where Franchino let them into an apartment overlooking the East River. The premises were clean and spacious, but ascetic; it hardly seemed to Corso as if anyone even lived there. But Franchino quickly put the lie to that impression by ushering him through to the living room, where a lone priest sat at the window, staring out at the river.

This is Father Hackett, Franchino murmured respectfully. *The chosen Sentinel of this place.*

Sentinel? queried Corso. But any further questions died in his throat when Hackett turned around to face him. The priest, he saw, was completely blind, the irises and pupils of his eyes eerily leached of all colour.

No man can see what Father Hackett sees and retain his sight, Franchino murmured reverentially.

Regardless, Corso couldn't shake the impression that Hackett still seemed able to perceive him somehow, in a manner that made the dealer extremely uncomfortable.

Hackett nodded sightlessly at him. *Mr Corso. Thank you for coming.*

I'm afraid I don't really know why I'm here, Corso replied.

I believe you are something of a traveller, Hackett said.

I, ah, get around, Corso said fumblingly. *It's the nature of my work, you see.*

Hackett smiled blankly. *All the way to Hell and back, I hear.*

Corso looked over at Franchino. *What is this?* he demanded. *Who are you people?*

Franchino shrugged. *Merely humble servants,* he said. *It is our duty to watch over this place.*

And what's so special about this place?

It stands upon one of the seven doorways to Hell, the monsignor replied.

Corso's stomach gave another sickening lurch, and he groped instinctively for his cigarettes, lighting one without waiting for permission. Inhaling deeply, he closed his eyes. *Seven doorways,* he whispered.

Indeed. The Church learned of this particular portal many years ago, and a Sentinel has guarded it ever since, ensuring that it is not breached. But the location of the other six doors has always been a mystery to us. I'm sure you can understand why this would be a matter of some concern to the Church.

Yes, said Corso distantly. *I'd, ah, be concerned too…*

Then Hackett spoke again. *Have you ever heard of the Book of Eibon?*

Not thinking, Corso only offered him a despairing shrug in reply, but somehow picking up on the visual cue, the priest continued. *It tells of the location of the seven doorways. Not only that, but it has the power to open or close them. We need to obtain that book.*

Corso found he was starting to give serious consideration to some career retraining. Possibly as an accountant, or something equally tedious. *I'm afraid I don't see how I can help you,* he told the priests. *I'm not familiar with the work in question, and all of the esoteric collectors of my acquaintance are…indisposed.*

Oh, but you see, we have recently learned of its whereabouts, Franchino assured him happily. *All we need you to do is go and collect it.*

And where would that be? Corso said, fully expecting the worst.

New Orleans.

That didn't sound too bad, at least.

There is just one problem, Franchino added, his face turning grave. *We believe the building in which the book is located stands upon another of the seven doorways. And it is quite possible that doorway has already been opened…*

Franchino had told him to seek out an abandoned hotel in New Orleans called – what else? – The Seven Doors Hotel. His recent encounters with the ineffable had taught Corso that occultists were often fond of hiding things in plain sight, a lesson that the Catholic Church had apparently completely failed to take note of. Still, what did he expect? The Vatican was a lumbering, bureaucratic beast, mired in centuries of dogma and tradition, whereas Corso prided himself on being quick-witted, adaptable and extremely light on his feet. And this time, there would be no treacherous *femmes fatales* to hinder his efforts. Doorway or no doorway, he intended on being in and out of that hotel and back on a plane to New York faster than an atheist's prayer; there to be richly rewarded and absolved of all his numerous sins.

And if there was any truth to the saying about rich men and heaven, well, he would worry about that later.

The first problem, Corso soon discovered, was that no one seemed to have heard of the Seven Doors Hotel. The cab driver who drove him from the airport insisted he had no knowledge of such a place; similarly the receptionist at his hotel, and even the woman at the New Orleans tourist information centre. As an accomplished liar of many years' standing, Corso knew the pungent aroma of bullshit when he smelled it, but no amount of wheedling or cash inducements could persuade anyone to part with the slightest scrap of information. It were as if the entire city had taken a collective vow to pretend that the hotel simply did not exist.

The dealer wandered the streets for hours, exploring every alleyway and cul-de-sac he passed, hoping without success that he might eventually manage to stumble across the building he sought. As the sun gradually sank lower and lower in the sky, Corso was about to admit defeat for the day, when he happened upon what looked to be a relic of old New Orleans, a dingy-looking herb store named Mammy Carter's. From the outside, the establishment appeared to be almost completely frozen in time, as though the proprietors had shunned the encroaching modernity taking hold of the rest of the city and simply decided to remain in the 1940's.

It had to be worth a try.

Inside, Corso was greeted by an ancient Creole woman seated behind the counter. She was blind in one eye, her face scarcely any less wizened than some of the preserved ingredients hanging up around the store. *Nice place you have here*, he said, in what he hoped was an approving tone. *Very authentic.*

With her one good eye, she managed to give him the sort of look Corso normally reserved for evangelists and small children. *What you want?* she croaked.

The dealer could see there was little point wasting any charm on her. *I'm looking for a place*, he said. *The Seven Doors Hotel.*

Her eye bored into him. *Thassa bad place.*

Yes, I know. I'm here on, ah, holy business.

The old woman began to wheeze with laughter, an rather alarming noise that put Corso in mind of poison gas escaping from a canister. *You see dat?* she said, pointing towards some kind of animal fetus preserved in a nearby jar. *It know more about holiness than you do.*

Corso shrugged. *It's a job, not a vocation.*

She sniffed. *Don't matter. You got no business goin' there. No one does.*

Please, he said, producing his wallet. *It's very important. I can pay you.*

You might as well go out there and throw youself under a streetcar, she scowled, folding her arms across her chest.

In reply, Corso laid a fifty dollar bill on the counter. *Please*, he murmured.

The old woman looked offended. *What you think I am, takin' a man's money to send him to his death?*

Another fifty.

She stared down at the money. *Look here, mister,* she said finally. *I tell you how it's gonna be. You buy a gris-gris from me to protect you, and I'll tell you how to find dat place.*

A gris-gris? Corso suppressed a look of contempt. *Sure, okay. How much?*

The old woman named a eye-watering sum. Seeing the expression on Corso's face, she shrugged. *You wanna go there or not.*

Begrudgingly, he paid up, exceptionally grateful that the store's sole concession to modernity was a credit card machine. In return, she gave him an old leather pouch filled with god-only-knew what, and a laboriously written set of instructions for finding the hotel. When Corso thanked her, the old woman waved him away like a lingering odour. *Don't be thankin' me. You never gonna make it outta dat place alive. And if somehow you do, don't you ever be comin' back here. You got the smell of evil about you, mister.*

During the long, complicated walk to the hotel, during which Corso had to double back and retrace his footsteps more than once, he mulled over what the two priests had told him about the place. According to them, a painter named Schweik had been killed there in 1927, executed in his room by a vigilante mob who believed him to be a sorcerer. The room in question – number 36 – had been rumoured to be haunted ever since. And as far as the Church was concerned, the mob had been entirely correct in their murderous assessment of Schweik.

He was an evil man, who created evil works, Franchino had insisted. *He painted visions man was not meant to see. The book you seek belonged to him.*

But when Corso had raised the not-unreasonable point that he could hardly expect the Book of Eibon to still be present in the hotel almost a century later, the monsignor had quickly dismissed his objection. *The book is the key, Mr Corso. It cannot be separated from the door for long.*

The ground was awash with shadows by the time Corso eventually located the hotel. The building was situated in an area of dense woodland neighbouring the nearby Mississippi River, its white clapboard outer walls filthy with accumulated grime, the surrounding air thick with humidity and mosquitoes. By now, the dealer was perspiring heavily and quite out of breath, and the sight of the old hotel squatting there in the gloom, crepuscular and foreboding, left him considering whether to postpone his quest and return the next morning.

On the other hand, he'd come this far, which right now felt like very far indeed. Not to mention that Corso couldn't quite rid himself of the irrational notion that if he did come back tomorrow, it might be to discover that the hotel was no longer here.

Girding himself, he lit another cigarette, partly in the hope that it would help ward off the massing mosquitoes. Perhaps between the clouds of tobacco smoke and the gris-gris, he might just make it out of the building unscathed.

Corso gingerly climbed the steps to the front porch. The hotel's front door was hanging open by a single hinge, and the dealer immediately noticed a sickening smell emanating from within: the unmistakeable reek of decomposing meat. Gagging, Corso turned his face towards the river, inhaled a lungful of marginally fresher air, then plunged inside.

Stepping into the interior was akin to submerging himself in cold porridge. The inner walls of the hotel were clogged with black mould and rot, rendering the atmosphere soupily dank and vile. The dealer suddenly became convinced that the old woman from the voodoo store had been right; he would never make it out of here alive. Not due to any ancient curses or infernal portals, but because he would simply choke to death before he could take another step.

Scanning the lobby area, Corso noticed a large oil painting sitting propped against the wall. Something about it drew his attention, and, squatting down before the canvas, he began to wipe at the layers of dust and grime obscuring the image. Strangely, underneath the surface dirt, the painting seemed to be entirely undamaged by the rank humidity in the air. From what Corso could make out, it seemed to depict some kind of hellscape; barren and empty, save for a scattering of dessicated corpses.

Schweik's work, no doubt. Well, if this particular example of the painter's art was anything to go by, Corso couldn't honestly say that the world had been deprived of much by his untimely demise.

Putting the canvas to one side, he decided to begin his search in Schweik's old hotel room. The dealer didn't believe for a minute his task would be quite that simple, but as much as he was temperamentally disinclined to trust the word of the Catholic Church and its adherents, he had to start somewhere. Coughing like an asbestosis patient, he began to climb the treacherous-looking staircase, taking great care to step on the outer edges of the stair risers.

Corso arrived at room 36 to find the door ajar, almost as if he were expected. As he warily pushed it open, the dealer couldn't stop himself from calling out to see if anyone was inside. His voice sounded flat and unfamiliar in the desolate emptiness of the hotel, and for a moment the dealer was seized by a irrational urge to seek out a mirror and check that he was still the same person. This damned place was getting to him.

Inside, the room's furnishings were all covered with mildewed sheets, the air fogged with dust and mould spores. Flapping his hands in front of his face, Corso noticed an uncovered dresser in the far corner, a selection of cobwebbed items piled on top of it. Upon closer inspection, he could make out an open book lying amongst them. His heart lurched excitedly. Had the universe finally decided to cut him a break for once?

He reached down for the book and carefully closed it. The front cover, discoloured and shrivelled with water damage, read, simply, *Eibon*.

Corso pulled the book to his chest and hugged it with glee. Two more minutes and he'd be out of this godforsaken shitpile. He'd jump in a cab, find a quiet bar somewhere, relax with some good whisky and the best the local cuisine had to offer...

It was then that he heard the noise behind him. A wet, rasping sound that sounded like some dreadful imitation of breathing, by something that had forgotten how to breathe and perhaps no longer even needed to.

Corso whirled around just in time to see the dead thing shambling towards him. Doubtless it had once been a man, but now only barely resembled one, looking more like a golem crudely sculpted from decomposing meat. The lifeless flesh of its face was swollen and shapeless, forming a grim parody of human features. It possessed no functioning eyes that Corso could see, but moved unerringly towards him regardless, quickly hemming the dealer in amongst the maze of cluttered furniture. The creature's arms lunged greedily for him, a strangled moan escaping its flaccid lips.

He had nowhere to run.

Shuddering with revulsion, Corso shrank back against the wall, simultaneously cursing the men who had sent him here and praying that his death at the creature's hands would at least be quick.

But when it reached in to seize him, sparks of blue flame immediately erupted around the dead thing's fingertips, quickly rising to engulf the whole of its arms. Corso watched in astonishment as it wheeled away, letting out an agonised, high-pitched wail.

His hands flew to the leather pouch hanging around his neck. The old woman's gris-gris had saved him.

Tucking the *Book of Eibon* safely under one arm, Corso shoved his way past the creature and bolted from the hotel room. In the corridor outside, more of the zombies were starting to emerge from the other rooms. Banking on their clumsiness and lack of speed, the dealer lowered his head and charged through them, hoping that his protective ward would do the rest. In this fashion, he managed to make it back to the hotel's central staircase, which Corso proceeded to charge down full-tilt, hoping that one of the rotting steps would not give way underfoot and break his ankle. Both the stairs and his luck held, at least until he reached the bottom. There, Corso looked around to see more of the dead things spilling in through the hotel entrance. There were already hordes of them blocking his path, the lobby reverberating with their mournful cries. In order to escape the same way he had come in, he would have to plunge into their ranks and hope that the power of the gris-gris could still protect him against them en masse.

It was not a chance Corso was particularly eager to take.

Behind him, the zombies from upstairs were continuing their pursuit, lurching awkwardly down the staircase. If he waited much longer, he would be completely surrounded.

In desperation, Corso threw himself through the only exit currently available to him – the doorway leading to the hotel's cellar. Slamming the door closed behind him, he hurriedly barred it against his pursuers, aware that he was probably sealing himself in with no means of escape.

Perhaps it would hold them off. Perhaps there would be another way out.

And if not?

Well, Corso mused fatalistically, at least it gave him time for a condemned man's last cigarette.

Hurriedly lighting said cigarette, he descended the rusted spiral staircase leading to the basement. Noticing a pervading stench of stagnant water, he peered down to see that the cellar was heavily flooded. Reaching the bottom of the steps, Corso kicked out at a nearby crate in bitter despair. Was it too much to ask for a man to at least be warm and dry when he died in screaming abject terror?

Upstairs, he could hear the dead battering against the door. The dealer doubted it would hold for very much longer. He supposed he should probably try and search the cellar in the forlorn hope that there might be a way out, but Christ, he was tired. The thought of simply sitting here and smoking for whatever remaining time he had left seemed so much more appealing.

Then he heard a man's voice from the shadows. *Hey, you! Over here!*

Eyes straining against the darkness, Corso thought he could discern a gaping hole in the opposite wall, through which a figure was gesturing to him. Keeping a careful distance, the dealer took a few steps closer, before igniting his Zippo and holding it up so that he might see the stranger more clearly.

He turned out to be a nerdish-looking man with an alarming shock of black curly hair. He wore a pair of round spectacles perched on the end of his large nose, their lenses obscured by mud and dirt, and held a sealed box under one arm.

Continuing to gesture to Corso, the man peered short-sightedly over the rim of his glasses. *Come on!* he hissed, in a broad Bronx accent. *Follow me! Quickly!*

Hearing the sound of splintering wood from upstairs, the dealer decided he didn't really have the time to question any of this, and hurriedly followed the man through the hole in the wall.

For a few seconds, everything was a haze of bright light and white fog, and when Corso's vision finally cleared, he found himself in a naggingly familiar-looking landscape; a seemingly endless wasteland devoid of life or presence.

The other man stood before him, his face urgent. Now that Corso could see him more clearly, he realised that his rescuer was wearing clothes that had to be half a century out of date. But before he could ponder this matter, or indeed the question of exactly where he was and why his surroundings seemed so familiar, the man darted forward and plucked Corso's glasses from his face.

When the dealer responded with a surprised curse, the man cried, *No time to explain!* Without his spectacles, Corso was rendered almost entirely blind, and could do little more than stand there helplessly. He heard frantic scuffling sounds from around his feet, before the glasses were carefully placed back onto his nose. Only now, the lenses had been completely obscured with dirt.

Squinting at the dim shape of the man standing before him, Corso grabbed him by his lapels. *What the fuck?* he snarled.

The man began to gibber. *You don't understand, I'm trying to help you! If you look at this place too long, you'll go blind!*

A faint voice echoed in Corso's mind: *No man can see what Father Hackett sees and retain his sight…*

Now, the dealer realised why he recognised the surrounding landscape. It was the same infernal place Schweik had depicted in the painting he'd stumbled across in the hotel lobby.

So was this yet *another* region of Hell…?

Oh Christ, not again, Corso moaned, He let the man go, and began to fumble for a cigarette.

As he busied himself lighting it, the other man spoke again. *Hey, I'm really sorry about all of this,* he said. *I had to get you outta there, and there was just no time to explain.* He sighed. *Not that I'm sure where I'd start…*

Maybe you could just start by telling me who you are, Corso replied wearily.

Oh, sure, the man said eagerly. *My name's Barton. Barton Fink. I'm a writer.*

Now Corso was certain this all had to be some kind of sick cosmic joke. Not only had he managed to get stranded in Hell – *again* – he was stuck here with a fucking *writer*, of all people. As much as the dealer had come to despise books, he'd be the first to admit he'd made a comfortable living from them over the years. But as for the people who actually *wrote* them, well. As far as Corso was concerned, the only good writer was a dead one. That way, he didn't have to stand around and listen to them drearily expound on the agony of the writing life. Not to mention the fact that once they were dead, their books might actually be *worth* something.

Okay, Barton, the dealer muttered. *My name's Corso. So, now that the introductions are out of the way, you mind telling me how you got here in the first place?*

I don't really know, Barton replied. I was in Hollywood, you see, working in the pictures. I'd written this script, the best thing I'd ever done, about this common man, this poor wrestler…

You can skip the synopsis, Corso said bluntly.

Sorry, sorry. I know I get carried away sometimes. Barton took a deep breath. *So, anyway, the studio, the goddamn philistines, rejected my script. I guess I was in a pretty bad place…things hadn't been going too well for me… so I went down to the beach. And there was this girl there. No surprise, right? A beach, a pretty girl, they go together like ham and eggs. But this girl looked like she was straight out of this painting I'd had hanging on my hotel room wall. It was like I'd stepped into the painting, understand?*

He giggled madly. I mean, I couldn't figure it out either. But all of a sudden, it was like I had nowhere else to go. I was in this painting, and it was my whole world, everything. So, in the end, I just walked into the sea. It seemed like the only thing I could do. I let the waves come over my head, and everything went dark. The writer paused. *And the next thing I knew, I'd washed up here. Wherever here is.*

Corso thought back to his first impression of Barton's oddly out-of-date outfit. *And just how long have you been here, Barton?*

The writer's face grew distant. *I don't really know. Sometimes I think it's only been hours, but at other times it seems more like…*

Barton tailed off, his silence telling Corso everything he needed to know. Was that to be his fate too? Marooned in this blasted purgatory, wandering aimlessly for all eternity?

No. He'd escaped Hell once, he would do it again.

Somehow.

The first thing to do was keep moving. *Come on,* Corso told the other man. *There was a way into this place, there's got to be another way out somewhere.*

He marched away, leaving Barton to scuttle along behind him. As they walked, the writer began to drone on about his life's work; his attempts to create a theatre for the common man, and his unspeakable treatment at the hands of the barbarians in Hollywood. For the most part Corso ignored him, but neither of them seemed to care. Barton was just happy to have someone to talk to, and as far as Corso was concerned, the constant background chatter at least served to drown out the crushingly oppressive silence.

The two men walked for hours, the landscape around them never changing, seemingly frozen in time. Corso thought back to Schweik's hellish painting, and imagined himself pictured as a small figure in the artist's vista. Eternally trapped in two dimensions, so that when he reached one side of the canvas, he would simply reappear on the other. He hurriedly dismissed the thought. Allowing it to gain any purchase in his mind would be to submit to madness, he knew.

Suddenly desperate for distraction, Corso glanced over towards Barton. *What the hell's in that box you're lugging around with you, anyway?* he demanded.

I don't know, came the oddly reticent reply. *It was given to me for safekeeping.*

By who? Why don't you open it to see what's inside?

Barton's voice rose to an agitated whine. *Look, I don't* want *to know what's inside, okay?*

And that, it seemed, was the end of that particular topic of conversation.

Sometimes they would hear other people wandering in the distance, moaning and sobbing in desolation. Corso thought it far better to avoid them; there was nothing they could do for such lost souls, and even listening to Barton's self-absorbed prattle was preferable to being subjected to the eternal despair of the damned.

But a short time later, they came across a lone figure, lying on his back in the middle of the wasteland and staring up at the fogged, tea-coloured sky. At first, Corso thought the figure must be another of the shrunken, wizened corpses that were scattered everywhere, but as they drew closer, he could see that the man was in fact alive, his obese frame very far from being wizened.

We should go around him, Corso murmured to Barton.

But the writer shrugged him off, peering over his spectacles to snatch a better look at the man blocking their path. *Charlie, is that you?*

The man looked blindly around and sat up. *Bart?*

Barton darted forward, seizing Charlie's meaty hand between his own. *It is you! Oh boy, it's good to see a familiar face!*

Likewise, brother. Charlie smiled broadly. *Not that I can actually see you, but hell, you catch my drift.*

Corso cleared his throat, prompting Barton to introduce them. *Oh, so this is Corso, who I met a little while back. Corso, this is Charlie.* His voice became hesitant. *Well…Karl.* Another pause. *I, uh…listen, what exactly am I supposed to call you, Charlie?*

Charlie laughed heartily. *Hell, Bart, what's in a name? That's what that Shakespeare fella said anyway, and I'll bet you didn't think old Charlie Meadows would know a thing like* that.

Oh, you're just full of surprises, Charlie, Barton snivelled.

So, compadre, how'd you get to be here? Charlie asked him. *Still just a tourist with a typewriter, huh?*

I don't have the typewriter anymore, Charlie. But look, I still have your box! The writer proudly brandished the box like a winner's trophy, before remembering that Charlie was blind and shamefacedly pulling it back to his chest.

With the mention of the box, Corso felt something instantly shift in the air. Charlie hauled himself to his feet, where he towered over the pair of them. *The box, huh?* he said in a low, threatening voice. *That was my special gift to you, Bart. You mean to say you haven't opened it?*

Barton cowered. *I…I was afraid to, Charlie.*

You're afraid of a lot of things, aren't you, brother? Charlie whispered. *And look just where it's got you. So much for the life of the goddamn mind.*

Charlie reached out and laid one huge paw on Barton's shoulder, the writer buckling under its weight. Corso was suddenly certain that if he didn't intervene somehow, things were about to go even more horribly awry than they had already.

It took every remaining scrap of courage he had left, but the dealer hastily inserted himself into the gap between Barton and Charlie, the larger man's face looming up nightmarishly before him.

Say, Charlie, Corso said, as casually as he could manage. *You seem to know the lie of the land. Any idea how we might go about getting out of here?*

For a moment he thought the other man was about to raise a fist and strike him down to the dirt. But then, turning on a dime, a wide grin split Charlie's face. He averted his head and spat into the dirt, as though ridding himself of a foul taste. *Hell, where are my manners?* Charlie bellowed. *Here's me and Bart talking about old times, without a single thought as to our guest! Forgive me, friend. I'm just a big old dumb lug and sometimes I truly forget myself.*

That's okay, no harm done, Corso assured him. *So, do you have any thoughts about a way out…?*

Charlie's sightless eyes gazed back at Corso for a moment, and then he laughed, gesturing at the book the dealer still held underneath one arm. *Jesus, well, you've got the book, don't ya? That's all you need, friend.*

Accepting Charlie's apparent knowledge of the volume the same way he'd accepted every other inexplicable thing that had happened to him in the course of the last twenty-four hours, Corso carefully opened the *Book of Eibon,* tugging his dirty glasses down so that he might scan the pages. But the passages within seemed to be written in a hodgepodge of Greek, Latin and some other ancient language the dealer didn't even recognise. *I can't read it,* he finally admitted.

Not a scholar, huh? Charlie said. *Hell, I sympathise. I was never much for reading myself. But listen, you don't need to know what a sign on a door says to go where it'll take you, am I right?* He extended one hand towards Corso. *May I?*

Hesitantly, the dealer passed him the grimoire. Clutching the *Book of Eibon* between his hands, Charlie eased himself down onto his knees, spreading its pages open before him.

Say, would one of you fellas happen to have some matches or something? he said brightly.

Corso immediately grew alarmed. *Matches? What do you –*

Charlie's face darkened once more. *Do you want my help or don't you?!?* he roared. *Maybe you're just like old Barton here, someone else who DOESN'T LISTEN!*

Not in any great hurry to find out what Charlie might do to such people, Corso fumbled for his lighter and passed it to the other man, watching dumbfoundedly as Charlie ignited it and held the flame to the book. As the fragile pages began to blacken and shrivel, the dealer let out a small whimpering sound. In his mind's eye, he imagined all of the zeroes on the Vatican's cheque popping like so many soap bubbles.

Quit your griping, compadre, Charlie snapped. *Look, the pair of you.*

Corso and Barton did as he instructed. Unbelievably, the flames from the book had now spread to the ground below, and it, too, was rapidly scorching to ashes, opening a black tear in the earth as though it were nothing but paper…or a canvas painting.

If you come across a locked door, sometimes you just gotta kick it down, Charlie mused with satisfaction.

Corso watched as the tear continued to widen, its blackened edges curling back with the heat of the flames. His brain could not properly process the optical disconnect between the two-dimensional appearance of the rupture and the three dimensions of the surrounding wasteland, and he began to feel dizzy, his legs growing weak underneath him. He might even have fainted, were it not for Charlie's steadying hand on his shoulder.

No time to take a powder, the other man urged him. *You gotta get out of here before that thing seals itself up again.* He turned to Barton. *You too, brother.*

But what about you, Charlie? Barton replied querulously.

Ah hell, Charlie said. *I've been here awhile now, and I guess it's starting to feel like home. Besides, you meet some damned fine people around these parts. But it was a pleasure to run into you again, Bart.*

There seemed little more to say. The two men shook hands, then Charlie stepped aside, allowing Corso and Barton to access the newly-opened portal. A impenetrable void gaped within, looking as though it might lead anywhere…or nowhere at all.

Fuck it, Corso said, and threw himself into the rupture.

For a few horrible moments, the dealer felt as though he was being turned inside out, his stomach and intestinal tract torn through his screaming mouth. But in the next instant, the sensation abruptly ceased. Plunging forwards, his face then encountered some sort of unseen barrier or obstruction. Under the weight of Corso's momentum, the barrier quickly gave way with a loud ripping sound, sending him sprawling to the ground.

Hurriedly wiping the dirt from his glasses, the dealer looked up to find himself in a dingy hotel room. The atmosphere was oppressively hot, and he could smell smoke in the air. Glancing around, he saw that he had somehow emerged from within one of the room's walls, a gaping tear in the dreary-looking wallpaper marking his passage.

As he watched, Barton materialised from within the same hole, and fell to the ground beside Corso.

So where the fuck are we now? the dealer groaned.

Barton knew the answer immediately. *We're in my hotel,* he told Corso, reaching up to polish his own spectacles clean. *It must only be minutes since I left. Charlie set it on fire, you see. The whole building is about to burn down.*

Christ! Corso leapt to his feet. *Do you know a safe way out of here?*

They ran from the room, and Barton led them to the back staircase. Hurtling down the steps two at a time, the pair quickly reached the ground floor. They burst through the lobby doors, only to instantly recoil from the savage wall of heat that greeted them there.

The whole area was ablaze, snaking towers of flame climbing the walls like ivy. The hotel entrance was a roaring furnace, rendered completely impassable. Corso realised they had simply exchanged one hell for another. He wondered whether he should simply cast himself into the fire now, or run back upstairs and throw himself off the roof instead.

Barton seized his arm. *This way!* he shouted.

Corso allowed the writer to drag him behind the hotel's reception desk, where Barton dropped to his knees and wrenched open a trapdoor in the floor. *Down here!*

Another hotel, another basement. And that hadn't really worked out so well the first time, had it?

Corso shook his head. *It's suicide. We'll suffocate down there.*

Barton grinned maniacally. *Trust me! I think I'm starting to get the hang of this!*

Without waiting for Corso, he turned and plunged into the darkness below, his hunched figure soon disappearing from sight.

The dealer glanced back at the burning lobby. The inferno was almost upon him, his hair and eyebrows already crisping with the heat. Perhaps, he rationalised, suffocation would be less agonising than being burned alive.

He turned and followed Barton down the steps, closing the trapdoor securely behind him. As he descended into the shadows, Corso could feel the air quickly growing cooler. He picked up his pace, but the staircase seemed endless. On and on he walked, past the point of all possibility. Just how deep could this cellar be?

Suddenly, Corso felt another wave of physical dislocation sweep over him, similar to the sensation he'd experienced while crossing over from Schweik's hellscape to the hotel. All at once, his senses became utterly scrambled, and the dealer found he could not discern up from down, nor left from right. He stubbornly forced himself to continue descending the steps, but his brain was now telling him he was somehow upside down, his feet moving above his head.

Then, everything abruptly seemed to right itself, only for Corso to realise that he was now walking *up* a set of stairs, rather than down. A short distance above him, an open trapdoor mouth promised freedom. But was it a false promise? Would this mirage of escape simply lead him back to a fiery death in the flames?

Still, he could not feel any trace of the same suffocating heat he had just escaped from, and so continued to proceed cautiously up the remaining steps.

Upon reaching the top, Corso carefully poked his head through the trap door and looked around. He seemed to be in some sort of log cabin, dusty and cobwebbed with disuse, its furnishings faded with age. A Tiffany lamp burned in one corner, and Corso could see Barton standing there, examining an old book. The sight of yet another book made him immediately nervous, and the dealer wondered if he might, quite understandably, be starting to exhibit the first symptoms of bibliophobia.

Hearing the creak of the stairs, the writer turned to look at Corso. *Ah, you made it!* he said with a smile. *Didn't I tell you we'd be okay?*

Corso extricated himself from the cellar opening and moved towards a nearby window in an attempt to get his bearings. *We're not out of the woods yet,* he told Barton, instantly cursing himself when he subsequently peered out through the glass and saw that they were now indeed situated in the middle of a dense twilit forest somewhere. As to precisely where, who could say?

The dealer reached for his cigarettes, finding he had but one remaining. Once again feeling like a condemned man, he quickly lit it, huffing at the cigarette as though it were an asthma inhaler.

Corso's mind raced. Where the fuck had they ended up now? For all he knew, they could be stranded in the middle of the Russian taiga. Surely there had to be a clue in the cabin somewhere. He glanced back at Barton, still engrossed in his discovery.

The book! That might serve to give some idea of roughly what country they were in, at the very least.

Corso marched over and snatched the volume from the writer's hands. Ignoring Barton's aggrieved protests, he began to flick through the pages, his disquiet rapidly mounting as he did so. The book was all in Latin, written and illustrated entirely by hand. The illustrations in particular filled him with a nagging dread; detailed etchings of unspeakable obscenities and hideous abominations.

Another grimoire.

His hands trembling, Corso turned back to the title page, to find a single word inked there: *Necronomicon.*

The very same volume Walter Paisley had been so desperate to acquire.

According to what Walter had told him, that could mean they were in Tennessee somewhere. Not high on the list of Corso's preferred destinations, but it certainly beat the Russian taiga.

He closed the book, turning it over in his hands. The front cover of the *Necronomicon* depicted a grotesque demonic face that seemed to leer directly out at the reader, and the material used to bind it felt sweatily unpleasant to the touch. For a moment, Corso almost fancied he could feel the book throbbing beneath his fingertips.

Fascinating, isn't it? Barton said from over his shoulder. *It seems to be some sort of spell book or something…*

That's precisely what it is, Corso told him, tucking the book safely under one arm. *And if I've learnt one thing, it's that you don't fuck about with black magic.*

He should probably pay better attention to his own advice, he knew. Part of him wanted nothing more than to toss the *Necronomicon* down into the darkness of the cellar, but Corso remained mindful that Walter would pay a pretty price for it, enough to ensure that this whole miserable caper wasn't a complete write-off.

The dealer strode to the front door of the cabin, throwing it open and peering out into the encroaching gloom. There was a car parked right outside, a battered-looking Oldsmobile covered in grime and fallen leaves. It seemed to Corso as though the only place the vehicle might be capable of going in a hurry was straight to the nearest wrecking yard, but it was still the best chance they had of getting out of here.

The dealer turned back inside, hurriedly scanning the room and finding a set of car keys lying on a small side table. Snatching them up, he glanced over at Barton, only to find him poised with his finger over the 'Play' button of an old reel-to-reel tape recorder. *I wonder what's on this?* the writer murmured.

Don't touch that! Corso screamed, sprinting the length of the cabin and violently shoving Barton away from the machine. *Don't touch* anything, *for Chrissake!*

Jeez, okay, the writer said sulkily. *You don't have to get so pushy about it.*

The dealer took a deep breath. *Look, we don't know what this place is. But if you found this book here, the smart money says it's no particular place we want to be. So just come outside with me while I try and get this car started.*

His point made, Corso turned on his heels and strode outside, Barton slouching along behind him. There, they both began to clean some of the accumulated filth from the Oldsmobile's windows, until Corso was satisfied it was in a semi-reasonable state to be driven.

Barton took a step back and peered curiously at the car. *Say,* he enquired to Corso. *Exactly what year is this, anyway?*

I'm not sure I even know any more, Corso replied, before handing Barton the *Necronomicon. Look after this while I see if I can get this damn thing started*, he ordered the writer.

Barton happily accepted the book back into his safekeeping, and began to pour over it once more. Meanwhile, Corso popped the hood of the Olds and proceeded to examine the engine, his eyes straining in the failing light. While the dealer was admittedly no one's idea of a mechanic, a short inspection satisfied him that everything at least appeared to be in its right place.

Closing the hood, Corso walked around to the driver's door and climbed inside. But when he turned the keys in the ignition, the car's engine did nothing but let out a sluggish, snoring sound.

Corso kept on trying, his nerves growing increasingly frayed, his attention focused solely on the task at hand. Barton was merely a hazy shape in the periphery of his vision, wandering back and forth in front of the car with his head buried in the book.

Finally, when the dealer had started to abandon all hope, the engine finally, reluctantly, turned over and started. Letting out a yell of triumph, Corso thumped the dashboard and glanced over towards his companion, only to see Barton standing facing the darkened forest, one hand raised in the air. As he looked on, the writer slowly began to intone: *Khandar estrada khandos thrus indactu…*

No! Corso shrieked, but Barton seemed not to hear his cry, the book's accursed spell having taken hold of him. *Nosfrandus khandar dematos khandar…*

The dealer immediately leapt from the car, but it was too late. Suddenly, several tree vines, animated by some unearthly force, exploded from within the forest and wrapped themselves around Barton's body like pythons. Screaming in horror, the writer looked desperately back at Corso for help, but the dealer could do nothing to prevent him from being dragged back into the black woods.

Struggling frantically against his bonds, Barton dropped the *Necronomicon* from his grasp and was gone.

Corso stood frozen by the car, inanimate with terror, torn between the primal instinct to run and the more considered fear that to do so might attract the attention of whatever it was lurking within the forest.

Then he felt it; a tremor in the air, signalling the approach of something huge and utterly dreadful.

Fuck this, he whispered.

Scrambling back into the Olds, Corso frantically restarted the vehicle and began to manoeuvre it down the long dirt road connecting the cabin with (he hoped) the outside world, pausing briefly to open his door and grab the *Necronomicon* from where it lay on the ground.

Throwing the book down onto the passenger seat, the dealer desperately gunned the engine, the clawing fingers of the overhanging trees scraping at the car's paintwork as it sped down the track.

Corso could hear something pursuing him over the noise of the vehicle; a presence unleashed from deep within the earth, roaring like a thousand caged animals driven insane by untold decades of captivity. He quickly glanced back through the rear windshield but saw nothing chasing him, although the dealer fancied he could make out the glass starting to warp and buckle under the heat of his invisible pursuer's infernal breath.

He tried to press his foot further to the floor, only to find that the car's squalling accelerator had nothing more to give. Corso stared out at the length of dirt track in front of him, leading off into what appeared to be nothing more than a gaping black abyss.

His hands tightened around the wheel. *No more books*, he vowed silently. *If I ever get out of this, not another…single…fucking…book.*

The Oldsmobile hurtled on into the darkness.

Christ, but he needed a cigarette.

LILY SAYLOR

Ruth Wilson in I Am the Pretty Thing That Lives in the House, 2016
written & directed by Osgood Perkins

IN TRYING TO UNPICK THE ENIGMA OF THE OLD HOUSE ON TEACUP LANE in Braintree, Massachusetts, of Lily Saylor and those who came there after her, I'm afraid my efforts will only end up contributing further to its mysteries. The property seems to resist any sort of rational explication, gathering riddles to itself like moss to a stone, shrouding itself within layers of paradox until its true nature is utterly obscured from view.

As an allegedly 'haunted' house (if indeed that's what it can be said to be), it is far less legendary than, say, its notorious Massachusetts neighbour Hill House, located only a short drive away. To the observer's eye, they could not appear any more different. Hill House is a sprawling gothic pile, squatting in place like a fearsome ogre; one almost dares not look at it directly, for fear of drawing its attention. The Teacup Lane house, however, is a plain white clapboard building; neat and primly presentable, but with nothing to differentiate it from any number of similar houses. And whereas the former property seems almost in revel in its infamy, brandishing its death toll like a war banner and positively daring the unwary to cross its threshold, the Teacup Lane house merely sits and waits, entirely innocuous and unobtrusive in its aspect. The history of Hill House has been exhaustively researched, written about (not least by myself) and even dramatised; the dread folklore surrounding the strange lives and deaths of Hugh Crain and his family, not to mention Eleanor Vance and however many others, is now forever entrenched in pop culture.

But as for Teacup Lane? Nothing. Not only that, but the harder one tries to look, the *less one sees*. It is as though the house's past has been written on a blackboard; one which is wiped clean after every occupancy. As a result, the stories of those unfortunates who have lived there are now nothing but motes of chalk dust: hanging suspended in the air for a short time before dispersing forever.

I had best try to explain.

I first became aware of the property when Mrs Wendy Saylor – previously Torrance (and yes, anyone familiar with the details of the Torrance family's own tragically haunted history can perhaps recognise a pattern emerging here; see how Teacup Lane accrues decades of stories to itself like sediment?) – knowing of my professional interest in such matters, contacted me about her daughter Lily's mysterious passing while she was employed at the house.

It turned out Lily Saylor had worked at Teacup Lane for several months as a live-in nurse to the author Iris Blum. A writer of gothic fiction, Ms Blum had enjoyed a quite significant readership during the 1960s and 70s, although public awareness of her work had seemingly dwindled in recent years. Stricken by advanced dementia, Ms Blum had nevertheless stipulated her desire to see out the remainder of her life at home, and thus required around-the-clock care. In August of 2015, Lily Saylor had been hired to provide that care. Originally from Altoona, Pennsylvania, where her mother Wendy now resided with her second husband, Lily had relocated to Braintree, understanding that her sojourn there would be an indeterminate one. Although Ms Blum was by now lost to the fog of senility, her health was apparently good in all other respects, and there was no way of knowing how much longer she might live for.

In my conversations with Wendy Saylor, she told me that she'd been extremely worried for Lily:

WENDY: When I spoke to her on the phone, she told me how lonely the house was, tucked away at the end of that little lane. And Lily was always such a nervous girl. I blamed myself for that. Ever since that winter at the, the… (*NB: Mrs Saylor could never bring herself to say the Overlook Hotel's name aloud*), in Colorado, I've suffered from all sorts of anxieties and phobias, and I feel as though I passed them onto Lily.

Although Lily's first year in the house passed largely without incident, she did confide in Wendy that she'd occasionally seen or heard odd, unexplained things – things that *might* have been down to her nervous imagination, but on the other hand, might not.

WENDY: That obviously worried me. I called Danny (*Torrance, Lily's half-brother*) and asked him to speak to Lily. He knows about these sorts of things. Apparently he did call her but I don't know what they said to each other.

(When I tried to contact Daniel Torrance afterwards, he refused to comment.)

WENDY: Lily also got creeped out because Ms Blum would always call her Polly. She didn't mind it at first – dementia patients often do that sort of thing, don't they? – but then she picked up one of Ms Blum's books and realised that Polly was the main character in the novel (*The Lady in the Walls*,

published 1960). Well, after that she told me she
started to feel as though she was actually living
in the novel _herself_, that Ms Blum had somehow
written her in there decades before she'd even been
born. It was at that point I vowed I was gonna go
up there.

Tragically, Wendy Saylor never got her chance. Shortly afterwards, all communications from Lily Saylor ceased, and before much longer her lifeless body was found in the downstairs hallway of the house by the manager of Iris Blum's estate, one Mr Waxcap. Sadly, Iris Blum had also perished of neglect during the time that Lily's body lay undiscovered. The subsequent autopsy determined that Lily's death had been caused by an undiagnosed congenital heart defect.

An highly unfortunate tale, but nothing particularly *outré*, you might think. However, this was only the start of it – or if not precisely the *start* (in truth, unsettling stories have surrounded the house ever since its construction in 1812), then perhaps it would be more accurate to say that this was where I came in.

This is the transcript of my telephone conversation with Mr Waxcap, when I contacted him while carrying out background research on Lily's time at the house:

WAXCAP: Hello, yes?

ENSLIN: Mr Waxcap? My name's Mike Enslin. I'm
calling you about Iris Blum's old house on Teacup
Lane.

WAXCAP: Oh, it isn't me you need to speak to any
more. The house is now administered by a grant
foundation, House of Stories. You'd need to apply
for a residency through them, although I warn you
now, the house is only open to female authors.
Those were Iris Blum's specific wishes, I'm afraid.

ENSLIN: I wasn't looking to apply, Mr Waxcap. I'm actually researching Lily Saylor's story.

WAXCAP: Who?

ENSLIN: The young nurse who passed away in the house.

WAXCAP: I don't know what you mean.

ENSLIN: Lily Saylor? She looked after Ms Blum for the last year of her life. Until she sadly had a heart attack and died suddenly, right there in the house. Surely you remember. You <u>were</u> the one who found her.

WAXCAP: What nonsense.

ENSLIN: Excuse me?

WAXCAP: Is this meant to be some sort of <u>joke</u>?

ENSLIN: I assure you it isn't, Mr Waxcap. Lily Saylor died in the house in 2016. As in fact did Iris Blum, from neglect - caused by the sudden death of her carer. This is all a matter of public record.

WAXCAP: I don't know what you're talking about. I hired all Ms Blum's nurses myself, and there was never anyone called Lily. And Ms Blum died peacefully in her sleep, not through <u>neglect</u>. The very idea! Now what exactly is this supposed to be about, Mr Enslin?

ENSLIN: Then who <u>was</u> the last live-in nurse you employed there, Mr Waxcap, if not Lily?

WAXCAP: Oh god, I can't remember. I think her name was Polly. Polly…Parsons. Yes. That's it.

ENSLIN: Polly Parsons?

WAXCAP: But she left suddenly. You can't trust these young girls. They get their heads turned by a boy and poof, they're gone. I had to hire a temporary nurse after that, and it was <u>then</u> Ms Blum died.

ENSLIN: Mr Waxcap. Polly Parsons was the name of the character in Iris Blum's book. *The Lady in the Walls*.

WAXCAP: [*Pause*] Look, Enslin, I don't know what kind of damn fool game you think you're playing, but I've had quite enough. No one died at Teacup Lane except for poor Ms Blum herself. And it is entirely down to her generosity and goodwill that the house is now run as a charitable trust, offering long-term residencies to female writers. I won't see such a fine legacy dragged through the mud by hack writers like yourself. Good day. [*Hangs up.*]

Now, what are we to make of that, I wonder?

At the time, I told myself that Waxcap was merely stonewalling, trying to protect Iris Blum's legacy from damaging, scurrilous rumours. I couldn't even say I particularly blamed him. Using the name of Iris Blum's character as a smokescreen was admittedly a little odd, but in all other respects, there wasn't very much here to go on. Two women – one young, one old – had died under tragic circumstances, and now the estate was trying to brush the whole affair quietly under the carpet. If there was any sort of a story there, it didn't really appear to be of the variety that I've made a career out of uncovering.

But I'd made a promise to Wendy Saylor. Wendy believed something was very wrong in the house on Teacup Lane, and given her undoubted familiarity with such matters, I was inclined to give her the benefit of the doubt. So I kept on digging.

I soon learned that the current beneficiary of a residency at the so-called House of Stories was apparently a writer named Jennifer Hills. Something of a recluse, Hills had suffered a violent sexual assault as a young woman and, in the decades since, had written a series of gritty feminist-leaning crime novels. While the books had never quite crossed over into the mainstream, she enjoyed something of a cult reputation, which was only heightened by her reluctance to conduct interviews or PR. Realising that any attempts to contact Ms Hills would probably meet with a wall of silence, I decided I would travel to Teacup Lane to try and find out whether she had experienced anything untoward during her time in the house.

But upon my arrival, I found the house empty; closed up and uninhabited, apparently for some time. Had Hills cut short her stay? And if so, for what reason? I contacted the House of Stories foundation in an attempt to obtain some answers. Initially, the woman I spoke to there was understandably reluctant to provide me with any information pertaining to the house or its residents, past or present. But when I said I was urgently trying to speak to the house's current occupant, she (rather sniffily) informed me that the Teacup Lane property was closed for renovation work and would not be open again for residencies until later in the year. When I subsequently told her that this ran entirely contrary to my information, and I in fact had it on excellent authority that the crime author Jennifer Hills was currently in residence there, she informed me that she had no application on file from any such person, and indeed had never even heard of Ms Hills.

This was obviously rather hard to swallow. But then, an even more curious thing happened. My subsequent attempts to trace Ms Hills myself were quickly stymied – not by any unwillingness on her part to be found, but by the plain and simple fact that she *did not exist.*

Despite my prior checks into her background, any research I conducted after my abortive conversation with the House of Stories foundation was now met with the same result: <u>there was no writer named Jennifer Hills</u>.

At least, not in the real world.

For what I subsequently discovered was that actually yes, there was indeed a writer named Jennifer Hills – but she was a *fictional character*, featured in a series of unpleasant-sounding 'rape-revenge' exploitation movies entitled *I Spit on Your Grave*.

Do we see a pattern starting to emerge here? Lily Saylor – died in Teacup Lane under mysterious circumstances; afterwards, her very existence is denied by the man who first employed her, who appears to confuse her with a character appearing in a novel written by the very woman Saylor had been hired to care for. And then Jennifer Hills – who, according to my original sources, was a recipient of a writing residency in Teacup Lane, but has now vanished without a trace. Unless you wish to define a 'trace' as an apparently fictional existence as a horror movie character.

I decided to update Wendy Saylor on my bizarre findings, but when I contacted her, the following conversation took place:

ENSLIN: Hi Wendy, it's Mike Enslin here.

WENDY: Yes? Sorry, who?

ENSLIN: Mike Enslin. You asked me to look into the death of your daughter Lily.

WENDY: My <u>daughter</u>? I'm sorry, what is this?

ENSLIN: I...I'm sorry, Wendy, I'm a little confused here.

WENDY: I've never had a daughter. I think you must have the wrong person.

ENSLIN: I'm speaking to Wendy Saylor, yes? Previously Torrance?

WENDY: [Pause] OK, I don't know who the hell you are, but if this is just some attempt to get me to dredge up the past and talk about Jack again, you can forget it.

ENSLIN: So it _is_ you. Wendy, you were married to Jack Torrance. He went crazy that winter in the Overlook Hotel and tried to kill you and your son Danny. Afterwards you remarried and had your daughter Lily--

WENDY: I never _had_ a daughter. I don't _know_ any Lily. And I'm certainly not discussing my previous marriage with you, whoever you might be.

ENSLIN: That...that's just not possible. Wendy, you approached _me_--

WENDY: I want you to leave me alone, you hear? Whoever the fuck you are, just fuck off and leave me alone. [_Hangs up_]

Given these events, it is difficult not to conclude that anyone who stays too long in the old house on Teacup Lane will not only be, for all intents and purposes, erased from existence, but also somehow rendered *fictional*, folded into the pages of the house's grand narrative. 'House of Stories' has never seemed like a more apposite name for Iris Blum's foundation – surely her final, sly joke on us all.

I say 'us all' because I am now writing this from what was once Iris Blum's office in her house, the same house that has claimed the – lives, souls? – of Lily Saylor and Jennifer Hills and who knows how many others. Ironically enough, there are still visible traces of Iris preserved here in the room, perhaps in an attempt to help inspire those writers granted residence: her old typewriter and office stationary, her iconic horn-rimmed spectacles, even her nicotine-stained ashtray.

The irony being, of course, that Iris is apparently the only person to have ever occupied this house and left any discernible trace of themselves behind.

Determined to navigate my way through this hall of mirrors, to penetrate to the very heart of the labyrinth of realities that is the old house on Teacup Lane (excuse me shamelessly mixing my metaphors, but that seems somehow appropriate under the circumstances), I bribed someone at the House of Stories foundation to give me the keys to the property and allow me to spend a single night here. I knew I might be taking a significant risk, but people told me exactly the same thing when I stayed in room 1408 at New York's Dolphin Hotel. And yet I survived, and even thrived (certainly my book sales did). Yes, I still suffer from recurring bad dreams, but that seems a relatively small price to pay for being permitted to peer beyond the veil, as it were. I now know that there are things we do not, perhaps *cannot*, understand in this existence, and yet I have dedicated myself to the pursuit of trying to do exactly that. I craved an answer to the mystery of Teacup Lane, and so here I sit, in the same chair that Iris Blum once occupied, writing about this house, just as she herself once did.

My first few hours here passed uneventfully. While the building certainly possessed a somewhat funereal atmosphere, I've found that such aspects are not uncommon in old houses, especially isolated ones like this. I would argue that it's impossible for a succession of lives to blossom and wither within a building's walls and not leave some lingering impression of themselves behind, whether you choose to believe in actual ghosts or not.

With nothing preternatural to distract me, I was free to cook myself a hearty dinner, enjoy a couple of glasses of wine, and retire to bed early with one of Iris Blum's books (*Underwater Housewife*). I had only read a few chapters when the words began to swim and blur on the page, and so I turned off the light and went directly to sleep.

Before long, I began to dream. I dreamt that Lily Saylor came to me, still wearing her white nurse's uniform. She knelt down by my bed to whisper in my ear, and this is what she told me, in a dry, cracked voice that sounded like the pages of an old book turning. She said: *Our bodies may rot, but our stories never will. A mere life can be forgotten, but not a truth. Such as we are not made from memories, but the tales they tell about us.*

That was all. When she got up from the bedside, I could see that her head and torso were twisted completely around, somehow facing in the opposite direction from her lower body.

The next moment I woke up.

At least, I *think* I did. Although the house around me certainly suggested waking reality, entirely solid and corporeal to the touch, when I got out of bed to fetch myself a glass of water, I felt curiously weightless and insubstantial, as though something ineffable had been stolen from me. Although the vision of Lily in my dream had left me shaken, I knew it had been just that: a dream. There was not the merest suggestion of anything untoward in the house now that I was awake once more. It was just an old building, filled with memories.

Such as we are not made from memories…

I went to the bathroom and drank a glass of water. Then, knowing I would not be able to get back to sleep right away, I came back into Iris's office and sat down at the desk. Opening my laptop, I began to idly browse the internet. But the odd sensation that a part of myself was somehow *missing* persisted, and it was then that I was seized by a nagging, insistent urge to Google myself.

Now, I am not trying to be self-aggrandising when I say that my name normally returns page upon page of hits when typed into a search engine. I'm far from a habitual ego-surfer, but I do occasionally have good reason to look myself up, and can assuredly state that, as an author of several books (many of them New York Times bestsellers) and some small prominence, typing 'Mike Enslin' into Google will normally produce all manner of links to interviews, articles, gossip pages, hit-pieces, outright libel, and not least, my own official website.

But there was *nothing*. All of it was gone, wiped away.

I tried another tack, typing in some of the titles of my most popular books, but it was if I had never written them.

How can that be, when I can still quote entire passages from them verbatim? I *know* I wrote them. Christ, I did three drafts of each, plus editorial passes and proofs. Not to mention the promotion for them: the talk shows, the author profiles, the endless fucking book tours…

I WROTE THOSE BOOKS.

Without really realising it, I began to weep, already beginning to understand what had been done to me. I searched for my own name again, checking the results more closely this time, and it was then I found it.

A reference on Goodreads to a short story entitled '1507' by a popular horror author named William Denbrough. The story concerns a hack true-life ghost story writer named Mike Enslin, who checks into an allegedly haunted room in a hotel called the Whale, and is forced to confront the reality of the supernatural phenomena he has spent his whole career scornfully fabricating in search of a quick buck.

My own life, turned into cheap pulp fiction.

Insanely, my first thought was to sue, until I remembered that a man who does not exist can hardly claim defamation of character. It would set an interesting legal precedent for a fictional character to sue their own creator, however. I'm certainly not ruling the possibility out, hahaha

(you do have to see the funny side mike)

And then I tell myself that if I were to pick up my cellphone and call my lawyer – the same lawyer whose services I have retained for the past twenty-something *years* – he would claim not to know me. Just as my ex-wife Lily oh god *Lily*, see how this works? see what this fucking house DOES??

i'm going to finish writing this and send it out into the world and hope that it makes someone REMEMBER. If someone REMEMBERS me just one person maybe that will be enough to bring me back i pray it will be enough

i don't want to spend eternity with a bunch of fucking dead writers hahahahaha

wait

wait

are you reading this in a book??????
no
   no
   NO

thisisrealthisisrealthisisrealthisisrealthisisrealthisisrealthisisrealthisisreal
thisisrealthisisrealthisisrealthisisrealthisisrealthisisrealthisisrealthisisreal
thisisrealthisisrealthisisrealthisisrealthisisrealthisisrealthisisrealthisisreal
thisisrealthisisrealthisisrealthisisrealthisisrealthisisrealthisisrealthisisreal

   i can feel her watching me from the doorway
   how can she watch me with her head turned backwards

TRAVIS BICKLE

Robert De Niro in Taxi Driver, *1976*
written by Paul Schrader
directed by Martin Scorsese

EXCERPTS FROM THE DIARY OF TRAVIS BICKLE

October 30th 1968.
Two weeks leave. I thought about not coming home but I had nowhere else to go. I wrote Dad to ask him to collect me from the bus station but when I arrived he wasn't there. I waited for an hour then caught a cab. When I walked through the door he was watching TV. He looked away from the screen for a second and said 'Hi Travis' and then went back to watching his programme, like I'd only been away for five minutes.

The house feels strange. After everything that happened here, it doesn't feel like a home anymore. The air is slow and heavy and it's difficult to breathe. It feels like the jungle, like death might be waiting for you around every corner.

I don't think I will sleep tonight.

November 2nd 1968.

I went to visit Bobby today. I had to sneak out without Dad knowing, but that wasn't too hard. He was still sleeping off his drunk from last night. I guess that ever since the murders, all he does is sit in his chair and drink. The other night, he turned to me and said, 'Do you know what I think about doing, Travis? I think about visiting the sonofabitch in that hospital and just blowing his brains out there and then. That's what they should have done to him, if there was any goddamn justice. I'd shoot him dead and then put the barrel in my own mouth and pull the trigger. Wipe the goddamn slate clean. That's what I think about. I think about it a lot.' Then he just went back to drinking.

I thought the institution would be dirty, smelling of piss and shit and madness, but it was actually real clean. Bright and sunny, all the nurses constantly smiling like the smile was a part of their uniform, something they put on before they leave the house. It kind of made me uncomfortable. I felt as though there was nowhere to hide, like everyone was watching me everywhere I went.

Bobby seems happy there though. He got up and gave me a big hug the moment I walked in the room. He's a little skinny but looks well otherwise. He asked me how long I was home for, and I said I was going back to do another tour in two weeks. He seemed startled by that, but didn't say anything.

Then he said, 'I'm kinda surprised you came to see me, Trav.'

I just shrugged, so he carried on. 'I suppose you wanna know why I did it. I can't really answer that.' He thought for a minute. 'I used to get these bad thoughts in my head sometimes. At first that's all they were, just thoughts. But then they turned into pain, this sick, burning pain behind my eyes, like my brains were boiling. It got so bad I thought the only way to stop it would be to let the thoughts out. So I did.'

I asked him if the thoughts had gone away now, and he nodded. 'Yeah. They give me pills three times a day and now I don't have the thoughts anymore. I still get pretty bad headaches though.'

I get headaches sometimes too, but I didn't tell Bobby that.

'I'm sorry you didn't get to see Mom one more time though,' he told me. 'You know, she prayed for you every day you were over there.'

I didn't want to talk about Mom, so I asked him, 'What about if I'd been there? Would you have shot me too?'

He thought for a minute, then nodded again. 'I guess I would have, yeah. But it's nothing personal, Trav. You're my brother and I love you. It was just a sickness.' He leaned forward and whispered, his eyes darting from side to side. 'Sometimes I think they did something to us over there, you know what I mean? Put stuff in our food, experimented on us. I'm not the only one who says that. You should be careful, little brother. You might have a sickness too.'

'You're only as healthy as you feel,' I said, and he laughed. Then we just sat there for a minute, neither of us saying anything. I didn't really know what to say. What do you say to your brother when you haven't seen him for two years and then you come home and he's a murderer?

Then he asked me about how things were back home. I told him it felt strange. Everyone in the street watches me and I don't like it. All I have to do is walk down the driveway to take the trash out and I can feel all the neighbours staring at me, like they're afraid I'm just going to pull out a gun and walk from house to house shooting until they're all dead.

Bobby nodded. Then he reached out and put his hand on my shoulder. 'I'm real glad you came, Trav,' he said. 'It's real good to see you. But I don't think you should come here again.'

When I got up to leave, Bobby asked me how Dad was. I shrugged. 'You know. He doesn't say much. Mostly now he just sits at home and drinks.'

Bobby nodded. 'You know, if there's one thing I wish, it's that I'd got him too.' Then he grinned. 'Hey, Trav, if you ever wanna finish the job, be my guest!'

After I left the institution, I felt a little funny, so I just drove around for awhile. I guess I drove for longer than I thought, because suddenly I looked out of the window and it was dark. I was driving down Sunset and I could see all the hookers gathering on the sidewalks, crawling out of their holes like vermin, and I started to feel a pain behind my eyes, so I turned around and drove straight home.

When I got back, Dad had already passed out in his chair. I stood in the doorway watching him for awhile, then I went into his study. The police took all Bobby's guns away, but Dad still has his collection. I unlocked his gun cabinet and took out a pistol. Then I went to my room. I didn't turn the lights on, just sat there in the dark and thought about what Bobby had said. My head was hurting pretty bad by then but I put the gun barrel in my mouth and sucked on it and eventually the pain went away.

May 17rd 1973.
I got my honourable discharge today. I am not going back home as there is nothing there for me now. Instead I am going to move to New York. It seems like a good place to Start Again.

When I wrote to Bobby and told him this, he said he thought it was a good plan. In his letter he said, 'You should change your name too. Go incognito, so no one knows who you really are. Maybe take Mom's maiden name.'

I thought about that. Mom's maiden name was Bickle. Travis Bickle. I liked the sound of it. And I liked the idea of having a new name, like I was an undercover agent.

In New York no one knows who I am.

July 8th 1975.
I am home from the hospital now and feeling much better. Still a little sore but that will pass I guess. When I got home there was a Get Well Soon card from Bobby waiting for me. All it said was 'Good Shooting Travis!!!'.

While I was in the hospital reporters kept trying to sneak in to speak to me. I didn't want to see anyone and thankfully the nurses did a good job of keeping them out. I'm happy for them to write about me as long as they get their facts straight but I know if I talk to them they will probably twist my words. But so far the articles are mostly fair and I have started cutting them out and saving them.

There was this one guy who came to see me though. He wasn't a reporter and I don't know how he got past the nurses. I woke up one morning and he was there in my room, just sitting watching me. I guess I looked pretty surprised to see him there because he gave me a big smile and told me he was a friend and not to exert myself. Then he told me his name was Jack Younger. When I said I didn't have any friends by that name he smiled again and told me he worked for a company named Parallax. He said they were looking to recruit Unusual Personnel and had read about me in the newspapers. He said he thought that I might be just what they were looking for.

When I told him I already had a job he laughed and said the kind of work they offered was strictly on a freelance basis. He said I could easily fit it around my cab shifts. (I guess that's what they mean by moonlighting.) He also told me that it paid real well. I think 'extremely lucrative' were the words he used. That was how he talked, like an advertising brochure or something.

He was small and had these real dark eyes. He reminded me of a rat, scurrying around behind the walls without you even knowing it was there. I didn't trust what he was saying so I just told him that I was tired and in pain and couldn't think about working right then. He nodded and apologised and said he would come see me when I got out of the hospital. Then he told me that, as a gesture of goodwill, Parallax would pay all my hospital bills.

I suppose that was a nice thing to do but it still made me nervous, like they thought they could buy me or something. I wonder what I should do if he comes back. The cops took all my weapons for evidence so I have nothing to protect myself. I wonder what he really wants.

July 11th 1975.
Jack Younger came to see me again this afternoon. He said he was pleased to see me looking so much better already. I came straight out and told him I didn't know what he wanted from me, that I was just a cabbie and there was nothing special about me.

He said, 'Travis, that is the Big Lie that you and thousands of young men like you are being sold every day. Just because you're White and working-class and love your country, the people in charge want you to believe you're somehow inferior. Well, you're not. You just have a different outlook on the world, one that we at Parallax share with you one hundred percent. We're looking for people ready to make a stand, just like you did.'

That sounded pretty good to me, I guess. So I asked him what sort of work he had in mind. He said a lot of it was security-type stuff, that it could be dangerous at times but that I'd already proved I could function in high-risk situations. He told me they'd already had an offer for my services. He said, 'Travis, money can't buy talent and experience like yours, so we'll ensure that clients have to pay a premium rate to hire you.'

Money doesn't mean very much to me, but I liked the rest of what he'd said, so I nodded. Next thing he picked up one of the Vote Palantine flyers I still had lying around. 'We <u>Are</u> The People,' he said, and smiled like he'd said something funny.

I just shrugged.

He said, 'You don't like Charles Palantine very much, do you, Travis?'

So I told him, 'I don't like people who don't say what they mean, is all. This fucking city is full of them. There's so much lying and bullshit, rising up above the buildings like a filthy smog. I just want people to be decent.'

He nodded, and said, 'You are an admirable man, Travis. I truly believe that you and I can really help each other.'

Then he told me he'd be in touch soon and left.

After he'd gone, I picked up the Palantine flyer and stared at it awhile. I thought about who The People really are and what they want and then after a little while without even really meaning to I began to think about Betsy.

And then I started getting a headache so I burnt the flyer in the washbasin and went to bed.

(Newspaper clipping found in the
journal of Travis Bickle)

SENATOR PALANTINE SHOT DEAD JUST AFTER MAKING VICTORY SPEECH

NEW YORK (AP) – Sen. Charles Palantine was shot in the head early today by a gunman who turned a Manhattan victory celebration into a scene of terror.

Witnesses saw a man dressed as a waiter remove a gun from underneath his jacket and fire at the Senator as he was leaving the stage, shouting 'We are the people!'. Onlookers wrestled him to the ground moments later, one man receiving gunshot injuries in the process. There were unconfirmed reports of a second gunman concealed backstage, but these have so far been denied by police…

January 22nd 1978.
I've been feeling real good lately. The work I'm doing for Parallax gives me a sense of purpose at last. Everyone there seems to like me and says I am one of their Best Men. Obviously I can't talk about it with anyone but that's okay. When people ride in my cab I look at them and think I Know Something You Don't and then I want to laugh in their faces.

Today I saw something strange. I dropped off a fare in Columbus Circle and saw that there were all these cars piled up and on fire. Then I noticed that all these women were fighting around the cars. The women had hardly any clothes on.

A crowd of people had gathered to stare, and it took me a while to see that another woman was taking photographs of it all. So the undressed women were only models, I guess. I don't know why anyone would want to take photos like that.

February 14th 1979
Something funny happened today. I picked up this lady in Soho and took her uptown. She was beautiful but real nervous-looking. She reminded me of a china doll, too fragile to touch. She didn't say much at first but then she noticed my ID. She asked me if I was THE Travis Bickle, the one who'd rescued that girl a few years back.

So I just kind of nodded. I don't like to make a big thing of it. Then she got excited and told me she was a photographer and wanted to do a shoot with me. Well that just sounded crazy to me and I told her so. But she said no, she was a famous fashion photographer and people paid her a lot of money for her photographs.

Then I remembered that weird shoot up at Columbus Circle last year. She said that was her, and that she'd like to do something similar with me. That sort of made me uncomfortable, I don't like to have my picture taken. But she started pleading with me and said she'd make me look real handsome and pay me a lot of money. I don't care too much about the money but there was something about her, something in her eyes. She seemed like she needed someone to take care of her and I realised I'd like to get to know her better.

So I said I would think about it, and she got real happy. She gave me her business card and told me to call her office.

Her name is <u>Laura Mars</u>. I haven't really spoken to many women since Betsy so I guess I will give her a call. I don't trust women too much now but maybe Laura will be different.

She was very Beautiful.

June 17th 1979.
I woke up this morning with the feeling that my life was about to change. I do not know whether it will be good or bad, all I know is that it will be Different.

Today I had my photo shoot with Laura. She asked me if I still had the clothes I wore the night I saved Iris but I told her they were all bloody and the nurses at the hospital threw them away. So she said I should wear something similar. I asked her if she wanted me to shave my head again but she said no, they would give me a wig.

I picked out my outfit and then a car arrived to pick me up. It took me downtown to where they had hired a building for the shoot. It was not the same building which I heard they tore down, but it was only a couple blocks away and it looked almost the same. When I got out of the car Laura ran over to me and gave me a hug. There was a guy with her, I guess he was her agent or something. I didn't like him, he seemed like a Fag to me. But I didn't say anything to Laura.

She took me inside the building and asked me what I thought. It seemed okay but I told her there should be more blood on the walls, they had only used a little and it looked wrong. So she said fine and was there anything else? I said well, the real building stank real bad of sweat and cum. Laura looked nervous for a minute, then she laughed and said it was all an illusion anyway and no one would know the difference.

Maybe that was the wrong thing to say.

They took me off to make-up and put a mohawk wig on me. Then the girl started to make up my face and I got uncomfortable. I asked her if it was really necessary and she said, 'Sure honey, don't you want to look good for the camera? This will really bring out your cheekbones.'

Then Laura came in the trailer and said she didn't like what I was wearing and that I should go to wardrobe to change. I thought the clothes they wanted me to wear were all wrong and I told them, but Laura said that real stuff looks fake on camera and if you want it to seem real, you have to fake it. I don't know how I feel about being fake but I did as she asked.

The photo shoot was real strange. There were all these models there, giggling and smoking constantly. They were dressed like hookers but not real ones. Like someone's phoney idea of a hooker. Besides, real whores are not that pretty. I thought they looked ridiculous but I stayed quiet. They flirted with me at first but when I didn't respond they kept their distance and kept giving me funny looks. I think I heard one of them call me a creep.

We worked for hours. Laura kept changing the lights and fussing with the models' hair and make-up even though nothing ever seemed to really change much. I had to pretend to shoot these guys dressed as pimps even though they were all models too and faggots so they were nothing like real pimps.

Then Laura brought a new model on set and said, 'Travis, this is your Iris.' I looked at the girl and for a minute I thought she <u>was</u> Iris. The clothes were all wrong but her face looked just like sweet little Iris.

Then she held out her hand and said 'Hi, I'm Connie.' I guess she was older than Iris really but she seemed young to me.

My head started to feel funny then. They took a lot more photographs with me and Connie and in some of them she wasn't wearing many clothes. That felt all wrong. I didn't like the idea of seeing Iris naked or that people seeing the pictures might get the wrong idea about me. But when I told this to Laura she just looked nervous and said a lot of stuff I didn't understand about sex and art and foreign words I can't even remember properly to write down.

But it still felt dirty to me.

By the end of the day I had a terrible headache. I felt like I was back in the real building and the scar on my neck started to throb real bad. When they said it was a wrap I ran straight outside because I thought I might puke. Laura came out to find me a few minutes later and gave me another hug. She told me I was a natural and that she'd loved how In The Moment I was.

Then she asked me to go to dinner with her that night.

I really wanted to say yes but my head was hurting so bad I couldn't see straight. So I apologised and told her I wanted to but I had a headache. She said, 'Oh you poor Darling, I worked you too hard!' She told me a car would take me straight home and that we could take a raincheck for dinner. So I told her I was free for dinner on Friday and she said sure, call my office to confirm.

My head feels a little better now. It was a very strange day and I don't know what to think about any of it.

But I liked it when Laura called me Darling.

June 20th 1979.
I need to write this down quick so that I know it all really happened. Sometimes I get confused. Sometimes I get Bad Ideas and I don't know if they're real or I imagined them.

BAD IDEAS!!!

I went to dinner with Laura tonight. She suggested a restaurant and I said sure even though I didn't know it because I knew I would never be able to take her somewhere that was right. I offered to pick her up but she said her driver would take her. I wore my Best jacket and arrived at the restaurant early, but they wouldn't let me in until Laura arrived. The head waiter treated me like I was scum but I didn't make a Scene because it was a Fancy Place and I didn't want to make Laura look bad.

She was fifteen minutes late and I had to wait on the sidewalk in the rain the entire time. When her car pulled up I was real happy but then I saw that her fag agent was with her. He clings to Laura the entire time like a fucking leech. She is surrounded by fake people that use her and only want her money but I guess she is scared to be alone.

Laura hugged me and kissed me on both cheeks but when the fag offered to shake my hand I just looked at him until he took his hand away. This was Our night why did he have to ruin it? We went inside and were seated at our table and now the waiter was real nice to me. The menu was not in English and I didn't know what to order so I just had the same as Laura. The food was okay I guess, although I don't know why people pay so much money for small portions like that.

Laura looked very beautiful but there was a sadness about her too. I wanted to tell her it would all be alright, but we had no privacy to talk. Every time I tried to have a Serious Conversation with her the faggot would make some faggy comment and laugh like a girl. I do not know how she can bear to be around him.

I guess Laura got pretty drunk, and when we finished the meal the fag told her she should go straight home to bed. But she said no, the night was still young and we should all go back to her apartment for a nightcap. I guessed she did not want to be rude to her agent and tell him to go home.

I followed her car to her apartment building. Inside the place was real nice but cold somehow, like no one really lived there. It reminded me of one of Laura's photographs and I wondered if she would rather live in a photograph than the real world. She poured us all a drink and then the faggot excused himself to go to the bathroom. At last we were alone.

I knew I had to take my chance so I said, 'Laura you are a Very Special person but I think you are surrounded by people who don't take you seriously. But I believe you and I have a Connection. I could feel it the first time you got in my taxi. I know that there is a Sadness within you but I know I can help make it go away. I only wish that leech hadn't followed you here so that we could have some time together. I'm sorry to call him that but I think that's what he is.'

She didn't say anything for a minute, just looked at me. I figured she wasn't used to people talking to her like that, just being straight and honest.

Then Laura started to laugh. For a minute I told myself she was laughing because she was so happy but I soon realised she was laughing at <u>me</u>. I guess she could tell I knew that because then she made an effort to stop. She said, 'Oh, I'm sorry Travis, I'm not laughing at you, honestly.'

It was then I knew she wasn't an honest person.

She said, 'Darling, listen to me. When people work together in my business, the work is very short and intense, and because artists are in touch with their emotions, sometimes we form strong attachments to each other. And I know that you are

in touch with your emotions too, I can see that in
your eyes. But these attachments soon pass. It's
just a fleeting thing, you know?'

I told her that it wasn't for me. I said I was a
serious person and I would never treat someone like
a passing thing, like they didn't matter.

'Oh dear,' Laura said. 'I don't really know what
to tell you, Travis. I don't feel the same way about
you, I'm afraid. And Donald came along tonight
because I asked him to. I suppose I didn't want you
to get the wrong idea.'

Then the faggot came back in the room and asked
why everyone was looking so serious. And then Laura
said, 'Travis was just telling me about his feelings
for me.'

The faggot started to laugh. He reminded me of how
the girls in school used to sound when they laughed,
all high-pitched and nasty. He gave me a look like I
was just dogshit on the sidewalk. I guess I should
have just walked out then but my body would not obey
my commands. All of a sudden the Bad Ideas were
filling my head and there wasn't room for anything
else. And when it gets like that you just have to
let them out, there is No Other Way.

I don't carry a gun around any more but I still wear
a knife in my boot. So I quickly pulled it out and
stabbed the fag in his throat. He stopped laughing
then and started squealing. He still sounded like
a girl but frightened now and not nasty.

Laura just sat there with her eyes wide. The
faggot fell to the carpet, his blood spilling out
everywhere. I pointed the knife at him and told
Laura, 'This is what it really looks like. Not like
your stupid photographs. This is what you wanted
all along.'

Then she started to beg. She told me she was so sorry about everything, that she was my friend and that we could work it all out if I just put down the knife. But the Bad Ideas were still inside my head, swarming and screaming and biting like an ants' nest. I knew they would never be quiet until I let them out.

So I did.

There was a lot of blood afterwards. I knew I would never be able to clean it all up so I just left them where they were. I cleaned myself up as best I could and found an old raincoat in Laura's closet to hide the bloodstains. Then I hurried downstairs and out of the building. I tried not to look at the doorman as I went.

But I knew it was hopeless. Too many people had seen me and Laura together in the restaurant. Soon the police would find her body and then they would come for me and put me in an institution like Bobby. There was only one thing I could think to do.

I parked near a payphone and called Jack Younger at Parallax. When he answered, I said 'Jack, this is Travis Bickle. Are you my friend like you always said?'

He told me he was, and to tell him what I needed. I explained what had happened in Laura's apartment. Jack didn't get mad or anything, just listened carefully. Then he told me that he would take care of it. He said, 'I understand that these things happen, Travis. You were right to call me. I am your friend and I promise it will be okay. Go on home now and don't speak to anyone until I give you the all-clear.'

I did just as he told me.

I hope I can trust Jack.

TWILIGHT'S LAST SCREAMING

September 4th 1979.
I haven't written here in awhile. I was waiting to
see what happened about Laura, and my stomach has
been hurting so bad I could barely think. The day
after I went to her apartment the reports of Laura's
murder were all over the TV news. The police said
they were following up leads and were confident they
would be making an arrest soon. Every time I heard
a sound outside my door I thought it would be the
cops coming here to take me away. But they never
came.

Eventually they arrested some crazy artist called
Reno Miller for her murder. They said he had sent
Laura abusive letters about her photography and
killed a bunch of other people too, some of them
with a power drill. So I guess I didn't feel too
bad about him taking the rap for what I did.

Jack came to see me afterwards. He said he hoped
I was happy with how things had turned out and I
said yes and thanked him. Then he said, 'Travis,
you know you are one of our Best Men and we're
very happy with your work for Parallax. And we do
understand that accidents happen. But I hope you
understand that nothing like this can ever happen
again. It costs us a lot of time and money to clear
situations like this up. I know that you are a very
unique person and that is precisely why we employ
you, but if you can't control these urges that you
feel then I'm afraid Parallax will have no choice
but to terminate your employment.'

Jack looked at me funny when he said that, and
I wondered exactly what he meant by it. So I gave
him my word that it would never happen again and he
clapped me on the back and told me I was a Good Man
and there was no real harm done.

I meant it too. Laura was only an accident just like Jack said and it has taught me never to trust another woman again. I thought I had learnt that lesson after Betsy but I guess not.

It reminded me of what Dad always used to say: Fool me once, shame on You. Fool me twice, shame on <u>ME</u>.

20th September 2015.
It has been a long time since I wrote in this journal. I am old now and I guess I don't have too much to say any more. I quit driving a taxi a few years back. I had some money put away so I retired and bought a little apartment out in Queens. The city wasn't so bad by then because the mayor finally cleaned up the streets but I'd started to see things. Maybe they were ghosts or maybe I was just imagining them but I would see a passenger hailing me down and the next time I looked it would be Betsy or Laura or sometimes Iris, staring at me with black insect eyes, their faces all cold and dead. And I knew if I let them inside the cab they would never go away and it got so I was scared to pull over. So in the end I just quit.

That turned out to be a good thing because soon after my stomach started hurting again and eventually it turned out I really <u>do</u> have cancer. They tried to treat it at first but now the doctors say it is Inoperable and they tell me I don't have too much longer now. When they first told me I guess I didn't really react because the doctor asked me if I understood and I just shrugged and said yes. I guess it's hard for them to understand that a person might not care about dying but if I am being truthful (and I always Try to be) I don't really do much except sit here and watch the TV. And sometimes I sit here for hours and then I realise I have forgot to turn the TV on.

Sometimes I think maybe I died saving Iris that night all those years ago and the rest of my life has just been a dream.

So I guess I never really became a person like other people like I used to say but that's okay. I used to look at the faces of the people who rode in my cab and they didn't seem happy to me. So if the world is full of people who are Unhappy why should I want to be like them?

Anyway something funny happened yesterday and I thought I should write it down. Like I said I don't do too much of anything any more. I don't drive a taxi and after a while Parallax stopped contacting me. I guess I got too old to be Useful to them. So I figured I would just wait until the cancer took me or else if the pain got too bad I could end it myself.

But then yesterday I had a Visitor. No one ever calls here so I wondered who the hell it was. When I opened the door I saw it was a woman and I figured she probably had the wrong apartment. But no she had had come to see Me. She said her name was Girder and that she worked for Parallax.

I felt bad because I was only dressed in my underwear but she laughed and said it was okay. So I invited her inside and fixed her a drink of water. I asked her how Jack Younger was doing these days and she thought about it for a minute and said, 'I think he's dead.' Then she said 'I know it's been awhile since we used you Travis but as you know you were always one of our most Valued Operatives and something has just come up which we thought you would be Perfect for.'

I said I was surprised they would need an old man like me and she smiled and told me that this was Top Secret but things were changing at Parallax. She said that real soon they would have a machine that could send their operatives inside someone else's head and it would make their Work much easier. But until they'd finished testing it they were still stuck doing things the Old Way and who better for that than an old guy like me haha?

Well this all sounded pretty crazy to me but I don't understand the world anymore so what do I know anyway? So I just said okay sure what do you need me to do.

Then Girder told me they would set me up with a job at a television studio, just as a janitor or something like that. She said 'I know you're sick so don't worry, it won't be anything too strenuous and it won't be for long.'

I never told anyone at Parallax I was sick but I figured out a long time ago that no one has any secrets from them.

Then she showed me a picture of a man and asked if I recognised him. I said sure I do, I see him on TV all the time. That's the U.S. Vice President.

She smiled again and said, 'We know we can always rely on you, Travis.'

We talked some more and she told me exactly what would be needed and then said she would be in touch again soon. It's a shame Jack is dead as he always seemed to Understand me but Girder seems like a nice lady.

After she'd gone I immediately felt much better. My stomach stopped hurting and I had more energy than I have had in years. I had a Purpose. I might not have much Time left but my life now had somewhere to go.

I was Ready.

The last thing Girder told me before she left was this. She stood on my doorstep and said 'I want you to understand one thing, Travis. If you do this job for us, if everything goes as we've discussed, you will literally be changing the world. How many people can say that about themselves? Just think about that.'

So I came back inside and sat down and thought about it.

And I decided it sounded pretty good to me.

GREG STILLSON

Martin Sheen in The Dead Zone, *1983*
written by Jeffrey Boam
based on the novel by Stephen King
directed by David Cronenberg

WHILE IT IS NOT SURPRISING THAT A GREAT MANY BOOKS AND ARTICLES have been devoted to the life and career of Greg Stillson, given how thoroughly he has disproven F. Scott Fitzgerald's famous dictum that there are no second acts in American lives, what is particularly noteworthy is the degree to which Stillson has been able to establish his own narrative in recent years. Perhaps we should expect no less from a man whose early political ambitions seemed to have been decisively capsized by a media tempest of scandal and ignominy, but, Scott Fitzgerald be damned, clung onto the wreckage and eventually found his way back to dry land, there to build a second career as a controversial television pundit, and now, perhaps, as the next President of the United States.

Stillson himself likes to credit his unlikely comeback as being down to 'a lot of hard work and humility', and 'the unparalleled decency and capacity for forgiveness of the American people', but such PR homilies do nothing to advance our understanding of what enabled such a remarkable turnaround. Some pundits have derisively dubbed Stillson's second act 'the greatest confidence trick ever pulled on the United States of America', but if it is indeed all nothing but a colossal grift, why has no one yet succeeded in exposing it?

Certainly, Stillson's camp maintains an iron grip on his media profile these days; the infamous 'No Future for Stillson' *Newsweek* cover still lingers in a lot of people's memories, even some three decades later. But that can hardly be the only reason. The instant the disgraced former politician first embarked on his quest for public rehabilitation, a veritable locust storm of press attention descended upon him. The reporters covering the story ran the gamut from Pulitzer Prize winners to gutter hacks, but regardless of their byline or credentials, they all wanted the same thing: dirt. Given that Stillson had been exposed as an opportunistic coward once already, how could they possibly fail to find the *real* story behind his comeback?

But fail they did. Some would have us believe that was because Stillson truly has nothing to hide any more; that, as his frequent (and often tearful) talk show appearances at the time had it, he'd undergone a life-altering series of spiritual revelations and embraced a higher power. As we shall see, there may indeed be some partial truth to that statement – albeit a perverse one – but it is very far from the complete story.

I should state for the record that many of those reporters were tireless and extremely diligent in their attempts to uncover the full truth of the matter. Nevertheless, their attempts still ended in failure. Not, however, the sort of everyday failure any journalist might expect to encounter during the course of their career – leads going cold, sources refusing to talk – but of a much darker stripe. Simply put, anyone who tried to get too close to Stillson, and – perhaps more pertinently – the shadowy figures who facilitated and backed him, were met with intimidation, violence, and worse. Over the past few decades, a number of reporters covering the Stillson story have died under suspicious or violent circumstances. Nothing that could ever be connected to the man himself, of course. A high incidence of freakish accidents, or simply someone being in the wrong place at the wrong time; a botched robbery here, a hit-and-run incident there. Other journalists, perhaps less fatally devoted to the cause of getting their story, suffered 'only' violent threats or some form of bodily harm. Regardless, the net effect was entirely successful. The only profiles published of Stillson in recent years have been puff pieces and hagiographies. Any scrutiny or criticism of the current Republican presidential candidate has been restricted solely to his public positions and statements. Simply put, the real Greg Stillson story has not yet been told.

Am I, then, proposing to reveal it here?

Well, while this book is undoubtedly Stillson's story in a great many ways, it is not *only* his story. He is but a single part of it, a featured player in the drama being devised and set in motion by dark actors who crave the limelight to a far lesser degree than Stillson. And it is my unhappy task to tell their stories too, as best as I am able.

So no, I cannot restrict my attentions to the man who currently seems likely to be the next American president, whatever the dire implications of that eventuality may be.

Nevertheless, there are some hidden corners of Stillson's life that might permit us some small insight into the greater narrative unfolding within these pages. So allow me to present to you a series of excerpts from Greg Stillson's unwritten biography, in lieu of the full volume that will probably never be published.

1. 1970

One period of his life that Stillson is generally happy to allude to is the time he spent working as a travelling Bible salesman in the American South. It plays into both his folksy man of the people routine and his often shameless courting of the evangelical vote. Still, the references Stillson commonly makes to that particular time are anecdotal and little more; corny slices of homespun wisdom he picked up from his time spent amongst the 'plain folks' of the country he loves.

He has never certainly never spoken of the day in July 1970 where he unexpectedly came face to face with the dark underbelly of America. Even a man of Stillson's less-than-scrupulous character was shocked by the unbridled depravity he witnessed that afternoon, and yet it was an encounter that served to set him on the same path he walks to this day. A chance meeting that revealed to him the seething rage and discontent lying at the heart of the country. A discontent he has subsequently been more than happy to spend his entire career coaxing and prodding, as if he were taunting a vicious fighting dog trapped in a cage.

It was the height of a Texas summer, some distance east of Austin. Stillson had been on the road for the best part of the day, and his battered pickup was running short on gas and in serious danger of overheating. The stretch of countryside he was travelling through was desolate and seemingly without end. Indeed, the only sign of life he had seen for several miles was an old slaughterhouse adjoining the highway, and the stench of cowshit and screams of the cattle on the killing line lingered in his senses for quite some way down the road afterwards.

So when he came upon the old gas station, Stillson felt as though all his prayers had been answered at once, although given his decidedly opportunistic relationship with religion, he was not often given to communing with his Lord and Saviour. He could fill up the gas tank, have the water checked, get a cold Coke and maybe make a quick sale or two to the sorry cracker assholes running this place while he was at it. There was one of them now, sitting out in the middle of the merciless heat and staring blankly up at the sun, as though any minute he might ascend to Heaven and get his just reward in time for supper, if he only stared long enough and hard enough.

He pulled up in front of the gas pump and climbed out, nodding to the attendant. *Howdy*, Stillson said. *Fine afternoon, ain't it?*

A voice came from behind him. *Don't waste your breath on him. He ain't got the sense he was born with.*

Stillson turned to see a buck-toothed older man in work overalls peering at him from the shade of the station entrance. *Good afternoon, sir*, he replied. *Do I take it you're the manager?*

You can take it any way you please, the man said. *Fill 'er up?*

If you would. And I'd be grateful if you could check the water while you're at it.

Hotter than a hog roast in Hell, ain't it? The man busied himself filling up the tank. *You just passing through?*

Stillson made an expansive gesture. *Passing through, and spreading the Word of God while I'm at it.*

The older man snorted. *Folks round here don't have much use for God.*

Well, this could be your lucky day, sir! Stillson darted towards the back of the pickup, and produced a gilt-edged Bible from one of the several boxes placed there. *This here Good Book could change your life. Like I always say, you never know what you've got a use for until you try it.*

The man fixed him with a suspicious glare. *You a preacher? Or a salesman?*

Stillson flashed him a beatific smile. *I am merely a humble servant of God. But I'm afraid even the Lord's servants incur certain unavoidable living expenses. So I could let you have this Bible for, say, a mere seven dollars ninety-five. And let me tell you, sir, at that price, I am barely breaking even.*

A scowl. *A salesman, then.* Grumbling to himself, the older man rounded the truck and hoisted open the hood.

Stillson moved to his side, his voice dropping to a murmur. *Between you and me, sir, my present occupation is merely a pit stop along life's long highway. One day, I aim to be a U.S. senator. And, God willing, perhaps even president.*

The man squinted at him. *You a politician? You famous?*

Not yet. But give me a little time.

A sniff. *Don't have much use for politicians neither.*

Stillson clapped him on the back. *And why would you, sir? Why would you? Listen, I'll tell you the truest thing I know.* He paused for effect. *Capitol Hill is a cesspool, filled with liars and thieves. They care nothing for the honest folk of America, good people like yourself who strain and struggle just to put a hot meal on the table.*

Well, that's for damn sure, the man spat. *Nothing round here was ever the same after they automated the slaughterhouse, and did those politicians give a damn about all the men they put on welfare? No, they did not. My daddy and my youngest boy, they both lost their jobs.* He angrily slapped the side of Stillson's vehicle. *For as long as I can remember, my family's always been in meat, and now we got squat.*

You see? Stillson exclaimed. *This is exactly what I'm talking about. Decent people like your family, left out in the sun to rot. And do you know where all those American jobs are going? To foreigners overseas. To communists, most likely.*

The other man's eyes grew distant. *I don't much care for foreigners. They have a curious smell about them.*

Me neither, Stillson confided. *And that is why my mission is to go up there to Washington and throw all of them thieves right out of the temple, just like Jesus did. I'm gonna give America back to the Americans.*

The man looked at him with wary interest. *You talk pretty good sense, mister.* Gazing off into the distance, he thought for a moment. *Say, how'd you like to come up and meet my family?*

Stillson smiled apologetically. *Well, I'd love to, but you see, I have a busy schedule to keep…*

Oh hell, won't take long. Now it was the other man's turn to clap Stillson on the back. *Don't you want to get to know the honest folk you're fixin' to represent? I mean, if you do want them to vote for you someday. And listen, we'll serve you up a plate of fresh home-cooked barbecue while you're there just to seal the deal. Best damn barbecue in the county, if I do say so myself.*

Stillson raised his eyes to the heavens. '*He doth loveth the stranger, in giving him food and raiment,*' he murmured reverently.

Oh, our door is always open to strangers, the older man replied with a grin.

What followed was amongst the most bizarre and depraved experiences of Greg Stillson's entire life; a mealtime of the mad and the macabre. Although there would be many subsequent horrors to follow in the years to come, he would never forget that July day in Texas.

The gas station manager took him to a large white clapboard house nearby, set some distance back from the highway. *Like it's lying in wait,* Stillson thought as he navigated his pickup up the dirt track leading towards the building.

From the moment he set foot on the porch, he could smell it: a fetid porcine stink of carrion and shit. Despite the dry heat of the day, the air inside the house was clammy with it, as though they were stepping inside the rotting corpse of some great fallen beast. Stillson immediately clamped a hand over his nose and mouth, but his companion barely seemed to notice the stench, merely gesturing vaguely and saying, *You'll haveta excuse the state of the place. My boys ain't much for housekeeping.*

The 'mess', Stillson soon discovered, was so much more than that. The floor of the first room they came to was covered with a thick carpet of chicken feathers and bones, some animal, some apparently human. That last impression was confirmed by a quick glance around the rest of the interior: several grinning skulls dangled from the ceiling, and much of the old wooden furniture dotted around the room had been decorated with elaborate arrangements of skeletal human remains.

Ohmigod, Stillson whispered, fighting the urge to puke, to run screaming from the house.

The other man looked at him and shrugged defeatedly. *I know, it's a damn mess is what it is. This is what happens when young folks don't have jobs to keep them out of mischief. I've told my oldest boy a thousand times to stay outta them graveyards, but does he listen?*

With that, he turned and hollered into the shadows of the house: *You boys get your asses out here! We got company!*

The next moment, Stillson heard an animalistic squealing, and the metal sliding door at the rear of the downstairs hallway screeched open to reveal an entirely fresh horror: a hulking brute dressed in a bloodied butcher's apron and wearing a crudely stitched homemade mask, assembled from skinned human faces.

At the sight of their visitor, the creature immediately let out an array of grunts and snorts, gesticulating wildly.

Stillson thought he might be about to lose his mind. He only wished he'd thought to bring a Bible with him from the truck; never had he longed more fervently to believe in a higher power. *There are no atheists in slaughterhouses*, he thought wildly.

The older man stepped forward and slapped the brute roughly around the head, despite their sizeable difference in build and height. *Shaddap, you idiot! This here's our guest, and we're gonna show him some old-fashioned Texas hospitality! One day this man's gonna be president!*

The creature squealed and cowered, standing back to allow them passage into the house. Stillson's host led him into the nearby dining room, the décor of which was mercifully restrained when compared to the previous room, save for a couple of lampshades that looked to have been fashioned from human skin.

Make yourself comfortable, the older man told him. *I been smoking some meat all day, should be just about ready now.*

He pulled back a chair, inviting Stillson to sit. Too late, the visitor noticed that the seat's armrests had been decorated with the decayed arms of a corpse. Fighting back nausea, Stillson forced himself down into the chair, keeping his own arms tightly crossed over his chest.

During the meal that followed, the family's dinner guest honestly believed he was in the midst of his own personal Last Supper. Surely, Stillson thought, there was no way that this wretched tribe of deviants would ever let him leave the house alive. As well as the gas station attendant and the masked brute (whom the rest of the family had apparently christened Leatherface), they were joined at the table by the brute's brother, a gibbering long-haired imbecile who spent the whole of the meal cackling and playing with a straight razor. Even worse, the final diner to join their number was what at first glance appeared to be a wizened corpse, but which eventually turned out to be the family's grandfather: a grotesque, barely sentient parody of human life.

Stillson was quite certain the two younger members of the clan would have gleefully killed him without a second thought, but thankfully his host was taking his social responsibilities seriously, and viciously berated his boys for their bad manners whenever they treated the guest with anything less than good old Texan hospitality. *This here's an important man!* he bellowed at them. *One day he'll be in charge of the whole damn country, and then things'll finally be different around here!*

Stillson did his best to nod enthusiastically, trying as he was to swallow a chunk of barbecued meat. His nagging nausea was making it difficult to eat, although the lurking question of what the penalty might be for not cleaning your plate in this particular house compelled him to keep on doing so. Still, he was forced to admit that the meat was everything its cook had claimed it would be: moist, tender, and beautifully seasoned.

Is that right? the long-haired brother asked him. *You gonna be president?*

If God is willing, yes, Stillson assured him.

Damn! I need to get me a picture!

The imbecile hurried off to fetch a Polaroid camera, and upon his return, made the assembled family pose with Stillson for a portrait. When he was satisfied with the group composition, he set the camera timer and joined the others, he and his brother giggling and squealing as they waited for the click of the shutter.

Stillson felt as though he had never smiled so hard, for so long.

When the camera spat forth the photograph, the imbecile duly presented it to their visitor. *That'll be two dollars*, he told Stillson.

His father promptly erupted. *Goddamn bitch boy! That man's our guest!*

Sullenly, his son blew a raspberry. *Alright, one dollar!*

Stillson fumbled hastily for his wallet. *It's fine, it's fine, I'd be happy to pay…*

When the meal finally drew to a close a short time later, the older man asked Stillson if he'd care to join him for a cigar on the porch. With as big a show of regret as he could muster, his guest declined, explaining that it was already late and that he had to be back on the road in order to make his sales appointments the next day.

His host nodded. *I hear that. Working men like us, we always got to keep one eye on the next dollar. Well, I sure hope you enjoyed your barbecue.*

It was delicious, Stillson assured him. *Practically melted on my tongue. But what meat was it? I couldn't quite tell.*

The older man grinned broadly. *Funny thing is, I think it was the last guest we had over to visit. Like I said, our door is always open to strangers.*

To his credit, Stillson managed to make it back to his truck and down the full length of the driveway before pulling over to expel the contents of his stomach. He then drove for the rest of the night without stopping, vowing never to set foot in that part of Texas again.

But to this day, he keeps the framed photograph of him and the deranged cannibal family displayed on his study desk; a macabre reminder of the left-behind 'ordinary folks' he would owe much of his future political success to.

2. 1982

Shortly after Greg Stillson announced his third-party Senate candidacy for the state of New Hampshire, he received a mysterious telephone call at home one evening. The man on the other end of the line, who spoke with a broad Boston accent and called himself Dillon, was entirely unknown to Stillson, whose home telephone number had been unlisted for quite some time.

When Stillson demanded to know exactly how the caller had obtained his number, the man just laughed. *I know people, Mister Stillson. I know a lotta people.* There was a pause on the other end of the line. *But what's more important to you right now is what else I might know.*

So this is a shakedown, is that it? Stillson snarled.

Another laugh. *That ain't quite the word I'd use. I'm trying to help you out here, Mister Stillson. Let's just say I know something you don't.*

Stillson's hand tightened around the receiver. *And what the hell might that be?*

I know who your daddy is. More to the point, I know where he is.

Greg Stillson had never known his father. He had grown up in the household of Rachel Cooper, a middle-aged woman who'd devoted herself to taking in orphaned and unwanted children during the long years of the Great Depression. His mother Ruby Stillson had been the oldest of Rachel's foster children, and of that bothersome age where boys had started to turn her head. She had recently taken to sneaking into town of an evening to loiter around the drugstore, encouraging the attentions of the local boys that congregated there like hungry crows. Rachel was fond of saying that *One day she'll be losing her mind to a tricky mouth and a full moon, and I'll be saddled with the consequences,* and in no time at all, her prediction proved to be entirely correct.

When Ruby did indeed go and get herself into trouble, the result was one Gregory Ammas Stillson, born in mid-1940. A forgiving woman by nature, Rachel never held Ruby's youthful indiscretion against her, and Greg went on to enjoy the same manner of upbringing as her other young wards: disciplined but loving, with a strong dose of Bible education to set them on the right path in life. As Greg grew older, he would occasionally try and quiz Ruby as to who his father was, but she always adamantly refused to speak of the man. And when he attempted to ask Rachel instead, the result was exactly the same. She pursed her lips and looked off into the distance, simply telling Greg that, *He was no good, is who he was. And he's dead now anyway, so it don't matter a bit what name he went under.*

Dillon's call had brought all these memories flooding back. *My father's dead,* Stillson curtly told the other man. *Has been for years.*

Well, could be you were misinformed, Mister Stillson, Dillon chuckled. *This guy I know, he sure seems to know a lot about you and your mom. Ruby, wasn't it? He told me she was a real peach.*

What do you want from me?

I think maybe we should have a talk. Face-to-face. See, your daddy, he's kind of a colourful character. I reckon your voters would be real interested to find out what sort of a man he was. Like people say, the apple don't fall far from the tree. Course, I could be persuaded to forget all about him…

Stillson agreed to meet Dillon at a bar in Boston the following week. Taking his trusted fixer Sonny Elliman with him, they travelled down to the city, following Dillon's directions to a nondescript dive bar in Boston's Back Bay area. As they entered, some of the more inquisitive patrons gave them a quick sidelong glance, before immediately looking away. It was the kind of place where people knew to mind their own damn business.

Moving over to the bar, Stillson signalled to the bartender, a heavyset bald man. *I'm looking for Dillon,* he told the man.

The bartender looked at him critically. *You Stillson?*

I am, yes.

I thought you'd be taller. He grinned. *I guess it's because you're always up there on a stage, huh?*

Dillon.

The man's grin widened. *That's me.*

Stillson climbed onto a bar stool, Sonny preferring to linger unobtrusively in the background. *What have you got for me, Dillon?*

Dillon gestured towards Sonny. *Who's that, your muscle?*

Sonny works for me. But never mind him. Talk.

Wiping his hands on his apron, Dillon leaned forward on the bar. *Well, it's like this. I did a short stretch in West Virginia a while back. Moundsville Penitentiary, you know it?*

Never had the pleasure, Stillson said coldly.

Course not, important man like you. Dillon's voice dropped to a murmur. *Well, see, they stuck me in a cell with this old guy. He'd been in there for years, some kinda wife killer. A real Bluebeard, they said. Anyway, he liked to talk. Mostly he'd go on and on about God, all sorts of Old Testament bullshit, ya know? But sometimes, sometimes he'd talk about you, Mister Stillson. Talked about how you were his boy, and he knew it even if you didn't. Just to look at you, he could tell you were his blood. He was real proud of you. Said you were gonna be president one day, and didn't that just go to show?*

What does that prove? Stillson scoffed. *Some senile old lifer in a prison cell.*

Like I said, he knew your mommy. Little Ruby Stillson, he said. She couldn't have been more than fifteen or sixteen at the time, right? He was her first, he said. Dillon flashed him a conspiratorial smile. *But he told me he'd always remember just how bad she wanted it.*

Sonofabitch! Stillson grabbed Dillon by the lapels and hauled him across the bar.

Easy there, Mister Stillson. I might forget what a good mood I woke up in today. Dillon reached up and carefully removed Stillson's hands from his shirt. *Anyway, I figured his name might be worth something to you. If not, it might be worth something to the press. Either way, I'm fixing to get paid, ya know?*

Now it was Stillson's turn to lower his voice. *That's a nice little plan you've got there, Dillon. But the thing is, you see Sonny here? Well, he takes real good care of me. He fixes any problems I might have, big or small. And the way I see it, you're not that big.*

On cue, Sonny stepped towards the bar. Ignoring the fixer, Dillon's eyes moved to peer over Stillson's shoulder. *Look around you, Mister Stillson.*

Stillson did as he was asked. No one in the bar met his eye, but, quietly and unobtrusively, a number of the patrons had shifted in their seats just enough to reveal various firearms concealed about their persons.

Like I said, I know a lotta people, Dillon said amiably. *And a lotta people might be kinda upset if anything were to happen to me, ya know?*

Stillson sat unmoving in his seat, thinking. Finally, he motioned for Sonny to back off, then reached inside his jacket for a thick envelope, which he handed to Dillon. *Will this be enough?* he asked.

Dillon thumbed through the contents, then nodded. *Sure, okay. Way I look at it, I'm a simple man with simple tastes. And I figure I can cut you a break, seeing as how you're such a man of the people and all that.* He laughed uproariously.

Now give me his name, Stillson demanded.

It was Powell, Dillon told him. *Harry Powell. He reckoned he was some kind of a preacher, but seemed to me the closest he ever got to a church was stopping to take a piss in a graveyard.*

The name was familiar to Stillson, and probably would have been even if Powell's life had not already intersected so dramatically with his own.

Harry Powell was a notorious conman and murderer responsible for the deaths of over twenty women. He was finally arrested in 1939 for the murder of his wife Willa, after subsequently terrorising and pursuing her two children in an attempt to steal ten thousand dollars that their late father had concealed in a toy doll. The children had escaped in a rowboat up the Ohio River, which eventually brought them to Rachel Cooper's doorstep…and following close behind them, Harry Powell too.

Like the sly fox that he was, Powell did not immediately mount a direct assault on the henhouse, but chose to bide his time. One evening, when Ruby Stillson slipped away on one of her frequent sojourns into town, Powell approached her, plying her with gifts and ice cream. Ruby quickly became enraptured by the man's charm and charismatic patter, which seemed so worldly compared to the catcalls and innuendoes of the boys that normally hung around the drugstore. So when Powell abruptly abandoned her, having confirmed to his satisfaction that Willa's children had indeed taken sanctuary in Rachel Cooper's house, she decided to give chase.

Ruby never told anyone the details of what else happened that night. Quickly catching up with Powell, she clutched at his arm and begged, *Please don't leave me! I'm so lonely stuck up in that old house. There's a whole world out there and I ain't seen none of it.*

Powell gazed down at her, an animal stirring behind his eyes. *You want to know more about the world, is that it, child? About the lustful ways of men?*

Ruby nodded hesitantly.

Why then, allow me to show you.

The so called preacher dragged Ruby into a nearby alleyway, where he proceeded to force himself upon her. The only small mercy of it was that the act was over quickly, the twin engines of Powell's lust and misogynistic rage combining to work him into a complete frenzy. He climaxed within seconds, stumbling away with his pants down his ankles and moaning to himself, *Whore…filthy, dirty whore.*

Ruby slumped to the ground in a daze. It all happened so quickly that her mind had not yet caught up with the brutal actuality of what had been done to her. Hearing a stealthy click, she glanced up to see a knife blade glinting in the glow of a nearby streetlight.

Powell's looming shadow took a step towards her, then stopped and looked upwards. *Yes, Lord?* he crooned. *Please grant me the wisdom of Solomon, so that I may know what I must do.* He raised his arms towards heaven. *Yes, I understand. Not this one, not now.*

His hand extended towards Ruby, brandishing the knife at her. *The Lord in His wisdom has seen fit to spare you this night. But never come near me again, harlot, or it will be the worse for you!*

With that, Harry Powell pulled up his pants and ran from the alleyway.

Ruby cleaned herself up as best she could and hurried home. She only confessed to Rachel what had happened when it became clear she was carrying her assailant's child. Nine months later, she gave birth to a healthy baby boy, whom she christened Gregory.

And Powell? After he'd been caught and tried for murder, the judge had sentenced him to death without a moment's hesitation. And yet that was still not quite the end of it. Some might have surmised that the Lord did indeed look favourably upon the Reverend Powell and his murderous calling; others would simply have said that Harry was as slippery as a basket of freshly-caught eels. Either way, he had the good sense to both dedicate himself to holy works within Moundsville Prison and hire a particularly unscrupulous lawyer named Katz, who had enjoyed some success defending known murderers in the past. With Katz's aid, Powell was able to successfully appeal to the West Virginia state governor for clemency and have his death sentence commuted to life without parole.

So it was that the old snake was still rotting there when Dillon came to serve his own stretch in Moundsville, some thirty-odd years later.

Of course, Greg Stillson could not know any of this. But he'd heard plenty of stories about the infamous wife killer Harry Powell while growing up, and his mother's stubborn refusal to ever discuss his father or the circumstances of her only son's conception rendered it but a short mental leap to imagine the rest.

He got up from the stool and nodded brusquely at Sonny. They were done here.

Dillon smirked. *Hope you got your money's worth, Mister Stillson. Say, how about a drink on the house?*

I'll take a raincheck, Stillson replied. *Because I do definitely look forward to us meeting again someday.*

Well, you know where to find me, Dillon said companionably. *And hey, good luck with the election. Us working stiffs are counting on ya.*

The next day, Sonny Elliman telephoned Moundsville Penitentiary, only to be informed that Harry Powell had contracted cancer and was currently a patient in the prison hospital. He was not expected to live much longer. Upon being told that his only son wished to see him, the prison agreed to sanction an hour-long visit the following week.

When Greg Stillson subsequently arrived at his father's bedside, he found a large, imposing man, visibly diminished by illness but still formidable, like some great old bull elephant. Harry's sleeping face was sunken and jowly, reminding his son of a slowly deflating balloon. His hands were pulled up to his chest and clenching fitfully in his sleep, revealing the fading words tattooed there: 'LOVE' and 'HATE'.

Stillson pulled up a chair by the bedside, its legs squeaking upon the tiled floor. The noise awoke Harry, who looked around and peered at his son through clouded, piss-yellow eyes. It took a few moments, but Stillson eventually saw surprise register there.

Truly, the Lord doth move in mysterious ways, Powell rumbled.

His son was forced to admit that He did.

You found me, after all these years.

It wasn't easy, Stillson said. *I guess maybe the Lord did have something to do with it.*

Truly, I blame myself. Powell let out a hammy sob of regret. *I'll be honest with you, boy, you were the product of a moment of sinful weakness, a moment I've long regretted. But it was an act of love, nonetheless. And love has a heaven-sent power all its own.* His eyes moved to the ceiling. *Do you know the story of left hand, right hand?*

Stillson shook his head, prompting his father to weakly raise his left hand in the air.

H-A-T-E! It was with this left hand that old brother Cain struck the blow that laid his brother low. Then, Powell raised his other hand. *L-O-V-E. The right hand, the hand of love! Now watch and I'll show you the story of life. These fingers is always a-warring and a-tugging, one against the other. Now, watch 'em. Ole brother left land. Left hand, he's a-fighting. And it looks like love's a goner. But wait a minute, wait a minute! Hot dog! love's a-winning? Yes, siree. It's love that won, and ole left hand hate is down for the count!*

The effort of telling the story left Powell coughing uncontrollably. Stillson sat and watched his father struggle for breath, his face betraying no visible emotion.

When the old man's coughing fit had finally subsided, Stillson reached over and took Powell's right hand in his own. *That's a real nice story, Daddy.*

Wheezing, the old man squeezed gently at his son's fingers in grateful response.

His son looked him square in the eye. *Not a damn word of it's true, though,* he whispered.

Abruptly, Stillson viciously twisted his father's arm, snapping the wrist like a wishbone. Powell began to scream, but his cries were immediately muffled as his son seized a pillow and clamped it down over his face. Resolute, he held it there as the old man jerked and thrashed, and for quite some time after he finally stopped.

When Stillson was satisfied that Harry Powell had gone to meet the maker he had always claimed to serve so assiduously, he removed the pillow and carefully tucked it back underneath his father's lifeless head.

Personally, I've always found that hate gets you a helluva lot further in life, he said.

3. <u>1984</u>

It was over.

He'd been so close. The polls had shown him consistently gaining on the Democratic Senatorial incumbent, more and more voters won over by the voice of the common man schtick Stillson had spent so many years perfecting. Of course it had all been a long con, little more than a nightclub impressionist's routine he'd worked up in front of the bathroom mirror, but apparently it was precisely what the poor suckers wanted to hear.

And then the freak had wandered into his path. Johnny Smith, a crippled loner, eyes like a beaten, half-crazed dog. Christ alone knew how he hadn't been locked up years ago. Apparently he'd worked as a private tutor, and as to what sort of right-minded parent would ever consent to leave their child alone with a man like *that*, Stillson couldn't even begin to imagine. The tabloids said he was some kind of dime-store psychic; supposedly he'd helped the police out with that Castle Rock Killer business a few months back. Stillson could almost respect him for that; an act like that took a long time to perfect. But Smith had always refused to accept money for his 'gift', which suggested he'd gone and fallen for his own routine. And if there was one thing Greg Stillson understood only too well, it was that the moment you started buying your own bullshit, it was all over.

Anyway, the freak had gotten obsessed with him for some reason. Apparently he'd been stalking one of Stillson's female campaign volunteers for months, so Smith must have blamed him for not being able to have her; some kind of psychotic projection or something. Wasn't that exactly how Reagan got shot? Jesus, this country was full of psychos, angrily spilling out of the cracks like fire ants from a nest. It was, after all, a land founded on genocide, and at times Stillson wondered whether all of that blood and madness had seeped into the very soil of the country, poisoning the American people for generations to come.

So here comes Johnny Smith, seething with his own deadly poison, distilled over years of solitude and obsession. He'd followed the Stillson campaign to Jackson, New Hampshire, where Stillson was due to hold a town hall event. There wasn't even any great method to Smith's madness; the would-be assassin had merely broken into the venue the evening before the event and spent the night hidden up on the balcony, a loaded rifle by his side. Even the most cursory of security checks would have caught him, but that miserable asshole Elliman was apparently too busy checking out the ladies in the audience, of which there were several; Stillson always prided himself on his substantial appeal amongst female voters. If there was any justice whatsoever, one day Sonny Elliman would get just what was coming to him, but he'd vanished right after the clusterfuck went down. And he'd been entirely correct to; if Stillson could only live so long, he swore he would extract his pound of flesh out of Sonny's worthless hide, and never mind how much blood was spilt in the process.

But living that long wasn't on Greg Stillson's agenda, not any more.

For what happened next that day ruined several lives. Johnny Smith – no crank or fraud, but a genuine seer – had seen into the future and glimpsed the beginnings of an apocalypse. He'd witnessed a vision of the current third party Senatorial candidate for New Hampshire as an older man, one who'd succeeded in riding the wild horse of his ambition all the way to the White House. And from there, Johnny realised, he would bring about the end of the world.

Desperate to prevent this eventuality, the psychic waited for Stillson to begin speaking, then took his shot. But he was a bookish schoolteacher, certainly no marksman, and missed. Cursing himself, he prepared to fire again, and might even have succeeded if Stillson had not seized a nearby child and used it as a human shield. Johnny hesitated, giving Elliman enough time to return fire. Several bullets tore into the psychic's body, sending him plummeting from the balcony to the venue floor below.

As Johnny lay there dying, his own future spilling out of his body in crimson rivulets, Stillson had descended upon him. *Who the hell are you?* he hissed, barely able to resist the urge to smash the dying man's brains out against the floor.

Laughing, Johnny grabbed Stillson's hand and was rewarded by a vision of what he took to be Stillson's newly-altered destiny. He might have failed in his bid to kill the candidate, but Stillson's act of abject cowardice – witnessed by dozens of onlookers and caught on camera for millions more to see – would result in the candidate's national humiliation and the premature end of his political career. Unable to bear the weight of his own failure, the ruined man would then take his own life.

Or so Johnny Smith believed.

Alas, there were distinct limits to his gifts.

Johnny's visions were only ever oneiric shards: fragments plucked from a waking dream, like gold pieces salvaged from the ocean floor. He could not ever hope to see, nor understand, the totality of the future. And, as much as his preternatural gift granted him the capability to change the course of oncoming events, it did not ever occur to him that there might be others – perhaps with far greater powers – with the means and nefarious will to alter them yet further.

So when Johnny saw Stillson, alone and utterly bereft, aiming a pistol beneath his jaw, he believed he had won. That, despite his initial failure with the rifle, he had succeeded. In his mind, he heard the crack of Stillson's gun, saw the blood splatter. It was enough to tell him everything he needed to know about the man's future, Johnny thought. A huge darkness lifted from him, and he died at peace.

But as Stillson himself could have told Johnny, a week is a very long time in politics. What then, are months, or even years? After all, Greg Stillson was still a relatively young man. And while it is certainly the case that, as a consequence of his actions, the erstwhile Senatorial candidate for New Hampshire quickly found himself reviled and savaged in the arena of public opinion, his career ambitions apparently destroyed, the actual truth of what occurred next is this.

While Greg Stillson did indeed come within a hair's breadth of taking his own life, it soon transpired that other forces were watching over him, and working to ensure a very different future than that which poor Johnny Smith had foreseen.

So, when Stillson raised the pistol to his jaw and prepared to make that final, irrevocable gesture, in the very next instant something swift and dark hurtled into his office window, splintering the glass with a loud crack.

The shock of the sudden noise caused Stillson's gun to slip, and when it went off, the bullet only creased the side of his face. The wound would leave a visible scar for the rest of his life, but proved far from fatal. Stillson slumped to the floor, merely dazed.

And somewhere, Johnny Smith was screaming.

Clutching at his bloody face, Stillson crawled over to the window, all thoughts of suicide temporarily forgotten. All he cared about in that moment was seeing who or what had been responsible for saving his life.

On the windowsill lay a dead raven, its neck broken. He couldn't imagine what had possessed it to fly directly into his window. Was this some kind of sign, or omen?

Behind him, the telephone on his desk began to ring. One might have expected the injured man to ignore it, but in his shock and bewilderment, it seemed to Stillson as though this was all somehow connected: the suicide attempt, the dead bird, and now the unknown caller.

He hauled himself upright and stumbled over to the desk, fumbling to pick up the receiver. *W-who is it?* he said groggily.

There was a low chuckle on the other end of the line. *Good. You're alive.*

Who the hell is this?

Another chuckle. *Who the hell indeed. Just call me an interested party, Mr Stillson. There will be time enough for introductions later. For now, you should get yourself to a hospital. That wound could be unpleasant if you don't get it seen to quickly.*

The caller hung up, leaving Stillson staring mutely at the receiver.

The sudden understanding that he was being watched over by unknown forces left him feeling like the pawn in a much bigger game, and this chill realisation of his own inconsequentiality was almost more painful than the gunshot wound in his face.

Later, when he was recovering in a private hospital room, the blinds closed against the hordes of reporters camped out in the grounds outside, Greg Stillson received a visitor. He looked up from his copy of that day's *Washington Post* to see a well-dressed, darkly handsome young man entering the room.

Good afternoon, Mr Stillson, the man said. *I hope you're recovering well?*

He immediately recognised the sly voice of the mysterious phone caller. *It's you,* Stillson said.

I promised you we'd be introduced, didn't I? My name is Damien Thorn.

Stillson knew the name, of course. The Thorns were an American dynasty, their power and influence extending into the upper echelons of political and corporate life. Infamously, however, they had been dogged by ill-fortune in recent years, the tragic deaths of several family members leaving the various Thorn assets under the control of the young man standing before him, the sole survivor of a once-great family.

I know who you are, Stillson said.

Do you, now? Damien smiled inscrutably.

What do you want?

The younger man stared at him closely. *More to the point, have you thought about what* you *want?*

Damien's unblinking gaze was beginning to make Stillson nervous. He quickly averted his eyes. *It doesn't matter what I want,* he muttered darkly. *It's over, all of it.*

Ah. Far better you should take your own life, then.

And what the hell else should I do? Stillson picked up his newspaper and flung it angrily at Damien. *You've seen the goddamn press. I'm all they can talk about. Every headline, every op-ed, every fucking cartoon is about me.*

Calmly, Damien pulled up a chair and sat down at Stillson's bedside. *What if I were to tell you that one day, none of that will matter?* he said.

Stillson snorted with derision. *I'd say you were fucking crazy.*

But it's true. Damien leaned closer. *A storm is going to blow through American politics, Mr Stillson. It may take another two or three decades, but I guarantee you this: a time will come when, should anyone mention that unfortunate day in Jackson, your supporters will cry 'conspiracy!' They'll shout 'fraud!' They'll insist that whatever you may have done, the other side have committed crimes a thousand times worse. As far as they'll be concerned, Jackson never even happened. A chasm is going to tear the centre of this country apart, and all that will be left are two crazed tribes screaming threats at each other across an unbridgeable void.*

It was a nice pitch, Stillson had to admit. *And how do you know all that, Mr Thorn?*

Another smile. *Because I'm going to make it happen.*

Stillson stared over at his visitor. This Thorn kid was crazy, he had to be. Another goddamn Howard Hughes, trying to run the whole world from his palatial bedroom.

But crazy or not, he had money, power…and he was here in the room, talking…instead of sitting outside with a telephoto lens trying to get a shot of Greg Stillson showing his bare ass to the world. Again.

And that had to count for something, didn't it?

So what does any of this have to do with me? Stillson asked.

A smile. *A new day is dawning. This country is going to need the right man to lead it through some very uncertain times. I think that man could still be you.*

God willing, murmured Stillson reverently, old habits dying hard.

Oh, I don't think God will have an awful lot to do with it, replied Damien.

4. <u>Now</u>

Fifteen minutes, Adam Cramer told him.

Stillson nodded, and his campaign manager gave him a thumbs up. *You're gonna kill tonight, Greg.*

Tonight was the second of three scheduled presidential debates between Bill McKay, the Democratic candidate for President and current Vice President, and Greg Stillson, the Republican challenger. The contest so far had been rancorous and bitterly fought, with Stillson frequently being accused of dragging politics into the gutter. But as the Republican candidate liked to retort, *There's a lot of people who have been swept into the gutter by this administration. Decent, hardworking people. So I don't apologise for hunkering right down in the gutter with them. Better that than cruising by without a second thought for the folks you've abandoned, right down the middle of the damn road.*

Such rhetoric had proven effective, but only up to a point. With the campaign entering its closing stages, Stillson was still lagging behind in the polls. As Adam Cramer was given to observing, *The problem is this, Greg. When the voters look at you, they see themselves. When they look at McKay, they see whatever they damn well please. It's like trying to lay a glove on the fucking Invisible Man.*

The presidential debates were seen as Stillson's best chance to turn things around, but his first encounter with McKay had, it was commonly agreed, ended in stalemate. The Vice President had steadfastly refused to rise to Stillson's incendiary taunts, frustrating those who had tuned into see a reasoned argument, rather than a schoolyard confrontation between the class bully and the teacher's pet.

Would tonight's debate be any different? The Stillson camp were confident their strategy would prove to be a decisive one. As Cramer turned to leave the make-up room, his parting words to his candidate were, *You know just what to do, Greg.*

Stillson did not reply, his eyes fixed on the reflection in the mirror before him. The harsh lights of the make-up room seemed to deepen the lines in his face, whiten his already steely hair. He was an old man now. If he won, he'd be the oldest man ever to be elected President. Would he have enough time to do what needed to be done? Christ, his aborted run for the Senate seemed like – *was* – half a lifetime away. Where had all those years gone?

When Damien Thorn first approached him in the hospital, he'd come complete with a plan to rehabilitate Greg Stillson's public image. *Thorn are diversifying,* he'd said. *We're going to be launching a number of cable channels, amongst them Thorn News, a twenty-four hour news channel. We think the time is right for an altogether different approach. Broadcast regulations are loosening up, and people now want to see the news reported in a way that reflects the way they already view the world, rather than having some liberal journalist try and shape their worldview for them. We'd like you to join us in remaking the news, Greg.*

He'd agreed, of course. When you've just been rendered the most unemployable man in the country and someone suddenly offers you a job, you don't turn it down. So when Thorn News had finally launched, Greg Stillson had relaunched himself right along with it. The channel executives had been careful not to overexpose him at first, rationalising that the public needed a chance to get used to seeing Stillson as something other than a cold-hearted coward. So for a time he'd simply been employed as an occasional guest, booked to appear on talk shows and news discussion panels. A very thoroughly coached guest, of course; his handlers insistent on the need for him to be seen to walk a careful tightrope between penitent and opinionated. His audience approval ratings had been closely monitored, and once they were deemed sufficient, Greg Stillson had been rewarded with his own show.

Within six months he was the most popular personality on the network; a conservative firebrand unafraid (as his publicity would have it) to speak truth to liberal power, to lift up the rocks of consensus and shed some light on the real facts concealed underneath. Within a year he had married the glamorous head of the network, Diana Christensen, forging a union as a right-wing power couple who were at the top of every rich Republican's invite list. Everything Damien Thorn had promised him was coming true.

Indeed, the only thing missing by that point was Damien himself. He'd been severely wounded in an attack by a crazed ex-girlfriend, and had completely withdrawn from public life. It was rumoured that he was now a crippled recluse who saw or spoke to no one save his personal manservant. Certainly Stillson was no longer in touch with him. The time was they would talk regularly on the telephone, or have dinner whenever Damien was in the States, but all that was ancient history now. Without the backing of his primary sponsor, the man he privately referred to as his guardian angel, Stillson had come to accept his presidential ambitions were most likely dead in the water. This loss hurt him for a time, but he eventually came to terms with it. After all, he had money, influence, a beautiful wife. When he thought about how close he'd come to destroying everything, wilfully hurling himself into the void…well, a man should always count his blessings.

And then, over two decades later, the call had finally come. Stillson picked up the telephone to hear a familiar voice, still recognisable despite the discordant notes of age and infirmity.

Are you ready? Damien had asked him.

He was.

They'd begun positioning Stillson as a prospective Republican presidential candidate immediately. He would no longer be the third party disruptor; now he would strike at the system from within. Despite, or perhaps because of, his television fame, large swathes of the GOP viewed him as a loud-mouthed upstart, an unserious novelty act. *He's just trying to boost his ratings*, they sneered.

None of it mattered, Damien insisted. He'd returned to America after his years of exile in England, seemingly renewed and ready to fulfil his final promise to Stillson. As they were en route to the campaign's first fundraising dinner, Damien turned to Greg and assured him, *All the GOP give a damn about is winning, any way they can. So the moment you start winning – and you will – they'll fall in behind you like kids on a school outing. The people you really need to impress are the ones you'll meet tonight.*

That night, Damien had introduced him around the room to people he'd only ever read about in *Forbes* or the *Wall Street Journal*, figures with surnames that carried an almost mystical, incantatory weight: Corleone, Kane, Plainview, Cross, Cord. Stillson had smiled and shaken innumerable hands and grown hoarse telling his prospective donors exactly what he thought they wanted to hear. He might have been back in the Deep South selling Bibles again. As he told Diana as they lay in bed together later that night, *I've travelled a helluva long way and ended up right back where I started.*

But the money poured in, the Stillson campaign managing to raise millions more than his closest rivals. And of course Thorn News vigorously supported him, giving Stillson a public platform the other candidates could not hope to emulate. He'd won Republican primary after primary. By the time the party conference came around, his nomination was all but assured. Oh, there were still whispers of discontent amongst those who saw Gregory Ammas Stillson as nothing but a vulgarian outsider, but they were in the extreme minority now. The rest of the GOP had lined up behind him, just as Damien had predicted. They were ready for him to win.

The only question was, could he?

It was one thing to beat a field of grey-faced party hacks to the nomination, lifeless men who couldn't wish you good morning without it sounding like a funeral elegy, but in Bill McKay he was facing an incumbent Vice President, a man whose personal approval ratings remained high despite the country enduring two decidedly lame duck years with the outgoing Commander-in-Chief. As Stillson saw it, McKay had spent his entire career standing for nothing in particular, but he had to admit it made the Vice President a hard opponent to beat. The Republican campaign tried everything, they occasionally went high, mostly they went low, but nothing quite seemed to stick.

After the dead heat of the first debate, the campaign's inner circle had gone out for dinner to discuss what was to be done next. Stillson, Diana, Adam Cramer, and Damien Thorn had all assembled in a private room in the best restaurant in town, with an extra place set for the bodyguard who now never left the candidate's side; a tall cold-eyed man named Callaghan, who had joined the Stillson camp after a personal recommendation from Damien. The bodyguard tended to be implacably taciturn at the best of times, so Stillson certainly did not expect him to contribute much to that evening's discussion.

The candidate himself was in a foul temper. *Fuck Bill McKay in his fucking ear,* he spat. *The whole goddamn country's going into the shitter under his watch, and he doesn't have a fucking thing to say about it. When are people gonna wake up?*

Darling, it's your job to wake them up, Diana murmured.

Stillson slammed the tabletop with the flat of his hand. *I've been busting my balls trying to do just that! But listening to eight years of liberal bullshit has sent this country into a goddamn stupor.*

We've been talking about our strategy, Adam interjected. *Our message clearly isn't getting across as well as we'd like. But there is a solution. Perhaps a fairly radical one, but it should put us over the top.*

And here I thought radical was a dirty word, Stillson joked sourly.

Have you ever heard of the Parallax Corporation? Damien asked him.

Stillson folded his arms. *What are they, more PR consultants? I've had it up to here with those assholes.*

A smile. No. They're a bit more…specialised. Damien nodded towards Stillson's bodyguard. *Before he came to you, Harry here used to work for them.*

Stillson gave Callaghan a brief sideways glance. If he was being completely honest – admittedly an unusual position for the candidate to adopt – the bodyguard gave him the goddamn creeps. He could never quite rid himself of the notion that Callaghan's preferred approach to his work would simply be to kill anyone else in the room first and worry about whether they posed any threat to his client later.

He waited for his bodyguard's response, but Callaghan said nothing. Christ, it was like talking to a goddamn waxwork. *Well, Harry?* Stillson said finally. *Care to share?*

The bodyguard exhaled slowly through his teeth, the sound reminding Stillson of a cobra's warning hiss. *I still know some people there. They can take care of your problem.*

Okay, but what exactly are we talking about? Stillson complained. *More ratfucking? We've tried that, and nothing seems to work.*

Callaghan stared at him blankly. *I said they'll take care of it.*

And that was all he'd had to say on the matter.

Adam had assured Stillson that they'd handle all the details, he himself wouldn't have to worry about a thing. Once the final arrangements were made, Stillson would just need to do his bit. Everything else would be taken care of, exactly as Callaghan had promised.

And now here he was, striding out onto the debating stage to respectful applause from the audience. A few whoops here and there from his base support, Stillson acknowledging them with a wave of the hand. Over to his left, McKay approached his own podium. Each candidate stood in silence, listening to the moderator's opening remarks. The opening topic of the debate was to be inequality in America, with McKay speaking first. Stillson stood and listened, silently bridling at the man's hypocritical piety. During their first debate, he had frequently interrupted and heckled his opponent, but this time, there was an entirely different plan.

You know just what to do, Greg.

After two minutes, McKay finished speaking, and the floor was turned over to Stillson. He gazed out at the studio audience, his eyes growing moist with emotion. *The first thing I'd like to say is this*, he declared. *I grew up poor, during the Great Depression. I lived in a house full of orphaned and unwanted children, not in some liberal college town, and I saw the true face of inequality in Amer...*

There was a sudden commotion from the opposite wing of the stage, cutting Stillson off mid-sentence. With a collective gasp, the audience looked over to see a elderly stagehand dashing onstage, directly towards Vice President McKay.

He's got a gun! someone cried out from the audience.

The man raised his arm. There was a flash of light and a loud crack. Amid screams from the watching crowd, McKay collapsed.

Seconds too late, security guards were everywhere, wrestling McKay's attacker to the ground.

Stillson's gaze moved to the assassin, now pinned helplessly to the floor. He quickly took in the name on the man's ID badge: 'BICKLE, TRAVIS'. The assassin must have been in his late sixties or early seventies, but his dark eyes were gleaming, filled with life. Meeting the candidate's gaze, Bickle flashed him a broad, shark-like grin.

Members of Stillson's team appeared at his side, trying to drag him to safety. But the Republican candidate shoved them away. *I have to see whether he's alright!* he shouted.

Sprinting across the stage towards McKay's podium, Stillson jostled past a sobbing woman to see the Vice President lying on the stage, blood pumping from a gunshot wound in his throat. Instantly, he was down on his knees, cradling the dying man's head in his arms. *Give him some air*, he bellowed at the crowd pressing in around them.

McKay stared up at him, his eyes slowly emptying of life, like the last vestiges of water evaporating from a scorched river bed. Raising his voice so that the rest of the crowd might hear, Stillson began to recite a half-remembered prayer: *May the Lord who frees you from sin save you and raise you up...*

Then, he leaned in to whisper in the dying man's ear. *You lose, motherfucker.*

A sudden bright light bleached out his field of vision. Blinking, Stillson looked up to see a battery of camera flashes going off around him. He immediately pulled his mortally wounded rival closer to his chest, glancing up towards the nearest lens.

Why, he could just see the next cover of *Newsweek* now.

ALICE SPAGES

Paula Sheppard in Alice, Sweet Alice, *1976*
written by Rosemary Ritvo & Alfred Sole
directed by Alfred Sole

LIKE SO MANY OTHER STORIES, IT BEGAN WITH A MURDER. HER SISTER Karen's murder, in fact; pretty, perfect Karen, the younger of the two Spages sisters and the apple of their mother Catherine's eye. And as much as Catherine always insisted that she loved both her daughters equally, everyone knew the real truth; that surly, spiteful Alice was most definitely the pallid little worm in that apple.

So when Karen was brutally murdered in church that day, strangled and left to burn in a fire, suspicion naturally fell upon Alice. It was no secret just how much she envied and resented her younger sister, and there had always been a lot of talk in their New Jersey neighbourhood about how Alice wasn't quite right in the head. *She's probably gonna grow up to be one of them nymphos*, people would say. *Have you seen how she flirts with men? And her only twelve years old. Girls like that are capable of anything.*

In the end, her parents had sent her away to a children's centre for psychiatric evaluation, where the doctor had primly informed them that Alice had deep-seated violent tendencies, and was quite probably schizophrenic. Although her neighbours never would have admitted it to Catherine, they would have been quite happy for her daughter to remain institutionalised indefinitely, and when Alice was later exonerated of the murder and released, much chagrin was discreetly expressed behind her mother's back. *Well, maybe she didn't do it after all, but she definitely coulda done, you know what I mean? They shoulda kept her there for her own good, it's only a matter of time.*

Given all of this, what chance did Alice Spages have? Despite being innocent of any crime, she had already been deemed guilty. In a world already filled with sinners, her sin was somehow greater. Alice began to wonder what difference it would have made if she *had* killed Karen. No one could have hated her any more than they did already, and at least Alice would've had the satisfaction of shutting up her sister's incessant whining for good. She'd been taught that God's eyes were on her always, but how could that be true? Because if He'd known that Alice was innocent all along, why had He let His faithful bully and punish her, and lock her away in the nut hatch?

And so if God didn't care whether she'd done right, then why should He give a good goddamn if she did something wrong?

There had been more murders after Karen, Alice's own father being one of the victims. When old Mrs Tredoni had finally been unmasked as the real killer, she'd gone crazy in church and stabbed Father Tom in front of his whole congregation. It was then that Alice finally decided it was all bullshit. The Father had been a decent, kind man, everyone knew it, and right there in His own house, God had still let him die bleeding like a stuck pig. The way she saw it, Father Tom had been just as innocent as Alice, and still *they* were the ones that had been made to suffer. Meanwhile Mrs Tredoni would probably see out the rest of her days in the crazyhouse, which Alice figured was probably no picnic, but on the other hand, they'd give the old lady three square meals a day and she'd never have to scrub another floor for as long as she lived. There was no justice to any of it, divine or otherwise. So why shouldn't Alice do whatever the hell she wanted?

In all the commotion in the church that day, no one had seen her grab the knife Mrs Tredoni had used to stab Father Tom. People were screaming and crying, the priest's bright red blood running down the aisle in rivulets, and for once in her life, no one cared what Alice Spages might be getting up to. So she'd slipped the bloodied blade into her bag and walked out of the church, easy as you please. All the way to the door, she'd gazed up to the rafters and muttered *Whydontyoustopmewhydontyoustopme* and still nothing happened.

Not only was God not watching her, He wasn't even *listening*.

As soon as Alice reached the bottom of the church steps she'd run all the way home and gone down to her private place in the basement, where she'd taken out the knife and held it in her trembling hands. How many people had it killed? At least two, maybe more. There was a kind of power in that, Alice decided. *The life of the flesh is in the blood*, the Bible said.

This knife had tasted that precious blood, drunk of that life for itself. She could sense the metal of the blade humming with the force of it, singing its need to her. It wanted more.

But she would wait. The recent spate of killings had left the city of Paterson reeling in shock, and now its streets were charged with a sort of dreadful, morbid excitement. If nice old Mrs Tredoni had really been a bloodthirsty lunatic all along, what *else* might their neighbours be concealing? The windows of the local streets were now constantly aflutter with nervously twitching curtains, and a neighbourhood watch scheme was hastily organised. There was a pungent, simmering paranoia in the air, and Alice knew it would take very little to make it boil over. She consequently took great pains to stay out of trouble, only ever leaving the apartment to go to school, or to fetch something from the store for her mom. The murders of her youngest daughter and ex-husband had caused Catherine Spages to withdraw into a deep fugue of melancholia, adrift in a haze of grief and tranquillisers. And it was just the two of them now; Catherine's shrewish sister Annie, once such a persistently meddling irritant in their lives, had become a neurotic shut-in after her own narrow escape from Mrs Tredoni's knife.

So Alice dutifully went about caring for her mother's needs, all the while silently resenting the crummy hand life had once again seen fit to deal her. She finally had Catherine's attention all to herself, but could barely even get her mother to look away from the tube long enough to acknowledge her. Even when she did, all Catherine ever had to offer Alice was the fleeting ghost of a smile, a muscle memory of happiness and nothing more.

The months passed, and Alice's thirteenth birthday came and went without ceremony. She spent most of that day alone in the basement, muttering her discontent to the shadows. It was what she did now instead of praying; no doubt the doctors would say she was talking to herself and diagnose it as another symptom of Alice being a hopeless schizo, but that wasn't it, not at all. Alice had grown convinced someone was listening to her down there – she could feel their stealthy presence, lurking just out of sight in the darkness – she just wasn't sure exactly *who*.

She was becoming a young woman now. The changes in her body were drawing attention to her, the eyes of all the dirty old men on the block crawling over Alice as she walked home from school every day. She could just imagine their lustful, gurgling voices: *look at that dirty little tramp rubbing it in our faces i'd like to give her exactly what she has coming to her.*

God, but she hated this lousy dump. She wished she could just burn it all down and walk away. It suddenly occurred to Alice that Mrs Tredoni had been exactly what this neighbourhood deserved. It was like she'd crept out of the city sewers, the inevitable by-product of all the lies and sins and religious hypocrisy that everyone here flushed down the drain on a daily basis. She began to think about getting out, and what she might do to make them all sorry before she did.

Alice always did her best thinking in the basement, so later that night, she crept down the staircase and descended into the waiting darkness below. She could feel the watchful presence lurking there beside her, but she was not afraid. She knelt down in the shadows and pleaded for its guidance.

And then, for the first time in her young life, she received an answer. The voice she heard murmuring in her ear was as cunning and elusive as a spider, certainly not the Voice of God; anyone could tell that, even someone as crazy as Alice.

But it didn't matter, because she had finally been listened to.

The voice told her, simply: *Do it, Alice.*

A sudden warmth blossomed in the pit of her belly, her skin prickling with ecstasy. Was this how other people felt in church, she wondered? All those tired, pancake-faced housewives, was *this* the sensation that kept them coming back to prostrate themselves before the altar week after week, month after month? Was this what it meant to be touched by the Divine?

She quickly stole back upstairs to her apartment. Her mom was sound asleep in her room; Alice had made sure to give her two sleeping pills tonight. She tiptoed to Catherine's bedside and leant down to gently kiss her goodbye. As much as her mom had always let her down, Alice didn't want her to suffer. They'd both be much better off this way.

Closing the bedroom door behind her, she went into her own room and threw some belongings into a bag, nothing but clothes and a few small keepsakes. Then, reaching under her mattress, she removed the knife which lay hidden there, dried flecks of Father Tom's blood still clinging to the blade.

At last it was time.

Moving into the kitchen, she went to the top shelf and took down the jar in which Catherine kept the spare key to Aunt Annie's house. Pocketing it, Alice grabbed the set of matches sitting next to the stove, as well as a bottle of cooking brandy from the cupboard, then proceeded into the dining room and doused the furniture and carpet with the alcohol.

By the time anyone noticed the fire, it would be gone, all of it. She shivered with a potent mixture of fear and delight. Was she really going to do this? Burn her own mother in her bed? Alice reassured herself that Catherine would never even know; she'd die of smoke inhalation before she ever felt a thing. And everyone else in the apartment block could roast in Hell as far as she was concerned.

With any luck, everyone would assume Alice died in the fire too. Because if they caught her after this, she knew they'd toss her in the nuthatch until she rotted.

Fuck it, she whispered, the forbidden curse word delicious on her tongue. Striking a match, she tossed it down onto the carpet. The resulting explosion of flame lit her fleeing shadow up on the corridor wall, dancing gleefully away in search of a new life.

Next, she walked the twenty or so blocks to her Aunt Annie's house, carefully avoiding the pooled light of the street lamps so that no one had cause to wonder what a thirteen-year-old girl might be doing out in the small hours of the night. *The darkness is where you live now*, Alice told herself, feeling a small, exquisite thrill at the notion. No longer would she be watched for every single second of the day, adults forever sticking their goddamn noses in her business and telling her what to do. She was invisible, immaterial; she might as well not even exist.

Arriving at her destination, she unlocked the front door and slipped inside. The house was quiet as a tomb; so absolute was her aunt's tyranny that her family dared not even make a noise in their sleep. Mounting the staircase, Alice paused outside her cousin Angela's door. She bore the girl no particular malice; Angela was a timid, overweight child, cowed into almost permanent silence by her overbearing mother. But neither could she take any chances, not when she was so close to escaping for good. Taking out her knife, Alice eased Angela's door open and entered the room.

A wash of moonlight illuminated the sleeping girl's face, bathing away the perpetual anxiety that creased Angela's features whenever she was awake. Alice stood over her, blade at the ready. She fancied she could feel the weapon straining with its impatience to draw blood, but she would not be hurried. The angry little girl she used to be would always rush blindly into situations, acting impulsively with little thought as to the possible consequences. But Alice knew she was poised on the threshold of something far greater. The deed she was about to commit was, in its own perverse way, a rite of adulthood, and there could be no turning back once she took that final dreadful step.

The next instant, Angela stirred and opened her eyes.

The two cousins gazed at each other for a moment. Without thinking, Alice raised her finger to her lips and motioned for Angela to be quiet. Drowsy with sleep and conditioned to always do exactly what she was told, the other girl remained silent, and continued to stare unblinkingly up at her cousin.

Alice heard a quiet hiss from the darkest corner of her mind. *Do it.*

Without hesitation, she brought up the knife and slashed it across Angela's fleshy throat, swiftly stepping back so that the resultant gush of blood would not splatter her. Her cousin let out a halting gurgle of shock, but otherwise died as she had always lived: in complete silence. Within seconds, her head slumped lifelessly back to the pillow.

Alice exulted in her newfound power. *This is how Mrs Tredoni must have felt*, she thought, and then just as quickly banished the realisation from her mind. The old lady had believed she was enacting some kind of moral vengeance upon a corrupt society, whereas Alice intended exactly the opposite. Steadfast in her belief that she was living in a godless universe, she would now set out to prove the utter amorality of existence, acting in violent defiance of the meaningless, oppressive piety that had dominated her life so comprehensively until now.

The intended subjects of her next demonstration lay sleeping in the next room. Creeping along the hallway, Alice entered her aunt and uncle's bedroom, marvelling at the array of religious chintz that festooned the interior. Christ bared His heart to her from the wall, imploring her to accept His divine love. Alice removed the framed portrait from its hook and gazed at it silently, her eyes studying the details of its bloodless, anesthetised mutilation.

She began to wonder what a human chest would *really* look like if it was opened to the air.

The act itself did not take long. Once again, she chose to slit her uncle Jimmy's throat, having no great interest in prolonging his suffering. As he slowly bled out, his wife lay snoring beside him, cocooned obliviously in a sleep mask and doubtless content that her Lord and Saviour was watching over her from on high.

Alice leapt onto her aunt's stomach, legs straddling the older woman's torso. Quickly, she ripped away the sleep mask from Annie's face, then grabbed the haft of her knife with both hands, raising it high in the air.

Are you washed in the blood of the Lamb? she howled, before bringing the weapon down with all the force she could muster.

After she was finished, Alice left the Sacred Heart portrait lying at the end of the bed, her Aunt Annie's own oozing organ placed carefully upon Christ's chest.

Once she'd showered off the blood and changed her clothes, Alice took whatever money and valuables she could find, then carefully locked up the house behind her. Jauntily humming a hymn to herself, she headed downtown to the Broadway bus terminal, where she caught an early bus into New York City. As she watched the town she'd known all her life elide and change into streets and neighbourhoods she'd never ever seen, Alice began to think about what she was going to do next, and realised she had absolutely no idea. The sly presence at her shoulder seemed to have now gone quiet – perhaps forever? – and so it seemed she had little choice but to abandon herself to whatever fate might have in store for her.

She alighted in Manhattan and set off to explore the city streets, marvelling at the sights and sounds of the Big Apple. Alice had visited Manhattan before, but always under the careful supervision of her parents. Now, coming here alone, everything seemed bigger, louder, more imposing. Unlike her snooping neighbours back in Paterson, no one here gave a damn about her. Everyone in Manhattan had their own problems – Christ, even drawing breath in the big city required an effort – and they had no time to worry about a young girl roaming around on her own.

Eventually, her wandering brought her to the East Village. Alice soon discovered that the streets of the area were filled with young, odd-looking people, so unlike her peers back home. The kids here spoke weird, dressed weird, sometimes even smelled weird. But many of them appeared to be barely any older than herself.

Perhaps there might be a place for her here. But how should on earth should she go about finding it?

Alice began to feel very tired, and very, very small. It was all too much, the relentlessness and sheer scale of the city bearing down on her like a landslide. She realised just how hungry and thirsty she was, and paused to peer enviously through the windows of a nearby restaurant. It seemed impossibly grand to her: fancy paintings all over the walls, well-dressed people laughing and drinking, dinner plates piled high with rich, exotic food. She knew she could never dare set foot in such a place.

Longingly, she glanced up at the restaurant sign. Even the name was fancy: *The Dante*. As Alice gazed upwards, her head began to swim, the letters of the sign blurring into fog.

She stumbled backwards, on the verge of fainting. The next moment, she heard a nasal voice exclaim behind her. *Ohmygawd! Roman, quick!*

As Alice's legs crumpled beneath her, a pair of hands grabbed her underneath the arms, easing her fall. Her rescuer gently lowered her to the sidewalk, where her head immediately began to clear.

A kindly, well-spoken voice said, *Take a moment to get your breath back, my dear.*

Opening her eyes, she looked up into the face of an elderly man, smiling down at her. *There, that's better,* he said. *It was very fortunate we were passing. Eh, Minnie?*

Destiny! squawked the nasal voice. Seconds later, a second face appeared alongside the man's: an old lady, her shrunken features garishly daubed with rouge and eyeshadow. *Look at the poor little mite. She's pale as milk!*

The man helped Alice to sit upright. *Now, my dear, how can we best assist you?* he asked gently. *Can we put you in a cab home? Or is there someone we should call?*

Alice shook her head. *There's no one,* she mumbled.

Minnie elbowed the elderly man impatiently. *Roman, that poor kid needs a hot meal inside her before she can even start to think straight!*

Alice climbed unsteadily to her feet. *Thanks for your help, but I'm okay now,* she told the couple. *I won't bother you any more.*

What the hell are ya talking about, I never heard such a lotta nonsense in my life! Minnie's claw-like hand seized her by the upper arm. *You're gonna have dinner with us, and I don't wanna hear another word about it, young lady!*

Alice found herself propelled inside the Dante, and within moments she was sitting in a dinner booth with her elderly saviours. Minnie poured a glass of ice water and shoved it across the table at her, while the old man sat back and observed Alice with a thoughtful smile.

We haven't been properly introduced, he said politely. *I'm Roman Castavet, and this is my wife Minnie. We're very pleased to meet your acquaintance, Miss...?*

Alice supposed she should probably give them a fake name, but found herself entirely too discombobulated to think straight. So instead, she told them, *My name's Alice and I ran away from home today. I don't wanna go back so please don't call the cops.*

Minnie pulled an appalled face. *Hell, we wouldn't dream of it, would we, Roman?*

Roman looked grave. *Indeed we would not, my dear. Alice, my wife and I believe very strongly in personal choice and individual freedom. If you have chosen to leave your home, then that was entirely your decision and we have absolutely no right to interfere with it.* His eyes twinkled. *My only wish is that you will also choose to join us for dinner – on me, of course! – so that Minnie and I might get to know you a little better.*

Alice nodded in bewilderment, prompting Minnie to thrust a menu in front of her. *Order whatever ya want, the food's delicious.*

So, for the next few hours, she found herself enjoying a three-course meal in the company of Roman and Minnie Castavet. The old lady babbled away constantly, randomly careening from one topic of conversation to the next, like a pebble bouncing down a steep slope. Roman, meanwhile, sat back and listened quietly, offering occasional thoughts and interjections, and carefully coaxing their guest out of her shell.

For her part, Alice realised she had better offer her benefactors some kind of a story, and figured the closer to the truth she could stay, the better. So she told them of her father and Karen's murders (Minnie clucked sympathetically), the arrest of Mrs Tredoni (Roman muttered darkly about the iniquities of the Catholic faith), and her mother's subsequent breakdown. By this point, Alice figured the old couple were eating right out of her hand.

So then they packed me off to live with my Aunt Annie, she said. *Only she's crazy, a real nut, and used to beat me just for looking at her the wrong way. And my uncle? I caught him peeping at me in the bathroom once. Finally I just couldn't take it anymore, ya know?*

Minnie snorted. *You poor baby. Those God-fearin' types, they're the absolute worst. You're lucky you ran into us. Whaddaya say, Roman?*

Her husband signalled for the cheque. *What I say is that Alice should come home with us tonight,* he said firmly. *We have a guest room all made up, and you're quite welcome to stay for as long as you need.*

Alice became flustered. *But, I…I mean…I don't…*

Minnie shushed her. *Look, it's just till ya get things figured out. And it's no trouble, I swear! We'd love the company.* She flashed the girl a conspiratorial smirk. *Tell ya the truth, I'm getting a little bored of Roman's stories.*

Alice didn't know quite what to say. After a lifetime of being berated and punished, she wasn't at all accustomed to acts of kindness. Did the Castavets want something from her in return? Was this some weird sex thing? Did old people even *have* sex? She had no idea.

Dumbly, she nodded her head in mute acceptance of the offer.

The next thing she knew, she was being ushered into a cab and driven uptown to a large gabled apartment building. As their taxi pulled up outside, Alice's eyes moved to the sign mounted above the entrance: *The Bramford.* The very name sounded wealthy and important to her, unknowably alien in its affluence. A doorman welcomed them into the building, his gaze registering Alice's unfamiliar presence but betraying nothing as to what he thought of it. Suddenly seized by anxiety, she kept her eyes fixed firmly to the floor as they rode the elevator upstairs, fearful that she might at any second be identified as a trespasser and thrown back out onto the street.

The Castavets guided her down a long beige-walled corridor towards their apartment door. Inside, Alice was admitted to a whole new world, crammed with books and paintings and antique wooden furniture. The dining room alone was practically bigger than her old apartment. She looked around in wordless awe, wondering if there could possibly be a place for her here.

Ya like it? Minnie asked casually, barely even pausing to draw breath before she added, *Cocoa?*

Alice nodded quickly, then nodded again. *Y-yes to both, I mean,* she stuttered. *Thanks, Mrs Castavet.*

Minnie made a face. *Ah hell, call me Minnie. Mrs Castavet makes me sound like somebody's mother, and me and Roman never had no kids.*

Perhaps that was all there was to it. The Castavets were just two lonely old people who had no children of their own. Alice began to think she might really have lucked into something here. Although she had not heard the voice of the mysterious voice since leaving New Jersey, maybe it was still at her side, looking out for her?

She waited while Minnie fixed everybody cocoa, after which the couple showed her to the guest bedroom. It was airy and comfortable, spotlessly decorated all in white, unlike the reddish-brown hues which dominated the rest of the apartment. The double bed looked so vast and soft that Alice thought she might never find her way out of it again.

Minnie turned to her husband and made a shooing motion. *Let us girls talk for a minute, willya, Roman?*

The old man nodded. *Goodnight, Alice. I hope you sleep well, and be sure to rest for as long as you need.*

He withdrew from the room, closing the door quietly behind him. Immediately, Minnie sat down on the mattress and patted the spot beside her. *Come on over here and sit yourself down,* she told Alice. *Tell me alla your troubles, why don't ya?*

Alice duly followed the first part of Minnie's instruction. But as for the second, what could she possibly tell her?

She turned to the old lady, doing her level best to keep her face expressionless. *What else do you wanna know?* she responded. *I told you about my aunt and everything.*

Minnie sighed. *Roman sneaked a peek in your bag while we were in the kitchen,* she said softly. *He saw the knife.*

Oh, but that's just to protect myself, Alice said hurriedly, before Minnie cut her off with an impatient gesture.

Save it, kid, she said bluntly. *We saw all about those stabbings on the news. Roman said the knife still had blood on it. You didn't clean it too good afterwards, huh?*

Alice felt the ground falling away underneath her. A voice in her head screamed at her to run. Leaping to her feet, she was going to make a break for the door when she felt Minnie's hand close around her arm. The old lady's grip was surprisingly strong, pulling her back down onto the bed.

Calm down, calm down, she cooed. *No one here is gonna make any trouble for ya. Me and Roman, we unnerstand that ya musta had your reasons for what ya did. Like he toldya, we believe everyone should be free to make their own choices. I just wanna know why ya did what ya did.*

Alice felt her cheeks burning. Once again, she'd been caught being bad. But this was by far the worst of all. *Is it really important?* she said in a small voice.

Minnie was unyielding. *Damn straight it is, young lady.*

Alice turned to gaze out of the bedroom window. The twinkling lights of the city beyond promised freedom and escape, but seemed as impossibly distant as the stars in the night sky.

She slumped, defeated. *I heard a voice*, she whispered. *It told me to do it.*

The old lady relinquished her grip on Alice's arm. *A voice?* she said thoughtfully. *That's inneresting. That's really inneresting.*

You think? Alice couldn't tell whether Minnie was humouring her. *You don't think I'm crazy?*

Aw hell! Minnie made a dismissive gesture. *One minute they call you crazy, the next you're a goddamn prophet.* She leaned in closer. *Wanna hear a story? Back when I was a kid, I heard a voice too.*

You did?

She nodded emphatically. *When I was away at Catholic school. Goddamn fanatics. Big old place upstate called the Bramford Academy.*

Something sparked in Alice's mind. *Bramford? Like this building?*

Exactly! Minnie exclaimed. *Now, some people would say that was just a coincidence, but we know better, don't we? And ya know why that is, Alice? Because names have* power.

Alice absorbed this. She wondered if it was the same kind of power she'd felt after killing Aunt Annie and the rest. Darkly seductive, utterly irresistible.

Anyway, the kids there all said the place was haunted by the Devil Himself, Minnie continued. *They said the school basement was an entrance to Hell, and if ya got real close to the furnace down there and listened, you could hear the sound of souls screaming in torment.*

Alice smirked, wanting to show Minnie she was above such childish stories. But the old lady was being entirely serious. *And they were right,* she told Alice. *He started coming to me in my room at night, whisperin' things in my ear. At first I was just like you, I thought I was going nuts…but when I listened, really listened* – Minnie paused, and Alice saw the awe blossoming in her eyes *I realised they were the truest things I ever heard.*

The old lady suddenly grew silent, and Alice felt frustration mounting in her chest. *So what happened next?*

Minnie cackled, and climbed stiffly to her feet. *My whole damn life changed, is what happened. Now, let an old lady go to sleep, willya? It's way past my bedtime.*

But Alice still had one more question, so dreadful she almost couldn't bear to ask it. *Minnie…is the Devil talking to me?*

The old lady merely shrugged, as casually as if Alice had asked her whether she thought it might rain tomorrow. *Who knows? He don't talk to everyone, unnerstand?* She paused. *But Roman might be able to help ya out, if ya want. He knows all about this stuff. Ya gotta take it seriously, though. No kidding around, I mean it. This is life or death, Alice.*

Alice nodded solemnly.

Alright then. Now, sleep. Minnie turned off the light and left her to the darkness.

Alice hurriedly undressed and crept into bed. She lay there listening to the sounds of the city, waiting to see if the voice would speak to her again. But if the presence was there with her, it chose to remain silent.

Alice sat up in bed, eyes straining to see in the shadows. *Are you there?* she hissed impatiently. *Whaddaya want from me? Are you really the Devil like Minnie said?*

The only reply she received was the shriek of an ambulance siren from the street below. Exhausted by the events of the past twenty-four hours, Alice soon gave up and sank into a black dreamless sleep.

The next day, she began her induction into the ways of the Left-Hand Path. After enjoying a hearty home-cooked breakfast, Roman took Alice into his study and told her to take a seat. *Now then. Alice,* he said, taking the chair behind his desk. *Minnie tells me that you believe you're being visited by Satan.*

Alice immediately became flustered. *No, I dunno,* she said. *I do hear a voice, but I don't know who it is!*

And the voice told you to kill those people?

Her eyes fell to the floor, and she nodded.

Very well, Roman said, apparently unperturbed. *I want you to listen to me, Alice. I can help you, but the path ahead is long and difficult. We will have to study together every day, and you must do exactly as I tell you, without question. Can you do that?*

Yessir.

Because there could be terrible consequences for you if you don't. Roman rested his chin on his hands, studying Alice closely. *I do believe you have been touched by something ineffable, Alice. I could tell that the first time I saw you outside the restaurant.*

Alice didn't know what ineffable was, but she wasn't sure she liked the idea of it touching her. Still, she figured it was better not to interrupt Roman.

The old man sat back in his seat and clapped his hands together. *And who can say for certain? Perhaps it was the grace of our dark lord that delivered you into our hands after all!*

Whether it was fate or simply mere coincidence that had brought her together with the Castavets, Alice recognised an act of providence when she saw one. Over the next few weeks, she worked harder than she ever had done in her life. Roman was a stern and meticulous teacher, and insisted on schooling his new pupil not only in the Black Arts, but also in the more quotidian disciplines of English, Mathematics and Latin. *The world is full of idiots,* he would tell Alice. *And when Satan finally takes possession of our world, do you really think he will have any use for idiots? Christ is quite welcome to both the meek and the stupid.*

Alice was perfectly aware that in accepting Roman's tutelage, she was merely exchanging one faith for another, but found that the idea didn't bother her. For one thing, despite her disavowal of her Heavenly Maker, she still harboured a need to believe in something greater than herself, a thirst for supplication that, ironically enough, the Catholic Church had instilled in her at a very early age. And she couldn't deny that Satan now felt present to her in a way that the Christian God never had. When Alice looked at the world around her, she saw evidence of the Devil's pernicious works everywhere. But what possible proof was there of Jehovah? Oh, she knew that some believers would argue that the wonders of the natural world were nothing less than divine miracles, but when she mentioned this to Roman, he just scoffed in derision.

Yes, and see how easily those so called miracles are being swept aside by the forces of modernity! he exclaimed. *We are remaking the Earth in Satan's image, Alice. The world that God made is long past.*

However, some nagging doubts remained. Despite her naivety as to the exact rules and codes of the sinister new realm she now occupied, Alice was already well versed in the art Satan liked to proclaim Himself a master of: lying. And as such, she was minded to agree with the old dictum that it takes one to know one. So, when her instincts told her that the Castavets were not being entirely truthful as to their motives for taking her in, Alice grew wary.

She would often catch them giving her occasional sidelong glances, or making muttered comments that she couldn't quite fathom. Minnie in particular began taking a great interest in the way Alice looked and dressed. *You're gonna turn some heads when ya get a little older*, the old lady told her, and when her young ward insisted that she didn't care how she looked, Minnie's manner became impatient. *Ya may say that now, young lady, but you're gonna want to find yourself a man eventually*, she lectured Alice. *Someone powerful and important. And men like that know exactly what they want, lemme tell ya.*

One night Alice awoke to hear the Castavets engaged in deep discussion. The quirks of the ventilation system in the Bramford tended to carry sound an unexpectedly long way, and she realised she could eavesdrop upon them speaking within their own bedroom.

She heard Roman's voice first: *But she's so young, Minnie. Is she really ready?*

Then Minnie: *Ah, she's ready. She's started her periods and everything. There won't be any problem with that, lemme tell ya.*

Do you think He will accept her?

Minnie scoffed. *Why the hell not? You've seen how pretty she is once you get her in a nice dress and some makeup. He'll jump at the chance.*

Alice lay there unmoving, willing herself not to breathe in case the sound carried back to the Castavets' bedroom and they realised she was eavesdropping. What were they planning for her? It sounded like they intended to offer her to some man. Did they mean to turn Alice into some kind of hooker for their creepy friends? She felt sick at the thought, and although the Castavets concluded their discussion and turned in shortly afterwards, Alice lay awake tossing and turning for the rest of the night.

Matters came swiftly to a head the next morning. Minnie announced to Alice that she was going out for a few hours, but that Roman wanted to see her at her very best that day. So before the old woman left the apartment, she spent an hour dressing Alice and fastidiously doing her makeup. Alice didn't like the way Minnie made up her face – you only had to look at Minnie's own makeup to see that she had very little sense of how much was too much – but she'd learned to keep her thoughts to herself by now.

When she'd finished the task to her satisfaction, Minnie clucked in approval. *There, you look like a proper young lady now. Roman's gonna be real impressed.*

After she left, Roman ordered himself and Alice some Chinese takeout for lunch. When they sat down to eat together, she found that the old man was uncharacteristically taciturn that day, and Alice was sure she could sense him giving her furtive glances whenever she wasn't looking.

Once they finished their meal, Roman sat back in his chair, now openly staring at Alice, who soon began to squirm under his gaze. She'd grown comfortable with Roman over the course of the preceding weeks, but this was different. *He* was different.

Then she realised what it was; Roman was looking at her the same way the old guys back in Paterson used to. Like she was just a piece of meat, laid out on a butcher's slab for their private delectation.

Stand up, Alice, he told her.

She was so used to doing what Roman said by now that she did it automatically, without questioning.

That's good, Roman said quietly. *Now, give me a twirl. Show me how nice you look in that dress.*

Alice felt her cheeks growing hot, but did as instructed, stumbling slightly as she turned.

Very good. Now, do it again. But lift your skirt up slightly, so that I can see your legs.

A fist clenched in her belly. *I don't wanna!*

Roman's voice dropped to a murmur. *Are you defying me, young lady?*

Alice had never previously gone against Roman's word. She'd never even felt the need to before; this, after a lifetime of stubbornly resisting all authority. In truth, she'd enjoyed not having to fight any more. But now the old instincts were rising up inside her once again, only with one significant difference: Alice realised she was deathly afraid of defying Roman. She had no idea what he might be capable of if she tried, but quickly decided she didn't want to find out.

Her hands trembling, she reached down and grabbed the edge of her skirt, pulling it up a few inches.

Excellent. Now twirl.

Awkwardly, she did as she was told. She was starting to grow dizzy, although not from the twirling.

Are you a virgin, Alice? Roman suddenly asked her.

She froze in immediate outrage, her hands dropping her skirt back into place and balling into tight little fists. *Course I am!* she cried.

Roman frowned. *There's no need to shout. It's a perfectly normal question to ask a young girl. Especially one who's gone…astray.*

They stared at each other in complete silence.

I want you to come over here and sit in my lap, Roman told her.

Alice didn't move.

Roman sighed. *Am I going to have to come over there?* he asked softly, his eyes like cold fire. Recoiling from their gaze, Alice could feel herself growing brittle, as though she might shatter into tiny fragments at any moment.

Slowly, she walked over to where the old man was sitting and eased herself down into his lap.

There, he said, satisfied.

Neither of them moved. Behind her, Alice could hear Roman's breathing growing heavier. She wanted to scream at her own stupidity, claw out her own eyes as punishment. She'd believed Roman to be caring and wise, considered him a friend, when in reality he was just another dirty old man.

And where was her mysterious guide, that wheedling, disembodied voice that had got her into all this in the first place? It only ever seemed to speak up to encourage her to get into trouble, never to help her out of it.

In that moment, Alice felt truly and utterly alone, as though she had awoken to find herself the last person on Earth.

Roman shifted underneath her, letting out a soft sigh. *Sweet little Alice,* he breathed.

Alice felt his hands close gently around her waist, gradually sliding upwards to cup her breasts.

So, she was all alone in the world? So be it. She would just have to look after herself.

Her hand snapped out and snatched up the discarded fork from Roman's plate. Before the old man could react, Alice turned and plunged it into his meaty thigh.

Roman screeched in pain. *Bitch!*

Instantly, she was up and away, haring through the apartment. Alice had nowhere else she could possibly go, no clothes, money or possessions, but all that mattered right then was getting away from Roman.

Because she truly believed that if the old man succeeded in catching her, he might very well kill her.

She skidded around a corner, bringing the apartment's front door into view. Only a few more steps remained between her and and safety.

Then Alice heard the sound of a key scraping in the lock. Moments later, the door opened to reveal Minnie.

Alice lurched to a sudden halt, nearly overbalancing and falling to the ground.

Minnie stared at her, astonished. *What the hell's –*

Alice heard Roman roar from behind her, cutting his wife off. *Stop her, Minnie!*

With a rapidity that belied her age, Minnie immediately turned and grabbed a stout-looking walking stick from the umbrella stand next to the front door. Raising it above her head, she advanced upon Alice. *I knew you were gonna be trouble, you little tramp*, she growled.

Alice started to back away, only to feel Roman's hands clamp painfully around her upper arms. Helpless, she could do nothing to protect herself from the old woman rapidly bearing down on her.

The walking stick rose and fell, and Alice Spages abruptly parted company with the world that had caused her so much misery.

Eventually, broken snatches of conversation began to drift through the darkness enveloping her. *Found her on the street…offered her a hot meal… had no idea…try to help someone in need and this is what happens…*

Alice opened her eyes to find herself lying on the floor of the Castavet's dining room, both hands cuffed tightly behind her back. Two surly-looking cops were stood over her, busily taking the couple's statement. Roman was sitting in a chair holding a cloth to his bleeding leg, while Minnie stood behind him weeping theatrically, one hand clutching at her husband's shoulder.

Wincing at the pain in her head, Alice rolled over onto her side. *Excuse me, officer?* she said.

One of the cops glanced down at her. *That man tried to molest me,* she told him earnestly. *And you should know that both of them worship the Devil.*

The cop looked over at Roman quizzically. The room was silent for a moment, before everyone in it except Alice erupted into derisive laughter.

Yeah, that's quite enough outta you, the cop told her.

It did not take the policemen long to discover that there was an outstanding warrant for Alice's arrest, and she was promptly taken into custody. After the judicial system had eventually finished with her, she ended up right back where she had started, in New Jersey. There, she was committed to a juvenile detention centre. Alice's talk of Satanists and disembodied voices, not to mention her unspeakable crimes, had convinced the authorities that she was unquestionably psychotic, and so a psychiatrist was appointed to visit her for regular treatment sessions. The doctor, a middle-aged English man named Bain, was an eccentric, unconventional sort, much given to talking about Alice's 'journey'. Dr. Bain treated Alice for nearly three years, and although he came to view her with a great deal of sympathy, he was eventually forced to concede that the young patient was not responding to his care. In their sessions together, Alice would repeatedly insist that the voice she'd heard had been entirely real. Not only that, but she firmly believed it might even have been the Devil Himself talking to her.

And what do you think the Devil wanted with you, Alice? Dr. Bain would ask her.

I don't know, Alice admitted. *But one day I'm gonna ask him. I know right where to find him, see?*

Eventually Bain turned to a trusted colleague for assistance, one Dr. Samuel Loomis. Loomis already had one notorious child murderer in his care, and so Dr. Bain sought out his professional opinion on Alice.

Loomis spent one hour alone with the patient. When he emerged, his face was grave. *We need to see that she never gets out,* he bluntly informed Bain. *She reminds me of Michael. It's uncanny, really. She has the same blank stare, the same lack of affect, but it goes far deeper than that.* He paused, a look of dread clouding his features. *Believe me when I say that I get the exact same sense that there's something inhuman hiding behind that stare. Alice needs to go into a proper facility. There's nothing anyone can do for her here.*

When Alice turned sixteen, a court petition and supporting statements from both doctors were filed recommending that she be indefinitely committed into secure psychiatric care. She subsequently found herself being transferred out of state, to the Danvers State Hospital in nearby Massachusetts.

Upon her arrival at the hospital, Alice understood immediately that Danvers was not somewhere they sent you to get better. Vast and foreboding, the building looked like something conjured up out of the collective nightmares of the patients who slept there. No, they only sent you to Danvers when they knew you weren't *ever* going to get any better. In other words, it was what her mom used to call a *snake pit*. Alice remembered how, after she'd had her breakdown, Catherine Spages would occasionally have bouts of extreme paranoia. Her eyes would suddenly snap into focus and she'd look up at her daughter with a burgeoning, palpable terror. *Don't let them put me in the snake pit,* she'd beg, and Alice would hold her tightly until she quietened down and drifted off into a narcotic daydream once more.

But now her mom was dead, and Alice was the one they'd put here, to writhe and hiss and spit with all the other serpents.

Alone in her room that night, Alice could feel the weight of the long decades of misery and loneliness that had accumulated here bearing down on her, choking the air from her lungs. Limbs twisting in her coarsely starched bedsheets, she thought of voices in a darkened cellar, of damned souls screaming in a basement furnace.

This was Hell, she finally realised. She'd set out to find the Devil, and this was to be her punishment for such presumption. What conceivable right did some upstart girl from New Jersey have to seek the counsel of the

Prince of Darkness? He didn't care about her, any more than God did. And now she was shut up with others just like her, people who no one cared about. They were all nothing but a bunch of dirty little secrets, locked away in a box and buried deep underground.

She would die here, she knew. Maybe in sixty years' time, maybe even tomorrow, but she would die here, and no one would ever know. Fingers clawing at her mattress, Alice began to scream, and soon the other patients on her ward began to scream too, and as their chorus of suffering echoed through the empty corridors of the hospital, the dreadful sound at least made her feel slightly less alone, if only for a brief moment.

It was not until some nine years later, when she encountered Mary Hobbes, that Alice finally found her way back onto the path she'd strayed from as a child. Now thirty-seven, Mary had first been taken into care aged fourteen, after she'd stabbed her parents and brother to death. She'd been diagnosed with Multiple Personality Disorder and treated by several doctors over the years, apparently without much in the way of success. When Mary arrived at Danvers, word of her case history spread quickly amongst the other patients, and Alice immediately grew intrigued. Here was someone whose crimes were very similar to her own, who had also spent her entire adult life in care. Alice wondered what had driven Mary to commit such acts, whether there might perhaps be some kinship between them. Alice's memories of her own childhood were growing ever more hazy and indistinct, and after spending nearly a decade at Danvers, she'd reluctantly begun to accept that the doctors had been right all along. There were no voices, no Devil, and never had been. Like the kids at school used to say, she was looneytunes, crazier than a run-over dog. But deep down, part of her still yearned for some kind of affirmation, a sense that there was indeed something larger than herself.

One morning, Alice sought Mary out in the rec room. The woman was pale and wraithlike, almost insubstantial; she reminded Alice of a wavering reflection on the surface of a pond. She sat alone in the corner of the room, the fingers of one hand crammed in her mouth. When Alice cautiously took the seat next to her, Mary did not react, just continued sucking on her fingers and staring into space.

Eventually, Alice broke the silence. *Hello, Mary.*

There was a short pause, and then a light suddenly sparked in the other woman's eyes. Mary turned to look at Alice, who couldn't help but recoil. There was something watchful and predatory in Mary's gaze. Something inhuman.

Taking her fingers from her mouth, Mary smiled. She began to speak in a high-pitched, childish voice. *Mary isn't here right now, Miss Alice,* she trilled. *My name is Princess.*

Alice was surprised to find that the other woman knew her name, but she supposed someone must have told it to her; perhaps Mary wasn't always quite as absent as she first appeared.

Hello, Princess, Alice replied. *I'm very pleased to meet you. When will Mary be back, do you think?*

Mary pulled an exaggeratedly thoughtful face. *Mmm...I dunno. Mary doesn't really like meeting new people, Miss Alice.* Her expression brightened. *But I do! I like meeting people and having con-vers-ayy-tions. What would you like to talk about? We can talk about the sky, or dinosaurs, or what your favouritest dessert is...*

Alice tried to mask her sense of disappointment. This was obviously a waste of time. There was nothing she could learn from Mary Hobbes. The woman was clearly even crazier than she was. *That's okay, Princess,* she said hurriedly. *I'll just come back another time.*

Mary's features darkened. *Well, if you don't wanna speak to me, I know someone else who wants to talk to you...*

Alice was by now regretting ever having initiated this conversation. She forced a smile. *Oh, and who's that?*

The other woman's voice dropped to a frightened whisper. *His name's Simon.* She winced at the very mention of the name. *But are you sure you wanna speak to him? He's real bad. He does real bad things.*

This was intriguing. *I swear I'll be careful, Princess,* Alice whispered back.

A look of the profoundest sorrow flashed across Mary's face. Then, her features began to shift and change, a malevolent vigour seeping into her normally languid demeanour. Watching the transformation, Alice's breath caught in her throat. This was not merely a shift in personality; it almost appeared as though Mary was becoming another person entirely.

The other woman showed her teeth, her eyes gazing hungrily at Alice. *Hello...Alice,* she said.

And there it was. The voice she'd feared she would never hear again.

The same voice that had spoken to her in that darkened New Jersey basement. The same voice that had encouraged her to kill, and then to kill again. There was no mistaking it, even after all these years. Alice had simply never heard another voice like it: simultaneously sly and wicked and ruthless and wise. It might have belonged to a chorus of demons, all speaking as one.

It's you, she breathed.

Mary grinned craftily. *And who am I?*

I dunno. She said your name was Simon.

Maybe it is…and maybe it isn't.

Please, begged Alice. *You have to help me. I did what you said, and now I'm trapped here.*

Were you bad, Alice?

I was.

Her lips smacked with relish. *Were you…real bad?*

Yes! Alice half-screamed the word, far louder than she'd intended, and was suddenly aware that several of the other patients were now staring at her curiously. Not only that, but an orderly was weaving his way through the clusters of tables and chairs towards them.

Mary seized her forearm, long fingernails digging into Alice's flesh. *I'll come to you tonight, once it's dark. We can have so much more fun in the dark, Alice.*

And then, swift as death, Simon was gone. Mary's eyes drifted out of focus, her fingers releasing their grip on Alice's arm and slowly creeping back into her mouth.

Moments later, when the orderly demanded to know exactly what she had been doing with Mary, Alice innocently told him that they'd been praying together.

After sundown, Alice laid in bed and nervously awaited Simon's arrival, as though she were a virginal bride on her wedding night. It had taken her so long to find him again, and she had so many questions. So when she felt his watchful presence gathering in the corner of her cell, she immediately leapt up from her mattress.

Hello…Alice, Simon said.

Where have you been all this time? she cried. *I've waited for so long!* Alice remembered how alone she'd felt ever since the murders, and felt bile rising in her throat. *I thought you were my friend, and you abandoned me!*

I like to travel, Alice. A chuckle. *Wherever I lay my hat…is my home.*

With her? Is that where you've been all this time?

Mary…needed me. You didn't.

Alice's shoulders slumped. *I'm sorry about the Castavets! I made a mistake. I thought they were gonna help me find you again.*

But now I found you. Simon sounded pleased. *It's gonna be…real nice, Alice. We're gonna have fun.*

Alice gazed around at her cramped room, the walls pale and cold in the moonlight. *I don't wanna be here. Help me get out, Simon. We can be together on the outside. Then I can do whatever you want.*

Simon's voice took on a sneering, dismissive tone. *I…like it here, Alice. So many toys…for me to play with.*

No!

We're gonna have time to…play together, Alice. A real long time.

Reverting to the same angry child she'd been in Paterson, Alice turned her back on him, laying down in bed and pulling the covers tightly around herself. It had been so long since she'd heard his voice that she'd forgotten Simon only ever wanted things for himself, and never for her.

You're…no fun, Alice, the voice chided. *I guess I'll go find someone else…to play with.*

She lay there in silence for a few seconds, then turned over. *Simon, wait.*

What?

Are you the Devil?

Another chuckle. *Maybe. I have…lots of names, Alice.*

Tell me!

But Simon had gone.

He didn't visit her again for a week, and as much as Alice was hurt by the entity's games, the knowledge that he was somewhere nearby, ignoring her, was far more painful. So when Simon did eventually return, she did not bother to mask her gratitude. At last, she had a friend.

They would talk through the long nights, Simon telling her spiteful stories about the Danvers staff and inmates. In return, Alice would occasionally play tricks for him. Nothing too serious, mind – it would suit neither of them if she got into any *real* trouble – but she would sometimes arrange for little accidents to befall the other patients, small mishaps that the hospital staff would chalk up to clumsiness or misfortune. Most of the patients were so easy to bamboozle, and had no earthly idea how they'd ended up in the infirmary. But Alice and Simon knew, and their delighted laughter would echo through the empty corridors after dark.

And night after night, Alice would ask Simon the same question: *Are you the Devil?* And night after night, he would never offer her a straight answer.

This state of affairs continued for quite some time, until the day Arletty Long arrived at Danvers. She was a sad, tormented woman, carrying a terrible unwanted knowledge behind her eyes. But despite her melancholia, or perhaps even because of it, she possessed an undeniable beauty. Alice would watch her from afar, knowing that Simon was watching her too.

Simon always liked the pretty ones.

The entity made Alice tell Arletty that he was going to visit her that night. Despite the simmering jealousy she could feel bubbling in her stomach, Alice did as she was asked, knowing that Simon was liable to punish her severely if she refused. She wondered if she could arrange for Arletty to suffer one of her little accidents without Simon knowing.

That night, she waited for Simon for hours, tossing and turning in her sheets. What if Arletty became his new favourite? She would have no one to laugh and play tricks with. Once again, she'd be left all alone.

Alice decided that she would kill herself if Simon abandoned her again.

But then, just before dawn, Simon came to her, seething and cursing. *That bitch*, he snarled. *She shut me out. No one does that. Not when I want to play.*

But how? Alice asked, bewildered. The idea that someone might be able to resist Simon was inconceivable to her.

Simon's anger made him unguarded. *There was…something else. Helping her. Something from…outside.*

It suddenly occurred to Alice that this must mean there were limits to Simon's power. Which meant, in turn, that he couldn't be the Devil after all. After all these years, Simon was still not what she had been looking for.

I want you to hurt Arletty, Alice. I want you to hurt her…real bad, Simon hissed.

The idea was not altogether unappealing, but Alice's mind was clearer now than it had been for a long time. She gazed defiantly into the darkness. *If I do that, Simon, there'll be an investigation. And if they find out it was me, you know what they'll do.*

She'd watched the lobotomised patients shuffle blankly about the hospital, eyes like clouded glass, broken puppets with half their strings cut. They reminded her of the old horror movies she used to watch on TV with her mom.

What do you want? Simon said sullenly.

I want you to get me out of here.

The voice was silent for a moment. Alice knew how much Simon hated to give up one of his toys before he'd finished playing with it. *If you leave me, Alice…I'll never visit you again,* he threatened. *You'll be all alone.*

She would not budge. *That's the deal, Simon.*

The next moment, he was gone from the room. Alice took this to signal his begrudging assent.

Throughout the next day, she felt energised, filled with the same dark power she recalled from her childhood. Alice thought back to killing cousin Angela, her Aunt Annie and Uncle Jimmy, and how inexpressibly alive she'd felt. She might yet feel that same ecstasy again. Despite the years she'd spent in captivity, she was still a young woman. There was so much more she could accomplish, if only she could find the right mentor.

When the orderly unlocked her cell door that night, Alice was ready. She could feel Simon hovering at her shoulder, thirsting for revenge. Making her way into the next cell, she discovered Arletty lying expectantly on her cot, mute and unresisting. She found herself strangely comforted by the other woman's almost beatific acceptance of her fate, and as Alice pressed a pillow down onto her face, a part of her hoped Arletty might find the peace she herself had always been denied.

Afterwards, she made her way out through the deserted hospital, slinking through the shadows like a fox. Acting under Simon's influence, the orderly had left her an open window through which to escape.

As she prepared to climb through, Alice paused for a moment, once again sensing Simon at her shoulder. She waited for him to speak.

You don't have to go, Alice, he coaxed. *Think of all the fun we could still have together.*

Alice did not look back. *You're not the Devil, and you never were,* she told him.

As she hoisted herself through the window, she heard Simon's thwarted snarl behind her, the sound gradually dissipating into the air.

Hurrying across the hospital lawn, buds of dew bursting against her bare feet, Alice thought about how far she'd come, and how far she still had to travel. Upstate New York was probably about two hundred and fifty miles from here, she figured.

Then she thought back to the last time she'd fled from everything she'd known, and how bad things had gotten after that.

But now she had somewhere to go. A place where she might find that which she'd always sought.

A name burned in her brain. *Names have power,* Minnie had told her.

The Bramford Academy.

Alice wondered if He was still there, waiting for her.

She started to run.

ROSEMARY WOODHOUSE

Mia Farrow in Rosemary's Baby, 1968
based on the novel by Ira Levin
written & directed by Roman Polanski

THE KID'S A RETARD, SAID MINNIE CASTAVET. WOULD YOU BELIEVE IT? AFTER *all that goddamn work!*

The child in question, two-year old Andy Woodhouse, sat on a rug in the middle of Minnie's apartment, staring open-mouthed at the collection of toy cars scattered in front of him.

Don't say that, murmured Rosemary Woodhouse, the boy's mother. *He's just different, is all.*

You can say that again, Minnie howled. *He was meant to be different, but not like this! I don't know what the hell went wrong. Maybe the goddamn bloodlines weren't compatible or something. Christ, I wish Roman were here, he'd know.*

Minnie's husband Roman had died suddenly some months after Andy's birth, long before any developmental issues with the boy had been detected. As he lay on his deathbed, he'd exulted in the success of his plan to bring about the birth of the Devil's child on Earth. *Now, the world shall be His!* he cried. *Satan is Lord!*

Then he'd collapsed back to his pillow and hurried off to meet his diabolical master.

As for Rosemary – the helpless catspaw in Roman's grand Satanic scheme – it's fair to say that the nine terror-filled months of her pregnancy had left something of a mark on her. Betrayed by her husband Guy, raped by the Devil, surrounded by malign conspirators, and weakened by the rigours of carrying Satan's inhuman spawn to term, she had been transformed from a carefree flower child to a bitter, paranoid shadow of the girl she once was. Guy had hoped that, once the pregnancy and all the attendant fuss was out of the way, he and Rosemary might be able to repair their marriage and go back to the way things were, maybe even have another kid – a normal one this time. After all, he was a successful actor now.

But when Rosemary pulled a knife and lunged at him at dinner one evening, Minnie had advised him to spend some time away from the apartment. *Give the poor girl some time*, she'd told Guy. *She's been through a helluva lot. She'll come around, just like she did with Andy.*

Nevertheless, it had now been two years since Guy packed his bags and left, and given that Rosemary had since changed all the locks to the apartment, it did not appear as though she was likely to come around any time soon.

However, Minnie was quite correct in one respect: Rosemary doted on her little boy, the same child whose quasi-demonic appearance had so horrified her when she first beheld him lying in his crib. *What have you done to his eyes?* she'd screamed.

As Roman Castavet had so proudly pointed out to her, Andy did indeed possess his Father's eyes; a rather unfortunate genetic inheritance which had left the child with two goatish pupils and amber-coloured sclerae. To any outsider, he would appear deformed, even monstrous, and while the question of how Andy might eventually pass in the outside world remained as yet unanswered, Rosemary loved him with all her heart nonetheless. He couldn't help how he'd been born, or who his real father was. He was just her little boy.

So, even as Andy grew older, and the first developmental problems began to manifest themselves, Rosemary initially refused to acknowledge that there was any sort of an issue with her son. *Oh, he'll grow out of it in time*, she would insist. But while that might perhaps have been true in regards to the boy's continuing reluctance to talk, or his seeming inability to be toilet-trained, it was more of a stretch to argue that case in regard to Andy's growing proclivity for dismembering (and occasionally eating) any small animals that crossed his path. Two cats had already gone missing in the building, and Minnie and the rest of her coven feared for the consequences if the disappearances should ever be traced back to Rosemary's door.

In truth, Minnie had by now all but washed her hands of Andy. It was difficult to see him being any use to Satan whatsoever; indeed, there were growing rumours amongst the faithful that the Devil had successfully sired another child, one that He was now grooming to be His prince on Earth.

Maybe you were just a one night stand, she told Rosemary. *Wham bam thank you, ma'am.* Minnie sniffed. *I guess it shouldn't be much of a surprise when the Devil turns out to be a deadbeat dad.*

That's fine, Rosemary said. *Andy and I don't need anyone.*

But it wasn't fine, anyone could see that. By rights, the boy should be in a home – Rosemary's gynaecologist Dr Sapirstein, who'd delivered the baby, had said as much himself – if only the home existed that would take a child like Andy. But that was impossible.

So Minnie quietly began to consider the alternatives.

As she and Rosemary stood watching Andy, he picked up one of the toy cars and raised it to his mouth, enthusiastically crunching down on it with his baby teeth.

Andy, no! Rosemary cried, rushing to his side and gathering up the toys before her son could do any more damage. *I told you not to give these to him*, she muttered reproachfully at Minnie.

He's a little boy, he's supposed to play with toy cars! the old lady snapped back.

Well, he's not like other little boys.

Yeah, I think we've established that. Minnie rolled her eyes. *So anyway, while we're on the subject...*

What? said Rosemary suspiciously. She'd learned a long time ago not to trust anything Minnie said. If only the old lady weren't her only feasible option as a babysitter.

You gotta face facts, Rosemary, Minnie continued. *The kid's never gonna get any better. Something went wrong, and that's all there is to it. The older he gets, the worse it's gonna be. One day they might just take him away from you, and you know what'll happen then. He'll spend the rest of his life in a cage, like a goddamn freak.*

No! whimpered Rosemary.

And even if you keep him hidden, what happens after you're gone? There'll be no one left to take care of him, no one who understands.

So what exactly are you saying? the younger woman whispered.

A shrug. *I'm saying it might be a kindness if we ended it now.*

End *it?*

Minnie's gaze moved to Andy. *We won't hurt the boy or nothing. I've got herbs that'll do the job, totally quick and painless. Assuming, you know, we can do it that way.* She made a gesture with her hands. *I mean, the Devil's kid, who the hell knows? I heard there's some special daggers that would definitely do the trick, but they're stuck in a museum somewhere...*

Rosemary raced over to Andy and scooped him up in her arms. *You want to kill my boy?*

Minnie looked hurt. *I don't* wanna *do it, Rosemary, I'm not a monster. I'm just saying it'd be for the best, is all. For everyone. Andy included.*

Stay away from me! Rosemary pushed past the old woman, nearly knocking her to the floor. *I don't want you coming anywhere near me or Andy!*

Steadying herself, Minnie heard the slam of the front door as Rosemary fled the apartment. The old woman sighed. Screw it, she would have to come around to Minnie's way of thinking eventually. Give it time. A kid like that, there's absolutely nothing you can do.

Back when Minnie was a little girl, folks would look at a boy like Andy and say, *He's got the Devil in him, that one.* And in his case, they'd be righter than they knew. In her day, they'd always try and beat it out of a child, but you can't beat the Devil. Not the real one, you can't.

So the old woman went about her business, confident that Rosemary would soon be back at her door begging for help. But in that, she was quite mistaken. Back in her own apartment, Rosemary was already frantically packing for her and Andy to go away. She had no idea where on earth they'd go or how they'd live, but it was obvious they couldn't stay here. Rosemary had allowed herself to be convinced that her fears were simply paranoid delusions once, but wasn't about to let that happen again. After all, she'd been right all along, hadn't she? And this wasn't even paranoia. Minnie had directly threatened Andy's life!

Knowing that her neighbour always turned in early, she waited until she was sure the old woman would be asleep, then quietly stole from her apartment, Andy toddling compliantly along behind her.

With no particular destination in mind, Rosemary impulsively booked them seats on a Greyhound headed south. The New York winters were beginning to draw in, and while her son was oblivious to most things in life, he could be noisily vociferous in his objections to the cold. Rosemary had taken care to dress Andy in a hooded coat and scarf to help obscure his face, and when they boarded the bus, she led him to the very back, so that they might keep a safe distance from prying eyes. For once, her son seemed mildly interested in what was going on around him, and when their bus was about to enter the Holland Tunnel, both he and Rosemary turned around in their seats and waved goodbye to Manhattan.

They would never return to the city.

And so the pattern for the rest of their lives together had been set; rootless, forever on the move. They would travel from place to place, perhaps staying for a few months, sometimes for a matter of weeks or only days. In her sunnier moments, Rosemary would tell herself that she and her son were merely drifters, free spirits, whereas in the darker corners of her mind she harboured a desperate certainty that they were in fact little more than fugitives. She was forever on guard for the merest suggestion of anything suspicious; even someone glancing at her and Andy for a beat too long in the queue for the grocery checkout might prompt her to instantly up sticks and run again. She would then select their next destination at random, her sole criteria whatever whims, fears or superstitions happened to be foremost in her mind at that particular moment. Rosemary had taken to praying before bedtime every night, a ritual she had not observed since her days at Catholic school. Neither was she blind to the contradiction inherent in the act: her, the mother of the Devil's child, praying to God! But what else could she do? She had not asked to become pregnant with Andy, any more than he had asked to be born. Perhaps there could still be mercy for both of them.

But sometimes her constant terror would allay itself for a short while, permitting them to stay in one place just long enough to catch their breath. Guy would wire her money for Andy's care (she had half-expected him to object that the boy was not in fact his son, but he never did), and she would pick up a few dollars here and there doing sewing jobs for people. They survived. Sometimes, Rosemary would even tell herself that they might be close to living a normal life again. After all, Andy had shown some improvement in his development; he was talking now, and seemed somewhat more attuned to his surroundings. At one point she even went as far as placing him in a daycare scheme for special-needs children, making sure to outfit him with a pair of tinted safety goggles first (she told the teacher that he had an extreme sensitivity to light). But by the end of his second day there, one of the other children had ripped the goggles off and promptly collapsed into a screaming fit at the sight of Andy's eyes, so that was very much the end of that.

And in the end, sooner or later something would always start Rosemary running again, like an electric shock jolting a lab rat through a maze. For instance, there was the small Texas town where *everybody* seemed to be watching her, especially the local sheriff, a pig-eyed man named Taylor. He had taken to stopping by Rosemary's motel room to enquire about her welfare, and had shown a particular interest in Andy. *He's a special one, ain't he?* he'd told her with a knowing grin. Rosemary and Andy had hitched out of town under cover of darkness that very same night.

Or there was Stepford, Connecticut. One of Rosemary's old schoolmates had moved there some years back, and had always spoken of the town in glowing terms. Although her letters had grown infrequent and increasingly bland in tone in recent times (everything in her life was just 'the best'), Rosemary thought it might be an opportune time to look her up. But although Stepford itself was practically the epitome of the perfect little American town, almost uncannily so in fact, she found her friend somehow changed: her demeanour eerily blank and affectless. And although Rosemary would have shuddered to think of herself as any sort of feminist, even she was appalled at the woman's total subservience to her husband. *You know,* her friend confided in her while they shopped together one morning, *There was this one time we were having a cocktail party, and he told me to blow him in front of everyone. And I did! Isn't that just the best?*

But it wasn't just her friend – every woman in town was the same way. And they were *all* married, there were no single women anywhere to be found in Stepford. No divorcées, nothing. Thinking back to her own marriage, Rosemary wanted nothing more than to slap her friend across the face and scream, *You can't trust them, you know! None of them!* But it would do no good, she knew. After a time, Rosemary grew convinced the men of the town – who all seemed to belong to some sort of creepy association – were plotting against her, and so, once again, she and Andy fled.

Years passed. Rosemary entered middle-age, and Andy grew into a young man. He was the centre of his mother's world, but even she would admit something was missing. It wasn't just Andy's limitations as a companion – although her son spoke more frequently now, he would never be called loquacious – no, Rosemary was lonely. She missed having someone to hold her at night, someone to love. After New York, she'd thought she would never want to be close to a man again, but advancing age and constant terror had steadily worn down her resolve. Still, she knew that finding a partner was impossible – as well as the obvious impracticalities of hers and Andy's shiftless lifestyle, how would she ever be able to explain her son's unique nature to anyone? So, she always tried to push such thoughts away, usually managing to keep her melancholy at bay for Andy's sake, at least until the small hours of the morning, when she would frequently find herself overcome with tears.

But one afternoon, everything changed. Andy could be left alone for short periods now, and Rosemary often found it easier to pop to the grocery store without him in tow. On this particular afternoon, she returned from shopping and surprised her son in the act of playing with himself. They stared at each other mutely for a moment.

Oh, Rosemary said softly.

I'm sorry, Mom, mumbled Andy, although he made no move to cover himself up.

It's okay, honey, Rosemary assured him. *I'm sorry I startled you.* Slowly, so as not to alarm him, she moved closer. *If you like, I can finish that for you.*

Andy stared at her, saying nothing. Gently, she reached out and took him in her hand.

Like this, she said.

Her son moaned quietly.

See? Rosemary whispered. *Isn't that better?*

Afterwards, she took him into her arms and they lay down together. Rosemary had never felt closer to her son. Eventually, she turned to him and said, *You know, Andy. If you liked that, there are plenty of other things we can do together. Maybe I could teach you?*

And she did.

Rosemary felt as though she had at last achieved a rare kind of happiness. She no longer wanted or needed for anything. She and Andy had each other, and that was all that mattered. She knew that the outside world would shun and scorn them if it ever suspected the truth, but so what? It was just one more secret mother and son could share between themselves. It wasn't as though the need to conceal Andy's origin wasn't already paramount; despite all the so-called progress being made in the world, Rosemary had little doubt that her son would end up tied to a burning stake should the matter of his true parentage ever come to light.

Together, they grew older. Rosemary would study herself in the mirror – the deepening lines on her face, the flourishing crop of grey hair on her head – and wonder at the fact that she and Andy had ever made it this far, for this long. Perhaps she was simply paranoid after all. Despite her perpetual terror that they were being watched and followed, no one had ever tried to harm them. No one even seemed particularly interested in them any more. They were just an eccentric old lady and her disabled son, a subject of casual pity more than anything else.

Regardless, old habits died hard. When Rosemary began to notice the same black bird – she couldn't tell whether it was a crow or a raven – appearing at the kitchen window of their rented apartment every morning, she could not help but consider it some sort of ill omen. The very next day they were back on the interstate again, searching for a fresh sanctuary. By now Rosemary had learned to drive, but her worsening eyesight made it troublesome to stay on the road for too long. By mid-afternoon, she had decided to stop at a motel on the outskirts of the Sonoran Desert for the night. There she would study the map and try to decide exactly where they might go next.

Once they were both settled in their room, she ran a bath for Andy and sat on her bed watching Thorn News as he splashed about happily in the tub. The channel was showing footage of a speech given by the current Republican candidate for the presidency, Greg Stillson. Rosemary had never previously considered herself a conservative – back in Manhattan, her and Guy's circle of friends had been steadfastly and impeccably liberal – but she had seen a great deal of the rest of America since then, and understood just how hard life had become for so many of its people. Stillson, whatever his other failings, also seemed to recognise that. He had an unruly energy in him that Rosemary responded to, and, despite his advancing years, retained a certain boyish quality in his looks. Had she been a registered voter, she would have given him her vote without hesitation.

Absorbed as she was in Stillson's speech, it took Rosemary some time before she noticed the rhythmic tapping coming from the motel room window. When she finally registered the sound, she looked around to see a black bird – the *same* bird she had seen earlier that morning, she was absolutely convinced of it – watching her from the windowsill.

Andy! she screamed instantly.

Moments later, her son emerged from the bathroom, naked and dripping wet. *Mom!'*

Get dressed! Rosemary leapt up off the bed. *We have to leave, right this minute!*

Fifteen minutes later, they were back on the road once more. The motel, the bird, all of it, was receding in the distance behind them. Up ahead, there was nothing but desert. The sight of the barren expanse soothed her somehow; at least there was nowhere for anyone to hide out here.

After they had been driving for about an hour, Rosemary gradually began to relax. Part of her even started to consider whether she'd been a little hasty, even foolish, in her impulsive urge to flee. It was just a dumb old bird, after all. And there had to be *millions* of crows, or ravens, flying around. The idea that it had been the very same one was ludicrous, wasn't it?

The next instant, the engine of their car began to sputter and stall.

Rosemary felt a deep chasm of dread open up inside her. Pulling over to the side of the road, she leapt out of the car and moved to pop the hood, despite her dawning realisation that their predicament was hopeless. Rosemary knew next to nothing about car engines, or indeed how to fix them. The ensuing hiss of steam only served to confirm her despair.

They were stranded deep in a desert, without any means of summoning help. (Given her overpowering fear of being watched and followed, Rosemary refused to own a cellphone.) All they could do now was sit, and wait, and hope. *It'll be okay, Andy*, she assured her son. *Someone will come along eventually.* Closing her eyes, she offered up a silent prayer, asking God for deliverance. So when the pickup truck appeared in her rearview mirror about thirty or so minutes later, Rosemary was initially delighted. *We're saved!* she cried to her son.

But when the old man climbed from the truck's cab and sauntered over to her window, something about him put her immediately on her guard. It was nothing he *did*, exactly – he seemed friendly enough – there was just something about him that reminded Rosemary of Roman Castavet. That same ingratiating, anything-to-please manner, but masking an inner poison: like a rattlesnake concealed within a gift-wrapped package.

The old man peered in through her window. *Afternoon, ma'am. My name's Caleb. Got yourself a spot of engine trouble?*

It seems so, Rosemary said reluctantly.

Well, look, he replied. *We've got a little town just a short ways down the road, name of San Melas. I can tow you there and have your car looked at, while you and your friend here –*

My son, Rosemary interjected.

And a very fine young man he is too, laughed Caleb. *So, like I was saying, we can have your car seen to, and then you and your son can get out of this damned heat and have yourself a cooling drink. What do you say?*

What *could* she say? *I don't want to be any trouble*, she stammered.

Why, no trouble at all, Caleb said. *Wouldn't be the first time this happened. Damn cars overheat all the time in this infernal heat.*

She looked on helplessly as the old man took a tow line from the back of his truck and attached it to the front of her car. When the task was complete, Caleb gave her a thumbs up and returned to his driver's seat.

Rosemary turned to her son. *I'm scared, Andy,* she whispered.

Andy, not understanding what could possibly be wrong, and not knowing what to say to make it better, reached out and took his mother's hand. Together, they watched silently as the car crept into motion and the endless desert vista began to roll by their windows once again.

After a few more miles, just as Caleb had promised, they came to a turning and a sign announcing 'San Melas'. The turning soon brought them to the town's main street, a stretch of weathered-looking wooden buildings, untouched by much in the way of modernity or architectural progress.

After they had pulled to a halt, Caleb came to help them out of the car and spotted Rosemary surveying her surroundings. *Quaint little place, ain't it?* he said. *Hasn't changed much in, oh, three hundred years, just the way we like it.*

To the casual tourist, San Melas's retrograde appearance might have seemed charming, a signifier of old-fashioned American values and authenticity, but Rosemary found it deeply unsettling. Just like Stepford, there was an underlying *wrongness* about the place she could not quite put her finger on. Regardless, she allowed Caleb to lead her and Andy towards the nearby hotel, where he promised them iced tea and a comfortable place to unwind while they waited for Rosemary's car to be seen to. She reminded herself that she found a great many things in life unsettling, and yet she and Andy had survived for this long, decades after they had first fled New York in fear of their lives.

The iced tea was cold and refreshing, the hotel lounge peaceful. Rosemary must have been more tired than she knew, because her head soon started drooping towards her chest. Struggling upright in her seat, she looked over towards Caleb.

How long do you think the car will take? she asked him.

Oh, not too long, he replied. *But long enough for you to take a quick siesta, if you'd like.*

Oh, I really shouldn't, said Rosemary. *We have to get back on the road.*

Well, it sure looks like Andy here needed one. Caleb motioned towards Andy, who was now slumped sideways in his chair and snoring softly. *Don't you worry about a thing, now. I'll wake you just as soon as everything's ready.*

It didn't matter what he said, Rosemary *was* worried. Not least about how Caleb knew her son's name when she was quite certain she hadn't told it to him. But her concerns seemed more distant by the second. She felt simultaneously heavy and feather-light, as though her body was an anchor tethering her weightless spirit to the earth, when all it wanted was to float free.

Very soon her fears disappeared into nothingness, and Rosemary knew nothing more of them, or indeed anything else.

She was awoken some time later by the distant buzz of a light aeroplane engine circling overhead. Her body still felt too heavy to respond to her commands, and so she simply sat and listened as the engine noise slowly grew louder, the plane coming into land somewhere nearby. Hearing footsteps and murmured voices, Rosemary finally managed to force her eyes open, recoiling from the sudden intrusion of light.

She found herself in an old wooden church, painted white from floor to ceiling. In fact, almost everything here was white, even the large cross suspended behind the altar. Only Rosemary knew she must still be half-asleep, because the cross looked as though it had been hung upside down, and who on earth would make such a silly mistake as that?

Then she glanced down at the altar itself, and her breath seized in her chest. In stark contrast to the rest of the church's decor, the altar cloth was entirely black.

Lying upon it was Andy; bound there naked and spreadeagled.

Rosemary thought her heart might stop. She tried to will herself to move, but her limbs felt as though they were filled with wet sand. A soft whimper escaped her lips.

She became aware of Caleb bending down next to her and patting her gently on the hand. *There now, mother,* he murmured. *Won't be much longer, and then all your troubles will be over.*

Then she heard the church doors open behind her, and more voices approaching.

The first voice was loud, insistent, and somehow familiar: *What the hell is this place, Damien? I've got a campaign rally in Ohio at eleven tomorrow morning, and here you are dragging me off to Bumfuck, Arizona!*

Then a second, assured and calculating; the quietly measured voice of a man who never needed to raise it: *These are loyal friends of my Father's, doing me a small service.*

Rosemary sat unmoving in her seat, helpless to do anything but listen and wait. Moments later, three more men entered her field of vision. The first two she didn't know: a tall, wiry man, with a face carved of stone and two frozen pools for eyes, and an older man in a wheelchair, frail-looking and yet somehow dreadful; imposing enough that Caleb immediately bowed before him.

The third man she recognised immediately: Greg Stillson.

He peered down at her in evident confusion, the fingers of his right hand nervously playing with the 'It's Still Stillson!' button affixed to his lapel. *Who's the old lady? She looks like she's drunk.* Then, he turned to regard Andy. *And what the fuck is this freakshow? Damien, you said I wouldn't have to deal with any of the weird shit! I'm just here to win a goddamn election!*

The man in the wheelchair responded, never once taking his eyes off Andy. *Remember when I told you that, in exchange for my patronage, I would one day ask you for a service? That day has come.*

He wheeled his chair forward, bringing him eye to eye with the prisoner. Studying Andy for a moment, the man leaned closer and hissed one word: *Mongrel.*

Another whimper issued from Rosemary's lips. The sound prompted the man in the wheelchair to glance around at her. She suddenly felt a familiar terror, one she remembered from a long ago dream: the stark, instinctive terror that comes from having attracted the attention of something inexpressibly malevolent.

The man slowly moved across to her, the wheels of his chair squeaking against the polished floorboards. *Hello, Mrs Woodhouse,* he said. Reaching out, he held her chin gently between his fingers and smiled. *Forgive me. It isn't often you get to look what might have been right in the face.*

Rosemary finally managed to summon up the ghost of her voice. *Who are you?* she whispered.

Me? The man laughed. *Why, I'm Andy's brother.*

An awful knowledge filled her, a realisation of exactly who this man must be and what it meant for her little Andy. She tried to scream, but managed only to gasp, the air hissing from her lungs like a slow puncture.

The man span his wheelchair back towards Stillson, motioning for their companion to step forward. The tall man presented him with a metal case, opening the lid to display a red velvet interior, into which seven ancient-looking daggers had been set.

These are the Daggers of Megiddo, the man in the wheelchair told Stillson. *They're the only thing in the world that can harm me…or those like me.* His eyes moved towards the altar. *Those who could pose a threat to me.*

Fascinated, Stillson reached down and took one of the daggers from the case, testing its heft in his hand.

The first dagger must be thrust into its chest, to extinguish all physical life, the man told him. *Then the others must be placed to form the pattern of the cross.*

Wait, Stillson said in disbelief. *You expect* me…?

As always, you have the freedom to refuse me, the other man replied with a reptilian smile.

Stillson gazed back at him, then over at the tall man. His body slumped. *Fuck,* he said quietly. Then again, shouting it to the rafters. *FUCK!*

Rosemary felt hot tears searing her eyes. She prayed that they might burn and blind her, so that she might not have to witness what would happen next. But they were only tears, and lacked all power to do so, no matter how much they hurt.

Reluctantly, Stillson accepted the metal case, carrying it over to the altar and placing it down beside Andy. Gazing down at his anointed victim, he suddenly recoiled. *What the fuck is wrong with his eyes?*

He has his father's eyes, Rosemary mumbled automatically.

Stillson shot a look in her direction. *And what about her?* he asked worriedly.

The man in the wheelchair said nothing, but the look in his eyes told the candidate all he needed to know.

Your father…saw fit to choose her once, Caleb suggested haltingly.

The other man sighed in faint irritation, but eventually nodded. *If she remains here, she can live.*

Caleb nodded. *It will be our honour.*

Rosemary barely heard them. She could not tear her eyes away from Andy. He was conscious now, and staring back at her: the only living creature who had ever cared for him. Even as Stillson raised the first of the daggers in the air and prepared to extinguish his life, Andy held her gaze unswervingly.

And in those monstrous, golden eyes, bequeathed to him by his diabolical father, Rosemary realised that, for the first time she could remember, she could see the light of her son's love for her burning there.

KENDRA

Lynne Frederick in Phase IV, *1974*
written by Mayo Simon
directed by Saul Bass

IN HIS DREAM, HE IS NO LONGER ALONE. INSTEAD, HE IS ONE OF MANY: A restlessly swarming mass, as quick and pervasive as an outbreak of fever. His mind is no longer tormented by stories and unbidden knowledge; now, he exists only to serve the colony, his consciousness but a single grain of sand in the midst of a great desert. There is something comforting about such utter mindlessness, and even as his sleeping brain begins to wake, part of him wishes he could remain in the dream forever, freed from the tyranny of self.

The Narrator awakens, his sleep-clogged eyes blinking in the early morning desert light. Even before he takes his first waking breath, his hand is instinctively reaching across to his nightstand for the packet of cigarettes waiting there, the tobacco and nicotine they contain as vital to his continued existence as light or air.

As his hand closes around the packet, he feels something moving beneath his fingers. Dropping the packet with a jolt, the Narrator glances over at the nightstand, finding it covered with a bustling carpet of ants.

With a startled yelp, he sits up in bed and pulls his legs protectively against his chest. Bewildered, his eyes dart across the room, attempting to trace the line of scuttling insects back to its source.

He quickly sees that the entirety of his small shack is swarming with ants. They are everywhere the Narrator looks, mapping every last nook and cranny, busily prying into his most secret places. It is as though his mind cracked open during sleep and they came spilling out of his dream in their thousands.

What should he do? Run? Burn the entire shack to the ground?

Gingerly removing a cigarette from the ant-encrusted packet, the Narrator lights it with fumbling fingers, and inhales deeply. With a cigarette burning between his lips, he can at last start to think clearly.

As best as he can make out, the ants do not seem to mean him any harm. If anything, the long black procession of insects stretching across the room and out underneath his front door seems to be signalling for him to join them.

There is a story here, he thinks.

And where there is a story, the Narrator is always bound to follow.

Outside, the line of ants stretches off across the desert for as far as his eyes can see. How many millions of them must there be? All acting in complete, unquestioning harmony, with but one goal. There's something quite beautiful about such single-minded purpose, the Narrator decides.

His humanity seems petty and insignificant in the face of it.

Picture a man, he thinks. *A storyteller, a man who lives almost entirely in his own head. He awakens from a dream one morning, only to find that the dream is apparently real. So did his dreams come true, or was the whole world just something he conjured up in his sleep to begin with? And if you follow a dream, where does it lead you? Maybe, just maybe, along the long and winding pathway that leads only to the shadowed realm known as...*

Fuck it. He lights another cigarette and climbs into his pickup.

Following the ant trail, the Narrator drives for several hours. Like a mountain stream, the flow of insects ebbs and flows in volume over the course of its journey, but he never loses sight of it.

If their colony can achieve such a feat as this, what else might the ants be capable of, he wonders?

Eventually, he arrives at the outskirts of a small Arizona desert town named Happiness, where the Narrator at last finds the source of the long formic river that led him here. A cluster of tall structures, each one two or three times as tall as a man, have sprouted from the desert earth outside the town, reaching up for the heavens like miniature Towers of Babel. Thousands more ants pour from openings near the top of the structures, swarming down to the soil below.

Climbing out of his vehicle, the Narrator stands beneath the towers, squinting up at them through the desert haze of light and dust. They must be some form of anthill, he realises, although he has never before in his life seen one that looks remotely like this. The towers appear almost entirely alien, hinting at an otherworldly significance that is quite beyond his ability to fathom.

The Narrator scowls and lights another cigarette. As a rule, he dislikes such narrative ambiguities, but as the years have passed, he has found himself increasingly forced to tolerate them nonetheless.

Perhaps he will find answers in the town itself, although he already doubts it.

He is climbing back into his truck when he first hears it: a distant, high-pitched sound, carried to him on the wind. The Narrator imagines it must be some form of animal or bird call, although the sound is eerily absent of any discernible life or expression. Once again, he finds the word *alien* rising to his lips.

Driving into Happiness, the air is choked with whirling sand. Perhaps this is the reason why there is not a living soul to be seen on the streets, but the Narrator doesn't think so. Like a tuning fork, an inhabited town will continue to resonate with the accumulated energy of its populace throughout the day and night, but the atmosphere here is silent and lifeless. Arriving in Happiness is like entering a graveyard immediately before a funeral.

He parks his pickup outside a diner. The glass front of the building has been smashed to pieces, the shattered fragments of the window littering the sidewalk like sharply edged hailstones. Carefully, the Narrator picks his way inside. The interior is a jungle of upturned chairs and tables, and he navigates it warily, half-expecting some predator to come leaping out at him from the undergrowth. But the diner is seemingly as devoid of life as the rest of the town.

Quite how devoid only becomes apparent when the Narrator reaches the diner's counter and peers over the edge, to find three dead bodies piled on the other side.

The corpses have all been violently mutilated, although by exactly who or what the Narrator cannot be sure. If he had to guess, he would probably say some form of wildlife must have been responsible, but as to the question of what genus of creature would invade a town and attack human beings in such a manner, he is at a complete loss.

As he looks closer, the Narrator notices that the mutilations were not the only injuries suffered by the victims. Large areas of their skin are reddened and ulcerated, as though they had been drenched in some type of toxic substance.

Some form of acid, perhaps…?

Normally, the Narrator prides himself on having been gifted with a fairly sturdy constitution, but this grisly discovery has left him suddenly craving fresh air. Although this need perhaps has less to do with the condition of the bodies and is more related to his growing paranoia that his previous assessment of the ants' apparent benevolence might have been made in error.

Stumbling out through the wreckage of the diner, he notices one last thing before he reaches daylight: a catering-sized package of sugar cubes lying torn open on the floor, its contents removed or eaten. Kicking the disembowelled package aside, the Narrator shoves open the diner door and lurches out onto the sidewalk. Gulping for air, he remembers too late the amount of dust whirling around upon the breeze and inhales an arid lungful of grit and sand. Now seized by a violent coughing fit, the Narrator staggers over to his truck and leans down upon the hood for support. Another cough explodes from his aching throat, sending a spray of blood misting across the vehicle's paintwork.

An omen of his impending mortality. A reminder that, whatever the consequences of his strange trip to Happiness may be, the Narrator's own story is fast reaching its final fade-out regardless.

He removes a handkerchief from his breast pocket and dabs at his bloodied lips, his coughing starting to subside. It is then that he hears the strange high-pitched noise again, louder and closer this time. Suddenly, the link between the eerie sound and the scene he has just discovered seems all too apparent, and the Narrator hurriedly leaps back into his vehicle, no longer quite so curious to see how this particular tale turns out.

Heading back along the town's Main Street, the haze of dust in the air seems to have visibly thickened, and as much as the Narrator would prefer to step on the gas and get the hell out of Happiness as quickly as possible, he is forced to keep to a more moderate speed. It is only this fact that saves him from driving headlong from the looming, monstrous shapes that abruptly rise up at him out of the thick fog of sand.

The Narrator screeches to a halt, his bowels turning to water. The shelves of notebooks back in his hut are filled with feverish descriptions of nightmarish, impossible things, but he has only ever glimpsed those nightmares in dreams and visions, never in the flesh, never in the cold light of day.

But the three chitinous monstrosities barring his way are all too real. Their twitching antennae probe at the swirling air, scenting the truck that sits stationary in front of them. As they slowly advance upon the vehicle, their vicious-looking mandibles begin to snap open and closed, in eager anticipation of prey.

Sitting motionless in his seat, the Narrator stares into the lightless black eyes of the three giant ants and what he sees reflected back at him is nothing less than the entirely of the universe itself: an empty, pitiless void that is utterly indifferent to everything that he holds dear.

The Narrator bursts into terrified motion, looking to reverse the truck away down the street and search for another escape route. But as he glances over his shoulder, what he sees are three more of the creatures, lumbering up behind him.

He is trapped.

It wasn't meant to end like this, he thinks. Although not quite foolish enough to ever believe he was fully in control of his own story, he always had faith that his unique existence must have some larger purpose in the narrative of the world he inhabits. But it seems his life was just as meaningless as so many others.

As the Narrator sits there and begins to contemplate the fact of his own imminent demise, he sees the girl.

She emerges from the miasma of dust like a dream taking shape, young and beautiful and as impossible in her way as the monstrous ants that cluster around his vehicle. Walking slowly through their ranks, she appears entirely unafraid of the creatures.

Then the Narrator notices her eyes: bottomless black pools, just like those of the ants that tower above her.

She motions for him to exit his vehicle and join her.

Pausing to shakily light another cigarette, the Narrator opens his door and swings his legs out onto the asphalt, trying hard to suppress the tremble in his knees. He tells himself that there has to be more to this story, that he is not in fact simply rushing to his own death.

Inhaling deeply upon his cigarette, he approaches the girl. Her dark eyes stare impassively back at him. *You are the Narrator*, she says.

He nods. *Not much of a name, but it's all I have. And yours?*

We do not possess a name, but this body was once called Kendra.

The Narrator thinks back over the thousands of stories he has committed to paper over the decades, page upon page upon page written in a pinched scrawl that he can barely even decipher himself.

Then it comes to him. In his mind's eye, he sees a little girl wandering numbly out of the desert, her eyes blank and afraid. *Kendra Ellinson*, he says.

The ants took Kendra's family that day, she replies. *The humans believed she had escaped from the ants, but in truth we had spared her. She was already a part of us, although she had not yet joined our consciousness.*

The Narrator thinks back to the rest of the story. A colony of giant ants, mutated by nuclear radiation. *But those ants were killed*, he insists.

Some. Not all. Another colony survived and remained in the desert, waiting for the day we would ascend.

Ascend? he asks.

Kendra's gaze moves past him, to the empty streets of the town. *This planet will soon belong to us. Humanity's time is almost over. Already two scientists tried to stand against us and failed. One died, the other merged with us.*

More men will come. They'll fight you.

It does not matter, she says tonelessly. *It is not the ants that will end humanity. We have foreseen this. You will cease to exist, and we will ascend. It is the way.*

Once again, the Narrator's legs threaten to give way underneath him, and he stumbles back against his truck. *Christ,* he mutters, taking a final drag on his cigarette. Dropping the butt to the ground, the Narrator violently stamps it out with his heel.

Something unreadable flickers across Kendra's face. *You seem surprised. You are the Narrator. You have already seen this yourself.*

The Narrator laughs bitterly. *Yeah,* he snorts. *I suppose I just don't like hearing it from an insect.*

Still you pretend superiority over us.

Behind Kendra, the giant ants twitch and chitter.

The Narrator gives them a wary glance. *Is that what I'm doing?* He thinks about it, then sighs. *Yeah, I suppose I am. Well, you're just ants, for Chrissake. Once upon a time, all it took was a couple of cans of Raid to shut you up. So why the hell am I standing in the middle of the street arguing with you?*

It was not us who conjured your gods and devils into existence. Humanity created the means of its own destruction. We do not dream of such things. We are our own dream.

He reaches for his cigarettes, only to find the packet empty. Cursing, he screws it up and tosses it away across the street. *Okay, fine,* the Narrator says. *Stick a fork in us, we're done. So why did you call me here?*

Kendra steps forward and gently takes his hand. Startled, the Narrator looks up into her dark eyes. He would have guessed such tenderness was entirely beyond her.

Come with us, she tells him. *Ascend.*

Me? He stares at her, dumbfounded. *What the hell do you want me for?*

We wish to understand. We desire your knowledge.

For a moment, the Narrator is confused. Then, he realises. *My stories?*

Yes.

But why? What possible use are they to you?

They are part of the fabric of the earth we will inherit. It is necessary to our continued existence that we understand.

The Narrator stares over Kendra's shoulder at the looming giant ants and lets out a despairing cackle. Was *this* the whole reason for his existence? Had he spent his entire lifetime as a repository for the world's stories simply so that he could pass them onto the planet's new dominant lifeform?

It seems like some bitter cosmic joke. He can almost hear the closing narration now.

No, he says, simply.

Kendra's eyes widen slightly. She lets his hand go. *You refuse?*

Any moment now, he expects the giant ants to swarm in and tear him to pieces. *Look, Kendra…* The Narrator frowns. *And yeah, I know that's not your name but I have to feel like I'm addressing someone, okay?*

She nods slowly.

This is your story, he continues. *But it's not mine. This may be the last story I ever tell…but I have to tell it nonetheless. That's why I'm here. I don't know what reason or purpose there is to it, but that makes no real difference to me. If you want them, my stories will still be there after I'm gone. But I have to see this through to the end, if you'll let me.* He clenches his fist and lets it fall against the hood of his truck. *Because, dammit, what good is a story without an ending?*

Steeling himself, he waits for her response.

Kendra stares at him for what seems like hours. Finally, she speaks. *Very well, Narrator.*

That's it?

What else do you want from us?

I thought… His mind flashes back to the diner. *Christ, I don't know.*

We offered you a chance to ascend, she says. Her voice remains emotionless, but the Narrator thinks he discerns a trace of disappointment there. *If your mission prohibits you from taking that step, then that is your choice to make. But you are not our enemy, Narrator. We will leave you to whatever ending awaits you.*

For an instant, he thinks about the dark figure he has already glimpsed in his dreams, the nameless stranger striding purposefully out of the desert towards him. The Narrator pushes the thought away. If that is to be his ending, let it arrive in its own good time.

Kendra turns and glances back at the giant ants, which immediately retreat to the sides of the street, clearing a path along the road.

The Narrator suddenly feels drained. As grateful as he is to be leaving Happiness alive, the thought of the long drive back to California is almost enough to make him reconsider and accept Kendra's bargain. Thank God he has an extra packet of cigarettes sitting in the glovebox.

Unsteadily, he makes his way around to the driver's door, then glances back at Kendra.

Goodbye, Narrator, she tells him.

The Narrator gives her a resigned nod. *I'm only sorry I won't be around to see how it all turns out,* he replies.

Kendra gazes at him for a moment with those impenetrable insectile eyes. *It will be a happy ending, of a sort,* she says at last. *Isn't that the way stories are supposed to be?*

THE CREATURE

Ben Chapman & Ricou Browning in The Creature from the Black Lagoon, 1954
written by Maurice Zimm and Harry Essex & Arthur Ross
directed by Jack Arnold

THE CREATURE AND THE VAMPIRE SAT ON THE BANK OF THE RIVER TOGETHER, waiting for the end of the world.

After his previous encounter with human civilisation, the Creature had escaped into the Atlantic Ocean, eventually finding his way to the mouth of the St. Mary River. He'd then swum inland until finally arriving at the Okefenokee Swamp, which had subsequently served as his home for several decades. Here, he had been able to live untroubled by mankind, once again the apex predator of his environment. Only the more aggressive of the swamp's alligators had ever attempted to challenge the Creature's supremacy, and were very quickly put in their place when they tried to do so.

For years he had lived in peace, successfully managing to avoid the men and women that would occasionally venture into the wetlands. Ever since his initial confrontation with the world of man, the Creature had found himself hunted, imprisoned, and tortured, and now that he had at last regained his freedom, was in no mood to surrender it again.

So, when he first came across the girl bathing, he'd kept a wary distance and remained safely out of sight. However, the Creature's fascination was such that he could not help but watch her as she happily splashed and frolicked in the black waters of the Okefenokee. The girl was pale and red-headed, and although she appeared normal enough, the Creature's instincts told him there was something strange about her nevertheless. For one thing, she was swimming in the moonlight, and no matter the muggy pall of the summer evening and the tempting cool of the water, to come swimming here in the darkness was foolhardy at best, given the nocturnal feeding habits of alligators. But the girl seemed quite unconcerned about the prospect of encountering a hungry gator, or even a stray water moccasin, and for their part, the swamp's other reptilian inhabitants seemed entirely disinterested in her.

He had been observing her for about a quarter of an hour when the girl suddenly happened to glance around in the Creature's direction. Her eyes immediately fixed upon him, and here was another undeniably strange thing: given the level of darkness in the swamp and the distance between them, there was no way any normal human being should have been able to catch sight of him lurking in the shadows.

But see him she did. Not only that, she did not scream in terror or attempt to flee. Instead, she regarded the Creature with a calm, unruffled interest.

They both stood there in silence for several moments, until the girl cocked her head to the side and called out, *Hello there.*

Cautiously, the Creature began to swim towards her, until only a few feet separated them. Normally, human females reacted to him only with fear or revulsion, and he had little idea of how he might best communicate with this strange girl. Mimicking her cocked head gesture, he let out a low gurgle.

The girl smiled. *My name is Abigail,* she said. She turned to survey the surrounding swamp. *Is this your home? I hope I'm not intruding.*

Not wishing to alarm his visitor, the Creature began to slowly glide back and forth in front of her, hoping that she would take it as an invitation to join him in a swim. He wanted the girl to feel welcome in his presence, and, keenly aware that they had no shared language with which to communicate, the Creature instead relied on his physical movements, which in his natural aquatic habitat were of a supple grace and ease entirely at odds with his monstrous appearance.

Abigail laughed. *Oh, do you want to play?*

Instantly, she dove beneath the dark surface of the swamp. Following her into its depths, the creature saw her swimming swiftly away into the shadows, seemingly as at ease there as any turtle or water snake. He gave chase, and they quickly fell into a game of underwater tag, each of them darting between the trunks of the submerged tupelo trees as nimbly as the native jackfish. After they tired of that game, they took to chasing alligators, the sweetness of Abigail's laughter as she watched the alarmed reptiles scuttle away onto dry land helping to assuage the sour humidity of the swamp air.

The only interruption to their shared enjoyment came when the Creature manhandled Abigail too roughly at one point, and she reacted by baring a set of sharp fangs and hissing viciously at him, confirming the truth of his instinct that there was something odd about this pale, elusive girl.

Afterwards, they rested on a sand bank together, watching the colours of the dawn drift across the sky, and it was then that Abigail turned to the Creature and asked him, *I think I like it here. Do you mind if I stay awhile?*

He did not, of course. The Creature, as far as he knew, was the last of his kind, and although he could not possibly have known the word *loneliness*, he would have understood the cold, insistent ache that accompanied it; the crushing claustrophobia that came from being the last survivor of a long-forgotten species. True, Abigail was not like him either, but she was *different*, and that was enough.

She stayed.

Together, they lived in the Okefenokee for many years. Although the Creature still preferred to avoid humankind, Abigail relied upon them for sustenance, and would prey upon any unwary hunters or tourists that came their way, leaving the flesh of their drained carcasses for the creature to feed on. So began the legend of the dreaded White Lady of the Okefenokee, and after a time, fear of her grew so prevalent amongst the local inhabitants that many refused to venture into the wetlands, meaning she was forced to go further afield to feed. Sometimes she would be gone for days on end, and that familiar aching anxiety would begin to stir at the pit of the creature's belly, only to be quelled again when Abigail finally returned – as she always did – rosy-cheeked and satisfied.

But then, as they always must, things began to change.

One night, Abigail arrived back in the swamp wearing an expression which, if it could not be described as *concerned*, exactly – the vampire was far too impassive a creature for that – was at the very least thoughtful.

Something is happening, she told her companion. *There is unrest in the streets. People are protesting, and fighting amongst themselves. You can taste the blood in the air.*

The Creature thought little of it. Humans were always arguing and fighting, he had witnessed that much himself first-hand. And doubtless they would continue to do so for as long as there were other humans for them to disagree with.

In that, he was more correct than he knew.

He dived into the waters of the river, hoping that Abigail would join him for a swim. Instead, she simply sat down upon the riverbank and began to gaze searchingly up into the darkened sky, although as to what she was searching for, the Creature had no idea.

She sat there staring for the rest of the night and the whole of the following day, until the Creature began to grow quite frustrated. Being a realm so far removed from his own, he had little enough interest in the sky at the best of times, and he could not begin to see what there might be in the tediously predictable shift of dark into light and back into dark again to hold her attention so. Climbing out of the water, he shambled off into the swamp and started tearing up trees in a fit of pique, only for an annoyed Abigail to tell him to be quiet.

That same evening, the lights appeared in the sky. At first, they were only the flashing lights of planes, droning back and forth across the heavens like great insects. The noise of their engines was enough of an anomalous irritation to prompt the Creature to at last pay attention to what was happening thousands of feet above him. He surfaced from the river and slowly waded into the shallows, a questioning gurgle rising in his throat.

Up on the riverbank, Abigail got to her feet, never once looking away from the sky. *It's beginning,* she said quietly.

Then, alongside the lights of the planes came the bright flashes of air-to-surface missiles being fired, dozens of them in quick succession, each spiralling down to earth with a dissonant screech of triumph. The two of them began to hear the sound of explosions in the distance, their dull, rhythmic thud reminiscent of an impatient summons.

Hauling himself from the water, the Creature joined Abigail on the bank. Ageless predator that he was, he was not accustomed to feeling fear, and yet an unfamiliar feeling of trepidation, some primordial fight-or-flight instinct, began to gnaw at his insides. He had experience enough of mankind and the limitlessly cruel potential of their technology to understand that whatever was happening in the skies above them was an almost certain indication of imminent devastation and suffering.

Abigail slipped her small pale hand into the creature's webbed claw. *It's the end,* she said simply.

Somehow, the Creature knew this to be the truth. He had witnessed one apocalypse already, seen his own kind perish all around him, and although his memory of those long-distant events was by now as dim as a guttering candle, the mark they had left on him was indelible. He could already discern the mounting terror in the air, an acrid taste he recalled with a cold stark clarity.

The pheromonal discharge of a species that senses its own looming extinction.

After a time, the constant thud of the explosions slowly began to tail off, and the Creature and the vampire settled down to wait.

They did not have to wait for very long.

When the sun rose the next morning, Abigail finally abandoned her vantage point on the riverbank, preferring the cooling murk of the water to the warmth of the new day. But after diving beneath the surface of the river, she quickly resurfaced, an expression of puzzled distaste on her face.

Something's different, she told the Creature. *The water tastes…bitter.*

Struck by curiousity, her companion joined her in the river. Immediately, he knew that Abigail was correct. His amphibious senses told him that some foreign element had been introduced to the water. The Creature could feel its telltale chemical tingle on his skin, and the normally brackish taste of the riverwater had acquired an oddly astringent quality. Whatever the unknown substance was, it did not seem to affect him or Abigail, but it had obviously been intended to affect *something*.

Just what became clear later that day. The pair of them had been resting at the bottom of the river, and when the Creature awoke from his doze, he decided to fill his empty belly with one of the many wading birds that inhabited the Okefenokee. But when he surfaced in search of prey, it was to find the sky above the wetlands clouded with thick black smoke, the stench of burning in the air, and the startled native birdlife fleeing en masse into the distance.

Moments later, Abigail broke the surface beside him, and they both gazed up at the swirling fog that was fast blotting out the late afternoon sun.

Listen, she murmured, inclining her head slightly. *Do you hear it?*

The Creature began to listen, quickly honing in on a shrill, unfamiliar sound that was being carried upon the breeze along with the drifting black cloud. Despite the fact that they were several miles away from the nearest city, the sound was clearly identifiable as the massed screams and shouts of hundreds, if not thousands, of terrified men and women.

Abigail pressed herself against him. *What should we do?* she asked. *Should we run?*

The Creature gave a low growl, and slapped at the water with his claws. He would not run from mankind ever again. This swamp was his place, his and Abigail's both, and he did not mean to surrender or abandon it. Whatever manner of catastrophe was taking place outside the Okefenokee was not their concern. The Creature would defend their sanctuary, with his life if necessary, but let the humans perish, if it was their time. Regardless of what might happen in the towns and the cities, life would continue to go on in these wetlands. He and the alligators served as ample evidence of that.

Then we'll stay, Abigail said.

The screams and the burning continued throughout the next few days. In time, Abigail and the Creature learned to tune out the distraction, and resumed their normal routines. On the second day, they were startled by a sudden burst of gunfire from nearby, somewhere on the outskirts of the swamp. Taking refuge in the river, they waited to see if any humans would emerge from within the trees, but none did. For the time being at least, their sanctuary was still safe and secure.

It was not until the fourth day, after the black cloud lifted and the screams had finally died away, that they saw their first survivor. Sometime around noon, a rowboat came floating down the river, idly drifting like a fallen leaf on the current. They might have even thought the boat empty, were it not for the mixture of hoarse cries and tuneless, fractured singing that emanated from within.

Swimming up alongside the rowboat, the pair hoisted themselves out of the water and peered inside. There, lying in the bottom of the boat, was a scrawny old man, dressed only in a filthy pair of striped pyjama bottoms. Dotted across his wizened torso were a number of pitted scars, and he wore two black patches over his apparently sightless eyes.

Oblivious to his two observers, the old man continued to sing, his voice a painfully reedy falsetto:

> *Shall we gather at the river,*
> *Where bright angel feet have trod,*
> *With its crystal tide forever*
> *Flowing by the throne of God?*

Abruptly, as if sensing the silent presence of the two monsters, he broke off and reared up at Abigail, his skinny hands clutching at the empty air. *The name of the star is Wormwood!* he shrieked. *Wormwood! The God of Israel gave them poisonous water to drink! Many people died! Wormwood!*

The old man's babbling was fast becoming an irritation, and it had been quite some time since Abigail's last meal. Avoiding his flailing hands, the vampire reached into the boat and seized him by his long grey hair. The old man let out a strangled squawk, but was helpless to prevent Abigail from battening down on his thin white throat.

After she had drunk her fill, Abigail offered the drained carcass to her companion, who dragged the body into the depths and feasted upon what little meat the old man's body had to offer. His gnawed bones might have remained there, scattered at the very bottom of the St. Mary River, had

Abigail not then dived to retrieve them. Gathering the remains up in her arms, she took them back to the rowboat, which she had in the meantime dragged ashore. Placing the assembled bones carefully in the boat's bottom, she began to arrange a array of colourful swamp flowers around them.

Once she had finished, Abigail stood back to assess her handiwork. When the Creature waded from the water to join her, she glanced over at him with one eyebrow raised. *What do you think?* she asked.

The Creature gurgled in confusion, quite unable to glean the point of the display.

I thought I should make a little memorial, Abigail said. *After all, I used to be one of them once. And who knows how much longer they'll be around?*

Together, they pulled the rowboat back into the water and set it free to drift downriver. They watched silently as it slowly bobbed away into the distance, vanishing from view like a coin falling into a well, a cherished wish yet to be fulfilled.

Would anyone catch sight of the boat during its long passage to the ocean? If so, would they take a moment to mourn its lifeless passenger, and all that he symbolised?

Was there even anyone out there who still cared?

Abigail could not say, but as small a gesture as it was, she had made it nonetheless, and that felt somehow important. Because something told her that this was now a world that had very little use for small, meaningful gestures.

The Creature and the vampire joined hands, and together they dived below the surface of the river. There, they quickly disappeared from view, leaving this world and whatever had become of it far behind them.

TASYA VOS

Andrea Riseborough in Possessor, 2020
written & directed by Brandon Cronenberg

Darkness, emptiness. Surrounding her. She swims in a vast pool of night. Is she floating, or falling? What is this place? Is she adrift in space? There are no stars about her, just a fathomless void. Is this even a place?

Perhaps she is lying comatose in a hospital bed.

Perhaps she is dead.

It will help if she can remember. Who she is, where she's from. How did she come to this place that is not a place?

She concentrates.

The first image that comes to her is of a red room, hidden somewhere deep underground. There are four men in the room, which itself is not familiar to her, although the face of one of the men seems to be. They talk of power, and nation, and destiny; the sorts of tediously grand matters men like to talk *about. But such things do not concern her, not right now. It suddenly strikes her that this is not in fact a memory, but a glimpse into the near future, and that she must turn herself around and go back.*

Back, back.

She concentrates harder.

Two faces gradually coalesce out of the void: a man, and a young boy. They gaze at her with a deep love, mingled with visible sadness. They, too, seem familiar, but with that sense of familiarity comes a swelling, irrepressible dismay, and she turns away, banishing them from view. These are not the memories she seeks.

She goes further back, pushing past jagged recollections of blood and pain, flashes of extreme violence that light up the surrounding abyss like muzzle flashes in a darkened room. Mutilated bodies, staring, bloodied faces. The horror of these images is self-evident, and yet it does not disturb her to see them. They are merely facets of what she is, not who she is, and as such they are of little interest to her at this time.

No, she must venture even further, in search of abandoned memories she cast into shadow a long time before.

The darkness swallows her, and she begins to wonder whether those recollections are lost to her forever, devoured by the void. Then, at last, she finds the memory she seeks, floating up out of the endless night: a pale, wraithlike woman sprawled upon a filthy mattress.

The woman is clothed in nothing but a pair of grubby panties, and her sallow, wasted body is like a Francis Bacon painting made flesh. But despite her evident degradation, the woman is wearing a broad, beatific smile. She stares up at the ceiling, gazing far beyond the tobacco-stained paintwork and the cracked plaster. Her eyes are wide open and filled with a divine light, as if hosts of heavenly angels were setting off fireworks inside her skull.

Here, *Tasya Vos thinks.* This is where I came from.

——

Before Tasya Vos, before Parallax, there was only this woman, a nameless junkie whore strung out on synthetic Aylmer juice. Time was, that shit was everywhere. I'm sure you've heard the old rumours about how the CIA and

Big Business cooked it up in a lab together and then flooded the ghettos with it to see what happened next, because hell, it sure beat the fuck out of lab rats.

Well, what happened next was this.

At the time, the Parallax Corporation were working on something very big: a device that would allow their assassins to psychically occupy another person's mind and control their host's actions. Which, no prizes for guessing, inevitably involved the helpless stooge assassinating a stipulated target, someone close to them in everyday life. Once the job was complete, the assassin would simply force said stooge to blow their own brains out, and leap back to their own body. It was perfect. There would no longer be any need for Parallax to recruit a patsy they could frame for the killing, because the assassin *was* the patsy.

If all this sounds vaguely familiar, it's because the original tech was developed way back in the sixties by a man named Professor Marcus Monserrat. That device was later repurposed by the British secret services for use in covert black ops, and only a select few people were ever meant to know it even existed. But H.M.S. Britannia is a leaky old boat at the best of times, and Parallax's corporate spies soon made away with as many of the machine's specs as they could lay their light-fingered hands on.

There were just a couple of teething problems. The first was that the original process had only ever worked for short periods of time, and moreover, could prove to be extremely hazardous to the psychic occupant. (Monserrat himself had died when his own test subject was involved in a fatal car accident.) Parallax, requiring that their assassins be given a long enough lead time to properly prepare their hit, and generally preferring their expensively-trained personnel to remain alive beyond the length of a single contract, needed to refine the process further. This they did via the means of developing an implant that could be inserted into the host's brain, which would both allow the assassin to control them for longer, and to safely eject their consciousness upon the subject's death. So far, so good.

The second problem was that the overall process took a heavy psychic toll upon its users. During the initial testing process, many of the early guinea pigs went hopelessly insane after only one or two interfaces.

Spending too long inhabiting another person's mind inevitably resulted in a form of psychic disassociation, and ultimately, schizophrenia.

This issue would never entirely be resolved, but in Parallax's particular line of work, occupational hazards were something of a given. However, what they discovered was that a very select group of people found the whole experience of interfacing rather less traumatic than others: namely, habitual users of Aylmer juice. Scientists working on the project surmised that because juiceheads were accustomed to hallucinogenic out-of-body experiences – indeed, craved them uncontrollably – their brains were far more able to acclimatise to the mental rigours involved in the psychic transference process.

Parallax immediately began a concerted recruitment drive amongst the juicehead population of America. They would recruit users off the streets, give them aptitude tests, and if the results were positive, clean them up, give them new identities and train them to kill.

Which brings us right back to our nameless junkie whore.

Before Parallax found her, she was only ever straight for a few hours a day; just enough time to suck or fuck her way to just enough cash to score her next fix, which in turn would be just enough to see her through to the next day. *Just enough* was how she lived her life, and doubtless this state of affairs would have continued until such time as she fried her brain completely, had a Parallax operative not approached her on the street one afternoon and offered her enough dough to score for an entire *week*, if she would only take the time to sit a few basic psychological tests.

As it turned out, she scored off the charts. Some of the best results the company's shrinks had ever seen. So before our nameless junkie whore knew what was going on, she was taken away and put into lockdown, there to undergo several days of extremely painful cold turkey. Oh, how she fought and screamed! Even as she lay there in her cell, convulsively spasming and puking and shitting, she denounced her captors as *lying cheating motherfuckers* and detailed the agonisingly extensive punishment she was going to visit upon them just as soon as she got the hell out of there.

But Parallax gave her the best medical treatment money could buy, and they finally got her through it. And once she was clean enough to think straight, they offered her a deal: money, a home, a career. In short, a whole new life.

And a junkie whore she may have been, but everyone has their reasons, and while she might have done some stupid-ass things in her life, her ass wasn't stupid.

So she took the deal, and Tasya Vos was the result.

I mean, you didn't think Tasya Vos was anyone's *real* name, did you?

Skip ahead a few more years, and Tasya is now Parallax's number one assassin. She, it is fair to say, gets shit done. Nevertheless, however good she may have been, and however much Parallax might have got the whole interface process down to a fine art, when all's said and done, they were still fucking around with the infinite, and that tends to extract a very high price indeed. Over time, her handler Girder began to notice some bumps in the road, symptoms of incipient psychic burnout. And then, one particular job went all to hell in a hurry. Tasya ended up trapped in a subject's body, engaged in a psychic tug-of-war for control with her host.

Emergency contingency plans were activated, and although it was touch and go for a while, Girder managed to get Tasya out of there in one piece, give or take. Sure, her whole family had been slaughtered in the process, but as was previously noted, occupational hazards were part of the job. And besides, as far as Parallax were concerned, her loved ones had been nothing but dead weight, an albatross tied around their number one assassin's neck. With them out of the way, Tasya seemed much less distracted by the quotidian details of her day-to-day life, and far more focused on the task at hand. All things considered, it could have turned out a lot worse.

It was only on the next job that things *really* started to get weird.

Not wishing to overtax Tasya after the rigours of her previous assignment, Parallax tossed her a bone: a straightforward in-and-out hit, just to get her back up to speed. Once the initial interface had taken place, Girder and the doctors monitored her closely, but there appeared to be no cause for concern. Tasya successfully completed the contract within a matter of hours, and subsequently terminated her host without any undue issues.

The only problem was, when she returned to her body, she wasn't alone.

As was standard procedure, Tasya was taken to a recovery room to rest before her usual debriefing session with Girder. However, as she lay there in the darkened room, the soft hum of the air-conditioner lulling her into a pleasant doze, she suddenly heard a man's voice addressing her.

Good afternoon, Ms Vos.

Tasya opened her eyes and looked around, only to find herself alone in the room.

Please don't be alarmed, the voice said, speaking in a rich, authoritative baritone. *I am indeed here with you, just not in the literal flesh. A small matter of my not actually possessing any flesh to speak of. But neither of us are the type to permit the old mind-body problem to stand in our way, are we, Ms Vos?*

Tasya made a lunge for the panic button installed next to the bed, but found her arm frozen in mid-movement. Try as she might, she could not will it to move any further; the limb just hung there in the air, utterly paralysed.

Ah ah, the voice said reprovingly. *I'm afraid I can't permit that. No, you're just going to have to sit here and listen to what I have to say. A taste of your own medicine, as the old cliché goes. But do look on the bright side. I am at least willing to offer you a degree of autonomy, provided you don't try and interfere with my plans at all. That's rather more freedom than you ever allow your unfortunate hosts, isn't it, Ms Vos?*

Who are you? Tasya replied, trying to mask the quiver in her voice.

My name is John Morlar.

Do you work for a competitor, or....?

Morlar laughed. Tasya thought to herself that if a cello were to somehow possess the power of mockery, Morlar's laughter was exactly what it would sound like. *Not exactly, no,* he said, still chuckling. *I suppose you might call me a free agent.*

Then what do you want?

The amusement vanished from Morlar's voice. *What I want, Ms Voss, is the man – or to be more precise, the abomination – that you work for.*

I work for Girder, Tasya protested.

Not your handler, he shot back dismissively. *The man who owns all this. The man who wields Parallax like a stiletto. The name he goes under is Damien Thorn.*

She knew who Thorn was, of course. But she still didn't understand. *Damien Thorn owns Parallax?*

Not on paper. But yes. Parallax is indeed a part, however secret, of the rapacious conglomerate of unbridled greed and corruption that is Thorn

Industries. He has a great many weapons at his disposal, Ms Vos, but your little troupe of assassins has been amongst the most trusted and effective. And while you are doubtlessly untroubled by the morality of your rather squalid profession, I wonder if you would feel the same if you understood the actual ends you and the rest of your merry band of marionettes are working to achieve.

Tasya listened closely as Morlar explained to her the nature of Damien Thorn's true identity and the apocalyptic Biblical prophecy he was plotting to fulfil. To her ears, it was all nonsense, nothing more than religious fairy tales. But there was something about Morlar that demanded you listened to what he was saying. Perhaps it was the sheer power he possessed, or perhaps it was simply down to his evident charisma and intelligence; the strength of will he wielded like a battering ram.

Or maybe, just maybe, it was because he was telling her the truth.

After Morlar had finished his speech, Tasya was silent for a time. To give the man some credit, he was long-winded to a fault, but nevertheless appeared to realise that there were some occasions when a degree of quiet was called for.

Eventually, she spoke. *What do you want me to do?*

I want you to come with me. To Thorn's inner sanctum.

You mean leave my body?

Yes.

Tasya felt a heavy stone sink to the pit of her stomach. *But I can't. Not without a subject to interface with.*

Morlar's voice grew impatient. *I will provide you with a subject.*

Was he trying to get her killed, or drive her completely insane? *It doesn't work like that!* she insisted. *They need to be implanted. Otherwise the entire process won't function. It's too dangerous just to force yourself inside someone's head. The device doesn't work that way, not anymore.*

All Tasya wanted to do was to run out of the room and keep on running, but there's no hiding from someone who's already picked all the locks safeguarding your own psyche. *That* much she understood.

A sigh. *You will need to trust me, Ms Vos. All you have to do is use the device to exit your body. I possess the necessary power to place your mind where it needs to go. On this occasion, you must do nothing but observe.*

Do not allow the subject to gain the slightest awareness that you are present inside his thoughts. Merely watch, and reconnoiter.

Trust! Tasya snapped. *If I don't do it, you'll just force me to. Where's the fucking trust in that?*

It's a little late in the day for you to be bemoaning your lack of agency, don't you think? Morlar sneered.

The next moment, there came a gentle knock at the door.

Girder.

She poked her head inside the room, peering into the shadows. *Tas? Are you okay?*

Morlar instantly relaxed his hold on Tasya, although she could still sense him lurking there, coiled within the fleshy folds of her mind. *I'm fine,* she told Girder.

Are you ready to debrief? her handler asked.

Tasya made a show of rubbing at her eyes. *Listen, Girder. I'm absolutely wiped. That jaunt took more out of me than I thought. Do you mind if I crash here tonight and we can debrief first thing tomorrow?*

Girder stepped into the room and quickly turned the lights on, suddenly alert for any signs of trouble. *How are you feeling? Shall I tell Dr Malus to take another look at you?*

Tasya forced a smile. *Honestly, I'm okay. I just want to sleep.*

Her handler looked at her closely. *Well, if you say so.* She glanced around the recovery room. *I suppose you can stay here, but we'll be closing up for the night soon. I'll have to ask one of the doctors to stay with you.*

Girder, please, Tasya begged. *There's nothing wrong with me, and I don't want to force anyone else to stay. It really isn't necessary. I just want to sleep, that's all.*

Girder moved to her side, and reached down to cup Tasya's chin in her hand. Gently raising the assassin's face up to the light, the handler peered down into her eyes. *Promise me you'd say if anything was wrong?*

Of course I would. You know that.

Okay. Girder let Tasya's face drop. *But things are getting pretty crazy out there. People are rioting on the streets, and no one really knows why. I'm worried about leaving you all alone.*

I'll be fine, Tasya said. *Lock all the doors when you go. This place is secure as hell, right?*

Girder nodded reluctantly. *But you call me if there's a problem. Anything at all.*

The assassin gave her a thumbs up, and laid back down on the mattress as her handler turned the lights back out and quietly exited the room.

Tasya remained motionless on the bed, listening to the distant sounds of the facility being closed up for the night. Before long, she was completely alone in the lab.

Well, not completely.

Good, Morlar said.

Without waiting for any further prompting, Tasya climbed up off the bed and left the recovery area, heading for the room housing the interface machine. There, she began to ready the device, wilfully trying to ignore the fact that she was violating every safety protocol in the manual. To do what Morlar was demanding was tantamount to committing psychic suicide. Using the machine without an implanted subject in place meant that she would essentially be hurling her psyche blindly into the aether. And if Morlar did not do what he had promised and guide her into a suitable host, then it would simply drift there for eternity, while the empty shell of her physical body was left here to atrophy and rot.

Tasya was, by now, entirely accustomed to dying. Every time she undertook a new contract, it was in the knowledge that it would always culminate in the same way: with the violent death of her host, and the dreadful, vertiginous sensation that accompanied it. That much, terrible as it was, she could bear. But the prospect of wantonly flinging herself into infinite nothingness, like a shipwrecked sailor who'd been left to drift on an endless ocean but found themselves quite unable to drown, was almost too much to countenance.

As if Morlar sensed her trepidation, she felt a slight pressure at the back of her mind, nudging her into action. *We have no time to waste,* his voice urged.

I'm ready, she said impatiently. *Do you want this done properly, or don't you?*

Morlar remained silent as Tasya made the last few necessary preparations. Donning the interface headset, she laid back into the protective cradle that would cocoon her body for the – hopefully finite – period of time she would be outside it.

Her hand trembling, Tasya's finger hovered over the button that would initiate the process of separating her mind from its physical shell.

Are you there, damn you? she hissed to the empty room.

Come to me, Morlar said, his irresistible will forcing her finger down.

Her existence exploded in a white-hot shriek, and then there was nothing.

———

No. Not quite nothing. First, there were the memories, and scattered and diffuse as they were, that trail of breadcrumbs was just enough for her to find herself again. Now Tasya has followed her way back to where it all began, and remembers exactly why she is marooned here in this nothing-place.

She thinks: I came here because of a man who does not exist.

And that thought reminds her of the old rhyme about the man on the stair who wasn't there, and then Tasya wants to laugh, or maybe scream, because the poem ends with the poet wishing that the man who wasn't there would just go away, and that's just what Morlar has done, isn't it? He has gone away and left her in this terrible void forever, with nothing but her memories for company, and what sort of company are memories of pain and loneliness and blood and murder?

And then Tasya remembers holding the lifeless body of her young son in her arms, murdered at her own hand, and she does finally scream, a guttural, animalistic howl of anguish and despair that is no less awful for being entirely soundless. This is not a nothing-place, she decides; it is a hell, her own personal hell, one she has freely consigned herself to. John Morlar probably didn't even exist. He was nothing but the personification of her own misery and self-loathing, a bilious flood of repressed guilt that has now come spilling forth to engulf her...

Then, the curt snap of a familiar voice cut her off.

When you are quite finished, Ms Vos, *Morlar told her.* We have rather more important matters to attend to than your own petty self-absorption.

The sound of Morlar's contempt was like a hard blow to her stomach, and Tasya suddenly wished she could vomit. Fuck you, *she said.* What took you so long?

You might not have noticed, but the infinite is a rather large place, *Morlar replied drily. I found you just as soon as I could. Now, if you will* kindly follow me…?

Tasya had a sudden impression of swiftly gathering momentum, her previous sense of aimless drift transforming into a propulsive surge of movement. Before she could prepare herself, she felt as though the fabric of her mind was being stretched – no, smeared – wiped across existence like wet ink on clean white paper. She tried to scream again, but she was travelling so rapidly that her agony was left trailing in her wake, and she found herself spiralling down towards a vast pulsing red cloud. As Tasya plunged into the cloud's midst, the stuff of her innermost being immediately began to fuse with it, each element quickly becoming indistinguishable from the other. For a moment, she thought she felt her mind disintegrating completely, and tried desperately to hold onto the merest fraction of who and what she was.

I am Tasya Vos, *she thought.*

I am Ta y V s.

I m T y V .

I

———

Adam Cramer was screaming.

You said Wormwood was just going to be targeted at ghetto areas! he shrieked. *You said we were going to start a race war!*

I admit that I might have misled you as to the precise scale of the Wormwood Project, said Damien Thorn calmly.

How much? whispered Cramer, looking on the verge of tears. *How much of the world's water supply have you poisoned?*

Oh, I don't have the exact figures to hand, replied Damien airily. *But let's say approximately a third. Yes, I believe that's probably an accurate estimate.*

Jesus fucking Christ. Visibly swaying with shock, Cramer slumped down into a chair. *People will be slaughtering each other in the streets, Damien,* he said dully.

That's the general idea, yes.

But why? Cramer was openly crying now, making no attempt to staunch the flow of tears. *It will mean the end of everything.* He gazed hopelessly across at the other man standing a few feet away from him. *Mister President? How much did you know about this?*

Greg Stillson coughed awkwardly into his hand. *What you have to understand, Adam, is that the* real *war has been underway for years,* he said hoarsely. *This is just the endgame. It was never about black against white, or native against immigrant. It's so much bigger than that.* His eyes gleamed with a sudden fervour. *We're going to wipe the whole damn slate clean and start over.*

The three men were all clustered around Damien's desk, while a fourth, President Stillson's head of security Harry Callaghan, stood silently by the office's entrance, gazing distractedly off into space. The room itself was part of Damien Thorn's private sanctum, a small subterranean complex located deep underneath Thorn Industries's New York offices. Very few people were ever admitted here, and of the select handful that were, even those possessing no knowledge of Damien's true nature would doubtless be quick to observe that there was something unnervingly infernal about the space. The overhead lights were always kept low, while the office walls were painted a deep crimson, and decorated with an array of priceless religious paintings, many of them depicting demonic figures or hellish landscapes. The only wall kept free of paintings was the one to the left of Damien's desk, upon were mounted several mounted widescreen monitors, silently tuned to Thorn News, CNN, and a number of other television channels. Currently, each channel was displaying much the same picture: shocking images of the rising carnage and violence erupting across the planet. A second doorway, protected by an electronic fingerprint scanner, was located to the rear of the desk.

Adam Cramer's eyes darted wildly up at the scenes unfolding upon the television monitors, then back at the two men he'd previously respected most in the world. Men who'd promised him the chance to reshape society into something right, and just, and pure.

And now it turned out that had all been a lie. No, not merely a lie; a lie masking a plan that was nothing less than unbridled insanity.

I won't let you do it, he said.

Damien scoffed. *Adam, it's already done. There was never any prospect of you stopping it. My Father's time is finally at hand, and no one will stand in His way this time.*

Cramer looked imploringly at Stillson. *Mr President,* please. *We can still warn people. I don't know what kind of hold he has over you, but you have to understand –*

Adam, listen to me, Stillson said gently. *Everything is going to be fine. Change is always painful, but our congregation are well prepared. We chosen few just need to wait out the coming storm, and then take possession of what is left. We want you by our side, Adam. This is what we've worked for all these years.*

No! With a speed born of panicked desperation, Cramer fumbled inside his jacket and produced a small .22 calibre pistol. Before anyone could react, he levelled it at Damien's chest and pulled the trigger. There was a small pop, the flare of the gunshot briefly lighting up the dimly-illuminated room.

For a second, no one moved. Then, Damien glanced down at the small black bullet hole punched into the breast of his shirt, and began to laugh uproariously.

Cramer's hand dropped. He stared dumbly down at the smoking pistol, unable to comprehend what was happening to him. This was all a nightmare, some kind of deranged fever dream. That was the only conceivable explanation, wasn't it?

Stillson shot his head of security a furious look. *Callaghan, fucking do something!* he hissed.

The other man, who, up until that moment had given little indication that he was hearing anything at all that was being said in the room, suddenly snapped into action. With a fluid, practised motion, he drew his own weapon and fired.

The gun bellowed like some furious rabid beast, and in the next instant, the side of Adam Cramer's face exploded into a scarlet fog.

Stillson's Chief of Staff fell lifelessly to the floor, a look of terrified incomprehension still frozen on whatever remained of his face. In the close confines of the small room, everyone's ears continued to ring with the echo of the gunshot for several more seconds.

And when their hearing finally began to clear, Damien Thorn was still laughing.

Furious, Stillson rounded on his bodyguard. *Callaghan, I could have been killed! The moment that asshole pulled his popgun, you should have blown his fucking head off!*

There was an uncharacteristic look of doubt in the man's cold blue eyes. *I-I'm sorry, Mister President,* he said quietly. *For a moment there, it was like I wasn't even in the room. I felt like I didn't have control of my own body. I…maybe I'm coming down with something.*

Stillson snatched up an ornament from Damien's desk and threw it violently to the floor. *Well, while you stood there with your thumb up your ass, I nearly came down with a goddamn bullet in my skull!*

Damien ignored the explosion of temper, his eyes studying Callaghan closely. *Well, no real harm done,* he declared.

Taking a deep breath, the POTUS gazed down at the small scorched hole in Damien's chest. *It's true, then,* he murmured in wonder. *You really can't be killed.*

Damien gestured at the locked door behind him. *Everything that can possibly hurt me is securely sealed away inside that room,* he said.

Spinning his wheelchair around, the Antichrist moved towards the doorway and pressed his thumb against the fingerprint scanner. There was a low hum followed by a beep, and the door slowly eased open. Propelling his wheelchair forwards, Damien disappeared into the room's shadowy interior.

Stillson followed his master inside, Callaghan staying close behind him.

The room beyond was kept in almost complete darkness, save for a set of mounted spotlights, one on each of the three interior walls. The first shone down upon a life-size statue of Christ crucified upon the cross. The second, a display case containing the seven fabled Daggers of Megiddo, nestled in a base of crushed black velvet.

Neither of these items elicited more than a cursory glance from Stillson. What immediately seized his attention was the object illuminated by the third spotlight. His jaw dropping, he moved closer to inspect the exhibit, a look of fascinated repulsion upon his face.

What lay before him was a human brain, housed in a reinforced glass tank. The tank was partially filled with a cloudy liquid, and a number of electrodes had been attached to the slowly-pulsing organ. Beside the tank, a small computer monitor displayed any extant brainwave activity.

What the fuck, Damien? Stillson whispered. *Is this fucking thing actually alive?*

The Antichrist nodded. *It belonged to a man named Morlar, an extremely powerful telekinetic. Such is his power, in fact, that he simply refuses to die. After I defeated him in our first encounter, the brain lay dormant for a time, but has recently begun to show signs of increased neural activity.*

Jesus Christ, Stillson said, appalled. *But it's just a lump of jelly. Even if it is still alive, what can it possibly do to harm you?*

Damien wheeled his chair closer to the tank and leaned forward to peer inside. *Trapped within this useless bit of flesh, not very much at all,* he said softly. *My concern lies in what Morlar might be capable of if he ever manages to transcend the flesh. It's for that reason I keep his brain safely housed here.*

Next to the tank, the computer monitor beeped, registering a sudden spike in activity. Stillson took a startled step backwards. *Fuck, it's like it actually heard you,* he said.

Smiling, Damien sat back in his chair. *Believe me, that's quite impossible,* he told Stillson. *Nevertheless, I do have certain safeguards in place.*

A few feet away, Callaghan stood observing from the shadows, as silent and immobile as the statue of Christ positioned just behind his shoulder. His job was solely to wield a gun, not to offer thoughts or suggestions, and so neither Damien nor Stillson paid him any mind, not anticipating for a moment that there was also a second observer present with them in the room.

Hidden deep behind the bodyguard's eyes, Tasya watched as Damien reached down to press a small green button located at the side of the tank. She just had time to glimpse a flash of electricity light up the liquid inside before her mind was filled with the sound of Morlar bellowing in agony.

Instantly, Tasya's consciousness was ripped from its hiding place and flung back into the infinite. She felt that dreadful smearing sensation again, which seemed to last for a split second and an eternity all at the same time, and her psychic scream rose to join Morlar's, the two of them howling their torment into the void.

The next moment, she was back on the interface table, scrambling to remove the headset in time for her to lean over the edge and throw up.

Eventually, the wave of nausea began to subside, but this provided little comfort, given the insistent ache coursing throughout her brain and body. She rolled onto her back and gazed exhaustedly up at the ceiling.

Fuck you if you're there, she whispered.

There was no response from Morlar.

In that moment, Tasya thought that she had never hated anyone more. Not least because he had been telling her the truth. As bizarre and unbelievable as it was, everything Morlar had said had seemingly been borne out by what she'd witnessed in those underground rooms.

Those men – the actual fucking President of the United States, a man she'd *voted* for, and those others, whoever or whatever they were – were plotting to end the world. Ushering in an armageddon which *she* – contract by contract, bullet by bullet, killing by killing – had unknowingly helped to bring about.

So what the fuck was she going to do about it?

Wincing with discomfort, Tasya sat up. As much as the notion appalled her, there was very little she could do about it right now. She had already made two interfaces in the space of a day, when the strain the process put on the human body was such that it was normally forbidden to make two within the same month. To attempt a third now would almost certainly kill her.

No, all she could do now was go home, rest, and try and prepare herself to make another leap. Perhaps in a few days she might be sufficiently recovered…

Her train of thought was interrupted by the soft click of the door opening. Alarmed, Tasya glanced up to see Girder standing motionless in the entrance.

For a second, neither woman spoke. Girder's eyes slowly took in the details of the room: the blinking lights of the recently-used device, the puddle of puke lying steaming on the floor.

Jesus, Tas, she murmured. *What the hell have you done?*

Tasya jumped down off the table, her face pleading. *Please, Girder, I can explain everything…*

With a sour laugh, Girder fumbled inside her purse and produced a pistol, which she levelled at her star assassin. *Don't move!* she commanded. *You so much as fucking blink and I'll shoot.*

Tasya froze.

I couldn't sleep, Girder said, a look of horrified amazement spreading across her face. *I was watching CNN and the world has gone fucking crazy and I couldn't sleep. And then I thought about you being here all on your own. So I told myself, just go back to the lab and check on Tas. Took me twice as long to drive here because of all the mobs on the streets. But I made it in the end. And what do I find?*

Girder, please…

Shut up! Girder's gun hand dipped slightly, her finger tightening around the trigger. *So what the fuck is it, Tas? Huh? Sabotage? Industrial espionage? Are you working for a competitor?*

No.

Then what the fuck is it? Girder shrieked, striding forward until the barrel of the pistol was only inches from Tasya's face. *You tell me the fucking truth or so help me, I'll, I'll…iiiiiiii*

Her voice died abruptly in her throat. Tasya saw the other woman's body stiffen into position, becoming as rigid as a marble statue. Her handler's eyes moved frantically from side to side, but every other muscle and sinew in her frame had somehow been rendered utterly, immovably, inert.

Tasya gazed at Girder in disbelief.

Take the pistol, Ms Vos, Morlar's voice instructed.

Slowly, Tasya did as she was told, carefully prying the weapon from between the other woman's paralysed fingers. She cradled the pistol in her hand for a moment, staring at it as though she had never held a firearm before.

You know what you have to do, Morlar told her.

Tasya gazed into Girder's terrified eyes. It was far from the first time she had seen someone confronting the spectre of their own inescapable death, but it was still somehow the worst.

As she watched, she saw a thin trickle of blood start to creep out from the handler's left nostril.

Ms Vos!

Tasya slowly raised the barrel of the pistol, pressing it into the soft flesh beneath Girder's jawline.

I'm sorry, Girder, she whispered. *But they're going to end the world, and you, me, all of us, we helped them do it.*

There was a momentary flicker of confusion in the other woman's eyes, a confusion that was swiftly dispelled by the dry snap of the pistol shot.

Girder's body slumped lifelessly to the floor.

Letting out a cry of anguish, Tasya hurled the smoking weapon across the room. Gazing mutely down at her handler's corpse, she watched as the slowly expanding pool of blood around the body spread across the floor to lap at the toe of her sneaker.

Then Morlar spoke, his voice almost gentle. *We have to go back.*

Tasya's eyes snapped back into focus. *W-what?* she said.

We have to stop him.

But I can't! If I try and interface again now the strain will kill me!

Morlar's tone hardened. *This is our last chance, Ms Vos. You've seen what's happening out there.*

Tasya's shoulders slumped in despair.

Or you could just stand idly by and watch the world tear itself apart.

It's too late, already, she murmured. *Isn't it? That's what they said.*

I won't lie to you. It is. He paused. *But if we kill Damien Thorn now, there will at least be a chance for the survivors to build something new from the ashes. If not, this planet will just become an extension of his Father's kingdom, and everyone inhabiting it will burn forever, their suffering beyond all measure, until such time as the sun finally dies out.*

She closed her eyes. *If I die…will I get to see my family again, at least?*

Morlar was silent for a moment.

I don't know, he said finally.

———

Stillson strode down the long hallway towards the nearby elevator, his head of security following at his heels. As the President walked, his hands gesticulated wildly in the air, like some insane conductor leading an imaginary orchestra. *I still don't know what the fuck happened to you in there, Callaghan,* he remonstrated. *You'd better wise up fast. Maybe you haven't been paying attention, but a big pile of Biblical shit is about to hit the fan. We're living through the fucking Book of Revelation here, and not everyone is gonna make it to the last page, understand?*

Callaghan gave a wordless nod.

So I'm gonna need someone to watch my back, now more than ever. Those of us that are left, we're gonna be sitting pretty once this shit is all over, but we've got some wild times to ride out first. You take your eye off the fucking ball again and I'll make sure it gets torn out and used for fish bait.

The other man's face was impassive. *I said I was sorry, Mister President.*

Stillson's finger jabbed angrily at the elevator call button, prompting the metal doors to slide back with a serpentine hiss. As they stepped inside the waiting car, the three mirrored walls reflected back an infinity of presidents, all wearing the same self-satisfied smirk.

The elevator doors slid closed behind them. Stillson began to examine his reflection, his hand reaching up to smooth back a stray lock of silver hair.

Hell, I always said I was gonna be the sort of president who got things done, he preened. *Like the man said, some of us are just born great. Can you feel it, Callaghan? Even the air feels different now. Charged, electric. I guess this is what achieving your destiny feels like.*

His eyes moved to the man standing at his side. Callaghan was also absorbed in gazing at his own reflection, his stony features creased into an expression of puzzlement.

Stillson poked him rudely in the shoulder. *Have you even heard a fucking word I've said?* he demanded.

Very slowly, Callaghan turned to face him, his cold eyes narrowing to thin slits.

The force of his glare was such that Stillson instinctively took a frightened step backwards, pressing himself against the elevator wall.

The bodyguard loomed over him. *The thing is, Mister President,* Callaghan hissed, *I think we've all heard more than enough out of you.*

His arm whipped out and seized the POTUS by the hair. Before Stillson could do any more than utter a startled squawk, Callaghan began to repeatedly smash his face against the mirrored wall, over and over and over again. He might have been a robot on a factory assembly line, tirelessly working until his day's work was complete.

Greg Stillson's last sight on Earth was of his own terrified face; first shattered into a fractured mosaic of silent screams, then reduced to a bloody, shapeless smear, from which two bright, horrified eyes still gazed out helplessly.

After the POTUS finally stopped twitching, Callaghan ceased his assault, allowing the man's body to fall to the floor of the elevator with a moist thud. Shaking the blood off his hand, he turned and made to exit the elevator.

At his feet, Stillson let out a choked gurgle.

A look of irritation flashed across Callaghan's face. He paused, then swiftly raised his foot in the air and brought it smashing down upon the President's skull. There was a loud cracking sound, and everything immediately grew silent.

Excellent, Morlar's voice gloated. *I think it's been far too long since we had a good presidential assassination. So much more efficient than having to wait to vote the bastards out.*

Saying nothing, Callaghan opened the elevator doors and stepped out into the corridor. Drawing his service weapon, he began to stride back towards Damien's lair.

Upon reaching the room, he threw the door open and burst inside, weapon at the ready. But the office was completely empty, the only signs of movement coming from the scenes of chaos and mob violence being displayed on the various wall-mounted screens.

Callaghan slowly scanned the interior, his gaze moving towards the open doorway leading to Damien's trophy room.

Hidden behind his eyes, Tasya felt a pinprick of doubt. She had killed more times than she could easily recall, taken the lives of countless men, but this wasn't a man she was facing now. As unspeakably corrupt as so many of her victims had been, the being she was about to confront was something quite different: an ageless, inexpressibly evil abomination.

Reason was asleep in the world, and now the monsters held sway.

Even monsters must die when their appointed moment finally arrives, Morlar told her softly. *And Damien Thorn's moment has been a very long time coming.*

Tasya said nothing, but began to creep stealthily forward, letting the darkness of the trophy room draw her in.

Inside, she found Damien sitting quietly in front of the tank housing Morlar's brain, staring into its murky depths. He did not look up as the bodyguard entered the room, merely smiled to himself.

Did you find a little helper, John? he said, addressing the tank. *That's very ingenious of you.*

Tasya raised her firearm. *I'm here from Parallax,* she said. *I think you understand what I'm here to do, Mr Thorn.*

Damien inclined his head. *Indeed. Your firm has done such sterling work for me over the years.* Another thin smile. *I suppose it's only fitting.*

Suddenly, his hand darted out towards the button that would send a burst of electricity flooding through Morlar's prison.

But Tasya's reflexes, honed over the course of countless assassinations, were too quick. Instantly adjusting her aim, she fired into the machinery wired to the tank. There was a loud pop, and a belch of black smoke.

The next moment, Damien's palm slammed uselessly down on the button.

With a roar of fury, he pivoted in his chair, his head snapping round in search of her. With horror, Tasya saw Damien's features begin to shift and eddy like a reflection in water, its surface parting to reveal the true visage concealed underneath.

Face contorted with hate, he extended a hand. Tasya felt a wave of pure energy slam into her, sending the gun flying from Callaghan's fingers and his body sprawling heavily back against the display case housing the Megiddo Daggers. Glass splintered beneath her host's hands, tearing his flesh to ribbons. But the assault was not merely a physical one. Such was its psychic strength that it threatened to eject Tasya's consciousness from her host body and send her spiralling back into nothingness. Desperately she clung on, but she could feel her grip on Callaghan faltering, his mind slipping away from her...

THOOOOOOOOOORRRRRRRRRRRN!

At the sound of Morlar's shout, Tasya glanced up to see what looked like a miniature thundercloud forming above the nearby tank, sparks of primal energy flaring within its roiling depths.

Damien saw it too, his lips drawing back in a canine snarl. Tasya felt his psychic attack instantly diminish. As she watched, an explosion of unearthly power crackled forth from the cloud and engulfed Damien, sending him toppling over in his wheelchair. The Antichrist crashed to the floor, helpless as a beached whale.

Morlar's voice, urgent in her mind: *The daggers, quickly!*

Fumbling amongst the shards of broken glass, she snatched up one of the knives.

Thrust it into the base of his spine!

Damien writhed on the floor. *No!* he shrieked.

For a moment, Tasya sensed his dark energies gathering once more, readying himself to redouble his assault on her, but then Morlar struck at him again, and the Antichrist's final opportunity was lost.

With a yell, she raised the dagger into the air and brought it whipping down into the small of Damien's back.

Tasya expected him to scream, but other than a momentary hiss of agony, he remained silent. As she released her grip on the dagger, she saw Damien turn his head, searching over his shoulder for her. His eyes were now completely black, two dark pools that threatened to suck her into their depths, drowning her within their bottomless wells of deceit and loathing.

He smiled weakly. *It isn't too late, Tasya. You can still join me and rule at my side. I can give you your family back. I have the power to do that, you know. I can give you the life you always wanted, anything you desire.*

You lie! she screamed.

Do I? Damien whispered. *Who's the liar, really? Me, or the Nazarene with his endless promises of a reward yet to come? Serve me, and I'll repay your loyalty now. My Father understands the value of gratification. Your little boy could be back in your arms in an instant.*

He paused. *But defy us, and we will see to it that he burns forever.*

Kill him, damn you! Morlar shouted.

Tasya ignored him. Slowly, with one trembling hand, she reached out towards the knife embedded in Damien's back, her fingers curling around its haft.

The Antichrist began to laugh triumphantly.

Gripping the dagger handle tightly, Tasya carefully began to pull the blade out of his flesh...before reversing her movement and violently thrusting it even deeper into his spine.

Damien's laughter died in his throat, and now, at last, he started to scream.

Climbing shakily to her feet, Tasya stumbled back towards the display case to collect another dagger.

My son is dead, she whispered. *I killed him. Him and my husband both. And maybe I'll burn for that, and for all the other rotten shit I've done in my life, but I'm damned if I'll let you get your filthy hands on him.*

And when the assassin drove the second dagger into Damien's back, it was finally her turn to laugh.

After it was all over, and the Antichrist lay lifeless on the floor, two intersecting lines of knives marking out a cross upon his back, Tasya slumped to the ground, vainly fighting against the uncontrollable twitching that was fast overtaking her borrowed flesh.

Back on the interface table, she knew that her real body was entering its final death throes.

But she'd won, hadn't she? Insofar as this particular battle could be won, she had triumphed. What became of the world was no longer her concern.

Still, she couldn't rid herself of the sense that she hadn't really won at all. She'd just been conscripted in the service of a long, bitterly-fought war. A war between two creatures that could hardly have cared less for pathetic little people like her, people with everyday lives and dreams and hopes and tragedies. After all, what was John Morlar, if not just another monster? And it was his planet now, him and the rest of the nameless things like him.

But then, wasn't she as much of a monster as Morlar? She'd spent so much of her life killing for money, with scarcely a thought as to the possible consequences. So now that those consequences turned out to be the destruction of everything she'd known, Tasya supposed she scarcely had any right to complain. Just as mammalian life had once replaced the dinosaurs, humanity would now be supplanted by a different form of predator. A new era was about to dawn on Earth.

Tasya gazed around at the wreckage of the room. *Morlar, are you there?* she asked quietly.

Yes, his voice replied.

We beat him.

Yes.

She paused. *So what will happen now?*

That's a story that's yet to be written.

And who's going to write it, you?

Morlar contemplated this for a moment. *You know,* he said finally. *I once thought I might be the one to bring about the end of the world. But now that it is at last ending, I actually find myself interested to find out what might happen next.*

It wasn't much, but it was the closest thing Tasya had to hope.

She tried to laugh, but all that emerged was a painful cough. *I think I'm dying, Morlar,* she whispered.

I have one last request to make of you, if you are able.

She wiped wearily at her borrowed face. *What?*

Take me out of this place. I have much to do in the world.

Hauling herself upright, she staggered over to the tank housing Morlar's brain, hurriedly tugging away the tangled wires at its side. She heaved it up into her arms, the cloudy liquid inside sloshing back and forth.

Jesus, Morlar, she said, straining to bear the weight of the tank. *I'm glad I'm not gonna be here to hump you around for too much longer.*

Careful, Ms Vos, Morlar replied wryly. *Or I'll show you what happened to the last woman I knew that wouldn't stop complaining.*

Tasya Vos and John Morlar, or whatever remained of them, limped slowly from the room. Outside lay the ending of one world, and the beginnings of another.

And, broken and incomplete as they were, it seemed as though there might be a place for them somewhere in between the two.

EPILOGUE

THE BOY

Kodi Smit-McPhee in The Road, 2009
written by Joe Penhall
based on the novel by Cormac McCarthy
directed by John Hillcoat

WHEN THE WHOLE WORLD WAS GONE, WHERE DID YOU GO NEXT? During the years the boy had spent on the road with Papa, he had trusted that his father would always know where to go, what to do. Papa was the one who had brought them to the coast, in the hope that it would be warmer and more hospitable here. But the coastal sky was the same lifeless grey it was everywhere, a sodden shroud laid over the corpse of the Earth. When he was younger, Papa used to tell him bedtime stories of blue skies filled with birdsong, remembrances of golden buttery sunshine and vibrant green meadows alive with brightly coloured flowers. He had promised that one day the blue skies would return, and the boy had never quite been able to admit to his father that he simply couldn't picture such a thing in his mind. Grey was all he had ever known; even his dreams were drab and colourless. He glimpsed the occasional flickers of joy that would flash across Papa's face as he recounted these tales, wistful remembrances of his earlier life with the boy's mother, and envied his father these small treasures.

But in time, Papa had stopped telling the stories. The boy was not sure why; was it because the memories were too painful, or simply because his father had started to forget them? Either way, he did not want to trouble Papa by asking him. So the stories were left to fade into the same pallid limbo that had consumed the rest of existence, and before long all the boy knew of them were the fleeting smiles he would sometimes see flash across Papa's face while he was sleeping.

And now Papa was dead.

The boy had sat with his father's body for several days, wondering what to do without Papa there to advise him. They had finally made it all the way to the ocean; where else was there left to go? For a time the boy had considered throwing himself into the sea's freezing black depths, and only the thought of his father's disapproval had prevented him. He had to carry the fire, just like Papa had always told him. But carry it *where?*

Then the man and his family had found him. The boy was terrified that the man intended to eat him, and although he'd claimed to be one of the good guys, the boy still could not quite bring himself to trust him. The man's front teeth were snaggled and uneven, and they made him look as though he was permanently snarling, like the sort of feral animal that would dearly love to feast upon the flesh of a young boy. But the man's wife had a kind face, and the tenderness with which she'd treated him had awakened a dormant maternal longing in the boy. A yearning that he'd never really suspected existed, because he had never before known a mother's love.

They invited the boy to join their family – aside from the man and his wife, there were two children and even a loyal dog – and in the end he'd agreed. A part of him worried he was betraying his father, but after all, Papa had left him first. Still, his Papa was the closest thing to a blue sky he'd ever known, and he would never ever forget him. The boy had made a vow that he would talk to his father everyday, and it was a vow he meant to keep. So after the man had helped him bury Papa on the beach, the boy had turned his back on the ocean they'd both struggled for so long to reach, and set out on the road with his new family.

It seemed to the boy as though the group were travelling with some definite sense of purpose, and he longed to know where they might be going. But the other children were shy and taciturn around him, and when he'd asked their mother where they were headed, she'd simply smiled and said, *I trust my husband, and you should trust him too.*

However, trust was as scarce a commodity as hope these days, and every time the boy tried to pluck up the courage to talk to the man, one glance at his fixed snarl and the rifle that never left his hand sent his tongue crawling back to the rear of his mouth. So for the present, the boy merely kept his eyes trained on his own perpetually shuffling feet and followed.

When they'd stopped to camp that night and the man had asked him to help gather wood for a fire, the boy had been seized by a sudden terror that the campfire was intended solely for *him*, that the main purpose of the flames was to roast his own carcass for the family's evening meal. If he did as he was asked and accompanied the man into the nearby woods, would he ever leave them alive?

The man's wife must have glimpsed something in his eyes, because she put a reassuring hand on the boy's shoulder and murmured, *Go on. You'll be safe with him.*

So he'd followed the man into the dark forest, and although he could not entirely rid himself of the sense that every twig he heard snapping was the sound of his own death approaching, the boy did not die in the woods, and when he returned with an armload of branches for the fire, the man had even offered him a gruff smile and said, *Good work.*

Later that evening, after they'd finished their meagre meal, the man had sat in total silence, slightly away from the rest of his family, gazing off into the darkness. To the boy, it seemed as though the man were trying to listen to something, his eyes narrowed in deepest concentration, like someone attempting to hear the squeak of a mouse in the midst of a howling gale.

After a time, the man's wife leaned across to him and quietly asked, *Are we close?*

For a moment, it appeared as though the man had not heard her, or perhaps was choosing not to, but then his eyes cleared, and he'd turned and offered her a halting smile. *Maybe*, he'd said. *A few more days, perhaps.*

So they *were* headed somewhere, it seemed, although the boy couldn't begin to imagine where. When they'd all laid down to sleep that night, huddled around the dying embers of the fire, the boy had closed his eyes and imagined that his father was there next to him. *Where are we going, Papa?* his mind had asked. *Do you know? I want to trust this man but I don't know if I can. Where can he possibly be taking us?*

But if the boy had hoped that his papa might reply to him in his dreams, he was to be sorely disappointed. All he dreamt of that night was the dark ocean sweeping in towards him, the soothing whisper of the tide cajoling the boy to throw himself into its embrace. And when he looked around for somewhere to go, there was nothing to be seen but endless beach and endless sea.

They travelled for two more days, and still there was no word of where they might be going, and still the boy could not bring himself to ask the man. Instead, he found his thoughts turning more and more to his absent father. His eyes would desperately scan the surrounding landscape as they walked, as if expecting his father to suddenly step forward and reveal himself. *Where are you, Papa?* his mind shouted. *I need you to help me!*

There was no reply.

The boy began to wonder whether his father was angry with him for leaving him alone on that freezing windswept beach. Or perhaps he was jealous that the boy had found himself a new family to travel with. It was true, he had quickly become close to the man's wife, and although the couple's son continued to keep the boy at arm's length, he had started to strike up a rapport with their young daughter, often playing with her whenever they stopped to rest. But he still missed his Papa terribly, and did not want his father to be jealous or angry with him.

So that night, after the family turned in for the night, the boy forced himself to stay awake, and once the sound of their collective breathing had grown heavy and even, he crept out from underneath his bedding and stole away into the nearby woods, in the hope that Papa might finally speak to him if he was alone.

The boy did not venture too deep into the forest, just far enough for the campsite to be out of sight. Warily picking his way through the darkness, he eventually settled down beneath a large old tree, resting his back against its sturdy trunk. Sitting there in the dark, he suddenly became aware of just how impenetrably black the surrounding woods were. Although the campsite couldn't be more than a couple of hundred yards away, he could no longer make out the distant glow of the fire. It were as though he had fallen through a crack in the world, and was now marooned in a vast nothingness. Anything could be hiding behind that towering wall of shadow, the boy realised. Anything at all.

He immediately closed his eyes. *Papa!* his mind called out. *Please speak to me! It's safe for us to talk now! Please!*

For a short time, there was nothing but the same absence, the same wordless silence he had grown accustomed to over the past several days. The boy was on the verge of bursting into tears when he suddenly heard a faint reply echoing in his thoughts; a soft voice calling out to him from the depths of the infinite night.

I am here…

The boy's eyes snapped open. *Papa?* he whispered.

Yes.

In his mind, the voice did not sound quite like his father. It had a dry, aged quality, and the boy realised he could not even tell whether it belonged to a man or a woman. But that did not mean it was *not* his Papa, he told himself. After all, Papa was no longer talking with his voice, because he no longer possessed one. And people might sound very different after they died, mightn't they?

If you're my Papa, show yourself to me, the boy said.

There was silence for a moment, then the voice said, *I cannot show myself, because you left my body back on that beach. I can only show you what is left of me.*

And what is that? the boy said.

Why, the fire, of course, the voice replied.

In the next instant, a sudden light flared in the depths of the forest; a single ball of warm reddish light, suspended in the darkness.

Come to the light, the voice told him. *Come to me, and we can be together once more.*

The distant light looked so beautiful, its welcoming glow only magnified by the surrounding blackness, that the boy did not pause to give it a moment's thought. In a flash, he was scrambling upright, ready to plunge into the shadows in search of his lost father.

Then, he heard a cry of anger and fear explode in his ear. *NO!*

An arm seized the boy and threw him roughly back against the tree, winding him. He looked on in astonishment as the man stepped from out of the shadows, his rifle at the ready. The dog stood crouched at his side, snarling into the darkness.

Raising the weapon, the man levelled it at the light. *Get away from him!* he yelled.

No! screamed the boy. *Don't shoot my Papa!*

That isn't your Papa, you little fool! the man bellowed, before squeezing off a single shot in the direction of the distant glow.

The next second, the light winked out and disappeared.

The boy let out a despairing shriek. Grabbing him by the scruff of the neck, the man dragged him from the forest, the boy sobbing as they went.

When they emerged back into the campsite, the man's wife was sat awake waiting for them, her face creased with worry. When she saw the boy, she leapt up to embrace him. *Oh, thank god*, she said.

We have to leave, the man said urgently. *He called something up out of the forest.*

The woman nodded, and immediately moved to wake her children. Together, they quickly gathered up their belongings and set back out on the road, hurrying away from the campsite as quickly as they could.

The boy lingered a few steps behind the rest of the group. He did not know quite what he had done wrong, or exactly what the man had been so frightened of back in the woods, but he felt bitterly ashamed nonetheless.

They walked for a couple of hours, the family members still yawning from lack of sleep. Once the man decided they had put sufficient distance between themselves and the strange light in the forest, he allowed them to stop and set up camp once more, alongside a small babbling stream. The woman and her two children gratefully began to bed down again, but as the boy made to join them, he felt the man's hand on his shoulder.

We need to talk, the man said, motioning for the boy to follow him.

The boy's stomach plummeted. He felt certain the man was going to tell him to leave. He would be cast out from his new family and left to wander the roads alone, where, without his Papa's protection, he would surely perish.

The man led him a short distance away, out of earshot of the others. He squatted down at the side of the stream and patted the earth beside him, inviting the boy to sit. The boy did as he was instructed, but could not bring himself to look the man in the face, lest he burst into uncontrollable tears.

I'm sorry, he whispered, staring down at the rippling water. *I'll never do it again. Please don't send me away.*

Listen to me, the man replied. *I will never send you away. I promise. But there are things you must understand.*

Finally, the boy mustered the courage to look at him. *I can stay?* he said.

The man nodded. *I know I can be stern, but I am not cruel*, he said softly. *I only want to protect you all.*

I'll never sneak off again, I swear.

That's good, the man said. He sighed, and picked up a pebble from the ground. The boy could sense that there were things the man desperately wanted to say, but didn't quite know how to. Turning the pebble over in his hand, the man tossed it into the stream, then turned back to the boy. *Did your Papa never warn you about the things that lurk in the shadows?* he said finally.

The boy wasn't sure exactly what the man meant. *I know there are people that want to hurt us*, he replied.

The man shook his head emphatically. *No. Not people. Things. Things much worse than any man.*

The boy looked at him uncomprehendingly. What could possibly be worse than the tribes of murderous cannibals that roamed the land?

Another sigh. *Perhaps your Papa didn't know*, the man said. *Or perhaps he simply didn't believe. Some people still don't, you know. Even though the entire world has been wiped away, I guess they're still wedded to the way life used to be.* He reached down and ground his knuckles against the soil. *Or the way they think life used to be, anyway. They don't understand that when our world ended, all the nightmares came crawling out.*

I don't understand, the boy said. *What do you mean, nightmares?*

Monsters, the man said after a pause. *Do you know what a monster is?*

A little, said the boy. *It's something that wants to hurt you.*

When I was a boy, the man said, *monsters were just something in the stories my father used to tell me at bedtime. But it turned out they were real all along. We stopped telling our children about them after the world stopped because we thought things were bad enough already, but what we didn't know was that the stories were actually more important than ever.* He paused for a moment. *Because the world belongs to the monsters now.*

Tell me.

The man's eyes glinted in the moonlight. *Remember what happened last night? The woods to the north are haunted by witches and the things that serve them. They like to prey upon small unwary children.*

The boy thought back to the light in the forest, the voice urging him forward. *Like me?* he whispered.

Just like you. When the boy said nothing, the man continued. *And you know all about the cannibals, I guess. But do you know about the demon they worship?*

The boy shook his head.

They call it the Wendigo. It's very old, and very, very hungry. And if you ever taste human flesh, it will sink its claws into you and never let you go. You have to serve it forever, and no amount of food is ever enough to satisfy it.

The man let out another sigh, and seemed to be wondering whether to continue. The boy wasn't even certain he wanted him to. The world was already so much worse than he'd ever imagined.

Eventually, the man spoke again. *There are vampires in the east, they say. Horrible dead creatures that want to suck the blood right out of your veins. Maybe in the west, too. I once heard a story about a dark preacher and the lifeless congregation that follow him, spreading their unholy gospel across the land.*

The boy shivered.

And that's not all, the man said. Looking across at the man's face, the boy was struck by how much younger he seemed, the years falling away until the man seemed like little more than a frightened child himself. *They say the deserts to the west are filled with armies of ants, some of them as big as a house,* he continued. *And one day soon they're gonna come swarming out and devour everything.*

Ants? the boy said, picturing the harmless little black specks that came scuttling out of the earth in search of crumbs every time he sat down to eat.

That's what I heard. A pause. *But that's only the start of it. There are other monsters out there too, some of them so terrible they don't even have names. But they're out there all the same, waiting there in the darkness.*

I'm scared, the boy said.

That's good, the man replied. *You should be scared. It helps to keep you alive.*

But how will we protect ourself against the monsters?

The man thought for a moment. Eventually, he turned to the boy and asked, *Do you trust me?*

Yes.

I believe there is a safe place. Somewhere where people have gathered together. People like us, who are afraid of the monsters.

But how do you know?

The man gave a hesitant smile. *I hear it calling to me.*

Like the light in the forest called to me?

The smile vanished. *No,* he said curtly. *At least, I don't believe so. Like I said, you'll have to trust me. I give you my word I will never knowingly let any harm come to you.* The man climbed back to his feet. *But if you ever feel like I'm doing the wrong thing, or am putting you in danger, you are free to go at any time. I won't stop you.*

The boy considered this. *Okay,* he said.

Together, they walked back to the campsite, where the rest of the family were already fast asleep. The man said nothing more to the boy that night, just gave him a solemn nod as they both climbed underneath their blankets. When he closed his eyes, the boy felt certain that the light from the forest would visit him again while he slumbered, but his sleep was deep and dreamless, and he knew nothing more that night.

They travelled for two more days, during which time they had to hide from cannibal gangs twice. Perhaps it was just the stories the man had told him, but the boy felt less and less safe on the road, as though the world were slowly closing around him like a gnarled claw.

He began to wonder how much time they had left.

And it seemed as though he wasn't the only one. On both nights, after they had set up camp, the man's wife turned to him and said, *How much further?* Come the second night, the boy thought he sensed a growing edge of anxiety in her voice.

But the man's answer was exactly the same both times: *It's close. Trust me.*

They walked for close to another full day, and as the afternoon light started to dwindle, the couple's young daughter suddenly began to sob inconsolably. The girl's mother took her in her arms and looked at the man. *She's losing hope,* she told him quietly. *We all are.*

The man's shoulders sagged. *But we're so close,* he said.

They decided to rest for awhile until the girl calmed down. The boy watched as the man and his wife walked away to talk in private, their body language tense and coiled. They stood talking for several minutes, the woman's movements becoming increasingly agitated. Finally, the man turned around and stalked off into the trees. His wife stood and looked after him for several seconds, then, her face pale and bloodless, she moved back to join the rest of them.

Her own children said nothing, but the boy could not prevent himself from worriedly asking, *Where did he go? Will he come back?*

Of course he will, the woman said, a little too quickly. *What a silly question.*

But an hour passed without any sign of the man's return. The boy began to panic that, even if the man's intention *was* to come back, something terrible had happened to him to make it impossible. On several occasions he caught the man's wife staring off into the trees, something close to outright terror blossoming in her eyes. But whenever she sensed him looking, she would always offer him a fraught smile and go back to fussing over her daughter.

At last, when the sun was dipping low in the sky, and all hope was threatening to vanish along with the light of the day, the boy heard a sudden crackle of undergrowth and looked around to see the man emerging from the treeline.

His wife leapt to her feet, her expression caught somewhere between anger and relief. But before she could even decide how best to react, the man began to laugh. He rushed over to the woman and took her in his arms. *I found it!* he cried. *I found it just like I said I would.*

The rest of his family began to bombard him with questions, but he waved them away, telling everyone to hurry up and follow him before it got too dark to find their way.

They quickly gathered up their belongings and made their way into the trees. After his recent brush with the dark things that dwelled in the forest, it made the boy nervous to be back there again. To his jangling senses, every leafy rustle seemed to be a threatening whisper; every stray branch that snagged on his clothing a grasping talon. But the man moved with an assurance and purpose that comforted him, and he told himself that their protector would never knowingly lead them into disaster.

After they'd walked for about half an hour, the trees began to thin out again, and they soon emerged onto a winding back road. Just a short distance away, over on the other side of the road, the boy could see a large gateway. A heavy iron gate sat between two tall ivy-covered pillars, a padlocked length of stout chain holding it securely in place. Behind the gateway, a track snaked off into the deepening shadows. To the boy's eyes, it seemed just as likely that the path would lead to certain doom as to salvation, but he pushed his fears from his mind and followed the man as he led them across the road.

The family stood before the entrance, their eyes straining to pierce the gloom beyond the entrance. The woman turned to her husband. *You're sure this is it?* she said.

The man reached out and grasped the iron bars of the gate. *I've never been as sure of anything in my life*, he replied.

But the woman seemed uncertain. Looking around, she noticed something on one of the pillars, and moved closer to inspect it. Her hands parted the clustered vines of ivy to reveal two words engraved into the stone: 'HILL HOUSE'.

Even in the failing light, the boy could see what little colour there was in the woman's face instantly drain away. *Ohmigod*, she whispered.

What is it? the man said impatiently.

I've heard stories about this house, the woman said. *It's a bad place. Everyone says so.*

The man checked the engraving for himself. *Bullshit*, he said.

I'm telling you. They used to write books about this place. People died here.

Christ, the man snapped. *I don't know if you've noticed, but the whole goddamn world is a bad place now.*

We should leave, the woman insisted.

Just as a full-blown fight seemed about to erupt between them, the boy glimpsed furtive movement beyond the gate. A hostile-looking middle-aged woman stepped forward out of the shadows, a rifle raised in readiness. *Who are you people?* she demanded.

Startled, the man and his wife both took a hasty step backwards, the man holding his own rifle up in the air, signalling his lack of violent intent. *Please*, he told the woman. *We've travelled a long way to come here. Can you help us?*

The woman did not lower her weapon. *There's nothing for you here*, she said curtly. Her eyes moved towards the boy and the other two children. *Why do you think I can help you?*

The man's wife stepped forward. *We're sorry to have troubled you*, she said. *We intended no harm. We'll just be on our way now.*

The man shot her an angry glance. *Please*, he told the middle-aged woman. *We were meant to come here.*

And how do you figure that? she snapped back.

Because the voice told me to. The voice I heard in my mind.

The middle-aged woman did not move, nor did her hostile expression alter, and for a second or two, the boy thought she might be about to empty her weapon into the man's chest.

Then, at last, she lowered the weapon. *All right*, she said begrudgingly. *If he's spoken to you then I guess it's okay. But set one foot out of line and we'll chop you up and feed you to the pigs.*

Producing a rust-flecked key, the woman unlocked the gate and admitted them inside. Keeping her weapon at the ready, she began to lead them up a long twisting driveway, bordered on both sides by looming trees that seemed to stealthily inch closer every time the boy glanced away from them.

A bad place, the man's wife had called it. And while it was true what her husband had said about the whole world being bad, as they drew closer to Hill House, the boy thought he could now recognise the difference. The world was a bad place because it was full of people who meant you harm. But here? At Hill House, it felt like the very ground itself was bad, as though the whole property was steeped with deadly black poison.

The dog could sense it, he saw. With every step they took along the driveway, the animal became more and more distressed, whining and barking at the empty air. The man attempted to comfort his pet, but it seemed to do little good.

As the main house itself came into view, the boy noticed the man's wife stiffen in alarm. And when he gazed over at the house himself, he understood exactly why. When you looked at Hill House, it was like it looked right back at you, looked *inside* you: the cold stare of a merciless hunter sizing up its prospective prey.

The decades had not been kind to the grand old building. Several of the windows had been smashed and were now boarded up, and the boy could see a number of gaping holes dotted around the roof. But the exterior damage did nothing to lessen the sense of malevolent will that Hill House possessed. It was scarred but still unbowed; indomitable, unmatched in its sheer wickedness.

At the sight of the house, the dog let out a sudden howl and fled into the trees. The woman wanted to chase after it but her husband held her back. *He'll come home eventually*, he assured her. *He always does.*

But the man's wife could not bear it any more. *Please*, she begged the middle-aged woman. *Tell me how you can stay here. I know all the stories about this house. It can't possibly be safe. I can feel its madness everywhere about us, in the ground, in the air.*

For the first time, the boy saw a flicker of compassion in the middle-aged woman's eyes. She reached down and took the younger woman's hand.

Hush now, she said. *He keeps us safe. The house cannot harm us while he keeps watch. It's the safest place we could possibly be. No one else dares set foot here, and if they do, the house will destroy them.*

I don't understand, the man's wife pleaded. *Who is he?*

If you come inside, I'll take you to meet him now, the middle-aged woman told her.

The man put his arm around his wife. *It's going to be okay*, he told her softly. *Trust me.*

She nodded reluctantly, and allowed their guide to lead them inside the house.

The interior of Hill House was vast and gloomy, and despite the decay that had taken hold of the building, it still seemed impossibly grand to the boy, who had never seen a house so big in his whole short life. Small groups of people were scattered throughout; men, women and children, both young and old. Looking at their assembled faces, the boy realised there was something different about them; something he realised he had never glimpsed on another human being's face before.

They were not afraid.

The middle-aged woman led them deeper into the house, and the boy could not help but feel as though they were willingly throwing themselves into the belly of a hungry beast. But despite his trepidation, he could not deny that there was something else at work in Hill House, pushing back against the building's inherent menace: an atmosphere of community and togetherness, like a lone beacon in the dark. Even the man's wife seemed to feel it, and when the boy caught her eye, he was relieved when she offered him up a tired smile.

As they moved past one open doorway, the boy caught sight of walls covered with towering shelves, each of them crammed to bursting with books. Stopping to peer inside, he saw several groups of people sitting grouped around tables, pouring over yet more books. Fascinated, he made to step inside, only for the man to sternly call out to him. *Hey!* he said. *Don't wander off.*

It's all right, the middle-aged woman said. *Let the boy look.*

She stepped into the library and gestured for the boy to join her. *Do you like books?* she asked him.

I…don't know, he replied.

Well, you'll have plenty of time to find out, the middle-aged woman said kindly. She led him to a nearby table, where two men sat studying a pile of notebooks. The boy noticed that the volumes all seemed identical: each one bound between black covers, and filled with page upon page of dense handwriting.

These books are priceless beyond words, she told him. *In them, the secret history of the world is written. He tells us that by studying them, we can learn exactly why the old world ended, and how we might begin to build a new one.*

The boy gazed in wonder at the books. *Did he write all of them?* he asked.

The middle-aged woman laughed softly. *No. He no longer concerns himself with such matters. Another wise man wrote the books. He merely told us where to find them.* Her voice dropped to a respectful murmur. *Many people died bringing them back here to us.*

Behind them, there was a sudden noise. The boy jolted instinctively, his head snapping around in alarm.

But it had just been the library door swinging shut. The woman smiled. *Don't worry,* she told him. *You'll find the doors have a way of doing that here.*

Reopening the door, she ushered the boy back into the corridor to rejoin the others. The family continued to follow the woman as she guided them to a dark staircase, leading down underneath the house. The man's wife glanced nervously at her husband at the sight of the staircase's gaping black mouth, but when their guide plunged blithely forward and disappeared into the shadows below, it seemed as if the family had little choice but to follow.

They made their way down the stairs and emerged into a cavernous basement. Much of the space was in complete darkness, and gazing around, the boy could dimly make out the scattered shapes of piled crates and old furniture. But at the far end of the cellar, there was the discernible glow of candlelight, and it was in that direction that the woman now led them.

As they moved closer, the boy realised that several dozen people were crowded into this part of the basement. They all sat cross-legged on the stone floor, their attention focused solely upon an object sitting atop a nearby table. The boy's eyes strained to see exactly what it was, but try as he might, he could not be exactly certain what he was looking at.

He glanced over at the man's wife, who seemed similarly perplexed, and reached for her hand. *What is it?* he whispered, his fingers closing around hers.

I don't know, sweetheart, she whispered back, a look of doubt creeping into her eyes.

It is him, the middle-aged woman murmured reverently. *It is Morlar.*

My god, said the man, taking a step closer.

The object that the entire room was fixated on was a clear glass tank, about a third-full of cloudy liquid. There, floating in the liquid, was a disembodied human brain.

Please, the man's wife said to the middle-aged woman. *I don't understand any of this. You said he would keep us safe, but…* She gestured helplessly towards the tank. *I just don't understand!*

You will, replied the woman. *Just open your mind and let Morlar show you the way. He has come to lead us out of the darkness. But you must give yourself to him freely. You cannot resist or fight.*

The man put his arm around his wife's shoulders. *Darling, we've come all this way,* he told her. *And look at these people. They're safe, and happy. Don't you want that for us, for our children?*

She wiped a tear from her eye. *Y-yes, of course I d-do, but…*

If we go back out there, we'll die. Sooner or later, we'll all die. You know we will. But here, we have a chance. To build something. To belong somewhere again.

The woman gazed at her husband for a moment, then slowly nodded. She turned to look towards her children. *Kids?*

The two children rushed to her side, and together with the man, they all eased themselves down onto the floor. When they were all sitting, the man's wife looked back at the boy and, giving him a hesitant smile, extended her hand.

The boy felt the middle-aged woman's hand gently urging him to join the rest of the family. *Don't you want to be a part of something?* she whispered. *Something far greater than you?*

He didn't know what to do. His Papa had always taught him to be careful, to rely only upon himself and those he loved, and now he was being asked to cast all that away. The boy gazed around the gathered faces. It was true that the people here all seemed peaceful and happy, but he wondered what would happen to them if they were suddenly thrust back into the terrors of the outside world. Would they even remember how to survive?

The boy recalled something his Papa had told him once, when he'd asked him if there was anything good about the way the world was now. His father had thought long and hard about the question, and had eventually replied, *At least there's no one around to tell me what to do any more. The world used to be full of people who thought they had a God-given right to push the little people around, and if there's one thing I know, it's that we're all much better off without them.*

He wondered what Papa would do in his place. He thought that his father would probably just walk away, still loath to let anyone push him around, just like the woman was trying to push the boy to sit down with the others now. But Papa had been big and smart and strong, whereas he really was just a little person, a little person who was all alone in a big bad world.

And the people here *did* seem to be happy, and right now, after losing his Papa and the light in the forest and all the other miseries and terrors he had experienced, the boy wanted nothing more than to know a single moment of happiness.

He sat.

Next to him, the man reached out and squeezed his shoulder in gentle encouragement.

The boy's eyes were drawn inexorably towards the lump of grey flesh in the tank. He felt as though he were being pulled towards it, tugged like a dog on a leash, even though he knew his body was still sitting motionless on the floor.

He heard the middle-aged woman's voice whisper into his ear. *Now, close your eyes, and open your mind. Just think of nothing. Let all your thoughts drain away, and he will fill your mind with understanding.*

The boy concentrated. For an instant, he glimpsed the image of his Papa's face in his mind, tired but still smiling, before his thoughts emptied in a sudden torrent and only blackness remained.

Then he heard it. A single word like a drumbeat, remorselessly sounding over and over again, until the rhythm rose to drown out everything, drowning out the surrounding people, the house, the world, rising and rising until it *was* the world, until the sound of the word was all that remained.

Morlar…

Morlar…

MORLAR.

THE END

AFTERWORD

My apologies, but it was never going to end well, was it?

The fact that the world was working through one vaguely apocalyptic scenario when I sat down to write this book was never going to be something I could keep from seeping into its pages, but I didn't think for a minute that we'd stagger out of one global disaster to almost immediately find ourselves mired in another.

And yet here we are, and here *you* are. So thanks again for following this through to the bitter end. *England's Screaming* was a book I had to teach myself how to write, and there were certainly times that I wondered whether I'd ever make it to the finish line. I entertained some similar thoughts this time around, but that was partly because I didn't *want* it to end. I felt as though I knew precisely what I wanted to do here, and there were so many films I wanted to think about and write about that I thought I could go on and on without ever quite reaching the end.

But end we must. As much as we're constantly told we're in the age of long-form storytelling, sometimes I just want to know how things turn out, be it good or bad. I knew they wouldn't end particularly sunnily here, but anything else might have felt rather dishonest these days, don't you think? And I'll admit, I was also wary of letting these books simply run on and on. There are other things I have to do, and other things I'd like to do, and besides, no one wants to be a bad guest and outstay their welcome.

Perhaps I should also mention that, at the time of writing this, I'm still reeling from my former publisher cancelling publication of this novel at the eleventh hour. Contracts were signed, a publication date agreed, and then, in the blink of an eye, everything went straight to hell. I don't really have the time or the inclination to explain exactly why here: suffice to say that certain parties suddenly developed cold feet about some of the content contained in the book. Steve J Shaw of Black Shuck Books has my undying gratitude for stepping in to ensure that *Twilight's Last Screaming* found a new home, but the whole affair has left rather a bitter taste in my mouth, to put it mildly.

So I'm calling time at the bar. There's one more adjunct volume to follow (*That Fatal Shore*, which should be published at around the same time), but otherwise consider this particular story told. Hopefully I told it well, or well enough, anyway.

(And maybe one day, once the dust has settled, I will decide to write more, in one form or another. I do have some vague ideas. Maybe another book, one that goes back into England's murky past. Maybe even a monthly Patreon, if enough people wanted to read such a thing. Maybe.)

Sean Hogan
Margate
March 2022

THE FILMS

1408 (2007)
Abby (1974)
After Hours (1985)
Alice, Sweet Alice (1976)
Alone in the Dark (1982)
American Psycho (2000)
The Amityville Horror (1979)
Angel Heart (1987)
The Bad and the Beautiful (1952)
Barton Fink (1991)
The Beguiled (1971)
The Beyond (1981)
Black Noon (TV) (1971)
The Blair Witch Project (1999)
Blue Velvet (1986)
Bone Tomahawk (2015)
Bonfire of the Vanities (1990)
Brain Damage (1988)
The Brood (1979)
The Burrowers (2008)
Cain's Cutthroats (1970)
The Candidate (1972)
Candyman (1992)
The Changeling (1980)
The Crazies (1973)
The Creature from the Black Lagoon (1954)

Creepshow (1982)
Curse of the Undead (1959)
Damien: Omen II (1978)
Day of the Locust (1975)
Dead and Buried (1981)
Dead Birds (2004)
The Dead Zone (1983)
Deathdream (1974)
Detour (1945)
Dirty Harry (1971)
Donovan's Brain (1953)
A Double Life (1947)
Driller Killer (1979)
Duel (1971)
The Evil Dead (1981)
The Exorcist (1973)
Eyes of Laura Mars (1978)
Eyes Wide Shut (1999)
Fade to Black (1980)
February (2015)
Five Easy Pieces (1970)
The Fog (1980)
Freaks (1932)
Friday the 13th (1980)
Friday the 13th Part 3 (1982)
The Friends of Eddie Coyle (1973)
Ghostwatch (TV) (1992)
The Goddess (1958)
Grave of the Vampire (1972)
The Great Silence (1968)
Halloween (1978)
Hannah and Her Sisters (1986)
The Haunting (1963)
Hellraiser (1987)
Henry: Portrait of a Serial Killer (1986)

High Plains Drifter (1973)
The Hills Have Eyes (1977)
The Hitcher (1986)
The Howling (1981)
I Am the Pretty Thing That Lives in the House (2016)
I Spit on Your Grave (1978)
In a Lonely Place (1950)
Inferno (1980)
The Innocents (1961)
The Intruder (1962)
It (TV) (1990)
It Follows (2014)
It's Alive (1974)
J.D.'s Revenge (1976)
Jacob's Ladder (1990)
Jaws (1975)
Jennifer's Body (2009)
Ju-on: The Grudge (2002)
The King of Comedy (1982)
The Last Seduction (1994)
Last Summer (1969)
The Legend of Lylah Clare (TV) (1963)
Les Diaboliques (1955)
Let's Scare Jessica to Death (1971)
The Lighthouse (2019)
The Living Dead at Manchester Morgue (1974)
Lost Highway (1997)
Mad Dog and Glory (1993)
Maniac (1980)
Mean Streets (1973)
The Medusa Touch (1978)
Messiah of Evil (1973)
Misery (1990)
Near Dark (1987)
Network (1976)

Night of the Demon (1957)
The Night of the Hunter (1955)
Night of the Living Dead (1968)
Nightmare Alley (1947)
The Ninth Gate (1999)
The Norliss Tapes (TV) (1973)
Nosferatu: Eine Symphonie des Grauens (1922)
The Omen (1976)
Omen III: The Final Conflict (1981)
The Other Side of the Wind (2018)
The Outlaw Josey Wales (1976)
The Parallax View (1974)
Paranormal Activity (2007)
Paranormal Activity 2 (2010)
Paranormal Activity 3 (2011)
Phantom of the Paradise (1974)
Phase IV (1974)
Piranha (1978)
Poor Pretty Eddie (1975)
The Possession of Joel Delaney (1972)
Possessor (2020)
The Postman Always Rings Twice (1981)
Psycho (1960)
Q (1982)
Race with the Devil (1975)
Ravenous (1999)
The Road (2009)
The Rocketeer (1991)
Rosemary's Baby (1968)
Salem's Lot (TV) (1979)
Seconds (1966)
The Sentinel (1977)
The Servant (1963)
Session 9 (2001)
The Seventh Victim (1943)

The Shadow of Chikara (1977)
The Shining (1980)
Silent Snow, Secret Snow (TV) (1966)
The Sorcerers (1967)
A Star is Born (1954)
The Stepfather (1987)
The Stepford Wives (1975)
Sunset Boulevard (1950)
Talk Radio (1988)
Targets (1968)
Taxi Driver (1976)
The Texas Chainsaw Massacre (1974)
Them! (1954)
There Will Be Blood (2007)
The Thing (1982)
True Romance (1993)
The Twilight Zone (TV) (1959-64)
The Twilight Zone: Nightcrawlers (TV) (1985)
Twin Peaks (TV) (1990-91)
Twin Peaks: Fire Walk With Me (1992)
Two-Lane Blacktop (1971)
Valley of the Dolls (1967)
The Velvet Vampire (1971)
Videodrome (1983)
White Hunter, Black Heart (1990)
The Wind (2018)
Wise Blood (1979)
The Witch (2015)
WUSA (1970)

ACKNOWLEDGEMENTS

I'm indebted to both The Society of Authors and the Authors' Foundation for their financial support during the writing of this book, for which I am profoundly grateful.

Very special thanks must go to Steve J Shaw of Black Shuck Books, without whom you wouldn't be reading this right now. This book was very badly let down by people whose job it supposedly was to support it, but Steve stepped up when it really mattered. People you can wholeheartedly rely on are sadly all too rare, but I couldn't wish for a more loyal friend and collaborator

Thanks also to Marc Bennett, Darrell Buxton, Alex Davis, Barry Forshaw, Chris Fowler, Paul Goodwin, Kier-La Janisse, Nick Harwood, Jim Hinson, Matt Hope, Graham Humphreys, Penny Jones, Adam J. Marsh, Paul McEvoy, Gary McMahon, Kim Newman, John Llewellyn Probert, Jonathan Rigby, Gary Sherman, Stephen Volk, Giles Ward, Ian Winwood, and everyone else who has assisted or encouraged me during the writing of both this book and the rest of the titles in the sequence.

And as always, much love and appreciation to Lynda E. Rucker for her unflagging help and support.